THE COMPLETE
Au Naturel
TRILOGY

Other Books by Anna Durand

Natural Passion (Au Naturel Trilogy, Book One)
Natural Impulse (Au Naturel Trilogy, Book Two)
Natural Satisfaction (Au Naturel Trilogy, Book Three)
Natural Obsession (Au Naturel Nights, Book One)
Natural Deception (Au Naturel Nights, Book Two)
Natural Temptation (Au Naturel Nights, Book Three)
Lachlan in a Kilt (The Ballachulish Trilogy, Book One)
Aidan in a Kilt (The Ballachulish Trilogy, Book Two)
Rory in a Kilt (The Ballachulish Trilogy, Book Three)
The American Wives Club (A Hot Brits/Hot Scots/Au Naturel Crossover Book)
Brit vs. Scot (A Hot Brits/Hot Scots/Au Naturel Crossover Book)
A Novel Secret (A Hot Brits/Hot Scots/Au Naturel Crossover Book)
The MacTaggart Brothers Trilogy (Hot Scots, Books 1-3)
Gift-Wrapped in a Kilt (Hot Scots, Book Four)
Notorious in a Kilt (Hot Scots, Book Five)
Insatiable in a Kilt (Hot Scots, Book Six)
Lethal in a Kilt (Hot Scots, Book Seven)
Irresistible in a Kilt (Hot Scots, Book Eight)
Devastating in a Kilt (Hot Scots, Book Nine)
Spellbound in a Kilt (Hot Scots, Book Ten)
Relentless in a Kilt (Hot Scots, Book Eleven)
Incendiary in a Kilt (Hot Scots, Book Twelve)
Wild in a Kilt in a Kilt (Hot Scots, Book Thirteen)
Unstoppable in a Kilt (Hot Scots, Book Fourteen)
Valentine in a Kilt (Hot Scots, Book Fifteen)
Electrifying in a Kilt (Hot Scots, Book Eleven)
The Dixon Brothers Trilogy (Hot Brits, Books 1-3)
One Hot Escape (Hot Brits, Book Four)
One Hot Rumor (Hot Brits, Book Five)
One Hot Christmas (Hot Brits, Book Six)
One Hot Scandal (Hot Brits, Book Seven)
One Hot Deal (Hot Brits, Book Eight)
One Hot Favor (Hot Brits, Book Nine)
One Hot Bash (Hot Brits, Book Ten)
One Hot Moment (Hot Brits, Book Eleven)
One Hot Chase (Hot Brits, Book Twelve)
Fired Up (a standalone romance)

THE COMPLETE

Au Naturel

TRILOGY

ANNA DURAND

JACOBSVILLE BOOKS · MARIETTA, OHIO

THE COMPLETE AU NATUREL TRILOGY

ISBN: 978-1-964417-39-4 (paperback)
ISBN: 978-1-964417-40-0 (ebook)
ISBN: 978-1-964417-41-7 (electronic resource : retail audiobook)
ISBN: 978-1-964417-42-4 (electronic resource : library audiobook)

Manufactured in the United States.

Jacobsville Books
www.JacobsvilleBooks.com

Publisher's Cataloging-in-Publication Data
provided by Five Rainbows Cataloging Services

Names: Durand, Anna.
Title: The complete au naturel trilogy / Anna Durand.
Description: Marietta, Ohio : Jacobsville Books, 2025. | Series: Au naturel trilogy.
Identifiers: ISBN 978-1-964417-39-4 (paperback) | ISBN 978-1-964417-40-0 (ebook) | ISBN 978-1-964417-41-7 (electronic resource : retail audiobook) | 978-1-964417-42-4 (electronic resource : library audiobook)
Subjects: LCSH: Nudism--Fiction. | Nudist camps--Fiction. | Man-woman relationships--Fiction. | Oregon--Fiction. | Romance fiction. | BISAC: FICTION / Romance / Romantic Comedy. | FICTION / Romance / Contemporary. | FICTION / Romance / Multicultural & Interracial. | GSAFD: Love stories. | Humorous fiction.
Classification: LCC PS3604.U724 A96 2025 (print) | LCC PS3604.U724 (ebook) | DDC 813/.6--dc23.

Natural PASSION

An Naturel Trilogy, Book One

Chapter One

Eve

On the well-mowed lawn in front of me, four nude people batted a tennis ball back and forth over a net by striking it with the wedge-shaped wooden boxes fitted over their hands. Each player had one thug, the official name for the box-shaped thingy. They were playing miniten, a version of tennis unique to the nudist community, and having a ball doing it. They laughed whenever someone missed the ball and cheered whenever they hit it and the ball went sailing over the net. Miniten was more relaxed than tennis, making it the perfect sport for people who preferred to stay au naturel. No sports bras or jockstraps required.

Ah yes, this was my life. I entertained naked people for a living. Running a nudist resort involved a lot more than keeping my guests entertained, though. It also brought a slew of boring, unpleasant tasks like bookkeeping, meal catering, laundry service, and anything else my guests required. This was Au Naturel Naturist Resort LLC, but I was the only member of the company. That meant my guests were solely my responsibility, whether they wanted to be called nudists or naturists.

I leaned back against a tree, my hands in the pockets of my shorts. My tank top and short-shorts seemed downright tame compared to the unabashed nudity of the folks enjoying a friendly game of miniten and the spectators observing from the lawn's periphery. Four of them were over sixty, one was over eighty, and three were younger. Only one belonged to the millennial generation, but Ollie Jackson wasn't exactly a buff specimen.

Not that I cared what they looked like. Not that they cared either. I admired my guests' attitude toward the human body and their carefree outlook on life in general. Besides, Ollie had the cuteness factor, both in his looks and his personality.

"Hey, Eve!" Sylvester Norris shouted to me, waving. The breeze ruffled his shoulder-length gray hair. Other parts of him flapped too, but the seventy-two-year-old didn't seem to notice or care. He grinned at me. "When are you going to join the party?"

Every summer Sylvester and his wife, Ruth, visited my establishment, and every year he asked me when I might "join the party," meaning when would I get naked along with my guests. Though I admired their unashamed attitude toward nudity, I had no desire to shed my clothes.

"Maybe another time," I called to him.

That was my standard answer to the obvious question: Why did a woman who refused to strip down own a naturist resort?

I supposed it was kind of like owning a tattoo shop but having no tats of my own. Still, being the proprietor of a nudist resort did not mean I had to strip along with my guests. I took care of them like any good innkeeper would, but I kept my clothes on at all times—in public, and in private while in the company of other people who were not my lovers.

Ruth slapped her husband's arm. "Leave the girl alone, Sylvester. We're not evangelists for nudism."

"Naturism," said Ollie, my youngest guest at twenty-four. The only item he wore on his body was a pair of eyeglasses. "Get with the twenty-first century, guys. The word nudist is totally an old fart thing."

Sylvester winked at Ollie. "We are old farts, pipsqueak."

I smiled. Couldn't help it. My regular guests who came back year after year were like family to me. Even Ollie had been visiting my establishment for four years, at least three times a year. Two of those stays consisted of weekend-only trips, but every summer he enjoyed a two-week holiday here.

Except this year he was staying for six weeks. I wondered why, but it wasn't my business.

"Catch you guys later," I said, pushing away from the tree. "Gotta fix lunch and get ready for the new guest."

Everyone waved and shouted goodbye to me.

I ambled back to my house. It sat fifty feet away from the two-story building that served as the guest quarters. My little ranch-style house didn't look like much on the outside, but inside it had a spacious kitchen and a photo studio. As I walked through the main door, straight into the kitchen, my gaze flitted to the framed photos on the walls. Every wall in my house featured samples of my photography. The older images were of normal stuff like animals and scenery.

Everything from the past five years was…less normal.

In the photos, nude people of every age, size, and color frolicked. Nudists playing miniten. Nudists playing chess. Nudists having a picnic. Nudists gathered around a bonfire toasting marshmallows. Nudists… Well, let's just say I had photographed human beings in the buff doing more activities than anyone who wasn't a nudist would've realized people of that ilk engaged in. None of the images were lewd or sexual in any way. Whether they called it nudism or naturism, these folks weren't in it for erotic reasons. They simply preferred to go clothes free.

Nope, no porn here. I took tasteful pictures of my guests, but only of the ones who signed a release form. I posted the images on the resort website and also on some stock photo sites to earn a few royalties, but I had no illusions I'd become a famous documentarian of the naturist lifestyle.

Photographing nudists. Who knew this was where I'd end up? Not me, for sure. This resort in the boonies of Oregon was a long ways from New York City.

I threw open the refrigerator, grabbing ingredients and tossing them onto the large butcher-block island. My guests would be hungry after their morning exercise. The ones who hadn't participated in miniten had chosen other forms of physical fitness, everything from weight lifting to jogging. After lunch, they'd want to relax in the hot spring. Oregon in the summer was usually pleasant, making the hot spring a year-round attraction.

We hadn't reached prime bug season yet. I checked my supply of insect repellent, then got to work on lunch.

Twenty minutes later, I'd whipped up the appetizers and salads and was about to start in on the main course when the house phone rang. I had a cell, but the landline offered more convenience when my guests needed something. All anyone needed to do was punch the green button on any phone in the guest house to ring the one in my house. The digital display on the base unit told me which room was calling, whether it was a guest's room or the dining hall. This one originated from the supply closet that doubled as my handyman's office.

I nabbed the handset off the wall, cradling it with my neck while chopping lettuce. "What's up, Quentin?"

"Got a problem," Quentin Smith said in his gruff voice. My sole employee wasn't known for his cheerfulness, but he performed magic on the plumbing and anything else that needed fixing. "The room for the new guest is toast."

"What?" I dropped the lettuce and my knife, gripping the phone in my hand. "There was a fire? I didn't smell any smoke."

"There's no fire," he grumbled. "A pipe burst in the wall, but nobody knew about it until I came in here to make sure everything was good for the new guest. The place is wetter than a moose after a dip in the hot spring. Don't think anybody wants to sleep in that bed. Might as well paint yourself green since you'd be covered in mold by morning."

"Shit. What are we going to do?" I glanced at the clock and cursed again, too softly for Quentin to hear. "The new guest will be here any minute."

"You'll have to use your spare room, at least until I can get the pipe fixed and clean this place up."

We were booked up in the summer with a waiting list to boot. I'd hosted the occasional guest in my house when there was a problem with their room, but the spare room was mostly for my friends and relatives. Maybe I should've felt weird about letting strangers into my home, but it wasn't any different than if I'd owned a bed and breakfast.

"It's your choice, boss," Quentin said. "I can put a canoe in here and tell 'em to get paddling."

"Hilarious." I rubbed my forehead and sighed. "Okay, I'll put him up in the spare room. But please, Quentin, get that room cleaned up as fast as possible. My house doesn't have all the amenities for guests and the decor is girlie. I don't think a man is going to appreciate the pastel bathroom or the pink sheets on the bed."

"The new guest is a man?" Quentin made a noise that reminded me of a growl. "Maybe you should send him to a motel in town until the room here is fixed."

"Everything's booked up. The Pioneer Days festival is this week."

"Yeah, forgot." He growled again. "I'll get to work right away and see how fast I can fix this puppy."

"Thanks, Quentin."

I hung up the phone.

A guest in my house. The new guy would be nice like all my guests, I was sure. I knew his name and where he'd come from—Valentim Silva from Los Angeles—but nothing else.

Outside, the crunching of tires on gravel alerted me to Mr. Silva's arrival.

I snagged a little remote from the counter and sprinted out of the house toward the driveway.

A black pickup truck was stopped at the gate.

Breathing hard from my sprint, I stopped fifteen feet from the gate and punched a button on the remote in my hand. The gate rolled open. The truck had dark windows on the sides, and the glare of sunlight obscured my view through the windshield as the vehicle passed me. I trotted after it, gesturing for my newest guest to park near my house instead of in the gravel area set aside for guests. He seemed to get the idea, pulling up behind my pickup.

His made mine look like something I'd gotten from a junkyard. My Dodge Ram was six years old and lacked the ooh-la-la factor of this guy's Ford F-250 Limited Super Duty. I recognized the model. I'd seen one at the car dealership in town, though I'd gone there strictly to window shop. No way could I afford a new truck, especially not an F-250 Limited. It cost at least eighty thousand dollars.

Great. A rich guest. My little place was not a luxury resort, and the last time I'd hosted a wealthy guest, the woman had bitched about everything.

The driver's door swung open just when I reached the truck.

Panting, I rushed up to meet my guest. "Hi, welcome to Au Naturel Naturist Resort. I'm—"

My voice ceased working the instant the man jumped out of the car and turned toward me.

A god had stepped out of the luxury pickup. My gaze insisted on taking in the full picture of my newest guest, wandering over his entire body. Tall and muscular in an athletic way, he boasted skin lightly bronzed by the sun. His dark hair curled around his ears to kiss the lower edge of the lobes. His cocoa slacks clung to his thighs, accentuating the powerful muscles underneath. The top two buttons of his white dress shirt hung open.

My attention stalled on his chest and the elaborate tattoos that covered the swath of skin I could see.

He ran a hand through his artfully mussed locks, and his full lips curved into a relaxed smile.

All of my guests arrived wearing clothes since airports frowned on nude travel, but this guy's clothes struck me as designer quality. Most people showed up wearing shorts and T-shirts.

The god offered me his hand. "Valentim Silva. But you can call me Val."

He spoke with a light accent I couldn't quite place. In fact, it was so light I wouldn't have picked up on it if not for the lilting way he said his full name.

I settled my palm in his, my gaze drawn to his warm brown eyes. "Eve Holt. I own the resort."

"Yes, I know." He held on to my hand for a second or two longer than necessary for politeness. "I have seen your website. Your photographs are wonderful, very artistic."

"Thank you."

None of my previous guests had ever looked like him. I'd hosted attractive men before, but they were dim stars in the far reaches of the hotness galaxy. This guy was a supernova standing two feet away from me.

He peered over his shoulder at the guest house. "Is my room ready? I'm a little early."

I fanned myself with one hand, suddenly hot despite the temperate weather.

"Ms. Holt?" he said. "Are you all right?"

Shit. What was wrong with me? I cleared my throat and stuffed my hands in the pockets of my shorts. "I'm fine."

He raised his brows. "My room?"

My mouth opened, a response on my tongue, but I froze before uttering a syllable. His room. The one that had been flooded. Double shit. This man, this human supernova in designer slacks, was going to be sleeping in my spare room. Oh no, this wasn't a disaster at all.

It wasn't like I had to sleep with him.

No, I didn't have to…

"Come with me," I said, waving for him to follow as I headed for the house. "Your room was flooded, so you'll be staying in my house until the cleanup is done."

He grabbed his bag from inside the truck and came up beside me, smiling in a way that made my heart skip. "In your house? That's very generous of you, Ms. Holt."

"Call me Eve."

"Thank you, Eve. I don't want to put you out, though. Maybe I should stay in town."

"All the motels are booked up."

"I could sleep in my truck."

"You are my guest," I said, flashing him my professional smile, "which means it's my responsibility to take care of you."

My body had some very, very wrong ideas about how to take care of Val Silva. I ignored those thoughts. I didn't sleep with guests anymore. Besides, I was way too busy to waste time on a roll in the hay with a hot newcomer.

I glanced back at his vehicle, the spiffiest rental any guest had arrived in. "That's one fine truck you've got there. Somebody who can afford a luxury pickup could afford to stay at a luxury naturist resort too, I'm guessing. I hope you won't be disappointed by the accommodations here."

"Not at all." He stopped to gaze out at the large lawn where the miniten net was still set up and where guests lounged in Adirondack chairs or on chaises. "It's beautiful here, very quiet too. I'm used to the noise and crowds in LA."

I stopped too. We were halfway to my house, but I had to let my newest guest enjoy the scenery a bit. He was paying for the scenery. A forest of conifers covered the property, though the two acres around the guest house and my home were open. Puffy little clouds dotted the blue sky. With a temperature in the seventies, we were enjoying perfect weather for nudists.

"Since we're out here," I said, "let me point out the main features of the resort."

He threw me a sideways glance. "Well, I can see there's badminton or tennis. Or could it be miniten? Nudists love that game."

"All of the above. But we have a lot more to offer." I pointed in the appropriate direction for each feature as I listed them. "The lawn also hosts flag football and other sports. That little brown building over there is the sauna, but that's mostly used in the winter. The big building is the guest house, and inside it you'll find rooms with private en suite bathrooms, an exercise room, a dining hall, a game room, and a self-serve pantry filled with snacks. There's a pop machine in the downstairs hallway, along with a coffeemaker and water cooler in the dining hall. Those are available twenty-four seven, along with the pantry."

"Sounds like you have everything."

"There's more." I pointed at the dirt trail that disappeared into the woods. "We have nature trails too, and a natural hot spring as well as a small private lake."

"Impressive. A resort with all these amenities should be more expensive."

"There are plenty of luxury resorts in the world. I want to offer an affordable, family-friendly place where naturists and nudists can experience the wilderness without sacrificing the creature comforts."

"And that's why I decided to come here." He turned toward me. "For the friendly atmosphere. Your website says I'll find that here."

"You will. My guests are good people." I eyed his truck again and couldn't hold back my curiosity any longer. "Where did you find a fancy truck to rent? I would've picked you up at the airport if you'd told me when your flight was arriving. You left that question blank in the online registration form."

"That's because I didn't fly. I drove here in my own truck, not a rental."

"You drove from LA? That's a twelve-hour trip."

He shrugged one shoulder. "I wanted the privacy and quiet."

Deciding I'd been nosy enough, I started for the house and waved for him to follow. "Come on. I'll show you the spare room."

Val smiled again, this time with a warmth that exceeded friendliness. Not that he was leering at me. Flirtatious seemed like a more accurate description of his expression.

No more sleeping with guests, Evie.

Val caught up to me, that smile deepening. "I appreciate your hospitality and plan on taking advantage of it often while I'm staying here. If you don't mind."

"That's what I'm here for."

"Are you a nudist, Eve?"

"No. I run the place, that's all."

"Too bad." He skimmed his gaze up and down my body. "I've never seen a woman more worthy of the nudist lifestyle."

This guy was trouble. Sexy, flirty, down-and-dirty trouble.

And I hadn't slept with a man in almost a year.

Val winked at me, still smiling.

Oh yeah. Big, big trouble.

Chapter Two

Val

I trailed Eve into the house, letting myself enjoy the view of her luscious ass cupped by the shorts that barely covered her bottom. The woman had a body any man would worship, even the ones who preferred other men. Her curves were a work of art, and the freckles on her lightly tanned skin hinted at creamy coloring under the surface. I wanted to lay her down in the grass and crawl up her body, exploring every inch of her with my tongue and lips.

We would be naked, of course. I was a nudist after all.

But she wasn't. Eve owned a nudist resort but kept her clothes on. Somehow, that made me want her even more. Fantasizing about what treasures she hid under those shorts and that tank top could keep me entertained for days.

Eve led me through a large kitchen, waving an arm to indicate it. "This is where I make the food for all my guests, but meals are served in the guest house. While you're staying here with me, you can grab a snack or a pop from the fridge anytime you like."

"Will I take my meals in the guest house or here with you?" *Please say with you.*

Eve paused on the threshold of a hallway, whipping her head around to look at me. The long locks of her strawberry-blonde hair bounced around her shoulders. Her bright-blue eyes widened briefly, and she caught one side of her bottom lip with her teeth. "I guess that's up to you. I eat here."

"I'll have my meals with you, then." I couldn't stop staring at her lips, full and pouty, and the way she was biting down on her lower lip. What would she taste like? The flavor of her mouth would be different from the flavor of her cream, and I wanted to sample all of it. All of her.

She sucked in a deep breath, her breasts lifting, and exhaled it in a rush. "Moving on…"

Already, I was deeply in lust with those breasts. Not too small, not too large, just right for holding in my palms while I suckled the tips.

My fantasies about her breasts ended when she spun away from me and started down the hallway. I counted four closed doors.

Eve pointed at the first door on the left. "That's the bathroom. We'll have to share." She twisted her head around to give me a sheepish smile. "Hope you don't mind girlie things. The bathroom is pastel-colored and full of my stuff."

"Doesn't bother me." My mind went straight to a fantasy of me shaving her legs in the shower. "I have two sisters, and they left their things everywhere in our house when we were children. I know more about feminine hygiene than most men would want to."

"I bet. Over there is my photo studio," she said, pointing to the door opposite the bathroom. "My bedroom is at the end of the hall on the right. You might have noticed the other doorway leading out of the kitchen. That's the living room, where you can relax and watch TV if you want." She walked up to the next closed door on the left, turned toward me, and pushed the door open. "Here's where you'll be staying."

"Directly across from your bedroom."

"Both bedrooms have locks on the doors, if you want to ensure privacy."

"Hardly seems necessary." I set down my bag and leaned against the jamb of the open door, probably standing closer to her than was necessary or appropriate. Fuck appropriate. The sweet, fresh scent of her enveloped me, and I wouldn't give that up one second sooner than I had to. "Thank you for sharing your home with me, Eve."

"No problem."

I tipped my head to the side, studying her. "May I ask a personal question?"

"Sure."

"Why does a woman who's not a nudist own a nudist retreat?"

"For the money." She hunched her shoulders. "I know that sounds crass, but it's true. I make a decent living catering to the clothing-optional set."

"That's not crass. It's smart." My attention stalled on her breasts and the faint lines of the bra that held them up in perfect position. I would get her naked as soon as possible. I had to. My cock insisted on it, and I'd never had much luck fighting my carnal urges.

Eve glanced into the bedroom. "Oh, I forgot your welcome packet."

While she sprinted down the hallway to the kitchen, I carried my bag into the little room and set it on the floor beside the bed. The mattress was a decent size, large enough for me—and for Eve too, if she should join me. A dresser with a large attached mirror was pushed up against the wall, and a pair of accordion doors probably concealed a small closet. A telephone, cordless and seated in its charging base, sat on a little round table tucked into one corner while an old-fashioned clock with large hands counted the hours, minutes, and seconds.

A window overlooked the lawn where the miniten net was still set up.

The distinctive clapping of sneaker-clad feet on the wood floors drew my attention to the doorway.

Eve, breathless and smiling, clutched a large basket in her arms. It was full of items I couldn't quite make out, thanks to the large, blue-satin bow tied to the handle with its long ribbons hanging over the entire basket.

She marched to the little table, set down the basket, and plucked a manila envelope from inside it. She waved the envelope at me. "Here's your welcome packet."

I strode up to her and accepted the envelope.

"You've got a map of the property," she said, "with all the attractions noted, along with brochures for things you can do away from the resort in the local area. You'll need to wear clothes if you go off site." She pried open the metal tabs that held the envelope shut. "There are also coupons for local restaurants. The national forest borders my property on three sides, but there's no fee to hike on that land."

She pulled the envelope's flap out, seemingly to encourage me to examine its contents. Her expectant look confirmed my assumption.

I slid the contents out and flipped through them. "You are thorough, aren't you?"

"Yep." She stepped back and gestured toward the basket. "This is your welcome kit with samples of everything you might need."

I leaned in to examine the items. "Sunscreen. Lip balm. Foot moisturizer. Body lotion. Aloe. Insect repellent. Calamine lotion." I glanced at her, my brows raised. "Are you expecting insects to be a problem?"

"Not usually, but twice we've had an invasion of no-see-ums." She feigned disgust. "It's not pretty. Then there was the year we had an outbreak of poison ivy." She tapped the pink bottle of calamine lotion. "You may never need this, but trust me, if you do, you'll be glad you have it."

"You take good care of your guests." I considered what she'd said a moment ago. "No-see-ums?"

"Teeny-tiny bugs that will eat you alive and you may never even see them. They're also called midges." She faked an exaggerated shiver. "The no-see-um attacks were like something out of a horror movie. You need super-strong insect repellent for that. It might melt your tattoos, but at least you won't get bitten up."

One corner of her mouth twitched upward, and I knew she was teasing me. I liked that. "My tattoos are made from molten steel. I think they'll survive your insects."

She waggled her eyebrows. "You haven't seen the mosquitoes yet."

I grinned. She was the most adorable, sexiest woman I'd ever met.

Eve leaned her bottom against the table. "Here are the rules. No staring at women's breasts or anyone's private parts. Maintain eye contact. You're welcome to wear clothes anytime you want since this is a clothes-optional resort rather than a clothes-free one. Footwear is fine, but do not walk around in your underwear."

"I never bother with underwear."

"Okay." Her brows crinkled, but if I'd shocked her, she shook it off quickly. Clearing her throat, she continued. "Always shower before using the sauna or the hot spring. Always put a towel on a chair or other surface before sitting down on it. No PDAs—public displays of affection—other than a quick hug to say hello or a quick peck on the cheek. Hand holding is acceptable. Oh, no barn doors open when you're sitting or lying down in the presence of other guests."

"Barn doors?"

"It means don't have your legs spread so everyone can see your privates."

"Ah, I see. You don't need to go through all of this. It's not my first time at a nudist resort."

She folded her arms over her chest. "Everyone hears the rules the first time they come here. It's protocol."

"All right. I'm listening."

"No reaching during meals. If you need something, ask someone to pass it to you." She waved a finger toward my groin. "Make sure none of your bits intrude on anyone else's space. And if you absolutely must relieve yourself outdoors, whether it's number one or number two, please find a secluded spot where you can take care of things. No photography without express permission from the people involved. Do you have a cell phone?"

"Yes."

She dug a small, folded sheet of paper out of the basket, handing it to me. "Put a red dot over the camera lens, please. If your phone has more than one camera, please put stickers over all of them."

I obeyed, applying red stickers to the tiny lenses on the front and back of my phone.

Eve nodded her approval. She started to push away from the table but stopped. "One more thing. Men tend to get embarrassed when I bring this up, but it's necessary. If you get an erection when you're outside of this house, please put a towel over your lap or roll over onto your side. If you're in the hot spring or the lake, you can just stay put until the problem subsides."

She watched me like she expected me to blush or get upset.

Most men probably would have, but no one who knew me, or knew of me, would think I'd ever get embarrassed about something like developing a hard-on in public.

I chuckled. "Don't worry. I'm shameless."

"No need to pretend you're cool with it. I'm used to my male guests getting flustered when that happens."

I studied her expression for some sign she was teasing me again but found none. "You really don't recognize me, do you?"

She raked her gaze over my body. "If we'd met before, I'd remember."

Eve Holt had no idea who I was. Her attentiveness and attraction to me had nothing to do with my reputation or my past behavior. It was…refreshing.

"You're good to go," she said. Her gaze flicked to the clock on the wall. "I need to finish getting lunch ready. Once you're settled in, come find me in the kitchen."

"Thank you, Eve."

"I'm just doing my job." She moved toward the door, hesitating on the threshold. "If there's anything else you need, just ask."

"Don't trouble yourself on my account."

"It's no trouble. I'll let you get settled."

She disappeared down the hallway.

I shed my clothes and shoes, then headed into the kitchen.

Eve stood at the island placing food items into plastic trays and closing up each tray with a red plastic lid. She glanced up when I walked into the room.

Her eyes flared wide. She stared at me for a moment before blinking furiously like she was waking from a strange dream. Her cheeks pinkened. She bowed her head to focus on her task. "I see you've made yourself comfortable."

"Are you carrying all that food to the guest house by yourself?"

"My handyman, Quentin, will be here any minute to help."

I approached the island across from her. "I would be happy to help too."

"That's not necessary. You're a guest." She kept her head down but lifted her gaze to me. "Besides, handling food in the nude is a health code violation."

"How many guests do you have?"

"The number varies." She slapped the lid onto a tray and laid her hands on top of it, swiveling her gaze up to me. "The guest house has ten rooms with two queen beds in each. Some people bring tents to sleep out, and others come in RVs and sleep in those. Currently, I have seventeen guests, including you."

"And you manage all of this on your own. Just you and a handyman."

"Well, I do outsource dinner. Tonight, it's pizza delivered from a restaurant in town, with salad for the vegans."

I arched a brow. "Town is eighteen miles away. I didn't realize anyone delivered that far out."

"Normally, they don't. I have special arrangements."

She stacked four trays and lifted them in her arms.

I rushed around the island, intending to take them from her. "Let me help."

"You're a guest, and you're naked."

"I'm also not the sort of man who lets a woman do all the work alone. My sisters would whip me for not lending a hand." I turned halfway toward the hall. "Let me put some clothes on, and I'll help you. Please, I insist."

She set down the trays and raised her hands. "I surrender. Knock yourself out."

I sprinted back to my room and yanked on an outfit that seemed more appropriate for serving lunch than my designer clothes—a T-shirt, jeans, and sneakers. When I got back to the kitchen, Eve was waiting with her elbows braced on the island. She moved to pick up those four trays again, but I hurried over to take them from her.

A knock vibrated the door as a male voice hollered, "It's me, Eve."

"Come on in," she said.

The door swung open. A well-tanned man in jeans and a T-shirt, with clunky boots on his feet, pushed a metal cart into the kitchen. He dragged another metal cart behind him, and I could see a third parked a few feet outside the door.

"Sorry I took so long," the man said. Deep wrinkles carved lines into his face when he squinted at my hostess in what seemed like a strained attempt at a smile. "We better hurry, Eve. The natives are getting restless and might start gnawing on each other if we don't get them their food pronto."

The man looked at me, his squint deepening. "Guess you've got help already."

Eve cleared her throat. "Quentin, this is our newest guest, Val Silva. Val, this is my handyman extraordinaire, Quentin Smith."

Quentin offered me his hand, realized I couldn't take it with the trays in my arms, and pushed his cart toward me. "You can set those down here."

I deposited the trays on the cart and offered him my hand. "A pleasure to meet you, Mr. Smith."

"Just Quentin." He shook my hand, eying me up and down. One corner of his mouth twisted downward, then smoothed out. "Welcome to Au Naturel Naturist Resort."

"Hungry people are waiting," Eve said, stacking four more trays on the counter.

When she tried to pick them up, Quentin and I reached for them at the same time.

I yanked them out of Eve's hands and slid them onto the cart's lower shelf.

Quentin's mouth tightened.

"No fighting, boys," Eve said. "There's plenty of work to go around."

Her handyman pursed his lips, his gaze narrowing on me.

Did he have a special fondness for my hostess? If he did, he'd have to take a step back. For the next two weeks, I planned to be the one monopolizing her attention and seducing her into sharing my bed.

Chapter Three

Eve

For the next fifteen minutes, Quentin and Val competed in a bizarre race to ferry their carts across the fifty-foot gap between my home and the guest house and get their trays into the dining hall and unloaded. I pushed the third cart but gave up on keeping up with the men. Val seemed to think their little race was funny, but Quentin was not amused. I supposed he'd gotten used to being my one and only assistant. It probably didn't help that we'd slept together last summer.

Oh yeah, *that* had been a mistake. Ever since, Quentin had developed an odd possessiveness toward me. The sex had been decent, but not worth this aggravation.

When we'd gotten all the food offloaded in the dining hall and placed on the buffet tables, I encouraged Quentin to stay there and get himself some food before the teeming horde of hungry nudists descended on the buffet. He got the hint and took it.

Back in my kitchen, Val helped me put the last of the trays onto a cart.

"Let me take the last cart," I said. "You'll want to get out of your clothes, I'm sure."

He opened his mouth, and by the look on his face, I knew he wanted to protest.

"Go on," I said. "I insist. This is a nudist resort, after all. You came here to enjoy yourself sans clothing. And I can manage to push one cart."

Val stared at me for a few seconds, then he whipped off his clothes. Stretching his entire body, he let out a long, satisfied sigh. "Much better."

I leaned against the island admiring the view. Damn, that man had a killer body—decorated with just enough tattoos to give him that bad boy look. I'd hosted plenty of athletic male guests, but Val made them all seem like couch potatoes with beer bellies. He was lean but well-muscled, with washboard abs and strong thighs. I let my gaze travel down his body, starting with his face, moving down to the corded muscles of his shoulders and arms and along the center line of his torso. His skin was smooth with only the barest hint of dark hairs. Near his hips, those hairs grew thicker and longer, tapering down to the most beautiful set of manly parts I'd ever seen.

Oh yeah, he was well-muscled and well-endowed. Spectacularly well-endowed.

His penis hung slack and soft but proved no less impressive for its lack of arousal. Veins rippled along its length, though the skin looked smooth otherwise. I imagined taking his thick girth in my hand, exploring his flesh, fondling his sac.

No more sex with guests, remember?

Val cleared his throat deliberately.

I tore my gaze away from his dick and intended to look him in the eye, but his impressive pecs and biceps distracted me. "Are you ready to go?"

"Yes, I'm ready."

He infused those words with enough innuendo that even a nun who lived in a remote Himalayan convent would've understood his meaning.

I couldn't resist glancing at his cock one last time.

"Let's go, then," I said, rolling the cart toward the door. "Can't let all those naked people starve."

He pulled the door open for me and smirked. "I'll be hungry even after lunch is served."

Once I'd wheeled the cart across the threshold, Val nudged me out of the way. "I don't think my nudity will contaminate the food when it's inside covered trays. Let me at least push the cart to the guest house door for you."

"I guess that would be okay."

While he steered the cart down the dirt path to the guest house, I granted myself permission to ogle him a bit more. His tattoos fascinated me. The black designs adorned the upper part of his chest as well as his right arm. The ones on his chest were abstract patterns, but the one on his arm represented a stylized dragon that curled around his biceps and spit black flames from its open mouth.

I let my attention wander to his ass and the way it flexed with his every step. With all those taut muscles, along with his easy sensuality and complete lack of shame, he definitely had the raw material to be a fantastic lover.

Not that I would sleep with him. Way too complicated.

We finished stocking up the buffet table while Quentin chomped on his food, watching us from a table in the back of the dining hall. He kept squinting at Val but avoided looking at me.

Just what I needed. A jealous ex-lover on the premises.

I hurried outside to ring the lunch bell. Literally. I had a big brass bell attached to the side of the guest house and rang it to alert my guests it was mealtime. A few straggled in from the direction of the hot spring, but most emerged from their rooms. I returned to the dining hall only to be waylaid by Ruth Norris.

"What a hunk," she said, nodding toward Val. "About time we got some real eye candy for the ladies."

Should a gray-haired woman with seven grandchildren be talking about eye candy? It seemed weird, but I'd gotten used to Ruth's un-grandma-like comments over the past few years.

I slipped my arm around her shoulders. "Don't tell Ollie that. He thinks he's our man candy of the month."

"That dear, sweet boy is fine looking. But he"—she rolled her eyes toward Val—"is prime, grade-A beefcake."

"Cool down, Ruth. Sylvester might hear you."

"Oh, he doesn't mind. My hubby knows I'm window shopping." She cast me an impish sideways glance. "I heard a rumor the new guest is staying in your house."

"His room got flooded by a burst pipe. He's in the spare room until Quentin gets the cleanup done."

"I see," she said with a bit too much emphasis. "At least you'll be close by to keep an eye on Mr. Tall, Dark, and Beautiful when the Kitten Brigade shows up. They'll eat that poor boy alive."

Val, done introducing himself to other guests, sauntered up to me and Ruth. "Shall we go, Eve? I'm looking forward to a private meal with my hostess."

Ruth's lips tightened in a knowing smile. "Private meal? My, Evie, I didn't realize you were expanding your services."

I stuffed my hands in my shorts pockets. "It's a special case. Val is staying in my house—by necessity, of course—and I invited him to have his meals with me."

Ruth winked at me. "I'm sure the Kitten Brigade has nothing to do with it." She caught sight of her husband, flapped her fingers at him in a mini wave, and said, "I'll leave you to your private meal. Nice to meet you, Val."

She patted Val's arm, then toddled off to join her husband.

I waved for Val to follow me out of the dining hall. We'd made our way down the long hallway and out the side door, heading toward my house, before he spoke.

"Kitten Brigade?" he asked.

"That's what the older ladies have named them. They're a group of twenty-something girls who started coming here on their spring breaks from college." I pushed open the outside door to my kitchen. "They've come here every summer for the past four years. They are, shall we say, very enthusiastic in their admiration for attractive men. The term Kitten Brigade came about because Ruth said those girls would be called cougars if they were older. Since they're young, they must be kittens. I pointed out baby cougars are called cubs, but Ruth insisted kitten was a better term."

"A cougar, meaning a woman who pursues younger men."

"Yes. But the Kitten Brigade does not discriminate based on age. They'll pounce on any man, old or young, as long as he's of legal age."

"They sound awful."

"Oh, they're not so bad. When they come here, they want to have fun. I know they all have steady jobs, though, and not as strippers. Some are in grad school studying law, anthropology, or psychology. Others are accountants, advertising copywriters, and other serious stuff."

"When will these kittens arrive?"

"Later this week."

The door clicked shut behind us, and I went to the fridge, pulling it open. "Want a sandwich?"

He moved up behind me, leaning around me to peer inside the fridge. "Let me make lunch for you. After making a meal for all those guests, you must be tired."

No, not really. Staring at his gorgeous bod kept me awake and energized.

The heat of him, so close against my backside, sent a tingly shiver through me. And God, the way he smelled. Spicy, woodsy, tempting as hell. My lids fluttered half shut as I drew in another lungful of his scent.

"Are you all right?" he asked in a sexy rumble, his lips grazing my ear.

"Mm, fine." I forced my lids to open all the way and wriggled away from him. "If you want to make lunch, be my guest."

"I am your guest." He bent to study the contents of the refrigerator. "But I'd love to feed you."

Conversation seemed like the best way to tame the desire simmering inside me or to at least distract myself from it. I perched on one of the stools on the other side of the island, my hands clasped on the wood surface. I wiggled my butt until I found a comfortable position. "May I ask you a personal question?"

"Go ahead." He smiled at me over his shoulder. "I'm not shy."

No kidding. I'd spent five years catering to the needs of people who preferred to go sans clothing, but none of them had the audacity of Val Silva.

"You live in Los Angeles, right?" I said. "But your accent, I can't quite place it."

"I've lived in Los Angeles for five years, but I'm originally from Porto Alegre, a city in southern Brazil." He grabbed packages of cheese and deli meat, tossing them onto the island. "I've spent a lot of time in America. When I was fifteen, my father was appointed the Brazilian ambassador to the US. We lived in Washington, DC, for three years. After that, I went to Harvard."

"The university?"

"Yes." He tossed a package of bacon onto the island, peeking at me over his shoulder. "Is there another kind of Harvard?"

"No, I guess not." Why had I asked such a dumb question? *Jeez, Evie, get a grip.* "What do you do for a living? Are you a lawyer? I only ask because you seem smart and well-off."

He turned toward me and set down the condiments he held in both hands. Head tipped to the side, he observed me like I was a confusing creature. "You honestly have no idea who I am, do you?"

"You're Val Silva." I folded my arms on the island. "Are you from a super-rich family or something?"

"No," he said slowly. "I was a football player—soccer to Americans—for years until an injury forced me to retire. Now, I take modeling jobs when I feel like it."

"When you feel like it? Guess you made a good living at soccer." I ran my gaze over his muscular, tattooed chest. "You probably get paid a lot for modeling, with a body like yours."

He chuckled. "Thank you for the compliment, but that's not why I get high-paying modeling jobs."

"Why, then?" Realizing I was being kind of rude, I held up a hand. "Sorry, never mind. It's not my business, unless you want to tell me. I swear I'm not normally this nosy."

"I don't mind your questions." He bowed his head, focused on sorting the items he'd procured from the fridge. "Most people don't need to ask questions. They know all about me before they ever lay eyes on me."

"Are you famous?"

He set his hands on the island, leaning into them, and lifted his head to look at me. "Infamous is more accurate."

The house phone rang.

Damn, I wanted to know why Val was infamous, but I couldn't ignore the phone. My guests only called when there was an urgent issue.

"Hold that thought," I said and rushed to grab the phone off the wall. "Hello."

"You forgot dessert," Quentin said. "The guests are not happy."

"Oh. Sorry. I'll bring it over right away."

"Not like you to forget anything."

"I'll bring the desserts," I snapped. "Get back to work on the burst pipe."

"Plumber can't get here until tomorrow."

"Fine, whatever. Goodbye."

I hung up, oddly flustered by my phone call with Quentin. He had interrupted my conversation with Val, and I was annoyed. Why? Val was just another guest, one I would not sleep with ever, under any circumstances. Been there, done that, had the mental bruises to prove it. My mistake with Quentin last year had done damage I hadn't realized until today.

Until Val Silva showed up.

My gaze flicked to him. "I forgot to take the desserts over to the guest house. Gotta do that now, sorry."

"I'll help."

"That's okay, I can manage. The desserts are in the guest house fridge, which is always locked. I have the only key."

And I needed a little break from being alone with a nude, intensely hot man.

I left Val alone in my kitchen and jogged over to the guest house.

Chapter Four

Val

Eve came back a little while later but insisted she had work to do in her office, which was in the guest house. She grabbed the lunch I'd made for her and took off again, though not before encouraging me to go out and mingle with the other guests.

I wanted to mingle with her. Alone. All day and all night.

She really had no idea who I was or what I'd done. I had no shame about any of it, but I always ran the risk new people wouldn't appreciate my infamous past. Maybe my football career alone wouldn't have made me a celebrity, but my affair with a movie star certainly had. Our scandalous public behavior had made us a favorite of the tabloids. I'd assumed Eve was flustered around me because she knew about my indiscretions. Everyone with an internet connection seemed to know.

Eve didn't.

I ate my lunch alone before wandering over to the guest house.

A cheerful older woman with gray hair rushed up to me the instant I walked into the dining hall. The other guests seemed to be finishing up their dessert.

The woman, whom I'd seen with Eve earlier, seized my hand with both of hers. "We weren't properly introduced before. I'm Ruth Norris. It's so nice to meet you, Val. Eve told me absolutely nothing about you except your name."

Because Eve knew next to nothing about me.

I smiled. "It's a pleasure to meet you, Ruth. Thank you for the warm welcome."

"Let me introduce you to everybody."

"No need. I met them earlier."

"But you didn't get the Ruth Norris special introduction." She leaned in and whispered, "I saved you dessert, but Sylvester had to stash it in our room so these chow hounds wouldn't gobble it up. I'll get it for you after the introductions."

"Thank you, but there's no need to go to any trouble."

"It's no trouble, dear." She patted my cheek.

Ruth shepherded me around the room, presenting me to every one of Eve's guests. They all had nothing but praise for their hostess, though some of them commented that she needed a "good man" in her life. Ruth stated outright she thought I was that man.

I wanted to fuck Eve, but a relationship could never work. She didn't belong in my world any more than I belonged in hers. For a week or two, yes. For life? No. Besides, according to all my new friends, Eve did not date.

Ollie Jackson, the youngest guest in residence here, kept staring at me, though not with jealousy. He seemed confused. When Ruth introduced us, Ollie pushed up his glasses and said, "Have we met before? You seem familiar."

"I don't think we've met, but I do run into a lot of people when I'm working."

"What do you do?"

Ruth gave Ollie's arm a casual slap. "Don't interrogate the boy. Let's not scare him off on his first day."

I thanked heaven for Ruth's interruption. Ollie's question didn't upset me, but I preferred to avoid answering. This vacation was supposed to be an escape from my life and sharing too much would ruin that. But if I were completely honest with myself, I didn't want to talk about my life because I didn't want Eve to know about my escapades.

What did it matter? I planned to have sex with her, as many times as possible, but I did not want a relationship.

Ollie scratched his head, ruffling his curly blond hair. "I'm sure I've seen you somewhere."

I cleared my throat and changed the subject, not so deftly. "Eve has had no boyfriends since you've known her?"

Ruth chortled and squeezed my shoulder. "Don't worry, sweetie, she's free."

Ollie contorted his lips. "Well, it's not entirely accurate to say Eve's had no boyfriends. There was that thing with Cody and Aaron two summers ago."

A threesome? Eve? She didn't seem like the type, so that must not have been what Ollie meant.

Luckily, he explained. "See, Eve had a thing with Cody in the spring, but that ended. Then, when Cody and Aaron were both here for the summer, she had a thing with Aaron. Cody got righteously ticked about that." Ollie gestured with his hands to emphasize his words. "He kind of assumed Eve was, like, his girl and nobody else's. She'd told him it was totally and forever done with, but the guy did not want to give up."

"Cut to the chase, dear," Ruth said. "You're boring Val."

"Not at all," I said. "What happened, Ollie?"

"Well…" Ollie leaned closer, his voice dropping to a whisper. "Cody started pushing Aaron around. You know, physically pushing him. They yelled and stuff. But finally, Aaron had enough, and he slugged Cody." Ollie held up two fingers. "Twice. That dude had a black eye and could hardly chew for a week."

Ruth tsked. "Ollie is exaggerating. The black eye is true, but Cody had no trouble chewing."

"Tell me, Ollie," I said, "what did Eve think of all that?"

He scrunched his face and puckered his lips in a silent *oooh*. "She was royally pissed. Told both of them to take a hike. She even banned them from the resort for life."

A man with salt-and-pepper hair, whom I'd met but whose name I'd forgotten, jumped up and waved his arms. "It's nature hike time!"

He spun toward the dining hall doorway. Everyone else looked in that direction too.

Eve stood there with an enormous backpack slung over one shoulder. She'd switched her sneakers for hiking boots. "That's right. I've got the bug spray and sunscreen, plus bottled water. Are you guys ready to go?"

Her guests nodded. Some shouted, "Yes!"

"We're heading to the lake, so grab a quick shower first. Don't want to spread any germs, do we?"

"Evie's a germophobe," Ollie quipped, grinning at our hostess.

"Ha-ha. It's resort policy, as everyone knows, and good hygiene. Let's meet up outside."

Guests started to move toward the door.

"Remember the shoes, people!" Ollie shouted. "You want blisters? I sure don't. And does anybody remember the Great Barefoot Disaster of last summer?"

The entire group hurried past Eve, headed for their rooms to retrieve their shoes, leaving me alone with our hostess.

"Do you want shoes?" she asked.

"It's probably a wise choice. Mine are in your house."

She turned and waved for me to follow. "Let's go get them. We'll meet the gang outside."

While we walked back to Eve's house, I asked, "What was the Great Barefoot Disaster?"

"Last summer, the Kitten Brigade decided to go barefoot on a nature hike." Eve winced. "They didn't see the ant colony until it was too late. Velvety tree ants were nesting under a rock. One of the girls tripped over it. Those ants bite if you disturb their nest."

I grimaced. "That must have been unpleasant."

"Since then, nobody goes into the woods without shoes."

Once I'd rinsed off in the shower and put my shoes on, Eve and I met up with the others in the area between the guest house and Eve's home.

"Everyone all sprayed up and sunscreened?" Eve asked.

The group nodded.

"I've got extra if you need it," she said. "Aloe and antihistamine spray too, just in case."

"You're a worrier," I said.

"I've been hosting nudists for five years. It's experience, not worrying."

Eve led us past the miniten net and down a trail into the woods. I took the backpack from her, despite her eye roll when I did it. We ambled down the trail with Eve pointing out various flowers and bushes, explaining what they were and how they fit into the ecosystem. She pointed out birds too, as well as smaller creatures on the ground. I couldn't focus on anything she said. The sight of her round ass moving, stretching her shorts with every sway of her hips, distracted me.

I had to keep imagining ants attacking my dick to prevent a hard-on.

Fifteen minutes later, we reached a small lake. Eve instructed me and Ollie to set out the picnic blankets she'd somehow stuffed into her backpack along with everything else. She unpacked bottles of water and a plastic box filled with single-serve bags of potato chips and tiny pink cakes nestled in a smaller plastic box with wax paper separating them.

She'd brought a snack for us. The woman thought of everything.

After lunch, the group took a swim. Well, everyone except Eve. She waded into the cool water up to her knees but stepped no farther.

"What's the matter, Evie?" Ollie asked. "Did you see *Jaws* one too many times?"

She smiled and shook her head. "There are no great white sharks in this lake."

Ollie splashed her, making Eve laugh. The water soaked her shirt, and her taut nipples became visible through her bra.

I had to stay in the water several minutes after everyone else retreated onto the shore. Eve's wet T-shirt had left me in a state that wasn't suitable for mixed company.

While we ate dessert, Ollie told me his version of why Eve didn't date. "I think she got sick of guys fighting over her. I mean, every hetero dude who comes here wants to crawl inside Evie's pants and make a home there."

"Every man?" I tipped my head to indicate Ruth's husband, Sylvester.

Ollie snickered. "Every dude who's not married or on social security. Then again, maybe Sly does secretly want to get up in Evie's shorts."

"Does everyone call her Evie?"

"No, man, only special peeps." He hooked a thumb toward Ruth and Sylvester. "Me and the old farts have been coming here for years."

I didn't normally ask strangers personal questions, but Ollie seemed comfortable with me, and my curiosity prodded me to ask. "Have you and Eve…"

"Done the deed? No, dude, we're just friends."

"Are you gay? It doesn't matter to me, but I wondered, since you said every straight man who comes here wants her."

"Not me. I like girls, but not older women."

"How old are you?"

Ollie shoved half of a little cake into his mouth and chewed it up before answering. "I'm twenty-four. Been coming here since I was twenty." He gave me a knowing smile. "Eve's thirty, since you're dying to know."

Maybe I was dying to know everything about her, and maybe that contradicted the idea of a fling. My curiosity didn't care about that. It pushed me to find out more but asking Ollie to tell me those things was not the way to go. I wanted in her shorts as much as anyone, but I didn't need to know all about her unless she chose to tell me.

After the nature hike, the group split up and spread out. Some went inside to play board games while others opted for sunbathing. Ollie offered to help Quentin with the repairs to the water-damaged room. Despite his every attempt to talk the boy out of it, Quentin wound up letting Ollie be his assistant. I didn't want to think about what disasters might befall a nudist who engaged in home repairs.

I participated in one game of hearts before I abandoned the card table to find Eve.

The door to her office on the second floor hung open. She was concentrating on her computer screen, one hand poised over the mouse.

Pausing in the doorway, I drank in the sight of her shapely legs and those lush breasts I longed to taste.

She noticed me and smiled. "Come on in."

I sat down in the chair beside her desk, resting an arm on the desktop.

"Bored with hearts?" she asked, her gaze returning to the screen.

"Card games have never appealed to me."

"Mm-hmm," she said absently as she moved her mouse around and clicked it twice.

"Take a break, Eve. Come to the hot spring with me."

"I don't swim with guests." She moved and clicked the mouse, moved and clicked, moved and clicked. Her eyes darted but stayed focused on the screen. "Maybe Ollie will go with you."

"He's entertaining, but I'd rather spend time with you."

"Too busy." She typed on her keyboard, her fingers clacking the keys in rapid motions. "Maybe later."

She was paying minimal attention to me, and that had to change.

I propped my ankle on my knee. "May I call you Evie?"

"Uh-huh."

"All right, Evie. I wanted to fuck you in the hot spring, but since you won't stop working, this desk will do."

She froze. Though her head did not move, her eyes swiveled toward me. "What did you say?"

"I want to fuck you, *linda*. Right now."

Chapter Five

Eve

T hat's what I thought you said." I slumped back in my chair, considering the man who'd announced in a matter-of-fact tone that he wanted to fuck me on my desk. "You weren't kidding about being shameless. And you seem to have confused me with someone else because my name is Eve, not Linda."

"*Linda* means beautiful in Portuguese. You are beautiful, Eve, and we need to fuck."

"Sorry, but I don't sleep with guests anymore. It's way too complicated."

"Because two men once fought over you."

"Who told you about that? It must've been Ollie or Ruth." I shook my head, trying to frown but not pulling it off. I couldn't really be mad at them. They meddled out of love. "I knew I should've had them sign a nondisclosure agreement."

"Ruth thinks we're a cute couple." He held up a hand the second I opened my mouth to speak. "Not that I agree with her. I'm not interested in a relationship, and if we have sex, I won't get into a fist fight over you."

"That incident was the last straw, yes, but I'd already started to think getting involved with guests was a bad idea, business-wise."

He rested his arm on the corner of my desk. "I've been told you don't date either."

"Who said that?"

"Your guests."

Ruth and Ollie, no doubt, blabbing again about my personal life. I appreciated their concern for my happiness, but it was misplaced.

"Were they mistaken?" Val asked.

"No, but not dating isn't a conscious choice. I live way out here and always have guests to take care of, even in the winter. Hunting for men isn't a priority." I picked up a pen and braced it between the index fingers of both hands, my elbows on my chair's arms. "I tried online dating, but men are such cowards these days. They only wanted to talk to me through what they saw as anonymous messages on the dating sites."

"What about the town near here?"

"I go into town to buy supplies, not troll for dates." I toyed with the pen, lifting one end and then the other repeatedly. "Besides, guys who aren't perverts or losers are like Bigfoot. Even if they exist, you're never going to catch one."

Val drummed his fingers on the desk, studying me with a curious expression. "Relax, Eve. I don't want to date you."

"You want sex. Yeah, I caught your drift earlier." I tossed the pen onto the desk. "Why did you say you're infamous?"

"Because it's true. Haven't you looked me up online yet?"

"I don't invade the privacy of my guests."

"Anything that's online isn't private."

"Most of it should be. The world really doesn't need to know what everyone ate for lunch today, with close-up pictures of the food."

"True." He studied me again, studied my face. "A young, beautiful woman like you should have a lover."

"And you're volunteering for that job? Thanks, but I'm good the way I am." I rocked my chair, clasping my hands over my belly. "I'm not that young anymore."

"You're thirty. Ollie told me. That is young."

"So you've been quizzing my guests about me, eh?" I smirked. "In that case, how old are you?"

"Thirty-seven." He leaned forward. "I know you want me, I can see it when you look at me. I want you too, and there's no reason why we shouldn't act on our mutual desire."

"I've known you for a few hours."

He shrugged one shoulder. "You know what I look like naked. What more information do you need?"

"Maybe we won't even like having sex with each other."

Val chuckled. "I've never had a complaint."

Yeah, I had no trouble believing that. His body seemed to have been designed by Aphrodite herself to be the perfect sex machine.

Still, I shook my head. "I don't sleep with guests."

"But you do sleep with your employees."

"What? Why would you think that?"

"It's obvious from Quentin's jealousy and the way he glares at me."

I was pretty sure my entire face scrunched up for half a second. "Okay, yeah, I did sleep with him last year. It was a mistake."

"Do you mind if I ask why you did it? Was it one time or an ongoing affair?"

"Nosy, aren't you?" I grabbed the polished rock that served as a paperweight on my desk and rolled it in my hand. What the hell. I might as well tell him. "It was once. I'd had one too many margaritas on Mexican Monday."

"Was he drunk too?"

"I wasn't drunk. A little tipsy, that's all." I wrapped my fist around the paperweight. "But no, he didn't drink that night."

A muscle ticked in Val's jaw. He hissed a breath out his nostrils. "He took advantage of you."

"No, I make my own decisions."

"You'd been drinking. He hadn't. The bastard should never have seduced you." Val's lips compressed into a line. "I hate men who take advantage of women."

"Chill out. It wasn't like that." When his lips flattened again, I added, "I take responsibility for all my decisions, good and bad. If it doesn't bother me, it shouldn't bother you either. And for all you know, I'm a slut who throws herself at every man she meets."

His mouth relaxed, and his jaw stopped ticking. "All right, it's none of my business. I'm sorry for getting upset about it. Growing up with sisters has made me overly protective of women in general."

"That's not a bad thing. It's sweet."

He ran a hand through his hair, leaning back in his chair. "Let's talk about something fun, like when you're going to strip for me."

A poorly stifled laugh snorted out of me. "Whoa there, cowboy. I don't sleep with guests, remember?"

"I'll be the exception."

He rose from the chair with panther-like grace, unfurling his nude body with a languor that I felt sure was purposeful. He wanted me to get a spectacular view of every inch of his skin, from those tattoos all the way down to his impressive dick, and farther down to his powerful thighs. The man had a mouthwatering body, for sure. And no shortage of confidence either.

Everything about him was sexy as hell.

Maybe I should break my rule this one time. With him. In my bed. For hours and hours and hours.

Slickness blossomed between my thighs.

He moved closer, placed one hand on the arm of my chair, and bent to aim those heated brown eyes straight into mine. His breaths tickled my skin. "I don't want to date you. I won't be jealous when we say goodbye and you find someone else to warm your bed. Relationships aren't in my wheelhouse. But I'm staying for two weeks, and I'd love to enjoy you while I'm here."

"Sounds like you don't care if I enjoy you."

"That's a given." He licked his lips. "You want to touch me, don't you?" With his free hand, he picked up one of mine and guided it to within inches of his cock. "I want you to do it."

He let go of my hand, leaving the decision up to me.

I closed my fingers around his cock. It was hot and firm, thickening in my hand.

Val took a slow, deep breath, his eyes going hooded. "*Te quero*, Eve, and when I'm inside you, I guarantee you won't be thinking about anyone or anything else. You won't be thinking at all." He covered my hand with his, pressing my skin more firmly to his erection. "In case you had any doubts, *te quero* means I want you."

He let go of my hand.

I held his cock for a moment longer, reluctant to give up the feel of his inflamed flesh. We stared into each other's eyes, my breaths growing heavier while desire tingled through my sex and tightened my breasts. When I finally withdrew my hand, I couldn't help myself. I thrust that hand into his hair and tugged him in for a kiss.

Our lips touched, gently at first, then with more and more pressure until our mouths were fused. I opened for him, and he plunged his tongue inside my mouth, sliding it over mine, teasing the roof of my mouth, consuming me while I consumed him, the flavor of his mouth electrifying me while the warmth of his lips seemed to blossom outward into my whole body. He tasted so good, like exotic things I couldn't describe but that I longed to savor for the rest of eternity. The delicious warmth engendered by our lip-lock suffused every part of me and penetrated deep into the core of my sex.

God, the man could kiss. I clenched my fingers in his hair, loving the silky texture of those wavy locks. He plowed deeper, coiling his tongue around mine, and groaned with intense pleasure.

Despite the fact I was sitting down, my knees got weak. My ears rang, and I realized I'd stopped breathing.

Someone knocked on the door.

Val jerked away from me, still bent over my chair, and glanced over his shoulder at the open doorway.

Quentin, his fist on the jamb, scowled at Val before looking at me. "Need to talk to you about the repairs in the damaged room."

He spoke through clenched teeth.

I wondered how long Quentin had been standing there, how long he'd watched me and Val together. The door had been open, but both Val and I had our eyes closed until Quentin knocked. Would he have spied on us? Yesterday, I would've said no without hesitation. Today, after witnessing Quentin's jealousy, I wasn't so sure. I didn't want to believe it.

No, he wouldn't do that.

Val straightened but did not turn toward my handyman, probably because his dick was at half-staff.

Pushing my chair back, I got up. To Quentin, I said, "I'll meet you in the room in a minute."

Quentin's lips twisted into an annoyed slant, but he stalked off down the hall.

I smoothed my shirt, like it mattered if my tank top got wrinkled. "I don't sleep with guests, Val. That's my final word on the matter."

I moved to the door but paused on the threshold when he spoke.

"You say that now," he said, "but a second ago you would've let me do anything to you. If your handyman hadn't interrupted us, I'd be fucking you on your desk."

He was right, but I wouldn't tell him that.

Instead, I walked out of the room.

My phone chimed, indicating a new text message, while I was trudging down the stairs to the first floor. Sheesh, I needed to install an elevator. Going up and down the stairs multiple times per day got exhausting. I stopped halfway down the stairs and dug my phone out of my pocket to check the new text. It was from my mother.

You OK? she asked.

I typed my response: *Yes. Why?*
No call last week.
Busy, not dead.
Not like you to stop calling.

I really had been busy, even before the pipe burst in the guest house. Doing everything myself, except for the handyman work, required a lot of time. I typed on my phone's screen. *I'm fine, gotta go, will call later.*

Maybe we need to come for a visit, Mom replied, *to check on you.*

Oh no, absolutely nooooooo way. Sure, my family knew I owned a nudist resort and had no problem with that. But the last thing I needed was my parents meeting Val and seeing how much I lusted after him. I was sure I failed miserably at hiding it. I cherished my privacy, and unlike Val, I wasn't shameless.

Part of me envied his total disregard for what others thought of him.

No visit necessary, I typed to my mom. *All fine, talk to you soon.*

Mom at last said goodbye, and I stuffed the phone in my pocket.

I glanced up the stairs, but I couldn't see Val or the door to my office.

That kiss. His lips on mine had sparked something deep inside me, a kind of hunger I'd never known with any other man. I craved him. When he'd announced he wanted to fuck me, I'd gone instantly wet.

My original assessment had been right. That man was sexy, flirty, down-and-dirty trouble.

Stay away, Eve, keep your hands and mouth off him. I could do that. No problem.

As I trudged down the stairs, my mind replayed the sensations of our kiss.

Not sleeping with him. No way.

Who was I trying to convince?

Chapter Six

Val

Eve had disappeared by the time I walked out of her office. I'd needed a few minutes to recover from our kiss, from the lust that had gripped me when our lips met and I tasted her mouth for the first time. Her lips were soft and flavored with a hint of peppermint, but her lip balm hadn't been the taste that left me halfway to hard and craving more of her. Eve's natural flavor intoxicated me.

When I was finally suitable for public viewing, I ambled outside and glanced at the lawn. The miniten net had been removed. Several guests were laying out yoga mats on the mowed grass while Ollie took up a position in front of the group as if he planned to lead the session.

He spotted me and waved. "Come join us, Val. You do yoga, don't you?"

"Yes, and I'd love to join in."

Maybe a good session of downward dogs would distract me from thoughts of Eve's lips and her luscious body. I loved fantasizing about her, but getting a hard-on wasn't conducive to socializing with the other guests.

"I don't have a mat," I shouted to Ollie.

"No problem. You can get one in the exercise room. We'll wait for you."

Nodding, I trotted back into the guest house and down the hall to the exercise room I'd spotted earlier. Yoga mats, rolled up and sealed with shrink wrap, were stacked inside a large wooden box. A sign on the box said, "New yoga mats. Write your name on the sheet and $10 will be added to your bill. The mat is yours to keep." Eve took every precaution to keep things sanitary and convenient for her guests. I admired that about her. Eve was beautiful, yes, but also smart and capable.

The sheet in question was hooked onto a clipboard that dangled from a chain attached to the wall. I scrawled my name on the sheet and took a mat, peeling the wrapping off and dropping the plastic into a trash can on my way out. Ollie and the rest of the yoga fans had already laid out their mats by the time I got back to the lawn. I spread mine out.

"We'll start with a warm-up," Ollie said.

"No glasses?" I said. "Don't trip over your mat, Ollie."

He rolled his eyes. "I'm not that nearsighted. Now, everybody assume mountain pose. Feet spread to hip width. Let your mind go and really feel your feet. Stretch your toes up and then relax them down again."

I followed Ollie's instructions without thinking about it, my mind wandering to other thoughts. Eve. Her lips. Her scent. Her flavor. The faint pinkness of her cheeks after our kiss. I wanted to do more than feel her soft lips on mine. I wanted all of her, naked and wet and—

Fuck. I had to stop imagining all the things I wanted to do to her, or this would turn into porn yoga.

With a great effort of will, I concentrated on Ollie's instructions and on attaining a relaxed and thought-free state of mind. Ollie might've been young, but he led our yoga session with all the composure and patience of someone much older. By the time we got to the headstand pose, I'd stopped thinking at all. Serenity took over, and I let myself enjoy the sounds of nature around us—the singing of birds, the whisper of the breeze fluttering through the trees, the gentle intonations of our teacher.

I was vertical and upside down when I noticed Eve hovering at the lawn's edge.

She watched me, her head tilted to the side, her lips curved in a slight smile.

Only a few of us had attempted the headstand pose since it was an advanced move. Maybe I wanted to show off for Eve, because I found myself lifting one hand to wave at her. Held up by one arm, I began to teeter just a little.

Eve's eyes widened. Her mouth fell open.

I dropped my hand back onto the mat before I tumbled over, an outcome that wouldn't impress Eve and certainly wouldn't make her want to crawl into bed with me. Still, I was never above showing off to impress a woman.

"Okay," Ollie said, his voice a bit strained from holding his headstand, "time to ease out of it."

Moving slowly, I bent my knees and pulled them down toward my chest, then lowered my toes to the mat and rolled into a kneeling position.

Eve clapped and grinned.

She definitely looked impressed.

I waved to her again and probably smirked, though I resisted the urge to run over there, throw her over my shoulder, and cart her off to the nearest private spot, indoors or out.

The second Ollie announced the session was over and thanked us for attending, I sauntered across the grass to Eve.

"Wow," she said, "you've got the strength of a superhero."

Her compliment made me smirk again. "I appreciate the comparison, but I can't lift a building with my bare hands."

"I'm thinking you could if you really wanted to." She stretched out a hand to fondle my biceps. "You've got some powerful muscles."

Her voice had turned huskier, infused with sensuality.

Mission accomplished. I'd impressed Eve.

"Hey, Val!" Ollie called out.

Eve's hand lingered on my arm, but I tore my gaze away from her to glance back at Ollie.

"Forgot your mat," he shouted, pointing at the one I'd abandoned.

"Sorry, I'll get it." I asked Eve, "When will I see you again?"

"Dinner, probably. I've got work to do, and I need to get back to the drowned guest room. Had to get a tape measure from the house for Quentin."

That's when I noticed the tape measure she held cupped in one hand, almost hidden inside her curled fingers.

"Do you practice yoga?" I asked.

"Yes, but not in public." She gave my biceps a squeeze, her gaze trained on my arm. Her tongue slipped out to moisten her lips. "And not in the nude."

"We should have a private session, just the two of us. I can help you master the one-handed headstand."

She pulled her hand away from my arm and met my gaze. "I'll see you later, Val. Have fun with the other guests."

I enjoyed the view from behind as she sashayed toward the guest house door.

After rolling up my yoga mat, I headed into Eve's house and down the hall to my room. I checked my phone for messages, discovering I had one voicemail from Wendy Yu. I groaned. The last thing I wanted to do on my vacation was talk to my agent, but I never ignored phone calls, emails, or texts.

I dialed Wendy's number.

"Val," she said in her usual cheerful tone, "so glad you called me back. We've got an offer for a magazine spread."

"Not interested."

"The shoot isn't for six weeks. Plenty of time for you to finish your secret sabbatical and come home."

Was LA home? It had been for years, but lately, I'd started to wonder.

"Still not interested," I said. "Turn down all offers until I tell you otherwise."

"At least tell me where you are."

If I did that, Wendy would make sure a gang of paparazzi descended on the resort within twenty-four hours. My agent had done wonders for my career when I'd switched from football to modeling, but I wasn't sure I wanted that life anymore. When I'd mentioned my doubts to Wendy, she had told me to "have a vacay, bang someone, and get over it."

"Please respect my privacy," I told her. "And give me time."

"Just tell me it's not someplace trendy like Ibiza. You have an image to uphold."

"No jobs, Wendy. Understand?"

She sighed loudly. "Fine. But if your sabbatical takes too long, your career might dry up."

I wasn't sure I cared if it did. "Goodbye, Wendy."

Before she could complain, I disconnected the call.

How had I gone from Olympic glory to preening for the camera? I used to enjoy modeling, but these days, I wanted…something else. Something more. What that meant, I still hadn't figured out.

For now, I'd settle for getting Eve Holt in my bed. Or in the grass. Or in the hot spring. Anywhere and everywhere I could have her, I would have her.

The rest I'd think about later.

Chapter Seven

Eve

After discussing the necessary repairs with Quentin and authorizing him to proceed, I returned to my office to finish my boring business tasks. That's what I intended to do. But my mind kept flashing back to that kiss, to the feel of Val's lips on mine and his tongue tormenting me. I couldn't deny he'd been right when he said I would've let him do anything to me if Quentin hadn't interrupted us. I thanked heaven he had, but I also cursed the fates for getting in the way.

It was for the best. I should not sleep with Val. He'd admitted he was infamous, though I had no idea why. He had all but told me to look him up online.

No, I would not do that. His past didn't matter since he was nothing more than a guest.

I returned my attention to the computer screen. The numbers in my accounting software blurred. My mind reeled me back to the moment when Val's lips had touched mine. He smelled so good. He looked so good. Damn, he was sex on a stick slathered with warm caramel sauce and whipped cream. Watching him do yoga in the nude, that had transformed my desire into a living, breathing creature scrabbling to get out and have its way. I would never forget the sight of Val in a headstand pose with one hand raised to wave at me, a sexy smirk on his lips.

How could he hold that pose? The man must have supernatural powers.

My mind conjured images of all the positions he might pull off in bed and how deliciously naughty it would feel to let him fuck me. *Get a grip, Evie.*

For ten more minutes, I tried to do that. Really, I tried. My fingernails tapped on the desk instead of the keyboard, and I couldn't focus on the screen for more than two seconds.

Oh, screw it. I could check him out. He'd clearly wanted me to, and Googling him did not mean I would crawl into his bed in the middle of the night.

I opened my web browser and searched for Val Silva. A bunch of results popped up, including several women with the same name, but the top five results were all about my Val Silva.

Not mine. My guest.

The titles of the web pages listed in the results solved the mystery of his infamy. "International soccer star shucks his clothes to celebrate winning game," said an American newspaper. A sports website stated, "Former Olympic football champ Val Silva bares all on the field to celebrate World Cup win." Browsing the articles, I learned Val hadn't received any severe punishment for his antics, since both times he'd stripped after the final whistle and not during the game. The first time, he'd received a warning. The second time, he'd been fined and suspended for one game as well getting arrested, though his influential father got him out of jail with no charges filed.

It was the fifth search result that stopped me.

The article came from a gossip website. The headline read, "Silva-Taylor sex tape: Football champion Val Silva and Hollywood star Marina Taylor caught with their pants down, again."

My mouse pointer hovered over the link to the full story. I shouldn't click the link. No, I really, really, really shouldn't.

I clicked the link, wincing at my inappropriate curiosity. Was it inappropriate? He'd sort of suggested I look up his infamous behavior. He must want me to see the tape.

The article talked about Val's history of stripping down during football matches, usually after he'd scored the winning goal. I skimmed through the description of his athletic achievements, including the fact he'd led the Brazilian Olympic team to a gold medal and had been the star player of his professional football club. Later, he'd been instrumental in his national team claiming three World Cup wins. Every time, Val had scored the pivotal goals.

Then I got to the part about the video.

All I saw was a still image from the video with all the sensitive bits blurred out. Val sat in a chair with a woman straddling him. Her head was thrown back, and his eyes were closed. According to the text, the sex tape went on for fifteen minutes, with Val enjoying his lady friend in various positions and giving her several "happy endings." His video sex partner was the movie star Marina Taylor, according to the article, though I'd never heard of her, since I paid little attention to celebrities. The story went on to explain Marina had become as infamous as Val was for her scandalously risqué behavior in public, and the two of them had even received their own celebrity couple nickname, Valarina. The couple had also sprinted across the stage—naked, of course—at the Oscars, but nobody bothered to press charges for the incident. It was Hollywood, after all, the land of outrageous behavior. Marina was quoted as saying, of their sex tape, "Val and I have nothing to be ashamed of. He's a god in bed, and I'm blessed to have enjoyed the pleasure of his company."

His company? She'd been lost in ecstasy in the image from the video.

Val had given no comment on the tape.

The fact I'd never heard of any of their escapades was hardly surprising. I avoided social media, tabloids, and gossip shows.

I browsed a bit more of the search results and glanced at magazine spreads he'd posed for since retiring from football. Damn, but he was photogenic. Not that the fact surprised me. In person, he was drop-dead hot and sex incarnate. In photos, he made every other male model look like an amateur. I searched for his sex tape too but couldn't find it.

Okay, enough snooping. I closed my web browser. Now I knew why Val had said he was infamous. He had flaunted his nudism in public and starred in a sex tape with a famous actress. Mystery solved.

Again, I tried to get back to work.

My mind wouldn't let me. I fantasized about being the woman in that video, about all the things he might do to give me multiple happy endings.

I gave up and went outside to check on my guests.

Ollie and Sylvester were playing checkers, their board lying on the grass though they sat on towels, while behind them, other guests played volleyball. Ruth sat beside Sylvester, observing the checkers game.

When Ollie spotted me, he patted the grass beside him. "Sit down, Evie. Take a load off."

I accepted his invitation. For the better part of an hour, I watched Ollie and Sly shifting the red and black disks around the playing board, each of them winning several games. We all joked and laughed and talked about what to do tomorrow. The Pioneer Days festival was up and running, so we decided that might be a nice change of pace. Yes, the nudists would need to wear clothes, but they were cool with that. The rest of the gang agreed it sounded like a fun outing.

Eventually, Val came up the path from the woods, alone. He smiled at me, then joined the volleyball game.

I tried soooo hard not to stare at his penis, the way it bounced whenever he jumped up to hit the ball. Really, I tried. But every girl has her limits, and eventually, I allowed myself to grab the occasional glance. That man had the best ass I'd ever seen, not to mention the best dick.

After the checkers marathon ended, Ruth and Sylvester retreated into the guest house, taking the checkers board with them. Val had disappeared into the guest house with his fellow nudists.

I got up and stretched.

Ollie stood too. He twisted his lips this way and that, scratching his nose. "Do you know where Val's from?"

"He lives in Los Angeles, but he's originally from Brazil. Didn't he tell you?"

"I didn't think to ask." Ollie folded his arms over his chest. "I know I've seen him somewhere before."

"Well, he used to play professional football. His teams won the Olympics and the World Cup."

Ollie's brows cinched together, wrinkling the skin above his nose. "Football. Val Silva." His eyes widened, and he snapped his fingers. "That's it. He's the soccer player who kept ditching his clothes during games."

"That's right. I'm not sure if he wants to talk about it, though."

Ollie gave me an *oh please* look. "I'm a naturist. I know how to be discreet. But nobody should ever be ashamed of taking their clothes off."

"I think it's a crime to do it in public, at least in the US."

He flapped a hand in a dismissive gesture. "Only because the authorities have sticks up their butts."

A crunching sound drew our attention to the gravel driveway. A car emblazoned with the logo of the pizza restaurant parked alongside the guest house.

"Dinner's here," I said, and Ollie and I headed for the guest house.

I tried to grab a few slices of pizza and duck out to go eat in my own home, but Val insisted I sit beside him throughout dinner. He didn't touch me and never reached for anything. That a shameless exhibitionist like him followed the house rules surprised me, but the way he included me in every conversation made me feel oddly happy. One discussion involved everyone gushing about how amazing I was for running the resort all by myself. I smiled tightly and thanked them for their kind words. I wanted to bow my head and pull my hair over my face to hide. Their effusive praise made me uncomfortable.

During the entire meal, I resisted the frequent urge to slide my hand up Val's muscular thigh under the table. It would've been a violation of the rules, but I had a feeling he wouldn't have minded. Still, I stuck to my decorum.

By the time the pizza party ended, it was nearly ten o'clock.

When I told Val I planned to get some work done in the living room before going to bed, he shook his head and retreated into his room.

Half an hour later, I'd had enough work. My eyes were tired and gritty, so I shambled barefoot through the living room doorway into the kitchen. There, I paused to shut off the light and then made my way down the darkened hallway toward my room.

A wedge of light shined through the partly opened door to Val's room, spraying its glow across the wood floor in the hall. I did not peek through the opening when I walked past his room.

Hooray for my self-control. I almost pumped my fists in the air.

I had just pushed the door to my room open and was reaching for the light switch inside when a noise from across the hall caught my attention. A thump, that's what it had sounded like.

A long, low groan originated from Val's room.

Staring across the hall, I considered what to do. Should I go check on him? What if he'd fallen and hit his head? I couldn't have a guest dying of a cracked skull. I needed to check.

Decision made, I approached the door.

It hung open about six inches, enough to let the wedge of illumination spill out—and enough to grant me a view of him. My belly quivered, and my skin came alive with a tingling excitement that raised every hair on my arms and my nape.

Val reclined in the wooden chair by the desk completely naked, as usual, his feet on the floor and his big body slouched. He had his head thrown back, resting on the chair. His full lips were parted, his eyes closed. With one hand, he gripped the chair's arm. With his other hand…

Heat ripped through me.

With his other hand, he pumped his rigid cock in a leisurely, decadent rhythm. His chest rose and fell with his heavy breaths. Little grunts and groans escaped his lips. Every so often, he would lift his hips into the thrusts of his hand, and the chair would tip back a smidgen only to smack down again when his ass slapped onto the chair.

That explained the thump I'd heard. And the groan.

He raised his head, eyes still closed, his face tight with need.

I sidled up to the wall, hidden in the shadows but with a clear view of him. I should've walked away. Should've gone to my room and…masturbated while imagining what he was doing in his room. Shit. A good host would leave right now. Then again, he had left the door open. He must've known I would hear him. Maybe he wanted me to watch.

Or march in there and mount him.

God, I wanted to climb astride him and drive us both to screaming orgasms.

My sex had grown so wet I felt the slickness every time my legs shifted the tiniest bit. I could smell the scent of my arousal, and my clit throbbed. Oh, did it throb. I couldn't remember the last time I'd been this turned on. Maybe I never had been before.

He threw his head back once more, his mouth wide open, and hissed in a breath. He groaned it out, the sound resonating deep in his throat and chest. That hand stroked his length faster while the fingers of his other hand clenched the chair's arm harder.

I unhooked the button of my jeans and slid the zipper down inch by inch, so the sound was almost inaudible. Powerless to resist the urge, I slipped my hand inside my damp panties and stroked my mound.

His hand pumping, pumping. His rock-hard cock glistening. His palm and fingers encircling his shaft. The tip so red, begging to be sucked.

My mouth watered. I plunged a finger between my folds, rubbing my nub.

His back arched. He rocked his hips up, thrusting into his own hand, his breaths harsh and fast. The need to come wrenched his features, and as he pumped wildly, he sucked in a breath and held it.

Hunger pulsated through my clit, and holy fuck, I was on the verge of coming already. I rubbed faster, rougher, desperate to hit my release with him, but I couldn't stop it. The orgasm seized my body. I mashed my face into the wall to muffle my strangled whimpers. I squeezed my eyes shut, rubbing until I'd milked every last spasm of pleasure from my body.

I opened my eyes, still stroking myself lightly, and looked at Val.

A milky jet erupted from his cock.

He let out a hoarse cry, pumped twice more, and slumped in the chair. Sweat sheathed his tattooed arm and chest and dampened his hair. He grabbed a towel from the desk and began to wipe down his shaft.

Watching Val clean himself up after beating off, it got me all hot again. I couldn't stop myself. I ground my finger into my clit until another orgasm barreled through me, hard and fast. Flattening my back against the wall, I gritted my teeth and swallowed my own cries. Once the climax subsided, I could breathe again.

My cheeks flamed, not only from my climax. What had I done?

I tiptoed back to my bedroom and shut the door behind me. When I flopped backward onto the bed, the springs squeaked. What on earth had I been thinking? Spying on Val while he masturbated was bad enough, but I'd gotten myself off while watching him. Twice.

Damn if those hadn't been the best orgasms of my life.

I changed into my nightie and crawled under the covers. For a long time, I lay awake reliving those moments in the hallway and remembering the look on his face when he'd come. We couldn't work as a couple, I knew that much. Val and I had nothing in common. He was a celebrity with a checkered past, the kind of man who relished the spotlight and loved the big city. I liked my quiet life in rural Oregon, running my family-friendly naturist resort. Of course, he'd made it clear he didn't want a relationship with me and that he wouldn't start a brawl if another man expressed interest in me. He wanted sex, pure and simple.

Even that seemed like a bad idea. He was so…naughty. And I had a feeling if I got it on with him, one taste would never satisfy me.

No sex with Val. Decision made. He never needed to know I'd spied on him.

If I could just get my body to go along with that resolution…

Chapter Eight

Val

Eve was cooking breakfast when I walked into the kitchen the next morning. Instead of those very-short shorts and that tank top, the outfit I'd loved yesterday, she wore tight pink jeans and a loose-fitting white blouse. Her curves looked no less enticing in this outfit. She couldn't be frumpy even if she'd tried, not with that body.

"Good morning," I said, taking a seat on a stool at the island. Eve had already laid out place settings on the island, one on either side.

Across the island from me, she paused in frying up something in a skillet and glanced my way. "Good morning. Breakfast is almost ready."

"What about your guests? Don't they eat breakfast?"

"Their food is hot and waiting for them in the dining hall of the guest house."

I raised my brows. "It's seven o'clock. When did you get up?"

"Five thirty." She turned back to her cooking, stirring whatever it was with a wooden spoon. "I hope you like scrambled eggs, bacon, and pancakes."

"You didn't need to cook all of that for me. Especially not after making breakfast for sixteen other people."

"Oh, it's no trouble. I made the same thing for the other guests, so all I had to do was save a few pancakes for us. The bacon was precooked and warmed up in the microwave, so that was no trouble. I made fresh eggs, though." She smiled at me over her shoulder. "I hope you're hungry."

"*Estou verde de fome.* It smells delicious."

"Thanks, but I have no idea what that first thing meant."

"I said I'm starving." I winked. "In Portuguese."

"Wish I knew another language, but I barely passed high school Spanish."

"Maybe I'll teach you Portuguese—or Spanish, if you like. I'm fluent in both."

"Wow. I'm impressed." She shut off the stovetop burner and carried the frying pan to the island, then portioned out the eggs onto our plates. "Eat up. Can't have a guest starving on my watch."

I pointed at my plate. "You gave me more than you gave yourself."

"You're a big, strong man who can do a one-handed headstand. I assumed you'd need more protein than I do."

"That sounds rather sexist," I teased.

"I'm committing sexism against myself? Not sure how that works. If you don't want the eggs, I'll dump them down the garbage disposal."

"No, I'll eat them."

She set the frying pan in the sink.

I watched her reheat the pancakes and bacon in the microwave, though my attention frequently wandered to her ass. Her loose-fitting shirt seemed to make those perfect cheeks even more enticing.

Once she'd portioned out the rest of our meal, she perched on her own stool and picked up her fork, spearing a chunk of eggs.

"Did you sleep well last night?" I asked.

She froze with the forkful of egg poised between her open lips. Her eyes rolled up to stare at me. "Huh?"

"I asked if you slept well."

"Oh. Yes, fine." She shoved the food into her mouth and chewed it. "How about you?"

"Very well." I ate some of my food while keeping an eye on her, trying to gauge when would be the right time to bring up the subject of last night. After eating half of a pancake, I couldn't wait any longer. "Did you enjoy the show last night?"

Eve dropped her fork. It clattered onto her plate, and the chunk of pancake impaled on the tines broke in half. "Excuse me?"

"Last night. When you watched me. Did you enjoy it?"

Her eyes flew wide, and her cheeks turned slightly pink. "I—well—"

I picked up a slice of bacon and bit off a piece.

She sat up straighter, staring down at her lap, and took a deep breath that she exhaled little by little. At last, she raised her face to me. "How did you know I was there?"

"I saw you in the mirror."

"Mirror?" She winced as realization hit her. "The one on the dresser. I didn't think about that."

"That mirror was angled just right to let me see you." I bit off another piece of bacon and chewed it so I could take a moment to savor the pinkness of her cheeks and the way her breasts rose and fell. "You came, didn't you? I heard the little noises you tried to muffle by pressing your face to the wall."

To her credit, she didn't look away or try to deny it. Despite the faint blush coloring her cheeks, she stayed calm and resolute.

"Why deny it?" she said. "Yes, I came. Twice."

I couldn't help smirking. "Eve Holt won't go nude in front of her guests, but she is a voyeur."

"How is it voyeurism when you left your door open? I bet you did that on purpose, hoping I'd see you."

"Do you?" I chuckled. "All right. Yes, I did. I wanted you to see what you're missing."

She shook her head, her lips stretching into a closed-mouth smile. "I'd already seen that. I Googled you yesterday. Unfortunately, I couldn't watch your sex tape since I found only a still photo from it."

"The leaked video was taken down by the site where the thief uploaded it. At least half the world had already seen it by then." I dipped my finger into the syrup on my plate and thrust it into my mouth, drawing my finger out slowly, loving the way Eve's breath caught when I licked it and sucked the tip. Maybe she guessed that I was imagining doing the same thing to her. "I have the original on my phone if you'd like to see it. Marina and I recorded it on my phone, and I didn't bother to delete it. I never imagined my assistant would leak the tape. After that, everybody had seen it anyway."

"Did you watch your own video last night? Is that why you were jerking off?"

"No, I was fantasizing about you." I reached across the island to rub my thumb over her lips. "You can kiss me again anytime you want, anywhere you want. And I don't mean you can do it in the kitchen or in the bathroom. I mean anywhere on my body."

As her gaze traveled over me, the parts she could see above the island, the stiff peaks of her nipples jutted against her shirt. When her eyes met mine again, her pupils had enlarged.

I swirled my fingertip in the syrup on my plate, keeping my gaze nailed to hers. "How hard did you come for me last night?"

She touched the fingers of one hand to her throat, grazing them down to her collarbone. When she spoke, her voice had gone sultry. "Those were the best orgasms I've ever had."

"It'll be better when I'm inside you."

We studied each other for a moment, her lips parted and her cheeks rosy, while my cock stiffened. I had to have her soon or I'd go insane. Never in my life had I hungered for a woman the way I hungered for Eve Holt. Our kiss yesterday had only heightened my lust for her.

She cleared her throat, wriggled on her seat, and set her hands on her lap. "No, Val, I will not be kissing you again. I won't sleep with you either."

"Don't want to sleep, Eve."

"I'm not getting involved with you in any way." She shoved a piece of pancake into her mouth and devoured it, her throat muscles working as she swallowed. "I like my simple life out here in the woods. Nothing and no one is going to derail that." She stabbed her fork into her pancake. "You are trouble, Mr. Silva. You strip naked in public and save your sex tapes on your phone. I wouldn't be surprised if you leaked that tape yourself."

I licked the syrup off my finger and leaned into the back of my stool. "My personal assistant leaked the sex tape. The second I found out, I fired him. I'm not ashamed of what the world saw, but I can't have an assistant who betrays me for money. As for stripping in public, those were publicity stunts. I knew my football career wouldn't last much longer, and I wanted to see what kind of offers I'd get if I did something outrageous to make myself more of a celebrity."

"What offers did you get? Starring roles in porn movies?"

"Some of those, yes, but I turned them down. The offers I liked the best were for modeling work, so I accepted a lot of those."

She leaned back too, eying me with a renewed interest. "I saw a few of the spreads you did for magazines. You look good in print."

I raised a brow. "But not in person?"

"You know the answer to that."

"Mm, yes." I couldn't help smiling. "I gave you the best orgasm of your life without laying a finger, or a tongue, on you. Imagine what I can do when I'm touching your body."

"As intriguing as that sounds, the answer is still no. We are not getting involved."

"I don't want to date you, *linda*. I want to have sex with you."

She hopped off her stool. "And I told you no. You are the hottest mess I've ever seen, and I don't need the complications. A notorious athlete turned model who likes to strip in public and who starred in a sex tape. No thank you, Val."

"Not interested in complications. Just sex, nothing else."

"Uh-huh." She carried her plate to the sink. "I've heard that before. Quentin swore sex wouldn't change anything and we could go back to being just friends after. Instead, he's jealous of you even though I haven't slept with you yet. The last thing I need is you getting jealous of every man who speaks to me."

"I'm not the jealous type."

"Heard that before too." She turned around and braced her bottom against the counter. "No sex, Val."

I got up and strode around the island to stand in front of her. Inches separated our bodies. I placed my palms on the sink counter at either side of her hips, bending my head to meet her eyes. "You say that this morning, but last night you came twice from watching me get off. You want me. I want you. There's no reason to make this more complicated."

She wrinkled her nose. "Yeah, right. Guys always think they mean that, but they don't."

"I do. Sex only, *bebê*."

"Yeah, I can guess what that one means. You called me baby, didn't you?"

"That's right." I brushed my lips over hers, and she sucked in a breath. The feel of her mouth on mine brought my cock to attention, but she didn't seem to mind the hard length rubbing against her belly. I nipped her lower lip, then brushed my tongue across it. "Let's do it right now, right here in the kitchen."

"What if paparazzi show up and snap lurid pictures of us through the window? You are a notorious celebrity, after all."

"My life won't touch yours. No one knows I'm here, I made sure of that." I slipped my hand under her shirt, finding the waistband of her jeans and hooking a finger inside it. "I told only my parents and my sisters where I would be, and they're in Brazil. No one will find me. I drove instead of flying partly to keep anyone from tracking me. Mostly, I wanted to escape from my life for a while."

"What, did you release another sex tape?"

"No." I skimmed my finger along the inside of her waistband until I found the button on her jeans. Unhooking it slowly, I licked at the seam of her lips. "Let's enjoy each other, Evie. That's all I want and all you want too."

I tugged her zipper down and pushed my hand inside her jeans, inside her panties, to palm her mound. Her desire had drenched the soft, curly hairs that tickled my skin.

She sucked in another breath. "I don't have time for this. Gotta clean up the breakfast dishes from the guest house and—" She exhaled a breathy moan when I dived a finger between her slick folds. "We're all going to the Pioneer Days festival after lunch, so there really isn't…oh…time."

I thrust my whole hand between her folds, rocking it to rub her flesh. The scent of her desire wafted around us. She smelled incredible.

"Val, we can't," she said, though her voice was a throaty whisper and her head had tipped back, exposing the delicate column of her throat. Her fingers gripped the counter's edge harder, making tendons rise on the back of her hand. "I have to get to work. This place doesn't run itself."

"No, you're not leaving yet." I dropped to my knees in front of her, then dragged her jeans and panties down to her ankles. "Not until I've tasted you."

I grasped the backs of her thighs and lifted, hoisting her ass onto the counter.

Movement outside the window pulled my attention to the view, and for a second, I swore I noticed a shadow out there. It disappeared so fast I decided it must've been a cloud passing over the sun.

And I had more important concerns at the moment.

Eve glanced around as if expecting to see paparazzi outside one of the windows. "We can't. I can't. What if—"

"No one will know what we're doing. Unless you scream."

I shoved my head between her thighs, burying my face against her mound and thrusting my tongue between her folds. Her cream tasted sweet and tangy, and the musky scent of her drowned my senses. I draped my arms around her hips while I lapped at her flesh, circled my tongue around her taut nub, and raked my tongue down her cleft and back up to suck her clit into my mouth.

Her fingers plunged into my hair. "Oh, Val, yes."

A knock rattled the door.

I kept licking and suckling her nub, too inflamed by the flavor and heat of her to give up her body or to care who the fuck was knocking.

She whimpered, her nails scraping my scalp.

A more forceful knock rattled the door.

"Eve?" Quentin called. "You in there? I need your input with the repairs."

"Stop," she hissed to me.

I pulled back enough to look up at her. The blouse she wore had gotten bunched around her hips. "Tell him to go away."

"Can't do that." She planted her feet on my chest and pushed me away. "This is my job, Val."

While I sat back on my haunches, she shimmied her hips as she pulled her jeans and panties up, then zipped up and hurried to the door.

Her hand on the knob, she glanced back at me. "Better, um, go into another room or something."

She nodded toward my groin and the erection waving at her.

I leaned against the island. "Afraid your handyman will be jealous?"

"Unlike some people, I don't flaunt my sexcapades for the world to see." She flapped her hands, shooing me away. "Go."

I moved behind the island where Quentin wouldn't see the state Eve had gotten me into here in the kitchen.

She slipped her feet into the flip-flops she kept beside the door, pulled the door open partway, and sneaked outside. She yanked the door shut after her.

I shook my head, smiling. Stubborn as she was, Eve wanted me as much as I wanted her, and we would be fucking soon.

Very soon.

Chapter Nine

Eve

I ordered him not to do it, but Val insisted on helping me clean up the dining hall, take the dishes back to my house, and wash them. He even rushed back to the house to put on skintight jeans and a T-shirt, in accordance with the health code. Quentin tried to help too, but Val kept swooping in first to do everything. He seemed impervious to Quentin's hot glare and his snide comments. My handyman called my newest guest "a human bulldozer" and "an exhibitionist with a one-track mind" as well as "a mosquito buffet waiting to happen." The last one didn't make sense since Val was currently wearing clothes, but Quentin chortled at his own joke anyway.

The three of us carried the dishes back to my house. When Quentin tried to squeeze in to claim the sink first, Val casually asked whether my handyman had finished the repairs "you keep needing your employer's input on."

Quentin's face turned beet red at that comment. His nostrils flared—something I thought human beings couldn't do, but Quentin sure could. He fisted his hands, seeming about to erupt.

A fist fight was the last thing I needed, so I shooed Quentin out of the house, telling him to get back to work on the repairs.

I tried to shoo Val away, but the man was so large and strong I couldn't budge him. Even kicking his feet didn't make an impression. He flashed me a smile and went back to washing the dishes. That meant I stood beside him drying those dishes and trying not to stare at his ass. Those tight jeans didn't conceal much, though I couldn't see the bulge of his dick since he was leaning into the counter.

My mind kept flashing me back to earlier today when he'd shoved his face between my thighs. God, that had felt incredible. His hot, slick tongue working my flesh. His lips sucking. His fingers pressing into the backs of my thighs. I'd been so close to climax. If Quentin hadn't knocked on the door, I might have enjoyed a rockin' orgasm. Instead, I had to take care of the breakfast mess while my body throbbed from thwarted bliss.

Oh, and I remembered the glimpse I'd gotten of his aroused cock. When I'd pushed Val away from me, I'd seen it. Damn, the man was beyond well-hung. His erect penis was bigger, thicker, and even more impressive than when it hung slack. I wanted that inside me. I wanted him. More than anything, I'd wanted to tell Quentin to go to hell so I could mount Val right here in the kitchen.

Too complicated, I reminded myself. He was a notorious celebrity.

Well, I didn't have to get attached to him or get enmeshed in any kind of relationship. We could have sex, period. I could satisfy this outrageous craving for him that had me acting like a horny teenager and then move on.

Letting him go down on me in the kitchen? For pity's sake, I was thirty, not sixteen.

Once we'd finished with the dishes, Val turned to face me and leaned his hip against the counter. "Why don't you have a dish-washing machine?"

"Those things are expensive, and you have to practically wash the stuff before you put it in the dishwasher anyway." I replaced the dish towel on the little hanger attached to the counter, only in part as an excuse to look away from him and his hot bod, not at all disguised by his clothing. "I'm not above manual labor."

"You need more than a handyman. You need a team of employees."

"I've done fine so far."

He touched my arm. "When was the last time you took a day off?"

The warmth of his hand on my bare skin set off a flurry of goose bumps. My nipples went hard. I struggled to keep from sounding breathless when I told him, "My work habits are none of your concern."

He moved closer.

Too close. I could smell him, that indefinable essence of man that made everything inside me perk up and take notice. No, it wasn't the essence of man as in any old man. It was the essence of him.

His fingers curled around my arm. "Why haven't you hired anyone else? Why only Quentin?"

I noted the way his voice took on a faint sharp edge when he spoke my handyman's name. "It's complicated."

"You can tell me. I won't post it on Twitter." He winked. "I save that for sex tapes."

"Uh-huh." I considered walking away but decided I had no reason not to tell him the truth. I faced him and said, "When I started this business five years ago, I didn't have much money. My dad inherited this place from his great uncle, but he and my mom wanted to retire to the Florida Keys, not to the Oregon wilderness. They gave me this property. My parents also gave me ten thousand dollars to get started with, and I took out a loan for the rest, mainly to pay for building the guest house. I paid off the loan six months ago, which means I don't have enough left over to afford more employees or the other improvements I'd like to make."

"I would be happy to invest."

Folding my arms over my chest, I squinted at him. "Invest? That would mean you get your money back eventually, but I don't think that's what you really mean."

"Call it a gift, then."

"Oh-ho, no." I shook my head, wagging a finger at him. "I don't accept payment for sex."

A smirk stretched his lips. Amusement sparkled in his eyes and crinkled the skin around them. "That almost sounds like an invitation to fuck you."

"You think everything I say is an invitation."

"Because it is." He wrapped an arm around my waist, tugging me into his big, firm body. "We both want the same thing, sex with no strings. Stop fighting it. At the end of two weeks, I'll go home and we will never see each other again. What have you got to lose?"

My sanity. My self-respect. My heart.

I wouldn't fall for him. I barely knew Val, and I had no intention of getting to know him better. Sure, that's why I'd explained my financial situation to him. Ugh. As much as I would've loved to take a wild roll in the hay with him, I needed to shut this down ASAP.

"Sorry," I said, wriggling out of his hold, "I don't sleep with guests. Right now, I have to do some stuff in my office and then I need to make lunch. After that, we're all off to the Pioneer Days festival." I scrunched my lips, trying not to smile. "You'll need to keep your clothes on for that."

He tapped a finger on my lips. "I know that, Eve. I'll help you with lunch."

"No way. You are a guest, so go mingle with the rest of the gang."

Val stared at me for a moment, his full lips twisting into a half frown. He gusted out a sigh and nodded. "All right. I will mingle."

"Good."

He sauntered to the door, pausing there to glance back at me. "But I won't give up on seducing you."

Val walked out the door.

Once it clicked shut after him, I almost sagged into the counter. Whew. One calamity averted. For now.

He wouldn't give up. I believed that. For some bizarre reason, an infamous football star and unabashed nudist who liked to tape himself having sex had set his sights on me, the non-nudist proprietor of a low-rent resort who refused to sleep with guests.

Maybe a roll in the hay with him would be worth the risk of repercussions. He kept telling me he wasn't the jealous type and he didn't want a relationship. So maybe, just maybe, I could take the roll with him. Oh yeah, my body loved that idea.

Chapter Ten

When Eve strolled out of her house at one fifteen, her guests were waiting for her in the grassy area between her home and the guest house. I'd made sure to be in the front line. Eve stopped a short ways from us, gripping the strap of the huge purse she'd slung over one shoulder.

Her brows lifted a touch when she saw me.

I'd changed clothes for the occasion, though I doubted Eve would appreciate my ensemble. She had, I was sure, hoped I'd keep my entire body covered so she might feel less inclined to ravish me. Though I hated disappointing her in any way, this one time I had to do it.

Her gaze traveled the length of my body. Her raised brows lowered and cinched together over her nose.

Maybe my clothing surprised her. I was, after all, wearing swim shorts with a brightly colored zigzag print, a sleeveless T-shirt, and the latest, impossible-to-get style of Nikes that featured a bright pattern not unlike my shorts. I'd taken off my bucket hat and my Ray-Bans so I could see Eve clearly, though I held them in my hands.

She looked incredible in her pink jeans and white blouse. Here in the sunshine, the blouse became semi-transparent, revealing the outline of her bra that barely covered her gorgeous tits. She wore white sandals that exposed her toes and the shiny pink polish on them that matched the polish on her fingernails. She'd painted her nails since I had left her in the kitchen.

Just looking at her pink nails made me want to fall down at her feet and suck her perfect little toes one by one.

A straw hat with a wide brim perched on her head at a slight angle, shading her face. She adjusted the strap that held the hat in place and smiled at me. "Nice outfit, Val. I suppose that's the latest fashion in summer menswear."

"It is, but I augmented it with my own style."

"Naturally." She eyed my clothing again. One side of her mouth kinked upward. "Your style is definitely unique."

Every other man in our group wore subdued clothing—khakis, denim, shirts in earth tones. Ollie had opted for a bright-blue T-shirt, but even that was subdued next to my clothes.

"Why blend in?" I said to Eve. "I enjoy standing out from the crowd."

"No kidding." She feigned a surprised face. "I never would've guessed."

Ruth patted my arm. "This is a good sign, sweetie. Eve is flirting with you. I've never seen her do that with anyone else, not even the gentlemen she had flings with."

"I am not flirting," Eve said. She darted her gaze around the crowd, gripping her purse strap in both hands, and cleared her throat. "Not that it would be anyone's business if I were."

Her cheeks had turned a lovely shade of mottled pink. It almost matched her jeans.

Ruth hurried over to Eve and hooked an arm around her shoulders. "It's okay, Evie. We're all glad you found a man who excites you. Maybe you'll even let him take you on a date."

The idea of exciting Eve excited me, but Ruth would be disappointed about the dating suggestion. Neither I nor Eve wanted that.

"Thanks," Eve muttered. She stepped away from Ruth, lifted her chin, and called out, "Everybody in the bus. It's field trip time."

We all piled into a decommissioned school bus, once a yellow monstrosity but now painted sky blue. I hadn't noticed the bus on the property yesterday, but Ollie had explained that Eve kept it on the far side of the guest house, hidden in the shadows of tall trees. She didn't want a bus to be the first thing her guests saw when they arrived at the resort.

The afternoon had turned warm but not so hot we would be uncomfortable in the bus during the drive into town. Besides, someone—Eve, I suspected—had opened all the windows some-time earlier to let in fresh air. The vinyl bench seats had been re-upholstered with soft beige fabric and seemed to have acquired more cushioning than any school bus I'd seen before. The benches featured seat belts too. Eve did everything she could to make her guests feel comfortable and safe. It was no wonder they kept coming back to this place.

Every bench seat had at least one person occupying it by the time I stepped onto the bus. I scanned the interior, looking for a good place to sit.

Ollie waved at me. He had taken the front seat on the left side.

I nodded to him.

He scooted closer to the window and patted the seat beside him. "Take a load off, Val. This bus isn't exactly a Ferrari, or even a Chevy Volt, so it's a longer ride to town than if you were in a car. That's why Eve made the seats cushier and had better shock absorbers installed." He patted the spot beside him again. "Take a load off."

"Thank you." I settled onto the seat. "Does Eve organize a lot of field trips?"

"At least one a week. She likes to give us something to do other than sit around naked and contemplate our navels."

"Can't say I've spent much time doing that. My navel isn't that interesting."

"Belly buttons are weird, aren't they?"

I hadn't seen Eve's belly button yet, but I had a feeling her navel would be as sexy and fascinating as the rest of her body. The thought made my cock stir.

Quentin stomped onto the bus and dropped into the driver's seat. He flashed me a tight frown.

Eve bounded up the steps and faced her guests. "Everybody ready to go?"

Heads nodded. Voices murmured.

"Good," she said. "Buckle up, guys."

While everyone else secured their seat belts, she glanced around as if looking for something.

"Forget something?" I asked.

"I'm looking for a place to sit."

I patted my thigh. "My lap is available."

She clamped her lips between her teeth, clearly struggling not to smile.

Ollie hopped up. "Take my seat, Eve. I'll hang with Fred."

Before Eve could respond, Ollie squeezed past me and trotted toward the rear of the bus.

"Well," I said, "looks like you're sitting with me. Do you prefer the window or the aisle?"

"I'll take the window."

She sidled past me, and I got a close-up view of her bottom sheathed in those skintight pink jeans. Resisting the urge to palm her cheeks tested my willpower, but I managed to restrain myself.

Quentin started up the bus. It lurched forward.

Eve grasped the metal bar that separated our seat from the steps.

I placed a hand on her hip to offer support.

She raised her brows at me but settled onto the seat, sticking close to the window, careful to keep a gap between us.

"I'm not contagious," I said. "And I'm not even naked. Should I be offended that you're hugging the wall?"

"Sorry." She relaxed, moving a little closer. Her blue eyes studied me. "You must be rich, right? I mean, your truck is ultra-expensive and you're a famous athlete slash model."

"I have more than enough money, yes."

"Why did you come to my little bargain-basement resort? You would've been more comfortable at a luxury club."

"I like your resort. Besides, I value privacy and friendliness more than luxury."

Her lips curved into a sweet smile. "Well, you definitely came to the right place if you're looking for privacy. We're in the boonies."

"That's part of why I chose your place for my vacation."

"What's the rest of the reason?" She winced. "Sorry, I'm being way too nosy."

"Not at all." I draped my arm across the seat back, angling a few degrees toward her. "I told you I've seen your photographs. Your talent impressed me, Eve. I've done a fair bit of modeling, and you are better than the fashion photographers I've worked with. Do you sell your pictures?"

"Yeah, on stock photo sites."

A gray head popped up behind our seat. Ruth peered over the seat back at us and winked at me. To Eve, she said, "Don't forget to tell Val about the sessions tomorrow. I bet he'd love to pose for you."

Ruth's gray head retreated.

I looked at Eve. "Sessions?"

She focused on the floor, scratching the back of her neck. "Uh, yeah, I do private portrait sessions for my guests. Nude portraits. It's an add-on. The guests who want it pay an extra fee."

"How much?"

"A hundred dollars."

"Sign me up."

Her fingers froze mid-scratch. She rotated her unblinking eyes toward me. "You've posed for famous photographers. Why would you want me to take your portrait? All those other pictures of you ought to be enough."

"Those photos weren't for me, they were for magazines and billboards." I leaned closer, lowering my voice to a whisper. "I'd like to have an intimate portrait, and I would love for you to take it."

"Billboards? Jeez, you really must be famous."

"I was, briefly. It's not important." I leaned in more until my lips hovered an inch from her ear. "Will you photograph me?"

She stared straight ahead for a minute or more until, at last, she rolled her shoulders back and announced, "Yes, I'll photograph you."

"Thank you. I'm looking forward to it."

She swiveled her head toward me, those lustrous eyes zeroing in on mine. "Me too."

For the rest of the trip, we talked about nothing of importance. She told me funny stories about her past guests, and Ruth joined in to share her own stories. Soon, everyone on the bus was chiming in with tales of the shenanigans at the resort. None of it was salacious, though the antics of the Kitten Brigade skirted the line. I was both looking forward to and dreading the day when those young women arrived.

The Pioneer Days festival was fun, but I would've preferred to have Eve all to myself. Our group stayed within sight of each other the whole time. Ruth, Sylvester, and Ollie stuck close to Eve and me. Quentin had opted to stay in the bus at Eve's suggestion. I got the impression she was growing tired of her handyman's jealousy. About damn time, I thought.

When we got back to the retreat, a delivery car from a local bistro was waiting in the driveway. Somehow, Eve had arranged to have our dinner hot and waiting for us. When I asked how she pulled that off, she shrugged and said, "The restaurant has an app. I placed an order while everybody was getting back on the bus."

She thought of everything for her guests. I wondered when she'd last done something for herself.

Naturally, I asked her that question.

"I keep telling you, it's my job to take care of my guests," she said. "My needs are last on the list."

"What needs of yours aren't being met? Maybe I can help."

"I don't need any help."

Eve joined the group for dinner in the guest house. She enlisted Ollie to assist with the cleanup, waving me away when I tried to join in. Was she avoiding me? That wouldn't work for long. Tomorrow, I'd be posing for her. A private session with Eve Holt was worth a lot more than a hundred dollars.

Eve retreated to her office after cleaning up the dinner mess.

I waited in my room, lying on the bed, with the door halfway open.

At eleven o'clock, Eve sashayed down the hallway. When she spotted my open door, she leaned in to peek at me. "Thought you'd be asleep."

"I'm a night owl." I stretched and sighed. "Why don't you lie down with me?"

She shook her head, her lips twitching up at the corners. "Thanks for the offer, but I'm used to sleeping alone."

"Who said anything about sleeping?"

"Good night, Val."

She moved away from the door.

I sighed again, this time with disappointment. "Good night, Eve."

After a few minutes of trying to read a book on my phone, I gave up. Eve's curves kept invading my thoughts, driving me crazy with visions of what I could do to that body. I set my phone down and took my rock-hard cock in my hand. If she wouldn't join me, I'd take care of things on my own. Maybe she'd overhear and decide to join me.

By the time I'd come, I realized Eve wasn't going to walk through the door and beg to take my dick in her mouth. Just the thought of her doing that made me hard again. I tried to sleep, but the sensual woman slumbering across the hall from me tormented my dreams.

Tomorrow. We would fuck tomorrow.

If we didn't, I'd need tranquilizers to get through another night.

Chapter Eleven

Eve

"Oh, Val, yes." I slipped my hand between my drenched folds, stroking myself while remembering the dreams I'd had last night. Dreams about him. About us together. Naked and writhing and devouring each other in every way imaginable. I whisked my fingers up and down my cleft, and my breaths grew shorter and sharper.

A fist rapped on my door.

I froze, halfway to my happy ending, panting and burning for release. "Who is it?"

"Val. I've made you breakfast."

"What time is it?" I could've glanced at the clock on my bedside table, but I'd lost the ability to move even a single muscle. My hand was still between my legs.

"It's five thirty," he said. "This is when you normally get up, so I made sure to be up first. It's the only way I'll get the chance to do something for you."

Oh, he'd done something for me all right. He'd turned me into a sex-obsessed idiot who spied on him while he masturbated and got myself off repeatedly while thinking of him. I hadn't watched him last night, though I had my suspicions he'd done himself a favor at least twice. His bed had been thumping, and I'd heard his grunts.

Big mystery why I'd endured intensely erotic dreams last night that forced me to do myself a favor…or two, or three. Maybe this was the fourth time. I'd lost count.

"May I come in?" Val asked.

"Uh…just a minute." I snatched a tissue off the box on the table and wiped my fingers with it. Jumping up, I straightened my nightie. "Come in."

The door opened. Val sauntered inside.

He swept his gaze over my rumpled sheets and then up to my face. "Your cheeks are pink. Aren't you feeling well?"

Alive, that's how I felt. Aching and tingling in all the right places. The sight of his nude body did not help matters.

"I'm fine," I said. "Thank you for making me breakfast. I'll be there in a minute, after I get dressed."

"Don't dress on my account." He raked his hot gaze over my body. "You can wear nothing at all. I'm a nudist, remember?"

Right. Hard to forget that fact. Even if I'd been tempted to go naked this morning, with him, it was a bad idea.

Tempted? I wanted to tear my nightie off right this instant.

"I'll, ah, see you in a few minutes," I said. "In the kitchen."

"Whatever you want." He sauntered out of my bedroom.

How would I survive two weeks with him? Quentin had better finish repairing Val's room in the guest house fast.

I dressed in my favorite shorts and a mint-green crop top, then joined Val in the kitchen.

He'd cooked me a huge breakfast—an omelet stuffed chock-full of veggies, sausage, and three kinds of cheese. A plate of buttered toast waited beside my breakfast platter, with jars of every kind of jam and jelly I owned lined up next to it. He'd made hash browns too, plus adorable silver dollar pancakes.

I didn't even mind that he'd made breakfast while naked. Since this was a private meal, rather than one for the other guests, I decided he hadn't violated the health code.

After gobbling up my breakfast, I insisted on washing the dishes.

"I'll allow it," Val said, "only if you let me help you get breakfast ready for the guests."

"For the millionth time, you *are* a guest."

"No, I'm your slave."

The tone of his voice, deep and rumbly, told me he meant "slave" in a different way from what most people would've meant. Later today, I'd photograph his gorgeous, nude body—just the two of us in my little studio, inside this house, away from the other guests. Having him as my slave? That made my tummy flutter.

"Fine," I said. "You can be my breakfast assistant if you get dressed first. Straight after that, though, I have to prepare my studio for the portrait sessions."

"I can help—"

"You're sweet to offer, but I prefer to get things set up on my own." I hopped off my stool. "You came here to be nude and free, but you've spent half the time in clothes because you insist on helping out. I feel like I've cramped your style."

"There's no cramping. I like assisting you."

"As a favor to me, why don't you hang out with the other guests until it's your turn in the studio?"

He bowed from the waist. "If that's what you want, *linda*, your slave will obey."

Since he'd been the last to sign up for a session, he'd gotten the last time slot. I would photograph him after everyone else, meaning I would have no easy excuse to cut the session short. Did I want to cut it short? Why was I trying so hard to avoid having sex with him? We were both adults. No one but his family knew he'd come here. His wild life would not tarnish mine, which meant I had no excuses left.

Right, because that had worked out so well before.

The last time I'd engaged in casual sex, it had triggered a hairy situation. Quentin still seemed to think he owned me. And the more I thought about what Val had said, about Quentin taking advantage of me in my tipsy state, the more I wondered if he was right.

Val wouldn't be like Quentin. He would stay for two weeks and go home. We would never see each other again.

Quentin I had to look at every day.

Maybe I should've fired Quentin, but firing an employee I'd slept with might trigger legal ramifications I couldn't afford. Besides, Quentin did his job very well and was the only handyman I'd found who didn't mind working at a nudist resort.

Five hours later, Val and I had taken care of breakfast for the guests and I had photographed a dozen of them. The portraits weren't sexual, but rather just like regular portraits somebody might get at a regular photo studio. The only difference was my subjects were naked.

My little studio occupied a space that had originally served as a bedroom. The room featured one curtained window, various lights plus an umbrella, several backgrounds I could set up and swap out quickly, a fan to offset the heat from the lights, and extra power outlets

I'd had installed to accommodate my equipment. If my guests needed a drink during our shoots, I went to the kitchen to get it for them. A stereo tucked into the corner provided mood music. I preferred something relaxing to keep my guests in a good mood.

The centerpiece of my whole setup was my camera, of course. A couple years ago, I'd upgraded to a Canon EOS 5D Mark IV DSLR that cost over three thousand dollars. It had seemed like an extravagance at the time, but I'd earned back the cost and then some thanks to these photo sessions. My guests loved getting tasteful images of themselves to take home.

Right on time, Val strode into my studio.

He turned his head left and right, admiring the room like it was the inside of the Sistine Chapel. "Very nice. This is a professional studio."

"Mm-hmm." I gestured toward the chair set up in the center of the room. "Have a seat."

"In the chair?" He walked a circle around it, scrutinizing the piece of furniture, then stopped and shook his head at me. "I won't be posing in a chair."

"Well, I guess you can stand for the whole session."

"No, Eve." He moved the chair out of the way and sat down on the floor. "This will do."

"Okay, if you really want to sit on the floor the whole time, I guess—"

He stretched out on his side, his head propped up with one hand. "I'm ready."

"Uh, people generally sit or stand for portraits."

"No boudoir photos? I'd think at least a few people would want that."

I couldn't resist skimming my gaze over his body and licking my lips when I reached his groin. "Only a couple of people wanted sexy photos. My guests like that my pictures are tasteful and respectful. The ones who wanted boudoir stuff were older couples looking to spice up their love lives." Somehow, I managed to tear my attention away from his manly bits to meet his gaze. "Are you sure you wouldn't rather sit on the chair like everybody else?"

"Would you want me to be like other people?"

No, absolutely not. "The floor is awfully hard to lie on for very long. I've got an idea."

Racing into the corner of the room where I'd stashed various props and background screens, I retrieved a padded mat, more like a cushion really. Val got up when I started dragging the bed-size cushion toward him. He grabbed one end and took the thing away from me, laid it down where he'd been a moment ago, and stretched out on his side again—this time on the crimson cushion.

"Comfy?" I asked.

He patted the cushion. "Yes, very."

"Normally, I use the padded mat for photographing babies and toddlers." I drank in the sight of Val the human supernova laid out across the crimson mat, and my mouth watered. Seriously, it did. "The color suits you."

"How would you like me?"

The erotic rumble of his voice, molten and decadent, rippled heat through me. I gripped my camera against my belly, and though I tried not to ogle him anymore, I failed. His nude body standing up or sitting down was breathtaking. Lying there stretched out like a Roman emperor awaiting his concubine… God, he was beyond hot. Especially the way he kept looking at me. Brown eyes warm as melted caramel. Tongue flicking out to moisten his lips. And that penis, so thick and long. Holy hotness. I'd never seen anything as gorgeous and tempting as Val Silva.

Why was I resisting the urge to get horizontal with him? I knew there'd been a reason, but suddenly, I couldn't remember what it was.

His lips slid into a sensual smile. "Are you going to photograph me? Or would you rather join me here on the floor?"

My mouth opened, but I couldn't summon any words. Join him? Yeah, oh hell yeah, I wanted to do that.

Why shouldn't I? Maybe he was the kind of bad boy I tried to avoid, but it wasn't like we had paparazzi way out here in the boonies of Oregon.

Screw it. I wanted him, he wanted me, and we were both consenting adults.

"Let me take a few shots first," I said. "You are paying for this session, after all."

He tipped his head to the side, not blinking when he asked, "And then you'll join me?"

I wandered over to the stereo and the iPod docked to it. Yeah, I was old school. I didn't like listening to music on my phone the way a lot of people did these days. Flipping through my playlists, I found an album that fit the mood, a collection of songs by Delerium. An ethereal feminine voice crooned to a sensual, exotic rhythm.

"Yes," I said, returning to Val and raising the camera, "after I take some shots, I will join you."

He skated his palm over the velvety cushion beneath him. "Naked?"

I regarded him through the LCD screen on the back of my camera, framing up a good shot. "Since we'll be having sex, yes, I'll take my clothes off."

A grin spread across his face, lighting up his entire expression.

I pressed the shutter button, capturing a shot of him in that moment when he'd realized I wanted to fuck right here, right now. My heartbeat sped up, and my nipples pearled. He had a killer grin, for sure.

"You should be a model," I said, taking another picture. I peeked at him over the top of my camera, though he couldn't see it. "Oh wait, you already are."

As I moved around him, snapping shot after shot, I got more and more aroused by the sight of him. He didn't preen or do any of the silly poses hotshot models might do. He followed my directions, lifting an arm or sliding a hand into his hair. Honestly, the man looked incredible doing nothing at all. He didn't need to pose, he simply needed to be.

"On your back," I said.

He rolled onto his back and linked his hands under his head.

After one more shot, I set my camera on the chair he'd moved out of the way.

"Is the session over?" he asked.

"Yes, the photography session is." I took hold of my shirt's hem and flipped it up and over my head, letting it sail down to the floor. "But we're just getting started."

He stared at my flimsy bra, and his dick began to swell.

The thin lace of my bra left most of my breasts exposed and revealed the dusky pink of my nipples. They pushed against the fabric, aching for his touch. I shimmied my hips more than necessary as I eased my shorts down over my hips. They fell to the floor, and I stepped out of them.

Val groaned.

My panties were as flimsy as my bra.

I reached behind my back to undo my bra one hook at a time. Once I'd freed them all, I shrugged the bra off my shoulders. It fluttered to the floor, joining my shirt and shorts.

His dick rose up like a flagpole.

Licking my lips, unable to tear my gaze away from his cock, I wriggled out of my panties.

A groan resonated in his chest.

I dropped to all fours and crawled toward him until I straddled his body. My face hovered over his groin and the beautiful, rosy-tipped erection I craved.

"Eve," he said, turning my name into the most erotic thing I'd ever heard, "you surprise me at every turn. I'd expected I would have to seduce you. Instead, here you are climbing up my body with a ravenous look on your face."

"Mmm, I am ravenous." I licked the head of his cock. "For this."

No more excuses. No more waiting.

I gave his erection another long, slow lick. "I want you in my mouth, Val."

Chapter Twelve

I must've been gaping at the woman crouched over the lower half of my body. I couldn't help it. Eve Holt, the woman who'd sworn she wouldn't get naked with me, wanted to take my cock in her mouth. She had already surprised me with her sudden announcement she wanted to have sex. Her little striptease had made me hard, but her desire to give me a blow job stunned me. Wasn't this the same woman who'd said she didn't sleep with guests anymore?

Not that I was complaining. The most enticing woman I'd ever laid eyes on wanted to suck me like a lollipop. What man in his right mind would say no?

I slid a hand into her hair. "You're incredible, Eve. You can be sure I'll go down on you next."

She laved my crown with her tongue, making me suck in a breath. "I look forward to that. But first, I've got to eat you up."

"Don't make me come. I want to save that for when I'm inside you."

"Whatever you want."

"Already have everything I wanted—you, naked, about to let me fuck you."

She puckered her lips and blew a stream of air across my crown. I groaned.

Eve opened her mouth wide, lowering it to within millimeters of my cock, and exhaled a long, hot breath onto the tip. She raised her head to look at me. "You've got the most beautiful dick I've ever seen."

What else could I do? I grinned like a fool. This woman drove me wild and turned my brain to mush. I combed my fingers through her hair, amazed by her unabashed enthusiasm and by the sheer beauty of her body and her spirit. Other women had gone down on me, but none did it with the tenderness and enjoyment Eve displayed.

"So big too," she said in a husky tone, her breath teasing me with each syllable. "Can't wait to have this inside me."

"Neither can I. Let's skip the foreplay and—"

She ducked her head, pressing her mouth to my inner thigh, and dragged her lips up my flesh. Her silken hair had fallen over my cock to tickle my skin as she moved.

"Fuck, Eve," I growled, my fingers clenching in her hair.

The vixen lifted her head to switch to my other thigh, this time licking and nibbling her way toward my groin. When she'd almost reached it, she raised her head to hit me with a wicked little smile. "I love an ice cream cone before the main course."

"Ice cream?" I said, sounding as baffled as I felt. Baffled and intrigued, not to mention so hot for this woman I was fighting the impulse to flip her over and bury my face between her thighs.

She dragged her tongue up my dick, from the base to near the tip. Humming with pleasure, she did it again. Her eyes drifted partway closed. "Better than ice cream. Better than dark chocolate cake with cream cheese frosting, which I thought I loved more than sex." She took another long, sensuous lick. "May have to re-evaluate that. You are the most delicious thing I've ever tasted."

No woman had ever talked to me the way she did while doing what she was doing to me. Maybe I'd died and this was the afterlife, with Eve as my angel guide. She certainly seemed determined to kill me with pleasure.

Her lips sealed around my cock and sank down, down, down until she'd taken as much of me as she could into her mouth. She moaned, the sound vibrating my flesh.

A choked sound spluttered out of me.

She grasped the base with her fist and began to move her mouth up and down, sucking gently, moaning like I was her first meal in weeks. I thrust both hands into her hair, shut my eyes, and let the sensations flood over me. Her soft, warm tongue. The heat of her breaths. The way her hair teased my skin. Every time she pulled her mouth nearly free of my flesh, the dampness left behind by her lips and tongue sent a rush of coolness over my skin. I levered into a sitting position, keeping one hand in her hair, and spread my other palm on her back to caress her in long, slow strokes. The pressure escalated, little by little, with every swipe of her tongue and brush of her hair.

Every muscle inside me went taut. I teetered on the edge, and if she kept going…

She sat up and swept her tongue across her lips.

I almost came just watching her do that.

"Mmm," she said, "I enjoyed that way more than I usually do. Loved it, actually."

She'd loved it. I couldn't comprehend the full meaning of those words, not in my current condition.

"On your knees," I said. "It's your turn."

"My knees?"

"Yes." I lay back on the velvet cushion. "Move this way."

I curled my finger repeatedly, gesturing her to move closer. She rose to her knees and crawled toward me. Her brows crinkled in the sweetest way when I kept crooking my finger, but still she inched ever closer.

"Stop," I said. "That's perfect."

Her glistening pink cleft was positioned above my head. I stretched my hand up, sliding my fingers into the soft, curly hairs on her mound. She bit her lip. I caressed her with my fingertips. She released her lip gradually, her gaze hooded, and my cock throbbed. Eve Holt was beautiful, yes, but she was also the most sensual woman I'd ever known. Whether she realized how her every movement and expression fired up my libido, I didn't know. Her sensuality seemed innate, a part of her she couldn't have hidden if she'd tried.

I skated my other hand up her thigh to curve it around her hip. "You're incredible, Eve. Your body is stunning, but it's what I see inside you that makes me want you so badly."

She smirked. "You're only saying that because you're staring at my vagina."

"No, I'm staring at you." I palmed her mound, my gaze exclusively on her face. "I've never met a woman like you before. I doubt I ever will again."

She stopped blinking. Stopped breathing too, I suspected. Her gaze locked onto mine, the color of her irises seeming deeper and bluer.

"What is it?" I asked.

"That sounded almost…romantic."

"Almost? I must not have said it right."

"This is casual sex, remember?"

"I know, but I can still pay you a compliment. Can't I?"

What I'd said did sound a lot more romantic than the things I usually told women. I would compliment their bodies, not—what had I called it?—the things I saw inside them. This woman made me lose my mind. Anything I'd said to her was instigated by lust, nothing more. I'd met her the day before yesterday, for fuck's sake.

"Sure," she said carefully, "compliments are fine. But don't go getting the idea we might be dating or whatever."

"No worries." I grinned, hoping she would believe what I was about to say. "Relax, Eve. I want your body, that's all. I'm even less interested in dating than you are."

To prove my point, I shoved my hand between her legs, nestling it between her slick folds. The heel of my hand covered her clit. I ground my hand against that erect little nub until her eyes fluttered shut and her mouth fell open on a throaty moan. The hunger evident in that sound sent any blood that was left in my brain rushing south. I kept rubbing her clit while I stretched my fingers out to stroke her flesh, my longest finger nudging her opening.

She slapped a hand over mine on her hip. "Oh Val, I want you. Now. Please."

"You've got me." My voice had gone as husky as hers, strained by the need we both endured. I'd never been so aroused by a woman, so desperate to thrust into her moist heat and lose myself inside her. "In a minute, I promise."

I gazed up at her belly, the way it quivered the slightest bit, and higher still to those perfect breasts rising and falling with every breath she sucked into her lungs.

She gazed down at me, her lips parted. They'd turned a deeper shade of rose. She rocked her hips, pushing the heel of my hand harder into the rigid tip of her clit. "Don't stop. Please don't stop."

I would in a moment, but not yet. The longer I watched her, the more turned on she got, the harder I fought to hold back my raging need for her. I wanted to fuck Eve like I'd never wanted to fuck any woman. And I didn't want her to come until I was deep inside that lush body.

Her head fell back. A long, luxurious moan resonated through her.

I shifted my hand lower and plunged two fingers inside her. With my thumb, I worked her nub.

"More," she begged, "more, please, more."

Her plea shattered my willpower. I lunged my head up and gripped her ass with both hands, latching my mouth on to her nub, suckling and nipping, scraping my tongue over the rigid tip while my fingers dug into her cheeks, relishing the sound of her panting breaths. She clutched my head, her nails raking my scalp, and bucked her hips every time I sucked on her nub. I gazed up at her face while I worked her body, my breaths shortening and blustering through the hairs on her mound. Urgency gripped her features. She stopped breathing, and her body went stiff.

"Oh no," I said, pulling my mouth away from her flesh, "I'm not letting you come yet."

Her head snapped up, and she gaped at me. A delicate flush colored her cheeks.

I skimmed my hands up and down her thighs.

She kneed me in the side. "That was a dirty trick."

"Maybe, but I think you like it dirty. Besides, you didn't make me come."

"You told me not to." She bent her knees to sit on my lap, her wet and swollen flesh inches from my cock. "Do you have a condom?"

I patted my chest and hips like I was searching for one. "Sorry, I don't have any pockets to keep anything in."

"Right. You're always naked." Her gaze flicked down to my erection. She licked her lips. "Do you have any condoms anywhere? I don't. I'm on the pill, but…"

"Have some in my room." I ran my hands up her thighs again. "You'll need to move off me so I can go get one."

She glanced at my erection again and sighed, then slid off my lap.

I sprinted out of the studio.

Chapter Thirteen

Eve

I lay on my back on the velvet cushion, waiting for Val to come back with a condom. If I'd planned for this to happen, I would've stashed an entire box of Trojans in this room. Despite my reckless craving for him, I'd vowed I would not sleep with Val. So much for that resolution. Lying here, burning with desire, I couldn't remember any of the reasons why I'd sworn to avoid sex with this man.

Minutes elapsed. A few turned into several. Several became an uncomfortably long time.

"Val?" I called out.

When he didn't respond, I shook my head. Of course he wouldn't hear me. He was probably still in his room down the hall rummaging around for his box of rubbers. I got up and moseyed out of the studio, intending to swerve right toward Val's room. A noise from the direction of the kitchen made me pause. I leaned to the side so I could get a peek into Val's room. Since I couldn't see him, I figured he'd gone into the kitchen, maybe to get some chocolate syrup we could drizzle over each other's bodies.

I walked into the kitchen—and gasped.

The door to the outside hung wide open, and Quentin had his fist clenched, ready to lash out.

Val slumped against the wall massaging his jaw.

No, this couldn't be what it seemed to be. Quentin couldn't have punched Val.

"Get the hell out of here," Quentin snarled. He shook his fist in the air between them. "Or I'll lay another one on you. And this time, I'll draw blood."

I gaped at my handyman. "What do you think you're doing?"

Quentin's gaze veered to me. First, his eyes bulged. Next, his jaw dropped. His shock morphed into something else, something darker. One side of his mouth slanted upward while his tongue traced the inside of his lower lip. His wide eyes narrowed as he took in the full view of me.

Totally naked.

Maybe I should have run out of the room or at least snatched up a dish towel to cover part of myself, but I was too pissed.

I focused on Val when I asked, "What happened here?"

"He hit me," Val said, his voice surprisingly calm under the circumstances. He straightened and narrowed his gaze on Quentin. "I was coming back from my room when I heard the knob on the kitchen door jiggle. Came in here to check it out. That's when this bastard crashed through the door and attacked me."

I suddenly noticed the box of condoms lying near his feet, open, silver packets scattered across the floor.

Quentin's mouth crimped. "He's taking advantage of you. Right here in the kitchen where anybody might see."

Val was using me? Seriously? I stomped up to Quentin, my breasts bouncing, and jabbed a finger into his chest. "You're the one who took advantage of me. Remember that night when I'd had one too many margaritas? A real gentleman would have seen me home and said good night. But you saw yourself into my bedroom and had your fun."

For months, I'd convinced myself Quentin hadn't taken advantage of me. Today, with him staring at my body with a lustful gleam in his eyes, I no longer believed it.

I stabbed my finger into his chest so hard he flinched. "You're fired."

His eyes went wide again, with shock this time. "I'm sorry, Eve. I'll apologize to your boyfriend if you want."

Val was not my boyfriend, but that was none of Quentin's business.

"It's too late," I said. "You crossed a line, a big old red one with flashing lights on it. Breaking into my house? Attacking my guest? You and I, we're done. Get in your truck and get the hell off my property."

"Let me get my tools first."

I smacked my palm flat on his chest, making him stumble backward half a step. "I bought those tools. The only thing here that you own is your clothes and your truck. Get out of here, Quentin."

Val took a step closer, but I shook my head at him. He stayed put.

"Go," I snarled at Quentin. "I never want to see your face again. Your final paycheck will be mailed to you."

Quentin sputtered like he was trying to form words but couldn't quite do it.

I slammed both my palms onto his chest hard enough to make him stumble and trip over his own feet. "Get out!"

He spun around and bolted out of the house, slamming the door.

Val touched my arm. "Are you all right?"

"Yes."

Adrenaline spiked through my blood like an electric shock, but I would not let Quentin's invasion make me cry. I was too angry for that anyway. This energy created by my confrontation with Quentin, it burned inside me. As I focused my attention on Val, on his naked body and half-deflated erection dangling between his legs, the searing anger transformed into a different kind of energy.

An engine roared to life outside, followed by the harsh grumble and clatter of a vehicle speeding away down the gravel drive.

I blew out a breath. "We should call off what we were about to do before the interruption."

"We should," he said, but his voice had deepened into that sensual rumble again. He inched closer to me, his gaze skipping down to my breasts and lower to the hairs between my thighs before returning to my face.

My gaze dropped to his swelling dick before lifting to his face. "We really shouldn't do this."

"No, we shouldn't."

"We ought to wait until we both calm down."

He moved even closer, his cock now hard and nudging my belly. "You're right, we ought to wait until later."

The weight of lust settled low in my belly, and the need throbbed in my sex from my clit all the way down to my entrance.

I seized his face with both hands and crushed my mouth to his. Our tongues clashed, our teeth clashed, and we consumed each other like nothing in the universe, not even a nuclear explosion, could've severed our kiss.

Val pulled away only long enough to snag a condom packet from the floor, tear it open with his teeth, and roll the rubber onto his erection.

His mouth found mine again, his tongue scraping mine while his hands grasped my hips. He lifted me off the floor. Spinning around, he pinned me to the wall with his body and thrust inside me so hard and fast I gasped into his mouth. He hesitated. With our bodies joined, neither of us moved a muscle, not even our tongues that remained coiled around each other. He clasped my hands and held them to the wall above my head. Letting out a deep groan, he pumped his hips.

I moaned, the sound muffled by his mouth. God, he felt so unbelievably good. I hooked my legs around his hips, pulling him deeper inside me, moaning again from the sheer bliss of his powerful thrusts. His tongue demanded a response, and my body was beyond willing to give in to anything he wanted. I couldn't catch my breath, but I didn't care. I clutched his hands tight enough to sink my nails into his flesh, but he didn't seem to notice or care. Flesh slapped on flesh, every thrust punctuated by a wet sucking sound.

The phone rang, but my brain had shut down.

He pumped faster, rougher, and ripped his mouth away from mine to bury his face against my neck. Grunts and groans burst out of him while I fought for breath, the power of my need growing and growing, escalating into a pressure so intense my ears rang and dark spots speckled my vision.

About to come, so close, almost there.

My release blasted through me in a tidal wave of pleasure. Every spasm in my sex gripped him like a vise. The only noise I could make was a desperate whimpering as he punched into me with ruthless strength, slamming me into the wall. My neck muffled his choked cry when he blew apart inside me.

Panting, we both hung there in a suspended moment with our bodies connected in the most intimate way. His breaths blustered against my neck. Sweat drizzled down our bodies. Time seemed irrelevant, but after a few moments, we emerged from our mutual comas and untangled ourselves.

Val kissed me sweetly, tenderly, then moved away to discard the condom in the trash can.

I pushed away from the wall, wobbling a tiny bit.

He caught my upper arms with his big hands. "How do you feel? I hadn't planned on taking you like that. Not the first time."

The buzz of adrenaline had lessened, but it still had me kind of wired.

"Wow," I said, fanning myself with one hand, "that was amazing."

"I hope I didn't hurt you."

Noticing the concern on his face, I laid my palms on his chest. "Don't worry. I'm tough."

His mouth quirked. "I noticed that when you booted your handyman off the property."

"Let's go to a bed—your room or mine, I don't care which—and do that again."

"I'd love to." He drew me into his arms and kissed my forehead. "Maybe you need a glass of water first."

"Sure, that sounds good. Water and a cookie." I rolled my eyes in the direction of the cabinet above the fridge. "I hide the best ones up there."

He padded to the fridge and reached over it to open the cabinet.

Damn, he was tall enough to reach that without standing on his toes.

The phone rang.

I grabbed the handset off the wall. "Hello?"

"Evie, what's going on?" Ruth asked. "We saw Quentin stomp out of your house looking fit to kill someone, but then he drove off. That was one big cloud of dust he kicked up."

"Yeah, I fired him."

"Why?"

"It's a long story. I'll tell you later."

A long pause followed before Ruth said, "Is everything okay? Are you okay?"

"Yes, Val's taking care of me." I glanced at him, where he stood beside the fridge holding a box of cookies, a question on his face. "We'll share the story with the whole gang at lunch."

"Sure. See you then."

We said goodbye, and I returned the phone to its cradle.

Val arched one brow. "We'll share the story?"

"Not everything, obviously." I ambled up to him and took the box of cookies. Flipping the lid up, I dived my hand inside to grab a fistful of chocolate-chip yummies. I shoved a crunchy cookie into my mouth and gobbled it up. "Maybe I should crumble these all over you and eat my snack off your skin."

He chuckled. "I've had women lick whipped cream off of me, but never cookies."

"You're a cookie-crumble virgin?" I started for the hallway, aiming for his room. "Let's go. It's my first time too."

I took off at a dead run.

Val's feet slapped on the wood floor as he sprinted after me.

<h1 style="text-align:center">Chapter Fourteen</h1>

Val

After Eve had her fun crumbling cookies onto my body, we made lunch for everyone and ate with the rest of the guests in the dining hall. Eve's playful, naughty side had surprised me, but only in the best way. I supposed I shouldn't have been surprised. She might've been a workaholic who refused to go nude in public, but she did like to wear sexy outfits that showed off her beautiful body.

When Eve and I strolled into the dining hall, she was waylaid by Ruth and Sylvester who wanted to discuss what activities were on tap for the afternoon. Ollie approached me. After the usual pleasantries, he eyed my chest with a strange expression.

He leaned in a touch and asked, "Is that a chocolate chip stuck to your chest?"

I glanced down and realized it was in fact a chocolate chip, half melted and pasted to my skin. Eve had missed one.

"Ah, yes," I said, grabbing a napkin off the buffet table to wipe off the chocolate. "I had cookies earlier."

"You got cookies?" Ollie faked a pout as if the news offended him. "Eve never lets anybody near her secret cookie stash."

"How do you know she has a stash if it's secret?"

Ollie's mouth formed a sly smile. "Sometimes I help carry her groceries into her house. I saw boxes of cookies once and asked her about it. She swore me to secrecy, said she'd replace my insect repellent with sugar water if I told anyone." He waggled his eyebrows. "She must really like you if she let you see her cookie stash. It's like her own little pirate treasure. Keep expecting her to install a security system on that cabinet like something a museum might have to protect a huge diamond."

Eve didn't share her cookies with anyone, but she'd shared them with me. She'd crumbled them in her hands, sprinkled them onto my chest, and licked the crumbs and chips off my skin one by one. Her tongue had been velvety and warm, her licks gentle and—

My dick was stirring to life again.

I changed the subject quickly by asking Ollie what he did for a living. For the next five minutes, I listened to every detail about his work as a computer systems engineer. It bored the fuck out of me, but Ollie clearly enjoyed talking about his work. I liked him, and I liked all the other guests, but I despised Eve's former handyman. Good riddance, I said.

But I didn't say that to Eve.

"How long are you staying at the resort?" I asked Ollie.

"Six weeks."

"That's a long stay. Your employers must be generous with vacation time."

He bunched his shoulders, staring down at the ground with his lips pinched. "Yeah, they're real generous."

The tone of his voice implied they weren't generous at all. I might've asked him more about that, but it wasn't my business.

Ollie waved to some of the other guests. "How about a round of miniten?"

My conversation with Ollie ended there since I didn't feel like donning a thug to whack a tennis ball back and forth over a net. I wanted to get Eve alone. Preferably with cookies. Maybe chocolate syrup too.

I had to wait for my chance, but after lunch, Eve and I retreated into her house for more private time. We enjoyed each other in every room in the house until a vehicle pulled into the driveway and Eve announced it was dinnertime. She had ordered Italian food from a local restaurant. I would've preferred to have dinner with her alone in the house, so I could eat my fettuccine alfredo off her body, but she insisted on socializing with the other guests.

"I've been ignoring them," she announced while I watched her dress. "Spent most of the day having sex with you instead of tending to the needs of all my guests."

"My needs are the most pressing." I was lying on the bed in her room, where only ten minutes ago I'd been ravishing her. She stood in front of her dresser. I loved watching her get dressed, if only so I could look forward to stripping her later. "I don't think I can survive an hour without fondling your body."

She dropped onto the bed beside me and patted my cheek. "I think you'll live."

I did survive dinner, though I couldn't stop looking at Eve. Sylvester and Ruth teased me about it, but I was immune to that kind of harassment. The entire world had seen me naked, on the football field and in a sex tape, and those incidents had eradicated what little shame I'd had before that. At least Sylvester and Ruth were kind people who teased me out of affection, not paparazzi hounding me or comedians turning me into a nasty joke.

Being here with Eve and her guests, I didn't feel like a notorious scoundrel anymore. I liked the way I felt here. I'd become an almost-normal human being.

Once dinner was over, Eve invited me into her bedroom again. We were lingering in the hallway near the door to my room when she posed the question.

She hunched her shoulders and angled her head down to peek up at me through her lashes. "Would you like to come into my bedroom?"

"I'd love to, but I'm exhausted." I skimmed a hand up and down her arm. "You must be exhausted too."

"Yeah, but—" She bit down on her lower lip and stared at the wall next to me. After a few seconds, she forced a smile. "Never mind. You're right, we're both too tired. I'll see you in the morning. Good night, Val."

She all but sprinted toward her room.

"Good night, Eve," I called after her.

The door to her bedroom swung shut.

Her shyness about inviting me into her room had been adorable, but I couldn't understand why she'd felt embarrassed. Had she wanted me to sleep with her more than I'd thought? I'd assumed it was a casual request. Maybe she'd meant it as more and surprised herself with that realization.

Did I want more?

Of course not. Neither did she.

I ambled into my room but left the door open. Part of me hoped she might sneak in here in the middle of the night and crawl under the covers with me. Why was I wishing for that? We were having sex, that was all. I didn't need to feel her warm, supple body tucked against mine while I slept. I didn't need to wake up and find her head on my chest, and I absolutely did not need to dip my nose into her hair and inhale the sweet, fruity scent of her shampoo.

No, I didn't need or want any of that. I loved her body, and I loved enjoying that body, but my desire for her ended there.

For the first time in years, I had trouble sleeping. I was positive it had nothing to do with Eve.

I got up earlier than usual in the morning—not on purpose like I had yesterday, but because I couldn't sleep anymore. A hot shower sounded good until I was in the shower and started wondering if Eve would sneak in to join me.

She didn't.

Wishing she would join me in the shower had nothing to do with emotions. I wanted her like I'd never wanted any woman, and I wanteded to be inside her as often as possible from today onward. Thoughts of Eve's body had me beating off in the shower, but that wouldn't tide me over for long.

By the time I walked into the kitchen, Eve was already making breakfast for everyone.

She waved toward the stool on my side of the island. "Have a seat. I'll give you first dibs on breakfast."

I perched on the stool, noting that she'd already set out plates and silverware for us. "Thought I'd beat you into the kitchen this morning."

And I might have if I hadn't needed to relieve my lust twice in the shower.

The outfit she'd chosen to wear today didn't help matters. Her tie-dyed dress held up by spaghetti straps barely covered her ass and breasts, and the gold anklet draped around her elegant ankle made me hunger to have that leg strapped around me again. The sandals she wore had the skinniest straps I'd ever seen and looked like they might snap if she took one step. The shoes didn't have me wincing and adjusting my position on the stool, though. It was the dress. Was she wearing panties under that thing? She couldn't be wearing a bra, not with that plunging neckline and those slender straps.

Eve's breasts. Naked under the dress. Her perfect tits swinging free.

My erection scraped against the underside of the island's lip.

I coughed into my fist and said, "Smells good. What are you making?"

"Sheet breakfast sandwiches."

"What is a sheet breakfast sandwich? I've never heard of that."

She smiled at me over her shoulder. "You've heard of a breakfast sandwich, right? The ones I'm making have a pancake layer on the top and bottom with sausage, eggs, and cheese in the middle. Instead of making each sandwich individually, I whip up one huge sandwich on a big baking sheet. I'm using three baking sheets today. Then I slice each big sandwich into smaller pieces."

"Do you pour syrup on it?"

"No, but I put syrup out on the buffet table for anyone who wants it." She glanced at me again, this time curling her lip. "I also have to put out hot sauce and jalapenos. Ollie and Sylvester love that stuff."

"Have you tried it? Hot sauce and jalapenos sounds good to me."

She wagged a large knife at me. "If you expect to kiss me later, better not eat any of that."

Kiss her? Yes, I wanted to do that—for hours. I loved kissing Eve.

"When can I eat one of those?" I asked. "*Estou verde de fome.*"

"You're starving, eh? Oh yeah, you look puny and weak, for sure." She turned around, holding a plate with three breakfast sandwiches on it. Setting it down in front of me, she slanted in to peck a kiss on my lips. "Can't have you malnourished, not with the things I want to do to you today."

"More cookies?" I half hoped she would do that again.

She shook her head. "I saved a bottle of caramel sauce and a tub of ice cream just for us."

"An ice cream sundae? I like those."

"Uh-uh, this one's all for me." She stretched out one delicate hand, trailing the tip of her longest finger down my chest. "You *are* the sundae."

"I like that even better." I caught her hand, lifted her outstretched finger to my mouth, and sucked on it. "But it's only fair that I should get my turn to have an Eve sundae."

She withdrew her hand, but her eyes had taken on the glossiness of desire. "Well, I guess it is only fair."

While she returned to portioning out the breakfast sandwiches, I abandoned mine and sneaked up behind her. The scent of her hair made me draw in a deep draft of it, my nose buried in her silky locks. I slipped an arm around her waist.

"Can't wait for dessert," I said. "Need you now."

"But I have to finish making breakfast. Hungry nudists are waiting, and they won't like their hot breakfast to arrive cold."

I fisted my hand in her hair, tugging her head back to expose her slender throat. Her mouth fell open. I raked my tongue up her skin from the base of her throat to the tender spot right under her jaw. "We'll heat up the food in the microwave."

She leaned into me, her hands landing on my thighs. "We can't. We shouldn't."

"Yes, we should, and we can." I glided my palm down her leg until I found the hem of her dress, then slipped my hand under it. Her skimpy underwear blocked me from touching her where I desperately wanted to, so I settled for stroking her through the fabric. "Say yes, Eve."

Her breasts heaved. Her panties grew wet.

She crooked her fingers into my thighs and whispered, "Yes."

I suckled her earlobe.

High-pitched screams erupted outside.

Eve jerked. "They're early."

"Who?"

"The Kitten Brigade." She shoved me away and whirled around, straightening her dress. "They never get here this early in the morning."

She raced out the door.

I followed at a slower pace.

There in the driveway hunkered a neon-pink motor home. Young women were still pouring out of the vehicle, every one of them wearing a simple white T-shirt dress.

Eve and I stopped ten feet from the group.

Once the last girl had exited the motor home, they all whipped off their clothes and shrieked. White dresses, the only items of clothing they wore, flew into the air and sailed down to land on the gravel of the driveway.

The gaze of every last member of their group zeroed in on me.

Whoops and shrieks exploded from them, and the throng descended.

Chapter Fifteen

Eve

Oh. Dear. God. The Kitten Brigade swarmed Val like they'd discovered a juicy T-bone steak after being on a liquid diet for a month. I got muscled out of the way as eight twenty-something women rushed at the man I'd spent most of yesterday screwing. They giggled and shrieked and barraged him with questions, all talking at once so there was no chance he could understand their questions, much less answer them.

Val stayed calm, though. He smiled and shook the girls' hands. How a naked man surrounded by nubile, nude women could remain so composed baffled the hell out of me. Most guys would've freaked out or gotten angry—or developed a raging erection. I supposed Val was used to this kind of attention. He had become a celebrity thanks to his outrageous public behavior.

When the Kittens continued to swarm Val after a couple of minutes, I shoved two fingers into my mouth and whistled. The sound pierced the babbling of the crowd, and everyone in the vicinity—the Kittens, Val, and the other guests—swung their attention to me.

"Girls," I said, "let the man breathe, okay? Having a guest suffocate under a pile of women wouldn't be good press for the resort."

The de facto leader of the Kitten Brigade, Heidi Mackenzie, sashayed over to me. She gave me a quick, firm hug and then feigned a pout. "We're sorry, Evie. But you can't expect us to ignore the hottest guy who's ever set foot on your property."

"No, but I can and do expect you to not assault him en masse."

Somehow, even while stark naked with her nipples jutting from her perky breasts, she pulled off an expression of pure innocence. Her angelic looks, with golden-blonde hair and pale-blue eyes, helped. "We didn't touch him. Not even an ass pinch. We kept our hands to ourselves even though he is a walking fudge pop begging to be licked."

Oh yeah, Val and Heidi had something in common—utter shamelessness.

Heidi leaned in to whisper in my ear, "Please tell me you've tapped that."

"You know I never kiss and tell."

"Sad but true." She backed up a step and waved her arms, summoning the Brigade. When every last one of them had abandoned Val, some adopting a fake pout like Heidi had done, she turned to address her group. "The new guy is off-limits, Kittens." The sassy girl winked at me over her shoulder. "Evie's got this one."

My mouth opened, a denial on my tongue, but I shut my trap. Nobody needed to know the details of my whatever-this-was with Val.

"And now," Heidi said, "Eve will introduce us to the new hottie."

I glanced at Val, my brows raised.

He shrugged.

And I took that as permission to tell them.

To the Kittens, I said, "This is Val Silva. He's originally from Brazil but calls LA home these days. He was a soccer star for years, even went to the Olympics, but now he's a model."

"And he belongs to Evie," Heidi said with mock gravitas.

Shelby Thomas, the shortest member of the Brigade, shook her head. "What a bummer. I was looking forward to a good cat fight. Oh well, at least I don't need to keep my hair tied up if nobody's going to use it as leverage."

The brunette ripped the scrunchy out of her, setting her long locks free, and tossed the scrunchy high into the air.

It landed on Val's shoulder.

He wrapped the strip of lavender fabric around his wrist.

Shelby giggled.

"Let me finish the introductions," I said, and pointed to each lady in turn as I told Val their names. "Heidi. Shelby. Taylor. Allison. Heather. Sydney. Jane. Leah."

Val smiled. "Nice to meet you, ladies. What a lovely bunch you are."

Some of them smiled shyly. Others grinned. A few gave him saucy looks.

Heidi rose onto her tiptoes to glance around the area behind me where the other guests had gathered. "Where's our Ollie? Isn't he here yet?"

I turned around, searching the crowd until I spotted Ollie.

At the instant I spotted him, Heidi did too. She hopped on her toes and waved her arms in the air. "Get over here, sweetie! We missed you!"

Ollie smiled sheepishly at the people around him, shrugged, and pushed through the crowd to reach Heidi and the gals.

Heidi grabbed him in a bear hug.

"Cut that out," I chided. "Do I need to recite the rules right here? I thought we could hold off on that until you get settled in."

"We know the rules," Heidi said, releasing a blushing Ollie. "But I couldn't help myself. This boy is cuteness squared."

The rest of the Kittens took their turns hugging Ollie, but in the permitted fashion. Shelby ruffled his hair. Several of them kissed his cheek. In fact, they paid more attention to him than they had to Val.

Well, they had known Ollie for years.

I walked over to Val, who now stood alone.

He draped an arm around my waist. "I seem to have lost my appeal. Can't compete with Ollie."

"Yes, he does have that adorable-nerd vibe women love."

"Would you rather be hugging and kissing Ollie?" he asked with a smirk.

"No, I prefer the notorious-exhibitionist type."

He tugged me against his side. "I'm glad to hear that."

The Kittens spotted us in our intimate pose and started cooing "ooooh." Several of them shouted various things at us—well, at me.

"Evie's got a boyfriend!"

"No, she's just licking that lollipop!"

"When's the wedding?"

"Look at those muscles! Woo-hoo, Evie!"

Ollie, still surrounded by women fighting for his attention, flashed me an impish grin. "Leave her alone, girls. If Eve wants to shack up with the new guy, it's her business."

"Shack up?" Heidi said, sidling up to Ollie. "Do tell."

"Val's staying in Eve's house."

I wagged a finger at Ollie. "Don't be a gossip. You know it's only because of the burst pipe in the guest house."

"Right, the pipe. How are those repairs coming?"

He knew damn well the repairs weren't finished. Since firing Quentin yesterday, I'd forgotten to call around and find a contractor to finish the work. If anyone would come out here. Maybe I didn't want Val to move into the guest house yet. Or ever.

Or maybe scorching sex was making me forgetful. Yeah, that was it.

Everyone stared at me and Val, their expressions running the gamut from amused to surprised.

Which might've had something to do with the fact Val had his arm around me and was hugging me to his naked body. I fought the impulse to shout, "He's not my boyfriend!" That would lead to more questions about why we were so chummy and what exactly we were doing together. In my house. Alone. Most of the day and all of the night.

I broke up the crowd by suggesting the Kittens get their tents set up. Ollie offered to help out with that, and several of the older men offered too, as did Val.

While the girls retrieved their equipment from the RV, Ollie approached me. Val and the other men had gone around the guest house to the camping area, so Ollie had me alone.

He put his arm around my shoulders. "Is Val treating you right? You're like a sister to me, and I don't want some Casanova athlete breaking your heart."

"That's very sweet, Ollie, but I'm fine. No danger of heartbreak."

"You sure?" He gave me a squeeze. "Because you two have that look."

"What look?"

"The one that usually means two people are falling in love."

"Oh please," I said. "Now you're an expert on human behavior?"

"Hardly, but I've known you for four years." He took hold of my shoulders and angled me to face him. His expression was serious. "I have never seen you act the way you do with Val. This isn't a fling, Evie. You really like him, and he really likes you."

"We met four days ago."

"You never heard of love at first sight?"

"Heard of it? Yes. Believe in it? No."

Val and I were enjoying multiple orgasms per day, not falling in love. Neither of us wanted a relationship. I wouldn't tell Ollie any of that because it was private and none of his damn business. Still, his concern for my well-being might have been the nicest thing anyone had done for me in a long time.

"Okay," he said. "If you're good, I'm good."

He jogged off to help with the tent setup.

I went into my house to finish preparing breakfast.

Ollie was wrong. No way, no how could I fall for a guy I'd met four days ago. I certainly wouldn't fall for a big-time womanizer who liked to strip in public to get media attention.

No way, no how.

Chapter Sixteen

Val

After breakfast, I observed while the other guests enjoyed a raucous game of miniten with the rules treated as suggestions and everyone laughing more than hitting the ball. Though the game was supposed to be played by two pairs, the Kitten Brigade insisted on having six players on each side strictly for fun. Eve had only four thugs on hand, so the other players took up tennis rackets. The Kittens lost to the Silver Foxes, the team name for the gray-haired guests, but no one seemed to care about the score.

Once the game ended, I followed Eve into her house. She'd announced to everyone she was going to make lunch. Considering she now had twenty-five guests to feed, she needed help. Of course, she wouldn't ask for it. The woman seemed to be allergic to admitting she needed a hand.

In her kitchen, she rounded on me. "Go back outside. You're a guest, not my sous chef."

"Don't want to be your sous chef." I looped an arm around her waist and pulled her close. "I'm your slave, remember? I do your bidding all day and all night."

"Even if I made you clean all the toilets in the guest house?"

"Yes, even then." I considered what she'd said, then asked, "Tell me you don't do all the cleaning yourself."

"I do."

"Eve, you need to hire more people to help you."

She wriggled out of my hold. "I don't have the budget for that. Maybe soon I will, now that I've paid off the bank loan, but not yet."

"I'll give you the money."

She settled a hand on the counter and drummed her fingers. "Thank you for the offer. It's very generous, but I can't accept. I'm not a damsel in distress waiting for you to rescue me."

"This is help from a friend, not charity."

Her lips ticked upward at the corners even as they puckered slightly. She shook her head. "We're screwing, Val, not knitting quilts together."

I grabbed a spatula off the island, unsure why I did it, and clenched my fist around the thing. Maybe I needed to throttle something other than Eve. Most women begged me to give them money or buy them clothes, but she would have none of it. I thumped the spatula's handle on the butcher-block surface. "Why won't you accept my help? I have more than enough money. Let me share it with you."

"Why not donate it to a good cause? Kids with cancer or abused animals really need your generosity."

Though I studied her expression, I couldn't decipher her true reasons for refusing my gift. Well, I'd known her for a matter of days, and we hadn't discussed our pasts that much. Maybe she always disliked accepting financial assistance, but the fact she'd accepted it from her parents suggested otherwise. Maybe she didn't like a monetary gift from someone she'd known for a few days.

"Please," I said, "let me do this for you. If you won't accept a gift, at least let me invest in your company."

Why was I so determined to give her money? She wanted nothing from me, and I kept pushing her to take my gift.

Eve sighed. "My God, you're stubborn. I don't want an investor who's sleeping with me. Isn't that a conflict of interest or something?"

What was the point in arguing anymore? She would never accept help of any kind from me. Maybe that was because we were sexually involved, or maybe because she didn't like my past. An infamous man made her uncomfortable. I couldn't fault her for that. Not many women, except the ones who craved fame, wanted to get involved with a man like me.

Yes, I'd made this bed for myself. Today, I had to sleep in it alone.

"Have it your way, *bebê*," I said. "I'll leave you to manage on your own."

"Thank you."

I retreated to the outdoors where the other guests were engaged in a game of charades. Nude charades might sound sexy, but in fact, it was rather awkward and silly. Tits and dicks bounced while the players tried to act out various themes, and falling down meant getting grass and dirt on their skin and in their hair. I knew from experience grass and dirt could get into many places where a person didn't want it to go. Sand was even worse, but luckily, we had no sand in the field behind the guest house.

Heidi stumbled while flailing her arms—to represent what exactly, I had no idea—and tumbled to the ground. When she got up, she had a small daisy stuck to her nipple.

Ollie snickered. "Look, she's wearing a pasty."

"The organic kind," said Willy, one of the Silver Foxes. "Very progressive, Heidi."

"Sexual harassment," I said, "is against the house rules."

Edna flapped her hand in a dismissive gesture. "Heidi knows we're joshing, and she gives as good as she gets."

"It's true," Heidi said. She plucked the wildflower off her skin and tossed it to Ollie, then blew him a kiss.

The boy blushed.

Lunch arrived a few minutes after the charades game broke up. Eve was pushing one metal cart overflowing with food while pulling another behind her. The strain of dragging them both across the dirt path between her home and the guest house crimped her whole face. She looked tired, most likely because she'd made all the food herself. Several of the men rushed to her aid. Though she tried to wave them away, Ollie took possession of the cart behind her while Willy wrested the other cart from her grasp. Sylvester hurried into Eve's house to get the third cart laden with food.

When I approached her, she managed only a half-hearted smile. "Thought you'd be first in line to wrestle for the carts."

"You wouldn't have let me, would you? I hoped you'd accept help from someone else." I glanced at the men hauling the carts toward the guest house. "I assume you aren't sleeping with any of them."

"No."

"Have you been with any of them in the past?"

One side of her mouth twisted as if she were trying not to smile. "No, I have not."

I felt strangely relieved to hear that. "Are we joining the others in the dining hall or eating in private?"

"The Kittens just got here. I'd like to eat with them so we can catch up."

Was she trying to avoid me?

I moved closer, loving the way her lips parted and her breath caught. "Heidi mentioned all of you keep in touch through email and social media. You don't need to get caught up on their lives or vice versa."

"Abandoning them on their first day here would be rude."

"Heidi ordered me to make sure you have fun. She suggested an intimate picnic at the hot spring."

"That girl needs a hobby."

"She cares about you. So—" I'd almost said *so do I.* "So let's not disappoint Heidi. Have lunch with me at the hot spring. I understand it's only a short walk away."

"That's true, but—"

"Say yes, Eve."

"Maybe tomorrow."

I lashed an arm around her waist and tugged her tight against my body, relishing the feel of her curves. "Soon enough, you'll figure out I can be much more stubborn than you. All I want is to make you feel good. Relax. Enjoy a beautiful day. You've earned it."

"This is a serious violation of nudist etiquette."

"Because I'm naked and I'm hugging you? Yes, I know." I tugged her even more snugly to my body. "In case you hadn't noticed, propriety doesn't mean much to me."

"No kidding." She gazed into my eyes, her tongue slipping out to moisten her bottom lip. "I don't have a handyman anymore, which means there's a lot of work for me to do."

"Forget about work for a while." I sealed two fingers over her lips when she started to protest. "Please, Eve, let me do this for you. It's lunch, not a handout."

She glanced at the nudists tramping into the guest house. "Okay."

We made sure the other guests had everything they needed, then grabbed some of the food and packed it into a picnic basket. From Eve's kitchen, we gathered a few more ingredients, including a bottle of wine and two glasses. Soup and sandwiches wasn't the most romantic meal, but I cared more about making sure she was well-nourished. I had a feeling if I didn't do that, she might forget to eat.

I grabbed a pair of sandals too. The trail to the hot spring was dirt, but as Eve had warned me, footwear was a necessity out in the woods. I carried the picnic basket and a blanket slung over my shoulder while she led the way, refusing to walk beside me and opposed to me holding her hand. When I tried that, she yanked hers away.

She had to be in front, naturally.

After a short walk, we arrived at the hot spring. Two wooden benches hunkered alongside the pool, and a wooden box with a latching lid held towels for any guests who might have forgotten to bring one. The box also offered bottled water. Eve thought of everything for her guests but neglected to take care of herself.

That changed today.

Steam wafted up from the blue pool, curling up into the air and dissipating. We laid out our blanket and relaxed there among the trees, listening to the birds singing while we ate and talked.

"I hope the Kittens haven't overwhelmed you," she said after consuming a large mouthful of her sandwich. "They can be a handful."

"Don't worry about me. They're sweet girls." I brushed a crumb away from the corner of her mouth with my thumb. "Besides, I grew up with two sisters. The Kittens are more exuberant than Maria and Aline, but I can handle it."

"How often do you see your family?"

"Several times a year. Sometimes I go home to visit them, and sometimes they come to America to stay with me."

"I know you live in LA, but how long have you been in the US?"

"Quite a while."

She consumed the last bite of her sandwich and wiped her fingers and mouth with a napkin. "I know it's none of my business, but I'm curious. You only have a slight accent, and you talk like an American."

Her curiosity about my life should have made me uncomfortable. After all, I wanted nothing more than a fling with her. But I discovered I liked knowing she wanted to know about me. It made me curious to learn about her.

"My mother is American," I explained. "Of Cuban descent, but both she and her parents were born and raised in Florida. She met my father when he was in Florida on spring break—he went to Harvard, like me—and they became infatuated with each other. My mother didn't go to college, but she's a very smart woman. Anyway, they kept in touch through letters and over the phone. She visited him in Massachusetts for three weeks in the summer. Six months after they met, my father proposed. She married him, and after he graduated, she moved to Brazil with him."

"It must've been hard to move to another country. Did she speak Portuguese?"

"Not at first. My father taught her." I took a sip of my wine. "She was always fluent in Spanish, but eventually, she became adept at Portuguese too. Still, she insisted I learn about America and Cuba so I would understand my heritage."

"You mentioned your father was an ambassador."

I nodded. "For three years. I told you I went to Harvard after that, but I spent summers at home. After graduation, I moved back to Brazil to join the Olympic football team. I'd played football before my family moved to Washington, and I played soccer in high school here and while at Harvard. My father wanted me to get a degree in business, so I'd be more levelheaded about financial matters, but all I cared about was football. We compromised. I got the degree, then went back to football. He was right, though. Having business training has helped me make better decisions."

"Didn't you say you moved to LA five years ago?"

"Yes, you have an excellent memory." Or was she memorizing everything I said for another reason? Did I want her to? "After the Olympics, I played for a professional club, and later for the Brazilian national football team until I retired seven years ago. My first modeling jobs were in New York, so I lived there for two years. Then, I signed a contract with an agency in Los Angeles. I've stayed there ever since."

"Wow, you're quite the international man." She took a swig of her wine. "My life can't compete."

"I've told you my story. Now tell me yours."

She swigged more wine, a bit of it dribbling down her chin. "I'm boring."

With my thumb, I wiped away the dribbling red wine. "I doubt that. You've told me very little about yourself, and already I'm enthralled."

"You're full of shit, that's what you are."

"At least tell me about your family. Do you have any brothers or sisters?"

She took another swig of wine. "Fine, if you insist. Yes, I have both. My brother lives in Portland, Maine, with his wife and their two children. He teaches high school, and she works at a community college. My sister is an accountant, and she's engaged to a great guy. She lives in Portland too. That's where we all grew up."

"How did you end up here?"

"I moved to New York, thinking I could become a professional photographer. The city didn't work out as well for me as it did for you." She gazed across the hot spring, though she seemed not to be looking at anything in particular. "I was broke. My parents had retired to Florida by then, and they wanted me to move there too. My brother and sister both wanted me to go back to Maine. I didn't want to do either, so I racked my brain for a way to make ends meet while still having time for photography."

"That must be when you had your idea for this place."

"Yeah, but it wasn't a eureka moment. It was an accident." She swung her attention back to me. "I was researching nature photography when I made a serendipitous typo. While I was typing the word nature, the search engine popped up with suggested searches, and I accidentally clicked on 'naturist.' I was going to click away from the search results, but I got curious. When I looked at the first page in the search results, I learned naturist is another word for nudist. I didn't close the browser window. I kept looking."

"A closet voyeur, eh?"

"Maybe at first," she admitted, her head bowed, looking up at me through her lashes. "But then I realized it wasn't all about sex. Some people prefer to be naked. Browsing various websites about nudism gave me an idea. It seemed like there weren't a lot of affordable retreats geared toward nudists. When my dad inherited this property, complete with a hot spring, I got my brilliant idea."

"You serve an underserved population of tourists." I traced a finger down her cheek. "You are brilliant, Eve. And hardworking. And a talented photographer, not to mention incredible in bed."

"So are you." She reached inside the picnic basket and dug out a box of cookies. "Ready for dessert?"

My cock loved the idea of Eve crumbling cookies all over me and licking them up crumb by crumb, but my curiosity pushed me to ask one more question. "How often do you see your family?"

With a soft little groan, she set down the cookie box. "We all go to our parents' house in Florida for Thanksgiving. For Christmas, we alternate between Maine and my place. This year, it's my turn."

"Are those the only times you see your family?"

"My parents like to surprise me every so often. My brother and sister have each visited a few times, and they keep pestering me to visit them." She leaned forward to settle her hand on my thigh. "May we please end the getting-to-know-you session?"

"Absolutely." I rose and offered her my hands, helping her up when she took them. "Take your clothes off, Eve, and join me in the water."

"I don't go naked in public."

"We're alone. Heidi promised to keep everyone away from the hot spring."

"Oh great. Everyone will know we're out here getting it on."

"No, I told Heidi we're having a picnic."

Eve gave me a skeptical look. "That's code for screwing each other's brains out."

I kissed her forehead. "Take a chance. With me."

"But—"

I ran for the pool and dived in.

The water was warmer than body temperature, but not too hot. Perfect for making love to a beautiful woman. By the time I surfaced at the pool's center, Eve had shed her dress and was slipping out of her panties. The sight of her nude made me hard. I'd seen her naked body before, had my hands and mouth all over her, but seeing her never failed to arouse me. It was different than with other women. I craved her more every time I had her, but with the others, I'd gradually lost interest. I couldn't imagine ever getting tired of Eve.

I swam to the shore, where a ledge offered a place to rest my arms. "Grab a condom, would you? They're in the basket."

"There aren't any—"

"Underneath everything else."

She dug around inside the basket and brought out the box of condoms. "You sneaked an entire box of them in here? Seems like overkill."

"Not with you. I can't get enough of your body."

"We don't really need these anyway." She threw me a sideways glance. "Unless you have a secret you need to tell me? About your health?"

"I'm clean, Eve. I get tested regularly."

"Okay, then. We don't need these." She tossed the box of condoms back into the basket. "I'm clean too, and I'm on the pill. Besides, I don't know if condoms work underwater. Do you?"

"No, I've never had sex in the water before."

She straightened, her brows wrinkling as she stared at me. "You have never done it in the water? But you're so adventurous."

I shrugged. "Never had the opportunity."

She approached the ledge and sat down on it with her feet dangling in the water. "You're introducing me to a lot of new things, so it's nice I can do the same for you."

"Time to get wet," I said, running a hand up her inner thigh. "Or are you wet already?"

"You know I am." She slid off the ledge into the water, dunking her head to drench her hair. "But now I'm wet all over, not just between my legs."

I pulled her into my arms and kissed her. The sensation of her silken tongue on mine, of her supple and slick body pasted to mine, made me even harder. I whisked my palms up and down her backside, from her shoulders to her ass, while she tangled her fingers in the hair at my nape and plunged her tongue deeper into my mouth. I grasped her bottom with one hand, and with the other, I covered her breast. She gasped when I flicked my thumb across her taut nipple.

When I pinched it, she clutched my hair tighter.

I gave up her lips and her tongue, dipping my head to nuzzle her throat.

"Val," she moaned, her head falling back. "Please, yes."

"Eve, you're so perfect." I slid my hand from her breast down her stomach, and lower, to push my fingers between her folds. "I love your body."

I stroked her until she wrapped her legs around me, wrapped her entire body around me.

"Skip that," she breathed into my ear. "I can't wait any longer."

Neither could I. Even touching her with my fingers, feeling how ready she was, made me throb for her. I clamped both hands on her ass and thrust into her body, groaning when her wet heat surrounded me. "You feel so good. I want you to come all over me."

"Hurry, please."

I punched into her again and again, tugging her bottom toward me to deepen every thrust. She drew her head back to look at me, her lips swollen from our kiss, her eyes half closed and her cheeks dusted with pink.

God, she was so beautiful.

With our gazes bound to each other, we gave in to the moment and to the sheer pleasure of joining our bodies. I slowed my pace, pulling out and easing back inside her, to prolong this feeling despite the desperate need to slam into her until we both exploded. Never in my life had I longed to stay inside a woman forever, to revel in the intimacy and the sensations. Her hot sheath glided along my cock, wavelets lapped around us, and her head fell back as her eyes closed. She clung to me, both arms around my neck, and locked her ankles behind my ass. Her breaths tickled my ear. Her hair tickled my cheek. I rotated my head to bury my face in that hair and fill my senses with the sweet scent of it, the scent of her.

"Faster," she murmured into my ear.

I bucked into her, gripping her bottom, yanking her into me every time I drove my cock deeper. She made a desperate noise, a cross between a gasp and a whimper, and I fucked her even faster, even harder, pounding into her while the water splashed around us and sprayed our faces.

Eve's entire body stiffened around me. She threw her head forward and sank her teeth into my shoulder when she came, her cry muffled by my flesh, her body clenched around my shaft. The pulsating waves of her climax pushed me over the edge. A hoarse shout erupted out of me as I thrust once more, the deepest and hardest thrust of all, and exploded inside her sweet body.

I'd never before come inside a woman without a condom. She'd let me. She'd wanted me to do it. A feral part of me loved the idea that I'd branded her in this way, but mostly, I loved the intense intimacy of spilling myself inside this woman with nothing separating our bodies.

We were both breathing hard and drenched. She laughed softly and tickled my nape with her fingertips. I chuckled and squeezed her ass.

"Mmm," she hummed straight into my ear, her lips vibrating against my skin. "Water sex is awesome."

I agreed, but I couldn't manage to speak yet. Being with Eve left me speechless. Maybe I should've worried about that. I didn't have the energy for worry, too relaxed to do anything except savor the warmth of her body and the afterglow of our lovemaking.

Footsteps slapped farther down the trail, coming closer.

Eve's head snapped up, and she craned her neck to peer down the trail.

Heidi emerged from the woods. When she spotted us, her eyes widened, and she stumbled to a halt.

"Oops!" she said, flinging a hand up to cover her mouth. "Sorry, guys, I didn't think—" She moved her hand away from her mouth to cover her eyes. "Didn't see a thing. I hate to interrupt, but some new guests have arrived."

"New guests?" Eve pushed me away and whirled around, sloshing water over me. "I don't have any new bookings until next week."

"Uh, they're not paying guests. It's your parents."

"What?" Eve virtually screeched the word. She slapped her palms onto the ledge and hoisted her body out of the water, scrambling to get to her feet. Water sluiced off her skin and poured from her hair, but she didn't seem to notice. "When did they get here?"

"A few minutes ago," Heidi said. She made a pained face. "They brought the whole gang."

Eve went rigid and motionless as a granite statue, her eyes wide and her mouth open. Her voice was hushed, almost a whisper. "My brother and sister? The kids? Everyone?"

"Yep."

I heaved myself up out of the water and got to my feet. Coming up beside Eve, I slipped an arm around her shoulders. "Why do you look shocked? I would've thought you'd want to see your family."

Only her eyes moved when she glanced at me. "I do, but not today. It's kind of a bad time."

She looked me up and down, her eyebrows lifting. Her appraisal stalled at my dick.

Ah yes, that. I wasn't fully aroused, but neither was I completely limp.

Eve raced toward Heidi, grasped her shoulders, and spun her to face the trail. "Don't look back. Just go. Tell my family I'll be there in a few minutes. And please, do not under any circumstances let them come out here."

"Aye-aye, captain," Heidi said with a smirk.

She lowered her hand and trotted down the trail.

Eve rushed to get dried off and get dressed.

"Relax," I said, observing her frantic movements while I slipped on my sandals and toweled off. "Your parents know this is a nudist retreat. They won't be shocked to see me."

She yanked her dress on over her head. It got stuck on her ear. She fumbled with it but seemed too frazzled to get it free.

I unhooked the strap from her ear, and the dress fell into position. "You're panicking. Is it because of me?"

She almost tripped getting her sandals on. "Ya think? I just had sex with a man I don't really know"—she flapped her arms, apparently to indicate the woods and the hot spring—"out here in the open. I took my clothes off outdoors where anyone might see me."

Eve flapped her arms again and made a face I couldn't describe. Her upper lip curled even as her mouth fell open. Her nose crinkled. She squinted her eyes and shook her head. Maybe it was shock or embarrassment, but I'd never seen an expression like that before. It was adorable. Bizarre, but adorable.

I grasped her shoulders. "Take a deep breath, Eve. This isn't as bad as you think."

"Sure, not as bad." She nodded her head with so much vigor it must've jarred her brain. "My entire family is here, everyone knows you and I are having sex, and you walk around naked twenty-four seven. My parents aren't nudists, but hey, what's to worry about?"

Her grin was sarcastic and slightly manic.

I did the only thing I could do. I gave her a quick, hard kiss and then grasped her hand in mine to lead her back to the guest house and her home. She didn't complain about the hand-holding, a testament to her frazzled state. We walked out of the woods hand in hand.

Eve froze, her eyes even wider.

An older woman with blonde hair sprinted toward us, followed by an older man with a rim of gray hair around his large bald spot. The couple halted a few feet from me and Eve, taking in the sight of us—Eve in her skimpy, tie-dyed dress and me in…well, nothing.

We'd forgotten the picnic basket, I suddenly realized.

"Mom," Eve said, struggling to catch her breath. "Dad. Hi. I wasn't expecting you."

Eve's mother squinted at me.

Or rather, at my penis.

Her lips quirked, and she puckered them like she was trying not to smile or maybe laugh. She aimed her eyes, bright blue like her daughter's, at me. "Who's your new friend, Evie?"

I kept hold of Eve's hand but offered the other one to her mother. "Val Silva."

Eve's mother shook my hand. "I'm Donna Holt. This is my husband, Larry."

Mr. Holt shook my hand vigorously. "Nice to meet you, Val. We didn't know Eve was seeing anybody."

The Holts smiled and tried very hard not to stare at my dick, though Mrs. Holt kept glancing at it, her lips twitching every time. I guessed Eve hadn't told them the resort rules.

"I'm pleased to meet you too, Mr. and Mrs. Holt," I said. "You've raised quite a woman in Eve."

The woman in question hadn't moved or closed her mouth. I wondered if she was breathing. Her chest was rising and falling, so I decided she wasn't in danger of passing out from lack of oxygen.

"Call me Donna," Mrs. Holt said. "Or maybe you should call me Mom?"

Eve roused from her catatonic state with a jolt, blinking rapidly. "Mom, honestly, I met Val this week."

"Mm-hmm." She swept her gaze over me again. "But you must really like him. You were holding hands when you came back from the hot spring, where you'd been all alone together."

"Yeah," Mr. Holt said, "and you haven't called us since last Thursday. When Mom texted you the other day, you claimed to be too busy for that. We knew something was up, and Donna bet me fifty bucks it was a boy."

No one had called me a boy in at least fifteen years.

Mr. Holt clapped me on the shoulder. "Call me Larry. Dad can wait until the wedding's arranged."

Eve spluttered for a moment before she managed to speak. "We're not engaged, for Christ's sake. I haven't called because I've been busy. A pipe burst in the guest house and then I had to fire Quentin—"

"Oh, we heard about that," Donna said. She threw an arm around her daughter's shoulders and urged her to walk. "Heidi filled us in on the soap opera, and on your new beau."

Larry gripped my shoulder hard. "Let's have a little man-to-man chat while the girls catch up. What do you say?"

What could I say? "Of course, let's chat."

Chapter Seventeen

Eve

My dad dragged Val away from the crowd that had gathered around us. I watched the two of them retreating from view behind the throng of guests and wondered what on earth my father was up to. He never interrogated my boyfriends. Not that Val was my boyfriend. What was he, then? My lover, I supposed. I did not want to tell my parents that, though I had my suspicions the other guests had spilled those beans long before Val and I traipsed out of the woods.

What should I say to my parents? *Hey, guess what, I'm screwing a virtual stranger who made a notorious sex tape and used to strip in public. You can probably catch video of both on YouTube.*

Since Val said he had the sex tape on his phone, I supposed my parents didn't need internet access to view my lover's past escapades. If they asked, he would show them. He was just that kind of shameless exhibitionist.

And I loved that side of him.

I must've lost my mind, right? Sleeping with a man I barely knew. Getting naked outdoors. Heidi had seen us in the hot spring. I hadn't been caught getting it on with a guy since my sophomore year of college when my brother Andrew had barged into my dorm room unannounced. He'd wanted to surprise me with a visit. Oh yeah, I'd been surprised all right. My brother had gotten a good look at my tits before his face turned crimson and he scampered back into the hallway. Andrew and I never told a soul about that incident.

Somehow, today had been more embarrassing. I was a grown woman, thirty years old, not a college sophomore. But this time, everyone knew what I'd been doing with a guy.

Bye-bye, privacy.

"Evie," my mom said, "why didn't you tell us you have a beau?"

I'd never been good at lying to my mom, so I told the truth—partially. "It's not like that. Val and I met four days ago. Please don't start planning the wedding."

Yeah, I omitted the fact neither I nor Val wanted a romantic entanglement, much less a commitment.

Mom slung an arm around my shoulders and gave me a good squeeze. "You might be my baby, but you're an adult. I won't judge your choices. Have I ever complained about one of your boyfriends, even the ones I didn't like?"

"No."

"I like Val."

"You met him five seconds ago."

She tipped her head side to side, then gave a decisive nod. "I can tell if a man is good or bad news in thirty seconds or less. Val is a good one."

If she knew about his past, would she feel the same way?

Why did I care? Val was fun to be with and gave me awesome orgasms. End of story.

My brother and sister ran up to us, all grins and chuckles. Andrew had that gleam in his eyes that always meant he was about to razz me big time.

"Hey, Evie," he said, giving me a quick hug. "Hope you don't mind the surprise visit. Didn't know we'd be breaking up your private party."

Krista's lips twitched like she was trying not to smirk. "Must've been some party. You're all flushed, Evie."

"Don't tease your sister," Mom said. "Can't you see she's embarrassed enough already? But Evie, really, you don't need to be embarrassed. I'm glad you've found a man who makes you happy."

"Mom," I moaned, "I told you Val is not my boyfriend."

Andrew's grin turned positively goofy. "Not your boyfriend? You run off into the woods with lots of naked guys?"

"This is a nudist resort."

"Sure, but you were out in the woods with him all alone." He pointed at my dress. "And your dress is on backwards."

What? How had I not noticed that? Val hadn't seemed to notice either.

Before I could snarl at my brother, our mom said, "Be nice, Andy. Oh, what is your father doing over there? I'd better make sure he isn't giving Val a hard time."

My brother snickered and grinned some more. "I bet Val can handle himself fine. Can't he, Eve?"

Our mom smacked his arm on her way past him. She headed for the secluded spot on the other side of the lawn where my father had cornered my lover.

Krista sidled up to me and murmured, "Good job, Evie. Val is smokin' hot."

I wasn't sure what good job I'd done and decided I didn't want to know. Krista had a filthy mind.

My sister adopted a sarcastically dramatic tone of voice when she whispered, "Ollie told us Val is staying in your house."

"Uh, yeah, his room in the guest house got flooded by a burst pipe."

Krista leaned in closer, her face millimeters from mine. "Was that an accident, or did the pipe have a little help bursting?"

"Very funny." I settled one hand on my hip. "The pipe broke before Val even got here. I had no idea what he looked like or who he was. All I knew was his name. He might've been a pudgy sixty-year-old who smelled like cigar smoke."

"But he's not. He is one guy who absolutely should be a nudist." She glanced in Val's direction and sighed wistfully. "I love my fiancé, but Jeremy wouldn't know a weight machine if it dropped onto his head."

"Muscles aren't everything," Andrew said. He clucked his tongue and spoke in a tone of mock chastisement. "Shame on you, Kris. Aren't you supposed to love your fiancé for who he is, not what he looks like?"

"Yes, but that doesn't mean I can't appreciate a beautiful man. Val is eye candy." She winked at me. "Except to Eve. I bet he's all sorts of other kinds of candy for her."

"Ech," Andrew said, feigning a dry heave. "Don't make me hurl."

With an inward groan, I resigned myself to my fate. Today was going to be a blast.

Of the atomic bomb variety.

I loved my family, but really, could they have a chosen a worse moment to pop in for a surprise visit? I guessed I ought to be grateful they hadn't all tramped down the trail to the hot spring with Heidi.

Andrew scanned his gaze over the lawn until he spotted Val and our parents. His brows squished together. "I'd swear I've seen Val somewhere before."

Oh God, don't let my brother have seen the sex tape.

Even if he hadn't, Ollie knew about Val's past and might've blabbed to Andrew.

"Man, I wish I could remember," Andrew said, frowning and shaking his head. "Is Val an actor or something?"

I kept my trap shut, sealed with invisible duct tape.

"Yeah," Krista said, "now that you mention it, he does seem familiar."

Jeremy, Krista's fiancé, jogged up to us. "Hey, Eve, great to see you." He hugged me and slipped an arm around Krista while still watching me. "Why didn't you tell us you have a famous guest?"

"Famous?" Krista said. "You know who he is? We've been trying to figure out why Val looks familiar, but Eve won't tell us."

"He's Val Silva, the soccer champ who took the Brazilian team to the Olympics and scored the goal that won them a gold medal."

Please, please, please let that be all he knows.

"An athlete?" Krista said. "Well, that explains the sizzlin' bod."

"Yeah, he was an athlete," Jeremy said. "I think he's a model now. He used to like to strip buck naked at the end of every winning game."

Aw, fuck. Why did I have such sucky luck? I'd met Jeremy several times before, but I didn't know him well. Why couldn't he be the kind of guy who played video games all day? No, of course he had to be a soccer fan.

Krista looked at me like she'd never seen me before. "Evie hooked up with an exhibitionist?"

Jeremy squinted like he was thinking hard. His expression brightened, and he lifted a finger. "I remember the rest. Val Silva was notorious for being a nudist, but he got to be really infamous after everybody saw his sex tape."

I winced. Double fuck with a side of shit and a goddamn on top. The universe was punishing me for all my past transgressions. Sleeping with Cody and Aaron. Sleeping with Quentin. Spying on Val while he gave himself a happy ending, getting naked with Val in public, doing him in the hot spring, the list went on and on. Since Val arrived, I'd become a sex-crazed moron.

No, I hadn't done anything wrong. So what if everyone knew about Val's sex tape? I had no desire to get entangled in a relationship with him. His past had no bearing on my life or anything we did together. A surprise visit from my family had knocked me off balance, that was all.

My sister gaped at me, though I got the impression it wasn't all horror. There seemed to be a bit of awe in there too. "Evie, you naughty girl. No wonder you're glowing. A man like Val could perk up any woman."

I crossed my arms over my chest and said nothing, hoping my small smile came off as enigmatic.

"Everybody thinks I'm the bad girl in the family," Krista said. "All I did was flash my tits during Mardi Gras. But Evie, you… Wow, I didn't know you had a wild streak."

She sounded impressed rather than disgusted.

I excused myself to mingle with my guests, claiming I needed to check on whether they needed anything. Really, I needed a break from the pseudo-inquisition from my smart-mouthed siblings. For the rest of the day, I juggled spending time with my family and struggling to take care of my guests at the same time. When Dad and Andrew heard about the burst pipe, they insisted on fixing things for me. Val volunteered to help them, but they needed supplies first.

Val insisted I go with him into town to get those supplies.

And yeah, he wore clothes.

Well, sort of. His shorts were so short and tight they could've passed for briefs. His short-sleeve shirt was looser-fitting. He'd opted to wear the same sandals he'd had on when we sneaked off to the hot spring. No matter what he wore, he looked good enough to lick and nibble and fondle from head to toe.

Mm, I'd done all of that this week.

I drove the truck, though Val tried to talk me into letting him take the wheel.

"You're a guest," I said. "It's bad enough you insist on helping with the repairs. I am not letting you drive. Enjoy the scenery like a good little tourist."

"Are you upset about what happened? Your family knows about us."

"Everyone knows." I glanced at him sideways. "I'm sorry about the parental inquisition. My dad has never done that before."

"Should I be offended or flattered he gave me special treatment?"

"Not sure." I steered the truck around a corner while I thought about whether to tell him what my sister and brother had figured out. What the hell. Val wouldn't care. "Andrew and Krista know about your, um, antics on the football field. Krista's fiancé, Jeremy, recognized you. And he had also seen the sex tape."

"I know. Jeremy, Andrew, and I had a good long chat. They're very protective of you."

"Yeah, Andrew is. I don't know Jeremy all that well, so I doubt he was being protective."

"He definitely was. Face it, Eve, everyone loves you."

My pulse sped up. Everyone loved me? He didn't mean to include himself in that statement, for sure. Did I wish he had?

No, of course not. We'd known each other for a matter of days.

At the hardware store, we ran into someone I'd hoped to avoid for the rest of my life.

Quentin Smith walked down the plumbing aisle toward us.

I tried to pretend I didn't notice him, focusing on the tools Val was examining. I even tried to block Val's view of the human disaster striding in our direction. I wasn't tall enough to block Val, though. Rats.

Quentin stopped an arm's length away from me. "Eve."

I pretended I'd just noticed him and pasted on a bland smile. "Quentin."

Val's eyes narrowed, and a muscle ticked in his jaw.

"Good to see you," Quentin said to me, actively ignoring the imposing man beside me. "I wanted to apologize again for the way I acted. I'm sorry. I'd like to come back to work."

Was he strung out on heroin? He couldn't seriously think I'd give him his job back.

"That's not going to happen," I said. "You firebombed that bridge."

"Any bridge can be rebuilt." He inched closer. "Please, Eve. Gimme another chance."

I didn't get the opportunity to tell Quentin to go to hell. Val beat me to it.

He moved between me and Quentin. "Eve said no. Walk away."

The dark tone of his voice implied he might resort to violence to convince Quentin to leave me alone. What happened to not being jealous? Val had sworn he wouldn't act this way.

I laid a hand on Val's arm. "It's okay. I can handle this."

His gaze flicked to me, then back to Quentin.

My former handyman glared at Val. "I'm talking to Eve, not you, Tarzan."

I squeezed between the two men, turning sideways to both of them. "Enough machismo. Val, I can take care of this myself. Quentin, I fired you and that's that. Goodbye."

Without waiting for either of them to speak again, I marched off down the aisle and swung left into the main aisle. I had no clue where I was going. Getting away from the Testosterone Anonymous meeting was my sole purpose.

Val caught up to me in the paint aisle. "Are you all right?"

"Fine. I love it when big, brawny men fight over me while completely ignoring the fact I'm standing right next to them."

"I'm sorry. I shouldn't have intervened."

A long sigh gusted out of me. "It's okay. Quentin has been a complete asshole to you."

"To you too." Val leaned against the shelves that held gallons of paint. "I won't get in your way again. Should we go back to buying supplies?"

"Yes."

The whole time we were shopping for plumbing stuff, I kept wondering why Val had been so protective of me when Quentin showed up. He'd been overprotective, actually. He despised Quentin, and my former handyman despised him. Quentin's reaction to Val made sense now that I realized Quentin had thought I belonged to him because we'd had sex once. But Val's reaction to Quentin...

He couldn't be jealous. Could he?

Nah.

On the drive home, I wondered.

Chapter Eighteen

Val

After spending the better part of a day with Eve's family, I couldn't understand why she'd been so upset when they arrived. They knew what kind of resort she owned. They knew she spent every day hanging out with naked men and women. Her brother and sister didn't mind at all, and Andrew and his wife had brought their two children who were eight and nine. The children had been here before, Andrew told me, and were comfortable being around nudists.

Eve's parents didn't mind either, so I had to wonder. Why was Eve so frazzled? Was she ashamed to have her family find out she'd been sleeping with me? I knew she cherished her privacy, so maybe that was the only reason for her behavior. Our encounter with Quentin in the hardware store hadn't helped, for sure.

I'd wanted to belt that bastard.

Just after lunch, the FedEx truck arrived. Luckily, Eve was busy entertaining her family and didn't notice the delivery I accepted from the FedEx driver. I planned to surprise her in the morning, but for now, the package I'd ordered would stay a secret.

For most of the afternoon, I worked with Larry, Andrew, Jeremy, and a couple of the other guests to repair the room in the guest house. I wondered if Eve would make me move into this room once we'd finished the work. The thought of being relegated to the guest house bothered me more than I'd expected. I had gotten used to being mere feet away from Eve's bedroom, within easy distance if I wanted to sneak into her bed—or vice versa. Skulking across the dirt path from the guest house to get into Eve's home in the dead of night did not appeal to me.

Oh, but I would do that if I had to. No chance in hell I'd give up making love to her because of geographic inconvenience. I would've traveled to Siberia barefoot in the middle of winter, swimming across the Bering Strait to get there, if it meant I could feel Eve's body around me.

I liked her. Very much. For more than her body.

The realization stopped me for a moment. I stood in the damaged room in the guest house, a hammer raised in my hand, holding a nail in position to pound it into place. Was this what people called an epiphany? I'd never had one before. I liked Eve. That shouldn't have been shocking, but I'd never wanted a woman for much more than sex. The occasional dinner, maybe. Never more. Never anything…serious. With Eve, I wanted all of it. All of her.

"You okay?" Larry asked.

His question startled me out of my thoughts. "Fine, yes. Just thinking."

About his daughter and all the nonsexual things I wanted to do with her. Ah, but I did think about sex too. I could take Eve out to dinner and then for a romantic walk along the river in town, followed by hours of sweaty, dirty sex.

"We're almost done," Larry said, oblivious of my carnal thoughts. He patted my shoulder. "You've done great, helping out with the repairs. I'm sure Eve really appreciates it. And it was a wise decision to put on coveralls."

Yes, I'd given up my preferred state of undress during the repair job. When I had thought about doing construction work in the nude, I'd suffered visions of taking a nail to the dick or the balls. Sometimes, even a nudist needed to wear clothes.

Everyone ate dinner in the guest house that evening. Eve had ordered a feast from the local Mexican restaurant in honor of her family's visit, since they loved tacos and spicy queso dip. More laughter and chattering voices filled the dining hall tonight than on any other night since I'd been here. Ollie, the Norrises, and some of the other guests already knew Eve's family.

Krista, Eve's sister, sat next to me during dinner. Eve had taken the seat on the opposite side of me, so I was sandwiched between the two lovely Holt women. I flirted with Eve and only Eve. Krista was equally beautiful, but she had a fiancé. Besides, I'd realized during our time in the hot spring I had eyes for Eve alone. No other woman, no matter how beautiful, could compare to her.

Heidi sat beside Krista. Eve's parents along with her brother and soon-to-be brother-in-law occupied the chairs across the table from us. The next closest table stood a few feet away, so we could chat with Ruth, Sylvester, Ollie, and several of the Kittens.

Eve had been right about the Kitten Brigade. They were sweet girls, but they got boisterous whenever three or more of them gathered together. Those girls made every occasion a party but never took things too far. I could see why Eve liked them so much.

Conversation stayed casual until dessert, when Krista turned to me and asked, "So, what are your intentions with my sister?"

"Intentions?" I intended to fuck her every night and as often in the daytime as possible. Her sister wouldn't want to hear that, though. "I like Eve very much, but it's a bit early to be having intentions of the kind I think you mean."

"Hmm." She eyed me like she was sizing me up. "You're hot, and you seem nice. But Evie is my sister, and I don't want her to get hurt by some has-been athlete who likes to make DIY porn."

On the other side of me, Eve was engaged in conversation with Ruth across the distance between our tables. She seemed unaware of her sister's interrogation of me. Larry and Donna Holt had gone off to mingle with the other guests, and Heidi had moved into the chair beside Andrew, regaling him and Jeremy with stories of the Kitten Brigade's antics.

Krista had me cornered.

"I have no desire to hurt Eve," I told her. "She's a special woman. I enjoy spending time with her, but I haven't known her for long."

"Yet you're sleeping with her."

"Well—" I fidgeted in my chair but resisted the impulse to look away from Krista. Her interrogation would not unsettle me, that I'd decided. "I can't discuss it with you. Anything that happens between me and Eve in private stays private."

Krista locked her arms over her chest. "Does that mean you're not secretly taping it when you screw my sister?"

"I have never secretly taped any woman. You've heard about the sex tape. I'm not ashamed of that, but the woman I was with consented to being recorded. In fact, it was her idea."

Eve's sister studied me, one finger tapping on her arm.

Her attention set my skin to itching. I fidgeted again and scratched my thigh.

"Your sister means more to me," I said, "than a costar for a sex tape. I would never knowingly hurt her."

Krista puckered her lips for half a second, then smiled. "Good. That means I don't have to get Andrew and Jeremy to tie a concrete block to your ankle and toss you headfirst into the hot spring."

The twinkle in her eyes confirmed she was joking.

I might not have been sure otherwise. Krista had seemed like a cheerful, easygoing person when I'd first met her. Here in the dining hall, she'd turned into a deadly protector of her older sister. I respected that. If I'd thought any man was using one of my sisters, I would've done the same thing.

Krista got up and walked around the table to sit in the chair beside Jeremy, which Andrew had vacated.

Eve was staring at me, unblinking.

"What's wrong?" I asked.

"I—I heard what you and Krista were talking about." She bit the inside of her lip and focused on my shoulder. "You must've been saying that stuff to make my sister happy."

Saying what stuff? With a start, I realized everything I'd said. *Your sister means more to me than a costar for a sex tape. I would never knowing hurt her. She's a special woman.* Had I sounded like a smitten man?

I'd meant every word, a fact that stunned me, but I couldn't tell Eve that. She might panic more than she already had today. But I didn't want to lie to her either.

"Yes," I said. "I, uh, didn't want your sister to think I'm using you."

"Sure, I get that." Eve relaxed, the shock dissolving into a casual smile. "Krista is my baby sister, but she likes to pretend she's my bodyguard. She likes you, though. She saves the inquisition for guys she thinks might be— Well, she doesn't do it to every guy I'm with."

Eve's parents came back to our table and spirited Eve away for a private conversation.

I wondered what she'd been about to say before she changed her mind mid-sentence.

And then I wondered why I cared.

Chapter Nineteen

Eve

After a day with my entire family and all my guests, I fell asleep the second my head hit the pillow. Val and I had both been too tired for sex, so he retreated into his room while I retreated into mine. If I hadn't been so exhausted, I would've sneaked into his room to crawl under the covers with him and go to sleep there. A couple days ago, I'd invited Val to share my bed. *Would you like to come into my bedroom?* I'd asked, the words tumbling out of my mouth before I realized what I was saying. Val had declined the offer, of course. He wanted a relationship even less than I did, but his rebuff had stung more than I expected.

The idea of sleeping with him—actually sleeping—appealed to me a lot. I tried not to think about why.

When I woke in the morning, I felt good. Wonderful in fact. I'd slept straight through the night without rousing once. Lying in my bed, I yawned and stretched my entire body. Refreshed and ready for another day of chaos, that's what I was.

"It's a stunning view from here."

Val's voice made me jump.

He leaned against the jamb of my open bedroom door, arms crossed over his chest, that gorgeously naked body on full display. His hair was mussed like he hadn't bothered to comb it yet, and his sizzling gaze gravitated to my chest. "I dreamed about those tits all night. That and other parts of your edible body."

I glanced down and realized my stretching had made the cover slide down to my waist, exposing my breasts. Not bothering to cover them, I sat up and stretched my arms above my head. "Good morning. You look edible as usual too."

"Did you dream about me?"

Oh yeah, had I ever. Sinfully hot, decadently erotic dreams about all the things I wanted to do to him and with him, not to mention the things I wanted him to do to me. I pushed the covers off the rest of my body. "All I dreamed about was you. I had half a mind to crawl into your bed last night just to sleep there."

Why on earth had I said that part about wanting to sleep with him? I hadn't meant to say it. Like the last time I'd suggested we spend the night together, the words had tumbled from my lips without permission. My mouth had a mind of its own when it came to Val and the notion of sharing a bed with him all night.

Yesterday, Val had told my sister I meant more to him than a partner for a sex tape.

A little shiver coursed through me, but not the sexy kind. Getting attached to Val was a bad, bad, bad idea. The man was a notorious exhibitionist, he made sex tapes that he kept on his phone forever after, and he loved the spotlight. I needed my privacy, would've fled from the spotlight if one had ever veered in my direction, and never took my clothes off anywhere except inside my house. We were completely wrong for each other.

Yesterday I had, for the first time ever, disrobed outdoors.

Sure, Val had been the only one there. Heidi's accidental glimpse couldn't have amounted to much. Why had I gotten naked at the hot spring? Why had I had sex outdoors? That wasn't me at all. So of course, the one time I'd done anything of the sort, I'd gotten caught in the act. At least my parents hadn't seen it.

Would it have been horrible if they had? I was an adult, after all. They knew, because my guests had gossiped about it, that I was getting it on with Val. They knew I ran a nudist resort. Would they have cared if I became a nudist? Not that I was planning to do that.

"*Qual é o problema?*" Val asked.

"Huh?"

"I asked what's wrong. You're puckering your whole face. So what is the problem?"

"Nothing, not really. I was reliving the moment when we walked out of the woods together yesterday. My family must've heard from the other guests that you and I are, um, you know."

"Fucking? Yes, I'm sure they did." He strolled up to the bed and settled his taut ass onto it in front of me. "But they would've guessed we're more than friends anyway. We were holding hands when we walked out of the woods."

Holding hands? He'd tried to do that on the way out to the hot spring, but I wouldn't let him. On the way back, I'd been too freaked out to notice anything short of Bigfoot leaping out to snarl at us. When I thought about it now, I remembered the soothing warmth of his hand in mine.

"Guess you're right," I said. "And I know I've been an idiot about all of this. I'm sorry. Please don't think I'm ashamed of having anyone know about us. I'm not."

He reached out to sweep a lock of hair away from my face, tucking it behind my ear, and grazed his fingertips down my cheek. "I tempted you to step outside your comfort zone. That wasn't easy for you, I know."

"It was easier than I'd thought it would be." That was the honest truth. I hadn't hesitated for more than a few seconds when Val suggested I strip and jump into the hot spring with him. Sex in the warm water, with him, had been one of the best experiences of my life.

Being with him was the best experience, period.

He moved closer, his hip pressed against mine, and looped an arm around my waist. "What else can I tempt you to try, *docinho*?"

Gazing into his sultry brown eyes, I forgot all about my inhibitions and silly worries about privacy. I wanted to do anything and everything with him.

I blinked rapidly as I realized he'd thrown another Portuguese word at me. "What did you say? *Docinho*? I don't know what that means."

He shifted his ass on the bed and cleared his throat. "It means sweetie."

Not long ago, I would've bristled at his use of endearments. He'd called me *bebê* and *linda*, and I hadn't minded at all. Hearing him call me sweetie in his native tongue…I liked it. A lot.

Because he meant more to me than a casual sex partner.

Holy shit. It was true. The revelation tingled over my skin, raising the hairs at my nape, but it wasn't fear triggering my response. All my anxieties over getting attached to Val and whether our lives could mesh melted away at the instant I'd realized he meant something to me, something more than the best lover I'd ever had. Sure, we still might not work as a couple. We lived in different worlds, different planes of reality. But here, now, for as long as he stayed with me, I would enjoy our fledgling connection and the silky warmth it engendered in me.

I glided my palm up his torso, from his waist to his pecs. "I think you could tempt me to do just about anything."

He tickled my bottom with one long finger. "In that case, I'll have to think about what I most want to seduce you into doing with me."

"I have an idea."

One of his dark brows lifted. "What is it?"

"Take a shower with me."

"You do realize if we take a shower together, I will ravish you."

"I'm counting on it."

We dashed into the bathroom and enjoyed a long, steamy shower. The actual steam from the hot water filled the stall, but we also created our own steam. I locked my legs around his hips while he backed us up to the wall, directly under the shower head, and drove into me again and again until we both hit that peak together.

Then we did it again.

Our morning sex might not have been the most creative ever, but it got our day off to a blissful start. By the time I'd gotten dressed and walked into the kitchen, Val was busy preparing breakfast—for an army.

"What's all that?" I asked as I perched on a stool at the island.

"Breakfast for the guests and your family."

"Making breakfast is my job, not yours. Guests don't do manual labor."

He paused in stirring scrambled eggs in my largest frying pan and glanced over his shoulder at me. "I thought I was more than a guest by now."

Had I hurt his feelings? I hadn't mean to, but it sure seemed like he was wounded by the fact I'd called him a guest.

I rubbed my forehead. "All I meant was that you are paying to stay here. You shouldn't be making breakfast for everybody. I get paid to do that."

"You need employees, Eve. Since you won't hire any, I'll fill in until you change your mind."

"Until you go home, you mean."

He was staring down at the eggs again, stirring them with a wooden spoon while they gradually congealed into fluffy masses of sunny-yellow goodness. His shoulders bunched the tiniest bit.

Why did I get the feeling I'd hurt his feelings again? I couldn't figure it out. Yes, I'd realized I liked being with him for more than sex. He'd told my sister something similar. But he hadn't expressed any interest in staying beyond the two weeks he had originally booked. I didn't know if he meant anything by the statements he'd made to Krista yesterday, or if holding hands meant anything to him either. He was a self-professed player who'd assured me he didn't want a relationship.

Since when did I sit around contemplating the status of my relationship, or lack thereof, with a man? Something about this thing between me and Val, whatever it might be, had turned me into a frazzled mess.

Until this morning. Today, I felt much calmer and more like myself.

I pushed off the stool and sidestepped the island to stand beside Val. "All I meant was that you had planned to stay two weeks. Are you changing those plans? Do you want to stay longer?"

He froze, his gaze nailed to the eggs. "Would you want me to stay longer?"

"Yes."

Only his eyes moved, his gaze homing in on mine. He didn't blink.

"Are you going to make me beg?" I asked. "I'll probably do that if you don't say something in the next three seconds."

He dropped the wooden spoon into the frying pan of full of eggs, whirled toward me, and hauled me snug against his body with his big hands spread over my buttocks. "Yes, Evie, I want to stay longer. Much longer."

"Like another week?"

"As long as you'll have me."

My pulse sped up, and I couldn't help grinning.

He grinned too.

I patted his ass. "Why don't you get out the breakfast sausages while I whip up some biscuits."

"Already did that. The biscuits and sausages are staying warm in the oven." He turned around to pick up the frying pan by its wooden handle. "I'll put the eggs in there too, while we eat the breakfast I made for you."

"How did you whip up a meal so fast? It didn't take me that long to get dressed."

Those luscious lips of his curved into a sexy smirk. "I got up before you. The biscuits were cooking while we were in the shower."

I hadn't smelled them cooking, but then, I'd been a little distracted by hot shower sex.

"You didn't have to do that," I said. "But thank you, Val. I really appreciate it."

"Sit. *Café da manhã* will be served in a moment."

"The what now?"

He smiled and laughed. "*Café da manhã* is what Brazilians call breakfast. It literally means morning coffee. This is a special variation known as Café Colonial."

I waited on a stool across the island from him while he gathered the delicacies he'd already whipped up for a separate meal, this one exclusively for the two of us. My stomach growled. Loudly.

He grinned at me over his shoulder. "Hungry?"

"Sorry for the rude noises my body made. I'm starving, and the food smells soooo good."

"You can start with this." He reached into the oven and brought out a small basket overflowing with golden muffins, or maybe they were biscuits. He set the basket down in front of me. "*Pão de queijo*, or cheese bread. It's a Brazilian specialty made with Minas cheese from the southeastern part of Brazil."

"Is that near where you're from?"

"Further to the northeast." He retrieved two glasses from the refrigerator and set them down on the island. "I've noticed you don't drink coffee, so I made chocolate milk. I've never been a coffee drinker myself."

"Thank you."

"You're welcome, but I'm not done yet." He spun around, grabbed a bowl out of the fridge, and spun around again to plop it down in front of me. "Papaya and açaí."

I barely had time to notice the dark-purple berries nestled among the orange papaya slices before Val produced another basket of some type of bread from the oven and placed it in front of me.

"*Pão francês*. Literally, French roll." He gathered jars of jam and jelly from the fridge and placed them beside the rolls. "I've already buttered them."

The hunks of butter melting on the rolls had already clued me in to that fact.

"Looks yummy," I said, rubbing my palms. "May I dig in yet?"

"One last thing." He grabbed a plate off the counter which had been covered with a dish towel and put it in on the island. "*Cuca de banana*. That means banana cake. It has German origins and is something like streusel."

"German? I thought you were making me a Brazilian breakfast."

"I am. Brazil has a deep German connection." He eyed the items he'd laid out before me. "I don't normally eat this much for breakfast but being with you has given me a powerful appetite."

"Me too." I picked up a piece of cheese bread and plucked a sliver off it, chewing the bite before I spoke again. "Delicious. You're quite the cook."

"I had wanted to make more, but I didn't have time. Couldn't resist making love to you in the shower." He smirked. "Twice."

Making love. Until this morning, he'd called it fucking or ravishing me. Should I ascribe meaning to his change of phrasing? Probably not. Lots of people called it "making love" even when no love was involved.

I ate some of everything—most of everything, actually—because Val's cooking was incredible. I loved all the traditional dishes he'd made me, and I loved learning more about his homeland through those foods.

"Where did you get all the ingredients?" I asked. "The grocery store in town doesn't have Amazonian fruit or Brazilian cheese."

"I had them rushed here by overnight delivery."

"All the way from Brazil? That must've been expensive."

"You're worth it, and I can afford it."

I gnawed on my lip for a moment before deciding to just ask him. "Do you go all out for every woman you sleep with?"

"No." He picked at a hunk of cheese bread, peeking up at me with his head down. "Only for you."

His statement set my tummy to fluttering and gave me a strange glowy feeling behind my ribs. To avoid thinking about why, I redirected the conversation to general topics unlikely to lead to accidental intimacy.

After we'd finished our breakfast, Val tried to wash the dishes. I shooed him away. Since he'd made breakfast, for us and for the guests, I insisted on taking care of the cleanup.

Val insisted on drying the dishes. The man was incapable of not lending a hand.

While he was drying the last thing I'd washed, the frying pan, he peered out the window above the sink. His brows scrunched together, crinkling the spot above his nose.

"Are the Kittens prancing around naked out there?" I asked.

"No, it's not them."

"What's so fascinating, then?"

He tore his focus away from the window and set down the frying pan. "It's nothing."

Did he really think that would staunch my curiosity? I rose onto my tiptoes and peered out the window. My jaw dropped. Seriously. It dropped, possibly down to my belly button.

Out there on the lawn, my family was prancing around in the nude playing miniten with the Kittens and Ollie. My niece and nephew had kept their clothes on, but my parents and my brother and sister, along with their significant others, had stripped. They all seemed to be having a great time and seemed oblivious of their own nakedness, like they'd always been nudists.

I dropped back onto my soles on the cold, hard floor.

"Well," Val said, "it looks like your family has no problem with nudism."

Chapter Twenty

Val

Out here on the lawn, I watched Eve while she watched her family enjoying a friendly game of miniten while in the nude. How could I look at anything but her? The dress she wore, with its thin straps and above-the-knee hem, barely covered her curvy body. The way the fabric swished around her thighs whenever she moved had me fantasizing about whether she wore anything under it.

When she'd first seen her family through the kitchen window, her expression had gone from relaxed to abject shock in a millisecond. I'd never seen anyone look as stunned as she had been at that moment. She saw nudists every day and didn't bat an eye, but seeing her family jumping into the lifestyle left her speechless.

Literally. Eve had not spoken a word since she'd gotten her first glimpse of her family au naturel.

When she had wandered outside, I followed. We loitered at the edge of the lawn where a group of smiling, laughing people engaged in a game of batting a tennis ball back and forth over the net with the wooden thugs that covered their hands. I'd never played miniten, but observing a game made me want to try it.

"Let's join them," I said to Eve.

She jerked and veered her wide-eyed gaze to me. "What?"

"Relax," I said, laying a hand on her shoulder. "I meant let's join the game. You can keep your clothes on."

She did relax, a touch, and her eyes were no longer bulging. "I don't play miniten."

"Neither do I. But how hard can it be? Senior citizens are doing it."

"Miniten isn't usually so vigorous, which is why nudists like it. This group is really going for it, though."

On the playing field, Sylvester leaped up to smack the ball with his thug. His own balls flapped along with his dick. The tennis ball sailed over the net. Krista tried to hit it but missed, succeeding only in making her tits flap.

Eve twisted her mouth into a look of half embarrassment, half amusement. "I've never understood how nudist women can stand having their boobs flailing around like that. It hurts, you know? Unless you're flat-chested, it can be rather painful."

"Have you tried playing sports in the nude?"

"No, but I do occasionally go without underwear."

"I know, and I love when you do that." I slipped an arm around her shoulders. "Makes it easier for me to get you naked. Or to fuck you while you're dressed."

"You haven't done that yet."

She was right, I realized. I'd done pretty much everything else with her, but I hadn't pushed up her skirt and taken her that way.

I bent my head to whisper in her ear, "Are you wearing a bra and panties?"

Her lips kinked into a sexy, mysterious little smile as she angled her head to look at me. "Neither."

She trotted toward the miniten field, shooting me a grin over her shoulder. "Come on, Val. Let's play."

I ran after her.

We joined the Holt family's team, but that left the Kittens and Ollie with two less players than we had. Krista and Jeremy offered to defect to the other team to even things out. Despite her lack of undergarments, Eve played with as much enthusiasm as the Kittens. She jumped up to hit the ball, raced back and forth, and even spun around once to hit her final shot. It seemed like she'd executed that move strictly to show off.

The Holts won the game.

Well, the Holts and me.

"You're an honorary member of the family," Donna told me when I joked that I was the odd man out on this team. "Besides, you might be an official member soon enough."

Her mother's words made Eve stop blinking, though her eyes didn't widen like earlier. Her gaze swerved to me.

Official family member? That could mean only one thing. Donna Holt thought I might marry her daughter. The idea surprised me as much as it seemed to surprise Eve. The implication that her family might want me as an in-law floored me. I'd never met a woman's family before, but I'd always assumed if and when I did, I wouldn't receive a warm welcome. What parents would want their daughter to be involved with a notorious show-off?

My lifestyle and my choices had never bothered me before Eve. Now, I wished I hadn't done those reckless and rather narcissistic things to get attention and find a new career. I wished I'd been the kind of man with whom a woman like Eve might want a future.

I wasn't. I couldn't change that.

After another game of miniten, I led Eve away from the group. She slipped her hand into mine, threading our fingers. I loved the feel of her warm little hand wrapped around mine. I loved the soft smile on her lips too, and the matching softness in her eyes. We meandered around the guest house to the backside where no one ever seemed to go. The Kittens had set up their tents in the makeshift campground, a grassy area screened from our view by trees.

Eve glanced at the rolled-up yoga mat lying on the ground. "Somebody left their mat here. I'd better take it into the guest house and—"

"I put it there, *amorzinho*. For our private use."

"Our use? I thought you brought me back here to get it on, not do yoga."

"Both." I picked up the mat and unrolled it, laying it out on the grass. "I'm going to fuck you while we do yoga together."

Her eyes flashed wide for a heartbeat, but then a sexy smile curved her lips. "Nude erotic yoga? I've never tried that."

"Let's start with a warm-up...kiss."

I pulled her into my arms and kissed her, gently at first, relishing the taste of her while my cock stiffened and her nipples hardened against my chest with only the thin fabric of her dress separating us. I devoured her mouth like I was drunk on the flavor of her. And I was. I couldn't get enough of her lips, her slippery tongue, her breathless moans that I swallowed.

"Get rid of your dress," I murmured against her mouth.

She stepped back a few inches, just enough to let her whip the dress off over her head. It fluttered down to the ground beside the yoga mat.

I set my hands on her hips and backed her up until she stood on the mat. "Ready for a workout?"

Glancing around, she bit down on her lower lip. "What if someone sees us?"

"Everyone is on the lawn, on the other side of this building." I skated my hands down to cup her ass. "Let go, Eve. Let me have you here, now, please."

She hesitated for only a second. "Let's do it."

I moved behind her, my cock brushing her ass, and skimmed my hands up her sides. When I reached her arms, I used my hands to encourage her to lift them and join her palms above her head. "Do exactly what I say. I'm the teacher, you're the student seeking bliss."

"Val the yogi? Sounds like bliss to me." She craned her neck around to shoot me a saucy smirk. "Not sure this will be standard yoga, but I'm all in for whatever you've got in mind."

"Good." I gave her bottom a light slap. "Follow my instructions."

"Yes, sir."

I laid my palms over her joined hands and guided them down, past her face, to her chest. "Place your palms on your breasts with the nipples sticking out between your fingers."

She followed my command, smirking the whole time, the expression carving out dimples in her cheeks.

I placed my hands over hers and flicked my thumbs across her rosy nipples.

She sucked in a breath.

"Now spread your legs to hip width," I said, scraping my thumbnails back and forth over the rigid peaks of her breasts. "Are you wet?"

"Oh God, yes."

I glided my hands down to her belly and tugged her tight against my body so she could feel the hard line of my erection against her back. Her body felt so good, so warm and soft and tempting, that I couldn't resist rolling my hips into her, grinding my cock against her, while I slid my fingers between her folds. A deep groan vibrated my chest. "You're so fucking wet."

The sensation of her slick heat on my fingers amped up my lust, that slender thread of control fraying. I'd wanted to take my time, but this woman drove me out of my mind. She would do anything

I asked of her, anything, and never question it. Eve might've been straitlaced on the outside, but she had a deep, hot wild streak like no other woman I'd known.

"Downward dog," I said, my voice rough and low, strained by my need for her and only her. "Do it now."

She bent from the waist, planted her hands on the mat, and walked them forward until she'd stretched her body into an upside-down V.

A perfect downward-dog pose. Her luscious ass was in the air, her legs spread enough for me to do what I needed to do. To her. With her. Because of her.

I grasped her hips. "You are the sexiest woman alive, *amorzinho*. No other woman has ever made me come as hard as I do with you."

"Same for me. Sex with you is the best ever."

"Don't move." Before she could say anything, I pulled my hips back and thrust into her. "Hold the pose, and don't come until I tell you to."

A laugh sputtered out of her. "Not sure I have any control over that, especially with you."

I pinched her bottom, making her gasp. "Give it your best shot."

"Yes, sir."

Gripping her hips, I pumped into her in a steady rhythm, slow and easy, giving her time to adjust to the new position before I unleashed my lust on her. Holding back like this was maddening. I wanted to shove us both over the edge right now. More of her, I needed more of her, needed to go deeper, harder, faster, until her body clenched me and I erupted inside her. Somehow, I maintained the measured pace despite the intoxicating feel of her slick sheath around me. The pressure in my cock, the pressure to let go and come inside her sweet body, had me gritting my teeth.

She twisted her head around to look at me, desire tightening her features. "Forget yoga. I need to feel you come inside me right now. Please."

The huskiness of her plea snapped the slender thread of my willpower.

"Hold on," I growled as I lifted her legs and shuffled forward until she hung upside down with her hands flat on the ground and her legs bent. I slid my hands up to her ankles, one at a time. "Okay?"

"Yes. Do it."

I thrust into her, sinking deeper than ever inside her lush body, and paused there for a moment, letting myself fall into the pleasure of taking her. Then I plowed into her fast and hard, her cream making a sucking sound and my balls slapping on her skin, every movement rough and hungry. If my eyes had been open, they would've rolled back in my head from the indescribable pleasure of her body around me, so wet and warm and supple. When she came, I let out a strangled cry at the sensation of her sheath tightening around my cock and her body milking me. I threw my head back and punched into her even harder, twice more, spilling everything I had inside her depths.

"God, Evie." I lowered her feet to the mat, carefully, and hooked an arm around her waist to draw her up into a standing position. With her body plastered to mine, I wrapped both arms around her and rested my chin on her shoulder. "That was incredible. You are incredible, *amorzinho.*"

"That was earth-shattering, I'd say." She wriggled around to face me, enfolding me in her arms, her cheek against my neck and her breaths tickling my skin. "What was that you called me? *Amorzinho?*"

"It means love or sweetheart." I kissed the top of her head. "You are sweet, and perfect, but you're also brave and wild and passionate. I love being the only one who sees this side of you."

Her fingers plunged into my hair while she whispered into my ear. "I love it too. And I love the way you keep calling me affectionate things in Portuguese."

"Can't help it. I feel affectionate toward you."

"Me too."

This time when I'd spent myself inside her, I had experienced more than a sexual release. Something inside me had let go too.

I held her for a long moment, caressing her silken hair.

She pulled her head back to look at me and smiled that sensual little smile. "Let's do more erotic yoga."

"Love to."

What we'd just done had been more than sex. We both knew it.

The sound of a car door slamming made us both freeze.

"What was that?" Eve asked. "There aren't supposed to be guests arriving or leaving today."

"I'll check. Wait here."

I trotted to the corner of the guest house and peered past it to the driveway.

Quentin Smith's truck was backing up, turning around at a dangerous speed. Gravel sprayed up when the vehicle rocketed down the driveway toward the road.

What the hell had Quentin been doing here?

Eve came up behind me, laying a hand on my shoulder. "What is it?"

"Your former handyman just left. Took off like he was running from an erupting volcano."

"He probably stopped by to pick up his last check."

I turned to face her. "I thought you mailed that to him."

"Planned to, but he called and said he'd pick it up. I told him not to." She pursed her lips. "He doesn't listen very well."

No kidding. The man heard only what he wanted to hear. He'd probably hoped to find Eve alone and try to wheedle his way back into her life.

"I left his check in an envelope taped to the door of the house," she said, linking her hands behind my nape. "He's gone. Let's get back to dirty yoga."

I grinned. "Lots more poses to try."

"Command me, oh wise and scorching-hot yogi master."

We both laughed.

After less than a week with Eve, I felt closer to her than I had with anyone else in my entire life. I might've dismissed it as nothing more than the thrill of tempting a straitlaced woman into doing things she'd sworn she would never do. Deep down, I realized what we'd done today had been more than a conquest. It had been more, period.

I had no idea what that meant.

Chapter Twenty-One

Val stayed, even after the Kittens left. The day before the girls took off in their RV, Val and I walked in on Ollie and Heidi kissing in the downstairs hallway of the guest house. Both of them blushed and stammered excuses they didn't need to make. Afterward, Val and I agreed that Ollie and Heidi made a cute couple and seemed perfect for each other. Later, Heidi confided in me that she had liked Ollie for a long time but thought he didn't like her. They were going to try a long-distance romance.

It was so sweet. They were so sweet. I loved seeing two of my favorite people find happiness together.

After the Kittens left, things quieted down. Some guests left, new ones arrived. The guest house stayed at full occupancy, thanks to the guys finishing the repairs to the water-damaged room. When they'd completed the job, Val sought me out to inform me it was done. He found me in the kitchen making lunch.

"The room is ready," he said, lingering by the door to the outside. "All the repairs are done, and no one will ever guess a pipe had burst in there."

"Great." I put a pan of muffins into the oven and shut the door, brushing my hands off on my apron. "It's a relief to have that fixed. Thank you for helping out."

He shrugged one shoulder. "We were all happy to pitch in."

The way he was loitering by the door made me wonder if he was anxious about something. When he began to shift his weight from foot to foot, I knew he was.

"What's wrong?" I asked, walking up to him.

"The room is ready." His mouth pinched at the corners the same way his eyes did. "The room meant for me."

"Originally meant for you."

"Yes." He scratched the back of his neck. "Should I…ah…move there?"

"What? No, of course not." I got anxious then, rubbing my arms. "Unless you'd be more comfortable there."

"I wouldn't." He pulled me into his body, dipping his head to nuzzle my nose. "I'm the most comfortable when I'm with you."

"Well then…" I looped my arms around his neck and tickled his nape. "Maybe you should sleep in my room from now on. It's silly for you to go back to your room after we have sex."

"Are you sure?"

"Positive. Are you okay with that?"

His lips eased into a grin. "Yes, Evie, I'd love to sleep with you every night."

"Good."

My heart did a little cartwheel every time he called me Evie.

Time zipped by. My family left after twelve days. Both my mom and my sister told me how much they loved Val and that we made a great couple. Even my dad and my brother liked Val. They saw through his infamous past and got to know the real man underneath, the good man who refused to let me handle chores on my own and who insisted on making me breakfast every morning.

He'd even started bringing me breakfast in bed.

During the day, in between prepping meals and otherwise taking care of the guests, we would head to the hot spring, take walks, go into town to buy supplies, or anything we felt like doing. We talked a lot too. I learned more about his childhood in Brazil and what it was like moving to America, first as a teenager and later as an adult. I told him all about my family, my childhood, everything and anything he wanted to know. Every time I did photo sessions for the guests, Val wanted me to take more portraits of him—in and out of clothes. He kept trying to convince me to pose while he took pictures of me. I kept saying no, mainly because he wanted naked pictures of me. Besides, though I was a photographer, I didn't like pictures of myself.

One afternoon, Val and the guests went on a nature hike. I bowed out since I had boring business stuff to do in my office, like the task of filing my quarterly taxes. Maybe I should've found it strange that I no longer thought of Val as a guest, but I'd stopped trying to rationalize everything. I enjoyed his company, and I hoped he'd stay for a good long while.

After I finished my taxes, I headed out across the lawn toward the main trail.

Feminine shrieks emanated from deeper in the woods.

I stopped at the trailhead and tilted my head to listen. Why were women screaming? Val had probably made an off-color joke or done something flamboyant like grabbing a Frisbee and leaping up to toss it high in the air and then catch it. He liked to show off his athletic prowess.

Footfalls pounded. Twigs cracked.

A large figure barreled toward me.

I ducked sideways right when Val rocketed out of the woods. He kept rocketing straight past me and onto the lawn. Gasping for breath, he stumbled to a halt and doubled over with his hands on his thighs.

"What's wrong?" I asked when I rushed over to him.

He held up a hand, one finger raised.

I waited while he caught his breath.

Guests meandered up the trail toward the lawn. Ollie, Ruth, and Sylvester approached me and Val while our newest guests, the young ladies who must've been the ones screaming, trotted off to the guest house. Their smiles and giggles suggested they hadn't been terrified when they shrieked.

"What happened?" I asked Ollie.

"Val should've listened. You and everybody else told him to use the bug spray. He said he didn't see bugs, so why did he need to spray chemicals all over himself?" Ollie shook his head at Val. "Humility, man. You've gotta have a little humility when you're a naturist out in the woods."

Sylvester snickered. "Ought to listen to your girlfriend too."

I realized with a start Sylvester meant me. Was I Val's girlfriend? Was he my boyfriend? I guessed those labels did apply to us. After all, we were essentially living together.

"The rest of us used the bug spray," Ollie said to me. "We only got a few bites."

"What was all the screaming?" I asked.

"Val started shouting and swatting at the air, then he took off down the trail like a rabid bull on a rampage."

The bull in question straightened and faced me.

And that's when I noticed the red marks all over his body.

I winced. "Oh honey, you ran into no-see-ums, didn't you?"

He nodded, looking miserable.

"Why didn't you use the insect repellent? I warned you about the no-see-ums."

"Didn't see any insects."

"That's why they're called *no*-see-ums."

He scratched at a swarm of bites on his chest. "Didn't hear them either."

I bracketed his face with my hands. "Poor Val. You're all bitten up. Don't worry, I'll take good care of you."

Ollie raised his hand. "I got a few bites. Do I get the Evie special treatment too?"

"Sorry, it's for ex-footballer guests only."

I shepherded Val back to the house and made him lie down on my bed on his back. It seemed like the no-see-ums had mainly bitten him on his front side. I snagged a bottle of calamine lotion, a box of cotton swabs, a pill bottle, and a glass of water from the bathroom. Thus armed, I straddled him on the bed.

"Take this," I said, holding out a pink pill and the glass of water.

He eyed the pill with suspicion. "What is it?"

"Don't trust me enough to take it no questions asked, hm? It's an antihistamine." I glanced at his bites. "Maybe you need two pills."

"One will do." He nabbed the pill and the glass, popped the pill into his mouth, and swigged the water. As he set the glass on the bedside table, he said, "Thank you for taking pity on me."

"It's not pity. I've been swarmed by no-see-ums. It's awful." I set to work daubing the lotion onto every single bite with the cotton swabs. "Besides, you're as pitiful and miserable as a lost puppy in the rain."

"Pitiful? The itching might drive me insane, but I am not a lost puppy."

"Relax. I wasn't insulting you. Your misery is cute."

"I'm glad my condition amuses you."

"Shush. I'm working here." I bent to kiss him. "Once I finish tending to your wounds, I'll distract you from your itching."

"How?"

"I was thinking a striptease might do the trick."

Despite his discomfort, he pulled off a naughty smile. "Yes, please."

"Followed by sex."

He grinned. "You're a genius, *meu amor*."

"I don't think they give out a Nobel Prize for sex."

"They should create one for you."

"Don't hold your breath for that one." I raised my brows. "What did you call me this time?"

He went stone-still, his eyes unblinking. After a few seconds, when I was about to check for a pulse, he relaxed and smiled. "Never mind."

I let him get away with that only because of his pitiful condition. And because I wasn't sure I wanted to hear the answer. We had developed some kind of bond between us, but we hadn't talked about it. I had no idea if all his endearments were nothing but smooth talk he used with all the ladies.

No, I didn't believe that.

And I was pretty sure whatever he'd said included the word love.

By the time I finished covering him with calamine lotion from head to toe, Val was gazing at me with sleepy eyes.

"Ready for a nap?" I asked.

"Yes. The antihistamine helps, but it's making me too groggy to enjoy a striptease."

"We'll do that later."

He patted the mattress beside him. "Lie down with me. Please."

I dutifully crawled onto the bed and stretched out alongside his body.

Raising one arm, he invited me to cuddle up to him.

How could I resist? He'd become as pink as a baby pig thanks to the calamine lotion, but I'd risk getting the stuff all over myself for the chance to cuddle with him. Tucked under his arm, I nestled my head into the hollow of his shoulder.

Five seconds later, he was snoring.

We never did get around to the striptease.

One afternoon about a week later, following a series of portrait sessions with guests, Val repeated a request he'd made several times before.

I had just taken the memory card out of my camera and was plugging it into my laptop to download the images.

He came up beside me—nude of course—and said, "Pose for me, Eve. Please. Keep your clothes on if you like, though I love your naked body. You have nothing to be ashamed of."

"Not ashamed."

"Why won't you explain to me why you won't pose for pictures?" He leaned against the wall, beside where my computer table butted up against it. "I keep asking, and you keep sidestepping."

"I know, I'm sorry." I scrubbed hands over my face, groaning. "Explaining the reasons why I don't want to pose might offend you, and the last thing I want to do is make you uncomfortable or unhappy."

When I glanced up at him, he was staring at me with a blank expression.

"See?" I said, dropping my forehead into my raised hand. "I've already hurt your feelings by saying I'm afraid I'll hurt your feelings."

"I'm not offended." He knelt beside my chair, peeling my hand away from my forehead. "I was surprised, that's all. But I love that you care about me, and I care about you the same way. You can tell me anything, Evie. Whether I like what you say or not, I will never lash out at you because of it."

"Yeah, I know that. I'm not good at sharing my feelings, though."

"Neither am I. We're learning together, aren't we?"

"Guess we are." I relaxed back into my chair. "I don't like pictures of myself. It's not that I'm ashamed of my body. You know I have zero problems with wearing short-shorts and tank tops and other skimpy stuff. I'm not comfortable in front of the camera, that's all."

"There's something else. I can tell."

I squirmed in my chair. "If I were to pose for you, what would you do with the pictures?"

"Nothing. They're yours."

"But you like to flaunt your nudity. I don't."

He studied me for a moment, his lips tightening. His lips curled into a little smile, and he shook his head. "I think I understand. I only publicize my own nudity. I would never share photos of you, in or out of clothes, without your explicit permission."

"Not worried you'll post naked pictures of me online. Your assistant leaked your sex tape. What if somebody leaks my photos this time?"

"I won't let that happen." He took my hands in his. "I care about you, and I will never let anyone hurt you. After my former assistant leaked the video, I not only fired him but also implemented new security measures. My phone can only be accessed with an iris scan, and my home computer requires a password." He grunted, one side of his mouth twisting into a sardonic expression. "My password used to be the word password followed by the number of my football jersey. Now, it's something no one will ever guess. Besides, like I keep telling you, I'm not demanding you pose nude. I would love to have a photo of you, that's all. You're beautiful, on the inside and the outside."

His words set off a lovely warmth in my chest that blossomed outward. He cared about me. He loved the way I looked no matter what I wore or didn't wear. In the three weeks that we'd known each other, he'd done nothing except protect my privacy and help me in any way I'd let him. Even that day at the hot spring when we'd made love in the water, he hadn't pressured me to undress. I'd done it because I wanted to do it.

I slanted in to touch my lips to his. "Okay. I'll pose for you."

"Thank you, Eve." He kissed my cheek. "You won't regret this."

"Can't regret anything we've done together." Rolling my chair back, I stood and picked up my camera, then offered it to him. "All yours."

He accepted the camera and rose, scrutinizing the various buttons and switches on it. "I've never used a high-end digital camera like this one."

"Don't worry, it's easy. I'll show you the ropes."

For the next ten minutes, I demonstrated the basics for him, and he mastered all of it right away. I tested the lighting by having him lie down on the crimson cushion. When I held the light meter near his hips, he smirked.

"Is it critical," he said, "to make sure my cock is properly lit?"

"Oh, absolutely." I withdrew the light meter. "Can't have your gorgeous dick hidden in shadows."

He lunged up to grab me around the waist and haul me down onto the cushion on top of him. "It's your turn in front of the camera."

"It'll be hard for you to photograph me while I'm lying on top of you."

"You're right, though I hate to give up fondling you." To prove he meant that, he cupped my bottom with both hands. "But I suppose I must."

He rolled us over and hopped to his feet.

I tossed him the light meter.

Catching it, he headed for the table where I'd set down the camera.

While he had his back turned, I got ready for my photo session.

Val, camera in hand, turned to face me. He stared at me for a moment, but then his mouth stretched into a grin. "Evie, you saucy little vixen. After everything you said—"

"What you said changed my mind." I stretched my arms above my head, petting the crimson cushion, and bent one knee. The velvet felt divine against my naked skin. "How's this pose?"

"Perfect." He raised the camera and began snapping pictures. "You are the most beautiful woman in the world. Your body deserves to be captured on digital film for posterity. In fact, I might call the Louvre to offer them the modern masterpiece that is Eve Holt."

He paused in his picture-taking to wink at me.

"Very funny," I said, rolling onto my stomach, propped up on my elbows. "I know you won't really do that. But if you should plaster my nakedness all over the Internet, I'll show everyone the picture I took yesterday."

"What picture is that?"

"You tripping over a twig, about to fall flat on your face. Your mouth was wide open, and I think your tongue was sticking out."

"Do you honestly think I'd be embarrassed?" He dropped to his knees three feet from the cushion where I lay. "You know me better than that."

"I do. And I love your complete lack of shame."

He set down the camera and crawled toward me, stopping at the cushion's edge. "I don't expect you to be shameless like me, and I'm not sure I'd want you to be. I want you exactly the way you are."

"That's the nicest thing any man has ever said to me." I plunged a hand into his hair, pulling him closer. "I want you just the way you are too, sex tapes and all."

"Just so you know, I deleted the sex tape from my phone two days after we met."

"Why would you do that?"

"For you, Eve. I don't need a memento of my liaison with another woman."

"Glad to hear it."

I drew his head closer until our lips met.

He fell onto the cushion, half on top of me, braced on his elbows. The kiss deepened swiftly, hot and sensual and imbued with more emotion than any of our previous kisses. I latched my arms around him, spreading my legs. I was all but begging him to take me, and I felt no shame at all about it.

"My camera takes video too," I mumbled against his lips.

Val pulled his head back. "No, Eve, I don't want to tape us. What happens between you and me is strictly private. I don't want to share our intimate moments with the world, and I don't need a replay to remind me of how much I love being with you."

"I love being with you too."

We made love right there on the crimson cushion, like we had started to do the first time he had posed for me. After that, he insisted I let him take more pictures of me—and he insisted I wear clothes. He told me he wanted a picture to put in his wallet and one to have as his wallpaper on his phone. I took pictures of him with clothes on too, for the same reasons. By the end of the day, we had both changed our phones to display the photos we'd taken of each other.

That night, while I slept with Val's body spooning mine, questions niggled at me. Was I in love with him? Was he in love with me? The most important question kept me awake until after midnight.

Could we, two opposite types of people from two different worlds, really work out in the long run?

Chapter Twenty-Two

Val

The day that marked one month since I'd arrived at Eve's place fell on a Saturday. I had plans to celebrate the date with a date—a real one this time. Dinner in the nude while seated at the kitchen island didn't count. Dinner under the stars on a picnic blanket on the lawn, also in the nude, didn't count either. I wanted a genuine, fully clothed date with her.

I wanted to romance the hell out of Eve Holt.

Since I'd never in my life tried to impress a woman this way, I resorted to calling my sister Maria. After the usual greeting and pleasantries, I got to the point. "I want to ask Eve out on a date, the kind that takes place in a restaurant and involves nice clothes. How do I do that?"

Maria laughed. "*Como*? I must have misheard. You couldn't have said Val Silva finally wants to ask a woman on a date."

I growled under my breath. "That's what I said."

She laughed harder. "*Ó pá*! It only took you thirty-seven years."

My whole family spoke Portuguese, of course, but both of my sisters spoke English as fluently as I did. We often conversed in that language since I'd gotten accustomed to it over the years. Our mother liked English too because it was her native tongue. Sometimes we reverted to Portuguese, particularly if Maria or Aline wanted to scold me or mock me.

"I'm asking for your help," I said. "Will you stop laughing at me and tell me what to do?"

"My big brother needs my help. Give me a moment to enjoy this."

Another, louder growl rumbled out of me. "Forget it. I'll call Aline."

"*Porque?* Aline knows nothing about dating. She married the first boy who asked her to a dance." Maria paused, no doubt for dramatic effect. "Here's what you need to do. Are you listening? Write this down so you don't forget."

"Get on with it."

"Speak these precise words. Eve, will you please go on a date with me?"

My sister burst into laughter again.

"Thank you, Maria. I'm glad my anxiety entertains you."

Her laughter faded away. "You really are anxious about this, aren't you? This woman must mean a lot to you."

"She does."

"Go with your heart and be yourself. She must like you the way you are, eh?"

"I think so." Though Eve had her doubts about my past behavior, I believed she accepted me the way I was. She'd told me as much, but still... "What if being myself offends her?"

"Then she's not the woman for you."

She was the woman for me. I'd known it for a while. Whether I could be the kind of man she needed remained to be seen. I'd try as hard as I could to become that kind of man.

Maria and I talked a bit longer, mostly about our family and what everyone had been doing since the last time we'd spoken. After we said goodbye, I wandered through the house until I found Eve in the living room, sitting in an armchair. She had her legs crossed with her feet on a footstool, and her laptop was balanced on one thigh. Shorts and a tank top concealed only the most private parts of her body. The parts she saved for me alone.

The light of the sinking sun bathed her in a golden, pinkish glow.

When I walked into the room, she smiled. "Hey, gorgeous. Were you on the phone? I heard you talking."

"I called my sister Maria."

Eve angled her head to the side like she was analyzing me. "What's wrong? You look nervous, which isn't like you at all."

She was right. I felt nervous, and that was a rare experience for me.

I perched on the edge of her footstool with her bare feet nudging my ass. "I need to ask you a question."

Clapping her laptop shut, she set it on the table beside her chair. "Shoot."

My pulse throbbed faster, thumping in my ears. I scratched my head, fidgeted, and avoided looking her in the eye. Maria would've found this highly amusing. I wanted to grab the nearest blunt object and hit myself in the head with the thing. *Snap out of it*, I commanded myself.

For the first time ever, I had clammy palms because of a woman.

I cleared my throat. "Eve, I was thinking about what we should do for dinner tonight."

"This is Chinese night, remember? I placed an order already."

"For the guests." I fidgeted again. "For us, I wanted to, uh, make some kind of, um, special arrangements."

"Special?" Her eyebrows cinched together over her nose. "Like what?"

Be yourself, Maria had advised.

Eve liked me the way I was. Right?

She poked me with her big toe. "What's the matter? Did Ollie beat you at soccer? Sorry, I meant to say football."

"I didn't play a game with Ollie today." I took a deep breath, straightened, and met her glittering blue gaze. "*Como vai, gatinha?*"

"Huh?"

"It's Portuguese."

"What does it mean?"

"The phrase is a Brazilian pickup line." I angled in and laid a hand on her bare thigh. "How's it going, baby? That's what it means."

She laughed. "That's your great pickup line? How did you ever become a ladies' man with material like that?"

"It's all in the delivery. *Gatinha* literally means kitten."

Her laughter bubbled out again, light and musical. "Kitten? You should try that line on Heidi and her gal pals."

Making her laugh had relaxed us both, so I forged ahead. "Will you go out on a date with me, Eve? In our clothes, at a restaurant, the right way."

Her cheeks dimpled with a lovely little smile. "Yes, Val, I will go out to dinner with you."

"Wear something nice. I want this to be a formal date."

Those dimples got deeper. "I don't have much in the way of fancy clothes, but I'll do my best."

"Anything you wear will be perfect." I skimmed my gaze up and down her delicious body. "But you do look best in nothing at all."

"Same goes for you."

We ambled through the house hand in hand, splitting off in the hallway so I could go into my room and she could go into hers. Though I slept with her every night, I'd kept my things in the other room to avoid cluttering up her space. Ten minutes later, I was ready. When I knocked on Eve's door, she told me to "go away, please" because "a woman needs more than ten minutes to get beautiful." I considered reminding her she was always beautiful, with or without prep time, but I had the feeling she was as nervous about our date as I was.

I waited in the kitchen, perched on a stool, my foot tapping a fast rhythm on the floor. My gaze stayed glued to the clock on the microwave.

Fifteen minutes later, Eve swept into the room.

And my heart stuttered.

I couldn't move or speak. Her dress, a rich shade of sapphire blue, draped over her curves like it had been made for her body and only her body. The off-the-shoulder design showcased her beautiful shoulders, and the neckline plunged low enough to show off the slopes of her breasts. The flowing skirt dropped almost to her ankles, but one side featured a slit that exposed most of her thigh. Her elegant dress sandals each had a single strap over her toes and another that encircled her ankle. Their blue color matched her dress.

Her hair cascaded over her shoulders in lush waves, and her makeup accentuated her beauty rather than overpowering it.

She was stunning.

Those bright-blue eyes found me and flew wide for a second, then her lips curved into a satisfied smile. "I prefer you naked, but that suit is really doing it for me."

I glanced down at my gray suit. "I've had this for years. It's not even designer."

"Who cares?" She sashayed up to me, her hips swaying, and spread her palms over my chest. "It's damn hot. That's all that matters."

"Glad you like it."

"I'd rip this suit off you right now, but I'm looking forward to our date."

"So am I." Peeling her hands off my chest, I clasped one and guided her toward the door. "Let's go. It's time to romance you, Eve."

Her dimples returned. "I like the sound of that."

Chapter Twenty-Three

Eve

When was the last time I'd had a real date? Years, for sure. I couldn't remember exactly. Once I'd started my business, it had consumed the majority of my time. The word vacation had no meaning for me anymore. Time off consisted of kicking back in front of the TV to binge-watch all the buzzworthy shows I'd missed because I was working seven days a week.

Val took me to the nicest restaurant in town, a steak house. Despite its designation, the place offered a superb atmosphere and superb food as well as live music and a dance floor. Val pulled my chair out for me and pushed it back in once I'd sat down, the way I'd seen men do in movies but had never experienced before in real life.

Oh, that suit. I loved it. As in "I want to tear your clothes off with my teeth, Val." The gray color suited him, and the fit highlighted every one of those muscles I adored. Why had I agreed to a clothing-on date? I wanted him naked this instant.

The restaurant probably didn't allow nudism. Damn.

Val ordered a huge T-bone while I ordered the filet mignon. My choice seemed to surprise him, given the way his brows shot up. Once the waitress had taken our orders and left, he rested his elbows on the table and studied me.

"What is it?" I asked. "Do I have something stuck in my teeth?"

"No. But you are the only woman I've ever met who would eat a steak dinner in my presence. Or eat much of anything."

"If that surprises you, be prepared for a real shocker when you see me eat it."

"Yes, I know how you eat with gusto. I love that about you."

"Can't help it. I love food." I unfolded my napkin and placed it on my lap. "I don't eat steak often, so it's a treat for me. That means I will devour it."

"I have firsthand experience with the way you devour something you're craving."

"Even filet mignon can't compare to the flavor of you."

He reached across the table to grasp my hand. "You are a one-of-a-kind woman, Eve. Meeting you is the best thing that's ever happened to me."

My cheeks grew warm. "You sure know how to compliment a girl."

"It's the truth. You've changed my life."

Though I tried to speak, whatever words I'd meant to say got stuck in my throat. My cheeks flamed, but it was the fluttery sensation in my chest that rendered me speechless.

His thumb caressed the back of my hand, and his tender gaze was focused exclusively on me.

"You've changed my life too," I said when I finally regained the ability to speak.

And it was true. Before Val, I would never have taken time to relax in the middle of the day, much less taken my clothes off outdoors. His shamelessness encouraged me to stop worrying about what people thought of me. The only opinion that really mattered to me these days was his.

The waitress arrived with our drinks, interrupting our moment.

Val withdrew his hand and sat back in his chair.

I wanted to crawl onto his lap and cuddle up there.

We talked about everyday things while we ate our meal. Val smiled every time I shoved a chunk of steak into my mouth and moaned with satisfaction. For dessert, we ordered the darkest, most sinful chocolate cake I'd ever tasted. When I moaned at the deliciousness of it, Val's smile turned hot and hungry.

I'd expected he would whisk me home immediately after dinner, but he surprised me again.

He stood and offered me his hand. "A dance, Eve?"

A few couples occupied the dance floor, swaying to the romantic melody played by a piano and a string quartet.

I placed my hand in Val's.

He led me onto the floor, raised our joined hands, and placed his other palm on my back.

And we danced.

With our bodies barely touching, his hands provided the most solid link between us. No, that wasn't right. Something else, something far less tangible, provided the strongest link. I rested my cheek on his chest and let him sweep me around the dance floor. The music seemed like a waltz, and we moved in time with the rhythm, round and round, my dress swishing around our legs and his hand on my back anchoring me to him. He smelled so good, like woods and spice and man.

I lifted my head to gaze up at him.

He kissed my forehead.

My pulse accelerated. A delicious tingle swept over my skin, chased by a warmth that originated in my chest and bloomed outward to suffuse my entire body, my entire being.

Once the song ended, we headed back to our table to pay the bill. I offered to pay half, but Val shook his head.

"No, Evie," he said. "A gentleman always pays for dinner."

"What if I invited you? I should pay then."

"Maybe, but you didn't invite me. I asked you out."

We made it to the car before we lost control. I started it, climbing onto his lap in the driver's seat and kissing him like a sex-starved nympho. His hands whisked up under my dress, and he pulled his head back to arch his brows at me.

I shrugged. I hadn't worn any underwear.

He made love to me right there in the parking lot. We took it slow, every stroke of his cock lush and intoxicating. I gripped his shoulders, and when I came, it hit me so hard I jerked into the steering wheel.

The horn blared.

Val punched into me one last time, choking back a shout.

I wrapped my arms around him, breathing too heavily to speak, with his semi-firm shaft still inside me. He kissed my throat and worked his way up to my jaw, and finally, to my mouth. I couldn't respond at all, too stunned by the pleasure he always gave me and by the fact I'd had sex in a car for the first time ever. Sex in the parking lot of the most popular restaurant in town. Where anyone might've seen us. Maybe that should've embarrassed me, but I realized it didn't. Nothing much embarrassed me anymore, not since Val.

We drove home and rushed into my bedroom, our clothes gone by the time we got there, and made love again with the same leisurely pace, like we both needed to memorize every sensation. I'd never felt more connected to anyone, or more at ease and fulfilled. Afterward, he pulled the covers over us and hugged me to his side. We fell asleep that way, contented and spent.

Our first date had been bliss

Chapter Twenty-Four

Val

I lay on a lawn chaise soaking up the sunshine, my eyes closed behind my Ray-Bans. The noises of the guests playing badminton reminded me of my first day here. Back then, the guests had been playing miniten, but the sounds were similar. Eve had greeted me at the gate on that day, and I'd been smitten from the first second I'd seen her. She was more than beautiful. She was smart, accomplished, determined, and beloved by all her guests. Even the new ones took to Eve as soon as they met her. She worked hard to ensure the guests had everything they needed, and she made a concerted effort to socialize with them too.

Three days had gone by since our first date, but I'd been here for over a month. I no longer thought of myself as a guest. Neither did Eve. She kept talking about "the guests" but not including me in that designation. I wanted to take her on another date, but I had no idea how to top our evening at the steak house. Dinner, dancing, and sex in the parking lot. That was hard to outdo.

"Shit!"

The hissed curse from nearby made me open my eyes and glance toward Ollie, who lay on another chaise a few yards away. He had been reading a paperback. Now, he held the book over his groin, his cheeks red, and darted his gaze around as if making sure no one was looking.

"What's wrong?" I asked, praying it wasn't no-see-ums again. I'd needed seven days to get over that episode—seven days of

Eve tending to me, but still, I had no desire to repeat the experience.

Ollie eyed me sideways. "I, uh, have a little problem."

He shifted in his chair, squinting his entire face and taking great care to keep the paperback positioned over his groin.

"It's embarrassing," Ollie muttered out of one corner of his mouth.

Ahhh, I finally understood. Every nudist male had the same problem once in a while, though not often. I grabbed my towel off the grass and tossed it to Ollie. "Here. This ought to help."

He caught the towel but didn't use it. Squinting his face even more, he said, "This won't help. The problem is too...big."

I flattened my lips to suppress a laugh. "You're a nudist, Ollie. These things aren't shocking to the rest of us, so it shouldn't bother you. Roll onto your side for a bit or go walk it off."

"Don't think that will help. This isn't the usual kind of problem."

Since I could see the tip of his dick sticking out from under the paperback, I decided he wasn't exaggerating. "What precipitated the problem?"

He tipped his head in the direction of the badminton game.

I glanced there and spotted our newest guests having a good time whacking the ball around with some of the older guests. Kelly and her husband Todd, newlyweds on their honeymoon, had arrived yesterday. Kelly was very sexy, though she couldn't compare to Eve. Still, every time Kelly jumped to hit the ball, her breasts bounced. Every time she scored a point, she did a little victory dance with her knees bent, pumping her fists in the air in time with the thrusts of her hips. The young woman didn't mean it in a sexual way. She was having fun. But her dancing exposed the area between her thighs.

Well, I did see Ollie's dilemma. What man wanted a beautiful woman to see him in that unfortunate state, especially with her husband watching? Ollie couldn't help it, and I sympathized with his plight.

Not that I had ever been embarrassed about such a thing.

Ollie's gaze flicked toward Eve's house. His eyes bulged right before he squeezed them shut. "Oh fuck. Kill me now."

I glanced back.

Eve was moseying toward us wearing her favorite short-shorts and tank top with a pair of flip-flops. She smiled and waved at Ollie before aiming her brightest smile at me. Eve blew me a kiss.

Ollie moaned pitifully and sank down in his chair.

"Put the towel over yourself," I told him, "then lay the book on top of that."

He straightened somewhat and followed my advice.

Eve reached us as Ollie got himself covered. She ruffled my hair. "Scoot over."

I scooted, and she squeezed in beside me.

"This is a serious etiquette breach," I said, pretending to be offended. "Physical contact? Shame on you, Evie."

"This is our resort, and we can do whatever the hell we want." She wriggled to get in a better position. "Besides, I am showing incredible restraint by not copping a feel."

"I stand corrected. You are behaving admirably."

Kelly scored another point and did her inadvertently erotic dance.

Ollie moaned, shaking his head and squeezing his eyes shut again. He ran a hand over his mouth, sat up, and announced, "I'm going for a walk."

"We'll go with you," Eve said.

Ollie's eyes bulged again.

She tried to get up, but I slung an arm around her waist to hold her in place.

Eve glanced at me. "What are you doing?"

"I…" How to explain this without embarrassing Ollie further? I patted her hip. "I'm too comfortable here. Let's stay put and talk about what our next date should be."

She relaxed and cuddled up against me again. "Sure, let's do that."

Ollie looked so relieved I almost thought he might collapse. Eve didn't notice because she had aimed her adoring gaze at me.

Rolling onto his side away from us, Ollie dropped his book and got up while holding the towel in front of him. He hustled off toward the nature trail.

By the time he'd disappeared into the woods, Eve's expression had turned expectant. "What will our next date be? When will it be? I'm liking the romantic treatment."

"Hasn't fucking been romantic?"

"Sure, but it was nice to go out to dinner. And I loved seeing you in a suit."

"But you tore it off me the second we got home."

"I loved doing that too."

"You were stunning in that dress." I stealthily palmed her breast with the arm I had draped over her shoulders, making sure no one else would see it. "But I loved taking it off of your body."

She drew figure eights on my chest with her finger. "You know, I still haven't given you that striptease I promised you after the no-see-um attack."

My cock woke up at her suggestion, and I was on the verge of developing a stiffer problem than Ollie had. "Let's go in the house and do that right now."

A scream reverberated through the clearing around the lawn and the buildings.

Eve jumped out of the chaise at the instant another scream echoed from the nature trail.

I leaped up too. We both stared in the direction of the nature trail, the apparent origin of the outbursts. The screams hadn't been pitched high enough to be a woman. It must've been a man.

"What the hell?" Eve said, squinting to peer down the trail.

Ollie barreled out of the woods, without his towel, flapping his arms in the air and screaming again. "Run! It's after me! Shiiiiiiiiit!"

The guests playing badminton froze, their gazes swiveling to Ollie.

He got halfway to Eve and me before we saw the thing that was after him.

A porcupine hustled out of the woods, quills raised, making a beeline for Ollie.

"Shiiiiiiit!" he hollered again.

Eve rushed toward one of the guests, grabbed the gray-haired woman's badminton racket, and bolted toward the onrushing porcupine.

Well, if you could call what the creature was doing "onrushing." Though he moved fast for such a large, bulky creature, he was in no danger of catching up to Ollie.

I hurried after Eve, but she didn't need my help.

Eve stopped, planted her feet wide, and swung the racket in the direction of the porcupine. She snarled and shouted and stomped one foot, all while brandishing the racket in sharp, whooshing swings.

The porcupine turned around and hustled back down the nature trail.

Ollie fell to his knees, breathing hard and red-faced. He collapsed onto his side on the ground and rolled onto his back spread-eagled. "I think I'm dead. That bright light must be heaven."

Eve approached him, thumping the racket on her palm. "That's the sun, Ollie. You're not dead, though you sure made an unholy ruckus. What happened?"

He shut his eyes. "I was walking down the trail, kind of distracted and not paying attention to where I was going." He opened one eye to peek at me and winced. "I was looking down, and I sort of stumbled into the porky. He wasn't happy about it."

"Why on earth were you staring at the ground?" Eve said. "You know better than that. Keeping an eye on your surroundings is critical in the woods."

"I was—" He flushed even redder, almost crimson, and couldn't quite look at Eve. "I had a problem and needed some alone time."

"But why—"

"Give him a break," I said to Eve. "He's embarrassed enough as it is."

She glanced at me as I came up beside her. "You know what his secret problem was, don't you?"

"Yes, but I'm not going to tell you. It's one of those secrets between men."

Ollie nodded solemnly. "Thanks, man."

Eve's mouth twisted into a half frown. "Manly secrets? What does that mean?"

"It's the bro code," Ollie said. "Don't mess with it, okay?"

Her attention flickered between me and Ollie for a moment before she gave up and shrugged. "Whatever. I guess the secrets of man are not for woman to comprehend."

Ollie pushed up into a sitting position. "Think I'll go take a nap. Getting chased by a crazy porcupine took a lot out of me." He exhaled, his shoulders sagging. "I'm having one crap day."

Eve watched him while he got to his feet. "Did something else happen? I mean, besides the porcupine and your secret manly problem."

He ran a hand over his cheek. "I got an email from Heidi. She's back with her ex."

"Poor Ollie." Eve wrapped her arms around him. "I'm so sorry."

Ollie grimaced.

I decided he was concerned about a recurrence of his manly problem, so I dragged Eve away from him. "Let's go do that private thing we talked about earlier."

She grinned. "Yes, let's."

While Ollie shuffled off toward the guest house, Eve and I headed into our house. Yes, I'd started to think of it as "our" house, which didn't bother me the way it might have a few weeks ago. We were living together after all.

And I liked it.

Chapter Twenty-Five

My clothes lay here, there, and everywhere in the bed-room. I'd tossed them away without a thought for where they might land, more concerned with getting Val hot and bothered with my striptease. Not that it took much to get Val in the upright position for takeoff. Sometimes all I needed to do was wink at him. His easygoing nature did not extend to our intimate times. He could be tender, sure, but he could also become the most scorching, inventive, and energetic lover.

That explained why I was currently lying half on top of him, my cheek on his chest, lazing in the afterglow of sweaty, mind-blowing sex.

I pushed up on one elbow to admire the tattoos on his arm and chest. The dragon that snaked down his biceps had intrigued me since the day we met, but I'd never quite gotten around to asking about it. I traced the tattoo's lines with my fingertip.

"Does this dragon have some meaning?" I asked.

"The design is inspired by Amaru, the winged serpent of Tiwa-naku, but it's a stylized version." He took hold of my finger, drag-ging it along the tattoo while he explained. "It has the body of an anaconda and the head of a bird. Amaru represents the power of nature, and to the Incas, it became a protective deity. No one knows what the people of Tiwanaku thought of Amaru, since their civilization died out many thousands of years ago. Tiwanaku is in the mountains of Bolivia."

"Wow, you're a history buff. I learn something new about you every day." I tickled his skin with the finger he still held. "Your love of ancient mythology is wicked sexy."

"I also know about legends of Brazil. Would it turn you on to hear about those?"

"Absolutely." I wriggled my finger free of his grasp. "Does touching your tattoo give me magical powers?"

"You don't need magic to entrance me."

I bent to lave my tongue over the lines of his tattoo, beginning with the tail and gliding my way up to the wings and the head.

He sucked in a breath.

I swirled my tongue around the dragon's head.

Val dived a hand into my hair, cradling my head, halting my exploration. "Don't awaken the beast unless you want to be devoured."

"As much as I'd love that, I should check on the guests." I hopped off the bed and started collecting my clothes. "I need to cheer up Ollie. He's really bummed about Heidi."

"What are you going to do? He has a broken heart, but it will heal."

"I should do something." While I pulled on my panties, I mulled the problem. By the time I got my bra on, no ideas had come to me. I paused, hands on my hips. "How does a woman console a man she's not sleeping with? I mean, I know how to make you feel better, but a blow job doesn't seem appropriate for Ollie."

"While I'm sure he would love that, I'd rather you didn't."

Tugging on my shorts, I pretended to be confused. "Really? And I thought you were such a bohemian."

He sat up and shimmied to the foot of the bed, reaching out to grasp the waistband of my shorts and pull me toward him. "I'm an exhibitionist, remember? Never claimed to be a bohemian. I'd share my sunscreen with Ollie, but I won't share you with anyone."

"I won't share you either."

"Good." He placed his open mouth over my belly button and swirled his tongue inside it. "Sharing is overrated."

"Have you ever done a threesome?"

"Twice. I prefer to have one woman all to myself."

"I do love your one-track mind."

Those lips traveled higher while his hands slid down my thighs. "How can I think of anything else when I'm with you?"

A breathy moan whispered out of me, but I gathered what little willpower I had left after spending more than a month with him and backed away. I wagged a finger at him. "No more sex. Not until after dinner. Well, maybe mid-afternoon. Oh, just let me talk to Ollie and then you and I can get back to getting it on."

Val laughed. "That's my insatiable girl."

"Me?" I shook my head at him. "You are the one who drags me into the woods for quickies, and drags me behind buildings for quickies, and—"

"I confess to the crime of being addicted to you, Evie." He held out his hands, wrists together. "Lock me up in your dungeon. I hope it's a life sentence."

Those two words stopped me. Life sentence. He'd been joking of course, but the term implied he wanted to stay with me for good. Or maybe he expected me to go to LA with him.

Did I want to go with him? What would I give up to have him in my life for good?

To avoid thinking about that, I finished getting dressed, kissed Val on the cheek, and hustled out of the house to find Ollie. He was nowhere in the guest house or on the lawn. I ran into Ruth and Sylvester, who were relaxing in chaises.

"Have you seen Ollie?" I asked them.

"Yeah," Sly said. "He went down the nature trail again, this time wearing clothes and holding on to a badminton racket."

"That dear, dear boy," Ruth said. "How could Heidi break his heart? She's such a sweet child. This doesn't seem like her at all."

"We don't have to hate Heidi because she dumped Ollie," I said. "Sometimes things don't work out between two people. I'm sure Heidi didn't mean to hurt him."

Part of me wanted to be angry with Heidi, the protective part of me that thought of Ollie as a little brother. Mostly, I wanted them both to be happy. Too bad that hadn't happened for them as a couple.

"Don't forget," Sly said. "Ruth and I are leaving tomorrow."

"Yeah, I know. I'll miss you guys."

Ruth leaned forward to clasp my hand. "We'll miss you too, Evie, but we'll be back for the fall color."

Sylvester chortled. "Maybe we should build our own little bungalow in the woods and live here. Sure would save us the trouble of driving or flying here."

His wife tsked. "You'd miss the alligators and the early-bird specials."

Yeah, they lived in Florida. Alligators were one reason I would never move there.

I chatted a little more with Ruth and Sylvester before I headed down the nature trail in search of Ollie. I found him at the hot spring. He was sitting on one of the benches, his gaze aimed straight ahead though his focus seemed to have retreated into a distance only he could see. His hair was wet, but his clothes were dry. Rather than looking melancholy, he seemed relaxed and content.

I sat down beside him and patted his leg. "Hey, Ollie."

"Hey, Eve." He turned his face toward me and smiled a little. "If you're worried I might drown myself in the hot spring, you can relax. I'm okay."

"Are you sure? Getting dumped sucks."

"Yeah, it does." He braced his elbows on his thighs. "I should've known better. Heidi and her boyfriend were always breaking up and getting back together. Being the rebound guy is never a good idea."

"No, I guess not. I still feel bad for you."

"Don't. I'm fine, really." He waved one finger toward the water. "Took a dip in the hot spring, did a lot of thinking, and realized I'm not as bummed as I thought. Sure, I like Heidi. We don't know each other that well, so what I was feeling was only a crush."

I bent forward too and rested my cheek on his arm. "I'm still sorry. You deserve to find a woman who appreciates you."

"Heidi dumping me wasn't what really bothered me." He frowned at the ground. "I got laid off."

"What?" I sprang upright and scrutinized him for a moment until the shock of his statement waned. "That's awful. When did it happen?"

"A week before I came here. That's why I wanted to extend my stay from two weeks to six weeks." He ran a hand over his mouth and sighed. "Thought I'd feel better if I got away from home. It didn't work. Knowing I have to go back there and look for another job... Man, that sucks way worse than Heidi dumping me."

"Wish I could help you out somehow." I got an idea and leaped to my feet. I grabbed Ollie's hand and tugged. "Come on."

He eyed me with suspicion. "What are you up to, Evie?"

"Let's canvas the guests for ideas on how to get you re-employed."

"Oh no, come on." He made a pained face, his voice evincing the faintest whine. "I don't want pity from the other nudists."

"Don't you mean naturists?"

His lips tightened into a smile he was trying to suppress. "Yeah. I still don't see how the other naturists can help."

"Won't know unless we ask."

For the next half hour, Ollie and I talked to everyone—except Val, who had sequestered himself in the spare bedroom claiming to have "important phone calls" to make. Everybody had an idea for Ollie, though none seemed quite right for him. He wrote down everything they said, accepted business cards from those who offered him one, and thanked each and every person who gave advice.

By the time I returned to the house, Val was in the kitchen. He perched on a stool at the island.

"I've been waiting for you," he said when I walked into the house.

Despite being naked, he managed to look serious. Not suicidal serious, but rather, contemplative serious.

"What's up?" I asked as I parked my butt on the stool beside his. We faced each other, our knees inches apart.

"I have a proposition for you."

"Don't you think it's a bit soon for a proposal?"

He rolled his eyes. "Not that kind of proposition. What I'm offering is a business proposal."

"Okay," I said cautiously. Whatever he was up to, I hoped it didn't involve a massive grant from the private foundation he'd spent the last few hours setting up for this purpose.

Val slanted toward me, his gaze intent on mine. "I want to be your business partner."

"Business?" I searched his face for some sign it was a joke, but he still looked serious. "Partner? Do you mean, like, an official partner? I have an LLC, you know."

"Yes, I know. I want to buy into it and become a full-fledged partner."

My mind seemed to have screeched to a halt. I couldn't form thoughts, much less words. When I managed to speak, I babbled and even laughed nervously while I did it. "My company is a single-member LLC. I'd have to, uh, redo it somehow. I mean, a partnership LLC is different and— Are you sure about this? I've made some strides with the business, but you might lose your shirt."

He smiled. "I lost my shirt years ago. Best decision I ever made."

"You know what I mean." I wrung my hands and bit the inside of my lip. "Risking my own money is one thing. Risking yours... If I bankrupted you, I'd feel awful."

"I wouldn't enjoy bankruptcy either, but I want to do this." He slanted in more, his gaze aimed straight into mine. "For you, I'll take any risk."

A rock hardened in my throat, its edges sharp and rough. Take a risk with Val? I'd done that already, several times over, and it had been the best thing I'd ever done. But personal risks were a whole other thing from professional ones. I might bankrupt us both, and we'd wind up living in a tent in the state forest.

I hadn't worried about losing everything until he'd announced he wanted to be my business partner.

"Trust me," he said, his tone as earnest as the look on his face. "I know the risks, and I want to take them with you."

"What about your modeling career? Your life in LA?"

"I've had enough of that. Earlier, I called my agent and gave her the news. I'm retiring from modeling. After that, I called a real estate agent and put my house up for sale."

My mouth dropped open. "Why would you uproot your whole life?"

"Come on, it can't be that hard to understand." He cupped my face in both his hands. "I'm doing this for you. I want my life to be here with you, running this resort together."

"But why?"

"You still don't understand, do you?" His lips formed the sweetest smile I'd ever seen. "I love you, Evie. You are *meu amor*, my love. That's what I called you the day of my unfortunate encounter with invisible insects."

"I love you too, Val." The words poured out before I considered what I was saying. His declaration had hit me like the mythical arrow fired by Cupid, sinking deep into my heart. I loved him. The idea might've scared me a month ago, but today, loving him felt like the most right thing I'd ever done. "I really do love you. An awful lot."

"Me too." He smirked. "I love you an awful lot, not myself."

"You're one hundred percent sure you want to run this place with me, as official business partners."

"I do."

"Well then." I peeled his hands away from my face and clasped them to my chest. "Yes, Val, I accept your proposition. I will be your business partner."

"I'll call my lawyer so he can get started on the paperwork."

"Sounds good."

He leaped to his feet, swept me into his arms, and carried me off to our bedroom. For the next hour, we celebrated the best way we knew how—with plenty of grunting and moaning, a few screams, and lots of enthusiasm.

Chapter Twenty-Six

Val

The next day, with our new partnership in the works, I drove into town to visit the hardware and grocery stores—as a business partner, not as Eve's lover. This was my first official outing to buy supplies for the resort. Eve had wanted to come with me, but I'd convinced her to stay home and take care of our guests.

Our guests. I liked that.

I wandered into the hardware store feeling better than I had in years, since before I'd made a public spectacle of myself for the attention and become the accidental star of a sex tape scandal. My old life no longer appealed to me. The thought of going back to LA to finalize the sale of my house and collect my belongings made my jaw tighten. None of that mattered anymore, because I had the right life now. My life with Eve, working with her and living with her, was all I needed.

Ten minutes after I walked into the store, I was talking with an employee who seemed very knowledgeable about paint. Eve had looked at the store's paint selection online and had given me strict instructions to buy only the colors white and seafoam green. If I came back with gray or bright blue she would, she'd promised, sick a horde of no-see-ums on me.

Jeff, the paint expert, was explaining the types of paint to me. I nodded and pretended I understood the differences, knowing I would buy whichever kind Jeff suggested.

Out the corner of my eye, I noticed a figure moving down the aisle toward us. I glanced in that direction and gritted my teeth.

Quentin Smith stopped in the middle of the aisle, looking surprised like he hadn't noticed me before. A muscle ticked in his jaw.

With a herculean effort of willpower, I relaxed my jaw and turned my gaze away from him, back to Jeff. The young salesman seemed unaware of the tension between me and Quentin and had not paused in his description of the types of paint.

"Like I said," Jeff told me, "the paint and primer in one is the easiest to use and has the best coverage. If you want stain protection—"

I swore I could feel Quentin's gaze burning into me. I glanced at him, moving only my eyes.

He had his fists clenched now, along with his jaw.

Fuck him. I would not give the bastard the satisfaction of goading me into a confrontation. I had Eve. He didn't. End of story.

Naturally, the bastard refused to walk away. He marched up to me and growled, "Shouldn't you be going back to where you came from? The worms in the swamp must miss you."

His insult sounded like something straight out of a schoolyard. I almost laughed but quashed it because that would inflame him more. Eve wouldn't want me to beat the shit out of her former handyman. As good as punching him would feel, it wouldn't solve the problem.

Quentin was obsessed with Eve.

I gave him my back and asked Jeff to explain the stain-protection options again.

A hand slapped down on my shoulder. "I was talking to you, nature boy."

"Please excuse me," I said to Jeff. "I need to deal with a personal matter."

Jeff glanced from me to Quentin and back again three times. "Uh, sure. I'll be at the paint counter when you're ready to order."

The young man hustled away.

I turned to face Quentin, maintaining a calm demeanor even while I imagined the various ways I might pummel him. "What do you want, Mr. Smith?"

His eyes narrowed to slits, and he squeezed the words out between his clenched teeth. "I want you to stay the hell away from Eve."

Quentin's attempt to intimidate me failed. I folded my arms over my chest, casually, like I didn't give a damn what he said or did. Well, as long as he was badmouthing me, I didn't care. If he said one rotten thing about Eve…

"I'm not leaving," I said. "Eve and I are partners, in every way."

"Fucking her doesn't make you partners."

"My relationship with Eve is none of your business."

His mouth flattened into a slash, and veins stood out on his neck. "She'll see through you eventually. Eve isn't one of you nudie freaks. She's a real lady."

I glared at him. "Yes, Eve is a lady. But a real gentleman would never seduce a woman who'd had too much to drink. What does that make you?"

Quentin jerked backward as if I'd kicked him in the nuts. "She wasn't drunk. A little tipsy was all."

"Any amount of impairment should have been enough to stop you." I jabbed a finger into his chest. "You are the one who's a worm."

He stared at me, his face blank, for a few seconds.

I hoped he might give up and go away, but of course, he didn't. Quentin snarled, "You son of a bitch. I won't let you ruin Eve."

He pulled his fist back and swung it at me.

I caught his fist in one hand and slugged him in the gut with the other.

Spluttering, Quentin doubled over and staggered backward.

"Never show your face to me or Eve again," I said.

He glowered up at me, still bent over hugging his midsection. "This isn't over."

"Yes, it is."

I stalked down the aisle and out of sight of Quentin. For fifteen minutes, I wandered the aisles collecting the rest of the supplies before I headed back to the paint department. Along the way, I passed the checkout aisles. Quentin was making his purchases there, engaged in conversation with the cashier, a perky young woman who seemed to think Quentin was hilarious. Her giggles faded as I hurried past the checkout lines. She eyed me like I was a cobra about to pounce and sink my teeth into her throat.

Who knew what lies Quentin had told the girl.

Once I'd paid for all the supplies, I drove home to Eve. The tension that had lingered ever since Quentin first approached me dissolved the instant I got out of the truck.

Eve raced out of the house and threw her arms around me. She crushed her lips to mine. With her feet dangling off the ground, she broke the kiss and grinned at me. "I'm so glad you're home."

"I am too. But you're acting like I was gone for months, not a few hours."

"Can I help it if I missed you?" She pecked my lips again. "Besides, I'm excited about having you as my business partner."

"That's obvious." I hugged her tighter to me, loving the feel of her warm, supple body. "I need to get out of these clothes."

"Yes, you do." She slid down my body until her feet touched down. "Let's get naked."

She stripped off her tank top and tossed it onto the truck's hood.

I gaped at her, sure I must've been hallucinating. Eve Holt stripping in public? Well, it wasn't exactly public. This was our nudist resort, but still, I'd never imagined Eve would join the natives.

She removed her shorts next, followed by her bra and panties. Her sandals stayed on since we were standing on the gravel driveway. She scanned me up and down. "Why are you still dressed?"

"Your striptease entranced me." I whipped off my clothes, ditching them on the truck's hood with her garments. I held out my hand. "Shall we check in on our guests?"

"Absolutely."

She settled her smaller hand in mine, and together we headed for the lawn where our guests were lounging on picnic blankets. Ollie was playing the guitar and singing a pop song I recognized but couldn't quite name.

"Ollie sings?" I said to Eve as we reached the lawn's periphery.

"Yeah," Eve said, smiling. "He's great, isn't he?"

"He is."

The whole gang suddenly noticed us. Every gaze swung in our direction, and a flurry of surprised sounds and expressions ensued.

Eve didn't blush or turn away. She faced the group head-on, smiling and waving to them, and called out "hello" to each and every guest. She used their first names, even for the ones who'd arrived today. The woman had an amazing memory.

Ollie set down his guitar and hurried up to us with Ruth and Sylvester close behind. The older couple were leaving this afternoon, but they'd stayed long enough to witness Eve's first foray into nudism.

"Evie!" Ruth said as she dragged Eve into a quick bear hug. When she released Eve, Ruth patted her arms. "You finally did it. Doesn't it feel wonderful to get rid of those itchy clothes?"

"Getting rid of my bra sure feels good," Eve said, then flashed me a sly smile. "Though there are certain benefits to wearing clothes."

I loved watching her strip. That was the unspoken benefit.

After everyone had their chance to congratulate Eve on taking the plunge, she and I returned to the house to make lunch for the guests. Unfortunately, that meant we needed to wear clothes during the food prep and while carrying it to the guest house. Once we'd done that, though, we shed our clothes and joined the other nudists for lunch.

For the entire afternoon, Eve stayed nude.

Though nudism wasn't about sex, I had trouble holding back my hunger for her when I spent hours admiring her naked body. By three o'clock, I couldn't stand it anymore. I asked Eve to take a walk down the nature trail with me, but she guessed my intentions as soon as we set foot on the trail.

"Will it be the hot spring again?" she asked. "Or do you have other plans for where we'll have sex this time?"

I patted the blanket I'd slung over my shoulder. "Thought we'd try it on the ground."

"Let's go to the meadow where all the wildflowers are in bloom."

"Perfect."

We made love there in the meadow, surrounded by colorful flowers with the sun warming our bodies and the birds serenading us. It was beautiful. She was beautiful. I loved her body, but I loved her heart and her mind even more.

That night, we made love again and fell asleep with our bodies entangled.

In the morning, I rose before Eve and performed my usual task of making a special breakfast for her. When she moseyed into the kitchen, naked, and stretched her arms above her head, I nearly vaulted over the island to ravish her. I'd developed an enormous amount of willpower since meeting Eve. If I gave in to my desire every time it seized me, we would've done nothing but have sex since the day I'd arrived here.

"Mmm," she hummed as she reached the island. "Smells wonderful in here. What did you make me today?"

"Your favorite. Café Colonial."

"Oooh." She rubbed her hands together. "Breads and cheese and sweet stuff. Yummy."

Eve took a seat on one of the stools, where I'd already laid out the place settings.

I served her a few minutes later and sat down beside her.

"You are an amazing cook," she said while chewing a mouthful of cheese bread. "I'm one lucky girl to have landed a guy like you."

"No, I'm the lucky one." I wiped crumbs from the corner of her mouth with my thumb. "You took a chance on me in spite of my past."

"The best decision I ever made." She glanced around as if she'd forgotten something.

"If you're worried about the guests," I said, "it's taken care of. I made the food, while clothed, and Ollie helped me take it all to the guest house."

She froze mid-chew. "What time is it?"

"Eight o'clock."

Her eyes went wide. "Why did you let me sleep so late?"

"Because you needed the rest. You have a partner now, which means you don't need to work so hard."

Her lips curved into a sweet smile. "I love you, Val."

I kissed her cheek. "I love you too."

A fist banged on the door, rattling it, and a familiar voice shouted, "Eve! Open the door. It's an emergency."

The tone of Ollie's voice confirmed his statement.

Eve and I both ran to the door. She yanked it open.

Ollie was breathing hard like he'd been running. He was wearing clothes too.

"What on earth is wrong?" Eve asked, laying a hand on his arm.

"Just got a call from Sam Walsh at the hardware store."

Sam owned the hardware store, but I couldn't imagine what kind of emergency would compel him to call Ollie.

"He tried to call you, Eve," Ollie explained, "but you didn't answer your cell and he didn't have the landline number."

Eve shook her head. "I don't understand. What's the big emergency?"

"There's a passel of reporters heading this way." Ollie glanced toward the driveway. "Some of them already made it to the outer gate. I ran there to check. Since the gate doesn't have a lock, I'm guessing they'll be through it soon enough."

"Wha— I—" Eve looked to me, her mouth open, then looked at Ollie again. "Why would reporters be swarming this place?"

Ollie held up a cell phone. Its screen displayed a social media post that read, "The bad boy of international football is at it again. Val Silva is living in a sex commune where all the guests pose for erotic photos and engage in orgies."

The post included a photo of me and Eve.

Naked. Behind the guest house. Fucking.

Chapter Twenty-Seven

Eve

My vision blurred and drifted back into focus as my mind struggled to comprehend what I was seeing. Me and Val. That day we'd had sex behind the guest house. How could anyone have photographed us? How could anyone have known what we would be doing that day? They couldn't have known, but if a tabloid reporter had followed Val here, that person could've been spying on us since the day he arrived.

Why not? The naked truth about Val Silva, bad boy ex-athlete turned model, would make for a splashy headline.

And there it was. The headline. The splash. The lies.

Ollie stuffed the phone back into his jeans pocket. "What should we do? If those paparazzi or whatever they are want to get in, they can climb over the outer gate. The inner gate isn't shut, but even if we close it, they can climb over that too. Should we call the police?"

I couldn't speak. My thoughts whirled, and I couldn't grab on to any of them.

"This is private property," Val said. "They have no right to invade the privacy of our guests. Yes, we will call the police."

"Sheriff's department," I mumbled.

Val slipped an arm around me, tugging me into his side. "It will be all right, Eve. Once they realize there's nothing to see here, they'll lose interest and leave."

A sour taste crept into my mouth. I needed to talk to Val about all of this, but not in front of Ollie. So I told Ollie, "Call the sheriff's department and then inform the guests of what's happening. I'll come to the guest house in a few minutes, as soon as I get dressed."

And figure out what the hell to say.

Ollie nodded and trotted back to the guest house.

I pushed the door shut with my foot and wriggled out of Val's embrace.

He shook his head slowly, his mouth open, and spread his hands. "Eve…I'm so sorry."

"How did paparazzi find out about my resort? How did they know you're here?"

"Only my family knows I came here, and they would never tell anyone." He reached for me, but I scuttled away from him. "Eve, please, let me help."

"Help how? A horde of gossipmongers are invading my home, my business. How can anyone feel comfortable staying here again? Privacy is paramount for a nudist resort."

"I know. I'll do anything I can to make this right." Head bowed, he rubbed his forehead. "I don't understand how anyone found out I'm here. Someone has known for weeks, based on the photo of us."

"You mean the one of us screwing." I backed up to the island and hugged myself, suddenly cold from head to toe. "What if my family sees that? What if these scumbag paparazzi track them down and harass them? Whoever took that picture of us might've photographed everyone who's been here lately."

Val scrubbed a hand over his mouth. "This is my fault, I know. Please believe me, Eve, I never meant for my life to crash into yours. I left all of that behind, or I thought I did."

"Obviously not. Maybe your new assistant blabbed to the tabloids."

"He didn't know where I'd gone." Val shuffled closer but didn't try to touch me. "Once this initial shock passes, we'll both be able to think more clearly and figure out how this happened. We're partners. Nothing will change that."

"Everything has changed. My business will be toast. My guests will never trust me again."

"Don't assume the worst. Nudists can be very understanding."

He almost smiled when he said that but couldn't quite accomplish the expression.

I had no fucking idea what I felt, what I should feel, what I should do. The numbness of shock had penetrated me to the core. He was right. I needed time to recover from the sucker-punch jolt of learning my privacy and the privacy of my guests had been shattered.

Was it Val's fault? I had no clue. Not yet.

He wouldn't do this, a voice in my head whispered. *He loves you.*

Yes, I believed that. Right now, it was the only truth I was certain of. But if his past had precipitated this disaster, I needed to reconsider whether a relationship with him was the best thing for me, no matter how much I loved him.

I straightened and cleared my throat. "I have to get dressed and talk to my guests. Everything else will have to wait until the dust clears."

"By 'everything,' you mean us."

"Honestly, Val, I don't know. This is all too much right now. I have to focus on protecting my guests."

Before he could say anything in response, I hurried down the hall to my bedroom, slamming the door behind me. Tears pricked at my eyes, but I had no time to cry. Later, maybe I'd collapse onto my bed and sob for a while. At this moment, I needed to minimize the damage as much as possible.

How was I supposed to do that?

I pulled on jeans and a baggy T-shirt along with socks and sneakers. I almost forgot underwear but remembered before I walked out of the bedroom. The last thing I needed was a photo of me, braless and panties-less, splashed across the Internet. Sure, it wouldn't be as bad as the porn photo already out there, but I refused to add fuel to the gossip fire.

On my way out of the house, I grabbed my phone. Val seemed to have retreated into the spare room, considering the door was shut and he was nowhere in sight. I had no time to hash things out with him. My livelihood was in critical condition, on the verge of death.

Val was my partner. Not officially, not yet, but yeah. My partner. Should I include him in my decisions? I paused on the threshold of the outside door. Sunshine spilled through the opening into the kitchen, dispelling the shadows. The darkness inside me crept closer and closer.

I rushed out and yanked the door shut.

Ten minutes later, I stood in the dining hall in front of all the guests. They occupied chairs at the tables, and all of them wore clothes thanks to Ollie convincing them it was the smart thing to do under the circumstances. Everyone watched me and waited to hear what I would say. Fabulous. I had to come up with a reassuring and inspiring speech that would convince everyone I hadn't fucked up royally. No problem.

Rolling my shoulders back, I lifted my chin and began. "Thank you all for being so patient. I know you're wondering what's going on. Ollie told you a little about it, but I need to explain exactly what's happened and what we—" I hesitated for a split second, realizing I'd used the word we, implying I had a partner. "What I am doing to ensure your privacy and security. Nothing matters more to me than providing a safe and comfortable environment for all of my guests."

I paused, scanning the crowd to gauge their reactions. No one glared at me, so I figured I was okay for the moment.

"The sheriff's department has been informed," I said, "and they are sending deputies. The state police are also sending two troopers. That's all they can spare, but I doubt we'll need more. The people trying to get into the resort are tabloid reporters who want a juicy story. We are not going to give it to them."

"Why are they here?" someone asked.

The voice originated from the rear of the dining hall, and I couldn't see the speaker's face through the crowd.

I didn't want to tell them Val had been the bait that lured the paparazzi here. I still didn't know how they'd found out he was here. Until I could tell them that, I would not mention Val's connection to the craziness about to descend on us.

"Because of me," a voice behind me said. Val's words echoed through the dining hall. "This is happening because of me."

My heartbeat sped up as I swiveled my head to glance at him. He wore clothes, dark-blue jeans and a conservative tan shirt. He looked edible as always, but I couldn't muster any lust. His expression made sure of that. Sorrow was the best description of what I saw in his eyes.

"You all know about my past," he said from just inside the doorway. Though he spoke to everyone, his gaze remained locked on mine. "I've never tried to hide it, and in spite of my past behavior, you have welcomed me into your family. I'm very grateful for that. I wish I could turn back time and make it so what's happening today never happened, but I can't. All I can do is make sure no one else is harmed by it."

I clutched my hands over my belly, my body rotating toward him like it had a mind of its own. The look on his face, it pierced straight into my heart. My throat went thick. My mouth went dry. I had a sinking feeling I knew what he would say next.

"That's why I'm leaving," he said. "To protect you."

He was talking to me.

I swallowed hard, but my throat got thicker, tighter, constricted by a terrible emotion I couldn't quite name. He was leaving me. For my own good. Just a few minutes ago, I'd wondered whether I should continue our relationship. He'd made the decision for me.

All the guests jumped up and swarmed us, babbling things I couldn't understand. My focus had telescoped down to me and Val. Nothing else got through the haze of a new, colder shock and the pain that swept in behind it.

Guests asked me questions that I tried to answer as fully and honestly as I could. Noise outside made some of them run to the windows. I could see vehicles pulling up between my home and the guest house, people tumbling out of them even as others ran up the driveway and through the open gate. There hadn't been much point in closing the gate. It had no lock, and besides, the paparazzi could've climbed over it.

By the time I'd fielded all the questions and the group had settled down, Val was gone.

I hurried outside, arriving as the sheriff's deputies drove up in one vehicle and the state troopers in another. Talking to them took more time. I kept glancing back at the house, wondering if Val was in there or if he'd already left. The paparazzi tried to surround me, but the law enforcement officers forced them back and escorted me toward the house. I noticed Val's truck parked behind the house as usual, so he hadn't left yet.

The paparazzi rushed for the door of the house.

I hopped onto my tiptoes, craning my neck to see what they had seen.

Val had stepped out of the house carrying his suitcase. He held up a hand to quiet the crowd. Once they settled down, cameras raised and mics positioned, he said, "I'm leaving."

Several voices shouted complaints.

Val held up his hand again. He grinned and said, "Follow me back to LA, and I promise you'll get a better show than anything you'll see here."

He winked and trotted toward his truck.

That grin and wink had been totally fake. Sure, his act had been a stellar performance. Nobody else would've noticed the slight clues to his true emotional state. He was luring the paparazzi away from this place, away from me.

I wanted to run after him, kiss him, tell him he didn't have to do this.

My feet wouldn't budge. It wouldn't have made a difference if I could've moved. Val wanted to be the hero who saved me and my business from shame and ruination. Maybe it was for the best. What we had might not have lasted.

Bullshit, a voice in my head snarled.

I ran toward his truck, ran as fast as I could, shoving paparazzi out of the way, elbowing the ones who hissed nasty curses at me. By the time I'd plowed my way through the crowd, Val's truck was gone. I couldn't even see it rolling down the driveway. He'd taken off, kicking up a cloud of dust in his wake.

The vultures descended on me. They fired off question after question, their voices overlapping.

I ducked my head and charged through them until I stumbled up to the door of my house. They tried to follow me inside, but I slammed the door in their faces.

The cacophony of shutters activating filled the air.

Stern voices shouted things I couldn't make out, but I realized it was the state police and sheriff's deputies attempting to wrangle the herd.

Keeping my head down, I ran through the house shutting any open windows and yanking all the curtains closed. I locked the windows and the outside door. I called Ollie and instructed him to keep the other guests inside the guest house until the cops drove the paparazzi away. After we said goodbye, I collapsed onto my bed and slung an arm over my eyes.

Val was gone.

Chapter Twenty-Eight

Eve

A little while later—I'd lost count of the minutes or hours—a crisp knock lured me out of my bedroom and to the door to the outside. When I peeked out the window beside it, I saw one of the deputies. I also noticed the herd had thinned. Only a handful of paparazzi loitered out there.

I pulled the door open.

"Ma'am," the deputy said, nodding. "We got the reporters to leave. Most of them, anyway. Once we threatened to lock them up overnight, they seemed to lose interest in harassing you."

"Yeah, it was really Val they wanted."

"That was Val Silva, wasn't it? The soccer player whose team won the Olympics?"

I was more grateful than words could express that he hadn't mentioned the sex tape or Val's flagrant nudity whenever his team won games. Maybe this deputy didn't know about that, or maybe he was being tactful. Either way, I could've kissed him for it.

"Thank you," I said. "I really appreciate you guys stepping in to clear out the vultures."

"No problem, ma'am. The state guys are heading out, but my partner and I will hang around for a bit to make sure the rest leave."

"Would you guys like a bite to eat or something to drink?"

"A drink would be great."

I listed all the beverages I had on hand. He chose pop, and I gave him four cans so the other law enforcement men could have some too.

They all smiled and waved to me.

I couldn't move away from the doorway. Though only a few paparazzi remained, the idea of stepping outside and into the fray again left me paralyzed. I shut the door and retreated into my bedroom, curling up on top of the covers with my knees pulled up to my chest.

Would Val come back? Did he want to?

More time passed while I lay there, not sleepy, but mentally exhausted. Thoughts ricocheted through my mind like ping-pong balls. Should I have tried harder to stop Val from leaving? He would call me. Wouldn't he? Once he got home, he'd let me know everything was okay.

A knock roused me from my lethargy, and I headed for the front door.

Ollie was there when I opened the door. "Are you okay, Eve? I've been calling, tried your cell and the landline, but you didn't pick up."

I had a vague memory of hearing phones ringing, but I'd left my cell by the island and there was a hallway between me and the kitchen. The noises had seemed far away.

Yeah, I'd also been in a semi-catatonic state on my bed.

"Sorry," I mumbled. "Needed a break after all the craziness."

He touched my arm. "You okay, Evie? We all heard what Val said and saw him leaving. When's he coming back?"

I hunched my shoulders. "Don't know if he is coming back."

"Of course he is. Val's crazy about you."

A half-hearted shrug was all I could muster in response.

"You're wiped out," Ollie said. "Get some rest. I'll take care of lunch and dinner. If you don't mind me invading your kitchen."

I shrugged again.

"Be back in a few minutes," he said. "Gotta put some clothes on to make the food. You always tell us we can eat naked, but you have to make and serve the food with clothes on."

"Uh-huh."

He gave my arm a squeeze and trotted back to the guest house.

I slept all afternoon. Though I'd missed lunch, I didn't feel hungry at all. Ollie insisted I eat, even sat there watching me to make sure I did eat something. The food tasted like cardboard. Ollie's cooking wasn't the problem. Nothing would've tasted right to me. Nothing felt right either. My home had been invaded, my privacy torn to shreds, and my reputation blackened. Would anyone come to my resort ever again? I'd probably lose my business and be forever known as the slut who screwed Val Silva behind the guest house. Maybe I was overreacting, but I couldn't stop the crazy thoughts from whirling inside my head.

None of that mattered half as much as the fact he'd walked out on me.

After I dutifully swallowed food I couldn't taste, Ollie hugged me and left. I grabbed my cell phone and called Val. His voicemail picked up. I left a stammering message, sounding like an idiot. Two hours later, I left another message. At midnight, I tried again.

When I finally went to bed, I didn't get much sleep. Crying kept me awake.

The next day, I picked myself up and got back to it. Though my eyes were gritty and puffy and had dark circles under them, I refused to wallow any longer. I showered, got dressed, and started working on breakfast for the guests. Ollie showed up and insisted on helping. It seemed strange to see him in clothes, but he turned out to be an excellent helper. He also insisted on taking care of the other guests, handling any problems or requests they had.

When I caught him cleaning the toilets in the guest-house rooms, I told him, "You are a guest, Ollie. You shouldn't be doing janitorial work."

He kept scrubbing the toilet while he told me, "I don't mind. It's nice to do something constructive instead of being stuck in a cubicle. Besides, this place is like a second home to me. You're like a sister, and the other guests are my crazy aunts and uncles." He paused in his scrubbing and looked up at me. "I love you, Evie. Anything you need, I'm here to help."

I didn't know what to say to that other than the truth. "I love you too, Ollie."

We went on like that for a week. Ollie served as janitor, handyman, sous chef, receptionist, and guest coordinator. He had no official job here, but he worked as hard as any full-time employee. He wore clothes most of the time since the health code required him to wear clothes while cooking and serving food and, well, it would've been icky for him to go nude while cleaning toilets. In his duties as my receptionist and guest coordinator, he preferred to go au naturel.

Every day, at least five times a day, I tried to call Val. I gave up on leaving voicemails since he ignored them. I texted and emailed, but he ignored that too. After ten days, I gave up. Val was never coming back. My chest ached and tears blurred my vision every time I thought about him. Part of me wanted to hunt him down and kick his ass for running out on me. The rest of me, the larger and far less brave part, preferred to hide.

Another week dragged by with no contact from Val, not even a piddly email offering a half-assed explanation. The biggest excitement I had that week was of the unpleasant variety. I had decided to repaint the dining hall and went to the hardware store for the necessary supplies. Ollie had offered to handle the supply run, but I needed to get away from the guests for a while.

I was holding a gallon-size can of paint, reading the fine print on it, when I spotted a figure approaching in my peripheral vision. Glancing up, I nearly dropped the paint can.

Quentin nodded and offered me a tight smile. "Eve."

My brain couldn't generate any response to his appearance. Since I didn't care to stammer like an idiot, I opted for the silent treatment accompanied by what I hoped came off as a hard stare.

He hunched his shoulders and jammed his hands in his pants pockets. "I, uh, ought to explain."

I clutched the paint can to my belly. "Not interested in any explanations from you."

"You'll want to know this." He scrunched up his face and refused to look at me. "I'm the reason the paparazzi found out about you and Val."

The room did a pirouette around me. I hugged the paint can tighter, unable to speak until the spinning stopped. Even then, I opened my mouth but couldn't muster words. Quentin had called the paparazzi? How had he even known who to call?

He bowed his head, his shoulders hiking up even higher. "I'd been kinda jealous of Val. Started talking to the pretty new cashier Sam hired. More than once, I talked about Val and how he's a nudist, how he did all kinds of crazy shit that anybody can see online."

"You were blabbing about my private life to the checkout girl."

"Well..." He coughed and peeked up at me before averting his gaze again. "It was kinda like therapy for me. I got all my frustrations out and, after the third time, I realized I'm not jealous anymore."

"Hooray for you." I shoved the paint can onto the shelf where I'd found it and rounded on Quentin. "You feel better, so you decided to call in the hell hounds?"

"No, I—" He raised his face to me. "The cashier girl did. Just now, I was talking to her. She was upset the paparazzi didn't hang around for longer since she was looking forward to our little town getting on the evening news. That's why she told them about Val. She went to the website of one of those tabloids and submitted a tip. I think she got paid for it too."

We hadn't made the evening news. Not even our sex photo had gone that wide.

"Did you take that photo of me and Val?" I asked.

He covered his eyes with his hand, wincing. "Yeah. I went back to the resort to grab my last paycheck and a few tools I'd left behind. That's when I saw you two. I showed the cashier the picture on my phone. She wanted me to text it to her, so I…did."

You bastard, I wanted to scream. Shock paralyzed me, though, and I could manage only to stare at him. "Those tools belong to me. I bought them."

"After I saw what I saw, I left without taking any tools."

I glared at Quentin. "Let me get this straight. First, you beat up Val. Then, after I fire your ass, you start blabbing to the hardware store cashier. Next, you take a dirty picture of me and Val. Finally, you give that photo to the fucking cashier so she can sell it and all the gossip you told her to the first scummy tabloid she can find online. My life got blown up, and it's all because of you."

"Yeah, it's my fault. I'm sorry, Eve. I'm so sorry."

"I never want to see your face again. Not in the hardware store, not in the grocery store, not even when I drive past your truck on the street." I jabbed a finger into the air near his face. "Do you understand?"

"Don't worry, you'll never see me again. I got a job in Salt Lake City."

Maybe I should've felt relieved hearing that. All I really felt was sad. I'd lost a friend because he betrayed me and proved he'd never been a friend at all. I'd lost my privacy and my sense of security thanks to the invasion of the tabloid vultures.

I'd lost Val.

Maybe I couldn't change any of that stuff, but I could sure as hell change one thing. I pushed past Quentin and marched straight to Sam's office at the back of the store. The door hung open as usual, so I walked inside and dropped onto the empty chair beside his desk.

Once I'd explained the situation, I didn't get a chance to demand he fire the cashier.

"She's gone," Sam said. "I'll inform her right away."

Getting the cashier fired didn't make me feel better. Well, not a lot better. At least one person who'd screwed with my life had paid for it. When I got home, Ollie suggested I talk to a lawyer, but suing Quentin or the stupid girl who'd tattled to the paparazzi wouldn't help anything. I'd spend money I didn't have in an attempt to get restitution from a girl who earned minimum wage. Quentin wasn't rolling in dough either.

So, I took the high road and let it go.

A good wallow sounded awesome, but I had no time for that. The attack of the rampaging paparazzi had triggered an unexpected side effect. The resort was now fully booked for the next six months.

When the calls had started to pour in, I'd contacted my regular guests to find out when they might want to return, to make sure they got a spot reserved.

Ruth had told me, "We're coming right away, sweetie. You need all the support you can get."

"I'm fine, really. Ollie's sticking around to help out."

"We're coming, Eve. No arguments."

A few days later, Ruth and Sylvester arrived in a chartered bus.

When I saw the huge vehicle, I gaped at it and at the gaggle of people disembarking. I knew all of them. There was Ruth, Sylvester, my parents, my brother and sister and their significant others, my niece and nephew, and the entire Kitten Brigade. Well, almost all of them. Heidi wasn't among them. Shelby told me Heidi had gotten engaged and was too busy to come, but she'd sent a care package. It contained fancy things that might be found at a spa, things like goat's milk soap and bath beads. I loved Heidi in spite of the way she'd dumped Ollie. He still cared about her, I knew, but he'd recovered from their breakup better than I was recovering from mine.

Every member of my family hugged me. Even Krista's fiancé, Jeremy, hugged me.

Surrounded by my family and Ruth and Sylvester, I studied the vehicle they'd arrived in. "Why did you guys charter a bus? I would've picked you up at the airport. My old bus isn't luxurious, but it would've fit all of you."

"We didn't charter the bus," Mom said. "Val bought it for you."

"Yeah," Sylvester said, "he seems to think he's your business partner."

"What?" I started gaping again, my gaze flicking from Mom to Sly and back again. "But he went home. I haven't heard from him in two weeks."

"Don't know anything about that," Sly said, "but I heard him saying, clear as day, he bought this bus for your business."

"He said 'our business,' honey," Ruth corrected. "He meant the resort because he and Eve run it together."

"But—" I couldn't finish the thought because it had already fled my brain. Val bought me a bus. He called it "our" business. And yet he hadn't responded to a single damn voicemail, email, or text since the day he'd left.

"Give her the papers," Ruth said to her husband.

Sylvester pulled a sheaf of papers, folded in half, out of his back pocket and offered it to me. "Val said to give you these."

I took the sheaf and unfolded it. An envelope fell out and fluttered to the ground.

Krista snatched it up and handed it to me.

"You go inside," Mom said, "and look through that stuff alone. We'll join you in a little while, after we get unpacked and settled in."

"I don't have enough rooms for all of you," I said. "I was expecting Ruth and Sylvester, not a small army."

"An army of people who love you," Krista said. "It was a surprise. We knew if we told you all of us were coming, you'd tell us not to."

I couldn't argue with that. I probably would have told them to stay away.

But I loved them so much for being here.

"We brought tents," Jeremy said. "And the bus is pretty sweet too, comfortable enough to sleep in."

My surprise guests headed for the guest house, and I returned to my house to read the papers Val had sent. Seated at the island, I set the sealed envelope on the wood surface. I wasn't ashamed to admit I was afraid to open that envelope, afraid of what I'd find inside it. The papers consisted of legal documents that altered the structure of my LLC to allow for a partner and that also iterated the terms of our partnership. Val had signed the documents. They required only my signature to become real. Little sticky flags marked the places where I needed to sign.

I stared at the envelope for a couple minutes after I read the legal documents. Then, finally, I summoned the nerve to rip it open. The envelope contained a single sheet of paper, a letter written in Val's hand. I read slowly, making sure I didn't miss a single syllable. A tingle chased over my skin, a kind of excitement I hadn't experienced before or since Val had been in residence here. I read the note three times, despite the fact the damn thing consisted of only eleven words.

"Wait for me," he said. "Thirty days and I'll be coming for you."

Coming for me? What, like I was a dog he'd sent to a kennel? He couldn't not call me for two weeks and then expect me to be thrilled he might come back for me in another month. He could've called or texted or emailed. Instead, he left me hanging.

And he expected me to sign the papers.

The sound of bare feet slapping on the wood floors pulled me out of my contemplation. I glanced over my shoulder to see Ollie racing out of the living room.

"You've gotta see this," he said, breathless.

He hugged my laptop to his chest.

I waved a dismissive hand. "I trust you to handle whatever it is."

Ollie had become my de facto assistant manager. He handled everything from paying bills to cleaning toilets, so I didn't understand what could be so important that I needed to see it.

"Not this," he said as he plopped onto the stool beside me and flipped up the laptop's lid. He pointed at the screen. "Look. Somebody sent you money."

I bent forward and squinted at the screen. It showed the company PayPal account, and there was indeed a new transfer. It had come from Valentim Silva.

"Val sent you ten thousand dollars," Ollie said.

The amount sounded familiar, and I grabbed the legal papers to flip through them again. Yep, there it was. Val's initial investment in the company, required to become a partner, was ten thousand dollars.

Why would he send the money before I signed the papers? Was he trying to force me to accept him as my business partner? I couldn't believe he would do that. Maybe I didn't know everything about Val, but I knew him well enough to realize his investment in the company was his way of showing he still wanted to be a part of my life.

So answer your damn phone, Val.

"Thank you for showing me this," I told Ollie as I leaped off the stool and grabbed the papers. "I have some private calls to make."

"No problem."

I turned to leave the room but hesitated. I looked at him over my shoulder. "Could you handle everything if I, um, took a vacation?"

"Sure, but maybe you should hire a real assistant manager for that."

"No time." I clutched the papers to my chest. "I'm leaving as soon as I can make the arrangements."

Assuming my first phone call went the way I hoped it would. I needed answers, and I was sick of waiting to receive them. Time to go get them myself.

My family wouldn't mind me leaving them right after they'd arrived. Once I explained why I was doing this, they'd understand.

"Where are you going?" Ollie asked.

"California."

Chapter Twenty-Nine

Val

aves swelled and broke on the shoreline outside the picture windows, seeming dark and foreboding under the gloomy sky. Slouched in an armchair, I stared at the breakers and sipped my glass of bourbon. I'd always loved the view from my living room. Ever since I'd left Eve, nothing was beautiful anymore. I hated my house, I hated the ocean, and I hated the fucking paparazzi. Most of all, I hated myself for hurting Eve.

I would get back to her. If she'd have me.

A large breaker crashed onto the shore, spraying the beach.

Whatever I had to do to make this up to Eve, I would do it. Somehow, I had to make her understand why I'd abandoned her. Maybe I shouldn't have sent her the legal documents without at least calling first to explain. A phone call wouldn't be enough. I needed to look into her eyes when I told her.

I hoped I'd be kissing her seconds after that, but it might've been wishful thinking.

God, I missed her.

Why the hell did you leave her, then?

The doorbell chimed.

I groaned and swigged the last of my bourbon. Seeing anyone appealed to me about as much as wrestling with a porcupine. Poor Ollie had almost done that. A smile tugged at my lips but couldn't quite take hold. I missed Ollie too, and Ruth and Sylvester, even the Kitten Brigade. They'd become like family to me. Eve had become so much more.

The doorbell chimed again, three times in quick succession.

Christ, whoever it was had a hard-on for talking to me.

I slapped my glass down on the table and shoved myself out of the chair. The wood floor chilled my bare feet, but I didn't care. When I reached the front door, I swung it wide open. A wave of shock broke over me, but it swiftly transformed into a warm and welcome relief.

Until she spoke.

"*Você partiu meu coração.*"

A pain tightened the back of my throat, roughening my voice. "I know I broke your heart. I'm sorry, Evie, I'm so sorry."

"Yeah, I know you are."

What could I say? What could I do? I'd abandoned her. Now she was here, standing on my doorstep, and I was paralyzed.

"You know," she said, "we haven't seen each other in more than two weeks. I think it would be appropriate for you to kiss me."

That was all the invitation I needed.

I threw my arms around Eve and dragged her into me. She tried to speak, but I silenced her with my lips. She melted against me, moaning, opening her mouth and welcoming my tongue. She tasted even better than I remembered, sweet and sexy—if "sexy" were a flavor. With Eve, it definitely was. The taste of her and the feel of her body intoxicated me more than any alcohol.

Finally, I relinquished her lips. I held on to her body, though. No force on earth could make me let go.

"Well," she said breathlessly, "that answers one question."

I arched a brow. "What question is that?"

"Did you miss me."

"Of course I missed you. *Penso em você o tempo todo.*" I brushed stray hairs away from her face. "That means I think about you all the time. Missed you so much I want to drag you down to the floor and fuck you with the door wide open."

She laughed. "Same old Val."

The words she'd spoken a moment ago replayed in my mind. "Where did you learn Portuguese? You pronounced that phrase perfectly."

"I talked to your sister Maria. She suggested I ought to tell you in Portuguese how much you'd hurt me by taking off like that." Eve hunched her shoulders. "I figured what the hell. My voicemails and texts in English weren't getting through to you."

Yes, I'd done that. I'd taken off, then I had ignored her attempts to contact me. How could I explain the reasons for my behavior? I'd convinced myself I was protecting her.

We both fell silent for a moment, our gazes bound to each other, neither of us knowing quite what to say.

At last, I broke the silence. "You know I'm glad you're here, but why are you here?"

"Did you really think a crappy eleven-word note was enough?" She tapped a finger on my chest. "You ought to know better. Wait and I'll come for you? Please."

"Hmm." I grasped her bottom with both hands. "I suppose you're right. The Eve I know would never sit still for that."

"Damn right." She pulled out of my grasp. "What the hell were you thinking? Running away without even saying goodbye? I get a deafening silence for weeks, then legal papers and a half-assed note. I deserve better than that, Val."

"Yes, you do." I noticed my neighbors across the street staring at us and clearly whispering to each other about the scandalous sight at the home of the infamous footballer. "Come inside, Eve. Public nudity is still illegal in California."

A slight smile tightened her lips as she scanned me up and down. "I had thought you were exaggerating when you said you always go naked at home. But here you are, answering the door in your birthday suit."

I stepped back, and she walked inside. As I shut the door, I asked, "How angry are you?"

She ambled down the hallway toward the living room, visible at the hall's end. Glancing back at me, she gave me a sarcastically sweet smile. "Angry? Why would I be angry? Just because I fantasized about castrating you, that doesn't mean I'm mad."

I followed her into the living room, wondering how I was going to make this right. My plan had sounded reasonable and even noble at the time. Looking back, I realized how stupid I'd been.

Eve sat down at one end of the sofa.

After a brief hesitation, I settled onto the opposite end.

She watched me, her mood unreadable.

It was a challenge for me to explain, but I forged ahead. "I'm sorry, Eve. I did what I thought was necessary to protect you from the paparazzi, but I realize now it was a stupid idea. I'd intended to lure them away from your home for long enough that they would get bored and move on to the next pop star who goes into rehab. Did it at least work? Have the paparazzi left you alone?"

"Yeah, they're gone."

"This was all my fault."

She snorted. "No, it was all Quentin's fault. He blabbed to the cashier at the hardware store, and he took that photo of us. The cashier sold it all to a tabloid."

"Christ, I can't believe it. After all of that, and considering what I've done since I left you, I'll understand if you never want to see me again."

Her steady gaze remained fixated on me. "What have you done?"

"You must've seen the photos and videos."

"What photos? What videos?"

"On the internet."

She flapped a hand, dismissing the suggestion. "Oh, I don't look at stuff like that online. I don't even use social media."

How had I not known that about her? I'd learned a lot about Eve Holt over the past six weeks, but I still had much more to learn.

Eve angled sideways, leaning back into the sofa's corner. "What kind of trouble have you been getting into without me?"

I scratched my cheek. "Well, I needed to distract the paparazzi, to keep them away from you. That required…a splash."

"And by 'splash' I'm guessing you mean 'tsunami.' Right?"

"Yes." I crossed my ankle over the other knee, fidgeted, and tucked my foot under my knee. "I danced naked on the beach in broad daylight while singing Brazilian pop songs. And I did that every day for a week."

Her expression blanked. For a few seconds, she neither spoke nor moved.

Until she burst out laughing.

By the time she stopped laughing, her eyes were watering. She grabbed a tissue from the box on the coffee table and wiped her eyes. "Honestly, Val, I was expecting something more scandalous than that. What, no sex tape this time?"

"Of course not. I'm in love with you, Eve. I would never sleep with anyone else."

The humor washed out of her expression. She blew her nose and crumpled the used tissue. "I know you wouldn't do that. I was joking."

"I'm glad to hear that, but you must be upset with me for making a spectacle of myself."

"Why would I be upset?" She held up the tissue, glancing around like she was searching for something. "Where's the trash can?"

"Under the table behind you."

She twisted around, spotted the trash, and tossed her tissue into it. Straightening, she squared her shoulders and looked at me. "If you really love someone, you accept them the way they are."

"But the things I've done—"

"Are part of what makes you…you." She scooted a little closer. "I wouldn't change who you are, and I don't want you to do it because you think that's what I want. All I want is you."

"We haven't known each other that long."

She tilted her head to the side, studying me. "I know enough. We might be different, but we have a lot in common too. I may not ever strip naked in a packed sports stadium, but I love that you are the kind of man who might do that. I know you would never do anything to humiliate me or hurt me. I trust you, Val."

"But I flaunted my nudity in front of the paparazzi."

"I get that you expected me to castigate you for that, but I'm not the least bit embarrassed by anything you've done."

Entranced by her eyes, so clear and bright and focused on me, I couldn't think of anything intelligent to say. "Why not?"

"Why am I not ashamed of you?" She shook her head, her lips curling up at the corners. "Because I love you. How many more times do I need to say that before you believe me? I love you, and that means I accept all of you—your past, your present, and anything flamboyant you might do in the future." She scooted closer still, halfway across the sofa now. "I don't even care that your neighbors, some of whom are celebrities, saw me talking to a hot, naked Brazilian sex maniac."

I chuckled. "Sex maniac?"

"Maybe sex god is more appropriate."

"Yes, I prefer that one." I inched nearer to her. "Does this mean you'll have me?"

"I've already had you. Many times, in many positions, indoors and out."

"Eve, you know what I meant."

"Yes." She slid closer. "Of course I'll have you. I signed the legal papers on the plane. Why did you send the money before I'd signed?"

"To show you I'm serious. About being your business partner, and about our relationship."

"In that case…" She swung a leg up and over to straddle my lap. "We'd better seal the deal."

"That's it? I was expecting to jump more hurdles before you would forgive me."

She linked her hands at my nape. "I forgave you on the plane too."

I touched my lips to hers. "Thank you, *meu amor*."

"You're welcome." She raised her brows. "Dancing naked? That was the best you could come up with?"

"My only other idea was to lie on the beach masturbating."

She threw her head and laughed.

I pulled her shirt up. When she raised her arms, I tugged it over her head.

As the shirt landed on the coffee table, she grinned. "You like stripping me, don't you?"

"No, I don't like it. I love it." To prove my point, I unhooked her bra and stripped it off her body. "Clothing does have its purposes."

I flipped us so she lay stretched across the sofa with me on top of her.

She unfastened the button on her jeans and eased the zipper down. "Let's see how fast you can get the rest of my clothes off."

"A challenge? All right." I hooked my fingers inside her waistband and yanked off her jeans and panties in one sweep. They got stuck on her shoes, so I yanked those off too along with the socks. All of it fell to the floor within ten seconds. "Fast enough for you?"

"Very impressive." She bent one knee, tipping it to the side, exposing her slick, pink flesh. "I do have one more question."

"Now? I'm about to fuck you."

"Then answer quick." She clasped her hands above her head. "Are you moving to Oregon?"

"Yes. You already knew that." Though her body tempted me to forget everything else, I sat back and said, "I have an offer on my house, so I need to settle that and some other financial matters before I can move. That's why I said I'd come for you in thirty days."

"There's no need to wait. Your lawyer, your real estate agent, and your financial manager can handle that stuff."

"How do you know?"

"Because I talked to your lawyer. His name and phone number were on the documents you sent." She nudged me with her big toe. "How do you think I found your house? You never told me the address. The legal papers had your lawyer's address, not yours."

"I should've known I can't hide from you."

"Did you want to hide?"

"No, not anymore. Not from you." I lowered my body onto hers, and my cock brushed against her wetness. "Thought I'd have to work harder to get you ready for me."

"Honey, all it takes is your naked body. One glimpse of that, and I'm beyond ready."

"You must be very frustrated since I'm naked most of the time, often in front of other people."

"I would never describe the way you make me feel as frustrated." She locked her ankles behind my ass. "With you, I feel alive and free."

"So do I, Evie. Because of you."

Chapter Thirty

Eve
Ten months later

I tore my gaze away from the glowing screen of my laptop and surveyed the beach around me. A few mare's tail clouds wisped across the blue sky. Nude men, women, and children cavorted on the sand and in the water while delicate swells lapped at the shore. It was May, but here in southern Brazil, below the equator, that meant autumn. Porto Alegre boasted a subtropical climate that made it hot in the summer and temperate in the winter. Being in the southern hemisphere felt strange, but today it was in the seventies. I could get to like it here.

My gaze drifted away from the frolicking strangers and settled on the very familiar figure lying nude on a large beach towel beside me. Val wore sunglasses and nothing else, his bronzed body stretched out and on full display. This was a clothing-optional beach, after all. I was the only person wearing a swimsuit, though my bikini barely qualified as clothing.

I admired Val for a few more seconds, then returned my attention to the computer on my lap. I sat cross-legged, the laptop balanced on my thighs. On the screen, my half-written email awaited me. I typed the rest of my response to the newest guest at Au Naturel Naturist Resort LLC. She would arrive tomorrow. "Sorry I won't be there to greet you," I typed, "but my assistant manager will take great care of you. I'll be back from vacation next week. So glad you've chosen

Au Naturel for your holiday." After clicking the send button, I shut down my laptop and slipped it into its protective case.

Ollie had become my official assistant manager as well as the secretary and treasurer for the LLC Val and I owned together. Thanks to Val's resources, we could afford to expand and update the resort. The interior of the guest house had undergone major renovations, we had a real tennis court, and over the summer we planned to build guest bungalows and other stuff to make Au Naturel a top-notch nudist resort while keeping it affordable and family friendly.

I yawned, stretched, and said, "It's time."

Val lifted his sunglasses enough to peek at me. "Time for what?"

"This." I rose and stripped off my bikini. "I'm making my nude debut in Brazil."

He smiled in that sexy way that made me shiver with heat, not cold. "I wondered how long it would take you. Eve Holt going nude at her own resort is one thing but doing it on a public beach in another country is something else."

Yes, I'd finally embraced naturism. Since we'd recently hired people to cook and serve the food at our resort, Val and I were free to go without clothes whenever we liked. I still wore clothes when I greeted new guests—and I made Ollie and Val do the same, though they groused about it—because it seemed like the most professional way to go. A lot of our guests were new to nudism and needed to ease into it.

Val did on occasion walk down the driveway while naked to get the mail. He enjoyed the hike, and I was pretty sure he enjoyed the risk of someone seeing him. His exhibitionist streak might have gotten narrower, but it would never disappear. I didn't want it to either. I loved him exactly the way he was.

Here on the only nude beach in the vicinity of Val's parents' house, I twirled to give him the full view of my nakedness.

Val smirked. "Bringing you to a nude beach might have been a mistake. The sight of your naked body always makes me hard."

"Let me take one dip in the water before we go back to your parents' house."

"Make it quick." He licked his lips, and his voice turned huskier. "Or I'll be forced to drag you behind the nearest tree and make you scream."

I sprinted for the water and leaped into it. Water sprayed up around me. I ducked under the surface to get thoroughly drenched and bobbed up again. My breasts emerged from the water, bouncing. Brushing my hair back, I glanced toward Val.

He was sitting up, holding my laptop case over his lap.

I had a feeling he was experiencing the same kind of problem Ollie had suffered from once upon a time. I took pity on Val and got out of the water to pull my towel around my body.

He stood but kept the laptop case in front of his groin. "I suppose we should be going. My family is waiting for us."

I slipped on my bikini. "Ready to go."

"But are you ready to meet my sisters?"

We'd been here for a week, and I had yet to meet Maria and Aline, though I'd spoken to Maria on the phone back when Val had been avoiding me. Based on that conversation and the stories Val had told me about his sisters, I had a feeling I'd like them.

He glanced up and down the shore, seeming anxious. "Let's go farther down the beach to see if we can find a secluded spot."

"Thought we needed to go."

"A few minutes more. Please." He set down my laptop case and offered me his hand. "Come with me, Eve."

I shrugged and took his hand, dropping my towel on the sand so it covered the laptop.

He guided me down the beach past the smattering of people who lounged on towels or splashed in the water. We came to a stand of palm trees, and he led me into its midst. Shielded from view, we seemed to have satisfied his desire for seclusion.

Eying the palm fronds above our heads, he nodded as if he were satisfied with the location, but he still looked anxious.

"Is everything okay?" I asked.

He dropped to one knee, still holding my hand. My left hand. "I love you, Eve. All I want is to spend the rest of my life with you, running our business and, I hope, raising our children together." He hesitated, swallowing visibly. "Will you marry me?"

"Yes, Val, I would love to marry you."

He blew out a breath, the anxiety flooding out of him.

"Did you actually think I might say no?" I asked.

"I am a notorious exhibitionist, and I abandoned you for two weeks."

"We talked about all of this. I love you the way you are." I knelt in front of him, looping my arms around his heck. "As for the ditching-me thing, I'm way over it."

"Glad to hear it." He nuzzled my nose. "No one will believe I'm getting married."

"The bad boy bachelor settling down. Yeah, that might make news all around the world." I held up my left hand, wiggling the third finger. "Aren't you forgetting something?"

His grin disintegrated. "Fuck. I forgot the ring."

Val scooped me up and carried me all the way back to our towels, where he set me down on my feet. He unzipped a small pocket on my laptop case, a pocket I never used, and dug around inside it. With an "ah-ha," he brought out a small velvet box.

When he started to kneel, I said, "No need to do that again."

He did it anyway. "I'm doing this the right way."

"Nude on a beach? Not sure that's the traditional method for proposing."

"For nudists it is." He plucked the ring out of the box and held it toward my left hand. "Your finger, please."

I stretched out all my fingers.

He slipped the ring onto the correct one, kissed my palm, and rose. "Now it's official."

"Time to meet your sisters and make the big announcement, eh?"

"Yes, it is."

We drove back to his parents' house, which perched on the side of a hill and overlooked the coastline, though it had no beach access. Val's parents had neighbors who owned a private beach, but nudism was not allowed there. Val had put his clothes on before we left the beach since he couldn't go nude at his parents' place. They had no problems with his lifestyle, but their house featured many large picture windows that their neighbors could see. Not all of them were okay with nudism, and he understood that.

His sisters were already there when we got to his parents' place. Both Maria and Aline hugged me and oohed over the gorgeous diamond ring Val had given me. Thankfully, he hadn't bought a ring with a diamond so large it might blind astronauts in space if the sun hit it right. He'd chosen a tasteful yet beautiful ring.

Over dinner, I got to chat with Val's sisters. Maria laughed with gusto and loved to tease her brother affectionately. Aline was more subdued than her sister but also loved to tease Val. Both his sisters and his parents were thrilled he was getting married, and they didn't mind at all that he planned to live in America for good. They knew he and I would visit Brazil as often as possible. They also vowed to visit us often.

When we said goodbye to Maria, she pulled me into another hug and whispered in my ear, "I've never seen Val so happy before. Thank you, Eve. Now have some babies, would you?"

She kissed my cheek, winked, and left.

Babies? Val and I hadn't talked about that yet.

Once Val's parents had gone to bed, he and I lounged on the sofa. With his arm around me, I nestled into him and sighed with pure contentment.

He kissed the top of my head. "Exhausted?"

"Yes, but in a happy way. I love your sisters."

"They love you too." He hugged me a little tighter. "Maria and Aline both asked me when we'll start having babies."

"Yeah, Maria mentioned that to me too." I bent my head back to look at him. "Do you want kids? We never talked about that."

"I would love to have children with you, Evie. But if you don't want that, I understand."

"Oh Val, you really are the most unbelievably sweet and considerate man." I spread a palm over his cheek. "I would love to have kids with you."

"Should we wait a while to start a family? We do have all the changes at the resort to deal with."

"Do you want to wait?"

"No. Do you?"

I wriggled around until I was on my knees with his arm still around me. I kissed him softly. "Let's start right now. I'm still on the pill, but we could practice."

"Right here on my parents' couch?"

"No, I guess not." I tapped my chin, considering the options. "Let's do something naughty."

"What do have in mind? You know I'm up for anything."

"Let's sneak onto your neighbors' beach and have sex in the moonlight."

He pulled me onto his lap, wrapped both arms around me, and got to his feet while maintaining his hold on me. "Let's do it."

And we did just that. On the beach, in the moonlight, we made love for an hour. The naughtiness factor made it a little more exciting, but it was Val who made our time on that beach a night to remember.

When I'd first met Val, I had thought he was the wrong man for me. On the surface, we seemed like complete opposites. In the months I'd known him, I had realized how much we had in common and that our differences made our relationship stronger and more exciting. When my instinct was to play it safe, he encouraged me to take risks. When his instinct was to go a little too far,

I reined him in, but only enough to keep us both from getting arrested. I loved his wild side, his caring side, his intelligence, his humor, his body. I loved him, period.

Naked or clothed.

Epilogue

Ollie
Six Days Later

I scratched my chest through my shirt, not used to wearing clothes. Eve had instituted a new policy that decreed not only did employees have to wear clothes when greeting new guests, but we also had to wear a uniform. The fabric was itchy. She swore she'd order better ones soon, but for today, I had to act friendly while my whole body begged to be scratched.

A taxi rolled up the driveway, gravel crunching under its tires. The driver parked but did not get out to help the woman in the backseat get her things out of the trunk.

Everybody in town knew Au Naturel was a naturist resort full of naked people. Most locals didn't mind, but some thought it was a freak show. I recognized the taxi driver. Phil Johnson didn't mind sneaking a peek at the female guests whenever he drove someone out here, but he refused to set foot on the property. His shoes stayed firmly in the taxi.

As usual, he peered out the windshield hoping to catch a glimpse.

Since the other guests had gone inside for lunch, the perv was disappointed.

I hurried forward to pull the back door open.

The woman inside had her head down, focused on fiddling with her purse. Auburn hair fell over her shoulders and curtained her face.

Offering her my hand, I said, "Welcome to Au Naturel."

She slipped her hand into mine and climbed out of the taxi. Her head lifted, and she smiled a little. "Thank you. I'm Mara Severins."

I already knew that, but I couldn't manage to say anything in response. She was beautiful. Her almond-shaped eyes, an amazing shade of jade green, sparkled in the sunshine. Her skin was a golden tan, like it was her natural complexion and not made in a tanning bed or the result of a sunbathing addiction. The form-fitting dress she wore showcased her slender body and especially her breasts. They weren't large, but they weren't small either. Just the right size, I decided.

Her pouty lips tightened, and her brows drew together. "Is something wrong? Is this the wrong day? Sometimes I do that, I get the dates messed up and show up at the wrong time."

"I— whuh—" Yeah, those were the first syllables I spoke to the prettiest girl I'd ever seen. Shit. What was wrong with me? I still held her hand in mine, and her skin was so soft.

She squinted at my chest, then swung her gaze up to mine. "It's nice to meet you, Oliver."

How did she know my name? I glanced at my chest. Duh. The name tag pinned to my shirt told her.

Time to suck it up and act like a mature adult.

I rolled my shoulders back and released her hand. "Yes, I'm Oliver Jackson, the assistant manager. You can call me Ollie if you want. Let me get your bags for you."

"Thank you, Oliver."

"Open the trunk," I said to Phil. The lid popped up right when I reached the trunk. Inside it lay four large suitcases and one smaller case. Who brought this much clothes to a naturist resort? Maybe she had a shoe fetish and brought her entire collection. I hefted the suitcases out of the trunk and set them down alongside the driveway. Shutting the door, I called to Phil, "Thanks, man. See you next time."

Phil backed up and turned around, waving as he headed off down the driveway.

I waved back. Picking up two of the large suitcases, I stifled a grunt. Damn, these things weighed a ton each. I'd have to come back for the rest.

"Follow me," I said and started lugging the bags toward the guest house.

Mara Severins toddled after me, her high heels making it harder for her to walk across the gravel drive and the dirt path to the guest house.

I slowed down to let her catch up. "Might be easier if you take off your shoes."

"Right." She smiled shyly and removed her shoes, carrying one in each hand. "I'm not used to the outdoors since I live in Philadelphia, but that's why I came here. To commune with nature or whatever."

"You can definitely do that here."

When we reached the guest house door, she held it open for me.

"Sorry, that's supposed to be my job," I said, lugging the suitcases across the threshold.

"My fault. I overpacked. Always do."

The door shut behind us.

She pulled in a deep breath, her eyelids sliding half shut, and blew out the breath she'd held. "Mmm, I smell food. Haven't eaten since I left Philly early this morning."

"The other guests are having lunch. Why don't you join them while I take your things upstairs? They're nice people, and they love meeting new guests."

"You don't mind? I mean, I'm leaving you to carry my bags. I know they're heavy."

"It's my job." I nodded toward the door a dozen feet down the hall. "Dining hall's in there. Go on, have fun."

She smiled, and her cheeks dimpled. "Thank you, Oliver."

I readjusted the load I was carrying, unable to stop myself from admiring her backside while she trotted toward the dining hall door. She had a great ass.

Mara swerved into the dining hall.

And screamed.

I dropped the suitcases and bolted to the doorway.

Mara had stopped a few inches inside. Her shoes lay on the floor where she must've dropped them. Her mouth gaped, and her eyes bulged.

The other guests stared at her but seemed more confused than scared.

She stammered wordlessly before she managed to squeak out, "W-what is this place?"

I came up alongside her, touching her arm. "What's wrong? Are you having an epileptic seizure or something? I can take you to the hospital if—"

"No, I'm not having a seizure." Her voice sounded breathy. She squeezed her eyes shut and turned toward me. "Why is everyone naked?"

"Oh. Yeah, that. I know at some naturist resorts the guests dress for meals, but here we have a less formal way of doing things." I studied her face, which she had scrunched up tight. "Are you sure you're okay?"

"Fine. Yes." The syllables were clipped. She pried her lids apart to look at me. "Why would birdwatchers eat in the nude?"

"Birdwatchers? Some of our guests enjoy doing that, but what's clothing got to do with it?"

"Everyone is naked."

"Uh, yeah, that's kind of the point." I laughed, trying to sound casual though I'd started to feel uncomfortable. "This is a naturist resort."

She threw her hands up, huffing. "Like that explains it?"

"Well, sure it does."

Mara stalked out into the hallway where she couldn't see into the dining hall.

I followed her. "I'm confused. Why are you so upset that all the naturists are naked?"

"Because—" She flapped her arms and huffed again. "Public nudity is illegal."

"This isn't public. It's a private resort." I held up my hands, trying for a conciliatory tone. "Listen, you can dress for meals. Nobody will care."

Jeez, I'd never met an uptight naturist before. She was beautiful, but I'd started to think she might have a few screws loose.

"Oh, how generous," she said in a haughty tone. She scrunched up her face harder than before, her lip curling. "I'm allowed to wear clothes if I want. Shouldn't you be more concerned about disturbing all the other guests who don't want to eat surrounded by naked people?"

"Um, those are all the other guests in there."

"Everyone eats in the nude?" She grasped her head in her hands, her eyes wild, seeming on the verge of a nervous breakdown. "What kind of place is this?"

"It's a naturist resort." I touched her arm. "Relax. This is a clothing-optional resort, not a clothes-free one. You can take your time getting acclimated before you ditch the clothes. You haven't done this much, have you?"

"Done what?"

"Gone nude."

She lowered her hands, her gaze narrowing. "What do you mean it's a clothing-optional resort? I thought this was a naturist retreat."

"It is." A realization dawned on me, and I raised my brows. "What exactly do you think a naturist resort is?"

"A place where people go to enjoy nature and see the wildlife."

Seriously? I stifled a groan. "Miss Severins, you're at a nudist resort."

Her eyes bulged again as her face went pale. Her knees began to wobble.

And she fainted.

I caught her. "Miss Severins?"

Her lids fluttered open. "Nudist?"

"Yeah, that's right. Some of us prefer naturist, though."

She closed her eyes and moaned.

I helped her to her feet. "How did you not know? It says right on our website, and on every travel site where we're listed."

"Never saw any website. I hired a travel agent to book my vacation. She said this was a place where birdwatchers and other nature lovers come to enjoy the outdoors."

"Sorry. I don't know where she got that idea." I glanced at her suitcases. "You want to go home right away?"

"I can't." She threw head back and moaned again. "I bought non-refundable, round-trip airline tickets. Are there any motels in town?"

"Sure, but they're all booked up. The Renaissance fair is this week."

Mara slumped against the wall.

"I'll take your bags up to your room," I said. "And if you still don't feel comfortable eating in the dining hall, I can bring food to your room."

She managed a weak smile. "You're a good man, Oliver. How did you ever wind up working at a nudist retreat?"

I tried not to wince. She must've assumed I always wore clothes since I was wearing them now. The rude awakening could wait until later, after she'd calmed down and gotten used to the idea everyone else around here was naked.

"Never know," I said as I hefted her suitcases off the floor. "You might decide to give naturism a try."

She straightened and smoothed her dress. "I doubt that."

Mara Severins lifted her chin and marched off down the hallway barefoot.

I snagged her shoes from the dining hall and hurried after her. An uptight city girl at a naturist resort? Oh yeah, this would be tons of fun.

Not.

Natural IMPULSE

An Naturel Trilogy, Book Two

Chapter One

Mara

The forest raced by in a blur of green and brown, the blue sky seeming to melt into it, while I stared out the window of the taxicab without really seeing anything, too absorbed by my own thoughts. My life had become a blur too. Days bled into each other the way the sky bled into the trees, impossible to hold on to or to differentiate. This vacation was supposed to cure me of that.

Could two weeks at a birdwatching retreat do that for me? Maybe I was asking too much of the universe. Maybe I shouldn't moan about my life when so many other people had so much less than I did. But I needed a change. Something drastic. Nothing else might have a chance of breaking me out of these doldrums.

So here I was in Oregon, far, far away from my home in Philadelphia.

Where was I? Au Naturel Naturist Resort. Even the name sounded relaxing and blissful. When my travel agent had suggested I come here for my vacation, I'd jumped at the chance. The resort was for people who loved nature, she'd told me. It offered things like birdwatching and nature hikes. I could learn about the wildlife.

I had never left the city before, not in my entire life.

About time I expanded my horizons.

My parents would think I'd gone insane, so I hadn't told them where I was going.

The gray-haired cab driver leered at me over his shoulder. "So, you're one of those naturist freaks, huh?"

What about birdwatching was freakish? The driver had creeped me out from the moment I met him, but nobody else wanted to drive out here. Nobody at the airport would tell me why. They raised their eyebrows and smirked, like it was obvious and I was too dumb to understand.

"Not really," I said to the driver. "This is my first time at a naturist resort. I'm looking forward to communing with nature and stuff like that."

"Sure, communing." He leered at me again, snorting like he was trying very hard not to laugh at me. "Bet a pretty girl like you will commune with lots of other naturists."

Why did he say the word commune like it was filthy?

I returned my attention to the view outside the window. Out the corner of my eye, I spotted the driver still leering at me. It made my skin itch.

My phone made a blooping noise, indicating a new text message.

Sighing, I checked the text.

Nico: Where are you, Mar-Mar?

I growled under my breath. He knew I hated being called Mar-Mar. Hadn't he humiliated me enough? No, he had to taunt me with obnoxious texts. I typed, "None of your business."

Another bloopety-bloop. Another text from Nico. This one said, "I miss you."

My thumbs flew over the on-screen keyboard. *Should've thought of that before you dumped me.*

I made a mistake. Let's talk.

Another growl burst out of me. *Leave me alone.*

Talk later, then.

If I could've figured out how to block his number, I would've done it. I'd never been tech-savvy.

Another text came through, but I ignored it. At least they had cell coverage way out here in the boonies. Would the resort have Wi-Fi? Not that it mattered. I was getting away from the world, which meant no checking social media. Maybe I should've left my phone at home, but then what would I do in an emergency? What if there was a wildfire? An earthquake?

"Here we are," the driver said while he steered the cab down a gravel driveway that snaked through the woods. "Just a few more minutes until you can commune with the other freaks. You can get started now if you want."

I caught his leering gaze in the rearview mirror.

What was this guy's problem?

The cab rumbled down the gravel drive, emerging into a big, sunlit clearing. A modest-size house occupied the prime spot at the driveway's end, while a much larger, two-story building squatted to the right of that, a little further away. Other, smaller structures were barely visible behind the large building. I saw tents too, set up nearer to the woods.

I'd have to work up to sleeping in a tent. *Give me a soft bed and a plush pillow, please.*

The cab stopped near the small house.

"Here ya go," the driver said, leaning forward to peer out the windshield, squinting like he was trying hard to see something.

Someone rushed up to open the back door of the cab, but I couldn't see the person very well. The sun glinted on the windows, obscuring my view. Plus, it was so bright out and I'd left my sunglasses in one of my bags. Which were in the trunk. *What a hopeless ditz you are.* Maybe I had my spare pair in my purse.

I dug around inside it, hoping to find sunglasses. My hair fell around my face, tickling my cheeks and my nose. I scrunched up my nose, wishing with all my might that I would not sneeze on whoever was standing outside the car.

"Welcome to Au Naturel Naturist Resort," a male voice said.

A hand reached out to me. A hand that had been toasted in the sun, but not so much that the skin looked like leather.

I slung the purse over my shoulder and settled my hand into the stranger's, letting him help him out of the cab. His palm felt warm and soft. I lifted my gaze to his, and my tummy did a silly little flip-flop.

The gentleman holding my hand wasn't a drop-dead gorgeous hunk with enormous muscles, but I liked that he wasn't. He looked like a normal guy, though a uniform disguised his physique somewhat. The blue polo shirt had short sleeves that exposed a good bit of his biceps. This man wasn't ripped or shredded or whatever people liked to call it when a guy had bulging muscles rippled with veins. His physique seemed fit, but in a normal way.

He had the most beautiful face I'd ever seen, though I couldn't see his eyes with the sun glaring on his eyeglasses.

"Thank you," I said. "I'm Mara Severins."

Still holding my hand, the man stared at me. Not in an unsettling way, like the cab driver had. He stared like he couldn't believe what he was seeing.

Did I have lint on my dress? Or—*oh God, please say no*—did I have toilet paper stuck to my shoe? I had stopped at the restroom before leaving the airport.

"Is something wrong?" I asked. "Is this the wrong day? Sometimes I do that, I get the dates messed up and show up at the wrong time."

His lips worked for a second before he stammered, "I—whuh—"

A tag pinned to his shirt told me his first name.

I met his concealed gaze. "It's nice to meet you, Oliver."

He blinked several times, then glanced down at his shirt. Rolling his shoulders back, he let go of my hand. "Yes, I'm Oliver Jackson, the assistant manager. You can call me Ollie if you want. Let me get your bags for you."

"Thank you, Oliver." I liked the way his name slid off my tongue as smoothly as warm chocolate sauce.

He gestured to the cab driver. "Open the trunk."

The lid popped up, and Oliver hurried to get my bags. His brows shot up when he looked inside the trunk.

I winced. Yeah, I'd brought too much luggage. Four big suitcases and two smaller ones that held all my makeup and hair stuff, not to mention moisturizer and other necessities.

Oliver hoisted my bags out of the trunk and set them down alongside the driveway. He shut the trunk and the back door of the cab. "Thanks, man. See you next time."

The driver backed the cab up and turned it around, waving as he drove away.

Oliver waved back.

I eyed my luggage. My Prada luggage. Did nature lovers usually arrive with designer bags? Probably not. I also doubted they showed up wearing a designer, body-hugging dress and stilettos.

Such an idiot, Mara.

Oliver picked up two of my large bags, half stifling a grunt. He grimaced, but bravely soldiered on with my overstuffed bags. "Follow me."

I tried to navigate the gravel drive, but my heels kept tripping me up.

"Might be easier if you take off your shoes," Oliver said, slowing down so I could catch up.

"Right." I smiled sheepishly as I tugged my shoes off and held one in each hand. "I'm not used to the outdoors since I live in Philadelphia, but that's why I came here. To commune with nature or whatever."

"You can definitely do that here."

We were aiming for the two-story building, so I hurried ahead of him to open the door.

"Sorry, that's supposed to be my job," he said, lugging the suitcases across the threshold.

"My fault. I overpacked. Always do."

The door swung shut behind us.

Dragging in a deep breath, I let my eyelids ease half closed. The aroma of succulent foods wafted past me. Was that hamburgers? God, I'd kill for red meat. And did I smell fries? Maybe even sweet potato fries? *Please, yes, let it be.*

I blew out the breath I'd held. "Mm, I smell food. Haven't eaten since I left Philly early this morning."

"The other guests are having lunch," Oliver said. "Why don't you join them while I take your things upstairs? They're nice people, and they love meeting new guests."

"You don't mind? I mean, I'm leaving you to carry my bags. I know they're heavy."

"It's my job." He nodded toward the door a dozen feet down the hall. "Dining hall's in there. Go on, have fun."

A real smile stretched my lips. "Thank you, Oliver."

I trotted toward the doorway to food heaven, inhaling more delicious aromas, my eyes drifting partway closed again. My tummy grumbled. Oh lord, I was starving. At the doorway, I paused and opened my eyes all the way to survey the dining hall.

Men and women sat at tables, chatting, smiling, and stuffing fries in their mouths.

Naked men. Naked women. Not a scrap of anything resembling clothing on any of them.

A wave of ice cold flooded through me. I couldn't breathe. Couldn't budge even one-thousandth of a step.

Totally naked people.

Suddenly, the gaze of every single person in the dining hall veered to me.

And I screamed.

God, had I turned into the dumb chick in a B horror movie? Screaming? For heaven's sake, I was a grown woman. But I couldn't shake the ice-cold shock. What kind of birdwatchers ate lunch in the nude?

Pretty sure my jaw dropped. My eyes bulged too.

Something thumped behind me.

Everyone stared at me. They looked confused.

I stammered but couldn't piece together whole words, much less sentences.

Oliver appeared beside me, touching my arm. "What's wrong? Are you having an epileptic seizure or something? I can take you to the hospital if—"

"No, I'm not having a seizure." Why did my voice sound breathy? I squeezed my eyes shut and turned toward him, praying I could get a grip soon. "Why is everyone naked?"

"Oh. Yeah, that. I know at some naturist resorts the guests dress for meals, but here we have a less formal way of doing things. Are you sure you're okay?"

"Fine. Yes." The syllables were clipped. I pried my lids apart to look at Oliver. "Why would birdwatchers eat in the nude?"

"Birdwatchers? Some of our guests enjoy doing that, but what's clothing got to do with it?"

"Everyone is naked." Why did he not see how horribly wrong this all was?

"Uh, yeah, that's kind of the point." He laughed, sounding and looking a bit uncomfortable. "This is a naturist resort."

I threw my hands up, huffing. "Like that explains it?"

"Well, sure it does."

Seriously? He thought that explained the naked people scarfing down burgers and fries.

I stalked out into the hallway where I couldn't see into the dining hall anymore. Were my eyes on fire from what I'd seen? No, they were dry and hot because I'd been gaping at those people for…how long? An hour was what it felt like.

Oliver followed me. "I'm confused. Why are you so upset that all the naturists are naked?"

"Because—" I flapped my arms and huffed again. "Public nudity is illegal."

"This isn't public. It's a private resort." He held up his hands, his tone conciliatory. "Listen, you can dress for meals. Nobody will care."

"Oh, how generous." Christ, I sounded like a haughty bitch. How was I supposed to react to all of this? I scrunched up my face so hard my eyes watered. My lip probably curled. "I'm allowed to wear clothes if I want. Shouldn't you be more concerned about disturbing all the other guests who don't want to eat surrounded by naked people?"

"Um, those are all the other guests in there."

"Everyone eats in the nude?" What bizarre alternate reality had I stumbled into? I grasped my head in my hands, struggling to make sense of…anything. "What kind of place is this?"

"It's a naturist resort." He touched my arm again. "Relax. This is a clothing-optional resort, not a clothes-free one. You can take your time getting acclimated before you ditch the clothes. You haven't done this much, have you?"

"Done what?"

"Gone nude."

What on earth was he talking about?

I lowered my hands, narrowing my gaze on him. "What do you mean it's a clothing-optional resort? I thought this was a naturist retreat."

"It is." He raised his brows. "What exactly do you think a naturist resort is?"

"A place where people go to enjoy nature and see the wildlife."

He gave me a long-suffering look. "Miss Severins, you're at a nudist resort."

My eyes burned again, probably because I'd gone bug-eyed again. A new wave of icy shock crashed over me. My knees wobbled, and my face went subzero cold.

And I fainted.

Oliver caught me. "Miss Severins?"

My lids fluttered open, and I gazed into his eyes, now visible thanks to the lack of glare inside the building. He had gorgeous amber eyes. Cradled in his arms, I said, "Nudist?"

"Yeah, that's right. Some of us prefer naturist, though."

I closed my eyes and moaned.

He helped me to my feet. "How did you not know? It says right on our website, and on every travel site where we're listed."

"Never saw any website. I hired a travel agent to book my vacation. She said this was a place where birdwatchers and other nature lovers come to enjoy the outdoors."

"Sorry. I don't know where she got that idea." He glanced at my suitcases, where he'd dropped them on the floor when he hurried to my rescue. "You want to go home right away?"

"I can't." I threw head my back and moaned again. "I bought nonrefundable, round-trip airline tickets. Are there any motels in town?"

"Sure, but they're all booked up. The Renaissance fair is this week."

Oh great. I slumped against the wall. Sure, I could afford to buy another airline ticket, but that would mean crawling home with my tail between my legs to tell my parents I'd screwed up again.

"I'll take your bags up to your room," Oliver said. "And if you still don't feel comfortable eating in the dining hall, I can bring food to your room."

I managed a weak smile. "You're a good man, Oliver. How did you ever wind up working at a nudist retreat?"

His expression tightened a smidge, but only for a second.

"Never know," he said as he hefted my suitcases off the floor. "You might decide to give naturism a try."

I straightened and smoothed my dress. "I doubt that."

Then I lifted my chin and marched off down the hallway barefoot, having no fucking idea where I was going or how I would handle two weeks at a nudist resort.

Chapter Two

Ollie

I followed Mara down the hall, admiring her ass the whole time instead of watching where I was going. She had a great ass. I mean, epically great. Somebody should've sculpted a statue of her bottom, it was that fantastic. What wasn't great? Not paying attention to where I was walking.

Mara started up the stairs, but I didn't notice.

Holding on to two enormous and unbelievably heavy suitcases, I stumbled straight into the bottom step. My fingers popped open. The suitcases whumped down, and her shoes that I'd tucked under my arms clattered to the floor, but I tripped and tumbled forward right into Mara's fine behind.

She shrieked.

My face landed smack on her ass. I'd knocked her down, and now her legs were under me, but I wound up face-planting in her butt cheeks with only her dress and, I assumed, her underwear separating my nose and mouth from her body. Damn, she smelled good. Did she spray perfume on her dress or something? Nah, that wasn't a phony scent. It was all her.

"Get off me!" she hollered, trying to kick at me but not having any luck, what with all of me on top of half of her.

"Sorry," I mumbled into her ass.

I planted my hands on the step and pushed myself off Mara,

then offered her my hand. "Let me help you up."

The girl with the awesome ass glowered at me for a second. But then her features relaxed, and she accepted my hand. "Thank you, Oliver. I'm sorry I freaked out and kicked you."

"No problem. Sorry about the face-in-your-ass thing." Believe it or not, that wasn't the most embarrassing thing that had ever happened to me. I still remembered the day a porcupine had chased me out of the woods. Yeah, I'd screamed like a girl and run away from a pudgy creature that moved slightly faster than a snail. Not my finest moment.

"It's okay," Mara said, smiling shyly. "Probably my fault for making you carry those bags."

"Carrying whatever crap you bring is part of my job. Once, I had to haul a giant pet carrier with a Saint Bernard inside it."

Mara's eyes widened. "You allow pets here?"

"Sure. Only well-behaved ones, and they have to be on leashes."

"But Saint Bernards are…" She went pale, like she might faint again. "Their heads are huge. And their teeth…"

I grasped her elbow. "Whoa, take it easy. Don't pass out. There are no dogs here at the moment. Are you afraid of them?"

She squashed her lips between her teeth and squeezed her eyes shut, then sucked in a deep and noisy breath through her nostrils. Shaking off whatever it was, she squared her shoulders. "I am not afraid of dogs." She winced. "Most of the time."

Jeez, this girl was a tangled mess of phobias. Dogs. Naked people. What next? She was hot, and kind of sweet in a bat-shit crazy way, but completely neurotic.

I considered the stairs and the rooms they led to, rooms occupied by naturists. Lots of naturists. All of whom would be stampeding out of the dining hall anytime. How would Mara react to nude people playing miniten? She might freak when saw the thugs, the wedge-shaped boxes used to bat the tennis ball around in miniten. A thug kind of sort of resembled a Saint Bernard's head. If you squinted hard, and if you were an outrageously uptight city girl who was terrified of nudity.

"Tell you what," I said. "Why don't you stay in the little house, the one on the other side of the driveway? Val and Eve aren't here right now, so you can hang at their place until we sort out what to, uh, do with you."

Mara picked up her shoes. "Who are Val and Eve?"

"The owners of this resort."

She bit her lip. "Are you sure they won't mind?"

"Nah, they're cool. I've been staying in their house, but I can move if you'd feel weird about sharing a house with me."

"As long I have my own room, I'm fine with it."

"Yeah, you get your own room. With a door that locks." I hefted her bags off the floor, stifling a grunt. "Follow me. This is a family-friendly resort, so you don't have to worry about anything really crazy going on here. But it's probably best if you don't look into the dining hall."

She nodded gravely, still biting her lip.

Damn, I wanted to take that lip between my teeth and suck on it.

Instead, I led Mara out of the guest house and across the driveway to the little ranch house where Val and Eve lived. Until last summer, Eve had run the resort alone and cooked all the meals for all the guests in her kitchen. Ever since she and Val got together, and he became her business partner, they had loads of money to blow on improvements for the resort. Val was super rich, thanks to his previous careers as a soccer player and then a model. So now we had a big kitchen in the newly built addition to the guest house.

When we got to the door, I set down Mara's bags and dug the keys out of my pocket to unlock the door. I pushed it open, gesturing for Mara to go in first.

She peered inside with a hint of suspicion, but then smiled brightly at me and walked inside.

I lugged her bags across the threshold, kicked the door shut, and set the luggage down. "This is the kitchen."

Duh. Like she wouldn't know that if I hadn't told her. The room had a butcher-block island, two ovens, a double sink, a fridge, and pots and pans hanging from hooks.

Clearing my throat, I nodded toward the hallway. "Guest room's that way."

I headed down the hall with Mara behind me, pointing out the rooms as we went. The doors were all closed. "On the right is Eve's photo studio. Across from that is the bathroom. The other room on the right is Eve and Val's bedroom, which is where I'm staying, and this one on the left is the guest room."

Mara hurried past me to open the door.

"You've got a TV with satellite programming and DVR," I said. "There's also a clock radio with an alarm on the bedside table. This little desk here"—I ran my hand over the smooth wood surface—"has a drawer with notepaper and pens, plus a phone book. You also have a dresser with a big mirror on it, though I'm sure you figured that out on your own."

Yeah, the dresser was kind of hard to miss, being right there in plain sight. What an idiot I'd turned into today. It was her ass's fault. If she didn't have a shapely, enticing rear end, maybe I wouldn't act like such a dope around her.

Mara had stepped inside the room a few inches, but she eyed it with a hint of anxiety.

"Don't worry, nobody else is in the house." I tapped a finger on the phone on the desk. "If you need me, just press one. That rings the office in the guest house, which is where I'll be."

Her wide gaze flew to me. "You're leaving me alone here?"

"Relax, it's perfectly safe. You might not want to look out the window, but nobody will bother you here." I scratched the back of my neck. "Maybe I should hang around for a little while, to help you get settled."

Her tense shoulders sagged. "Oh thank you, Oliver. I'm so grateful there's one person here who isn't a nudist."

I almost winced. Not a nudist? She'd been assuming that because I was wearing clothes right now. If I told her I only dressed to greet new guests, she would panic for sure. Yeah, that was the reason I hadn't corrected her misconception about me. It had nothing to do with the fact I wanted to kiss her.

She inched toward the bed and cautiously settled her fantastic ass onto it. She bounced a little, like she was testing the mattress. "This feels wonderful. Very cushy."

Her breasts jiggled every time she bounced.

My brain went straight to a fantasy of Mara spread out on the bed, naked, moaning and begging me to—

"Oliver?" she said. "Are you all right?"

I coughed into my fist. "Yeah, fine."

The way she kept calling me Oliver made my balls tighten, but what the hell. Let's go with "I'm fine." If she called me Oliver again, I might develop a raging erection, but that was cool. I mean, it wasn't like she'd freak out and faint.

Ugh. At least this time, she would pass out on a nice soft mattress.

"Call me Ollie," I said for the sake of self-preservation. "Please. That's what everybody calls me."

My sister called me Liver, but she got away with it only because she was fourteen. No force on earth could stop a teenager from inventing insulting nicknames.

"Okay," Mara said. "Ollie."

That wasn't much better, but at least I'd averted a disaster. My dick had stopped twitching.

Until Mara stretched her arms above her head, smiled, and sighed. She flopped backward onto the mattress. "Mm, this bed is wonderful."

And then she glided her hands up and down her form-fitting dress.

Hard-on. Instant. Massive.

Shit, shit, shit.

I turned away from her, like I was about to leave. How could a woman who was terrified of naked people stretch like that right in front of me?

"You seem like you've settled in," I said, hugging the doorjamb to hide my hard-on. "I'll go make some calls to see if I can find a room for you somewhere else."

I made the mistake of glancing at her.

Mara, still lying on the bed, stretched her arms above her head again. "Thank you, Oliver."

Fuck. Would she ever stop saying my name?

I shut the door and ran out of the house.

Chapter Three

Mara

Ilay there on the bed for several minutes, luxuriating in the softness of the mattress and the seclusion of this cozy little room inside this cozy little house. Curtains shielded the windows, so I couldn't see if nude people were having an orgy out there. Not that I believed they actually would do that. Ollie had told me this was a family-friendly place, and I believed him. He'd been so sweet and kind to me. Thank goodness I'd found one normal, non-nudist person to talk to at this resort.

He was cute too. And sexy.

I sat up and reached behind me to unzip my dress. Why had I worn this thing? It was tight and made it hard for me to kneel or sit down. I longed to strip it off and put on something comfy.

But I couldn't reach the zipper.

How stupid are you, Mara? Wearing a new dress for the first time when you're traveling.

When I'd bought the dress, the woman in the clothing store had helped me get out of it. Maybe that should've been a clue, but I hadn't been thinking clearly about anything. Get out of town, that's all I'd had on my mind.

I struggled to reach the zipper, contorting my arms into positions that almost hurt, but couldn't quite reach the damn thing. *Shit.* I flopped back onto the bed, glaring at the ceiling.

Footsteps drew my attention to the open doorway.

Ollie stopped at the threshold with two of my large suitcases and the two smaller ones in his hands, plus the other two big ones under his arms. Panting, he said, "Almost forgot your bags. They were still in the kitchen."

His gaze skimmed over me, and he licked his lips.

I sat up.

Ollie walked into the room and set my suitcases on the floor. "There you go."

He started to leave.

"Wait," I said, pushing up off the bed. "I, um... It's kind of embarrassing, but I need help."

It was completely humiliating, actually.

"Help with what?" he asked.

I hunched my shoulders and pointed at my back. "Can't get the zipper undone."

"Oh." He licked his lips again, his hands curling into loose fists. "I guess I can give you a hand."

"If it's too weird for you, I'll understand."

"No, it's not weird."

He came up to me, gesturing for me to turn around.

I did, but he made no move to unzip the dress. I waited, feeling more anxious with every second.

"Nice dress," he said, his voice huskier. "You look really good in it."

My voice refused to work, but my body warmed, starting with my cheeks.

He took hold of the zipper and eased it down, inch by inch, his warm fingertip grazing my skin. A sensuous tingle trailed down my flesh in its wake, and suddenly, I had trouble catching my breath. When he reached my bra, he pulled his hand away.

"I think you can do the rest," he said, his voice gruffer.

When I turned around, he was staring at me. Lips parted. Chest rising and falling visibly. Eyes darker somehow, probably because his pupils had enlarged.

My breasts lifted with every breath I struggled to suck into my lungs, and I had the most inappropriate urge to kiss him. Cool air teased my skin where the dress gaped open, the sensation making me a little bit crazy. I wanted to touch him. Press my lips to his. Slip my hand inside his pants.

Ollie's gaze wandered down to my breasts, and he scrubbed a hand over his mouth. "I should go make those calls for you."

He moved toward the door.

I rushed forward to grab his arm. "Oliver."

Though he stopped, he didn't turn to look at me.

A reckless urge overtook me, one so irresistible I couldn't prevent myself from doing what my body wanted. I stepped in front of him, caught his face in my hands, and kissed him.

He held stone-still for a few seconds, while I kept my lips glued to his and reveled in the warmth and softness of them. God, his mouth. I wanted it. Now. Wanted him to thrust his tongue between my lips and ravage me.

Instead, he took hold of my upper arms and pushed me away. "This is really not a good idea. You're still freaked out about the naturist thing, and I don't take advantage of vulnerable women."

Of course he didn't. Oliver Jackson was a good man. I'd known that when I screamed and fainted and he'd caught me. Despite my stupid behavior, he'd taken care of me. Maybe I was not quite myself, but I knew I wanted him, and he didn't want me. Rejection felt like crap.

"Sorry," I said, feeling my cheeks heat up, with embarrassment this time. Ducking my head, I sidled out of his way. "I didn't mean to—Oh God, I really am an idiot."

"No, you are not. But you've had a big shock." He touched my arm. "Take it easy for a while. Watch some TV and chill."

I nodded.

He hooked a finger under my chin and urged me to look up at him. "You're sexy, Mara. I want to kiss you, but not like this."

Ollie ran his thumb over my bottom lip, then he walked out the door.

I stood there like a statue for a minute or two, maybe longer, wondering why I always did such stupid things. Of course he wouldn't want to kiss me. Why would he? I'd freaked out when I saw naked people.

After changing clothes, I ventured out of my room, heading down the hallway and into the kitchen. Ollie wasn't around. He'd told me he was going to his office in the guest house, so I hadn't really expected to find him here, but I had hoped for it. What should I do? Going outside seemed like a horrible idea. The nudists might be out there, and though I knew I wouldn't pass out this time, I still didn't feel up to facing a bunch of naked people who'd heard me scream and seen me faint. God, they must've thought I was a lunatic.

My stomach grumbled.

Should I rifle through the fridge for food? This wasn't my house. I didn't feel like I should poke around in someone else's kitchen. Ollie was letting me stay here instead of in the guest house out of kindness and probably a desire to make sure I didn't faint in his arms again.

I leaned my elbows on the butcher-block island.

And that's when I saw the tented card standing in the middle of the island. It had my name written on it. I picked up the card and looked inside. It said, "Eat anything you want, then kick back and watch TV. I'll bring you dinner tonight." Ollie had signed the card.

Now that I had permission to rifle through the fridge, I did. The owners of the resort had lots of food on hand, some of it things I'd never heard of, like Minas cheese. I made myself a turkey sandwich, even putting cheddar cheese on it in spite of hearing my mother's voice in my head saying, "Dairy will make you gain weight, Mara, and proper ladies don't get chunky." Screw that. I'd had a horrible day so far, not to mention the entire year before today, so I deserved cheese, mayonnaise, and sour cream and onion potato chips.

And milk. Mm, it tasted so good.

Consuming a forbidden sandwich and chips made me want to go all the way, food-wise. I'd seen a tray of cupcakes in the fridge too, so I retrieved the tray and set it on the counter. The cupcakes looked like dark chocolate, tinged with red, and with vanilla frosting on top. Could they be red velvet? I'd never had that, though I'd dreamed of cupcakes like this often after seeing a case of them at the bakery across the street from my condo. Red velvet looked so decadent. So yummy. So…forbidden.

I picked up a cupcake, peeled back the wrapping, and sank my teeth into the dark, succulent flesh. The deep, dark chocolate melted on my tongue. The flavor of the cream cheese frosting melded with the chocolate in the most delicious combination. Sweet. Tangy. Rich. *Mmmmm, yum.*

An actual moan escaped my lips.

Swallowing, I closed my eyes and bit off another chunk of dark-chocolate heaven. Then another. And another. Once I'd finished off that cupcake, I dived into a second one, moaning even more deeply when the flavor of it filled my mouth.

A throat-clearing behind me made me jump and glance at the door.

Ollie still had his hand on the knob, the door halfway open. He wore a tight expression that seemed almost pained. "Sorry, I should've knocked first so I wouldn't scare you."

I quickly chewed and swallowed my bite of cupcake. Dropping the rest of it on the tray, I wiped my mouth with my hand. "No, I'm sorry. I shouldn't be wolfing down all the cupcakes. Bill me for the cost of them, please."

"No way." He shut the door and approached the island, standing near me. "You're a guest. All the food is included."

I gazed longingly at the cupcakes. "I just found out I love red velvet."

"Yeah, I could tell."

His voice was deeper, infused with something I couldn't quite identify, something almost…hungry.

I offered him a cupcake. "Want one?"

"No thanks. But you go ahead and eat all you want."

He still had that touch of hunger in his voice, but he said he didn't want a cupcake. Why did he sound that way, then?

Ollie raked his gaze over me from head to toe, taking in my capri pants and short-sleeve top. His tongue sneaked out to moisten his lips, and his eyes seemed to darken. When I got to my feet, he pulled in a long breath and exhaled it slowly, rubbing his jaw. "Pink toenails. I like it."

My sandals exposed my toes, and I always kept them painted. When he'd said he liked my pink nail polish, his voice had gotten deeper and huskier.

He lifted his gaze to mine.

The heat in those amber irises could've melted the clothes right off my body. It didn't, thankfully. But I did feel hot and wet in the most intimate way.

I suddenly realized the truth. When he'd looked hungry a minute ago, it hadn't been for cupcakes. He wanted to gorge himself on me.

No, it couldn't be that. *Stupid, Mara, jumping to conclusions.* If he'd wanted me, he wouldn't have pushed me away when I kissed him earlier.

His gaze skipped down to my chest and the modest amount of cleavage my top revealed. He licked his lips again.

"I should go," he said. "See you later."

And he left before I could form any words. How bizarre.

The door clicked shut behind him, and I went back to devouring red velvet cupcakes.

Chapter Four

Ollie

Pink toenails turned me on. Who knew? Not me, that's for sure. I'd never thought of women's toes as sexy, but one glimpse of Mara's pink-tipped digits had me fighting off a hard-on. It didn't help that she'd been enjoying a cupcake when I walked into the house. The blissful look on her face made me imagine her looking that way when I was fucking her. And the way she'd opened her mouth to take a bite, then closed her lips around it…

I'd pictured her mouth sealing around my cock the same way.

And that's why I'd needed to run away. Christ, the girl was terrified of nudity. How would she react if I developed a raging stiffy?

Oh yeah, I had one of those now. Luckily, I'd gotten out of the house before Mara saw it. I managed to sneak back into the guest house and up to the office without running into anyone. Most of the guests were out on the lawn playing miniten.

After half an hour of calling every hotel, motel, bed-and-breakfast, and campsite in the area, I realized I was never going to find another place for Mara to stay. I expanded my search to a hundred-mile radius, but still had no luck. It seemed like every person on the planet had decided to visit this part of Oregon this week. Calling all those additional places took another forty-five minutes. By then, I was feeling stiff all over—but at least not in the way I had been when I saw Mara earlier. My dick might've been relaxed, but the rest of me needed a massage.

I pushed up out of the desk chair and stretched, groaning when my muscles protested. My skin itched too. I really, really wanted to ditch the clothes, but I couldn't do that with Mara around. She was so happy to have one non-nudist to talk to. How could I turn up naked? She'd freak like she had when she saw the nudists in the dining hall.

Moving to the window, I stretched again and glanced toward the miniten court. The game had ended, but the net was still up. Guests lounged on outdoor chaises. Some lay on blankets, sunbathing or just talking to each other. My focus wandered toward the little house, the one where Eve and Val lived when they weren't visiting Val's family in Brazil. All the curtains were closed.

A flash of movement made me look at the guest-bedroom window. The curtain was partway open, at an angle like someone was holding it that way. My curiosity got the better of me, and I grabbed a pair of binoculars off the cabinet beside the window. Eve kept them there in case we needed to scout for bears or other wildlife that might wander into the main resort area. I aimed the binoculars at the window of the guest bedroom of Eve and Val's house.

Mara was standing there, holding the curtain slightly open, peeking out at—

A laugh snorted out of me. She was watching the guests who were hanging out on the lawn. Not so terrified of nudity, after all, I guessed. Maybe she'd worked up enough courage to take a peek, but I doubted she would scamper out there to join in the fun.

My phone made that silly tinkling noise it always made when I had a new text. While still holding the binoculars, I checked, and yep, I'd gotten a text from my best friend, Damian. He wanted to know when he could come for a visit. With Mara here? I had my hands full already, and Damian was kind of a player. He loved the ladies, and he'd never been shy about flirting with them—or stripping naked in front of them. I wasn't sure how Mara might react to him. He wasn't a nudist, but we had gone to an adults-only resort a couple years ago. Damian loved that.

I liked it here. With guests who were like family.

So I typed, *Not now. Too busy.*

Damian replied, *Maybe I'll surprise you.*

Please don't.

Okay. I'll wait. He typed an emoji of a winking face. *See ya.*

Just as I finished saying goodbye to him, the desk phone rang. I set down the binoculars and answered.

"Hey, Ollie," Eve said. "How are things at home?"

"Fine." I leaned back against the desk, where I could still see out the window, my attention fixed on the guest-bedroom window and the barely visible shape of Mara. "You know, you don't have to check in on me five times a day. I'm a big boy, Eve. I can handle everything on my own."

Yeah, I wasn't quite sure I could, but Eve didn't need to hear that. I mean, I could handle the guests. But then there was Mara…

"I know that," Eve said. "You're highly capable and very smart. But I got a text from Ruth Norris, and she seems to think you've got a bit of a problem on your hands."

Shit. Had Ruth blabbed to Eve about Mara?

"And I hear that problem is very pretty," Eve added.

"What? Come on, Evie, I'm a professional." Sure I was. I'd become super adept at acting like I knew what the fuck I was doing when I actually wanted to scream and pull my hair out. My career in computer systems engineering had gone kaput. What did I know about running a resort? Not much, but I was learning. The hard way, sometimes.

Like when I'd seen Mara and her pink toenails.

"I don't get involved with guests," I said.

"Never suggested you were involved with Mara Severins. It's interesting that you assumed that's what I meant."

The teasing tone in her voice told me she was enjoying ribbing me about this. So I ribbed her back. "I remember when you swore off sleeping with guests."

"Yeah, I stuck to that resolution for about five seconds after Val showed up." She laughed. "Oh Ollie, don't make the same mistakes I did. If you like Mara, tell her."

"I can't." I shuffled to the window, leaning my forehead on the glass,. "She's terrified of naked people, and I kind of, uh, let her sort of believe I'm not a naturist."

Eve laughed again, much louder than before. "Honestly, Ollie, you're the cutest."

"This isn't funny, Evie."

A male voice said something in the background, but I couldn't make out the words.

"Hang on," Eve said. "Val wants to talk to you, man to man."

Oh great. The notorious playboy, the guy who used to strip naked on the soccer field when his team won a game and the guy who'd starred in his own sex tape, was about to give me advice about women. One woman. A nutcase.

A really hot nutcase.

"Ollie," Val said in his Brazilian accent that women all seemed to love, especially Eve, "I hear you have a woman problem."

"There's no problem. Everything's fine."

He chuckled. "You're infatuated with a girl who's afraid of nudity. How is that fine? I can give you advice, you know."

"Thanks, but I'm good."

"Are you sure? I do have experience in this area."

"No, man, that's okay. I can handle things with Mara."

"All right. If you're sure."

We said goodbye, and I stood there with my forehead on the glass. Movement caught my attention again, and I glanced at Mara's window.

She had pulled the curtains halfway open and now held a small pair of pink binoculars.

I lifted my head, sure I couldn't be seeing what I thought I was seeing. Mara, the anti-nudist, could not be watching the naturists with binoculars.

But she was.

Maybe she wasn't as uptight as I'd thought. If she had a naughty streak… Just thinking about that made my hard-on return. Oh fantastic. I'd be spending who-knew-how-many days around a woman who gave me the worst case of blue balls in the history of mankind.

I sat down at the desk and forced myself to concentrate on work. Accounting was pretty much the most boring thing on earth, next to watching a golf game, so I focused on that for half an hour. My stiffy softened up gradually the less I thought about Mara, distracted by the complicated accounting software, until I felt reasonably confident I wouldn't look like a total perv when I walked out of the office.

Ruth Norris cornered me when I got to the bottom of the stairs, so close to escaping the guest house that I could see the exit sign down the hall. Of course I couldn't get away without an embarrassing conversation with a seventy-ish woman who loved to razz me. In a sweet old lady way. Like she was my naughty grandma.

"Ollie," she said, hooking her arm around mine. "I've been looking for you."

"Did you need something?"

She fixed me with a grandmotherly look of concern. "Are you all right, dear? Everyone can see how much you and Mara like each other, but the poor girl is afraid of nudity."

"How do you know if we like each other? You saw her for thirty seconds and never even spoke to her."

Ruth's mouth kinked up at the corners in a sly smile. "She came out of the house while you were hiding in the office."

"She—what?"

"Mara sneaked outside to have a look, from a distance, and I met her." Ruth urged me to walk, taking us down the hall toward the exit. "She's such a lovely girl, but I'm afraid she's full of anxieties. Mara needs a good man to straighten her out."

I had a sinking feeling in my stomach, like somebody had dropped a head-size boulder in there and it was tearing a hole in my gut, that I knew what Ruth would say next.

She squeezed my arm and tapped my chest. "You, Ollie. You are the man who can help her."

"When did I become the house therapist?" I shook my head. "Mara is crazy. She's cute, yeah, but totally out there. What do you expect me to do about it?"

Ruth waggled her eyebrows. "I'm sure you can think of something."

Yep, no doubt about it. A senior citizen was encouraging me to have sex with Mara in the hopes that would "straighten her out." I wasn't self-conscious about my skills in bed, but honestly, I kind of doubted I could fuck sense into Mara.

But I'd have fun trying.

No, I would not. Sex as therapy? Jeez, the girl was so uptight she'd probably shriek and hit me over the head with a baseball bat if I tried to seduce her.

Well, she had kissed me.

Oh no, I could not be seriously considering Ruth's insane suggestion.

Even though I was absolutely *not* considering that, I heard myself saying, "I'll see what I can do."

"Try singing for her. Women love men who have hidden talents."

"Uh, maybe. We'll see."

Ruth led me out of the guest house, then peeled off to go find her husband, Sylvester. I spotted him playing checkers with another senior guest, Gil Foster. The two silver foxes had become good buddies right off the bat when Gil had arrived a few days ago.

Other guests were playing volleyball on the court that had been set up for miniten earlier.

A trio of twenty-something girls had brought out butterfly nets and were jumping around trying to catch the little critters. Even the bouncing of their breasts couldn't rev my libido.

I scanned the area, looking for Mara.

She hugged the corner of the little house, not far from the kitchen windows, her expression pinched. I couldn't tell for sure if she had her eyes closed, but I thought maybe she did. I hadn't expected her to come outside at all, so this was a huge step forward for her. I walked toward her, seeing more of her face the closer I got. She held her palms to her cheeks, then slid them up to cover her eyes, only to peek out between her fingers.

"Enjoying yourself?" I asked, coming up beside her.

Mara jumped like she hadn't noticed me approaching. "Ollie, I—Well, I thought immersion therapy might be the best thing for me."

"Sounds like a plan. How's it going so far?"

"Think I need to go back inside for a while."

"No rush. Take your time adjusting to the naked people."

She smiled, her lips sealed, then retreated into the house.

I went back to doing my job, but several times I glanced out the office window to see Mara outside the little house, cautiously watching the guests who were hanging out on the lawn. And yeah, I got out the binoculars so I could get a closer look—at her facial expression, not her body. Okay, maybe I enjoyed taking a peek at that too. She seemed less anxious about the whole naturist thing, since she didn't squeeze her eyes shut anymore, though she still didn't go out onto the lawn to socialize. Baby steps, I guessed.

At lunchtime, I got a great idea. Well, it sounded like a great one to me. Mara shouldn't hide in the little house all day. Fresh air and exercise, plus a few fun activities that didn't involve nudity, would make her feel better. I was sure of it. So I made us lunch in the big kitchen in the guest house and trotted over to the little house, setting my picnic basket and guitar case on the ground beside me. I knocked on the door to avoid scaring Mara again.

When she opened the door, she smiled. "Hi, Ollie."

This girl had the most beautiful smile in the history of smiling. I had no idea how long ago people first started making that expression, but it didn't matter. To me, her smile was the best.

"Hey, Mara," I said. "Made us a picnic lunch. Want to come out to the lake with me? All the other guests are in the big house, in the exercise room or the entertainment room, so we'll have the lake to ourselves."

"I've never walked in the woods before."

"You came here to commune with nature, right? And do some birdwatching?" When she nodded, I said, "I want to show you my favorite spot for seeing birds and other wildlife. It's also a nice place for a picnic."

She peered out the door at the lawn, where only a few guests still hung out. They were chilling on chaises and talking, not doing anything crazy.

I held my hand out to Mara. "Come on, it'll be good to get some fresh air. Trust me."

She bit her lip, but then slipped her hand into mine.

My gaze dropped to her feet and those sexy little pink toenails.

Veering my attention to her face, I cleared my throat. "You might want tennies instead of sandals. Better for a nature walk."

Mara hurried off to change her shoes and came back wearing pink tennies. She stepped outside and shut the door, saying, "Let's go."

I picked up the picnic basket and my guitar case. "Follow me."

We headed toward the nature trail, skimming the edge of the lawn maybe thirty feet from the naturists who were hanging out there. Mara glanced sideways at them but didn't even flinch. Maybe her immersion therapy was working. I hoped so, because I didn't want her to leave. I kind of liked her, neuroses and all.

"Want me to carry something for you?" she asked. "You've got your hands full."

"I'm cool. Don't worry about it."

But yeah, I had a feeling I did have my hands full with this girl.

Maybe that's what I needed in my life—something unpredictable.

Chapter Five

Mara

Ollie guided me down the wide dirt path, pointing out the trees and wildflowers while explaining what each one was. I'd never gone out in the woods before. City parks had been the extent of my nature communing. I hadn't needed to leave the city, except to fly somewhere for a vacation at a fancy resort, so I never had.

The trees were so big and beautiful here, and their branches formed a canopy above our heads. The sunlight filtered through them, creating a gentle glow. I heard birds tweeting and squirrels chattering. Ollie had to explain to me what that chattering noise was, since I'd never heard such a thing before. There must've been squirrels in Philadelphia, but I swore I'd never noticed them making noises.

Today I'd learned something. I loved the outdoors.

Once we got to the lake, Ollie set up our picnic by laying out a blanket for us to sit on and setting food items on it. We sat facing each other, so we could talk while enjoying our meal. Ollie had made sandwiches—the best I'd ever eaten. He also brought cupcakes like the ones I'd eaten earlier.

I munched on a potato chip before asking him the question I'd been wondering about all morning. "How did you wind up working at a nudist resort? And how long have you worked here?"

He seemed so normal, not like the kind of guy who would want to spend his days with naked people.

Ollie winced, though I couldn't understand why. He looked down at the picnic blanket for a couple seconds before aiming his gorgeous amber eyes at me. "How long? I, uh, started working here last fall. It just sort of…happened. They needed an assistant manager, and I'd gotten laid off from my job as a computer systems engineer, so it all worked out. To be honest, I was sick of my old job, anyway. Staring at a computer screen all day got really old really fast."

"That's quite a leap, from computers to a nudist resort."

"Maybe, but it made sense to me." He screwed up his mouth, looking away again. "But I'm boring. Tell me more about you. What do you do for a living?"

Oh, I hated that question. Whenever I told a man about my work, they wound up finding excuses to run away. Escape from the spoiled rich girl, that was all they wanted to do. Nobody understood that I took my job seriously. Maybe Ollie would understand, but I didn't want to chase him off before we really got to know each other.

So I played it safe. By sort of lying.

"Me?" I said as a lame delaying tactic while I considered my answer. "Well, I'm basically in real estate."

"Cool. Do you sell a lot?"

"No. I'm more into…management." I picked up a cupcake and bit off a big chunk, eating it as another delaying tactic. Then I swigged water from the bottle Ollie had given me and decided to offer him part of the truth. "I'm really good at the business side of real estate. I know that sounds arrogant, but I don't mean it that way. I love figuring out the best marketing strategies, testing them, refining them, all that stuff."

Ollie grinned. "I knew you were smart. I mean, I thought you were crazy at first, but I could still tell you had brains too."

"How could you possibly know that? I've been acting like a complete idiot since the moment we met."

"Nah. You had a big shock when you found out what this place really is, that's all."

Wow, he was absolutely the sweetest man on earth.

"If you don't mind me asking," he said, "how did your travel agent screw things up so bad? She must not have even looked at our website or read what's on the travel sites."

"Ugh, I'm so mad at that woman. She came highly recommended, but I have no idea why she thought this was a birdwatching retreat." I shook my head. "She'll be getting an earful from me, let me tell you."

"I'd love to listen in on that conversation." He leaned over to set a hand on his guitar case. "Mind if I play for you?"

"No, I'd love that. Do you sing too?"

"Sure." He opened the case and brought out his guitar, bracing it on his lap while he tuned it, plucking each string and adjusting the little knob doohickeys. "I do modern songs too, but my favorites are the classics. Stuff from, like, the fifties and sixties. Some even earlier."

"That sounds wonderful. I'd love to hear it."

He started to play a tune I recognized, but only when he began to sing did I realize it was "Bridge Over Troubled Water." He sang beautifully, with a natural voice that didn't seem like an affectation or an attempt to sound like popular singers. I found myself smiling and swaying to the gentle rhythm of the song.

"You can sing along," Ollie said, while performing an instrumental break in the song.

"Oh, I couldn't. My singing is awful."

"I doubt that. Maybe another time."

He started singing again, taking the song to its climax, then he strummed one last chord. "How about a little birdwatching now?"

"Will you sing for me more later?"

"Sure." He returned the guitar to its case, stood, and offered me his hand. "I know a great spot for birds."

I took his hand, letting him help me up.

He grabbed a pair of binoculars out of the picnic basket while still holding my hand, then led me down to the lake's shore. I heard a strange, fluttery call, and Ollie told me it was a loon. He handed me the binoculars so I could get a closer view of the birds that had just landed in the lake, further away from the shore.

"Look!" he said, pointing at the sky. "It's a bald eagle."

I swung the binoculars up, getting a fantastic view of the majestic bird as it soared over our heads. Jumping up and down, I pointed at the eagle. "It's so beautiful! I've never seen one before!"

Ollie grinned and laughed, watching me jump around and squeal like a goofball. He didn't look annoyed by my behavior. He seemed to think it was entertaining.

Something buzzed past me from behind, sounding like the Godzilla of bees. Before I could react, the thing buzzed right past my face, inches away from my nose. I shrieked and ducked, spinning around to find the monster that seemed bent on having me for lunch. My heart thudded. I didn't dare move, what with adrenaline burning through my veins.

A tiny bird hovered above my head, its wings beating so fast they became a blur.

It dived toward me.

"Help!" I shrieked, flinging myself at Ollie. "It's trying to kill me!"

Ollie caught me right as I tripped over my own stupid feet.

I wound up clinging to his body with my face in his crotch.

And I shrieked again. Honestly, I couldn't help it. A dive-bombing bird? Nobody warned me about that.

Ollie stared down at me, his mouth open, like he had no frigging idea what the crazy girl attached to his body was doing.

I shoved myself away from him, landing on my ass with elbows sunk into the sand and my legs over my head.

He kept staring at me for a couple more seconds, then he rushed forward to drag me up off the ground. While he brushed sand off my shoulders, he asked, "Are you okay? What happened?"

"Well—I—" I flapped my arms, rotating them like an insane windmill. "That bird tried to kill me."

The sweet man tried not to laugh, but he wound up sputtering and snorting. The spittle flying from his lips sprayed my face.

"Oh crap," he said, wiping my face with the hem of his shirt. "Mara, I'm so sorry. Didn't mean to laugh. I know you were scared by that bird, but it was just a hummer. He must've thought you're cute and came in for a closer look."

He smiled when he said that and tapped my chin.

"I'm the one who needs to apologize," I said. "Don't know why I keep freaking out. I mean, I've never seen a bird like that one before, but that's no excuse."

"You don't need to apologize. I get that all this nature stuff is new for you."

"What was that bird? I've never heard of a hummer. Is that some bizarre species of bomber birds only found in Oregon?"

"No, it's a hummingbird." He pushed my hair off my shoulders and combed his fingers through it, cleaning the sand out. "Hummers like to dive bomb people, but they're not dangerous. That one looked like a black-chinned hummingbird. You can tell by its black head and purple throat."

"I didn't get a good look at it." Because I'd been too busy screaming and hurling my body at him. When I remembered where my face had wound up… Oh God, it was humiliating. "I swear I'm not usually this much of a disaster."

"Everybody has a little accident now and then." He patted my arm. "Maybe you've had more than your fair share in one day, but don't be embarrassed."

"Hard not to be." I frisked my hands over myself to get rid of the rest of the sand. "At best, I'm a total klutz."

"You should've seen me last summer when a porcupine chased me. Now *that* was humiliating."

Ollie really was the sweetest man on earth.

"Ready for more birdwatching?" he asked. "Or would you rather go back to a nice, bird-free house?"

"Let's keep going. I'm okay, I promise."

I picked up the binoculars, which I'd managed to send flying so they landed a good fifteen feet away, and scanned the vicinity again.

"Look over there," Ollie said, pointing toward shore ahead of us. "See that bird with a rust-colored head and neck?"

I swerved the binoculars over there. The long-legged bird was wading in the shallow waters along the lake shore, lifting its skinny legs high with each step. The black and white wings made a striking contract to its rusty neck and head, and the bird had the longest, slenderest beak I'd ever seen. Not that I'd seen much more than pigeons until today.

"What is that?" I asked. "It's so pretty and so weird at the same time."

"It's an American avocet." He moved behind me, his body brushing against my backside, and placed his hands over mine on the binoculars, guiding me to shift it toward the trees. "If you look real close, you can see a golden-crowned kinglet."

Ollie lowered his hands but stayed close behind me, the heat and scent of him surrounding me.

I adjusted the focus on the binoculars and spotted a small, plump bird with a bright yellow head that was rimmed in black. Its wings had yellow and gray on them. "How did you see that without the binoculars? It's so little."

"Yeah, but I saw the kinglet flying toward that tree. The yellow crown is hard to miss."

He had bent his head to speak to me, his mouth so close to my ear that his breaths tickled my skin when he spoke.

I wanted to kiss him again.

Damn, what was wrong with me? He hadn't wanted to kiss me earlier, so I really shouldn't try it again now. But maybe he'd meant what he said before, when he told me he didn't want to take advantage of me when I was upset.

God, I loved having him so close, his body almost touching mine. I didn't know if he used aftershave or cologne, but he smelled incredible. I couldn't resist turning my head to look at him. With his cheek no more than an inch from my face, I got an up-close look at those beautiful eyes. The sun wasn't glaring on his glasses, so I had a clear view of them. I'd never seen irises that color before, a golden amber shade that seemed to glow in the sunshine.

"Ollie?" I said.

He turned his head toward me, and our lips brushed. It was the faintest touch, but that's all it took to make my lips tingle and my breaths shorten. We gazed into each other's eyes for several seconds while the most intimate parts of me awakened, growing warm and slick. I'd been attracted to men at first sight, but never in my life had I become so lustful that the thought of kissing a man got me this aroused.

Ollie cleared his throat and stepped back, checking his watch. "Oh shit. I have to get back to the guest house. We've got new people coming any minute." He met my gaze again, his tongue darting out to moisten his lips. "Sorry to cut this short."

"Don't worry. You can always show me more of the wildlife another time."

"We'll definitely do that."

He led me back to our picnic site. We gathered up the leftovers of our lunch, and this time I carried the picnic basket. Ollie let me do that because it weighed almost nothing now. He'd slung the strap of the binoculars over his shoulder and carried his guitar case in his hand. We got back to the resort just as a bunch of nudists swarmed the lawn.

I stopped at the end of the trail, at the edge of the woods. Could I handle being around these people yet? The ones I'd met seemed super nice, and I couldn't go on hiding inside the little house. I wanted to get used to their nakedness. I had to. Maybe I couldn't change all the dumb mistakes I'd made in the past, but I could get myself over the shock of hanging around with nudists.

"Will you be okay alone?" Ollie asked. "You can go back into Eve and Val's house if you'll be more comfortable there."

"No, I want to introduce myself to everybody. I need to do it."

"Okay." He glanced around, then pointed at the gray-haired woman I'd met earlier. "You know Ruth Norris, so start with her. She'll take good care of you."

"Thank you, Ollie. I really enjoyed our picnic and seeing the birds."

"You're welcome."

He trotted off toward the guest house.

And I marched straight onto the lawn full of naked people.

Ollie

For the rest of the day, I alternated between doing my job and keeping an eye on Mara, without seeming like I was spying on her. Even though I kinda was. But not in a creepy way. I hoped. Talking her into wearing tennies instead of sandals had spared me from seeing her pink toenails, but I'd neglected to take into account the fact that she was damn sexy all over, not just her toes. Every time she smiled, I felt my dick trying to firm up. When I sidled up behind her on the lake shore, to show her the kinglet, the proximity of her body had turned me on big time. Leaving her alone for the rest of the day seemed like the smartest choice.

Late in the afternoon, I headed outside and spotted Mara sitting on a lawn chaise, perched on its edge with her hands clasped on her lap. Her eyes were large, but she didn't seem freaked out like before. Some of the guests were playing miniten again, and she followed the players' movements with her eyes, flicking them left, right, left, right, up, down, right, left. Her lips curled up the tiniest bit at the corners, carving out the sweetest little dimples.

The goofy girls who'd been trying to catch butterflies this morning were at it again. One of them bumped into her friend, and the two tumbled to the ground, shrieking with laughter.

Mara smiled. Really smiled. Her teeth showed a little bit.

She was beautiful.

And just like that, my dick started to swell. Mara would freak out if she saw the lump in my pants getting bigger. I probably should've gone over there to remind those butterfly girls about the resort rules—like no body contact—but I couldn't do that when my dick thought this was a good time to get hard. Those dopey girls had wandered off toward the guest house, so I decided to give them the etiquette speech later. But I wanted to talk to Mara. Needed to. It was dumb but true.

I ducked back into the guest house to get a clipboard from the exercise room. It was the sign-up list for buying yoga mats. Didn't matter. I needed something to hold in front of my groin, and this would do. Armed with my clipboard, holding it in front of myself, I marched straight to Mara.

She noticed me and smiled, waving at me.

I clutched the clipboard to my crotch like it was glued to my body. No, that didn't look weird or pervy at all.

"Hey, Mara," I said, sitting down on the chaise next to hers. I kept the clipboard on my lap. "Seems like you're feeling a lot better about being out here with the naturists."

"I am, thank you." Her smile softened into a curling-up, dimple-carving expression that made my heart stutter. "Thank you again for our nature walk. It was amazing. And for the bazillionth time, I'm soooo sorry about the way I acted earlier. Honestly, I'm not terrified of naked people. But I was raised a certain way and taught to believe public nudity isn't proper."

"This isn't a public place. It's a private resort way out in the boonies." I tried to focus on her face, because her body looked so damn good in those pants and that top, but even her smile made me get stiffer in the one place I didn't want to get stiffer right now. "But I get that it was a shock. Glad you're feeling better."

Her brows knit together over her sweet little nose, and her gaze shifted to my lap. "Do you need me to sign something?"

I glanced down. Duh. I was holding a clipboard that had papers clipped onto it.

"No," I said, pushing my glasses up with one finger, "nothing like that. This is the sign-up sheet for guests who want to buy yoga mats from us. Do you do yoga?"

She nodded. "Not in public, though."

Of course not. Uptight city girls didn't do yoga poses in front of strangers, I guessed. But she hadn't seemed uptight when we had our picnic by the lake. The way she'd gotten so excited about seeing birds had made me want to kiss her. For a moment there, when we'd looked at each and our faces had been a breath apart, I'd been tempted to do it.

Until I remembered I was lying to her. Well, not outright lying. I let her believe I wasn't a nudist and gave her an evasive answer to her question about how I wound up working here. How could I kiss her, much less sleep with her, when I wasn't being honest with her?

Not that I intended to sleep with her. That would've been wrong. I was the assistant manager, and she was one of the guests. Even kissing her probably violated my professional ethics. I ought to avoid her as much as possible.

How could I do that when we were sleeping in the same small house?

Mara's smile had turned shy. She bowed her head, peeking up at me through her lush eyelashes.

And damn, even that made me harder.

I coughed into my fist and asked, "Did you want to buy a mat?"

"That's okay. I brought my own."

"Oh. Cool." I got up, careful to keep the clipboard in position. "I'll see later, then."

"Wait," she said. "Can I ask you a nosy question? Feel free to say no."

"Uh, sure." I sat down again. "Ask away."

She caught her lip between her teeth, letting it go little by little. "What do your friends and family think of you working at a nudist resort?"

"My parents are fine with it. They want me to be happy, that's all. My little sister doesn't care either." I tapped my finger on the clipboard, which I still held over my lap. "I don't have many close friends. But my best friend, Damian, thinks it's really funny that I work at a naturist resort."

"Funny? Why?"

"Because he dragged me to one of those adults-only naturist resorts for spring break during our first year of college. He said we needed to cut loose and get wild." I shook my head, though I couldn't help smiling a little when I remembered that vacation. "I hated that place. It was too slick and risque for my taste. I prefer—" I cut myself off before I announced I liked homey naturist resorts like this one. Maybe Mara would be okay with finding out the truth about me, but I wasn't sure. Better not to risk it. "I prefer more subdued vacation spots."

"It's nice you have a best friend. Don't think I've ever had one."

"Damian and I have known each other forever. He's lots of fun, but he really likes to play on the stereotype of gypsies."

Mara's brows crinkled. "Why would he do that?"

"Oh, I didn't tell you, did I? Damian's family is of Rom heritage. Most people call them gypsies." I rolled my eyes when I thought about my best friend's favorite pastime. "Damian thinks it's fun to play like he's a real gypsy, with supernatural powers and everything. He does palm readings, but I don't know how accurate his fortune telling is. Women seem to think his Rom stuff is hot."

"Doesn't sound all that hot to me." Mara smiled again, and my dick twitched. "I like normal guys who are reliable and don't pretend to have superpowers."

"Good to know." I stood up again. "Now, I really have to get back to work."

Like a coward, I sprinted for the guest house.

And though I took dinner to Mara later on, I ate mine in the guest house office and sneaked into the little house only after the lights went out in her bedroom. I'd have to rethink my avoiding-Mara plan, since I was in charge here until Val and Eve came home. But for tonight, I'd stay away.

Only a hallway separated my room from hers.

Sleeping right across from her room didn't ease my problem south of the equator. Of course, I didn't actually get much rest. My brain had other ideas. It tormented me with hot dreams about Mara and her pink toenails and all the dirty things I wanted to do with her.

Chapter Seven

Mara

The next morning, while I showered and got dressed, my thoughts rewound to yesterday and how Ollie kept running away from me—literally. Only during our nature walk had he stayed with me and not acted weird about it. After that, he'd raced back to the guest house within minutes after every time he came over to check on me, and I wondered why he'd seemed so tense when he was talking to me. Duh. I'd acted like a complete freaking lunatic since the second we'd met. Screaming and fainting because I saw naked people? No wonder he had to run away from me.

Once I'd gotten over the initial shock, I had decided to face up to my fears. Peeking out the window at the nudists had served as phase one in my desensitization plan. Once I felt okay about that, I'd ventured outside, staying right by the house at first. Eventually, after my walk with Ollie, I got brave enough to march over to the grassy area where the other guests were hanging out.

Everyone must have seen and heard me when I'd screamed. Still, they all treated me kindly. Ruth Norris, who described herself as "the busybody who helps spread all the gossip, but only in a loving way," seemed to have made it her mission to get me acclimated. She took me around the lawn, introducing me to everyone and putting her arm around my shoulders anytime I got anxious.

She intuitively knew when I needed a little support. Despite their nakedness and my lack thereof, every single guest treated me like an old friend.

Ruth had suggested I sit on a chaise and observe the nudists to get acclimated.

"Maybe after that," she'd told me, "you won't want to leave anymore. We'd sure love to have you stay, Mara. And I know Ollie would like that too."

She'd winked at me when she said the part about Ollie.

Ugh. How could he possibly want me to stick around? I'd acted like such an idiot, and I'd kissed him—which he clearly hadn't appreciated.

So stupid, Mara.

This morning, I decided to hide out for a while in the little house where Ollie had generously let me stay. He had left a note on my door saying he went to the office in the guest house and I should help myself to the breakfast he'd left in the fridge for me. Sure, I'd gotten somewhat accustomed to hanging out with naked people, but I needed a break from my immersion therapy. A little alone time. To decompress.

Nothing helped me relax more than a nice warm bath.

Unfortunately, this house had a shower, not a bathtub.

Did the guest house have a tub? I really, really, seriously needed some relaxation time, preferably with bubbles.

I peered out the kitchen window and spotted Ruth Norris right when she looked in my direction. I waved until she noticed, smiling, then gestured for her to come here. She nodded and hustled to the door. When I opened it, she walked right in.

"What can I do for you, sweetie?" she asked.

"Um, well…" I hunched my shoulders, feeling weird about what I wanted to ask.

She put her arm around my shoulders and gave me a gentle squeeze. "Don't be shy, hon. Whatever it is, you can tell me."

"I was wondering if there's a bathtub in the guest house. I'd love a nice, relaxing soak."

"There is a soaking tub attached to the exercise room. It's a jacuzzi-type thing, so it's great for relaxing."

"Exercise room?" I bit the inside of my lip, imagining all the ways I could be humiliated by someone walking in while I was soaking. Even if I wore a swimsuit, I'd feel embarrassed. "That sounds kind of…public."

"No-no, sweetie, you can shut the door. Nobody will go in there without knocking first." She gave my bottom a little pat. "Go on. Enjoy yourself. I'll let the other guests know not to use the exercise room while you're enjoying jacuzzi therapy."

"Thank you, Ruth. You've been so nice to me, in spite of the way I acted yesterday."

"Never mind that. We all have bad days."

Ruth gave me directions for how to find the exercise room, then left to alert the other guests that the room was off limits for a while. She even suggested I put a scarf or something on the door handle so I could take it off when I left the exercise room. That way, everyone would be sure to steer clear until I was done.

God, I loved that woman. I wished she were my grandma.

My real grandmother was just like my mom. If the people here thought I was uptight, they should meet my family. I loved them, but Mom and Grandma had high standards I never quite met.

I grabbed my conservative black one-piece swimsuit—along with a towel, a bottle of bath oil, and a silver scarf—before I trotted to the guest house and found the exercise room on the first floor. Like Ruth had promised, the room was empty. I hooked my scarf around the knob and shut the door. Once I got into the jacuzzi room, I discovered the tub was already filled and hot, with the jets turned on, bubbling away.

After pouring a small amount of bath oil into the water, I climbed in.

Only then did I realize maybe I shouldn't have used bath oil. Would it mess up the jacuzzi? Since it was too late to worry about that, I put the worry out of my mind.

Oh God, the water felt incredible. It was just hot enough to soothe me, but not so hot I'd sweat like in a sauna. I hated those. Getting drowned in steam made me nauseous. But this jacuzzi… Wow, I could live in it. The bath oil released its soothing scents while I leaned back and let the bubbles tease my skin. A jet pounded into my back, easing the tension there, and I moaned because it felt so damn good. I'd been stressed for a long time, with no real means of alleviating it. Nothing I did was good enough for anyone, and heaven forbid if I tried something that wasn't on the approved list of activities for a socialite.

Last year, I'd wanted to go to Disneyland, and my parents had said it was "too gauche for a lady like you." Well, my mom had said that. Dad let her do all the talking when it was slap-Mara-on-the-wrist time. No actual slapping was involved, though. Purely the verbal kind. My mom never yelled at me or insulted me. She simply reminded me of the rules for people in our echelon of society.

Sometimes, I really, really wanted to do something crazy, something totally opposite of what everyone expected. Something naughty. Something that might actually feel good.

That jet felt damn good pulsing against my low back.

Maybe if I turned around and lifted my hips...

I grinned, feeling deliciously wicked just thinking about it. Maybe the nudist resort setting had affected me, but I had an urge I couldn't resist. So I spun around and knelt in front of the water jet, letting the bubbly power of it pulsate on my body, right at the juncture of my thighs. It didn't quite hit the right spot, the one that would send me straight to the land of happy endings. I wiggled around, trying to find the sweet spot, but none of the jets had the perfect angle.

Shit. I was getting hot, and not from the water temperature. The second I'd thought about using the water jet to get off, I'd gone so hot and slick I almost couldn't stand it. Feeling the jet pounding into my thighs and hips ratcheted up my arousal until my rigid nub throbbed.

I lay back in the tub and slipped my fingers inside my swimsuit, straining to reach my clitoris. I couldn't get there. The suit was too snug for my hand to fit. *Ugh.* I tried rubbing myself through the swimsuit, but that wasn't working either. I kept getting wetter and more anxious, craving that release, but I couldn't reach that hard, aching nub to push myself over the edge.

Fuck, I needed to come. Needed it so badly.

Well, if I took off my swimsuit...

No, I couldn't. What if somebody saw me?

Ruth had sworn no one would disturb me. They'd stay away until I took the scarf off the door to the exercise room. And besides, I was inside the jacuzzi room with that door closed too. Two doors separated me from the rest of the guest house.

Whimpering, I slumped in the tub. I'd never needed an orgasm so much in my life, like I'd go insane if I couldn't hit that peak.

I glanced around, like I expected to see someone hiding behind me or on the floor. Nobody around. Nobody but me and the bubbles tormenting my sensitized skin.

So I peeled off my swimsuit.

While I relaxed against the tub's rim, slipping my fingers between my folds, I tried to think of a good fantasy to help me get off faster. I rolled my clit between two fingers while I stretched out my longest finger to rub up and down my cleft, coating my fingers with the evidence of my horny state, making my them more slippery with every stroke. Oh God, that felt goooood. Shutting my eyes, I let a fantasy play out in my mind, a vision of Ollie with his head between my legs, lapping and teasing, his hands pinning my hips down while I thrashed and thrust my fingers into his hair.

I came so hard and so fast a sharp cry exploded out of me.

"Oh shit!"

That exclamation had not come from me. The intensity of my release had robbed me of breath, allowing only that one small, wordless cry.

My lids sprang open—and I screamed.

Ollie was standing in the open doorway, his eyes wide and his mouth open. He whirled around to face away from me, throwing one hand up. "Sorry, shit, I'm sorry. Should've knocked, but— Fuck, I'm sorry."

He ran away.

Oh. My. God. Had Ollie seen me... touching myself? He had definitely seen me naked. But somehow, the idea of that didn't freak me out like I would've expected. Instead, I got more aroused again thinking about.

But he was shocked and humiliated.

My cheeks heated up, burning like a bonfire of shame. How could I get turned on by a virtual stranger seeing me naked? While I was giving myself a happy ending?

I should've known the one time I cut loose and did something naughty, I'd get caught.

With my cheeks on fire and my stomach churning, I pulled on my swimsuit and left the jacuzzi room. The exercise room door hung open, my scarf still hanging on the knob. I snatched it up, shuffling across the threshold.

Ollie was there. Standing beside the door. He leaned against the wall, his arms crossed over his chest, his lips crushed into a sharp line. The light glinted on his glasses, making it hard to see his eyes.

"I'm sorry," I told him. "What I did was completely inappropriate. You must think I'm disgusting."

"Disgusting?" He pushed away from the wall, coming closer, so close the natural, masculine scent of him surrounded me. "You are so fucking beautiful, Mara. And the look on your face when you come… It's incredible."

Oh no, no, no. He *had* seen me and known what I was doing.

"I've never done anything like that before," I said, edging sideways to get a little distance from him. His proximity was making me horny again. That and the hungry look on his face. "I mean, I've done *that* before. Everybody has, right? But doing it in a public place and getting caught…" I shook my head, squeezing my eyes shut. "That's so not me."

A shuffling sound made me open my eyes.

Ollie advanced on me, forcing me to back up to the wall. His hands landed on the wall at either side of me, penning me there. "Nothing wrong with getting off the solo way. I do it too. But you weren't in a public place. This is a naturist resort. Everybody gets naked around here, except you."

"But I was… you know… where anyone could catch me." I wriggled against the wall, getting warmer and wetter down below, more and more every second that he stayed so close. "Ruth said she'd tell everyone to stay away from the exercise room, but still, I should've known better than to do…that."

"I didn't get the memo. Haven't seen Ruth this morning." He leaned in, bending his arms, bringing his face within an inch of mine. "Wish I could say I regret what just happened, but I can't. I loved seeing your body, all wet and slippery, and seeing that look on your face when you came. I want to be the one to make you look like that next time."

"But you were horrified when I kissed you."

"No, not horrified. Surprised. And you'd been so upset about all the naked people, I didn't want to take advantage of you." He grazed his lips over mine, making me suck in a sharp breath. "You're not freaked out anymore, and I want to kiss you."

"I want that too."

And God, did I want it. His lips. On mine. *Yes, please, yes.*

Ollie groaned, the sound resonating with hunger, and claimed my mouth. His warm lips pressed hard against mine, demanding a response, and I couldn't resist letting him in, loving the silken glide of his tongue on mine and the way he thrust it deeper, over and over, pumping it with movements similar to how he might thrust his cock into me. The rhythm of it drove me wild with need, and my nipples hardened. I flung my arms around his neck, plunging my tongue into his mouth, moaning at the taste of him and the feel of my nipples rubbing against his firm chest.

He pinned me to the wall with his entire body, bending his head to keep our lips locked. The swollen length of him pressed into my belly.

I hooked my leg around his, all but begging him to take me right here, right now. Never in my life had I wanted a man this much, and for once, I felt no shame about wanting all the dirty things that my mind conjured up for me.

He pulled his head back, breaking the kiss, though his body stayed plastered to mine. "That's how much I want you. Get it?"

Speechless, I could do nothing more than nod once.

"Good." He backed away, the bulge in his pants like a flashing neon sign announcing how turned on he was. "The next time I see you naked, I'll be the reason you get that look on your face. I'll be the one making you come."

He hurried off down the hall and up the stairs.

The next time? I wanted that to happen right now.

But being me, I couldn't summon the courage to run after Ollie and tell him that.

Chapter Eight

Ollie

Naked Mara. *Fuck me.* She was beautiful and so damn desirable I wanted to jump in that jacuzzi and show her a much better way to get off. Instead, I kissed her and left. What kind of moron was I? Sure, my record with women wasn't exactly the stuff of legends—unless those legends centered on a loser who couldn't keep a girlfriend for more than six months. They all kicked me to the curb eventually, for a hotter guy who didn't wear glasses or work as a computer systems engineer.

These days, I was the assistant manager of a naturist resort. Didn't that make me cooler now? More attractive to girls?

Nope. Not one bit.

My last girlfriend, Heidi, had gone back to her ex to "give it one more try, just to be sure." I'd wanted to ask her why she'd dumped him in the first place if she wasn't sure about it. And why she'd hooked up with me before she made double sure. Christ, we hadn't even slept together, that's how brief our so-called relationship had been. I'd been the rebound guy, for probably the tenth time, the guy who cheered girls up after their dickwad exes broke their hearts. Once they felt better about themselves, they cut me loose. And how many times had I cringed while a girl gave me the heave-ho by saying I was like her gay best friend?

I guess they thought that was a compliment, but it sounded like an insult to both me and all the actual gay guys out there.

Behold the legend of the loser geek, see him on display at the Museum of Loser Geekdom. Buy your tickets today for half price.

At least I wouldn't have to see Heidi this summer. She and her friends usually vacationed here at least twice a year, but Heidi had stayed home last time and her friends said she wouldn't be with them when they arrived later this week.

I started to head for the office upstairs but stopped when I got to the second-floor landing. Why was I running away? Mara had seemed really into our kiss. I'd been so into it I had to walk bowlegged when I hustled away from her. Maybe I could still catch her.

Sure, I might be a loser in some ways, but I had total confidence in two of my skills. First, my computer creds. Second...

I vaulted down the stairs two at a time, sprinted for the exercise room, and froze in the open doorway, breathing so hard I had to slap my hands on my thighs for support.

Mara wasn't there.

Damn. Where did she go?

I waited a few seconds, until I caught my breath, then I took off down the hall and out the main door. Mara was just going into the little house, so I kicked it into high gear and barreled across the gravel driveway. Thankfully, I was still wearing shoes—and clothes, but I didn't thank anybody for the fact I was trapped in polyester—because if I'd run barefoot across the gravel, I'd have blisters the size of Texas later on.

"What's the rush, Ollie?" somebody shouted.

"Yeah," another somebody hollered, "where's the fire?"

"It's in Ollie's pants, that's where," the first voice shouted. "Guess Val's rubbing off on him."

I didn't bother to glance back or respond. Didn't give a shit who was razzing me or why. My mind focused exclusively on the vision of Mara naked and what I planned to do once I caught up to her.

At the door to Eve and Val's house, I had to stop. Bent over at the waist, hands on my thighs, I gasped for air like a ninety-year-old chain smoker. I exercised. I was in great shape these days, but now I could barely breathe. Well, I hadn't practiced barreling down a flight of stairs, through the guest house, and across the driveway. Never in my life had I literally chased after a girl.

What was up with me? This was not at all my style.

The one thing that had been up was now down. Way down.

I growled at my dick. "Wake the hell up, little buddy. We've got work to do."

Oh great. Now I was talking to my dick. Out loud. In public.

Shoving the door open, I hurried inside and stopped short of slamming the door shut. That might freak Mara out. So I eased the door closed and walked through the kitchen into the hallway that led to the bathroom, bedrooms, and Eve's photo studio. I should've announced myself. Really, I should have. It would've been the polite, not-a-creepy-stalker way to behave. My mouth still wouldn't work, though, what with my lungs insisting I wheeze.

In front of the bathroom door, I stopped to wait out the wheezing. Slow, steady breaths. Mara would scream again if I stumbled into her room sounding like a heavy breather on a sleazy phone call and looking like I might drop dead any second.

Soothing new age music came from her room.

Listening to the music, I closed my eyes and took those slow, steady breaths until I calmed down. Then I walked to Mara's door, which hung open—and my little buddy woke up fast.

She was doing yoga. Wheel pose. She lay on her back with her feet flat on the floor, knees bent, and her palms on the floor just above her shoulders. While I watched, paralyzed and speechless, she lifted her hips off the floor and held that position for a couple breaths. Slowly, she raised the rest of her body until only her palms and feet touched the floor. Her head hung down, her ponytail dangling. With her spine arched upward like that, her breasts jutted out, her stiff nipples obvious under her thin tank top.

Yeah, she'd changed clothes. No more capris or short-sleeve shirt. Now she wore snug yoga pants and a snug tank top.

She looked good enough to fuck. Right here. Right now.

My little buddy loved that idea, twitching like he was telling me to go get her.

Jeez, I really needed to stop calling it my "little buddy," even in my head.

I cleared my throat to let her know I was here.

Mara yelped and tumbled out of wheel pose into a heap on the floor.

"Are you okay?" I asked, rushing over to help her.

She was already helping herself, scrambling into a sitting position on her yoga mat. She laid a hand on her chest and blew out a breath. "Ollie, you scared me half to death."

"I know, I'm sorry." Why had I thought throat-clearing was a good way to announce my presence? Yeah, social skills weren't one of the two things I rocked at. I knelt beside her. "I hope you didn't sprain anything."

"No, I'm fine." She smiled at me in her shy way, which made me want to kiss her. "But you're so sweet for worrying."

Just once I wanted a girl to say, "Damn, Ollie, that was so freaking hot the way you scared the shit out of me." Okay, maybe I didn't want to hear that after all. It had sounded good when I thought it, but now I realized how stupid it was.

"Twice today I've surprised you," I said. "Swear I'm not stalking you or anything."

"I know that." She got up and stretched her entire body, making her tits jut out again. "I decided to do yoga to relax, but it wasn't really working anyway."

Somehow, I managed to get up without looking like a clumsy dweeb. "Are you still anxious about being around all the naturists?"

"No, it's not that. I mean, I still feel a little weird about it, but everybody's so nice here." She sat on the edge of the bed. "They're like a big, extended family."

"Yeah, we get the same people coming back every year." I settled onto the bed beside her, leaving a couple feet of space between us. "Some people come back several times a year."

"I can see why. It's beautiful here."

"You haven't seen the hot spring yet. It's amazing."

Mara caught her lip between her teeth and aimed those incredible jade eyes at me. "Would you show me?"

"Now?"

She nodded, still biting her lip.

I wanted to take that lip between my teeth and suck on it. Since I wouldn't tell her that, I said, "Sure. I can be your nature guide."

What the hell was I saying? I'd come here to show her the other thing I rocked at, but instead of seducing her, I was offering to be her tour guide.

"Maybe we could take the hike later," I said, leaning in closer. "I have something I want to show you first."

"What is it?"

I cupped her face in one hand, slanting in even more, brushing my lips over hers. "I want to make love to you, Mara."

Her breathing had become shaky, her eyes big and luminous. "You don't want to have sex with me, Ollie. I...get inappropriately excited about it."

I almost laughed but swallowed it. The look on her face convinced me she wasn't joking.

"Who told you that?" I asked, caressing her cheek with my thumb.

"My—my ex." She squeezed her eyes shut, scrunching up her face. "He said I need to temper my carnal urges because no man of good breeding wants a wife who gets too excited. Sex is for men, not for women. It's our marital duty."

"Why the fuck would he tell you that? Your ex sounds like an asshole."

"I'm sure my mom would agree with him if she knew about that part of my life. She very into what's proper, what society would approve of, stuff like that."

"No offense, but your mom sounds like an asshole too."

"She's not that bad, really. But my family, especially my mom, cares a lot about what's proper and what the rest of our peers think."

"Peers? Do you mean, like, royalty?"

"No." She opened her eyes to gaze into mine. "You're very sexy, Ollie, and I'd really like to be with you, but I couldn't stand it if you were disgusted with me."

"I won't be. But maybe we should talk a little first, so you'll feel more comfortable. I kind of sprang this on you." I pulled my hand away. "Or we could wait until later, or not do it at all. Your choice."

"Let's talk."

And then have sex, I hoped. Her family sounded pretty damn awful to me, but then, I came from a home where my mom and dad hugged us every morning and said, "Have a good day at school, sweetie, I love you." I would've bet good money that Mara's family didn't even shake hands without slathering on sanitizing gel first.

Maybe that explained why Mara had gotten so uptight.

"What did you mean when you said 'peers'?" I asked.

She bowed her head, gripping the mattress like it might fly up into the sky at any second. "My parents are wealthy. They circulate among the most prestigious social circles, they never say or do anything inappropriate, and they only kiss on the cheek in public. I've only seen them kiss on the lips three times in my entire life."

"But you love to kiss, don't you? And you're really good at it."

Her head came up, and those beautiful eyes focused on me again. "You think so? I do like it, a lot. I loved kissing you." She winced, then sighed. "And that's another thing that's not proper."

"Kissing me? Or liking it?"

"Both." She made a noise that was part growl, part whine, and covered her face with her hands. "I'm so sick of being proper."

"Then don't do it anymore."

She dropped her hands to her thighs, slumping her shoulders. "I'm already the family screw-up, so it probably doesn't matter what I do. Might as well go crazy, right?"

"I'm all for going crazy in moderation."

Mara stared at me like I'd gone totally insane. But when I winked and smiled, she seemed to get the idea I'd been kidding. Nobody went insane moderately. They went all the way or not at all. Or at least that's what I thought. I didn't have any experience with lunatics.

She almost smiled at my dumb joke, but the expression crumbled quickly.

"You're not a screw-up," I said. "Everybody makes mistakes. Even the uptight jerks who claim they never mess up."

"You don't get it." She made that noise again and flopped back onto the bed. "I can't even speak Japanese."

Okay, that was one thing I'd never heard on somebody's list of ways they'd screwed up.

I braced one hand on the bed beside her and leaned into it, gazing down at her face. "If that's the yardstick for being a screw-up, I'm just as bad as you are. I can't speak Japanese either."

"But nobody expects you to." She moaned pitifully, rolling her head side to side. "My mom is super proud of our Japanese heritage. So is my grandmother. My dad is half Dutch, half Welsh, but he doesn't expect me to speak Dutch or Welsh. My mom is so humiliated that I couldn't learn Japanese, even after years of lessons. I suck at it."

"It's a really hard language, huh?"

She moaned again, even more pitifully. "My mom learned it when she was a little girl. She's never been to Japan, doesn't know anybody in Japan, and the Kanda family has been American since my great-great-whatever grandparents moved here in eighteen eighty-three. But learning the language is like a badge of honor in our family." She pounded her fists on the bed. "And I can't speak Japanese."

"I won't hold that against you. I mean, I flunked out of high school Spanish and had to repeat it in summer school. Even then, I had to pay a girl in my class to tutor me so I could squeak by with a C minus."

"Are your parents Spanish? Do they think not speaking the language is shameful?"

"No, I can't say they do. And my family's part Scottish, part Italian, part French. That means we love plaid, we curse and spit at everybody, and we make awesome bread."

Her lips twitched like she might smile any second. "Thank you for trying to cheer me up. I'm sorry I went off on a rant about my family."

"Don't worry about it. Seemed like you really needed to get all that off your chest." I looked down at her chest, at those sexy tits barely hidden inside her tank top. "And I'd be happy to help you out by getting that shirt off your chest too."

She laughed, the sound completely feminine and melodic, like tiny bells tinkling.

First, I talked to my dick. Now, I was thinking about tinkling bells. Time to get off that track before my balls derailed for good and I turned into a girl.

It was also way past time I told her the truth about me.

"So," I began, in a not-at-all lame way, "are you really cool with the nudity? You can handle seeing more people in the buff?"

"Yes, I can handle it. You don't have to worry about me shrieking and fainting in your arms again." She crossed her heart with one finger. "Promise."

"Hey, I didn't mind the fainting in my arms part. But if you're really sure, there's something I need to tell you. Or maybe I should just show you."

"I'd love to see whatever it is you want to show me. I trust you, Ollie."

"You've known me for barely more than a day."

"Doesn't matter. I trust you."

"Well, uh…" I straightened, scratching the back of my head. "I kind of—Well, I didn't quite lie to you, but I wasn't completely upfront about something."

Mara sat up too, hitting me with a sweet smile. "Considering how much I freaked out when I first got here, I don't blame you for holding back anything."

"You really are the nicest girl I've ever met." I let my gaze travel down her body and back up again. "And the hottest girl I've ever met."

She waved her hands in a come-on gesture. "Tell me whatever it is. Or show me. Whichever."

"Okay." I got up and took off my shirt, trying not to smirk when her eyes widened and she bit her lip. When I ditched my pants and stood naked in front of her, I spread my arms wide. "I'm a naturist, Mara."

Her tongue slipped out to moisten her lips, and her gaze seemed to have stalled slightly south of my hips. "Oh. I see. No underwear? Whew, I *really* see."

"And you're okay with it?"

She nodded her head so vigorously her ponytail flopped around. "Absolutely."

I was so relieved my shoulders sagged.

Her tongue darted out again, and she looked up at me with her lips curled into the sexiest little smile I'd ever seen. "Can we get it on now?"

Chapter Nine

Mara

Ollie naked. Wow, wow, *wow*, he was hot. Maybe he didn't have an outrageously ripped physique all the movie stars did these days, but Ollie Jackson had more sex appeal than any of them. His chest offered enough muscles to make me want to run my fingertips over every single one of them, followed by my tongue. I wanted to taste his skin. Run my hands over those biceps, where they bulged a touch, enough to offer visual proof of how strong he'd be in bed. Strong and agile. A man who did yoga? Damn, that was the hottest thing ever—and he'd know all the best moves, the ones that required dexterity and agility. And those thighs. Powerful, but not overdone. I wanted to feel every sinew flexing while he thrust into me.

But I could not overlook the most incredible part of him.

His dick hung semi-hard, the shaft thick and long and sleek. No one would ever guess, seeing him with his clothes on, that he concealed one impressive package down there. The crown was reddening, the length swelling and rising.

"Your turn," Ollie said.

Sometimes, when a man wanted to have sex, I got embarrassed about undressing. Worried about what they'd think of my body. Not with Ollie. He'd already seen me au naturel, but even if he hadn't, I would never feel shame with him. He was sweet and sexy, strong and tender, all the best combinations of everything.

I stood and pulled my tank top off over my head, then stripped off my bra. Cool air teased my naked skin, but the way my nipples hardened had less to do with the air temperature than the gorgeous man standing proudly nude in front of me. I shimmied out of my yoga pants, dragging my panties down with them.

Ollie ran a hand over his mouth. "Mara, you're so damn beautiful."

"Thank you." I moved closer, splaying my palms on his chest. "You're the hottest man I've ever seen."

He slung an arm around my waist, tugging me into his body, his erection caught between us. "Time to show you the second thing I rock at."

"What's the first thing?"

"My tech skills."

I skated my palms across his chest in slow circles. "Wow. Hot and smart. I'm impressed."

"Wait till you see the second thing." He cradled my face in one hand and kissed me, slowly, deeply, with such erotic skill that I moaned. His eyes were hooded when he murmured in a sexy rumble, "Actually, it's more of a sensory experience than a visual one. An immersive sensory experience."

A tingle raced over my skin, and I couldn't breathe. The thought of having sex with Ollie got me more excited than I'd ever been before.

He ducked around me to pull the covers off the bed, then picked me up and laid me down on the soft mattress and the silky sheet.

I spread my fingers over the fabric, loving the smooth texture of it. "These sheets feel so good on my skin."

"*You* feel so good on *my* skin." Ollie grabbed his pants off the floor and dug a condom out of the pocket. He tossed it onto the table. "Can't wait till I'm inside you."

"Please, Ollie, hurry."

He straddled my body, his face hovering over mine.

A shimmering, sensual heat rippled through me, fanning out through my entire body like delicate waves on a sun-warmed pond.

"I've wanted to do this since I first saw you," he said, inching backward on all fours. "Can't wait anymore. Gotta eat you up."

He kept backing away until his head was above my hips, then he eased my thighs apart with one hand. When he lay down with his face inches above my mound, I sucked in a breath, knowing what he planned to do and craving it with a need so intense it made me a little lightheaded. He took off his glasses and tossed them onto the bedside table. I gripped my pillow with both hands, suddenly breathing hard, almost panting. Ollie smiled with a hunger that stole my breath as he lifted my legs to rest my knees on his shoulders.

The second his tongue touched my flesh, I gasped and jerked.

He nuzzled the hairs on my mound, darted his tongue out to tease my skin, and kept his gaze on mine the whole time. I clenched my pillow harder, my fingers punching into it. He thrust his tongue between my folds and circled it around my taut nub, his tongue so agile it encircled my clit, wrapping around it again and again, the silken warmth of it driving me wild.

"Oh, Ollie," I moaned.

"Call me Oliver."

"I thought…oh…you didn't like that."

"Now I do, while I'm feasting on you. I want to hear my full name when you come. Please do this for me."

"I will, Oliver."

He shoved his head as far between my thighs as possible and devoured me. His tongue lapped and swirled, his breaths blustered over my flesh, and his teeth scraped and nipped at me. I writhed wildly, panting and gasping and crying out, not giving a damn if anyone heard me. The pleasure mounted inside my body, a rigid coil winding tighter and tighter until my back bowed into the mattress and my head came up off the pillow. My knees drew up too, and I clutched his head while it bobbed as he tormented me with more and more demanding strokes of his tongue.

But when he stopped, I almost screamed—in frustration.

I gripped a handful of his hair and pulled his head up so I could see his eyes. "What are you doing? Don't stop. Make me come, dammit."

He chuckled. "You're so cute when you're sexually frustrated."

"Will you do it if I beg? Please, Oliver, please." It came out more throaty than pleading, but considering the way his eyes narrowed and he licked his lips, I didn't think he cared.

He drew in a ragged breath. "Fuck, that's so hot. Hearing you say my name that way."

"Oliver," I purred, letting go of his hair. "Make me come, please. Then I'll return the favor."

I swore his pupils blew right as I watched. His eyes became dark, shimmering pools of carnal need.

He pulled my clit into his mouth and rolled his tongue around it.

And I came, just like that. My fingers clenched his hair again, my entire body caved in, and the cry that exploded out of me echoed off the walls. The pleasure ripped through me in waves so powerful I lost my voice and my breath. He kept licking, kept tormenting me with the most wonderful blend of ecstasy and pain I'd ever experienced. My muscles spasmed with such intensity that I was sure I'd be sore later from the strength of this one unbelievable climax.

When it finally subsided, I collapsed onto the bed. "Oh. Wow. God. You weren't kidding. You absolutely do rock the sex."

"Glad you're satisfied." He sat back on his heels, kneeling near my feet. "But that was only phase one."

"Wait a minute so I can catch my breath and then it's my turn. I want to feast on you."

"Later. I'm on a mission right now."

I stretched my arms above my head, dancing my fingertips along the top of the headboard. "What mission is that?"

"To fuck you so long and so good that you'll never want to be with anyone else."

"Oh yes, please do that."

He rose onto hands and knees, crawling up my body, his expression one of pure hunger and determination. He wanted me that badly. I wanted him just as much, maybe more, so much that my pulse raced and my breaths came fast and short.

Growling softly, he skimmed a hand over my belly and up between my breasts, his fingers grazing them, setting off a flurry of excitement that tingled over my skin and made my clit pulsate. My skin grew so sensitized to his touch that I choked back a whimper, every brush of his fingers a beautiful torment. No one had ever touched me the way he did or made me feel the way he did. I'd known him for such a short time, yet I couldn't deny that I felt more comfortable with him than I ever had with anyone else.

Sex with a virtual stranger? Never, not me.

Except today. With him.

He dipped his fingers into his mouth one by one, moistening their tips until they glistened. When he swirled his damp fingertips around my nipple, not touching it, I wanted him so much I almost whimpered again. He circled his forefinger around and around, moving ever closer to my rigid peak, his focus intently on the task, until at last he brushed that finger over my nipple.

I gasped, my back arching.

"You like that," he murmured, his gaze shifting to my face. "You want me to take this"—he raked his thumb across my nipple—"into my mouth and make you squirm because it feels so damn good."

"Unh. Yes. Please."

He laved the peak with his hot tongue, leaving it aching and moist, the air chilling my skin, the sensation even more arousing. "You taste incredible, from your lips and your skin to your cream."

I could manage nothing more useful than a desperate grunt, since he'd latched his mouth onto my nipple again, suckling and swiping his tongue over it, nipping gently, all the while cupping my other breast in his hand. He massaged it and flicked his thumb over the peak, back and forth, on and on.

"Oh God, Oliver," I moaned. My voice grew strained and more desperate while his hand and mouth drove me to the edge of bliss. "Yes, oh God, yes, Oliver, I'm about to—"

He removed his hand from my breast and pulled his mouth away from the other one. A sexy smirk tightened his mouth. "Not yet, Mara."

I writhed, fisting my hands in my pillow, the pain of not quite coming so frustrating and yet so electrifying. "I can't take any more, please. Fuck me, Oliver."

"Damn, you just had to go and say that, with your voice all hot and sexy and needy."

"You sound hot and sexy and *hungry*." I glanced down at his cock, hanging between our bodies, and licked my lips. "Mm, I want your dick, Oliver. It's beautiful and big, and I'm sure it tastes even better than dark chocolate filled with caramel that melts on your tongue."

"I am hungry, but not for food." He hoisted my leg up, hooking it over his shoulder, and bracketed my body with his hands on the bed. "For you, Mara. I'll lose my mind if I don't do this right away."

"Do it." I set my palms on his chest. "Now, Oliver."

He thrust into me, filling my body, and began a sure, measured rhythm of strokes. I gripped his shoulders, hanging on while he pushed inside me and withdrew, over and over, every thrust a hot, silky glide of his flesh against mine, my body molding to his rigid length while I grew slicker and more sensitive. I experienced his every movement with a powerful surge of pleasure, not quite a climax, but getting closer every second. Never had anything felt as good as this. I clutched him with my hands and my body, and he lowered onto his elbows, bending my knee even further and giving him deeper access. I couldn't stop the words that tumbled out of me—desperate, greedy, lustful, wild cries.

"Ohmygodyes, Oliver! Please, yes. I love this, I love your cock, it's incredible, I love your body too. Oh God, you're the hottest man on the planet, please don't stop, don't stop, I'm about to—oh! God! Yes!"

My release struck so fast, and with such intensity, that I couldn't scream any more stupid words. I couldn't breathe, couldn't think, couldn't stop from sinking my nails into his shoulders and locking my free leg around his hip, needing him even deeper inside me while the waves of my climax thundered through me, shredding my self-control.

He came inside me while my body was still gripping him. I felt the pulsating rhythm of his release, even while I spiraled down from the heights of pleasure, dazed and beyond satisfied.

The mattress bounced, and I realized he'd collapsed onto it beside me. I had my eyes squeezed shut, tears trickling down my cheeks.

"Did I hurt you?" he asked, his tender voice close to my ear.

I shook my head, unable to do anything more.

"Can you open your eyes?" he asked, his tone becoming slightly amused. "I know I'm good, but I didn't think I was good enough to leave a girl paralyzed. Not sure that would be a good thing."

Pulling in a deep breath, I let it out gradually and forced my lids to open. My heart still pounded, but I managed to smile, as much as anyone could while stunned by the most amazing sex ever.

Lying on his side, he brushed sweat-dampened hair away from my cheek. "You are gorgeous when you come, especially the way you just did, like it was the first time and a sex bomb went off inside you."

"I think it did." I rolled onto my side, snuggling up to him, my head tucked under his chin. His skin was damp, and he smelled like sweat, but I loved it. "I said a bunch of stupid things a minute ago. Sorry."

"Don't be. I loved all the goofy things you screamed, especially the part about how I'm the hottest guy on the planet."

"What about when I said I love your incredible cock?"

"That was awesome too." He kissed the top of my head. "Everything you said got me going even more. I've never fucked a woman like the world was about to explode and it was my last chance to have sex. But damn, Mara, you made me that hot."

I looped an arm around him, skating my hand up and down his back. "Why don't you have a girlfriend? You're amazing."

"We met yesterday, so I'm not sure you have the info to make that announcement yet. But I appreciate." He sighed into my hair, his hands wandering over my body. "Truth is, I'm not that popular with girls. You wouldn't believe how many of them dump my ass by saying, 'You're like my gay best friend.' I mean, what the fuck? That's not what they screamed the night before."

Lifting my head, I gazed into his amber eyes. "I will never, ever call you my gay best friend."

His lips quirked into a crooked smile. "Thanks."

I studied him for a moment until I worked up the courage to ask. "What did those insanely stupid girls scream the night before?"

"Kind of what you did, but they weren't as good at it."

I was better than those silly girls. Maybe it was weird, but hearing him say that made me feel even better than I already did. My body had become deliciously relaxed, still warmed by our fantastic sex. I cuddled up to him again, but my tummy was starting to rumble.

"Hungry?" he asked.

"Mm-hm. But I don't want to move."

"I'll go into the kitchen and make us lunch." He wriggled away from my body, kissed me, and hopped off the bed. "Gotta call to check on lunch for the guests, but we've got great cooks. I shouldn't need to go over there." He leaned over the bed to run a hand along my thigh, sending an electric shiver down my skin. "That means I can focus on you."

Ollie walked out the door, stark naked.

And I lay on the bed, stretched out like a Roman empress. That man had given me the best sex of my entire life while making me feel sexy and powerful, not at all like a screw-up who couldn't keep a man.

Thank you, Ollie.

Chapter Ten

Ollie

I went into the kitchen and called to check on things at the guest house, then I gathered ingredients from the fridge to make lunch for Mara and me. While I whipped up my culinary creations, I thought about how this day had changed so completely from what I could've ever expected. I had sex with Mara. Holy shit, that happened. She'd freaked out when she first saw the naturists in the buff, but when she'd stepped out of that taxi I'd been dumbstruck by how beautiful and sexy she was. Mara had calmed down pretty fast after her freak-out. Though she swore was okay with naturism, I figured she must still have had some issues with it. She wanted to get past them. I knew that.

Not that I expected she'd ever become a naturist.

But damn, she had the body for it.

While I sliced cucumbers for a salad, I considered the problem of Mara. She had hangups, for sure. Her parents seemed to have done a bang-up job of convincing her she wasn't good enough—for anything. I'd never met them, but I already didn't like them. Mara seemed like such a sweet girl, and smart too. Not to mention amazing in bed.

I had fucked a woman I'd known for less than two days.

Yeah, I still had trouble wrapping my head around that one. I was a computer nerd who struggled to get dates and couldn't keep a girlfriend. As for one-nighters… Yeah, that never happened to me. How did I get so lucky today?

Mara wandered into the kitchen while I was finishing up. She'd put on the same outfit she wore earlier, with the capri pants and sandals.

"Sit down," I told her, pointing at the stools on her side of the island. "Lunch is almost ready."

She perched on a stool, folding her hands atop the island. "Thank you for making me lunch."

"It's the least I can do after the workout we just had." I couldn't help smirking when I remembered our time in the bedroom. "I've never had sex with a girl I barely know, but it was incredible."

Mara blushed a little. "It was wonderful. And I've never had sex with someone I barely know either."

"We're both first-timers, eh?" I slid two plates across the island, one for Mara and one for me, then I slid two glasses of lemonade over there too. The salads were on the plates, beside double-decker sandwiches. "Here you go. Figured we both needed a big lunch to catch up on the calories we burned in bed."

"I am starving." She pulled her plate closer and licked her lips. "It looks delicious."

"Dig in." I walked around to her side of the island and sat on the stool next to hers. "The sandwich is ham, turkey, and bacon with vinaigrette dressing and provolone cheese. I made the lemonade from scratch. The salad has thousand island dressing, but Eve made that. She always whips up a big batch of the dressing and puts it in glass jars herself so we can use them as needed."

"Wow, you don't get homemade dressing at a regular resort." She picked up her fork and ate a mouthful of salad. "Mm, yummy."

"Glad you like it."

She took her double-decker sandwich in both hands, biting off a sizable chunk. While she chewed, she closed her eyes and moaned.

My dick started waking up again.

"Uh, I'll go put on some clothes," I told her, sliding off my stool. "You're still getting used to the naturist thing, and I don't want you to feel weird about me sitting her in the nude eating a sandwich."

"That's okay. You don't need to do that on my account."

"It's no trouble."

Running back to my room gave me a chance to get a grip on myself. If I got hard every time I saw Mara, we were in trouble.

After putting on jeans and a T-shirt, I went back to the kitchen and to Mara. Her plate had the same amount of food on it as when I'd left.

"Don't you like it?" I asked, nodding at her plate. "You haven't eaten much."

"I was waiting for you."

She smiled shyly, which for some reason always got my dick excited, so I jumped onto my stool and started eating as a way to avoid looking at her. The food did taste pretty good. Maybe I couldn't keep a girlfriend, but I had three things I rocked at—computers, sex, and now food. Serving as Eve's sous chef, in the days before we hired actual kitchen staff, had taught me a lot about cooking.

Not that sandwiches and salad counted as cooking.

Mara moaned again while devouring her sandwich.

I shifted uncomfortably on my stool and focused on my own plate. Never in my life had I eaten as fast as I did now.

"Really hungry, huh?" Mara said.

"Kinda," I mumbled through the food I'd stuffed into my mouth. Swallowing, I said, "Tell me more about you. I know your family's rich, but what about you? Do you work?"

"Yes." She swigged her lemonade. "Mm, this is delicious too. I do have a business. Kind of. Like I said before, I'm basically in real estate."

"Right, I forgot you said that. What exactly do you do?"

She hunched her shoulders, staring down at her almost-empty plate while picking at the crumbs on it. "I sort of, um, own a building."

"You own a building?" I probably gaped at her like a moron, but jeez, I'd never met anyone who owned anything that big. "What kind of building is it?"

She winced. "An apartment complex."

I gaped some more. A minute, maybe longer, ticked by while I tried to cobble together words, any words, in the hopes I wouldn't come off as a total idiot.

"That's amazing," I finally said. "Do you run the place or just own it?"

"Everyone and everything in the building is my responsibility." She shut her eyes for a moment, then sighed and looked at me. "When I was twenty-two, fresh out of college, my parents bought the building and gave it to me as a graduation present. They said I needed to grow up and take responsibility for something, so I could prove to them I'm a mature adult."

"How did that go?"

"The building was empty, had been for a few months. My first job was to get the place in shape for tenants—the high-end kind, not the riffraff—and then attract those tenants."

"Sounds like a big project." I watched her face, though she'd turned it away from me to gaze toward the window above the sink. "You seem really smart, so I'm guessing you pulled it off."

Her gaze swerved to me, her eyes wide. "You assume I did a good job? That's not how anybody else felt. My parents were sure I'd screw up. They didn't say it outright, but I figured they must feel that way. I screw up all the time."

"Did you mess up with your building?"

She hugged herself, scratching her arms. "It wasn't easy. I hired contractors and decorators to fix up the place, always mindful of the fact I had to pay back the loans my parents had helped me get. Once the building was ready for occupancy, I came up with a marketing campaign to attract tenants. The complex was at full occupancy within two weeks after it opened."

"Your folks must've been proud."

She laughed, though it didn't sound cheerful. "My mom said she was glad I hadn't gone bankrupt yet, but that it would take several years to know whether I'd made the business successful. It's been years, and still she acts like it's a work-in-progress. Like I'm a work-in-progress."

"They never say they're proud of you, do they?"

"My dad does."

I studied her for a moment, trying to figure out why her Mom treated her like she was a mess. Mara was so sweet, not to mention funny and sexy and awesome at business stuff. I wished I had her skills at that. "I don't get it. You made your building a success, so why does your mom think you're a screw-up?"

"For all the reasons I told you earlier."

"Because you can't speak Japanese." I leaned over the gap between our stools, grasped her hands, and looked her square in the eye. "That's bullshit, Mara. I've known you for a day and a half, and already I can tell you're an incredible woman."

"It's more than not speaking Japanese." She glanced down at our hands. "I drove my husband away."

That sounded like bullshit too, especially considering what she'd told me earlier about her ex complaining she got too excited about sex. What kind of asshole was that guy? Mara was hot. More than that, she was a good person. She deserved praise, not insults from sniveling turds.

"I lied to you," she said, still staring down at our hands. "Well, maybe not outright lied. I let you believe I can't afford to buy another plane ticket to go home. The truth is, I don't want to go home because I'll get another lecture about how I screwed up yet again. Accidentally booking a vacation at a nudist resort? I'll never hear the end of it."

"Then stay." I lifted one hand away from hers to cup her cheek. "Hang out here with the crazy naturists. Chill out, enjoy the sunshine, go on nature hikes, whatever. I guarantee you nobody here will ridicule you or say you're not good enough. The guests are good people, like a big family, and they'll make you feel welcome."

And I'd never met anyone who needed a vacation more than Mara Severins.

She chewed on her lip, finally looking at me again. "I'd love to stay here. Is forever too long to book a room for?"

"I think we can arrange that."

"Thank you, Ollie." She gave me a tentative smile. "You're the nicest man I've ever met."

"Just doing my job." Now who was full of shit? I didn't say all that stuff to Mara because it was my job. I liked her, that's why I said it. "You can call me Oliver if you want. I usually don't like it when people use my whole name, but I love the way you say it. Especially when we're having sex."

Her cheeks dimpled with the cutest smile. "Okay, Oliver. I like your name, by the way. It's sexy."

My manly parts were about to get active again, so I had to make up a dumb excuse to get away from her for a few minutes. Just until I cooled down. Her smile, and her statement that my name was sexy, had way too much of an effect on me.

"Excuse me for a minute," I said, sliding off my stool. "Gotta hit the head."

The best I could hope for was that some time alone would let me figure out how to survive being around Mara, indefinitely, without walking around with a giant hard-on twenty-four seven.

Was that a pig flying past the window?

I returned to the kitchen a few minutes later, with my problem mostly under control, and found Mara standing at the sink. She was gazing out the window. I came up beside her to see what had caught her attention.

The guests were playing miniten.

Mara glanced at me, then returned her attention to the game going on outside. "What are they doing? I saw people playing that game yesterday, but I don't know what it is. Looks kind of like tennis or badminton, but they have bizarre boxes on their hands."

"It's called miniten. Naturists invented the game. Miniten is short for mini tennis." I pointed with my finger while I explained, "See, most naturist retreats don't have a lot of room for tennis courts, so they had to adjust the game to suit the space they had. Those wedge-shaped boxes are called thugs. Each player has a thug on one hand, which they use like a racket. Miniten is popular because it's more relaxed than tennis, so there's no need for jock straps or sports bras."

Mara leaned sideways toward me to whisper, "I think some of those people could use a little…support."

I chuckled. "Yeah, you're right. I'm sure the balls they're hitting aren't the only ones flying around out there."

"Not to mention the tits."

Her statement shocked me for about two seconds, then I grinned. "Mara, I love your sense of humor."

"Thanks." She grinned too. "You make me feel so comfortable that I can say all the things I would never say at home."

I slung an arm around her shoulders, tugging her close. "I'm sorry you feel that way at home. But here, you can be whoever you want to be."

The house phone rang.

Reluctantly, I gave up having Mara tucked under my arm and answered the phone. "What's up?"

"You're late," Ruth Norris said. "Yoga time was ten minutes ago, and the natives are getting restless. We might have an uprising if you don't get out there and lead them to serenity. And you know how Sylvester loves your yoga sessions."

Yeah, a seventy-two-year-old naturist did yoga. Why not? Sylvester was in better shape than he looked like he was. Having some flab didn't mean he had no strength or agility.

Just watching Sly play miniten proved that point.

"If they're dying for yoga," I said, "why is the miniten net still up? We need the space, unless everybody wants indoor yoga this time."

My outdoor yoga classes had become popular. I'd done the first one last summer when I was a guest, just for fun, but once I became assistant manager everybody begged me to make yoga a regular thing here.

"We'll take care of the net," Ruth said, "and you get yourself out here, cutie-pie."

"Be right out." I hung up the phone and faced Mara. "Sorry, I forgot about a yoga class I'm supposed to teach. Gotta go."

"I'll be fine, don't worry."

"Yeah, I know you will." I started for the door but stopped. "Do you want to come out with me? You can watch the class, and after, we can go for a walk down the nature trails."

"I'd like that."

"Cool." I swung the door open, waving for her to exit. "Beautiful, sexy ladies first."

She walked out, flashing me another shy smile.

And damn, my dick loved that.

Chapter Eleven

Mara

I felt hot all over, like I was in a sauna with the steam going full blast and those hot coals sizzling away. The coals were
inside me, though. Red-hot, smoldering lumps of lust. It was
completely Ollie's fault that I couldn't cool down. When he taught
a nude yoga class, he should've handed out flyers with a big warning written on them in bright-red letters: "ALERT: You will get
hot and bothered watching your gorgeous instructor move his sexy
body into all those poses."

Never had I thought of yoga as salacious. Today, I did.

And I wasn't even paying attention to the other attractive young
men in attendance. No one else interested me, only Ollie.

I might've thought that was because we'd had sex a little while
ago, but something told me it was more than that. I felt comfortable with him, even when he was naked. Talking to him, I didn't
feel like a loser who had let her family down over and over and over,
or like the girl who couldn't keep a husband. Honestly, I hadn't
wanted to keep Nico. Not at the end.

My phone chimed, indicating a new text.

When I checked it, I groaned. Nico. Did my ex-husband have
psychic powers? Or had he bugged my phone so he could tap into
the camera and spy on me? Neither, I knew, but he sure did have
perfect timing.

Perfect for ruining my day. Yeah, he'd always been great at that. The text said, "Can we talk?"

I started to type a response but stopped. Why was I indulging him? He wanted to make me feel like shit, but I did not have to let him. So I deleted his text and slipped the phone back into the little purse-like bag for it that hung from a belt loop on my pants. The hem of my shirt hid it, not that I was worried somebody might steal my phone. Nobody here seemed like the type. Ollie had been right when he said everybody here acted like one big family.

Ollie was currently in standing splits pose, with one foot on the ground and the other leg raised almost vertical. Both his hands lay flat on the ground, his arms were bent, and his head hung upside down. Before we came outside, he'd taken his glasses off and asked me to keep them in my shirt pocket. Since I sat on a chaise facing sideways to him, he could see me if he glanced this way.

He did, and he smiled and winked.

I smiled and waved.

"Okay," Ollie said to his class, "let's kick this up a notch and move into a headstand. Slowly straighten your arms. Then we're going to push up with the foot that's on the ground and ease into the headstand."

"Jeez, Ollie," one young man said, "that's way too advanced for me."

"Then skip it. Nobody will think you're a wuss if you don't do this one."

Ollie eased into the headstand pose with grace and agility, having no trouble achieving it.

Another young man tried to do the headstand but tumbled out of it, muttering a curse.

"You okay?" Ollie asked.

The guy sat up and gave Ollie the thumbs-up sign. "Totally good, man."

Ollie's ability to do a headstand impressed me, but the part that got me really hot for him came a little later when they all got into downward dog pose. The basic version of it wasn't super sexy. The pose involved planting the hands and feet flat on the ground and straightening the arms and legs to get into a kind of inverted V position. I could do that pose. It was pretty basic, not an advanced move.

But when Ollie raised one leg straight up, I got a great view of his manly parts. Oh wow, the sight of his dick and his balls made me flash back to earlier, in my room, when we'd gotten hot and heavy—and I'd come like a supernova. God, he was fantastic in bed.

What would it be like to have sex with him outdoors?

I froze, stunned by own thought. Holy shit. I wanted to have sex outdoors.

But only with Oliver Jackson.

No, I couldn't do that. It wasn't proper. And what if someone caught us? What if my family found out I'd not only done the deed with a virtual stranger, but I'd done it outdoors?

I let my head fall back against the chair and expelled a long sigh. Why did I still care what my parents thought? I'd always done what they wanted, what they expected, and it had gotten me exactly nowhere. Sure, I'd done okay with the apartment complex. But I was divorced. Another failure.

My phone rang.

The noise made me jump, and I fumbled to get my phone out of its little case. I twisted around, trying to dig the phone out, but my fingers slipped. I lost my balance, since I'd apparently been leaning too far over, and flopped onto the ground with a yelp.

Crunch.

I'd landed on my stomach. My phone stopped ringing just as my chest collided with the ground—and crushed Ollie's glasses in my pocket.

Pushing up onto my knees, I winced as I pulled his glasses out. The lenses were broken.

"Are you all right?" Ollie asked, rushing over to kneel beside me.

"Yeah, I'm fine," I said, kind of whining when I spoke the words. I squeezed my eyes shut and offered him his glasses. "I'll pay for replacing them. It's my fault, I'm sorry."

He took the glasses. "It's okay, Mara. I have a backup pair."

"I'm such a klutz. A walking disaster."

"Come on, it's not like you shoved that iceberg into the Titanic." He laid a palm on my cheek, his thumb brushing over my skin. "Relax. Everybody has accidents."

I moaned miserably.

"Open your eyes," he said. "It's okay. Look at me, Mara."

Though I didn't want to, I looked at him.

He smiled and kissed me. It was soft and brief, but the feel of his lips made my tummy flutter.

"See?" he said, waving his other hand to indicate our surroundings. "You didn't destroy the world. I'd call that a win."

I couldn't help smiling. How did he know exactly what to do and say to make me feel better?

Ollie set his broken glasses on the chaise and helped me up. "I'll get my backup glasses and then we can take that hike. Would you be more comfortable if I got dressed?"

"No, that's okay. I'm getting used to being around naked people."

He kissed me again, then grabbed his glasses and headed for the little house.

I slumped onto my chaise, frowning down at the ground.

My phone rang again.

This time, I carefully pulled it out of its case. The screen told me who was calling—Nico. Oh great, that's exactly who I wanted to talk to right now. I didn't want to talk to him ever again, but I knew he wouldn't give up until I did.

So I answered. "What do you want, Nico?"

"I miss you, Mar-Mar. When are you coming home?"

"When I feel like it. And my name is Mara, not Mar-Mar. You know I hate that nickname."

"But you used to love it when I called Mar-Mar while we were making love."

I huffed. "No, I hated it then too. You ignored me when I told you so."

"We were good together. Let's not throw that away."

Good together? Was he on drugs? And he had filed for divorce, so he had no right to imply I'd thrown our relationship away. He did that all on his own. I knew my ditsy behavior had pushed him away, but he hadn't even tried to work things out. Even when I'd learned about his infidelity, I tried to work it out with him. What an idiot. I was better off without him.

"You and I are divorced," I told him. "That's the definition of 'over.' Stop calling and texting me, Nico, or I'll get a restraining order."

I hung up on him. And I had no idea if I could get a restraining order because my ex-husband was annoying the hell out of me. I hoped the threat would convince him to go away.

A throat-clearing behind me made me jump and squeak.

"Sorry," Ollie said, coming around in front of me. He wore his backup glasses, which looked just like his wrecked ones. "Didn't mean to scare you, but I kind of thought you hadn't noticed me there. Guess I could've done something more smooth to let you know."

"It's fine." I got up. "Let's go for that hike."

He screwed up his mouth and hummed like he was trying to decide whether to tell me something.

"What is it?" I asked, sounding a touch more…touchy than I'd intended.

"I sort of accidentally overheard the last part of that phone call. Your end of it, anyway."

"Oh." My shoulders slumped. "I suppose you figured out I was talking to my ex-husband."

"Yeah." He took my hand. "Let's talk while we walk."

I let him lead me down the nature trail into the woods. Birds twittered and sang. The breeze ruffled the trees. Above us, the sunlight filtered down to the ground, muted by the foliage, and its warmth seemed muted too. The heat I'd experienced while watching Ollie do yoga had given way to a slight chill.

Ollie led me down the path until we reached a spot where a downed tree lay alongside the trail. He motioned for me to sit on it.

I settled my bottom onto the tree. It was surprisingly comfortable to use as a bench.

He sat right next to me and clasped my hand again. "You don't have to tell me anything."

"But I want to. Not sure why, but I feel like I should tell you."

"We hardly know each other. You don't owe me anything." He clasped my other hand too. "But I'm here if you need to talk."

"It's my ex. Our divorce was finalized six months ago, and I haven't heard from him since. Until the day I arrived here, and he texted me to say he wants me back." I turned my face toward Ollie. "Nico called me today to say he misses me and wants to give it another try."

"What do you want?"

"Not him." I moaned again, even more miserably this time. "He cheated on me. I mean, he used to tell me all the time how I don't behave like a proper lady, then he goes and screws the checkout girl at the grocery store." I gritted my teeth. "At the store."

"He sounds like a real prick." Ollie gave my hands a little squeeze. "And he's obviously a moron. He had an incredible woman like you, and he went and fucked some checkout girl? If I ever meet him, I'll punch his lights out."

Maybe his anger should have shocked me, possibly even disgusted me, but it didn't. I got a funny warmth in my chest when he threatened to deck my ex. Nobody had ever taken my side when they found out Nico had cheated, and definitely not when we got divorced.

"You're so sweet, Ollie," I said. "But how can you be sure he's the idiot? Maybe I messed things up."

"No way. I get that you've got this complex about thinking you're a mess and screw everything up, but I don't see that at all. You're amazing."

"I feel so good when I'm with you. The sex was incredible, and I really want to do that again, but maybe we should spend some time getting to know each other first." I hunched my shoulders, afraid he might say no to the next part. "Like maybe a week with no sex?"

"Sure. Let's do that."

Relief sagged my shoulders. "I'm so glad you said yes."

He got up and held out his hand. "Time for me to show you more of my world."

I took his hand and let him lead me away.

Chapter Twelve

Mara was so much fun to be with, which would've surprised me if we hadn't screwed each other's brains out earlier. She put on an uptight front most of the time, but when given the chance and some encouragement, she could cut loose like nobody's business. When we got to the hot spring, I made a joke about jumping in with our clothes on and how she was scared of nudity. She knew I was kidding.

"Is that a challenge?" she asked teasingly. "Because I'm not freaking out anymore, in case you haven't noticed."

"Oh, I noticed. But I'll bet you a free massage that you won't get in the hot spring even if you keep your clothes on."

"You're on."

She kicked her sandals off and took a running leap at the hot spring, splashing down with so much energy that the water sprayed up around her and splattered me where I stood six feet from the pool. She surfaced a couple seconds later, grinning and laughing.

I jumped in too, with my clothes on.

We got into a splash fight, both of us laughing so hard we had to stop to catch our breath. She was so fucking amazing. Anyone who met her for the first time would never realize she had so much joy inside her, just waiting to come out and play. I got to see it. She trusted me enough to show me the real Mara, the one she'd been afraid to show to anyone. I loved that. I liked her, a lot.

And I'd known her for less than two days.

Once I managed to drag Mara out of the hot spring, we headed down some of my favorite trails where we could see the birds and the wildlife, places I hadn't shown her yesterday. She got so excited when a deer trotted past us. The girl had never seen one in person. Never.

"How is that possible?" I asked.

We sat in a small clearing filled with wildflowers, their blossoms in full bloom—just like Mara, who had spread her petals today.

"I lived in the city, in Philadelphia, and never drove anywhere," she said, picking a small flower and studying it. "The few vacations I took were at big resorts. I've seen the beach in Tahiti, but not the woods in America."

"You never, ever left the city. Not even for a day."

"Well, I've driven through rural areas. But I never got out to do more than use the bathroom at a rest stop."

"Uh-huh." I was still struggling to wrap my head around that. Never seeing the woods? Or a freaking deer? "Guess I can't imagine living that way, but everybody's different. The city is your home. I found out a rural naturist retreat is where I belong."

She ran her fingers over the petals on the flower she'd picked, still focused on it. "Not sure the city is my home. It's all I know, but…" She dropped the flower and looked at me. "Being here, with you, I'm starting to wonder if I've missed out on what really matters." She sucked in a deep breath, her eyes fluttering shut. "I love the way it smells here, so fresh and clean and sweet. And the grass feels soft on my toes. It's wonderful."

I loved watching her face while she enjoyed all of those things and so much more. She seemed younger, and definitely freer.

We stayed in that clearing for a while, kissing and talking and kissing some more. I could've kissed Mara all day. Her lips were soft, and she tasted better than any woman I'd ever kissed before. Maybe I was kind of smitten. Maybe she didn't actually taste different from other girls. I didn't care, because I'd never felt this good in my life.

We went to the lake again too. Mara waded out into the water up to her knees, giggling when she realized how cold this water was compared to the hot spring. She waved for me to join her, so of course I did. At first, we held hands and splashed our feet in the water. Then, she slipped her arms around me, and I put mine around her, and we just stood there like that for a while. Eventually, we started kissing. Mara didn't seem to care anymore if someone stumbled onto us doing whatever the heck we wanted. Well, no tourists other than the resort guests could come here, since the lake lay on private land owned by Eve and Val.

While I gazed down at Mara, at her gorgeous green eyes and the cute smile on her lips, I found myself thinking about Eve and Val. They had seemed like complete opposites, and I supposed they still were, but their relationship worked despite that—or maybe because of it. They were business partners and partners in life. Spending every day with Eve and Val, seeing how their partnership encompassed every aspect of their lives and how they made each other stronger and better, it made me want that too. I wanted to find the right girl and share a life with her. I didn't know if Mara could be that woman, but I intended to find out.

A week of getting to know her. Yeah, that sounded perfect.

Except that I still had this little problem of getting turned on every time she smiled. When she'd jumped into the hot spring and emerged completely soaked, her shirt had gone almost transparent, and I could see her nipples. Oh yeah, hard-on alert.

I was an adult. I could handle this.

Probably.

We were relaxing on the beach, watching the gentle waves lap on the shore, when Mara asked me a question.

"Do you get along with your family?" she asked.

"Sure. My parents are good people, and they've always supported me in whatever I wanted to do." I winced, realizing how that might sound to Mara. "Not that I'm bragging or something. I'm sorry your family isn't like that."

"It's okay. You don't need to apologize for having good parents." She smiled shyly. "They certainly raised an amazing son."

Her compliment made me feel a little weird, or maybe I was embarrassed. Hard to say for sure. But I knew without any doubts that I liked the way she made me feel.

"My family isn't as bad as you think," she said. "My mom is always there for me when I need her. When I was growing up, anytime I got sick she would make me soup or get ice cream for me, and she'd sit by my bed reading stories to me. She and my dad would take turns doing that."

"Then what's up with the 'you have to be proper' garbage?"

She shrugged. "My mom and grandma worry about stuff like

that. We have to fit into the level of society we're in, where people care about appearances more than anything else."

"No offense, but that's dumb."

"Yeah, I know. But I'm stuck in that world, so I have to try to be what people expect. A proper lady."

I couldn't imagine how stressful that must've been. Constantly worrying about how other people viewed me and whether I'd lived up to their expectations sounded like the definition of hell.

No wonder Mara had been so uptight.

"Do you have any brothers or sisters?" she asked. "I don't. Only child here. But I always wished I had a brother or sister."

"I've got one sister, Bailey. She's fourteen and likes to call me Liver."

Mara laughed. "Liver?"

"Yeah, it's short for Oliver." I shook my head but felt my mouth tightening into a closed-mouth smile. "She's a brat, but I love her anyway. You have to cut teenagers some slack, because their brains haven't grown any common sense yet."

"When I was a teenager, I never did anything I wasn't supposed to do. I was the shy girl nobody wanted to be friends with."

"I would've been your friend. As the nerd with glasses who loved computers, I didn't fit in either."

"But now you do." She glanced around, her lips curving into a soft smile. "You found where you belong, didn't you? I can tell how much you love this place."

"I do love it. But it's more than the trees and the hot spring. I love the people too."

She aimed her smile at me. "I can see why. They're really nice people."

After our visit to the lake, we headed back to the main resort area. Nobody was using the lawn where the miniten net had been set up earlier, but I knew why. It was time for the weekly bingo competition. Everyone would be in the dining hall for that.

Mara and I joined the game. She won twice, earning two snack-size bags of candy. Afterward, we relaxed on the lawn watching one of the guests lead an impromptu tai chi session—nude tai chi, of course. Mara seemed fascinated by the slow, precise movements.

She tore open one of her candy packets and dropped one of the chocolate-covered peanuts onto her tongue. Sealing her lips, she smiled faintly while she let the chocolate melt in her mouth and hummed with satisfaction. Then she chewed the peanut, slowly, almost sensually.

I wanted to drag her down onto the grass, strip her naked, and give her a different reason to hum like that.

"Want one?" she asked, holding a peanut to my lips. "They're so yummy."

She said that like a chocolate-covered peanut was the most succulent, delicious thing on earth, like she wanted to devour the entire bag while writhing on the ground in ecstasy.

Okay, maybe that was my fantasy, not what she actually wanted to do. Licking melted chocolate off her body... Yeah, I wanted that.

"Are you allergic?" she asked. "To peanuts, I mean."

"No, not allergic." I closed my mouth around the candy and her fingers, lapping up every molecule of chocolate before I chewed and swallowed the peanut. "Mm, you're right. That's really good."

But it didn't taste as good as Mara.

We had sex this morning, but I wanted her. Right now.

I'd told her we should get to know each other better before we got naked again, so I had to keep to my own word. For the rest of the day, we talked and hung out with the other guests and fed each other peanuts until both of the bags she'd won were empty.

At the end of the evening, I kissed her cheek to say good night at the door to her room.

Did I sleep? Sort of. But I dreamed about Mara—that smile, that body, the way she felt wrapped around me.

A week without feeling that again. I might just go insane.

Chapter Thirteen

I'd learned a lot about Ollie in one day, but the next three days taught me even more about him. Not only did he teach yoga, but he also entertained the guests with music, singing and playing the guitar like he had for me on that first day. On the second evening of my stay here, everyone gathered around the fire pit behind the guest house to toast marshmallows and have a good time.

I'd never seen a fire pit like that one, but it was a nice way to have a small bonfire without worrying about how to contain it. A circular brick enclosure surrounded the pit itself, which looked like a large metal bowl. A mesh screen formed a dome over the fire, but Ollie took that off so everyone could toast their marshmallows.

The newest guests, who'd shown up the day after I'd come here, had brought their children with them. Those boys put on a hilarious play about a dragon and dueling knights, with the bonfire as their backdrop.

After that, Ollie took center stage.

Well, he took center lawn. Ollie sat on the grass, cross-legged, and played his guitar so beautifully that he ought to have been a musician, not a computer systems engineer. But when he started to sing, he enthralled me. I'd heard him sing before, but his talent still amazed me. His voice wasn't polished like he'd taken years of lessons. He sang in a natural voice that suited the low-key pop songs he'd chosen to perform. I loved listening to him. His voice made me feel warm in a very different way from the warmth he gave me the rest of the time. This wasn't lust. His singing gave me a good feeling deep inside, one that morphed into a glow in my chest.

After every song, the crowd clapped and whistled. A few people whooped. I was one of them. God, Ollie was incredible. I wanted to see him perform his musical act in the nude, but he still insisted on wearing clothes for my sake.

Though I had gotten used to the nudists, once in a while they surprised me.

On the afternoon of the third day, Ollie had to do some assistant manager work, so I headed down the nature trail on my own. Ollie and I had taken several walks together, and I knew the way. I'd asked him to meet me at the hot spring when he got done with his work, but on the way there, I decided to detour down one of the side trails where he'd shown me a meadow full of wildflowers that attracted lots of butterflies.

I loved that meadow. On this day, the sky was pure blue, and the sun beamed down on me to toast my skin. I spent some time there, enjoying nature, but I didn't keep track of the time. What did it matter? I'd wanted to escape from my structured life in the city, so here I was ignoring the clock and reveling in the beauty of nature.

After a blessedly indeterminate length of time, I returned to the main path and followed it until I reached the junction with the hot spring trail. I turned down that path, but only got a little ways before it happened.

I had just rounded a curve in the trail and when I saw a gray-haired man standing alongside the trail, maybe twenty feet away. He faced sideways to me and had his head down, focused on his hand that cupped his penis.

And he was urinating. Right there. In full view of anyone who walked down the trail.

In full view of me.

"Oh!" I said, slapping a hand over my eyes. Realizing how dumb that was—I'd been around nudists all day every day for the past several days—I lowered my hand and focused on his face.

The man smiled and shrugged. "Sorry. I didn't think anybody would be on this trail. Everybody's playing badminton or watching the games. Everyone except you."

Since this man was clearly in his seventies, maybe even eighties, I decided he wasn't a pervert. He just needed to pee.

I was very proud of myself for not screaming or fainting.

"Don't worry about it," I told the man. "Sometimes you can't fight the call of nature."

My new friend ambled back to the trail and approached me. He offered me his hand to shake—the hand he hadn't used to hold his dick while he relieved himself. "I'm Carl Weatherman. And no, I never worked as an actual weatherman."

He smiled when he said that.

I shook his hand. "Mara Severins. You just got here this morning, right?"

"Yeah, me and my wife got here today."

That meant he probably hadn't heard about me, the idiot who screamed and fainted when she got her first glimpse of nudists. He must've wondered why I wore clothes, but he didn't say anything about that.

Carl wanted to go back to the guest house, so I walked back to the junction with the main trail with him to keep him company. We chatted about how beautiful it was here and how all the other nudists were so nice. He finally asked the obvious question when we stopped at the trail junction.

"It's none of my business," he said, "but I'm wondering why you wear clothes. This is a naturist resort, after all."

"Yeah, I wondered when you'd ask me that." I bit my lip while I considered how best to answer. Well, he'd probably hear about my freak-out sooner or later. Might as well get it out there now. "My travel agent made a mistake and thought naturist meant birdwatching and observing wildlife. So when I got here, I wasn't prepared for all the nudists. I shrieked and passed out. I've gotten used to all the naked people, but I still don't feel comfortable going au naturel."

"This is a clothes-optional resort, so keeping your duds on is acceptable. Maybe one day you'll try it our way." He patted my arm. "Never know, kid, you might enjoy it."

Carl and I said goodbye, and I went back down the trail to the hot spring. Ollie wasn't here yet, so I kicked off my sandals and sat down on the rocky ledge that surrounded the pool, letting my feet dangle in the water. I swung my legs, splashing my feet in the blue water, loving the silky warmth of the hot spring. It felt so nice, but I wanted to experience it all around me like I had the first time, when Ollie brought me here. I'd dived into the spring with my clothes on, but today, I wanted to feel the steamy water on my skin.

I couldn't. I mean, I was the girl who went wacko when I saw naked people eating lunch in a cafeteria.

But things had changed since then. I had changed. Ollie had shown me how to relax and take pleasure in the simple things without worrying about whether other people thought I was an idiot. He'd helped me loosen up in record time, but I knew I still had a ways to go before I'd shed that part of me for good. Eventually, I'd have to go home—to my family and to the disapproval of those high-society idiots who turned their noses up at my sometimes ditsy behavior. Would this new version of me, the one I really liked, disappear when I left the resort?

God, I hoped not. But just in case, I wanted to revel in my newfound freedom as much as possible before I had to leave this magical place.

I got up, glancing around to make sure nobody was around, then I stripped off my clothes. A breeze tickled my skin, and my nipples went rigid from the cool kiss of the air. I walked to the very edge of the rock ledge that encompassed the spring, my toes curled over its rim, and gazed down at the beautiful blue water and the steam wafting up from it.

Then I dived in, cannonball style.

Water plumed up around me.

I sank beneath the surface, bobbing up out of it. Laughter bubbled out of me, and I dived under the surface again, springing up out of the water, laughing even more, squealing when a wavelet lapped against my face. I couldn't remember the last time I had this much fun. Well, fun that didn't involve Ollie naked on top of me.

And I had never felt this free, except with him.

Paddling around the pool, I flipped over to do the backstroke and then moved into the center of the spring to float on my back. The sun shined down through an opening in the trees, casting its glow on the water around me and on my face. I shut my eyes while I swirled my fingers in the water, letting the rest of the world drift away until nothing remained except the sound of the breeze rustling the trees and the birds twittering.

"Mara?"

Ollie's voice pulled me out of my meditation. He stood near the edge of the spring, looking down at me with a confused expression.

I swam to him, folding my arms on the ledge. "There you are. I thought you'd forgotten about me."

"That won't ever happen." He knelt to get closer to me. "You're swimming. Naked. In the outdoors."

"Mm-hm. It feels wonderful." I splashed my hand in the water, some of the spray landing on his face. "Have you ever made love in the hot spring?"

He swallowed hard enough I could see it, and his voice dropped to a husky register. "No, I've never done that. Everybody knows Eve and Val did that once. Probably more than once, but nobody's caught them since that first time. I wouldn't want to be a copycat."

"But I want you, Ollie. Want you so bad."

"I, uh…" He blinked several times and shook his head, like he was trying to clear his thoughts. "I want you too, Mara, but there's been a complication."

"What's wrong?"

"Your parents are here."

Everything inside me froze, mutating into solid ice. My parents? Here? At a nudist resort? *Oh shit, shit, shit, shit, shit.*

I scrambled out of the hot spring, pushing Ollie over in the process, and struggled to get my clothes on. Taking them off had been so easy, but now I couldn't seem to get them back on the right way. Words tumbled out of me while I fought with my clothes.

"They can't see me like this, they can't. Naked? In public? Oh God, they'll have me committed or arrested or—"

"Stop." Ollie grasped my shoulders, turning me toward him. "Take a deep breath and exhale out all that anxiety and panic. Come on, Mara, you can do it."

I drew in one shaky breath, letting it out slowly.

"Again," Ollie said, his voice so calm and soothing that I believed I could shake off the panic as long as he stayed with me.

I pulled in a less shaky breath, blew it out, and inhaled a good, deep lungful of clean air. No quivering breath this time when I exhaled. I released the air in my lungs little by little, feeling the anxiety melt away.

Ollie smiled tenderly and brushed hair away from my eyes. "There. See? You did it."

"Yeah, thanks to you." I moaned pitifully. "But my parents…"

He kissed me, hard and quick. "You are an adult, Mara. You don't need anyone's permission or approval. If your parents are dicks about it when they realize this is a naturist resort, that's their problem."

Easy to say… Not so easy to believe.

Dammit, girl, you can do this.

I squared my shoulders, lifted my chin, and nodded once with conviction. "Yes, I can do this. Once I get my clothes on the right way."

Ollie grinned. "I can help you with that."

He did help me, and I loved feeling his hands on my body again, even it was purely to get my clothes on right. He kissed me again, slower and hotter, giving me the boost I needed to face my judgment day.

Ollie took my hand, leading me back toward the guest house—and my parents.

Chapter Fourteen

Ollie

Nothing had prepared me for walking in on Mara swimming in the hot spring in the nude. Sure, I'd seen her naked before. Once. We'd done the deed, but somehow, seeing her frolicking in the hot spring without a stitch of clothing on had hit me harder than the first time I'd seen her naked. Surrounded by the blue waters, she looked so peaceful and so damn sexy.

But her tranquility evaporated when I told Mara her parents were here. Still, she was handling the news better than I'd expected.

The closer we got to the main resort area, the more we could hear the badminton game unfolding out on the lawn. Some of the younger guests, who were in their twenties like me, had wanted to make badminton a contact sport. The guys kept bumping chests and whooping, and the girls hopped up and down while giggling.

I told them to please calm down, but I guessed as soon as I'd left the vicinity, they'd gone wild again. Their screams and whoops echoed through the open area beyond the last bit of trees at the end of the nature trail.

Mara stopped us within sight of the trailhead. She chewed on her lip, staring at the vague shapes of human beings we could see through the trees.

"You okay?" I asked. "It's cool to take a minute before we go out there."

She sucked in a breath, rolled her shoulders back, and gave me a tight smile. "It's okay. I can do this. About time I stood up to my mom, anyway."

"I know you can do it. You're one amazing woman, Mara. Don't forget that."

"Thank you, Oliver."

Every time she called me Oliver, I wanted to tear her clothes off and make her scream my name. Since I couldn't do that right now, I settled for kissing her.

More whoops and shrieks erupted beyond the trees.

I led Mara out of the woods.

Some guy shouted, "Go for it, Tad! All the way!"

Just as Mara and I reached the edge of the lawn, maybe fifteen feet from the edge of the makeshift badminton court, it happened.

"Go for it for real, dude!" someone hollered.

Everything seemed to unfold in slow motion. I saw the shuttlecock, that comet-shaped ball, fly through the air. And I saw a muscular guy with buzz-cut hair leap high off the ground, his racket outstretched, determined to whack that shuttlecock. He missed and kept sailing, sailing, sailing through the air…

The guy slammed into Mara.

My hand was torn from hers. I tripped and hit the ground rolling.

And Mara screamed.

I came to a stop facedown on the dirt and lifted my head to see what had happened to Mara.

She lay on her back on the ground.

The shuttlecock guy had landed smack on top of Mara, but in the opposite direction. His face was between her thighs, and his dick was crushed to her face.

Mara screamed again, flailing her arms in an attempt to shove the guy off her.

I scrambled to my feet and rushed to her. "Get off her, you dickwad."

The guy seemed stunned, and he didn't move.

So I thrust my hands under him and pushed the shuttlecock ass off Mara. He ended up on his back beside her, laughing so hard his eyes watered.

"Are you okay?" I asked Mara, kneeling beside her. "Did that jerk hurt you?"

She shook her head, but her lips were trembling.

I picked her up and cradled her to me, kissing the top of her head.

And I glared at the dickwad.

He was still laughing.

"Shut up," I snarled at him. "Get your shit and get the fuck out of here. You're banned from Au Naturel Naturist Resort for life."

The idiot stopped laughing. "What? You can't do that, man, it was an accident."

"I told you to calm things down and behave like grown-ups. You and your pals think it's funny to act like lunatics, but we do not condone that kind of behavior here. Your broke all the rules." I hugged Mara tighter. "Get out of here. Right now."

The guy stared at me for a moment, then got up and slunk back to the guest house. His friends followed him.

Every single one of the remaining guests started clapping and cheering.

"Way to go, Ollie!" someone shouted.

Ruth Norris gave me an appreciative nod.

Mara, snug in my arms, was gazing up at me like I'd just defeated Godzilla single-handed. "Thank you, Oliver. You're my hero."

I opened my mouth but couldn't think of a damn thing to say.

Two people, a man and a woman, stood separate from the crowd, doing their damnedest not to look at all the naked guests. The woman lifted her chin and marched straight up to me and Mara. The man trailed after her. He had auburn hair and green eyes like Mara, and the woman had Mara's golden skin coloring and almond-shaped eyes. I'd met these people earlier, so I knew who they were—Peter Severins and Sheryl Kanda Severins.

They were Mara's parents. If I hadn't met them already, I would've guessed who they were based on their clothes. Mrs. Severins wore a navy pantsuit that I figured was designer, not that I knew squat about women's clothing, and her husband wore a gray suit and tie.

It was eighty degrees today.

Mrs. Severins puckered her lips, narrowing her gaze on me. "What have you done to our daughter?"

"Uh, I was just helping her—"

"She's filthy. And wet."

Yeah, Mara's dip in the hot spring had gotten her clothes wet when she put them back on, and her hair was still drenched. Since she'd gotten knocked down by that asshat, she now had dirt on her backside.

Mara wriggled in my arms like she was trying to get free.

I set her down.

She straightened her clothes and patted her hair, but apparently realized there was no hope of fixing that without at least a hairbrush.

"Ollie didn't do anything," she told her mother. "That jerk rammed into me, and Ollie dealt with the situation. That's all."

Mrs. Severins squinted at Mara. "Why are you wet? You're a mess. What's happened to my proper, ladylike daughter?"

"I…" Mara's expression fell, and her shoulders drooped. She spoke in a small voice when she said, "I was just having fun in the hot spring."

The word proper seemed to have been the trigger for Mara's change in attitude. I wanted to butt my nose into the conversation and tell Mrs. Severins to go jump in the hot spring headfirst, but it wasn't my place to do that. Mara needed to stand up to her parents on her own. I knew she *could* do it, but I had no idea if she *would* do it. She'd only just gotten used to being around people who played sports in the buff.

Mara slumped more and gnawed on her lip.

Sheryl Kanda Severins grasped her daughter's arm. "You're coming home with us this instant."

For a second, I thought Mara would leave with her parents.

But then she lifted her chin, straightened, and said, "No."

"No?" her mother repeated. "Mara Tamiko Severins—"

"I said no, Mom." Mara crossed her arms over her chest. "I'm staying here. With Ollie." She grabbed my hand, tugging me closer. "This is Oliver Jackson—my boyfriend."

This was news to me. Boyfriend? Sure, we'd had sex once and had been hanging out a lot since then. But she never told me I was her boyfriend. Not that I minded. Actually, I kind of loved the idea.

Mrs. Severins launched into a tirade that I couldn't understand, so I guessed it was in Japanese. Mara seemed equally confused, which confirmed my suspicion about the language her mom was speaking. That day when we'd gotten it on in her bedroom, Mara had moaned, "I can't even speak Japanese." That had been the cutest thing ever, until I realized she wasn't kidding. She felt like a failure because she'd never mastered that language.

Her mom knew Mara couldn't understand Japanese. So why was she barraging her daughter with words that made no sense to her?

"Stop it, Mom," Mara said. "I know you love to babble in Japanese when you're ticked at me, but you know I have no clue what you're saying."

Mrs. Severins shut up, though she still looked pissed.

Her husband cleared his throat. "Your mother is saying a lot of things that I won't translate. Honestly, Sheryl, I've never heard you curse so much. Mara is an adult, and we need to respect her decisions even when we don't agree with them."

Okay, I liked her dad a lot more now. Definitely more than her mom. But I supposed I shouldn't condemn Mrs. Severins right off the bat since she might've been in shock from finding out her daughter had been staying at a naturist resort.

Mr. Severins offered his hand to me. "I'm Peter Severins. It's nice to meet you, Oliver."

I shook his hand. "Nice to meet you too. You can call me Ollie."

"Thank you, Ollie. You can call me Peter." He glanced at his wife. "Don't be rude, Sheryl. Say hello to the man our daughter is dating."

Mrs. Severins shuffled closer to me and held out her hand, limply. "I am Sheryl Kanda Severins, Mr. Jackson."

"It's Ollie." I shook her hand, but she didn't clasp mine at all. "Mara's told me a lot about you guys. It's good to finally meet you."

"I'm sure."

Peter threw his wife a long-suffering look.

She rolled her eyes at him, then sighed, squared her shoulders, and aimed a polite smile at me. "Please call me Sheryl."

"Thanks."

I wasn't sure I wanted to call her Sheryl, considering her husband had goaded her into saying that.

Sylvester Norris walked up beside Mara's mom—completely nude, of course. All his manly bits were swinging free when he patted Sheryl's shoulder and announced, "It's a real pleasure to meet Mara's folks. She's such a sweet kid, and smart too. You must be proud of her."

Mara's mom turned her face toward Sly and forced a polite smile. But then she made the mistake of glancing down—a lot of newcomers who aren't already naturists make that mistake, it's like a reflex action or something—and her eyes bulged bigger than I'd ever seen anyone's eyes do. Her mouth gaped open, and a strangled gasp burst out of her. Her jaw flapped.

I swore she looked like a fish that got yanked out of the water. All she needed was a hook jammed into her cheek.

And I kind of felt sorry for her. She wasn't used to this sort of thing. I also finally understood where Mara got her fear of naked people. It wasn't proper, after all.

Sly, oblivious as usual, grabbed Sheryl's hand and shook it. "I'm Sylvester Norris. That's my wife, Ruth, over there." He nodded toward Ruth, who stood several feet away. "We're so dang pleased to welcome you to our home away from home, Au Naturel Naturist Resort."

Peter slung an arm around Sheryl and gently pulled her away from the naked man who was smiling at her. Sheryl's face had gone pale, and she looked like she was on the verge of fainting or throwing up. Jeez, it wasn't like a porcupine had jumped her. Having experienced that myself, I would've sympathized a lot more if Mara's mom had gotten chased by one of those buggers. But this was just an old fart who let everything hang out.

What was it with the Severins women and nudity?

"Calm down," Peter told his wife in a patient, soothing tone. "That nice man is naked, but he's not going to hurt you. He wants to say hi, that's all."

Another senior citizen nudist, Ralph Edwards, trotted up to Sheryl and offered her a bottle of whiskey. "One swig of this and you'll feel all better. Trust me."

Sheryl stared at Ralph's face for a few seconds, then swerved her attention down to his equipment. Her cheeks turned pink, which seemed like a step up from her pale-and-about-to-barf expression.

Finally, she took the bottle. "Thank you."

She sounded a little hoarse, but at least she was speaking a language everyone here understood.

"No problem," Ralph said, smiling. "A shot of Jack Daniels always makes me feel better."

Ralph moseyed off, disappearing into the crowd.

Sheryl took the cap off the bottle and downed one huge swig of whiskey. She ran the back of her hand across her mouth and gave her husband the bottle. "I would like to speak to my daughter in private, please."

"We can talk," Mara said, "but with Ollie there too."

Mara's mom pursed her lips, lifting her chin.

Peter waved the whiskey bottle in her face. "Maybe a few more gulps of this will loosen you up, Sher."

His wife flashed him a frown, then smiled politely at me. "Of course, Ollie. You may join us, if that's what Mara wants."

"It is," Mara said. "Thank you, Mom."

Sheryl tugged her suit jacket down and smoothed the lapels. "Where may we speak in private?"

"In the caretaker's house." Yeah, I'd just made up that name for the place, since I figured Mara's parents wouldn't understand if I called it Eve and Val's house. "Follow me."

Mara clinched my hand tighter as we led her parents away from the congregation of nudists.

Chapter Fifteen

Mara

Ollie and I sat on the stools at the kitchen island while my parents stood on the other side. My mom had refused to sit even when Ollie invited her to take the other stool. After that, Ollie had suggested we go into the living room, since it had plenty of comfy places to sit.

My mother said no. Curtly.

Dad threw her a chastising look, but she ignored it.

So here we were, Ollie and I on this side of the island and my parents on the other side. Dad leaned back against the sink counter, but Mom kept her spine straight and her backside away from the counter.

"Explain yourself, Mara," Mom said. "Why on earth would you want to vacation at a nudist camp?"

"I didn't know that's what it was."

"And you didn't even tell us," she went on, completely ignoring the fact I'd spoken. "If you want to sow wild oats, at least have the courtesy to inform us."

"Like I just said, I didn't know this was a nudist resort. The travel agent screwed up. She told me 'naturist' meant birdwatching."

"How could I have raised such a naïve daughter?" Before I could respond, she barreled straight ahead. "And why didn't you tell us once you found out what sort of…resort you were staying at?"

Only my mom could make "resort" sound like this place was Sodom, Gomorrah, and Caligula's palace all rolled up together.

Apparently, I said that out loud—probably mumbled it, but Mom heard.

She huffed. "You know I don't understand all that young person slang."

"That's not young person slang, Mom. Sodom and Gomorrah are from the Bible, so as a devout Methodist, you really ought to know what I'm saying." I sat up straighter, because finally standing up to my mother made me feel emboldened and strangely energized. "And Caligula was the most depraved emperor in the entire history of the Roman Empire."

Her cheeks turned slightly pink. "Of course I know about Sodom and Gomorrah. But I thought Caligula was a reference to—I don't know. That's not the point, Mara. You have a lot of explaining to do."

"No, I don't." Wow, was that me saying those words? I sounded so...confident. Hanging around with nudists was good for me. "I'm happy to tell you all the fun things I've done since I came here, but I'm not going to justify myself to you. I didn't call to let you know about the mix-up because I knew you'd go crazy over it. And really, it's none of your business. I'm an adult."

"Then act like one."

Dad laid a hand on her arm. "Calm down, Sher. Mara is a strong, capable woman. It's about time we let her know we appreciate that and stop treating her like a child."

My father had never, ever contradicted my mother. She seemed as stunned as I was.

He took hold of her arms and turned her toward him. "I love you, Sheryl, but you can be a bit of a dictator. I've never spoken up about it because you never went this far before. Cut Mara some slack. She's a good girl, and she deserves better than a dressing-down from her mother."

Dad was right. Mom never had behaved like this before, so overtly hostile to my life decisions or my mistakes. She would primly inform me of what I should have done, but she did not get angry.

"Relax," my dad said to my mom. He kissed her forehead and smiled gently. "Let's have a normal, adult conversation with our daughter."

Mom let her head fall back and moaned, the way I often did. I'd never seen or heard my mother do that, though.

"All right," she said. "Let's go into the living room and have an adult conversation."

Ollie led us into the living room, where Mom and Dad settled onto the sofa side by side. I took the smaller of the two armchairs in the room, leaving Ollie with the bigger, much puffier one. He looked kind of silly sitting in that oversize chair, like a kid in a furniture store trying out all the big recliners. Though he looked outwardly silly, his demeanor and posture made him all man. His clothes clung to his body just enough to provide hints of the muscles underneath, muscles I had vivid memories of feeling pressed against me.

What I wouldn't have given to sneak off to the bedroom with him.

Instead, I sat there in an armchair with my feet on the floor and my hands clasped on my lap. I looked at my parents, not Ollie. My gaze did keep gravitating back to him, but I forced myself to focus on my parents.

Mom stayed ramrod straight, her hands on her lap, though she clasped hers much more primly than I clasped mine. She threw Ollie a sideways look before aiming her disapproving gaze at me. "How long have you known this young man? A few days?"

"Yes. We met on the day I arrived here." The day I'd freaked out and fainted in Ollie's arms. Yeah, I didn't plan on telling my parents about that.

"Days?" Mom's eyes widened, but to her credit, she calmed down within seconds. "Mara, I'm trying to understand this, I honestly am. But it's difficult to reconcile my obedient daughter with the woman I see before me today. You have been keeping company with...nudists."

"Naturists," Ollie said. "Some of us prefer to be called naturists."

Mom veered her squinty gaze to him. "Some of *us*?"

Oh crap. If my mom figured out Ollie was a nudist, she would shanghai me back to Philly.

At the same moment I realized what he'd let slip, Ollie seemed to realize it too. He froze, not even blinking while he stared at me. After a couple seconds, he shook his head the tiniest bit and mouthed, "Sorry."

I shrugged, pretending to not panic about this even while my heart raced like an Olympic sprinter on speed.

And of course, Mom understood what was going on. She'd always had the uncanny ability to root out my secrets. Or in this case, Ollie's secret that had become mine too. We had kept the truth from only my parents.

Mom stared at Ollie. "You are a nudist. My daughter has been doing who knows what with a pervert who wears no clothes in public."

"This isn't a public place," Ollie said calmly. "It's a private resort. I wear clothes when I go into town, and also when I greet new guests."

"I see." Mom looked at me. "You are coming home with us, and that's that."

"No, I am not," I told her. "Ollie is a good man, not a pervert, and the fact he prefers to be naked has nothing to do with why you're mad at me. I screwed up again, didn't I? That's what you think. Stupid little Mara made another fuck-up."

She sat up even straighter. "Watch your language, Mara."

"No, I don't think I will." I jumped out of the chair. "And I am not going anywhere. I like Ollie, and I want to stay here with him to find out if we could have something together. He's helped me overcome some of my fears already. I plan to keep on doing that, getting past the things that used to make me a frazzled mess. I'm stronger than you think, Mom, and I don't need you to tell me how to live my life anymore."

Never had I spoken to my mom like that. I'd always cringed at the idea of telling my mom what I really wanted, what I needed. Standing up to her both invigorated and terrified me.

She opened her mouth, about to speak.

I held up a hand. "I'm not done yet."

My mother shut her mouth.

Dad's lips slid into a closed-mouth smile. He winked at me.

I rolled my shoulders back and forged ahead. "Mom, I know you love me. I know you're trying to look out for me, but you tend to forget I'm an adult now. I'm twenty-nine years old, and I can take care of myself. Please trust me to do that."

She wasn't staring at me anymore in that mother-knows-best way. Instead, she looked down at her hands and sighed. "I worry about you, Mara. You're my only child."

"Haven't I proved I can handle things on my own? You gave me an abandoned apartment building, and I made it a success. Doesn't that show I'm capable of running my own life?"

Mom fiddled with the cuff of her shirt, tugging it out from under her jacket sleeve.

Dad got up and hugged me. "Mara, I'm so proud of you."

"For what?" I asked.

"Everything. Standing up to your mother, turning the apartment complex into a real business, making your own decisions." He kissed my forehead. "You're a fine woman. And I already like Ollie Jackson more than I ever liked Nico."

"Really?"

"Yes. I never cared for Nico, actually." He rolled his eyes to indicate my mom. "I let your mother have her way most of the time, and she thought Nico was a catch. He acted like a decent guy, but something about him always bothered me. Maybe I should've spoken up about that. I'm sorry."

"Not your fault. I'm the one who married him."

I glanced at Ollie, maybe expecting him to look annoyed or disgusted or something, but he just smiled at me.

Mom cleared her throat. "It's possible I've been wrong about a few things."

"A few?" Dad said with a slight smile and a twinkle in his eyes.

"Possibly more than a few." Mom slumped into the sofa. "What do you think we should do, Peter?"

My father stared at my mother blankly for several seconds, then a broad smile broke across his face. "You know, Sher, I think that's the first time you've ever asked me that."

"I always ask for your opinion."

"No, I always give you my opinion. But then we do whatever you want." He settled onto the sofa again, taking Mom's hands in his. "I'm proud of you too. Mara's a grown woman, and we need to stop treating her like she can't do things herself. It's time we show her that we do trust her judgment."

"How do you suggest we do that?"

"It's simple." He lifted her hand to his mouth and kissed it. "We stay here with Mara for a while."

"What?" Mom gaped at Dad like he'd suggested she sign up for a nude mud wrestling contest. "You expect me to stay here with all those...nude people?"

"That's right. Maybe it'll be good for you to be exposed to a different way of life." Dad glanced at me. "It's sure been good for Mara."

Mom moaned and dropped her head onto Dad's shoulder. "Our daughter is a nudist."

"No, Mom, I'm not." Though I had jumped into the hot spring naked. She didn't need to hear about that. "I don't know if I'll ever want to be a nudist like Ollie and the others here, but I like these people. They're nice. Everyone here has accepted me as-is, and that's a new experience for me."

Though I'd kept my clothes on the whole time, staying here had turned into the most liberating experience of my life.

Dad murmured things to my mom that I couldn't hear, but it seemed to relax her a bit. She raised her head to look at me.

"All right," she said. "We'll stay here. Could someone please get my bags? I need Xanax."

I couldn't blame her for that. Maybe I needed some too. This conversation with my parents had been more stressful than when I'd gotten my first glimpse of nudists. The whole thing had left me on edge, and I needed to decompress soon, maybe by doing yoga—or doing Ollie.

Glancing at him, I couldn't help wetting my lips.

He caught me watching him and smiled in a sexy, yet oddly supportive, way.

I exhaled the breath I hadn't realized I'd been holding.

Ollie set his hands on his chair's arms, about to get up. "I'll grab your bags."

"No," I said, "let me. I know which one Mom keeps her Xanax in, so I can bring it to her faster. We can get the rest of their stuff later, once they're settled in somewhere."

"I'll stay in the guest house. Your parents can have the room here."

"Are you sure your bosses won't mind? It's their room, after all."

"Yeah, but Eve and Val are cool. They won't care." Ollie flicked his gaze to my mom and back to me. "Besides, I think your mother will be happier here than in the guest house."

With all the naked people. Yeah, he had a point.

"Thank you, Ollie," my dad said. "I appreciate that."

"No problem."

I marched into the kitchen, straight to the door to the outside, and swung it open.

An enormous naked man with wild hair and the most enormous penis I'd ever seen filled the doorway.

Every ounce of blood in my body seemed to evaporate. My heart pounded so hard and fast I couldn't catch my breath.

And I screamed.

Chapter Sixteen

Mara's scream echoed through the house. She didn't just scream once, though. She did over and over, with only a little gap between each outburst, probably to pull in more air so she could shriek again. What the heck was going on out there?

The shock of her screams kept me frozen for a moment, but then I leaped up and bolted into the kitchen.

Mara stood at the door that led outside, one hand on the open door, her body stiff.

Val Silva hunkered at the threshold, completely naked, his lips moving. He seemed to be trying to calm Mara down, though her screaming drowned out his words. He moved his hands like he wanted to grasp her shoulders but seemed to nix that idea. Instead, he held his hands up like he was in a bank during a holdup and Mara was the robber pointing a gun at him.

I raced up to them, inserting myself between her and Val. "Mara, it's okay."

Her last scream wound down into silence, the only noise her ragged breaths. Her chest heaved, and her lips quivered.

"Take it easy," I said, bracketing her face with my hands. "It's okay. This is Val Silva. I told you about him, remember? He and Eve own the resort. This is their house."

Over Mara's shoulder, I spotted her parents in the living room doorway. Sheryl had her hand over her mouth while she stared wide-eyed at Val. Peter watched everything with a slightly bemused expression. When Val shifted a little to the side, Sheryl got her first good look at his dick, and her eyes went even wider. Her husband, now smirking, slapped his hand over his wife's eyes.

"I'm sorry," Val said. "I didn't mean to scare her. Eve and I just came from the airport, and I couldn't wait to get rid of my clothes. I had no idea you were hosting guests in our house."

Val didn't mean "our house" as chastisement. He was stating a fact, that's all. And I hadn't called Eve or Val since I decided to let Mara stay here with me. So this was my fault.

I could explain that to Val later.

"Take a slow, deep breath," I told Mara, rubbing her arms. "Val usually has a strong effect on women, but you're the first one who's screamed at him."

She took my advice, hauling in slow, deep breaths until she calmed down enough to speak. "I'm okay. I promise."

Val snaked a hand around me to offer it to Mara. "It's a pleasure to meet you, Mara. I'm Val Silva, and I don't make a habit of terrifying women. I hope you can forgive me."

She shook his hand. "It's okay. At least I didn't faint this time."

"I'll get some clothes from the truck and get dressed."

Val left.

Mara's shoulders sagged, and she leaned her forehead on my chest. "That was so embarrassing."

"Nah, that was nothing. You should've been there when Val got attacked by no-see-ums."

She lifted her head to look at me, her lips kinking into an almost-smile. "I'd love to hear that story."

"Tell you later. When your parents aren't watching."

Mara glanced over her shoulder and smiled sheepishly at her parents. "I'm okay. He surprised me, that's all."

Sheryl still had her hand over her mouth, but her husband lowered his hand from her eyes. Mara's dad looked tickled pink by the commotion. Well, at least he was having a good time.

Peter took his wife's hand. "Why don't we go outside and let Ollie and Mara have a moment alone."

Sheryl's eyes flared so big this time that the whites seemed to glow in the sunlight that came in through the window. She said in an indignant tone, "I am not going out there with all those perverts. And with that…man who has…" She fake shivered and made a disgusted noise. "Walking around with no clothing on is not proper."

Yeah, I decided she must've thought Val was hot—jeez, what woman didn't?—and now she was embarrassed by that fact. Even Ruth Norris, a seventy-something grandmother, made no attempt to conceal her appreciation for Val's body. Val had been a model after he retired from football, so yeah, nobody could deny he had the looks women loved. He was also smart and a nice guy, but that was never the first thing anybody noticed about him.

He worked out. A lot. I worked out too, but not like he did. Compared to Val Silva, I looked like a puny geek.

Peter Severins all but dragged his wife outside, winking at me and Mara as they passed by us. "I trust you to take care of my daughter."

"Yes, sir, I will."

He closed the door behind himself and his wife.

Mara sucked in a big breath and blew it out. "Wow, that was totally not fun in any sense of the word."

I shrugged one shoulder, trying not to laugh. "I don't know. That was kinda fun for me."

She slugged my shoulder. "Hey! My boyfriend isn't supposed to laugh at me."

"Come on, I wouldn't do that." I grinned. "Now your mom's reaction is another story. I think she was drooling. Definitely devouring Val with her eyes, even while they seemed like they might pop out of her skull any second."

Mara's lips puckered like she was trying really hard not to smile. "Yeah, Mom was ogling him for sure. I don't think she's ever seen a naked man before. I always kind of assumed she and Dad have sex in total darkness. I wouldn't be surprised if she has no idea what a man's penis looks like."

"Well, she does now."

Mara held a hand to her mouth while half-suppressed laughter snorted out of her. "I shouldn't be laughing. Mom was horrified."

"Yeah, but your dad thought it was hilarious."

"He knows how to handle Mom, but today is the first time I've ever heard him disagree with her."

I cupped her face in my hands and kissed her forehead. "Maybe he's finally realizing how much your mom's 'this is not proper' stuff has affected you. I bet things will change a lot after this."

"Don't hold your breath for the day when Mom becomes a nudist."

"Yeah, that'll never happen." I chuckled. "But your mom might not mind being around naturists now that Val has come home."

"He is hot. Can't say I blame Mom for being flustered by him."

God, I hoped she wasn't about to call me her gay best friend. I knew Mara liked me, but she hadn't met Val until today. The guy was a god, according to every straight woman on the planet. Okay, maybe Eve was the only one I'd actually heard say that. I inferred the rest.

"What's wrong?" Mara asked. "You're scrunching up your face."

Shit. I didn't realize I'd been doing that.

"It's nothing," I said, totally lying to her.

Mara set her hands on her hips. "That's baloney. What's bothering you, Ollie?"

This time I knew I scrunched up my face, and I bowed my head to scratch the back of it. "It's dumb. And it's doesn't matter."

"Anything that bothers you matters to me." She rested her palms on my chest. "You matter to me."

I raised my head, stunned by her statement, though it really shouldn't have surprised me. Other good-looking men had visited the resort while she'd been here, and she had never paid much attention to them. She liked me, not them. So why was I worried she might get turned on by Val's ripped body?

Letting out a long sigh, I told her the truth. "Val is a sex god. He works out like crazy, and he used to be a model, had his picture in magazines and on billboards. Before that, he was an international football star. That means soccer, by the way. His team won the freaking Olympics, mostly because of him. He also made a sex tape that everybody saw."

"Not me. I never saw it. And I've never heard of Val Silva, never laid eyes on him before today, not even in a magazine."

"But he's to die for, according to Eve."

Mara laughed, the sound soft and gentle. "Eve is in love with him. Of course she thinks he's the hottest thing since the ghost pepper."

"What's a ghost pepper?"

She laughed again, and her delight tickled my senses. "It's the hottest chili pepper on the planet. At least it used to be. Not sure if it still is."

"Oh." I tried to grumble, but it came out a little whiny. "Well then, every woman who sees Val thinks he's a ghost pepper. Even the senior citizens drool over him."

"Are you jealous of Val? I thought he was your friend."

"He is. Val's an awesome friend and a great boss." I scrubbed my face with both hands, groaning. "I swear I'm not jealous of him. Not until today." I hunched my shoulders. "Not until you met him."

A radiant smile carved out dimples in her cheeks. "You are so incredibly adorable. How can you not realize how ghost-pepper hot you are? I'd much rather ogle your naked body than Val's."

"Seriously? You claim his ginormous muscles don't do anything for you."

"Of course I think he's gorgeous, but I don't want to sleep with him. Or go hiking with him. Or swim naked in the hot spring with him."

"We haven't done that yet. You did it by yourself."

She snuggled up to me, sliding her arms around my waist. "We could do that right now."

"Your parents are waiting outside."

"Dad can take care of Mom." She nuzzled my neck. "Take me to the hot spring, Oliver."

"You know how I get when you call me that."

She nibbled on my chin. "Yes, I know. Oliver."

I swept her up in my arms. "Let's sneak out the back way."

Mara grinned.

Damn, I was one lucky geek.

Chapter Seventeen

We snuck out the back door, which I hadn't noticed before. Ollie told me Eve and Val had installed a secondary door only this year, so they'd have a back entrance for receiving deliveries of supplies. The door blended into the wall and had no knob on it, another thing Eve had wanted because she thought a regular door wouldn't look good there.

Ollie pushed a button on the thermostat to open the door.

I asked him why the button was there, instead of on the wall.

"To be sneaky," he said with a crooked smile. "Eve and Val are the horniest people on the planet. They need a secret escape route so nobody will bother them when they run off into the woods to get it on."

"Can we do that?"

"What? Sneak off? I thought that was the plan before you saw this door."

"It is the plan." I bit my lip, trying to look sexy but not at all sure I pulled it off. "But I was talking about the getting-it-on-outdoors part."

"Oh." His smile turned into a grin. "Love to do that. And I've got all your favorite foods to feed you after."

He had packed a picnic lunch for us and held the basket in one hand, by its handle.

We ran out the back door, heading for a side path to avoid the main nature trail. Other guests might be using that path, and besides, my parents might see us if we went that way. I needed time alone with Ollie. Lots of time. Completely alone. After a stressful talk with my parents and the scare Val Silva gave me, I needed to do something wild and hot.

Didn't a girl deserve hot sex in the outdoors once in a while?

Nico would never believe I was capable of doing anything so brazen. Hell, he wouldn't believe I could do anything he or my mother disapproved of, including eating a hamburger with the works on it. That was too messy, and naturally, a lady didn't get mustard smeared on her face. Besides, it might make me gain weight.

I didn't hate my mother. I loved her, and I didn't even blame her for my hang-ups. But I'd realized lately that I didn't want to be like her anymore. Maybe she loved dressing just so and behaving just so and speaking just so. I didn't. Ollie Jackson had shown me how wonderful it could be to stop worrying what other people thought and follow my true desires. It was about more than sex. I'd been rethinking my whole life.

Ollie led me deeper into the woods than I'd been before, into a new area with a less-groomed trail. This path led into real woods, not the semi-manicured version of it. Birds chirped all around us, and only the occasional ray of sunshine penetrated the canopy of trees. The peacefulness of this area helped me shake off the remnants of the stress that had gripped me earlier. Ollie's hand in mine helped even more. I loved the feel of his palm on mine, his fingers curled around my hand.

He stopped us in front of a huge tree that had big branches high up. Lower down, a single thinner branch stretched out from the trunk. It hung a few feet higher than my head.

Ollie patted the branch. "Take your clothes off and grab onto this."

"What?"

"You heard me. Do what I said."

His bossy tone should've annoyed me, but instead, it made me shiver in the most delicious way.

I stripped off my clothes and moved under the branch, stretching my arms to grasp it.

Ollie removed his clothes and sauntered up to me. He settled his hands on my hips, gazing into my eyes with a lustful look in his. "I love that you did what I said without asking why. Girls don't usually do that."

"I trust you, Oliver."

"Damn, it's even hotter when you say my name right after saying you trust me." He skimmed his hands up my sides, then back down to my hips. He shifted them behind me, cupping my ass. "I trust you too. All the way. I've got an idea for something I've never tried before, but I had a feeling you'd go for it."

"Anything you want to do, I want to do too." I rocked my hips forward, grazing his erection. "*You* are the sex god, Oliver. Val Silva has nothing on you."

"I love that you mean that."

He kissed me, slowly, decadently, groaning his pleasure while I moaned into his mouth. Our tongues coiled around each other, slick and hot and hungry, while I hooked my leg around his and he skated his hands up and down my back. The sensation of his fingers dancing over my skin heightened my arousal until my flesh felt electrified, sensitized to his touch. And God, he tasted so good, like magical things I couldn't describe, things that made me want him even more. Maybe he had cast a spell over me so I would bend to his will, or maybe I just loved being with him. I'd do anything he wanted, because I craved the same things he did.

I craved him, period.

Ollie kissed his way down my neck, his tongue teasing my skin, while he traced his hands over my shoulders and along my arms. His lips traveled down my chest, between my breasts, until he reached my nipples, where he paused to lick and nip and suckle them, cranking my lust up a few more notches with every swipe of his tongue. I moaned and thrust my hips, but I couldn't reach his amazing dick, the part of him I hungered for most of all. God, I remembered how fantastic it felt to have him pushing inside me, filling me up, touching parts of me I'd never known existed until he found them.

He bent his knees as he kissed and licked a path down my tummy, inching closer and closer to where my body ached and throbbed for him, to where I was already drenched and ready for anything he might do to me.

"Oliver," I whispered, reaching down to tunnel my fingers into his hair.

Millimeters from my mound, he stopped and looked up at me. "Uh-uh-uh. Keep those hands on the branch."

I grasped it with both hands again.

And now I was completely on fire for him. If he didn't make me come soon, I'd lose my mind.

Before I could voice my need, he seemed to recognize it. He dropped to his knees and laid a hand on my inner thigh, pushing gently, urging me to spread my legs.

"Yes, Oliver, please."

He shoved his head between my thighs, latching onto my clitoris.

The first tug of his teeth on my flesh made me buck my hips and cry out. It felt incredible, so fantastic beyond words, and he'd barely touched me. When he began to swirl his tongue around my taut nub, I gripped the branch even harder and threw my head back. He pushed his hand between my folds, rubbing in an irregular rhythm, driving me so wild that I thrashed and cried out again.

Just when I thought I couldn't get more turned on, he thrust a finger inside me, then another, and another. He fucked me with his fingers while tormenting my nub, his own breathing ragged and labored, just like mine.

"Ollie! Yes, please, yes, yes, yes!"

He nipped my clit, and I erupted.

My scream reverberated through the forest.

But Ollie didn't stop until he'd teased every last spasm of pleasure out of me, until my arms quivered from the strain of holding me up and he'd robbed me of breath.

He rose in front of me, his expression the embodiment of sheer, unbridled lust. His voice sounded deeper and rougher when he said, "Breathe, Mara. Can't have you passing out before we get to the best part."

I did what he said, taking slow breaths until my heart stopped pounding like a jackhammer. I let go of the branch and stumbled a little, still weak from the power of what he'd done to me.

Ollie slung an arm around my waist and hugged me to him. "Let me know when you're ready for more. I can't wait to be inside you again."

"I want that too, and I'm okay now." I walked my fingers up his chest. "But I'd like to give you something special first."

"Just being with you is special enough for me."

"You're so sweet, Ollie. But I've been fantasizing about this all week." I wriggled free of his embrace and knelt in front of him. His cock curved up in front of me, making my mouth water. "I want this."

"Oh… uh… You don't have to…"

He blushed.

I couldn't help grinning and laughing. His embarrassment was the cutest thing I'd ever seen, and it made me want to do this even more.

"Relax, Ollie," I said, "I've done this before. My husband thought my enthusiasm for sex was unseemly, but he loved it when I gave him a blow job. Apparently, it wasn't unseemly to enjoy doing that for him. But I'll love doing this for you so much more."

He combed his fingers through my hair, gazing down at me with a tender smile curving his lips. "You're the sexiest woman in the world, Mara. I'd love for you to do that."

"Maybe you should hold on to the branch. I plan to make you come so hard your knees will buckle."

"Damn, that sounds incredible."

He moved to stand directly under the branch, clasping it with both hands.

I knelt in front of him and took his erection in my hand, closing my fingers around its girth, loving the heat and firmness of him. A drop of moisture formed on the head of his cock. I licked it away, making him shudder and suck in a breath.

"Are you ready, Oliver?"

"Fuck yes."

I pumped his length in a leisurely rhythm while I began to massage his inner thigh with my other hand, easing it upward inch by inch, moving closer and closer to his groin. His head fell back, the look on his face the epitome of pleasure. He groaned softly when I cupped his sac and gasped when I fondled the skin behind it.

"Mara," he said through gritted teeth. "You're so—uh. So hot."

"Can't wait to taste you." I rasped my tongue over the crown of his cock, flicking it out to taste the slit. His breathing turned rough and labored, and I grew even slicker than he'd made me when he put his mouth on me. "Oh Oliver, I'm going to eat you up."

Knowing he loved giving me oral sex as much as he loved receiving it from me made this even hotter, even more perfect. I took him in my mouth, sliding his length in as far as I could before I pulled away.

"Fuck, Mara, you better hurry." His face had become pinched even while it took on a look of sheer ecstasy. "I don't think I'll last long, not with you doing this to me."

"Look at me, Oliver. I want you to watch me feast on you and swallow everything you give me."

Chest heaving, he bowed his head to watch me. His gaze drilled into mine, and he licked his lips. "I definitely won't last long if I'm looking at you."

"Doesn't matter how long it takes, as long as your eyes roll back in your head."

I swallowed him, drawing his cock deep inside my mouth while I massaged his sac. He tasted so good, though I couldn't describe the flavor of his skin. No words on earth seemed right, but giving him this gift seemed like the most right thing I'd ever done with a man. Nico might've loved blow jobs, but only because of the pleasure it gave him. He'd always kept his eyes closed, focused solely on how what I did affected him. He never said anything until after he'd come, then he would tell me, "I really needed that."

Ollie called me sexy and wanted to watch me do this to him. I had no doubts that afterward he would compliment me in the sweetest way. He was that kind of man.

His breathing grew even heavier, and his lids drifted half shut, but he kept looking at me. Our gazes were tied to each other with an invisible thread, a link between us that I'd felt since the moment I'd met him.

I worked his cock with my mouth, my lips covering my teeth, while I stroked the skin behind his balls. He groaned and grunted and murmured my name, his voice rough and almost hoarse. I dragged my tongue over the tip of his erection, and he hissed in a breath. His entire face scrunched up with blissful agony when I began to slide my mouth up and down his length, sucking and laving him with my tongue even as I grasped the base of his cock and pumped there too.

"Shit, Mara," he growled. "God, I'm about to—"

With a shout, he came. His whole body jerked. The salty flavor of him filled my mouth, making me hum with pleasure. I kept going until he was done, completely done, and so spent he dangled from the tree branch with his head limp, his chin almost touching his chest. The most adorable look of dazed rapture came over his face.

He managed a lopsided smile. "You rock the blow jobs, Mara. Any guy who couldn't see what a hot, amazing woman you are is a total idiot and a complete dick. I've never been with a sexier, more exciting woman in my life."

I couldn't help smiling. "Anytime you want this again, let me know. I loved doing that to you, and watching your face while you came. It got me so turned on."

He peeled his hands away from the branch to kneel in front of me. Gliding his hands up and down my arms, he leaned in to kiss me.

I expected a lips-only kiss. I mean, what man wanted to taste himself in my mouth? But Ollie didn't care. He sealed his mouth to mine and thrust his tongue deep, letting out a groan of pure carnal delight. We kissed with languor, like we had all day to sit here on our knees, in the woods, enjoying each other's mouths until the sun set and the moon rose, and then we could make love by moonlight.

We didn't get the chance. A phone rang.

Ollie kept kissing me, wrapping his arms around me and crushing my breasts to his chest, crushing my entire body to him.

The phone rang again, and I pushed his face away with my palms on his cheeks. "Is that your phone or mine?"

"Don't know. Don't care."

He claimed my mouth again, devouring me so deeply and hotly that I forgot about everything else in the world.

But that damn phone rang again.

Ollie broke the kiss and huffed. "Can't anybody get along without us for one frigging hour?"

"I think it's only been, like, fifteen minutes."

"But I was planning to make love to you for another forty-five minutes, at the very least."

I grinned.

He scowled as he scrambled around on his knees to find our clothes, then dug in various pockets until he found the ringing phone. He handed it to me. "It's yours. Says 'Mom' on the caller ID."

"Oh." I took the phone and answered it. "Mom?"

"Mara, where on earth are you? Eve and Val let us into the house, but you're not here. We were getting worried."

"Ollie and I went for a walk. We'll be back in a little while."

"Mara..." Her voice took on a sheepish tone I'd never heard before. "There's something I meant to tell you, but after that naked man frightened you, I forgot."

"What is it?"

The silence that followed my question dragged on for several seconds. I knew we hadn't been disconnected thanks to the background noises of men's voices. I couldn't make out what they were saying.

"Mara," Mom began, still sounding slightly embarrassed, "it's about Nico. Before your father and I left Philadelphia, I called him."

"Nico? Why would you do that?"

"I was convinced you were in some sort of trouble, and I knew he wanted you back. So I thought he might be able to talk you into coming home." She hesitated, sighing. "Nico just got here. He's with us in the caretaker's house."

"What?" I almost shrieked that word. My skin went cold, and I was pretty sure my blood froze to solid ice. "You invited my ex-husband to come here? Like it's some kind of intervention for your crazy daughter?"

"Yes. I'm sorry. But you'd better get back here before Nico takes off into the woods to look for you."

Shit. He would do that, for sure. Nico was exactly the kind of jackass who believed he knew what was best for me, and finding out I'd come to a nudist resort would set him off for sure.

"Okay, I'm coming."

I hung up on my mom and rushed to get my clothes on.

"What's wrong?" Ollie asked.

"My—" I paused in yanking my clothes on and tried to calm my racing heart, but I failed. "My ex-husband is here. I have to get back to the house before he calls the state police or who knows what to come search for me."

I didn't wait for Ollie. Once I was dressed, I took off down the trail, headed for the house.

Nico. Here. Could things get any worse?

Chapter Eighteen

Mara took off at a dead run. I scrambled to get my clothes on and gave up on tucking my shirt in, determined to keep up with her. I had longer legs, so I caught up to Mara in a few seconds, despite the time it had taken to get dressed. Only when we reached the trailhead, behind the little house, did I realize I'd forgotten my shoes.

She slid to a stop, almost falling over in the process.

I grabbed her arms to keep her from tumbling to the ground.

Gasping for air, she laid a hand on her chest. Her eyes were big, her mouth hung open, and she stared at the house like it might turn into a giant monster and squash her with its foot.

"You okay?" I asked.

"Uh-huh, sure," she said, sounding sarcastic even while she fought to calm her breathing. "My mom invited my ex-husband to an intervention at a nudist resort, so they can set me straight. But sure, everything's peachy."

I grasped her shoulders and turned her to face me, though her gaze stayed trained on the house. "Look at me, Mara. Come on, look at me."

She rotated her wide eyes toward me.

"Take slow, deep breaths," I told her. "That's right. Keep breathing. Take it easy and keep looking at me. You don't need to panic because I'm here with you, and I won't leave you alone with anybody unless you tell me it's okay. Got it?"

Mara nodded, clamping her teeth over her lips. She kept taking deep breaths and exhaling them gradually, and the panic on her face relaxed into something more like mild anxiety mixed with a hint of annoyance. I was pretty sure she wasn't annoyed with me. Her ex-husband and her mom seemed like the most likely targets.

"Thank you, Ollie," Mara said once she'd calmed down. "You're better than Xanax."

I chuckled. "That's the strangest compliment I've ever gotten, but coming from you, it's also the nicest one." I thought about what she'd said and asked, "Do you take Xanax? Or Prozac? Anything like that?"

"Never took Prozac, or any antidepressant. But my mom insisted I get a prescription for Xanax." She squared her shoulders and stood up straighter. "I haven't taken one since I came here. Not even after the dining hall incident that first day."

"Good." I pecked a quick kiss on her lips. "I'm proud of you, Mara. Your parents showed up, and you didn't freak out. You stood up to your mom. Now your ex is here, and I know you can handle that too."

The start of tears glistened in her eyes. "You're the first person who ever really believed in me."

"Oh, I think your parents believe in you. Your dad for sure. But I think even your mom does, deep down, and maybe she'll tell you that sometime and explain why she told you all that shit about being proper."

"Maybe." She lifted her chin and cleared her throat. "Right now, I have to face my ex."

"I'll be right here with you, all the way."

She touched my cheek. "I know, Ollie, and that means more to me than you could possibly know."

I took her hand in mine and turned toward the trailhead. "Ready?"

She nodded.

We marched out of the woods and walked into the house via the back door, stepping into the kitchen.

Five people swiveled their gazes toward us.

Eve and Val smiled.

Peter Severins smiled too.

Sheryl glanced at her daughter but quickly averted her gaze, hugging herself.

The fifth person—Mara's ex, I assumed—glared at me for a couple seconds, then he rushed up to Mara. He pulled her into a hug and, like I wasn't standing right there next to her still holding her hand, he planted a big old kiss on her.

A long kiss. Like, loooong long.

I gritted my teeth and tried to be the understanding boyfriend, but honestly, how long would she let him keep doing that? The creep had treated her like dirt. She couldn't want him back. So why was she standing there while he kissed her?

Oh no, he couldn't have done what I thought he just did. He could not have shoved his tongue into her mouth.

Yeah, the asswipe had.

I was pretty sure I growled. My free hand clenched into a fist, and I had an almost overpowering urge to slug this creep.

Finally, after what seemed like an hour, he pulled his mouth away from hers. Giving Mara the smarmiest smile I'd ever seen, he said, "I was so worried about you, baby. Glad to see you're okay."

She gaped at him. Not moving. Not speaking. Her cheeks had turned pink.

I still held her hand even while my other one stayed balled into a tight fist.

Her ex glared at me again but quickly pulled on a cloak of civility, smiling politely and offering me his hand. "I'm Nico Marshall, Mara's husband. You must be one of her new friends."

Did this asshole really think I wanted to shake his hand? He couldn't be that stupid.

Mara was still standing beside me gaping at her ex. Was that stunned look because she couldn't believe he'd had the gall to show up here? Or was that a stunned "I want to get back with my douchebag ex-husband" expression?

"It was nice of you to take my Mara for a walk," Nico said. "She's always been afraid of the woods. You must be a great wilderness counselor."

Wilderness counselor? What the fuck was that? Maybe they had those in the big city, where people thought "wilderness" meant a patch of grass with a scraggly bush on it.

"Mara doesn't need counseling," I said. "There's nothing wrong with her."

The prick patted my shoulder. "You don't know her the way I do."

Okay, so he *was* as stupid as I'd thought. Only a moron would say that to me when I was holding his ex-wife's hand.

A breath blustered out of Mara, like she'd been holding it in and finally let it all out. Her stunned expression evaporated, blown away by her big sigh.

"Nico," she snapped. Once he looked at her, she rolled her shoulders back and said, "I do not need or want you here. Go home."

Okay, not an "I want my asswipe ex back" expression after all. I tried to keep my mouth from forming a smirk, but it happened anyway. Who cared what Nico thought? I had Mara, he didn't, and he could go jump into a volcano for all I cared.

"I can't leave," Nico said, "until we talk about what's going on with you. A nudie resort? That's the craziest mess you've ever gotten yourself into, and I've seen you do a lot of crazy things."

She puckered her lips, and I swore a little bit of steam erupted from her nostrils.

"Listen up, Nico," she said. "You don't know me at all, because you never bothered to ask me anything. That was the problem with our marriage. It was all about you, when it should have been about us. A shared life. But that's something you can't even comprehend."

He opened his mouth, but she held up a hand, her expression stern and determined.

That look was sexy as hell. Everything about her in this moment made me want to fuck her right here in front of everybody.

"I never did a single crazy thing in my life," she said, "and that's the problem. I always did what was expected of me, living by rules you and Mom and other people made up for me. Of course I turned into a neurotic mess. I never had any fun."

Nico eyed her like she might kick him in the balls any second.

I would've loved to see that.

Mara jerked her hand free of mine, spreading her arms. "Look at me. Do I seem anxious or neurotic? No, I don't. Know why? Because I stopped caring about those stupid rules and started listening to my heart. I love being here at this 'nudie' resort. I'm not leaving, but you need to go. Right away."

"Mara—"

"No. I'm not listening to you anymore." She made a shooing motion with her hands. "Go. Get out."

He stared at her for a moment, his mouth open, then got a sneakily determined look on his face. "You can't make me leave. I paid for a room here. For a week-long stay."

"What?"

I glanced at Eve and Val. Eve shrugged and shook her head. Val bowed his head, scratching it.

"Why don't I show Nico to his room," Eve said, "and give everyone a little time to decompress."

Nico didn't look like he wanted to go anywhere, but Eve knew how to graciously force someone to get the hell out. She and Nico left.

"I'm sorry," Val said to me and Mara. "He made the reservation online, and we didn't know—"

"Don't worry," Mara said. "I know it's not your fault. Let him stick around. He'll realize eventually that I'm not going home with him."

"If he harasses you, let us know. We will evict him and ban him from the resort for life."

"Thank you, Val. I appreciate that."

He left too, no doubt heading for the guest house to help Eve.

Mara's parents stayed put. Sheryl still hugged herself, her head down.

Peter smiled at his daughter. "Good for you, Mara."

High-pitched squeals erupted outside the house.

What on earth?

I stayed confused for about thirty seconds, until the house phone rang and I picked it up.

Before I could speak, Ruth Norris said, "Dear, the Kitten Brigade is here. And they're swarming Val with even more enthusiasm than usual. Maybe you should get out there and save the poor boy."

Val didn't need saving, but with Eve escorting Nico to his room in the guest house, I was the only other employee available to greet the Kittens. Val preferred not to get involved in guest intake. His forte was organizing sporting events.

I looked at Mara. "Will you be okay if I go? The Kitten Brigade is here, and I really need to get them settled in. Val isn't good at that, since those girls think he's a walking lollipop."

Sheryl's head popped up, her eyes wide. "Lollipop? Kittens? What kind of perverted resort is this?"

Peter hooked an arm around his wife's shoulders. "Relax, Sher, I'm sure it's nothing like that."

"No," I said, "it's really not. The Kitten Brigade is our name for a group of women in their twenties who come here at least twice a year. They all have serious, stable jobs, but visiting the resort gives them a chance to cut loose. And I was joking about Val being a lollipop. The Kittens think he's the cat's pajamas."

Mara snickered at my bad joke, and Peter smiled, but Sheryl kept gaping at me.

Yeah, she'd need more time to adjust to the naturist thing.

"Go on," Mara said, "I'll be fine. Sounds like Val needs a little help."

More screams echoed outside, confirming her statement.

"Why don't you go with Ollie?" Peter asked Mara. "I'll take care of Mom. Honestly, I think she just needs to lie down for a while. We had a long plane ride to get here, and a long drive from the airport."

"Okay, if you're sure."

"I am. Go." He glanced at me, then Mara. "It's nice to see you having a good time, honey."

Mara smiled shyly, and I led her out of the house.

Chapter Nineteen

Mara

A throng of lovely women frolicked in the area between Eve and Val's little home and the guest house. Well, frolicking wasn't the right word for it. They jumped and danced and chest-bumped and spun around and around. Every single one of them wore a pale-blue T-shirt dress and sandals, though each had her own version of the footwear. Some wore sandals with sparkly decorations on them, while others donned platform sandals or flip-flops.

They shrieked and hooted too.

My goodness, those ladies had powerful lungs.

In the middle of the throng, Val Silva stood there seeming quite calm and somewhat amused by the antics of the ladies around him. None of them touched him, but they danced around the man like they'd never seen a hot guy before—or like they were performing a bizarre ritual.

Suddenly, they all looked at each other and tore their dresses off over their heads. They hurled the garments high in the air, letting them flutter down to the ground.

The Kitten Brigade pumped their fists in the air and whooped.

Ollie shoved two fingers from each hand into his mouth and blew hard, emitting the loudest, most piercing whistle I'd ever heard.

I slapped my hands over my ears until he finished.

The entire Kitten Brigade froze. They swung their heads in our direction, all gazes zeroing in on Ollie.

A blonde girl broke off from the crowd and approached him. "Hey, Ollie, it's been a while."

He stared at her, not blinking and apparently not breathing either. His jaw fell open, then clapped shut. His eyes rotated toward me only to veer back to the blonde. "Heidi, hey. Wow. I, uh, didn't expect you to be here."

"I wasn't going to come, but then I realized it's silly not to. We're both adults. We can handle seeing each other again, can't we?"

Her innocent expression didn't seem fake, but Ollie eyed her like she'd suggested he drink that funny-smelling fruit punch she was offering him.

"Yeah, sure," Ollie said, "it's cool."

"So glad you feel that way."

Heidi flung her arms around Ollie and mashed her mouth to his, shutting her eyes, holding that position for several long seconds. Ollie kept his eyes open. His brows knit together over his nose, and he held his arms out like he was afraid to touch Heidi. When he glanced at me, he lifted his shoulders in the best version of a shrug he could manage with a beautiful blonde attached to him.

Finally, he pushed her away.

Wiping his mouth, he gave a nervous laugh. "Whoa, Heidi, we're not dating anymore. Remember?"

Heidi bit down on her bottom lip. "I missed you, Ollie. Maybe we could talk alone?"

"Talk?" His jaw fell open again, but this time it didn't clap shut for so long I started to wonder if bugs would fly into his mouth. Then he shook his head vigorously and swallowed hard. "Heidi, I have a new girlfriend. This is Mara." He slung his arm around me and pulled me tight against him. "Mara, this is Heidi Mackenzie. We dated for about thirty seconds last year."

Ollie's ex froze. Only her eyes moved when she looked at me. "New girlfriend? So soon?"

"I haven't seen you in almost a year," he said. "You went back to your ex. Was I supposed to wait around wishing you'd change your mind and come back? I moved on, and so should you."

Heidi gnawed on her lip, newly formed tears shimmering in her blue eyes. "Oh. I get it, sure."

It was totally bizarre to stand here with Ollie, both of us fully clothed, while his nude ex-girlfriend seemed on the verge of crying. Had Ollie hoped one day Heidi would come back and want to reconcile? He'd seemed shocked to see her, but that could mean one of two things. Maybe he was over her and hadn't expected to see her again, so he was caught off guard by her appearance. Or maybe he secretly wanted to get back with her, but he felt trapped by his involvement with me.

Which was it? I didn't know, and I couldn't ask him in front of his ex.

"Should I leave?" Heidi asked. "I mean, this is awkward, right?"

Ollie scrunched up his mouth, moving his lips like he couldn't quite figure out what to do in this situation. "You paid to be here, so you should stay. It'll be fine."

He looked at me, a question on his face.

What else could I say? "Sure, Heidi ought to stay."

"For real?" Heidi said. "You don't have to say that."

"It's all good," I said. "Don't worry about it."

"Yay!" Heidi flung her arms around me, squeezing me tight. "Thank you, Mara, you're awesome."

Why was she thanking me? I didn't own the resort, so my permission didn't mean much. When I glanced at Ollie, who'd been shoved away when Heidi hugged me, he shook his head and shrugged, a slight smile on his lips.

"Sure, yeah," I said. "You're welcome."

Heidi let go of me and rushed back into the crowd.

They had all remained silent during Ollie and Heidi's reunion, and they stayed like that after she rejoined them, waiting for whatever Ollie had been about to say after he whistled.

He raised his arms, spreading them wide. "Welcome back, Kittens. Get your tents set up and let's meet on the lawn for a game of miniten, okay?"

They shrieked.

All those beautiful, naked women split off in smaller groups and started gathering stuff from inside their big, neon-pink motor home.

"Wanna help me set up the miniten net?" Ollie asked me.

"Sure."

He kept a hand on the small of my back while he headed into the guest house to retrieve the net and the other equipment that went with it, like the thugs and the tennis balls. Ollie carried the rolled-up net while I lugged a bag full of thugs and balls, though he tried to convince me to carry just the balls and leave the thugs for him to get later.

"That's sweet," I said, "but I can handle it. They're not that heavy."

When I lifted the big canvas bag and hooked its straps over my shoulder, Ollie's brows rose.

"You're no wimpy girlie-girl, are you?" he said, smiling. "My Mara's a tough chick in disguise."

I loved it when he called me "his Mara." It gave me a warm, fuzzy feeling in my tummy.

After we set up the net, I lounged on a chaise at the periphery of the lawn. Ollie gathered the guests who wanted to play miniten and split them into two teams—the Kittens and the Silver Foxes, which meant the older guests. Val opted out, despite the Kittens begging him to play for their side, saying he and Eve needed to rest and recover from jet lag. They'd only just gotten back from Brazil.

As the two of them retreated into their house, Ollie leaned in to whisper in my ear, "Eve and Val have a different idea about what resting means. I hope your mom won't freak out if she hears them having a good time in their room. It's right across the hall from where I put them."

"It might be good for Mom to be exposed to inappropriate behavior."

He chuckled. "You're the best, Mara."

With Eve and Val home again, Ollie and I had to take rooms in the guest house. Val had moved my stuff there while Ollie and I got the miniten court ready, so I didn't need to do a thing except watch my hot boyfriend referee the game. Ollie had kept his clothes on, partly for my sake, I was sure. But I also suspected he did it so my mom wouldn't go ballistic.

My parents emerged from the main house not long after the miniten game started and took seats on the chaises next to mine. Mom sat right beside me, with Dad on the other side of her.

And Mom tried really, really hard not to look at the naked people knocking tennis balls around with wedge-shaped boxes on their hands.

I still had a little trouble with nudism. Whenever these people played sports, parts of them flapped that I didn't really need to see flapping. Sometimes they wore jockstraps or sports bras. Other times, they didn't. Ollie had told me, and my experience over the past few days had confirmed it, that naturists liked miniten because it was less strenuous than tennis and therefore didn't, um, flap their flappable parts as much.

The Kittens didn't seem to have gotten that memo. They played miniten with a vengeance, like they were competing for the Olympic gold medal in naturist sports. All but one of them had put on a sports bra. All but Heidi Mackenzie.

Her boobs bounced like crazy every time she leaped up to slam her thug into the ball. Good thing she had modest-size breasts instead of big jugs. I couldn't imagine how painful it would be to play so roughly with a huge set of tits.

My mom sat sideways on her chaise, hands on her lap, studiously avoiding glancing at the nudists frolicking off to her right.

"Dear lord, Mara," she said. "How can you stand to be around these...people?"

"You mean how can I stand being around super nice, friendly people who make me feel like I belong here? Who don't treat me like a screw-up who can't do anything right?"

"It's not proper, running around with no clothing on, where anyone can see you."

"Not anyone." I folded my arms over my chest. "This is a private resort in a secluded section of the woods. The only people who can see the nudists are the other nudists."

She rolled her gaze up to the sky. "What about satellites? Your father showed me Google Earth once. Did you know you can see into people's backyards with that website or software or whatever it is? It was horrifying."

"Oh come on, Sher," Dad said from where he reclined on his chaise, his baseball cap over his eyes. "You once sunbathed in the nude. And I remember that time at the lake when you suggested we skinny dip."

My eyes flew so wide the air dried them up. "Mom! You skinny dipped? And sunbathed naked?"

She threw Dad a chastising look. "Peter, you promised never to tell anyone."

He sighed and sat up, plopping the cap onto his head. "Mara's not anyone. She's our daughter, and I think it's about time she learned the truth about her mother."

"But—"

Dad tipped his head down to peer at her with an expression I'd never seen before. He seemed to be...almost scolding her with that look. "We both know why you've force-fed Mara all this nonsense about being a proper lady. You were humiliated once, and that's all it took. You stopped being the adventurous woman I'd married and turned into a prude." He winked and smirked. "At least in front of other people. You still love sex, don't you, Sher?"

My mom's mouth dropped open so far her chin might've touched her chest.

Okay, maybe not quite that far, but still really far. I watched for insects so I could warn her if any of them tried to fly into her mouth.

Dad moved onto Mom's chaise and clasped her hand in both of his. "Relax, honey. It's time we told her the truth. I let you instill your fears into our daughter, and today I realized how wrong that was. I should've made you stop. I should've helped you get over your fears before you ever started in on Mara. I love you, Sheryl, but things have to change."

Mom shut her eyes, exhaled a long breath, and leaned against Dad. "Maybe you're right. But what will Mara think of me?"

"She'll understand."

"I will," I said. "You can tell me whatever it is. I can handle it. Believe it or not, being here with all these nudists has helped me realize how silly all my fears were. If I can get over it, so can you, Mom."

She opened her eyes, fixing her uncertain gaze on me. "But I've done things you would never have done."

"You'd be surprised what I might do."

Nico strolled up to my chaise. "Hey Mara, let's go for a walk."

"I'm having a conversation with my parents. You're being rude, and I don't want to go anywhere with you." I faced my parents, blatantly ignoring him. "Take yourself for a walk, Nico."

Out the corner of my eye, I could see him watching me.

"Go," I said, waving a hand to dismiss him.

Nico headed for the nature trail.

Mom cleared her throat and said, "About the skinny dipping…"

Chapter Twenty

Ollie

I was keeping an eye on the miniten game—okay, mostly I watched Mara—when I saw Nico Marshall traipsing down the nature trail. Had that guy ever been in the woods before? I kind of doubted it. He seemed like the urban type, not the vacay-in-the-wilderness type. Maybe I ought to go check on him, to make sure he knew to stay on the trails and not wander off into who-knew-where. The last thing I wanted to do was talk to Mara's ex, but it was my job to look after the guests.

With Eve and Val "recuperating" from their big trip south of the equator, I was the only one who could stop Nico from getting himself into trouble. Not that I cared if he got bitten by velvety tree ants or quilled by a porcupine. In my opinion, he totally deserved that. But we had these annoying things called laws that required us to keep our guests safe. Letting Nico wander into a bear's den might be fun, but it would get us shut down for sure.

So, I tramped toward the nature trail.

I passed Mara and her parents, but they were too involved in their conversation to notice, and I didn't want to interrupt just to let Mara know I was stalking her douchebag ex.

By the time I got into the woods, Nico had disappeared down the trail.

Where had the moron gone? He clearly knew nothing about the

woods. If I were an arrogant ass who'd never left the city before, where would I go?

Nope. I had nothing.

When I got to the fork in the trail, where one branch led to the hot spring and the other toward the lake, I hesitated. Two signs announced where each trail went, but I had no idea which one Nico might've chosen. Was he a hot spring guy? Or did he prefer a lake? Maybe he didn't like water, in which case he could take one of the offshoot trails after he picked left or right at this junction. Which did not help me find him.

Damn. What would I tell Mara if her ex disappeared in the woods? Or got mauled by a wild animal?

"Help!"

The cry echoed in the distance. It sounded like a man's voice.

Oh great. What had Nico done now?

"Help me!"

I decided the cry was coming from the hot spring trail and hustled down that path. Not far in, I found Nico.

He huddled in a tree, clinging to a slender branch with his ass pushed into the trunk and his arms lashed around the branch. His eyes were big, and his lips quivered.

"Oh thank God," he said, almost whimpering, when he saw me standing a few dozen yards away. "I'm gonna die. You have to do something."

"Come on, man, you got yourself up there. I'm sure you can get your sorry butt back down again." I waved at the branch he clung to, then at the ground. "It's not that far. Jump."

He flapped his head. "I can't. It'll get me."

I glanced around but couldn't see any dangers. "What will get you?"

"That." He jabbed a finger toward the ground, pointing to the other side of the tree. In a hushed but hoarse voice, he said, "It's waiting to eat me."

Maybe I should've brought a can of bear spray. I hadn't, though, so I crept around the tree, keeping a good twenty feet between me and it at all times. As I rounded the backside, I saw the vicious wild beast that had treed Nico.

The raccoon sat up on its hind legs, holding its cute little paws up.

I looked at Nico and chuckled. "It's a raccoon."

He jabbed his finger toward the animal again. "That thing chased me. It bared its teeth, and now that monster wants to eat me alive. Do something, will you? Save me."

I stifled a laugh, which turned it into a snort. "You probably scared the little guy, so he bared his teeth. Raccoons don't eat people." I glanced at the critter, who was watching Nico with what I took for curiosity. "I think your yelling and fussing caught his attention. He's curious, that's all."

"Do something," Nico snarled. "It's your job to take care of guests, isn't it? That means you work for me. So kill that monster right now."

"Kill it? No way, man. It's a harmless animal." I rushed toward the raccoon, stomping my feet and clapping my hands. "Shoo, little man. Shoo."

The raccoon scampered off, out of sight.

"See?" I said to Nico. "It's gone."

He whimpered again, injecting a slight whine into it too.

"It's okay," I said, trying to sound encouraging. I wanted to tell him to man up and get his own dumb ass down here. Instead, I told him, "You can do it. Just slide off the branch, keeping your arms around it until you're ready to drop."

"Drop?" He almost shrieked the word. "I'll break my neck. You have to call the fire department and get them to bring their truck out here."

"A fire truck?" I tried not to laugh, but come on, the guy was acting like more of a scaredy-cat than my little sister had been when she saw a big old wolf spider for the first time. Bailey had been six, so I cut her some slack. The jerk in the tree didn't deserve any of that. "You can jump down. It's only, like, six feet to the ground."

"No way. It's at least twenty feet."

Oh jeez. Nico was freaking out more than Mara had when she walked into the dining hall and saw all the nudists for the first time.

Nico whimpered again.

"Are you afraid of heights?" I asked.

He glared at me. "No, I am not."

"Okay then, get some cojones and slide off that branch."

"Could you at least pile up some leaves to break my fall?"

I spread my arms, indicating our surroundings. "It's spring. There are no dead leaves, and I'm not denuding the frigging forest to make you feel better. Oh look, there's some moss down here. Aim for that. Time to suck it up, princess, and get your own ass out of the tree."

He scowled at me for a few seconds, then slid his body off the branch with all the lightning speed of a sloth. Which meant he did it so damn slow that I probably developed gray hairs watching it. Seriously. It took him at least a minute to get one leg off the branch. Finally, he was hanging by his arms. Which were wrapped around it like he was dangling over the open jaws of a great white shark. He gaped at the ground like it *was* a man-eating beast.

"Jump," I said. "Take a breath and just do it."

Nico squeezed his eyes shut, whined like a freaking dog, and let go of the branch. The second his feet touched the ground, his knees buckled. He fell into a heap on the grass.

And he started whimpering again.

"What's wrong with you now?" I asked.

He bent his leg toward his chest, bent his knee, and hugged it while whimpering some more. "I broke my ankle."

Yeah, right. Mr. Whiny-Ass broke his ankle.

"Let me have a look," I said, kneeling beside him. "You have to let go of your leg if you want me to check out your ankle."

He eyed me with deep suspicion, like I might rip his ankle clean off his leg. "Are you a registered nurse?"

I rolled my eyes. "No, princess, I'm not a nurse. But I've taken first aid classes, so I'm qualified to look at her your ankle without killing you."

Even though I'd kind of like to do that. Never in my life had I fantasized about murdering someone, but I did now. And the more time I spent around Nico, the more gruesome those fantasies got. The one that went through my head while I palpated his ankle involved a chainsaw.

He squealed. Seriously. Like a little pink piggy.

"Calm down," I said in my patient, professional voice, the one Eve had taught me. She'd told me everyone needed to have a voice like that for dealing with annoying people. Damn, she was right. I told Nico, "I'm barely touching you, so just try to relax while I gently feel your ankle to check for injuries. Okay?"

He nodded, his bottom lip quivering.

And yeah, he had tears forming in his eyes.

I focused on his ankle. Once I'd finished checking it out, I said, "No broken bones. But if it keeps hurting"—I held up a hand to stop him when he opened his mouth, to complain, no doubt—"I'll take you to the hospital. But only if it's super painful. Got it?"

"Yeah," he mumbled.

A squirrel chattered from high above us.

Nico screamed.

My ears hurt. I was kneeling right beside him, a few feet from his big mouth.

"That's a squirrel," I told him when he stopped screaming. "It won't hurt you."

"Are you sure?"

"Positive." I sighed. "I'll help you get up, and you can lean on me while we walk back to the guest house. If you can't manage that, I'll go get somebody to help me carry you. Okay?"

"Yeah. Thanks."

Nico was being polite. I'd known the guy for maybe an hour, but he'd acted like a jerk the whole time. I guessed getting injured while fleeing from a raccoon had made him humbler. At least for now.

I shoved my arms under his and hefted him up, careful not to bump his ankle or get it bent wrong. He threw an arm around me, and I kept my arm around him. Oh yeah, this was how I'd imagined spending my afternoon. Hugging Mara's ex-husband.

We started down the trail. It was slow going, with Nico limping, but we made gradual progress toward the trailhead. Nico got winded twice, and we stopped so he could rest. Maybe his ankle really did hurt a lot. I had to assume it did and give him the benefit of the doubt. When we trudged out of the woods, Val saw us. He'd been standing at the edge of the lawn, at this end, so he ran over to help me get Nico into the main house. It was closer than the guest house.

Nico didn't even bitch about a naked guy assisting him.

After a lot of wrangling, we got Nico on the sofa in the living room, lying lengthwise on it with his ankle propped up on pillows.

"We have Tylenol and Advil," Val said to Nico. "Would you like either of those?"

"Advil," he said. "Thanks."

I sat down on an armchair across from Nico. "How's your ankle?"

"Kind of better. Still hurts like a son of a bitch, though."

"Maybe I should get you some ice."

"That might help. Thanks."

By the time I got the ice, Val had given Nico the Advil, and Mara and Eve had come to see what was happening. We finally decided Nico didn't need a doctor—and he actually agreed. His room in the guest house was upstairs, so Eve and Val offered to stay there instead so he could sleep in their room here.

Mara's parents seemed kind of annoyed by Nico's needy, whiny behavior. Because yeah, the guy kept complaining and demanding everybody get him things, like water "not from the tap but with electrolytes" and "organic gluten-free crackers with sea salt." Luckily, we had bottled water and those funky crackers, though not organic ones, thanks to Eve's insistence we try to accommodate anything our guests might want. Some people genuinely needed gluten-free foods, but Nico just wanted that because it was trendy. I knew because I asked if he had any food allergies, and he said no.

When Mara and I finally got to our rooms in the guest house, we were so tired, mentally and physically, that we kissed each other good night and went to bed.

Man, what a day. Mara's parents. Her ex. My ex. Jeez, what would happen tomorrow?

Chapter Twenty-One

Mara

The next day passed in a blur, with Ollie too busy to spend much time with me and Nico constantly texting me to ask for food or a drink or whatever thing he decided he had to have at the moment. I didn't see my parents much either, since I felt like I had to take care of Nico so Ollie, Eve, and Val could do their jobs instead of catering to the needs of my annoying ex. By the end of the day, I needed a break from all of it.

Nico tried to get me to sit at his bedside all night to "watch over" him, but I said no. He had dumped me. I'd given up my day for him. Why should I tend to his needs all night? It wasn't like he was dying. He didn't need a twenty-four-hour nurse for a twisted ankle. Once I'd explained that to him, Nico pouted but stopped demanding I stay with him.

I met up with Ollie in the guest house, and we walked upstairs hand in hand.

At the door to my room, we stopped. I pushed the door open and leaned against the jamb while Ollie slanted in to kiss me. It started out sweet and soft but swiftly intensified as I thrust my tongue between his lips and slid my hands up his neck to link them at his nape, tugging him closer. He groaned and responded with increased hunger, but despite the need growing inside us both, he kept the kiss heated but slow, taking his time while we both savored the taste and feel of each other.

He pressed his body into mine, the rigid line of erection prodding my belly.

God, I wanted him. Naked. In my bed. Right now.

I moaned and wrapped my leg around his.

Without severing the kiss, he picked me up and carried me into the room. I heard the door slam shut—he must've kicked it closed—and the next thing I knew, I was sprawled on the bed with him on top of me. The weight of him felt so good. I moaned again, tunneling my fingers into his hair, wishing he would strip my clothes off and make love to me right now. We kissed and kissed and kissed, with Ollie driving me wild with the need to have him inside me, and the velvety heat of his tongue making me so crazed my moans turned into greedy little grunts.

He pulled his head back to look at me, breathing hard. "Mara, damn, can you kiss."

"Mm, I love kissing you. It's so much more fun than it was with any other guys." I trailed my fingers down his back and up again, cradling his nape. "Especially Nico. He thinks he's a great kisser, but ugh, he really is not. I'm so grateful I found you—or fainted in your arms is more like it."

"I'm glad too." He brushed his lips over mine. "You're the best thing that's ever happened to me."

The best thing that ever happened to him? Me? My throat grew tight and dry. No man I'd ever dated described me that way. Hearing Ollie say it gave me a warm feeling in my chest that bloomed outward, intensifying into a delicious, liquid sizzle.

"Make love to me, Ollie."

He kissed me again, and this time it didn't stop there. We shed our clothes without disentangling our bodies, which required quite a bit of twisting and pulling, but we got it done. He made love to me slowly, with a languid intensity that turned sex into more than physical pleasure. It became a joining of our bodies, our hearts, our everything, in a way I'd never experienced in my life. I'd known Ollie for less than a week, but I felt like we'd always known each other, like all the failed relationships and heartbreaks had been preparation for this moment, in this time, with each other.

We fell asleep together.

And we woke up together too. Ollie roused me with feathery kisses on my neck, moving lower and touching his lips to my skin more firmly when he realized I'd woken up. I lay there with my eyes closed, reveling in the decadent sensation of his mouth exploring my body, his tongue flicking out to taste me, his fingers following the same trail down my skin. By the time he got to my feet, I was wet and aching for him.

"Yes, Oliver," I moaned. "Please, yes."

He drew my little toe into his mouth and suckled it.

I gasped at the strangely exciting sensation. Nobody had ever done that to me before. It felt... "Ohhh, yes. Do more of that, Oliver."

Releasing my toe, he chuckled. "You like toe sucking. Who knew? I learn more things about you all the time, and every single of those things makes me hot for you."

"So fuck me, Oliver." I did my damnedest to mold his name into an erotic come-on.

And it worked, because he let out a soft growl and pounced on me. With his face an inch from mine, he said, in the sexiest voice ever, "Your wish is my command, baby."

Oh God, I loved the way he called me baby.

Someone banged on the door. "Ollie, are you in there?"

It sounded like Eve Holt.

Ollie rolled off me and groaned, but not in a sexy way this time. "Yeah, what is it, Eve?"

"Your friend is here. Damian Petrescu?"

"Damian?" Ollie sprang upright. "What's he doing here?"

"I don't know, sweetie, but he swears it's urgent."

"Okay, I'm coming."

"He's in the office."

Jumping off the bed, Ollie scrambled to find his clothes. "Tell him I'll be right there."

"Who's Damian Petrescu?" I asked, sitting up.

"My old high school buddy. I mentioned him before, remember?" Ollie yanked his pants on and began the hunt for his shirt. "We went to college together too, but we haven't seen each other as much since we graduated. I got a job in Arizona, and he got one on the other side of the country, in South Carolina. We keep in touch mostly by text and email, though Damian insists on at least one phone call a month."

"It's nice that you have a friend like that. I've never had that kind of person in my life."

Ollie paused in pulling on his shirt to look at me. "Never? You said that before, but it's still hard to believe."

"Most people think I'm weird."

"What's wrong with that? Weird can be awesome." He finished getting his shirt on, tucking it into his pants. "I love your weird hang-ups, your weird…everything. I'm not exactly normal either." He points at himself with both hands. "Naturist here. That's way weirder to most people than screaming when you see nudists in the buff."

"But I don't scream when I see you naked."

His lips eased into a smoldering smile. "Sure you do. But it's a different kind of scream, and it only happens when I'm fucking you."

I bit my lip, my cheeks turning slightly warm. "That's true. I don't mind screaming then."

Ollie leaned over the bed to kiss me. "I gotta go. Have a shower if you want, then meet me in the dining hall, okay?"

"Sure."

He hurried out of the room.

I lounged in bed for another few minutes, reminiscing about last night with Ollie. I hadn't screamed that time, but it had been the most incredible sex of my life. Everything with Ollie was a revelation. I'd learned things about myself I'd never realized before, like that I love getting it on in the woods. Being here, with Ollie and the other nudists, had forced me to face my hang-ups and figure out the root cause. I couldn't blame my mother for all of it. I had gotten more and more uptight over the years, because I kept listening to people like Nico who told me I wasn't good enough.

Ollie showed me every day how much he appreciated me, just the way I was.

After a quick shower, I got dressed and left my room, heading down the hall toward the resort office at the end. When I turned into the doorway, I froze.

He stood by the desk with a gorgeous, nude blonde leaning so close to him that her breasts nudged his chest.

The blonde was Heidi Mackenzie. His ex-girlfriend.

"Please, Ollie," she said, "can't you give me one more chance? I screwed up. I'm sorry, and I miss you, and I—"

"Stop, Heidi. You dumped me, remember?"

Neither of them had noticed me yet, since they stood at an angle to me, turned slightly away. I should've announced my presence, but I couldn't make my voice function. My muscles decided to stop working too, leaving me trapped on the threshold.

"That was such a huge mistake," Heidi said. She placed a hand on Ollie's cheek. "Can't we try again?"

"I'm with Mara now."

"But we have history."

She tried to kiss him, but he turned his head away.

And saw me.

"Mara," Ollie said, shoving Heidi away. "This isn't what it looks like."

Heidi stumbled and grabbed the desk to stop her fall.

I stepped into the room. "She's trying to seduce you, right? It's not that hard to figure that one out."

Ollie frowned at Heidi. "She might've been trying, but it was not working."

"Sorry," Heidi mumbled, then she raced past me, out into the hall, her bare feet slapping on the wood floor.

"I'm not into Heidi anymore," Ollie said, coming up to me, grasping my upper arms. "I'm with you, Mara. Only you. That's all I want or need."

I glanced around the office. "Where's your friend? I thought he was waiting for you here."

"Damian was here. I gave him the room I was going to sleep in, which actually works out great since I'd much rather bunk with you." He scrunched up his nose. "We shared a dorm room in college, and Damian farts while he's asleep. Really stinky ones."

"Ew. I didn't need to know that."

Ollie laughed, pulling me into his arms. He kissed the top of my head. "Sleeping with you is way more fun. Are you okay with sharing a room?"

"We'd better be sharing more than a room. I want you in my bed every night."

"Yes, ma'am." He skimmed a hand down my back, gliding it over my bottom. "It's my job to ensure guests get everything need."

"In that case, I need you twenty-four seven. Can you be my personal concierge?"

"Not sure Eve and Val would go for that, but you can always text me if you get…needy."

"Mm, good." I snuggled into him, my arms around his waist. "Why is your friend Damian here? I mean, if it's a super personal thing, you don't have to tell me."

"It's nothing like that. He wanted to get away from the city, and he knows how much I love it here, so he decided on a surprise visit."

"You must be glad to see him."

"Sure. It's always good to see him." Ollie crooked a finger under my chin and lifted it until I met his gaze. "Damian is my top guy friend. You're my number one best friend."

"That's the sweetest thing anyone's ever said to me." I hunched my shoulders and wanted to avert my gaze, but I made myself keep looking at him. "You're my best friend too. I've never had one before."

"About time, then." He cupped my ass in both hands, lifting so my heels came up off the floor and our eyes aligned. "Mind if I kiss you? I'm having a Mara craving, real bad."

I grinned. "Please kiss me. I'm having a serious Ollie craving."

He gripped my ass more firmly, and our mouths collided. Just when things started heating up, someone coughed from the doorway.

Ollie and I turned our heads at the same time.

A man stood there. A man about Ollie's age.

"Damian," Ollie said, not letting go of my tush. "Settled in already?"

"I didn't bring much luggage," Damian said. His attention settled on me, and the corners of hi mouth ticked upward. "Who's the sexy girl glued to you?"

While Damian swept his gaze over me, I did the same to him. He had a physique somewhere between Val's enormous muscles and Ollie's more subdued buffness. His skin had an olive undertone, accentuated by his dark eyes and hair. That hair flowed down to his shoulders in wavy locks.

Damn. Were all of Ollie's friends as hot as he and Damian were?

Ollie rolled his eyes at his friend and let go of me. He took my hand, clasping it in both of his. "This is Mara Severins. She's my girlfriend."

"Yeah, I figured. Good going, Ollie. She's bodacious."

"She's also sweet and smart and amazing."

Damian grinned. "Not trying to steal your girl. She seems one hundred percent attached to you. Physically. I'm surprised you didn't need a laser to separate your bodies, the way you two were going at it a minute ago."

My cheeks flamed.

"Sorry," Damian said to me. "I didn't mean to embarrass you. That was just guy talk. We can be real asses, you know?"

"Hey!" Ollie said. "Speak for yourself. I'm sensitive and charming. You're the douche who bangs women and never calls them back."

Damian strode up to me and claimed my free hand, raising it to his lips. He kissed my hand. "It's a pleasure to meet you, Mara. I'm Damian Petrescu, a Ludar prince."

"A what?"

Ollie sighed and planted a hand on Damian's chest, pushing him away from me. "Damian's family emigrated from Romania a way long time ago, when the Ludar people fled. They still like to call themselves Rom, but most people call them gypsies."

"Don't be so culturally insensitive," Damian said. "Do I call you a nerd?"

"No, but we nerds own the title. That means it's no longer an insult. It's sexy."

I giggled. Seriously, I did. I must've sounded like an idiot, but I didn't care.

"Ollie is definitely one sexy nerd," I said. "And so unbelievably hot in bed."

Damian's brows shot up. He slung an arm around my shoulders and tugged me away from Ollie, leaning in to speak in a pseudo-whisper. "Now, Mara, you'll need to tell me all about that. Tell me everything he does to you."

Ollie seized my arm and hauled me away from Damian. "Leave my girl alone. Haven't you got a dozen of them waiting for you to go home? Maybe you should do that."

I might've thought they were arguing, if not for their smirks and the humor in their voices. These two had a strange friend dynamic, but I could go with the flow. A week ago, I would've freaked. Today, I could take it.

And give it.

Hugging Ollie, I said, "Maybe we should tape ourselves having sex. Then Damian can see for himself how wicked hot you are."

"Oh no," Ollie said, "Damian does not get to see you naked."

"What if I become a naturist like you?"

"You can't do that until after Damian goes home." Ollie shook his head. "No sex tapes. Haven't you heard how that turned out for Val?"

"Oh yeah, Eve told me. It got leaked on the internet."

"Fantastic!" Damian said. "I'll wait for yours to come up on Cinemax."

"Let's go outside," Ollie said, towing me toward the door. "Lots of girls for you to sexually harass out there, Damian. Maybe you'll get arrested, and I won't have to look at your ugly face anymore."

I let him take me outside, with Damian following.

Today might turn out to be even more exciting than yesterday.

Chapter Twenty-Two

Ollie

Damian Petrescu was an awesome friend. I would never have called it a bromance, because that term was so lame, but we were absolutely best friends. So I was glad to have him here, especially since he'd never visited the resort before. Now he got to see where I worked and why I'd quit being a computer systems engineer—well, after I got laid off I decided to quit that line of work—and took a job at a naturist resort. He seemed cool with the idea.

And of course, he loved watching the Kitten Brigade play volleyball. All but Heidi wore sports bras. Damian paid the most attention to her, tracking her every movement with his gaze.

Fine by me. If he slept with Heidi, maybe she'd stop pestering me to take her back.

Heidi was a nice girl, but I didn't want her anymore. She chucked me overboard. Why would I want to crawl back onto that boat?

Mara and I sat on a chaise together, with her on my lap. Nude guests weren't allowed to do this, since it was a violation of the resort rules, but Mara and I were both wearing clothes. We could totally paste ourselves to each other in public.

Damian reclined on the chaise next to us. He'd ditched his clothes.

Mara's jaw had dropped when he did that.

I did not get jealous. She still hadn't gotten completely comfortable with naked people, and Damian worked out a lot, so I expected her to be surprised by her first look at his physique. But she only stared at him for a few seconds, then she went back to adoring me, her lips curled up in a sweet smile.

Yeah, that worked for me.

Mara tickled my lips with her fingertips. "You don't have to keep your clothes on for my sake. I know you'd rather be nude, and I don't mind."

"You sure? I'm cool with staying covered up. You've had a lot of surprises lately, and I don't want to add more stress."

She grinned. "Seeing you naked is the antithesis of stressful. I love ogling you."

"Good. But getting naked would mean I have to move you off my lap, and I'm not ready to do that yet."

Eve and Val had ordered me to take the day off to spend time with my girl and my best friend. How could I say no to that? I hadn't seen Damian in almost a year, and I wanted lots more time with Mara. Catching up with Damian and hanging with Mara seemed like the best day ever.

Except Nico decided to butt his nose into things.

The volleyball game had just ended when the jerk approached us. Mara was still on my lap, her arms around my neck. Damian was still distracted by watching Heidi.

"Could we talk?" Nico asked Mara, completely ignoring me and the fact she was sprawled over my lap.

"No," Mara said, without even looking at him.

She didn't sound annoyed, or even vaguely interested. With her focus on me, she just seemed happy and not the least curious about why Nico wanted to talk.

"Please, Mara," the jerk said. "It's important."

With a sigh, Mara turned to look at him. "Maybe it's important to you, but it's not even a teeny bit important to me. I don't care what you want. I've moved on, and you should do the same."

She focused on me again.

Yeah, I liked this. Mara on my lap, Mara smiling at me, Mara giving her dick of an ex the big brush-off.

Nico hunched his shoulders, shoving his hands into his pants pockets. "Mara, please. You have every reason to tell me to buzz off, but I just want to talk. That's all. I swear."

He sounded contrite and maybe a little sad.

Aw, hell. Being a total sap, I felt bad for the guy. He had gotten scared shitless by a raccoon, and though I hadn't told anyone about that, I still felt for the guy. Maybe he'd realized, after his humiliating tree-hugging incident, that he needed to change his ways.

Mara sighed and asked me, "Would you mind?"

"If you talk to Nico? It's none of my business."

She chewed on her lip. "But we're together now."

"We met this week. You don't owe me any explanations, and you sure don't need my permission." I patted her leg. "Go on, it's okay."

Mara slid off my lap. "All right, Nico, let's talk."

I watched them wander off toward the little house. Once they'd gone inside, I got up and stretched, trying to think of what I should do while Mara was gone.

Damian raised his brows at me. "You're one brave guy, Ollie. Don't think I would've let my new girlfriend run off with her ex."

"They didn't run off. They went into the house for privacy."

"How much history do they have? Did they date for a long time?"

I hesitated, not sure why, before I answered. "They were married for two years. Knew each other since college, though."

Damian's brows hiked up even more. "Damn, that's… Are you sure you're okay? I like Mara, but if she still wants to hear what her ex has to say, I'm thinking it's not as over as you might want to believe."

"You met Mara a couple hours ago. I know her better."

"Uh-huh." He sat up, straddling the chaise. "Look, man, I'm your best friend. It's my job to make sure you're not jumping headfirst into an empty pool."

"Mara is the most amazing girl I've ever met."

"Yeah, but is she really over her ex?" He held up his hands when I started to protest. "Hey, just doing my best friend job here."

"I know you mean well, but stay out of it. Okay?"

"Sure. Whatever you want. Keep your eyes open, that's all I'm saying. My Ludar lidar is pinging like crazy."

"Your Ludar lidar thought Trina was the perfect woman for me. But she dumped me for another girl."

"It's not a foolproof system."

Yeah, Damian loved to talk about Ludar lidar. He was a Ludar by heritage, but they didn't have lidar back when his ancestors fled Romania. That was a modern technology, like radar but with lasers instead of microwaves. Whenever Damian thought I was making a mistake, or stepping into iffy territory, he would tell me his Ludar lidar was pinging.

"You said your piece," I told him. "Let's drop the subject, okay? Help me figure out what to do to distract myself while Mara's having a heart-to-heart with her ex-husband."

Damian glanced at the Kittens, who were gathered at the other end of the lawn, laughing and making big hand gestures. "I wonder what those luscious ladies are up to."

"No frigging idea."

He got up, smiled, and slapped my arm. "Let's go find out."

Sure, I wanted to go hang out with my ex while Mara had a private meeting with her ex. Which meant I didn't want to do it at all. This day had started out so good, with my girl and my best friend. Now it seemed primed for getting flushed down the toilet, with all my good luck swirling and swirling until it dropped into the septic tank of life.

Yeah, that was my luck. A rotten shithole buried under my feet.

I could tell from Damian's expression that he really wanted to meet the Kitten Brigade.

"Sure," I said, "let's go see what they're up to."

Chapter Twenty-Three

Mara

Why was I inside Eve and Val's house talking to Nico when I'd rather be outside with Ollie? I felt sorry for Nico, I guessed. Which was ridiculous. He filed for divorce. He made me feel unworthy, like a total screw-up who didn't deserve to be with him. Sure, he never said those exact words. But I heard them between the lines.

Our marriage had started out good. I couldn't deny that.

But he trashed it, not me.

Nico sat on a stool at the kitchen island, while I stood on the opposite side of it. I wanted distance between us, to let him know I was not ready and willing to leap into his arms at the first chance.

He fidgeted, scratching his neck. "Look, I know I messed up big time. I had a great girl. I had you, and I threw it all away. It was the worst mistake of my life."

"You wanted a divorce, Nico. I gave it to you."

"Thought that's what I wanted, but I realize now I was just scared."

"Of what?"

He glanced down at his lap, then back up at me. "I love you so much, and I didn't think I deserved a woman as special and incredible as you. Kept thinking you'd leave me. So I, uh, decided leaving you first was the best way to keep from getting hurt later on."

"You said I was stifling you. That my neurotic behavior drove you crazy, and you couldn't stand being with such a screw-up."

"I know. I said that." He rested his arms on the island, keeping his head bowed. "That was my fear talking. Took me a long time to realize it, but I made a huge mistake that I need to fix."

What on earth did he expect me to say to that? Everything he'd said and done during the last six months of our marriage had shown me how little he cared about me. When he'd moved out, I had cried—but I'd been angry too. When he filed for divorce, I cried and languished in a blue mood for a week, but then I'd tried to get on with my life. Now he'd changed his mind. He wanted me back?

Oh come on.

I crossed my arms over my chest. "Why should I believe you?"

He knifed his fingers through his hair, letting out a long breath. Then he walked around the island to me, laying a hand on my shoulder. "I missed you so much, Mara. Not having you in my life for six months—eight including the separation—it made me realize how much I love you. I got scared, acted like a jerk, and fucked up everything."

"What do you expect me to say? You wanted a divorce."

"Because I was terrified you'd leave me for somebody better."

I tried to be angry. I should've been angry. But the look on his face, the tone of his voice, those things stopped me. He seemed so…sincere. Part of me wanted to believe him. The end of my marriage had been my worst screw-up ever, something my mom never let me forget. How could I let a catch like Nico get away, she'd asked over and over and over. I knew she'd been trying, in her own bizarre way, to help me with those comments. She honestly believed I would've been better off with Nico.

He had been a catch. An attractive, charming, successful man who owned his own restaurant. He'd been featured in the biggest restaurant-industry magazines as an up-and-coming entrepreneur and five-star-worthy chef. Of course my mom thought Nico Marshall was the perfect man for me.

"We used to be so good together," he said, rubbing my shoulder. "Don't we owe it to each other to give it another try? Come home with me. Please."

Yeah, Nico could be charming. But he was also the man who'd jabbed tiny pins into me with every sneaky little comment he made about my body, my enthusiasm for sex, the way I ate, and anything else that didn't conform to his standards for appropriate behavior.

"I've changed," he said. "Please, Mara, give me another chance."

My husband wanted my forgiveness. My ex-husband. I had loved him once upon a time, but I'd believed I'd gotten over that. Had I really? Did I still love him, even a little bit? God, I didn't know anymore. The week had been confusing and wonderful, almost like a dream.

This morning, everything had seemed crystal clear. Now I was trying to see through a fog of confusion.

Nico acted sincere.

What about Ollie? I adored him, but we'd met this week. I didn't know him that well, to be honest. I wanted to know him better, but now Nico had to throw this at me. Should I give in to his contrition and give him another chance? Should I tell him to buzz off and run back out there to find Ollie? All my old fears and anxieties came flooding back while I studied Nico's face. Maybe he would be different this time. Maybe Ollie would get sick of my neuroses and my hang-ups, and he'd leave me too. Maybe Nico was the best I deserved.

Dammit, that was Nico talking, getting inside my head.

And still…those doubts kept niggling at me.

"I don't know," I told Nico. "Give me some time to think."

"Sure. Take all the time you need."

Nico's smile seemed a little sad, but also a little hopeful. He wandered out of the house.

I waited a few minutes, standing there in the kitchen thinking about my life, the mistakes I'd made, the two men who wanted me. Was I a fling for Ollie? His ex-girlfriend wanted him back. They had history, while I was just the crazy girl who'd fainted in his arms.

Was fate trying to tell me something? If so, I had no idea what.

Finally, I went outside and looked for Ollie. I spotted him at the far end of the lawn with Damian—and the Kitten Brigade. They all seemed to be playing charades, so I walked over there.

The girl who had been making gestures to depict who-knew-what finished up right as I got to the group.

"How was that the Eiffel Tower?" Damian asked. "You looked like an uptight whooping crane."

Ollie snorted. "Like you've ever seen a whooping crane."

"I did see one. In a PBS documentary."

"Yeah, right." Ollie rolled his eyes. "The day you watch PBS is the day I join a monastery."

Ollie noticed me, smiled, and waved for me to come over to where he and Damian sat on the grass. I settled onto the ground beside him, my knees tucked under me.

He leaned in to whisper, "How'd it go?"

I shrugged.

"It's Heidi's turn!" one of the girls shouted.

Heidi trotted up to the spot the other girl had just vacated, positioned directly in front of the crowd. Another girl handed her a folded slip of paper. Heidi opened it and read whatever was written on the paper. Her brows crinkled, her nose too.

Must've been a hard one.

She crumpled the paper and tossed it into a large paper cup that seemed to be acting as a trash can. I could see other crumpled papers inside it.

Heidi began to pantomime. She waved her arms and tipped sideways, raising one foot off the ground.

Ollie watched her with a rapt expression.

A beautiful, naked woman showing off her body in front of her ex-boyfriend, the man I was currently sleeping with? No, that didn't bother me at all.

In the kitchen with Nico, I'd wondered if I should take him back. Now, I was jealous of Ollie ogling Heidi. I finally understood the concept of being torn between two men. Or maybe I was just crazy, like most people thought.

Heidi waved her arms with more enthusiasm, tipping left and right, making her breasts bounce.

Damian made a catcall.

The other girls clapped and shouted out silly things like, "You're a drunk astronaut!"

Ollie kept staring at Heidi, his lips parted and curved into a relaxed smile.

"Don Quixote," I called out.

Everyone froze and fell silent. All eyes turned to me.

Heidi's face blanked. "Wow, that's right. How did you know?"

"You were making like a windmill and tilting. Don Quixote tilted at windmills."

Heidi blinked several times, still seeming shocked. "You're really smart, Mara."

"Um, thanks."

Ollie looked at me, grinning.

And naturally, Nico appeared right then. He ambled over to the group and sat down beside me, sandwiching me between him and Ollie.

Nico patted my knee in a too-intimate way. "Hey, Mara. Thanks for listening, and I hope you'll think about what I said. It's not too late for us."

I scooted closer to Ollie.

And Ollie squinted at Nico, his lips flattened.

Nico smiled at me in a way an ex-husband should *not* be smiling at his ex-wife when she was with someone else. I wanted to deck him. Then push him into a colony of velvety tree ants. While he was naked. So yeah, I didn't want Nico anymore. His pleas in the kitchen might've made me doubt that for a while, but I was over it.

Ollie grabbed my hand, jumped up, and dragged me toward the guest house.

My heart pounded. My ears started to ring because I'd stopped breathing. Why was I letting men fight over me, like I was a prize heifer and they were in a bidding war over me? It was my life. A grown woman with a mind of her own did not let men make all her decisions for her.

I stopped dead halfway to the guest house.

Ollie tugged my hand.

I yanked it away.

We stood there staring at each other for several seconds, both of us breathing hard though we hadn't walked that far. His gaze burned into me, hot with lust and irritation, a potent combination that made me grow warm too—warm and wet. He clenched his fists, which made his biceps swell.

Peripherally, I noticed the other guests on the lawn, their attention glued to me and Ollie. But I didn't care what they thought.

I barred my arms over my chest. "Don't drag me around like a suitcase. If you want to talk to me alone, ask first."

He stared at me, his eyes narrowed, for a few more seconds while he took slow, deliberate breaths. "Please come with me, Mara."

The tone of his voice shivered heat through me. It was full of hunger, the dirty kind.

"Since you asked nicely," I said, "I'll go with you."

He claimed my hand and led me into the guest house, straight to the kitchen. It had stainless steel appliances and stainless steel counters, with pots and pans and utensils hanging from hooks above the counters and the stainless steel island. It looked industrial, but then, this kitchen did serve all the guests three times a day.

The kitchen was empty right now.

Ollie hoisted me up by the waist and set me on the island. "The cooks went to town to buy groceries. We've got the kitchen to our-selves."

His voice still sounded rougher, sexier, hotter.

"I'm not hungry," I said.

"Really." He pushed between my thighs and mashed his mouth to mine, plunging his tongue deep without waiting for my tacit permission to do it, making me moan and sag into him. When he pulled away, we were both breathing harder again. "Still not hungry?"

Gazing into his eyes, feeling his hard body between my legs, I couldn't deny the truth. "Starving."

"Thought so." His mouth slanted into a sexy smirk. "And here's how I'm going to feed you…"

Chapter Twenty-Four

Maybe I got a little jealous when Mara went off with her ex. Maybe I didn't like it when she came back and Nico followed her, then he touched her like he still owned her. Nobody owned Mara. I didn't want to, that was for sure. But I loved taking possession of her body so I could give her exactly what we both wanted.

Okay, I might've been a touch jealous.

Not anymore. I was the one who had Mara alone in the kitchen, where the erotic possibilities were endless. I'd never done anything like this before. Girls knew I rocked the bedroom, but they didn't like my adventurous suggestions.

Mara was up for anything. Our time under that tree in the woods had proved it.

I grasped her hips and pulled her closer, our faces aligned. "I know you're not a suitcase. Sorry I hauled you away without asking first."

"Apology accepted." She glanced around the kitchen. "You still haven't finished that sentence. You said 'here's how I'm going to feed you,' but you trailed off instead of telling me."

"I know. Here's the rest of it." I placed my open mouth on the base of her throat, dragging it up, swirling my tongue over her skin that tasted faintly salty. When I reached her earlobe, I pulled it into my mouth and sucked, making her moan. "I'm going to fuck you so good for so long that everyone will see it on your face that you're mine and I'm yours. You'll come so many times you'll think you can't take it anymore, but still you'll beg me to do it again."

"Yes," she breathed.

I nibbled my way along her jaw, then flicked my tongue out to tease her mouth. "I want to feast on you like I've never done with anyone else. That's why we're in the kitchen."

Her pupils had blown, and her breaths came hard and fast. The faint blush that colored her cheeks made me even harder. I wanted this woman like I'd never wanted anyone, like I'd never known I could want anyone. While I'd been pretending to watch the charades game, I'd been plotting the hottest ways to make Mara shiver and moan and writhe and scream.

Nico had better find another woman. Mara was mine. By the time I got done with her, she would never want anyone else. Yeah, okay, maybe I was getting a little caveman-ish. So what? Mara seemed to like it. And I would never force her to do anything.

I moved my mouth to her ear again. "You know what I want. What do you want?"

She yanked my shirt out of my waistband and shoved her hands under the fabric, whisking them up my chest. "You, Oliver. I want you."

Her hands traveled over my chest, exploring and arousing me. But when she pinched my nipples, I lost it.

"Fuck," I hissed, and I ripped her shirt off over her head. "I'm gonna feast on you for real this time."

I tore off her bra, and she wriggled out of her pants and underwear, kicking off her sandals too. Then she stretched out on the island with her legs dangling off it, her arms raised above her head. Stainless steel shimmered around her, and her auburn hair feathered over the shiny surface, a dark halo around her face.

A dirty angel. That's what she was, and I loved it.

"Get naked," she commanded, running her hands up and down the metal surface beneath her like she wanted to make love to it.

I stripped off my clothes faster than I ever had in my life. Gazing down at her body, at the curly dark hairs below her hips, I couldn't resist licking my lips. The scent of her lust overpowered my senses. I fought the urge to spread her thighs and dive in, because I had plans for that body.

"Do you have any food allergies?" I asked.

"No." She sounded a little confused by my question.

Pretty soon, she'd understand why I asked.

I opened the big fridge and got out the items I needed for the appetizer—strawberries, whipped cream, and vanilla ice cream. I set those items on the island beside Mara.

She watched me with a puzzled expression.

Puzzled and aroused. I got the feeling no one had ever done what I was about to do to her. Damn sure Nico never had.

I returned to the island, standing between her legs, and tugged her hips to get her ass resting on the very edge. Her puzzled expression melted into a smile so sexy it made my cock throb. I took a breath to calm myself—*cut that out, little buddy, we've got work to do*—and leaned over her body, looking straight into her gorgeous green eyes.

"Your cream is the sweetest thing I've ever tasted," I told her, "but I want to feed you a different kind of cream. Open that luscious mouth for me, baby."

She opened her mouth.

I grabbed a strawberry, dipped it in the bowl of whipped cream, and held it to her open mouth. "Take a bite."

She bit off half the strawberry, closing her lips around it, chewing slowly, sensuously, and then she moaned like she'd never tasted anything so good in her life. Her eyes half closed, she savored the strawberry until it was all gone. Her lips curved up at the corners, but her eyes stayed hooded.

"Mm," she hummed. "That tastes so delicious, but not as delicious as you."

Her words, the sultry way she spoke them, it made my cock throb again. I devoured the rest of the strawberry, but fruit wasn't what I wanted to consume right now.

Take it slow. That's the plan, remember?

Yeah, the plan. What was it again?

Mara stretched her tongue out, licking the strawberry remnants off my lips. "Mm-mm-mmmmm. Food tastes better on you."

I could barely catch my breath, but dammit, I would do this the way I'd planned. I straightened my arms, putting a little bit of distance between my body and hers.

She picked up a strawberry, dipped it in the whipped cream, and smeared cream all over my chest.

"Mara—"

"Oops," she said in a sexy tone, her smile just as hot as her voice. "Let me clean up the mess I made."

She lifted her head to lap up the cream she'd smeared all over me. Every flick of her tongue made it harder for me to breathe, and harder for me to ignore what my dick wanted so badly that I might just lose it and come all over her belly.

Not that it wouldn't be hot to do that. But I had these plans.

I pinned her wrists to the table. "Do I need to tie you up? Or will you let me do my thing before you make me blow my top?"

"You don't need to tie my up, but that might be fun too."

"Maybe another time." I let go of her wrists, sliding my hands down her arms, loving the feel of her silky skin and the fine hairs that dusted it. "I've got lots more I want to do to you."

I got another strawberry, loaded it with cream, and painted a trail down her body with it, starting at her throat. Every time my berry-brush ran out of cream, I dunked it again and kept painting that path down to her belly until I reached her mound. Then I used the berry-brush to drop a dollop of whipped cream on each of her stiff nipples.

Mara squirmed and bit her lip.

Tearing the leaves off the berry, I spit them out and held the strawberry between my lips, leaning in until my mouth hovered inches above Mara's. I swept the berry across her lips until she got the idea and bit off a chunk.

I ate the rest of it. Juice clung to my lips.

Before I could wipe it off, Mara sneaked her tongue out to lap up the liquid.

Damn, she was the hottest lover any man could ever want.

I licked the whipped cream off her throat, laving my tongue over her skin in leisurely strokes, and followed the trail I'd painted down her chest. When I reached her breasts, I drew one nipple into my mouth, licking and suckling until I'd cleaned every last speck of cream off it—and until she was writhing and gasping under me. I switched to the other breast, giving it the same attention, making her squirm and whimper.

"Oliver," she cried out when I nipped her rigid peak. "Yes, Oliver, please."

She knew how much I loved it when she called me Oliver, but I also knew she wasn't doing it on purpose this time. I'd gotten her so wound up she probably had no clue what she was saying.

Getting her turned on got me wound up too. But I focused on my task, licking my way down her belly, swirling my tongue inside her navel, lapping up every last bit of cream until I reached her mound. I nuzzled the soft hairs, inhaling a deep breath through my nostrils, intoxicated by the scent of her.

"Fuck," I groaned, fluttering those hairs. She smelled so damn good, and I knew she would taste even better.

"Oliver, please hurry."

"Uh-uh. Not rushing." I forced myself to give up the scent of her and grabbed the container of ice cream. I tore off the lid and dug a chunk of ice cream out of the tub with my fingers, holding it in my fist until it started to melt. With my other hand, I urged her to spread her legs for me.

Mara watched me, her head raised, her brows cinching together.

I chuckled. "Ready for phase two?"

She nodded so vigorously her hair flapped against her face.

Opening my fist, I let the half-melted chunks of ice cream fall onto her mound. The thick liquid oozed down her skin, between her thighs. I parted her glistening folds, letting the ice cream drizzle down between them.

Mara was breathing so hard her breasts jiggled.

I lowered my head and dragged my tongue up her folds. The flavor of ice cream and Mara deluged my senses, the taste so incredible I couldn't stop myself from groaning and devouring her with more hunger. She opened her thighs for me even more, diving her fingers into my hair. Ice cream. Mara cream. Nothing better in the whole world. I licked my way up to her clit, closed my lips around it, and sucked every last drop of everything off her flesh.

Her body tensed.

Licking, lapping, suckling, so drunk on the flavor of her that I couldn't stop.

"Oliver!" she shouted as her climax rocketed through her. She clutched my head so tightly her nails dug into my scalp.

I kept going until she went limp on the island. Then I lifted my head to look at her, breathing hard, my cock demanding I feed it some of Mara too. She lay there sprawled on the cold metal surface, her eyes closed, her mouth open, an expression of pure satisfaction on her face.

God, I'd never seen anything so beautiful.

Voices echoed from down the hall.

"Shit," I hissed. "It's game time."

"What time?" Mara said, sounding as blissfully dazed as she looked.

"Game time. It's a weekly event where guests play board games in the entertainment room."

I could not go out there in my current condition.

The voices got closer, but then faded as everyone veered off into the entertainment room. It was two doors down from the kitchen.

Mara sat up, draping her arms around my neck. "I don't care who's out there listening. You need to finish fucking me. Right now, Oliver."

If she hadn't called me Oliver, maybe I could've said no.

Yeah, I didn't believe me either.

Mara took my dick in her hand and raked her thumb over the head. "Do it now, Oliver."

How did she make my name sound like the dirtiest word on earth?

I pulled away from her just long enough to get a condom out of my pants pocket. Once I'd rolled it on, I nestled between her thighs, feeling her heat penetrate the latex. The sensation drove me crazy. And I hadn't even gotten inside her yet.

"Now, Oliver, please."

With a long, guttural groan, I thrust inside her, pushing in all the way until I couldn't go any further. Her hot body molded to my cock, and she latched her legs around my hips. With her breasts mounded against my chest, I couldn't hold back for one more nanosecond.

I spun us around, pinned her to the fridge, and fucked her.

She squeezed her eyes shut, her mouth open, that blissful expression taking over her face again.

Thrusting, thrusting, harder, faster. The sucking sound of our bodies colliding echoed in the kitchen while she flung her arms around me, her nails digging into my back. I flattened my palms on the stainless steel fridge, pumping and pumping, the pressure inside me so intense I knew I'd blow any second. *Wait for Mara.* I tried to do that, tried so damn hard I was gritting my teeth.

Just when I thought I'd go off before she did, Mara came with a strangled scream. I sealed my mouth over hers to muffle her cries—and my own. I came so hard I swore I saw stars flashing behind my eyelids. A couple more thrusts did me in. I sagged against the fridge with Mara crushed between my body and the steel surface.

I let my forehead fall onto her shoulder. "Oh God, Mara."

She hugged my head and kissed my temple. "That was incredible, Ollie."

No idea how I managed to move, but I did. I raised my head and kissed her softly. Then I withdrew from her body, set her down on the floor, and discarded the condom.

A throat-clearing drew our attention to the doorway.

Damian stood there with his hand over his eyes. "Didn't see a thing, I swear." He peeked through his fingers, smirking. "Well, not much."

I expected Mara to get embarrassed and run away.

She surprised me again, laughing as she said, "Oh well, this is a nudist resort. Damian was bound to see me naked sometime."

"Thought you didn't want to go nude in front of the other guests," I said.

"I've been thinking I might give it a try. As part of my self-liberation campaign."

Damian snickered. "Yeah, Mara, you get as liberated as you want."

I flashed him a scowl, which he saw since the ass was still peeking through his fingers. Then I pulled Mara into the corner farthest from Damian and whispered, "He might've seen what we were doing a minute ago."

She glanced at Damian. Though her cheeks turned a little pink, she shrugged and said, "So what?"

"You're seriously okay with that."

"Uh-huh." She wrapped her arms around my neck and smiled. "You make me feel brave and sexy and safe."

"You don't need me for that. You *are* brave and sexy, all on your own."

Damian pretended to gag. "If you two are going to make out, I'll head back to the games before I hurl all over this nice shiny floor." He looked at Mara. "I really didn't see whatever you two were doing. I heard weird squeaking noises and thought I should check it out. You were both standing there naked when I walked in."

Squeaking noises? I kind of remembered something like that, but my brain had been offline at the time. Mara's skin must've squeaked on the stainless steel fridge.

"Get out of here," I said, waving for Damian to leave.

He grinned and skedaddled.

"What should we do?" I asked Mara.

She puckered her lips like she was thinking hard, then she smiled again. "Let's take a shower."

I scooped her up.

Damian ducked back into the kitchen. "I've got a sudden yen for cleaning a kitchen."

My best friend was offering to clean up after the mess I'd made with Mara, which I hadn't even thought to clean up myself. My brain still hadn't ramped up to full power yet.

"Thanks, man," I said. "You're an awesome friend."

"Not really. I just don't want to eat food that was made on the counter where you two got it on."

He smirked and winked.

I carried Mara upstairs to our room, where a nice, big shower stall waited for us.

Chapter Twenty-Five

Mara

After our shower, Ollie and I headed back outside. Ollie had started to put his clothes back on, but I assured him he didn't need to do that for my sake. I'd gotten used to spending my days surrounded by naked people, and seeing Ollie in the nude was hardly a terrifying experience. I didn't blame him for thinking he shouldn't go naked in front of me, considering how things had gone when we first met, but I didn't want him to change his ways to suit me.

So now, we were participating in a game of miniten—Ollie in the buff, and me wearing shorts and a tank top. I wore sneakers, but Ollie chose to go barefoot. The game pitted the two of us against Ruth and Sylvester Norris. That sounded like an easy win for us. Two fit twenty-somethings against a pair of senior citizens? Piece of cake.

Not so much, as it turned out.

Today I learned never to underestimate anyone because they're over seventy. Ruth and Sly—Sylvester asked me to call him by his nickname—beat me and Ollie, barely letting us score two points in the whole game. Miniten might be a more laid-back version of tennis, but the Norrises decided to turn it into an acrobatic performance. They leaped up to smack the ball with their thugs.

I wondered why Ruth had bothered with a bra when we were playing an easygoing sport, but she did more than leap to hit the ball. She also spun around, dodged right and left, and even dived for the ground to hit the ball when I got my angle wrong and sent it barreling straight for the grass. Sly did the same and more, leaping sideways with his feet off the ground to whack Ollie's shot before it flew out of bounds. The Norrises won and celebrated by cheering and giving each other high fives.

Ollie had chastised the young guys yesterday who had played rough. But then, one of them had slammed into me. Ruth and Sly didn't do anything like that, and they never went overboard in their enthusiasm to hit the ball and win the game.

After the game broke up, I needed a trip to the bathroom. When I returned to the lawn, I glanced around to search for Ollie.

He and Damian were relaxing on the grass, talking. Ollie lay on his side with his head propped up with one arm, his cheek resting on his palm. Damian lay on his back, hands linked over his belly. Both men wore sunglasses. The sight of Ollie naked still made me tingle, which was highly inappropriate when other people were around. I couldn't stop it, though. He was hot.

And so was Damian. But his sexy bod didn't affect me the way Ollie's did.

I caught sight of Heidi on the other side of the lawn, hanging out with her girlfriends. She kept glancing at Ollie. Staring at him, actually. How much history did they have? She sure seemed hung up on him. Ever since Heidi had arrived here, I'd wondered if Ollie still had feelings for her. I'd also wondered if I still had feelings for Nico.

No, I didn't. But the thought made me a little queasy.

Did that mean I had no feelings for him? I supposed I would always care about him in some way, in spite of all his wheedling comments that had made me feel small and useless. But we'd had good times too, and I'd known Nico a lot longer than I'd known Ollie.

Why, then, did I feel closer to Ollie than to anyone else? Why did being with him give me a sense of relaxation and freedom I'd never experienced before? He came from a normal family and worked at a nudist resort. I came from an uptight family of rich snobs who were horrified I was staying at a nudist resort. That wasn't quite accurate. Dad didn't seem to care, and though he'd always gone along with whatever Mom wanted, he had never been uptight. He didn't tell me to act like a proper lady.

And yesterday, he'd told me he was proud of me.

No, I did not want Nico back.

But I wasn't sure I belonged with Ollie either. Could people from two different planets make it work? I wasn't even sure how this thing between us could work. He lived here. I lived in Philly. He had a job here, one that he loved. I owned an apartment building, which I'd built into a profitable business. Would I give that up to be with Ollie?

He might get sick of me. I mean, I was an uptight city girl.

But he made me feel free.

I sat down next to Ollie, still wondering about all of those things.

"Hey, Mara," he said, smiling at me. He patted the grass. "Come closer, baby."

Damian lifted his sunglasses to peek at us. "Isn't that against the rules? Getting friendly with your girl while you're naked?"

Ollie kneed Damian in the side. "We aren't going to make out. Mara can sit right next to me without it getting inappropriate."

Yes, we needed to be appropriate, didn't we? I understood the need for rules at a nudist resort, but I hated that word. Appropriate. And its synonym, proper. Both words made me cringe inside.

But I scooted closer to Ollie.

We spent the rest of the afternoon just hanging out, first on the lawn, and later in the entertainment room in the guest house. Damian and Ollie taught me how to play poker, but when Damian offered to show me how to cheat at it, Ollie intervened.

"Oh no," he said, laying a hand on Damian's chest to push him away from me. "You are not corrupting my girl. She's perfect the way she is."

I got a glowy feeling in my chest when he called me perfect. But a pit soon formed in my gut when I considered the ramifications of that statement. Did he expect me to be actually perfect all the time? No, of course not. I was being ridiculous.

My parents invited me and Ollie to go into town with them for dinner at a steak house they'd heard about from Val and Eve. My parents wanted to get to know Ollie better, and in an environment where my mom would feel more at ease. That meant a clothing-required outing. Ollie accepted their invitation with more enthusiasm than I would've expected. I mean, my mom hadn't exactly welcomed him with open arms. Ollie didn't hold a grudge, which made me like him even more.

And I'd already liked him a lot. Like, really a lot.

I put on my favorite dress, the only one I took with me everywhere I went because it suited any occasion and looked pretty damn good on me. The black halter dress hugged my curves, but flared out into a swishy skirt that stopped just above my knees. I wore my black heels too, though not the stilettos I'd had on when I first showed up at the resort.

Someone knocked on the door to my room right as I finished getting dressed. I already had my makeup on and my hair fixed. Ready to go.

I swung the door inward.

Ollie's eyes went wide, then slid half closed while he drank in the sight of me. "Damn, Mara, you look hot enough to melt steel."

"Thank you." I spun around so he could see my dress swishing around my legs. "You look sizzling hot too."

He wore a suit that showed off his sexy physique without seeming too tight. It fit him so well that I swore my mouth actually watered when I saw him. Oliver Jackson was one gorgeous man.

How could any woman have called him her gay best friend? How could Heidi Mackenzie have dumped him to go back to her ex?

All his exes had to be insane. No other explanation fit the facts.

Ollie offered me his arm, like a Victorian gentleman escorting a lady to a ball.

I slipped my arm under his.

He led me downstairs, where we met my parents, and all four of us got into a waiting taxi.

The restaurant was very nice, but my mom had to comment that it wasn't "five-star quality" like her favorite restaurant back home. She also curled her lip when she saw the menu.

"Red meat?" she said with a hint of horror in her voice. "I'm a vegan."

"Since when?" I asked. "You love escargot, which is snails. Little creatures that died so you could eat them."

My dad patted Mom's arm. "Sher, don't be difficult. I know steak and potatoes isn't your usual fare, but you can make do." He glanced at me. "Your mother is not a vegan."

So she was just trying to be a pain. *Ugh.* Would she ever get over the fact I wasn't married to her favorite guy, Nico? And that I liked staying at a nudist resort? I was positive what bothered her the most was that I'd broken all her rules of propriety.

Well, almost all of them. I hadn't become a nudist yet.

I doubted I ever would do that. I loved being naked with Ollie, but the thought of having other people look at me sans clothing made my skin itch. Everywhere. Really itch.

"Something wrong?" Ollie whispered to me. He'd leaned in so my parents wouldn't hear, though they sat across the table from us.

Realizing I had actually been scratching my arm, I forced myself to stop. "No, I'm fine."

"You sure? I know your mom can make you kind of crazy."

"I'm okay, really. You're so sweet to ask."

He kissed my cheek.

Mom finally ordered a steak, despite claiming she'd become a vegan after sitting down in this restaurant. She even enjoyed her steak. Dad and Ollie told jokes and talked about computers. My father had never been adept with electronic devices, so Ollie gave him pointers on how to make his phone work better and how to optimize his home computer.

Mom said nothing. She stared down at her plate while she ate, and when she'd finished, she stared down at her lap.

I wanted to ask if she was okay, but Ollie and Dad were still talking. It would've been rude to interrupt.

When Ollie excused himself to go to the restroom, I finally asked, "Mom, are you okay? You seem…not quite yourself."

She jerked her head up, blinking at me. "What?"

Dad hooked an arm around her shoulders. "Mara thinks you're unhappy, Sher. She's worried."

"Why? I'm fine," Mom said.

I chewed on my bottom lip.

Dad sighed. "Our daughter can see you're not happy. So can I. Why don't you tell us what's wrong?"

She fiddled with the napkin on her lap. "I don't understand why Mara wants to stay at that resort. Mr. Jackson seems nice enough, but he's not the right man for Mara."

"How do you know that?" I asked. "You've barely spoken to Ollie."

"I know, but—" She raised her head to look at me, her lips pinched. "He's a nudist."

She spoke those words in such a soft voice that I almost didn't hear her.

Groaning, I said, "And nudism isn't proper, right? Nothing I've ever done has been proper or acceptable, even though I was doing everything you wanted and making myself miserable in the process. I married Nico because you thought he was the right man for me. Well, guess what? He absolutely was not."

"I never told you what to do." Mom slapped her napkin down on the table. "I tried to show you how ladies need to act, so you wouldn't be embarrassed. The level of society in which we live is not forgiving of rash behavior."

"Rash? I never did anything without first considering how you would feel about it."

"You're dating a nudist."

"Ollie is the sweetest, kindest, most honorable man I've ever met. If you'd taken the time to get to know him, like Dad has, maybe you'd realize how amazing Ollie is." I grabbed my napkin and wrung it with both hands. "I've never been good enough for you, so why should I keep trying? Might as well strip naked right here in this restaurant. Maybe if I get arrested, you'll realize how much I've hated my life, until I came here."

Tears streamed down my cheeks. My eyes burned, and my gut twisted into knots. I had never spoken to my mother this way. Never. But the words had come pouring out, and I couldn't take them back. Did I want to?

Ollie returned from the bathroom.

He stopped at his chair, laying one hand on it while his gaze flicked back and forth between me and my mom.

"The ladies had a little argument," Dad said. "Why don't you take Mara out on the balcony for some fresh air?"

"Sure," Ollie said.

I got up, and he clasped my hand, leading me across the dance floor and out onto the empty balcony.

Then he pulled me into his arms.

With my head on his chest, pressed against his warm body, I felt all the anxiety sluice out of me.

"You don't have to tell me what happened," he said. "But I'm here to listen if you need it."

I sucked in a deep breath, exhaled it in a rush, and told him everything.

There was something about this man that made me feel free and whole and like the best version of myself.

But could we work out in the long run?

Chapter Twenty-Six

Ollie

We hung out on the balcony for a while, with Mara cuddled up to me and the music from inside drifting out here to us. The balcony overlooked the river that wound through town, but we couldn't see it in the dark, except for the pale glow of the moon shimmering on its surface, like a ghost hovering below us.

Mara's argument with her mom had really upset her. I couldn't imagine arguing with either of my parents that way. I'd never needed to, because my parents trusted me to make my own decisions and my own mistakes. Mara's dad seemed like a cool guy, but it was obvious he'd let his wife run the show for a long time. Now Mara wanted to take control, and Sheryl couldn't deal with it.

I actually kind of liked Sheryl. Maybe that was weird, considering she wanted Mara to get back together with Nico, but Sheryl Kanda Severins seemed like a smart lady who loved her daughter—but who went overboard trying to protect her from the world.

Mara lifted her head off my shoulder. "Thank you."

"For what?"

"Being so sweet and understanding. It's been a crazy week, and that's all my fault."

I cradled her cheek in one hand. "None of it's your fault. Your mom and your ex-husband threw you for a loop, and I think you're doing amazingly well under the circumstances."

"See? I was right. You are sweet and understanding."

"Just don't call me your gay best friend. Not sure I can handle that right now."

"I will never call you that." She kissed me, her lips lingering on mine as softly as a feather teasing my skin. "I've had sex with you. Lots. So trust me, I know exactly how straight you are."

"Glad to hear it." I linked my arms around her waist, tugging her closer to me. "Want to make out for a few minutes before we go back inside?"

She smiled, the expression brightening her from the inside out. "Yes, please."

For several minutes, we kissed. And kissed. And kissed. Her lips were soft and warm and tasted like steak sauce. Maybe that should've been gross, but the savory flavor of it just made me want her even more. Since we were in a restaurant, I couldn't do what I really wanted to do. I settled for making love to her mouth since I couldn't make love to her the right way.

When we finally went back inside, Mara's lips no longer had any lipstick on them. Luckily, I'd brought a handkerchief, so I wiped her lipstick off my mouth before we headed back to the table where her parents waited for us.

Sheryl seemed surprised when I pulled Mara's chair out for her and waited for her to sit down before I took my seat.

Yeah, I seriously doubted Nico ever held a chair for a woman or held a door for a woman or any other polite things nice guys did. Were all the guys in the Severins family's "level of society" as dickish as Nico? Nah, they couldn't all be like him. I'd met nice rich people. Maybe the Severins family liked hanging out with asshats. It was more likely Sheryl insisted they hang out with those people so they could be a part of that kind of society.

Whatever kind it was, I didn't want to go there.

I glanced at Mara. Could I stay with her and not join her world? She said she hated her life, but it was all she knew. I couldn't ask her to give that up for me. We'd known each other for such a short time. I already knew I wanted to be with her for the long haul, but maybe she didn't want that.

Sheryl cleared her throat. "Mara, I'm sorry. I shouldn't have gotten short with you, and it's none of my business how you live your life."

Mara's eyes widened. "Mom—"

Her mother raised a hand. "Let me finish, please. I have a lot to say."

"Okay."

I laid my hand over Mara's on her lap, giving it a quick squeeze. She flashed me a grateful look.

"Your father and I had a long talk," Sheryl said, "while you and Ollie were out on the balcony. I don't mean to make you feel unworthy. It's time I told you why I've been so hard on you and pushed you to be a proper lady, or what I thought was a proper lady."

Sheryl had her hands clasped tightly on the table.

Peter closed his hand over hers, giving her an encouraging smile.

"When I started dating your father," Sheryl said, "my mother disapproved. Peter wasn't an appropriate match for me, since his family was middle class." She looked at me when she said, "The Kandas have owned a string of high-end furniture stores for decades. When my great grandparents started the business, it catered to everyone, not just the wealthy. Over the years, as my family became more affluent, the business changed too. We lost sight of where we came from and stopped trying to appeal to anyone who wasn't in the right strata of society."

Why was she telling me this? Since she didn't want Mara dating me, she had no reason to explain herself to me.

But she kept looking at me when she spoke again. "I refused to stop seeing Peter. My mother put her foot down and threatened to disinherit me. I told her to go ahead and do it, because I would not break off the relationship."

Mara's mouth fell open. "Mom, you never told me any of this."

"I know. I'm sorry, Mara, I should have told you everything a long time ago." Sheryl bowed her head for a couple seconds, then met her daughter's gaze. "I stood up to my family, but it nearly cost us everything. Your father and I moved in together and got jobs. I worked as a cleaning woman, and he found work as a carpenter."

"What?" Mara said, gaping at her mother. "I thought—You always talk about the big check Grandma and Grandpa gave you as a wedding gift. Half a million dollars, that's what you said."

"And they did give us that gift." Sheryl glanced at her husband and smiled with genuine, deep affection. "Six months after we struck out on our own, my mother gave up. She agreed to accept Peter as long as we got married and both worked for the family business. The Kanda family business. You know your Severins grandparents aren't wealthy. My parents welcomed Peter and his parents into the family. It took a long time for the 'right' people to accept my new family, but eventually they did."

I still couldn't figure out what Sheryl was getting at with her story. Sure, I got that she was admitting she and Mara had more in common than Mara had thought. They both decided to be with men their mothers disapproved of, but I sensed Sheryl was trying to make some other point too. Damned if I knew what.

Mara's mom fixed her attention on me again. "I apologize, Ollie, for the way I've treated you. Peter has been telling me for days that I should look to my past for answers about the present. My husband likes to say cryptic things and then wait for me to figure it out. It's how he shows me what I've been doing wrong."

Peter patted his wife's hand. "You need a nudge in the right direction sometimes, that's all."

She nodded. "That's why I adore you, Peter. You're more than the love of my life. You're my conscience too."

"No, you don't need me for that. You always do the right thing, eventually."

"Because you show me the way." Sheryl turned back to her daughter, and her eyes glistened with what seemed like tears gathering in her eyes. "I'm so sorry, Mara. I love you, and I'm more proud of you than you could ever imagine. Despite everything I've done, you have grown into a strong and capable woman. You run that apartment complex without any help from me or your father, and you stood up to me when I went too far."

Mara opened her mouth, closed it, opened it. She did that several times before she managed to speak. "Thank you, Mom. But I'm far from perfect. I've screwed up so many times—"

"No, don't do that. Do not dismiss your accomplishments." Sheryl leaned forward, and the tears pooling in her eyes shimmered even more. "You are a better, stronger woman than I could ever hope to be. Don't let anyone, not even me, tell you otherwise."

"You've never told me I'm not worthy," Mara said in a hushed voice. "I decided that's what you meant every time you told me how to behave like a proper lady. I was so afraid of screwing up and embarrassing you and Dad that I never did anything I really wanted to do. That's my fault, not yours."

"I made you feel that way. It wasn't my intention, but that doesn't change the fact I made you feel unworthy." The tears rolled down Sheryl's cheeks. "If I ever say anything about being proper again, don't listen to me. Listen to your heart, Mara, always. I let my mother convince me that being proper was the only way to survive in this world, but she was wrong. Find your own way."

Mara started crying too, wiping the tears away with her fingers.

Peter draped an arm around Sheryl's shoulders and gave her a squeeze. "It's okay, Sher. Everything's okay. Now that Mara understands why you are the way you are, she won't be afraid anymore."

"That's right," Mara said, sniffling. "I might have accidentally wound up staying at a nudist resort, but being there has made me realize I need more out of life than being accepted by the upper-crust elite. I don't care about any of that. Not sure what I do want, but I know I need to change my life."

Peter handed his wife a napkin.

She blew her nose delicately. "I want you to do whatever makes you happy. Promise me you'll do that."

"I will, Mom."

The ladies excused themselves to go powder their noses, which I figured meant they needed a few minutes to stop crying and splash some water on their faces or whatever women did to freshen up after a round of tearful confessions. Guys didn't do tearful confessions, so I had no idea what happened after something like that.

Peter and I talked about sports while we waited for our girls to come back. We were in the middle of a debate about which baseball team would win the World Series this year when I spotted a waiter leading two people toward an empty table across from us.

I froze. That was Heidi and Nico.

They couldn't be on a date. Heidi would never go for a jerk like Nico Marshall. Would she? Nah, she had to be trying to make me jealous or something.

Jeez, was I really that narcissistic? Thinking Heidi wanted me so badly that she'd hook up with Nico to get my attention. That had to be the dumbest thing I'd ever thought.

Nico settled onto a chair at the table, not more than fifteen from where Peter and I sat.

The waiter pulled out a chair for Heidi, who smiled and said something to him, probably "thank you."

Of course Nico hadn't bothered to get her chair for her. What a douche.

Heidi noticed me, her eyes flaring wide for a heartbeat, then she smiled and waved.

I waved back.

She waved at Peter too, who reciprocated.

When Nico saw me, he puffed up like a baboon who'd claimed his mate and wanted every other boy baboon to know she belonged to him. He aimed a smug smile at me.

Did he really think I'd get jealous? Did he think I'd care if he dated Heidi? Well, maybe I would—but not because I still had feelings for her. She was a nice girl, and I didn't want to see her get tangled up with somebody like Nico. Heidi deserved a lot better.

Mara and Sheryl came back to our table, giving me a great excuse to stop wondering what Nico was up to with Heidi. She was an adult who could make her own decisions.

The music started up again.

I guessed the band had taken a break, though I hadn't really noticed the lack of music. The conversation between Mara and her mom had kept the four of us distracted from everything else.

Nico got up and offered Heidi his hand. "Let's dance. You look so beautiful in that dress, it's a shame to waste it by just sitting here. I'm so lucky to have a date with a woman of your caliber, and I want to show you off to the world."

What a load of bullshit. I could practically smell it, that's how deep he'd shoveled into the shit to dig out that smarmy line.

Heidi blushed and took his hand, letting Nico lead her out onto the dance floor.

No, she couldn't be falling for his bullshit. Heidi was smarter than that.

"Ollie," Mara said sharply.

I realized I'd zoned out on the conversation at our table and smiled at Mara. "Sorry. What were you saying?"

Her gaze sharpened on me like a laser beam zeroing in on its target. "Dad asked if you've ever gone fishing."

"Oh. Yeah, sorry, I missed that." I faced Peter. "No, I've never gone fishing. Is that something you like to do?"

"Yes," Peter said, "I used to take Mara with me sometimes, until she got older and lost interest in it. Maybe both of you could join me and Sheryl on the boat sometime."

"Sounds awesome."

I couldn't stop myself from glancing at Nico and Heidi as they walked onto the dance floor and he took her in his arms, smiling and saying something that made her laugh.

Mara jabbed me in the side with her finger and whispered, "What are you doing? You haven't taken your eyes off Heidi since she walked into the restaurant."

Leaning in close enough her parents wouldn't hear, I said, "I'm worried about what your ex-husband is up to with Heidi."

"That's their business, not yours."

"I know, but Heidi's kind of…too trusting for her own good."

"Maybe you should go tell Heidi you're still in love with her."

"Why would I do that? I'm not in love with her."

"Are you sure about that?" Mara said loud enough for her parents to hear. "You haven't been able to stop looking at Heidi since she showed up the other day."

Nico was watching us and smiling like the smug baboon he was.

He must've noticed Mara's angry expression. I needed to calm her down and explain things, but I couldn't do that with Nico the Numbskull watching. He'd probably break out a bag of popcorn and munch on it while he enjoyed the show.

"Let's go outside and talk," I said to Mara. "Please."

"Fine." She hopped up. "Let's go."

She half walked, half ran toward the front doors.

And I hurried after her.

Chapter Twenty-Seven

Mara

What was wrong with me? I never got hotheaded. I cowered in corners and got so anxious it made me nauseous, but I never confronted anyone. Well, I had tonight. I'd confronted my mom, and she hadn't blown up. Instead, she'd confessed the truth to me, about how Grandma made her feel and how she did the same thing to me. But nothing my mom said had upset me as much as the way Ollie kept staring at Heidi.

I shouldn't be jealous. Right? It was dumb. Ollie wanted to be with me.

So why did he care so much about Heidi going on a date with Nico? He ought to be glad about that, since it meant Nico was losing interest in getting me back.

Unless Nico was using Heidi as a ploy to make me jealous.

I marched halfway across the parking lot, having no idea where I was going, before I stopped and spun around to face Ollie.

He raised his hands, palms out. "I am not in love with Heidi. I never was. We dated for five minutes last year, that's all."

Before I responded, I took a moment to calm myself with slow, deep breaths. "You were staring at her. And it was obvious you didn't like her being with Nico."

"Yeah, but that doesn't mean I want her back."

"Even if you don't love her, you're still attracted to her and still feel something for her. During that charades game, you couldn't take your eyes off Heidi."

"Because I couldn't figure out what she was supposed to be acting out."

"You looked like you really enjoyed leering at her naked body."

"Come on, Mara." He threw his arms up. "We were all naked. It's a nudist resort."

"And I'm the uptight city girl who won't take her clothes off." I hugged myself, suddenly feeling chilled. "Maybe you belong with someone like Heidi, someone who's not tied up in knots with all these hang-ups and anxieties."

Ollie strode up to me, grasped my upper arms, and looked me straight in the eye. "I want you, Mara. Only you. But Heidi is a nice girl, and I don't want her to get hurt as part of some scheme Nico's cooked up to make you jealous."

"I'm not jealous."

He leaned in closer, his lips hovering a hair's breadth from mine. "I'm not jealous either, not of Heidi and whoever she goes out to dinner with. The only time I get jealous is when Nico looks at you." One side of his mouth slanted upward. "I didn't like it much when Damian looked at you either, and he's my best friend."

"I get jealous whenever Heidi snuggles up to you. It's awful, and I don't want to feel that way, but I can't help it."

He brushed hair away from my face, his finger grazing my skin. "Heidi never snuggled up to me. She tried to kiss me once, but I told her I'm not into her anymore. She gets it, I think. But even if she doesn't, I have zero interest in her—except as a friend."

"Oh. Good." Having him so close was making me…tingle. I should've moved away, but I couldn't convince my body to do it. "I have zero interest in Nico, in any context."

"Glad to hear it." He slid an arm around my waist, drawing me closer until our bodies met. "Maybe I better show you how I really feel."

I couldn't catch my breath, with his body molded to mine and the heat of him penetrating me. "That's not necessary. I believe you."

"But I've always been better at show than tell."

He thrust his free hand into my hair, cradling my head so he could tip it back, curving my neck. With a soft groan, he dragged his tongue up the column of my throat, leaving a trail of moist heat on my skin. The air cooled the moisture, making goosebumps raise all over my body and my knees go weak. I clutched at his shirt to keep from collapsing at his feet, but every thought fled my brain when he danced his tongue over the sensitive skin just under my ear.

"Oliver," I breathed.

He pulled my lobe, and my diamond stud earring, between his teeth and licked it.

My knees buckled.

Ollie held me up with his strong arms and murmured in my ear, "Do you understand now?"

"Yes. I—" My voice failed me when he sucked on my lobe and tugged on the diamond stud with his teeth. "Oh, Ollie…"

He lifted his head to look at me. "Told you I was better at showing than telling."

"Mm-hm." I laid the back of my hand on my cheek. "You definitely know how to set me on fire from head to toe."

"Because you show me what you like, without saying a word." He pushed a hand between our bodies, cupping my mound. "I love finding every way to drive you crazy."

I tilted my hips forward, pushing his hand more firmly into me. "You make me feel wild and free, like I can do anything and nothing bad will happen."

"How wild are you feeling right now?"

"Like I want you to throw me down on the hood of the nearest car and fuck me."

He glanced over my shoulder and sighed. "Better save that for next time. Your parents are coming this way."

"Oh." For the first time ever, I didn't panic at the idea of someone catching me in an intimate moment with a man. Instead, I turned toward my parents and said, "We'll meet you at the car."

They veered in that direction.

Ollie held my hand while we made our way to the car. He kept holding my hand on the drive back to the resort, and he didn't let go until we walked through the door to my room. Our room. I wanted to make love with him, but he suggested tonight had been emotional and everybody needed a good night's rest. I had to agree. The evening's events had taken a toll, and I was ready to sleep.

Once we got in bed, he kissed my lips tenderly. "Not sure I can control myself. I might wake you up five times overnight to make love to you."

"I wouldn't mind that."

"You need to rest." He kissed me again. "There's always tomorrow."

After another kiss, a long and sexy one that made me tingle again, we curled up under the covers together, naked. I'd always wanted to sleep naked, but it had seemed like an improper thing to do, so I never tried it. I'd slept naked all night with Ollie once before, but going to bed in the nude still seemed wild and sinful.

And I loved it. The feeling reminded me of Ollie.

I woke in the morning in a fantastic mood, well rested and energized for the day ahead. Ollie had left me a note explaining he had to get up early to handle office duties, so I should go ahead and have breakfast in the dining hall with the other guests. He promised to find me later. And he signed the note, "Love, Ollie."

Once I'd done my usual morning routine—face washing, moisturizing, putting on makeup, fixing my hair—I got dressed and headed for the door.

Someone knocked on it.

Was it Ollie? He'd implied I wouldn't see him until after breakfast, but maybe he'd gotten his chores done earlier than expected. The prospect of seeing him again made me almost giddy, so I flung the door open.

Nico leaned against the jamb. "Morning, Mar-Mar."

"I hate that nickname, and you know it." I tried to push past him, but he thrust out an arm to stop me, so I glowered at him. "Out of my way."

"We need to talk."

"No, we don't."

He moved in front of me, forcing me to shuffle backward. "I didn't sleep with Heidi."

"She turned you down? What a shocker. I knew she was a smart girl."

"Oh, I could've fucked her if I'd wanted to. I can spot an easy lay at a hundred feet." He stretched an arm out to take hold of a lock of my hair, twining it around his finger. "But I was more interested in your reaction to seeing me with Heidi."

"Get out of my way."

"Not until you admit you got jealous." He leered at me, roving his gaze up and down my body. "You and Ollie got in a big fight after that. He's jealous of me being with Heidi, and you're jealous of her for being with me. We've still got a connection, Mar-Mar. Stop fighting it."

"Oh please." I tried to squeeze around him, but he managed

to bar the entire doorway with his body by spreading his legs and arms. I glowered at him again. "If you don't move on your own, I'll make you do it."

He laughed. "Little Mara thinks she's a superhero. That's so damn cute. You can't even get in an elevator unless somebody pushes the buttons for you."

"You don't know me at all."

"I'm the only one you can be with. Ollie Jackson will get sick of you eventually, and you'll realize the truth."

Fisting my hands at my sides, I gritted my teeth and hissed, "Go. To. Hell."

Then I backed up a few steps and took a running start before swinging my leg up to kick him in the gut.

Nico flew backward, landing in the middle of the hall flat on his ass.

While he lay stunned, I rushed past him and down the hall to the office door. I knocked, but he didn't answer. I turned the knob, finding it unlocked, and swung the door open.

No Ollie.

I spun around just as Nico roused from his shock.

He lifted his head to look at me. "Damn, Mara, what's gotten into you?"

"Liberation."

I stepped over him on my way to the stairs. Just as I reached the landing, Nico called out to me.

At the bottom of the staircase, I swerved left to head for the dining hall. My feet stopped moving so suddenly I almost tripped over my own toes.

There, halfway between where I stood and the door to the dining hall, Ollie leaned against the wall with a naked Heidi plastered to his body. He wore his work uniform. Heidi was puckering her lips, leaning in for a kiss, all but begging for it. He held her head in both hands like he was about to lay one on her.

My heart pounded. My head grew light and wobbly, or at least it felt that way. My hand flew to my chest all on its own accord, and I couldn't breathe.

Ollie noticed me. His eyes bulged, and he shoved Heidi away.

She tumbled over backward, landing on her rump.

"Mara," Ollie said, hurrying toward me. "It's not what it looks like."

"What's going on?"

"She was trying to kiss me, but—"

"Looked like you were about to kiss her."

"No." He bracketed my face with his hands. "I was trying to push her away. Heidi's stronger than she looks, and she was really determined. I couldn't push her away too hard or I might accidentally hurt her." He glanced over his shoulder at Heidi and winced. "Looks like I hurt her anyway."

Heidi was sitting on the floor massaging her ass.

I guessed he had needed to be more careful pushing her away, but still, he'd taken who-knew-how-long to even try it. Was I being irrational? I had no idea. Nico had made me feel like a foolish, stupid girl for so long that I didn't know if I could trust my own instincts. They urged me to believe Ollie. I'd known him for such a short time. What if I trusted the wrong man again? Gave my heart and soul to the wrong man again?

The adrenaline from my confrontation with Nico had me wired. I knew that, but I couldn't do a damn thing to stop it.

Ollie gazed into my eyes with such earnestness that it made my chest ache. "I care about you, Mara, a hell of a lot. Please believe me, I don't want Heidi—or anyone else."

Heidi clambered to her feet and hugged herself, her attention on me and Ollie. She bit down on her lip so hard it turned white, veering her gaze away from us. Head bowed, she slumped her shoulders.

I had no energy left to feel bad for her. Why should I empathize with Heidi, anyway? She had repeatedly tried to steal Ollie away from me.

"Mara."

Ollie's voice drew my focus back to him.

I shut my eyes for a second, hauling in a deep breath and exhaling it slowly. When I looked at him again, I shook my head. "I can't do this. You've come to mean so much to me, Ollie, but I shouldn't have rushed into this thing with you. I'm fresh out of a bad marriage, clogged up with all these crazy anxieties and fears, and I had no right to drag you into my mess."

"What are you saying?"

Something I did not want to say but that I'd suddenly realized I needed to say—to do, for myself and for whatever this was between us. "I have to go home. Be alone, and try to figure out what I need and what I want. I haven't really lived my life on my own terms, what with my mom and Nico telling me how to behave and who to love. I get why my mom did it, and I'm not angry with her anymore. Nico's another story."

Ollie bent his head to level our gazes, his nose millimeters from mine. "What about me? Us?"

"I don't know. Honestly, I just don't know." I peeled his hands away from my face, though I loved his touch, because I had to start separating myself from him right now. "I know I love being with you, and I meant it when I said you make me feel free and wild and happier than I've ever been. But I need to live my old life, for real, before I can commit to anything else. I don't expect you to wait for me. I'll understand if you can't."

He stared at me for so long I wondered if he might be considering how to phrase "fuck you, bitch" in a polite way. But no, Ollie Jackson would never say anything like that. Maybe I was saying those words to myself. How could I walk away from an amazing man? Maybe I'd lost my mind, for real, but all I knew was I had to sort out my own life before I could share it with anyone else.

Ollie kissed the tip of my nose and rested his forehead on mine. "You go home and do whatever you need to do. I'll be here, waiting for you, for as long as it takes."

I took his face in my hands and kissed him. "You're a good man, Oliver. The best I've ever known."

Then I walked away.

Chapter Twenty-Eight

Ollie

Well, at least Mara hadn't said I was like her gay best friend. This time, I got dumped the old-fashioned way—face to face, with apologies and explanations. I supposed that was better than getting dumped by text message. Yeah, that happened to me too. A brush-off text was bad enough, but a brush-off text full of crying emojis was even worse. I still couldn't keep a girlfriend, no matter how solid and hot the connection was between me and the girl in question.

Mara hadn't exactly broken up with me. Had she? Sitting on a little sofa here in the entertainment room, alone—everyone else had gone to the dining hall for breakfast—I replayed in my mind everything she'd said. I remembered all of it, word for word. She needed time. She needed to live her old life for a while. She didn't expect me to wait for her, but she clearly hoped I would.

How long did it take a woman to sort out her life?

Maybe I shouldn't wait for her, but I'd meant it when I said I would. I knew we had a connection, a strong one, and it was based on more than sex. I'd gotten to know the amazing, smart, strong woman behind all those hang-ups. She'd gotten over all of that, anyway. Well, most of it. Maybe she did need to go home for a while to figure out how to be herself—her true self, the one I'd gotten to know—without the complications of hanging out at a naturist resort with me, my ex, my best friend, and a bunch of other wacky but lovable people.

And then there was Nico.

I picked up a deck of cards and shuffled it, not really paying attention to what I was doing. The sound of the shuffling cards became kind of soothing, and I relaxed back into the little sofa. Shuffle. Shuffle. I needed patience if I wanted to have Mara in my life, and I knew she was worth it. But what if she decided being with me didn't fit in her new life plan? Shuffle. Shuffle. The cards poured out of one hand into the other, over and over. Nothing I could do if Mara wanted to leave. Unless I tied her to her bed upstairs. As hot as that sounded, I kind of doubted holding Mara hostage would convince her we belonged together.

My hand slipped, and the deck of cards flew out of my hand, spraying across the table, the floor, and a couple of chairs.

Shit. Maybe I was cursed.

Peripherally, I noticed someone stepping into the doorway. When I glanced up, I groaned out a long, pathetic sigh. "What do you want now, Heidi? You've screwed up my life enough for one day."

"I'm sorry, Ollie." She shuffled up to the table, where I had my feet propped on it, and only then did I realize she was wearing clothes. "I know I screwed up everything, and I want to fix it. Or at least try to."

Could I really blame Heidi for the fact my life had been dumped into a shithole again? It wasn't fair to pile all the blame on her shoulders.

I sat up and scrubbed my face with both hands, groaning again. "I'm sorry too. You didn't help matters, but my life would suck even if you hadn't tried to lay a big, wet smacker on me in the hall."

"Mara's packing. I saw her when I walked past her room. The door was open." Heidi perched her butt on the table's edge. "I need to apologize and explain myself. It won't take long, I promise."

"Okay, fine." I made a go-on gesture. "Get it over with."

"I need to say this to Mara too." Heidi got up, grabbed my hand, and tugged. "Please, Ollie, come with me. I won't do anything crazy, I swear. But we need to go upstairs to catch Mara before she leaves."

As much as I did not want to do it, I let Heidi lead me upstairs. Mara was just zipping up her suitcase. By the looks of things, she'd already packed her multitude of other bags. The dresser drawers hung open, empty.

Heidi and I stopped a few feet inside the doorway.

Mara swiveled her head to look at us, her focus veering down to my hand which Heidi still held and then up to my face. Her lips tightened.

I ripped my hand free of Heidi's. "She grabbed my hand to drag me upstairs, that's all. I am not having sex with Heidi."

"Yes, I can see that." Mara's lips twisted to one side, then the other, like she was trying not to smile. "At least she's not super-glued to your body anymore."

She was teasing me, right? That had to be a good sign.

Heidi stepped between me and Mara. "I need to apologize to both of you. I've done stupid, awful things. I'm so sorry, and you have my word I will never bother either of you again. Maybe someday we can be friends, Mara, but I'll understand if that's never possible. And Ollie, I understand if you don't want me around either. I won't come back to the resort again."

I shoved my hands in my pants pockets. "I can't ban you because you dumped me and then tried to seduce me. Let's just forget that stuff happened and move on."

"That's really generous of you, Ollie." Tears welled in Heidi's eyes, and she sniffled. "Thank you. I don't deserve your forgiveness, but I'm grateful you can see a way to move past all my craziness."

"I forgive you, Heidi."

A single sob burst out of her. She flumped down on the bed, keeping her head down until she'd calmed her staccato breathing. Wiping at her eyes, she raised her face to Mara. "I am so sorry, Mara, for everything. I've been so horrible, trying to steal Ollie away from you. I convinced myself you two weren't serious about each other, that it was just a vacation fling. But now I see how much you two belong together. I swear I have never in my life tried to seduce a guy away from another girl. It's just not me."

"Yeah, it really isn't," I said.

Mara studied Heidi for a moment, her expression giving away nothing.

Heidi grabbed a tissue from the box on the bedside table and blew her nose.

Finally, Mara sighed and sat down beside Heidi. "I forgive you. I honestly don't know if friendship will ever be possible between us, but I won't rule it out. That's the best I can offer."

"It's more than I deserve. Thank you, Mara." Heidi blew her nose again. "I know there isn't any excuse for the way I behaved, but there is kind of an explanation. My boyfriend, Tim, he dumped me last summer. It was the fifth time he'd broken up with me. I kept going back because he kept swearing he'd never cheat on me again, that he loved me so much, that our relationship meant everything to him. And I kept believing him."

"Yeah, I know," I said. "You pushed me overboard so you could go back to him."

"But I regretted it almost immediately. It was too late, though, and I couldn't come crawling back here."

Mara handed Heidi another tissue.

Heidi dried her eyes with it while she said, "I believed I had to fight for my relationship with Tim, to keep trying over and over, because he's not a bad man. He cheated because I wasn't giving him what he needed. Which is bullshit. But I believed that for a long time, partly because he kept telling me it was true."

"I know what that's like," Mara said. "To have someone constantly saying you're not good enough, it hurts. And it burrows into your heart and soul, so deep it can be hard to get it out."

Heidi turned her head toward Mara and blinked rapidly. "How can you be sympathetic to me? I tried to steal Ollie."

"Yeah, but Ollie and I weren't officially a couple. Besides, I'm starting to think you tried to seduce him in public places because you wanted to get caught and be punished for it."

Heidi stared at Mara, her face blank. "How did you know? I just figured that out this morning, after I made myself the wedge that drove you and Ollie apart."

"Once I got over the anger, I realized you must have a lot of insecurities, just like I do." Mara laid her hand over Heidi's. "We have that in common. I understand how other people can mess with your head and make you feel like nothing you do is right. Maybe you should do what I'm doing. Live your life alone for a while and see what happens."

"That sounds like a good idea." Heidi managed a small smile. "You're a super nice person, Mara. I get why Ollie thinks you're amazing."

"He has nothing but nice things to say about you too." Mara patted Heidi's hand. "That's how I know your recent behavior isn't normal for you. And that's why I forgive you. I'm glad we had this talk."

"Me too." Heidi got up. "I'll leave you guys alone now. Please don't give up on each other because of what I did. You two are a perfect match."

She left.

And I was alone with Mara. My skin itched, but I knew it wasn't a physical problem. I had no idea what to say to Mara now. She was leaving. I didn't want her to go, but I couldn't make her stay.

"I get that you need time," I said, "but I meant what I said. I'll wait as long as it takes."

"Yeah, I know." She stood and surveyed her bags. "But I need to do this for myself."

"Let me help you with your luggage."

I reached for the nearest bag, but Mara shooed me away.

"You don't have to do that," she said. "I can manage."

"But it's my job."

"Okay, fine." She picked up one of the smaller suitcases. "I'd appreciate the help."

I picked up the biggest, heaviest suitcase.

Val had offered to drive Mara to the airport with her parents, so I said goodbye to her beside Val's big, super-expensive truck. I kissed her cheek, because anything more seemed weird when she was leaving me. Sure, we hadn't exactly broken up. We hadn't exactly been a couple either. I had no frigging idea what we'd been to each other, but I knew one thing for sure.

I would miss her.

Once Val's truck disappeared down the driveway, I walked over to the little house and knocked on the door.

Eve swung it open and pulled me into a hug. "Ollie, I'm so sorry. I thought you and Mara were perfect for each other."

"So did I. But she didn't really end things. She needs time, that's what she said."

Eve ushered me into the kitchen, waved for me to sit on one of the stools at the island, and took a seat on the one beside me. "Nico told everybody that you and Mara had a huge fight at the restaurant and that she told you to go to hell. I know that's garbage, but I thought I should make you aware of what he said."

"Is that jackass still here?"

"No, Val and I banned him from the resort for life." Eve smiled. "Val literally threw Nico into a cab, along with his luggage, and told Phil to dump him off at the airport."

"Wish I could've done that." I rested my arms on the island, my thoughts rewinding to the last thing Mara said to me before she climbed into Val's truck. "Mara says she needs to sort through all the emotional stuff that happened this week and that means she can't have any contact with me for a while. That feels an awful lot like I've been cut out of her life."

"She'll be back. I can feel it."

"I hope you're right." I drew random patterns on the butcher-block island with my fingertip, obsessed with the pointless task. "I don't have good luck with women. Don't have any luck at all, actually."

"This time it's different." Eve clasped my hand to stop me from drawing invisible lines. "I saw you with Mara. What you two have isn't a fling. It's real, and I know she'll figure that out too."

"Mara needs to learn how to stand on her own two feet, and I get that. But I can't help worrying she'll realize I'm not the right one for her, and I'll be out in the cold. Again."

"Give it time, but don't wait weeks like Val did with me."

I glanced at her sideways, smirking. "Yeah, I remember how you jumped on a plane to California so you could go smack some sense into him."

"When you love someone, you fight for them. That's what I learned last summer."

"First, I have to let Mara do her self-analysis thing. Right?"

"I can't tell you what to do, Ollie. You know Mara better than I do."

"Yeah, I guess." I checked my watch, groaned, and slid off the stool. "A new guest will be here any minute. Better get out there and greet them."

"Let me do it." Eve hopped off her stool. "You need a few days off. Go hang out with Damian and the rest of the gang." She tugged on one of the buttons on my shirt. "And get out of these clothes. That's an order."

"Yes, ma'am."

"Oh, and you're moving back into the guest room here." She tapped my chest. "That's also an order. You wouldn't leave me alone when I was down in the dumps about Val leaving, so I won't leave you alone either."

"That sounds vaguely like you'll be stalking me."

"Only if you try to get away from me." She smiled and patted my cheek. "Relax. I'll ask Damian to keep an eye on you when I'm not around."

"Great. I have a feeling I'll be stalked by everyone at the resort." I pumped my fists in the air halfheartedly and gave a phony whoop. "This is the awesomest vacation ever."

"We'll stalk you only because we love you."

She kissed my cheek and left.

I got my stuff moved into Eve and Val's guest room and got rid of my clothes, then headed out to the lawn. Damian and some of the other guests were playing badminton. I spotted Heidi slinking toward the driveway while lugging a wheeled suitcase.

So I hurried to catch up to her.

Heidi froze when she saw me. "Ollie? What are you doing?"

"Don't leave, Heidi. Not because of me."

"I'm not leaving because of you. Not completely. I need to go home and get my head on straight, somehow."

"Women are walking out on me all over the place today."

"Mara will be back. She's crazy about you." Heidi lunged toward me to give me a quick hug. "You deserve to be happy, Ollie."

"So do you. Promise you won't stay away from the resort on my account. You and the rest of the Kittens love it here."

Heidi rubbed her arms. "We'll see."

A cab drove up, but it wasn't Phil driving this time. He'd still have been on his way to the airport with Nico. I held the door for Heidi while she climbed in, then I bent to kiss her cheek.

"Have a safe trip home," I said.

She smiled a little. "You're a good man, Ollie."

I shut the door, then stowed Heidi's suitcase in the trunk. And for the second time today, I watched a woman I cared about disappear down the tree-shrouded driveway.

Chapter Twenty-Nine

Mara

"Make sure the new sign gets put up today, and change those lights in the second-floor hallway," I said to Roger, the head of maintenance in this apartment building. "I don't want any gloomy areas in the public spaces. This building needs to be light and cheerful and welcoming."

"Will do." Roger smiled. "You're really on fire these days, aren't you? A new sign, new decor, new furniture in the lobby. You even hired full-time, on-call child care so parents can go out to dinner and a show without needing to search for a sitter."

"Everyone deserves to have fun. That's something I've learned lately, and I want to ensure our tenants enjoy living here." An idea popped into my head, and I said, "Oh, I also want to have weekly pool parties, weather permitting, with free food and beverages."

Roger scribbled on the almost-full sheet of paper clamped onto his clipboard. "Danny says the tenants keep raving about you and all the changes you're implementing. They love the suggestion boxes you've put on every floor too."

Danny manned the front desk during the daytime, while his twin brother, Dave, handled things at night. Twenty-four-hour concierge service was another new perk. The suggestion boxes on every floor meant nobody needed to feel self-conscious about voicing their opinions, since they no longer had to drop off their suggestion cards at the front desk. They could still do that if they wanted, but they had other options too.

"Thank you, Roger," I said. "I couldn't have done any of this without you and the rest of the staff. It's a team effort."

"With one very smart, very talented woman at the helm. You're our captain, Mara. We follow your lead—not because we have to, but because we love you."

He smiled again and strode off down the hall.

I walked back into my office. Sitting down behind the desk, I got back to work on the new marketing campaign. This one needed more oomph, since it would promote not only this complex but also the two new buildings I'd purchased and planned to refurbish in the same vein as this building. I hadn't asked my parents for money. I hadn't needed to. This apartment complex had become successful enough that I could get a loan from the bank, one I knew I could pay off swiftly once I got the new buildings up and running.

Two weeks had elapsed since I left Au Naturel Naturist Resort—and Ollie. He called me every day, twice a day, and we talked for hours sometimes. I'd told him all about the changes I was making to my business. He often told me how proud he was and how I amazing I was, which always made me blush. Ollie could see that, considering that we usually turned our calls in video chats.

Once, we even turned it into video phone sex. Yeah, that had been soooo hot.

He never asked when we would see each other again. Ollie was too sweet to pester me about that.

I wanted to see him in person. Wanted it so badly I dreamed about it every night. But I needed to finish what I'd started here first. How long could it take to get my chain of apartment complexes going full steam? It had taken months to get this one complex rolling along smoothly.

Waiting that long to see him…

Focus, Mara. You'll never get there unless you finish this marketing campaign.

For the rest of the day, I worked my brain to its limits. Then I headed home to my condo—the big, empty one. Sure, I had plenty of furniture and even artwork on the walls, but this place didn't feel like home anymore. The nudist resort did.

After ordering dinner in, I cuddled up on the sofa with my favorite fleece throw and an action movie on TV. Watching a hunky man fight the bad guys, getting sexily covered in sweat in the process, usually cheered me up. Tonight, it just made me think of Ollie.

Halfway through the movie, I heard the doorbell ring.

I paused the movie and padded over to the door, my fuzzy purple slippers dragging on the wood floor, and swung the door inward.

Nico grinned at me. "Mar-Mar, baby, I've missed you."

"Yeah, I know. I made sure you missed me every time you showed up at my work or showed up at my home or showed up anywhere within a ten-block radius of me."

Had I been running away from my ex-husband? Hell yes. I'd had enough of Nico at the resort, and I did not need to see him ever again.

"Come on, Mara," Nico said in a wheedling tone. "We can still work things out."

I laughed too loudly, because really, his statement was the dumbest thing I'd heard in ages. "Which part of me kicking you in the gut made you think I might ever want to see you again, much less get back together?"

"Thought you'd cool down and get back to being yourself. You know, now that you've gotten away from that freak show."

"I'm looking at a freak show right now." I flapped my hand in a go-away gesture. "Skedaddle."

"We belong together." He slid a hand up and down my arm. "You know I'm the only one who'll put up with your neurotic behavior."

I hadn't been neurotic since I left the resort. I'd found a new focus and a new determination to make my life what I wanted it to be instead of what others thought it should be.

"Go away," I told Nico. "Or do I need to get a restraining order?"

He grasped my shoulders and tugged me closer, lowering his lips toward mine.

I slapped both hands on his chest, stomped my foot down on his, and shoved him away.

Nico stumbled but didn't fall down. "Shit, Mara, what's your problem?"

"You, obviously."

The clacking of high heels made us both glance down the hall.

My mother was marching toward us, looking like a general about to kick the ass of her most derelict soldier. A general dressed in designer clothes. And wearing stiletto heels.

She rammed her stiletto down on Nico's foot and kneed him in the groin. "Get away from my daughter."

Doubled over, he gasped for air.

Mom bent to aim her glare straight into his eyes. "If you keep harassing Mara, I will call in every favor I'm owed to have you arrested and charged with stalking."

Nico finally caught his breath and straightened, though he cupped his privates like he thought Mom might nail him in the balls again. "You attacked me."

"Did I?" my mother said in her most frigid tone. "There's only one witness. What did you see, Mara?"

"Looked to me like he tripped."

Nico gaped at me. "And did what, hit my dick on the doorknob?"

I shrugged. "All I know is you fell before my mom got within ten feet of you. Maybe you had a few beers before you showed up at my apartment to harass and assault me."

"Assault *you*? I'm the one whose balls got burst like a balloon."

My mother dismissed his claim with a hand gesture and a soft snort. "You'll survive and still be fertile. Unfortunately."

"You two are crazy." Nico eyed us like he thought we might both jump on him and start tearing the flesh off his body. "I'm done with you, Mara. Done for good."

"Hallelujah," I said, raising my hands to the heavens.

Nico scurried off down the hall, practically flinging himself into the elevator when the doors opened.

Mom ushered me into my apartment. We both sat down on the sofa.

"Is that a Bruce Willis movie?" she asked, glancing at the TV. Her eyes lit up the way they often did at the prospect of a *Die Hard* movie. "Let's rewind and watch it together from the beginning. I love it when he takes his shirt off."

Yep, my mother loved her man candy. It was the one thing we'd always agreed on, and the one thing that always brought us together. Mutual appreciation of hot, sweaty men beating the bad guys to a pulp.

"Sure," I said. "Let's do that. I'll make popcorn."

"First, I need to talk to you." She stared down at her lap for a moment, then raised her head to look me in the eye. "There's something I've never told you, and it's time I did. I hope it will help you understand my behavior a little better."

I tucked my feet under me cross-legged style. "Okay."

"You know your father and I were married for four years before we had you, our miracle baby." She hesitated, biting her lip the way I often bit mine. "Two years before you were born, I had a miscarriage. The doctors told us I couldn't have children. Your father and I were devastated, and we even started talking about adoption. Went to an agency a few times too. Then the miracle happened. We found out I was pregnant—with you."

"Wow, I never knew that." Miscarriage? No hope of having a baby? God, I couldn't imagine going through something like that.

"The point is that I worried about losing you, while I was pregnant and after you were born. I smothered you because I was terrified something might happen to you." She sniffled and paused to dig a tissue out of her purse, dabbing her eyes with it. "Even once you were old enough that I didn't need to worry about your physical well-being, I still worried you might get hurt in other ways. Emotionally. So I tried to shield you from all of it and prepare you for whatever I couldn't see coming. That's why I was hard on you."

"I get that, Mom, I do. And it's okay." I clasped her hand. "You've always been there for me when it counted. Who stood beside me during the whole divorce court thing?"

"That was the least I could do, after the way I've mistreated you."

"Let's not dwell on the past anymore. I forgive you, and I want us to move forward and start fresh. That's what I've been doing."

"I'd like that. Thank you, Mara." She took my face in her hands and kissed my forehead. "I love you. All I want is for you to be happy."

Tears pricked at my eyes, but I blinked them away. "I love you too, Mom."

She blew her nose, rolled her shoulders back, and said, "You love Ollie too."

"Yeah, I do." An image of Ollie flared in my mind, and my chest ached. "But I don't know if we belong together. We're so different."

"I don't think you're as different as you believe. Besides, your father and I aren't the same, but it works for us. Our differences balance out and complement each other."

"Ollie lives in Oregon. At a nudist resort." I sank back against the sofa. "I want to be with him, and I've kind of been planning for that, but sometimes I think he'll be better off if I let him go. What if my new outlook on life doesn't last? I might slip back into Neurotic Mara mode."

"You have never been neurotic. I force-fed you my fears, and I regret it more than you'll ever know." She slipped an arm around my shoulders. "Don't let my mistakes taint your future. You know what you want, so go and get it." She gave me a quick, firm squeeze. "Go and get *him*."

"I can't fly to Oregon right now. I'm in the middle of re-branding my business."

She patted my arm. "Oh, you won't need to go as far as you think."

"What are you talking about?"

The doorbell rang.

My mother stood. "Get up, Mara. You have a visitor."

"I've had enough visitors tonight. It's probably Nico again."

She shook her head. "No, dear, it's not. I guarantee that."

"Ugh, Mom."

"Get up." She grabbed my hands and pulled. "He's waiting."

He? That single word made my pulse speed up and my skin tingle. It couldn't be.

I jumped up and ran for the door, flinging it open.

Ollie smiled, holding out a bouquet of daisies. "These are for you, Mar—"

He didn't get to finish saying my name. I threw myself at him, latching my arms around his neck and kissing him.

"I'll leave you two alone," Mom said.

The clacking of her heels told me she was walking away, but I didn't pay attention to anything else. Ollie was kissing me back with a hunger I'd never experienced before, and I responded with the same passion. God, he tasted so damn good. He felt so damn good too. With my body crushed to his, I relished the sensation of all his muscles flexing against me, and when he lashed his arms around me, I loved the way his biceps flexed and his hands splayed over my back.

He scuffled into the apartment with me clinging to him, my feet dangling above the floor. We didn't separate our mouths until he backed me into the sofa and I tumbled onto it.

We were both naked inside of one minute.

And he was inside me seconds later.

"Oliver," I whispered into his ear while he made love me to tenderly, taking his time, letting us both revel in the bliss of being together again.

After we both came, and we lay there with Ollie on top of me, I realized the curtains were still open.

Ollie followed my gaze to the windows. "Well, I guess any snoopy neighbors who have telescopes got a good show tonight."

"Let them watch. Who cares?"

He arched his brows. "You really don't care anymore, do you?"

"Nope." I skimmed my fingers up his back, loving the way his breath hitched. "I'm so glad you're here. I'd been planning to wait until I got the business going full steam before I begged you to take me back."

"Begging sounds hot, but it's not necessary." He brushed hair away from my eyes. "I told you I'd wait as long as it takes. I love you, Mara."

"I love you too."

He rolled off me, sitting on the edge of the sofa. "Are you going to stay here in Philadelphia?"

"Only until the two new apartment buildings are ready to go."

"You have two new buildings?"

I nodded. "This time, I bought them myself. Got a loan and everything, without any help from my parents. I'm sure knowing I'm the daughter of Peter Severins and Sheryl Kanda Severins didn't hurt, though."

He laid a hand on my thigh. "You get more amazing every day. How long will you need to stick around here?"

Now that he was here, sitting naked beside me, I had trouble remembering why I needed to stay in Philly. I had employees—lots of smart people who could handle anything that came up. I could work on the marketing plan from anywhere.

"Actually," I said, sitting up, "there's no reason to wait."

"What are you saying?"

"Let's go home, Ollie. Tonight."

He grinned. "Seriously? I don't know if we can get a flight out tonight. Your mom arranged for me to fly here, but the return flight isn't until morning."

"Can't wait that long. I don't care if we ride the bus all the way to Oregon." I wrapped my arms around him. "Just take me home."

He kissed me, long and slow and hot.

"You know," I said when we finally separated our mouths, "I bet my mom and dad can help us get a flight ASAP. They know people."

"How's it going with your mom?"

"We had another talk, and I told her I want us to start fresh instead of focusing on the past. She agreed."

"Glad you two made peace."

I couldn't stop myself from admiring his body, which I hadn't seen in person for two weeks. "Why didn't you tell me you were coming here?"

"Your mom called me this morning and said I should get my ass to Philly. She booked and paid for my flight." He glanced at our naked bodies. "Think we better get dressed if we're going home tonight. Airlines still frown on nude travel."

"Promise me one thing."

"Whatever you want."

"Never, ever wear clothes unless you absolutely have to."

Ollie chuckled. "You got it."

Chapter Thirty

Ollie

Life was perfect. I had my girl, my best friend, and an amazing group of guests who had become like family to me.

Mara and I had gotten home early yesterday morning—predawn early—and slept so late we had breakfast for lunch. After that, we had excused ourselves to spend time alone. Eve and Val didn't mind me taking a few days off. They were happy for me and Mara, and they knew better than anyone what a reunion meant.

Lots of sex. Lots and lots and lots of it.

But today, we were kicking back on the lawn with the other guests. Damian had gone home only long enough to quit his job and move his stuff here. I'd suggested to Eve and Val that Damian would make a great concierge for our expanding resort. They agreed but insisted Damian take today off and start his job tomorrow.

Like I said, life was perfect.

Mara and I were sharing a chaise, with me naked and her clothed. Well, since she wore tiny shorts and a bikini top, "clothed" was a relative term. God, I loved her body. I loved her, period.

"I'm ready for a walk," she said, getting up to stretch her lithe body.

"Yeah, sounds good." I got up too. "Better get some shoes."

She unzipped her shorts and pushed them over her hips, along with her bikini bottoms. They fell to her ankles. She kicked them aside and stripped off her bikini top. Stretching again, she said, "Mm, that's better."

I gaped at her.

Damian raised one brow and smirked.

While he was looking at Mara. Naked Mara. My naked girlfriend.

"Hey!" I said, smacking Damian's arm. "Quit gawking at my girl."

"Chill, Ollie," he said. "If you get bent out of shape every time a guy looks at Mara, you'll need serious therapy. Like, today." He glanced at Mara again. "Especially if she's becoming a naturist."

Mara nodded. "I am."

Pretty sure my eyes bulged like a cartoon character's.

She walked up to me and settled her palms on my chest. "Relax, Ollie. It doesn't matter how many guys look at me because I'm only looking at you."

"You really want to be a naturist?"

"I do. We both have to stay clothed while we're doing our jobs, but the rest of the time..." Her lips curved into a sexy smile. "I'll be au naturel."

"Mara's got a job here?" Damian said.

"Oh yeah," I told him. "Didn't you hear? She's our new marketing specialist. And she's also an entrepreneur in her own right, since she owns three apartment complexes."

"Damn, you really lucked out. Didn't you, Ollie?"

"I sure did."

Mara slipped her hand into mine. "So did I."

We ambled down the nature trail hand in hand.

Before I knew it, a month went by. Mara and Damian settled into their new jobs and excelled at them. I'd never doubted they would. Damian being...Damian, he couldn't resist bringing some of his Rom sensibilities to the resort. When he suggested he could offer our guests palm readings, I wasn't sure about it. I mean, that seemed awfully carnivalesque for a family-friendly place. But Eve and Val both loved the idea.

And of course, Damian ran with it. He convinced Val that he needed a special place to do his palm readings, and Val agreed. With Val's backing, Damian bought a freaking gypsy wagon, the kind that was usually pulled around by horses. And oh yeah, Damian suggested we offer horseback nature tours too. Eve and Mara loved that idea, but it meant we needed more employees to clean up the literal shit the horses left behind.

The gypsy wagon sat parked by the guest house, on the opposite side from the lawn, where all new guests would see it. The wagon had a blue, barrel-shaped roof and ornate decorations inside and out. The interior featured a small table with a gold tablecloth and lots of fringe hanging from it. Damian dressed up like a gypsy too, in clothes that Mara described as "hot Rom chic." His outfit seemed a little overdone to me, but the guests really did love his fortune-telling routine. He wore his uniform the rest of the time, while handling his concierge duties.

Today, I was greeting new guests—a married couple who had brought their kids with them. The twin boys looked about ten, but I'd never been good at guessing ages. Damian could guess anyone's age with surprising accuracy, which he claimed was "God's gift to the Ludar."

Maybe he did have mystical powers. Who knew? I kind of doubted it, but I had to admit his intuition was often spot on. He'd been wrong about me and Mara, but hey, nobody got everything right all the time.

Just as I was giving the new guests my standard spiel, reciting the resort rules and pointing out all the amenities, the door to Damian's wagon swung open and he hopped down the steps.

"Who is that?" the wife asked, her expression turning very, very appreciative.

Yeah, I'd seen that look a lot since Damian started up his palm reading schtick. Women salivated over him. Mara claimed it was the outfit, and his body. But mostly the outfit.

Damian wore black jeans and a black, long-sleeve shirt with the top three buttons undone, revealing a swath of his tanned chest. The chicks dug that. He also wore big black boots with chunky bronze clasps, a braided hemp necklace, and a big silver ring. He'd kept his hair long like before but purposely made it messy, giving him that "I'm a wild gypsy" look.

"That's Damian," I said to the new people. "He's our concierge, but he also does palm readings, tarot readings, and fortune telling."

"Can he speak to the dead?" the wife asked.

"Oh please," her husband said. "It's all a big show. A bunch of hooey to get more money out of the tourists."

"I can't swear he has supernatural powers," I told them. "But Damian is a genuine gypsy, though they prefer to be called Rom. Damian is descended from a line known as the Ludar."

"He's gorgeous," the wife said. "I'd love to have him read my palm."

"Uh, let's move on to the guest house." I shepherded them in that direction, hoping to defuse the jealousy bomb ticking away inside the woman's husband. I'd gotten used to handling the side effects of having Damian here. Swinging the main doors open, I waved for the family to enter. "Here we are."

The next day, my family showed up. Mara hadn't met my parents and my sister yet, but I knew they'd love her.

My sister, Bailey, marched straight up to Mara and said, "Liver's totally gaga over you, so you better not be mean to him."

"I would never do that," Mara said. "Ollie is my favorite person in the whole world. He's my best friend too."

"Cool." Bailey offered Mara her hand. "I'm Bailey Mariel Jackson, but you can call me B."

"Since when?" I asked. "Last I heard, you wanted to be called Bay, like you're a city or a port or something."

Bailey rolled her eyes and sighed. "When I was twelve, I wanted to be called that. Now I'm B. Get over it, Liver."

"Don't you want to be called BM, for Bailey Mariel? You know, BM like a bowel movement."

"Gross! Grown-ups are so totally retarded." Bailey took Mara's hand. "Come on, let's go someplace private and talk. I need to warn you about all the gross things Ollie does. Like when he eats baked beans and—"

I slapped a hand over Bailey's mouth. "Don't scare Mara away with your disgusting teenage humor."

"Okay, fine." Bailey caught sight of Damian and shrieked. "D-Man! It's you!"

My sister raced over to my best friend and high-fived him. They started talking and laughing, and I really hoped they weren't exchanging stories about baked beans and me.

"Ignore my sister," I told Mara. "She's insane. Teenage boys are supposed to be gross, but Bailey decided she's being a trailblazer by becoming a teenage girl who has a disgusting sense of humor."

"Well, you did start it by calling her BM."

"Yeah, I did." I pulled Mara snug against my side. "My family fell in love with you at first sight. I think I did too."

"I fell for you right away too, but it took me a while to admit it to myself." She latched her arms around my waist. "I'm not afraid anymore. The future isn't a scary, dark place these days. It's bright and full of potential."

"Yeah, it is." I scooped her up in my arms. "Let's go for a nature walk."

"Mm, I know what that means." She wriggled, smiling with excitement. "Naked fun time in the woods."

"And I know the perfect spot."

"I'm all yours, Ollie."

Oh yeah, my life was absolutely perfect.

Chapter Thirty-One

Mara
Two months later

I slid across the wooden bench to make room for Ollie, Bailey, and their parents. My mom and dad sat on the other side of me, leaving me sandwiched between the Severins and the Jacksons, with Ollie right next to me. There was nowhere else I'd rather be.

Ollie slipped his hand into mine, threading our fingers.

The ceremony would start in a few minutes. Eve Holt and Val Silva would tie the knot today, in this beautiful little church eighteen miles from Au Naturel Naturist Resort, with friends and family filling the pews. Lots of people loved Eve and Val. I'd come to love them too, the way I loved my family and Ollie's and all the guests, even Damian too.

Eve and Val seemed like opposites, but they shared important things in common and brought out the best in each other. She was a no-nonsense businesswoman, but Val encouraged her to take time to enjoy life and let go of her inhibitions. He had been a playboy athlete and still had an exhibitionist streak, but Eve brought out the softer side of him, the Val who loved his family and wanted one of his own someday.

Ollie and I had similar effects on each other. I'd been a tangled mess of fears and pent-up desires, but Ollie showed me how to embrace my passions and stop worrying about what other people thought. He had been a loser in love who thought he couldn't keep a girlfriend, until I proved him wrong.

Everyone finished filing into the church, and the first strains of the wedding march filled the air, played by a string quartet. A saxophone added a sexier vibe. The sax had been Val's idea, naturally.

We all twisted around to see the doors, waiting for Eve to emerge.

She moved into the doorway on her father's arm, revealing her dress that was a gorgeous combination of sleekly modern and lacy traditional, with a neckline that managed to be both sexy and modest. Her strawberry-blonde hair fell in loose curls around her face, and her makeup enhanced her natural beauty without overpowering it.

Eve looked so beautiful, so happy, so ready to join her life with Val's.

Her groom stood at the altar, waiting for his bride. He and Eve had decided not to have groomsmen or bridesmaids, since they had so many friends and relatives that it would've been impossible to choose who should stand up there with them. Besides, all they needed was each other.

Larry Holt led his daughter to the altar, kissed her cheek, and winked at Val. Then he took his seat in the front row beside his wife.

I clutched Ollie's hand tightly while we listened to the minister recite the opening lines. "Dearly beloved, we are gathered here today..."

But I stopped listening then. I watched the expressions on Eve and Val's faces, fascinated by the joy and love they evinced and the commitment they were making to each other. It was beautiful, magical, emotional. Some people might've said marriage was irrelevant these days, but the looks on this couple's faces told a different story. They loved each other with everything they had and pronounced their intentions to love and honor each other with so much conviction that it made my heart swell.

Love was real. Marriage meant more than words spoken before an officiant. It touched something deep inside everyone in this church.

Eve and Val exchanged rings, and then they kissed.

Cheers erupted inside the church. A few people whooped or whistled.

I started to cry.

And I wasn't alone. While Eve and Val walked back up the aisle, heading for the doors, I noticed other people crying too—including Ollie. He hid it well, but I saw the way his eyes glistened and he swallowed visibly. I loved that he could get choked up by seeing two of his closest friends tie the knot. I loved him, period.

Everyone walked across the street to the restaurant that would host the reception. I met Val's parents and his sisters, and I danced with so many men that I lost count. Ollie got the first dance with me, but Damian waited until much later, after I'd taken a whirl with everyone else, before he asked me for a dance.

While we glided across the floor, Damian said, "I've been to weddings before, but this one has made me rethink whether I want to get married."

"Have you been against it until today?"

"Yeah. It seems like a silly tradition, but now…" He shrugged. "Maybe it's not so silly after all."

Wow. Eve and Val had made a convert without even trying. Well, a potential convert.

"I've known Ollie for a long time," Damian said, "and I've never seen him so happy. You did that. So thank you, Mara."

"You don't need to thank me. Ollie did the same thing for me, and no words can describe how grateful I am to him."

"Ollie has an idea for how to express his gratitude." Damian nodded toward something behind me and stepped back. "She's all yours, man."

I turned to see Ollie standing there, holding out his hand to me.

"Come on," he said, "let's go for a walk. There's a nice little park a couple blocks away."

"Not sure my shoes are good for walking. They're strictly designed to look pretty."

"That's okay. I've got your sneakers in the car. We'll grab them on the way out."

I settled my hand in his, letting him lead me out of the restaurant. We both grabbed our sneakers from the car and strolled down the sidewalk past cute, touristy shops, until we reached the little park. Flowers overflowed concrete planters along the asphalt path that led through the park, beneath a canopy of trees.

Ollie stopped in a secluded spot and dropped to one knee.

My throat went thick. I knew what he planned to do, but still I couldn't breathe from the anticipation.

"I love you, Mara," he said, pulling a small velvet box out of his pocket. "I want to spend the rest of my life with you. After all the bad break-ups and 'you're like my gay best friend' bullshit, I finally found the one woman in the whole world who understands me and makes me feel like the best version of myself."

He flipped the lid open on the little box, revealing a sparkling diamond ring.

The tears flowed, trickling down my cheeks, and my lips trembled.

"Mara, will you marry me?"

I nodded, because I couldn't speak.

"Should I take that as a yes?" he asked with a lopsided smile.

"Yes," I managed to say, though the word came out choked and almost inaudible.

He slipped the ring onto my finger.

Then we just gazed at each other, with me crying, both of us too overwhelmed by the emotions of this moment to move or speak. I swiped at my eyes and sucked in a big breath.

"Oh Ollie," I said, "I can't wait to marry you."

"Good." He surged up to crush me in his arms. "Because I'm not letting go of you, not ever."

I wrapped my arms around his neck. "Not letting go of you either."

We kissed, and we didn't stop kissing until I was lightheaded from lack of oxygen. I loved kissing this man, and I could do it for the rest of my life.

"Let's go," I said. "We need to celebrate our engagement the right way."

"You mean while naked and screaming each other's names?"

"Absolutely. Take me home, Oliver."

He grinned. "You know how I get when you call me Oliver."

"Well, stop dawdling."

"Yes, ma'am."

He swept me up in his arms and took me home.

Epilogue

Damian
Three weeks later

I loved my job. Working at Au Naturel Naturist Resort was the best thing that had ever happened to me, and I had my best friend to thank for it. Ollie had convinced me to quit my old job, since I was bored out of my ever-loving mind there, and join him here. He'd been pestering me about it for almost a year, ever since he quit his tech job to move to Oregon. I kept saying no. I mean, a nudist resort? How could I ever concentrate with all those hot, naked girls prancing around? Then I came here for a visit and suddenly understood.

Not that many hot girls on the premises. Well, except when the Kitten Brigade was here. I'd met those girls once so far, but they were coming back today. Most of our guests were families or senior citizens.

So yeah, no hordes of nubile hotties to distract me.

Too bad, but also good. I loved women, but this was my job now, not a sexy vacay at an adults-only nudist resort in the Caribbean.

Had I been to one of those? Absolutely.

I climbed out of my "gypsy wagon," as Ollie insisted on calling it. Since I liked playing up the Rom angle, I didn't care if everyone called me a gypsy. So what? It was just a word.

Hopping off the last step onto the grass, I stretched and closed my eyes while I soaked up the sunshine.

The rumbling of a vehicle's engine interrupted my moment of relaxation.

I glanced toward the driveway, about a hundred feet away, and smiled.

A big, pink RV was pulling up. The Kitten Brigade had arrived.

Hot, naked girls on demand. Wasn't I the luckiest jerk on earth?

I watched the Kittens disembark from their RV, all of them wearing pink T-shirt dresses. All but one. The blonde who exited last wore cargo pants and a baggy T-shirt, with a baseball cap covering her hair. I remembered that hair. Golden blonde, silky, glistening in the sun. She'd let it grow out, so now it tumbled over her shoulders in lustrous waves. I also remembered her breasts. Spectacular, they were. I'd seen all of her nude body, but I had never even flirted with her, much less kissed her. I didn't want to be the rebound guy.

Heidi Mackenzie had been hung up on Ollie the first time I'd met her. Maybe she still was.

One way to find out.

The other Kittens shed their dresses, tossing them high in the air while whooping with joy.

Heidi hunched near the front bumper of the RV. She didn't undress.

Weird. She'd been one of the most fervent devotees of nudism.

Eve, Val, Ollie, and Mara all emerged from the little house to greet the newly arrived guests. Mara approached Heidi, and the two women shared a brief conversation that ended with Mara hugging Heidi.

Even weirder. Heidi had tried to seduce Ollie away from Mara a while back. Now they acted like old friends. There had to be a story behind the change, but I'd need to ask Ollie about that.

While Eve and Val helped the Kittens carry their tents and bags to the camping area on the other side of the guest house, I snagged Ollie and Mara.

"Hey, lovebirds," I said. "What's the deal? I thought Mara and Heidi would have an epic throwdown when they saw each other again. I was hoping for a down-and-dirty girl fight, with mud wrestling and everything. Preferably in the nude."

Ollie rolled his eyes at me. "The girls made up a long time ago. They've been trading emails."

Mara nodded. "We've talked on the phone a couple times too."

I really didn't get it. If I had a girlfriend and some dick tried to steal her away from me, I wouldn't forgive the guy and become his BFF. But Mara and Heidi had become friends. Seriously? Had I stumbled through an invisible portal into *The Twilight Zone*?

Ollie clapped a hand down on my shoulder. "Mara and Heidi are being adult about it. Besides, Heidi's been bummed out and needs all the friends she can get."

Well, if sexy little Heidi needed a friend...I volunteered for the job.

"Leave her alone," Ollie said, giving me his stern face that always looked silly to me. He wasn't the tough-guy type.

"What?" I said, pretending to be clueless. "All I want to do is help her through this transitional period."

Transitioning into my bed. That would cheer her up, for sure.

"You're my best friend," Ollie said, "so I'm asking you bro to bro. Give Heidi some space."

"What if she jumps my bones? It would be rude to reject her. It might damage her self-confidence."

"Are you really going to wait for her to make the first move? If she does."

"Fine, yes, I'll wait until she's ready. I'm not a total dick, you know."

"Yeah, I know." Ollie put his arm around Mara. "We should go help the Kittens get set up."

I glanced toward the guest house and saw Heidi going inside. "Isn't the home-wrecker staying in a tent with her girlfriends?"

Mara rolled her eyes at me this time. "Heidi is not a home-wrecker. She's actually very sweet. And no, she's not staying with the other Kittens. She'll be in the guest house."

Ollie kissed Mara's cheek. "We'd better get going if we want to have time for today's Japanese lesson too."

"Can't miss that," Mara said with enthusiasm.

Yeah, Ollie and Mara were learning Japanese online, through one of those language websites. It didn't sound like fun to me, but they seemed to like it.

The lovebirds ambled off to assist the Kitten Brigade.

I wandered into the guest house to find Heidi. Not that I planned to hit on her. Not yet, anyway. But I was curious why she'd dressed like a female version of a college guy. I'd never dressed that way, but cargo pants had been the uniform of choice for a lot of the guys I'd met in college. Some of the girls too.

But not girls like Heidi. She had a beautiful face and a killer body, and last time I'd seen her, she wasn't shy about showing it off. She clearly loved stripping naked. So why hide all those curves now? And that creamy skin, with those cute little freckles sprinkled around just enough to make me want to count them all with my tongue.

I found Heidi loitering at the bottom of the stairs, her head tipped back, seeming to admire the carpentry or something.

"Hey," I said. "Remember me?"

She startled, her wide blue eyes swerving toward me. "Oh, it's you. Damian, right? You're Ollie's friend."

"Yeah, but I don't think we were ever properly introduced." I held out my hand. "Damian Petrescu, proud Rom and descendant of the Ludar line."

She shook my hand, though she looked skeptical of me. "Right. I remember now. You're the guy who loves to put on gypsy airs. I'm Heidi Mackenzie."

Airs? Hey, I might've enjoyed playing up the gypsy stuff, but it was no act. Not entirely.

Heidi raked her gaze over my entire body, and her tongue sneaked out to moisten her bottom lip. "Why are you dressed like Dracula's low-rent cousin?"

"Women love the way I dress." I smirked. "You do, that's for sure. I can tell by the way your pupils dilated when you saw me and the way you licked your lips."

"My lips are dry, and it's kind of dark in here. It makes everybody's pupils get bigger."

"Have dinner with me."

She blinked slowly, her brows hiking up. "Excuse me?"

"You heard what I said. Have dinner with me. I give awesome dating."

One side of her mouth tried to smile while the other side wanted to frown. "Yeah, I'm sure you think you're awesome at everything to do with women. But I'm not interested."

I leaned against the bottom post on the staircase, cocking my hip. "I bet you'll change your mind after a date with me. What have you got to lose? I'll buy you a nice meal, we'll have some laughs, and then you can decide how badly you want to get me naked."

"Oh please. Does that kind of talk really work for you?"

"Usually." I slanted toward her and lowered my voice. "I can give you the best time of your life, and I'll even talk dirty if you beg me for it." I grinned. "Actually, you won't have to beg. I love whispering filthy things into a woman's ear."

"I'm not into that." She crossed her arms over her chest, elevating her tits. "I'm not interested in dating or sex at all."

"Come on, you must be joking. Aren't you the girl who loves to be naked and loves to suck every ounce of marrow out of life?"

"I'm not a silly, wild girl anymore. I've changed, for the better."

Right. In the space of a few months, she morphed from a party girl into a serious, cargo-pants-wearing woman. Sure, she'd humiliated herself with Ollie last time they saw each other. But that was no reason to shun hot sex and wild times.

"Don't you miss having a good time?" I asked. "I guarantee I can make you feel good."

"I'm not having sex with you."

"We can start with a date, then."

She shook her head, trying to frown but not quite accomplishing it. "You really are persistent, aren't you? Maybe I'm not being clear enough. I'm done with men, at least for a while."

"Have you defected to the other side?"

"What?" She shook her head again, almost smiling. "Oh, I get it. I'm not a lesbian. I'm taking a break from dating, that's all."

"Hmm." I inched closer to her. "We can start with getting it on, and upgrade to dinner once you're over this no-dating thing."

"Do you have concrete for brains?" She made exaggerated lip movements to match her exaggerated enunciation when she said, "I am celibate. No sex. No dating. No men, except for platonic friends. Get it?"

"I can read lips, you know. You could've just mouthed all that, and I would've understood."

"You're so pigheaded, I figured you needed extra emphasis."

Heidi Mackenzie was off dating. Off men. But I wanted her *on* me. Something about her frumpy clothes made me want to rip them off even more than if she'd been wearing a skimpy outfit. And her celibacy vow only increased my lust for her.

Seducing her into breaking her vow could be lots of fun.

"How about a kiss?" I asked.

"No, Damian. We can be friends—platonic, which means no sex, no kissing, no fondling—but that's it."

I sighed with all the melodrama in my Rom soul. "Have it your way."

"Thank you."

"We'll be friends, until you drag me into the woods and ravage me."

Heidi smiled just enough to create dimples. Her eyes twinkled too. "You're going to be a handful, aren't you?"

"Oh yeah. I always am."

I kissed her hand and walked away.

Life at the Au Naturel Naturist Resort was about to get wild.

Natural SATISFACTION

An Naturel Trilogy, Book Three

Chapter One

Heidi

Today, I have returned to the scene of the crime, or rather, the scene of my worst humiliation. After making a complete fool of myself a few months ago, when I'd thrown myself at Ollie Jackson repeatedly, I let my friends convince me that coming back to Au Naturel Naturist Resort was a good idea. Face my fear, that was the mantra. Prove to the world I'd moved past my shame.

Easier said than done, as the saying went.

I was the girl who loved to have fun, who never let anyone or anything drag me down. But I did the dragging all on my own. Ollie and I had dated for, like, five minutes last year—then I dumped him so I could reconcile with my cheating ex. Later, I'd returned to Au Naturel and tried to win Ollie back, even though he'd been with Mara Severins by then. Had I really wanted Ollie? No, not really. I realized that on my last day at the resort. I hadn't wanted to admit I gave up a good man because I thought I didn't deserve him.

I stared out the window of the big, pink RV my friends and I always drove whenever we headed for the naturist resort. And yeah, naturist meant nudist. We always wore T-shirt dresses when we arrived at Au Naturel so we could whip them off the second we exited the RV.

But today, I wore cargo pants and a loose-fitting T-shirt.

My friend Shelby sat down beside me, wearing her standard concerned look—mouth tight, brows lowered, gaze targeted on the object of her cheering-up campaign.

That would be me. Heidi Mackenzie, the most upbeat member of the Kitten Brigade, had become the girl who needed cheering up. I didn't feel like I belonged in the Kitten Brigade anymore. The wonderful people at the naturist resort had given us that nickname because we were young and carefree, always ready to cut loose and have a good time. I didn't feel like doing any of that anymore.

So I ignored Shelby and kept staring out the window.

My friend poked my arm. "Time to start talking, Heidi. You've been Ms. Silent Treatment for the whole three-day trip to Oregon."

"You guys insisted I come along, so I came." I would've rather stayed home in Nebraska, doing my boring job and avoiding my parents.

Shelby poked me again. "But you've said, like, ten words since we left home. Come on, girl, this is our vacation."

I eyed her sideways. "We went to the resort a few months ago. This trip is strictly so you guys can convince me I need to get laid."

Yeah, they'd been saying that for a while now. Get back out there, get laid, get something. They weren't pushing me to have anonymous sex. They just wanted me to act like the girl I used to be. But I couldn't do that. No more silly, self-centered Heidi. I was a mature woman with a serious job, not a sorority slut.

"Heidi." Shelby almost whined my name.

I sighed. "I'm not trying to ruin you guys' vacation. But we are going back to the place where I made a total ass of myself. I'm having trouble getting excited about that."

"Sure, I understand. But things will get better."

"Uh-huh." I didn't see how that would happen anytime soon, but I wouldn't contradict her. She and the rest of our group needed to believe in happy endings. I'd stopped believing in those a long time ago.

Shelby threw her arms around me, squeezing hard. "I love you, Heidi."

"Yeah, I love you too."

My friend pulled away, giving me a sympathetic smile. Then she rejoined the rest of our group where they'd gathered at the front of the RV.

As the vehicle turned onto the gravel driveway that led to the resort, I dug a baseball cap out of my duffel bag and stuffed the hat onto my head. Sometimes I missed wearing girlie clothes, but I'd made a vow to become a mature adult. No more skimpy dresses. No more shrieking with joy at every little dumb thing. I was a grown-up now, not a goofy kid.

The closer we got to the resort, the more acid churned in my stomach.

And when we broke out of the woods into the large clearing around the resort buildings, I got so nauseous that saliva filled my mouth, a sure sign I was on the verge of vomiting. I took several slow, deep breaths until the nausea faded away.

You can do this. Breathe, girl.

I obeyed my own commands, and though I wasn't about to barf anymore, I still suffered from a creeping unease that made my skin itch.

Jane, who had driven the last leg of our journey, parked at the end of the driveway near the little house occupied by Eve and Val Silva, the owners of the resort. Eve and Val weren't the ones I dreaded seeing.

Through the RV's windshield, I spotted Ollie Jackson and his fiancée, Mara Severins.

Ugh. Why couldn't they have taken today off? Well, I'd have to see them eventually. Sure, Mara and I had become friends, kind of, and we talked on the phone and texted sometimes. But virtual friendship was nothing like the in-person kind.

Mara was such a sweetheart. She would never do the idiotic things I'd done.

Jane opened the door, and my friends tumbled out of the RV, grinning and laughing.

I heaved my butt off the seat and scuffled out of the vehicle. The sun seemed a lot brighter than it had a few minutes ago. I hunched my shoulders, letting my gaze wander over the people who had gathered to greet us. Eve and Val, of course, stood in front. Ollie and Mara waited just behind them, and Ollie had his arm around his fiancée. Behind them, on the big lawn, senior citizens played miniten in the nude. The game was based on tennis, but designed for and invented by naturists, aka nudists. Instead of tennis rackets, they had wedge-shaped boxes over their hands. Thugs were a bizarre addition to the sporting world, though not many people who weren't nudists knew about miniten.

No miniten for me. I used to love the game, but I wouldn't play it anymore because Mature Heidi did not jump around with a wooden box on her hand.

My friends whipped off their T-shirt dresses and flung them high into the air, whooping with joy.

Part of me still wanted to join them, to be like them, but I couldn't. Revamping my life meant revamping myself too.

So I hid out near the front bumper of the RV and watched them.

While Eve, Val, and Ollie greeted the Kitten Brigade, Mara walked up to me.

"There you are," she said. "I'm glad you came, Heidi. Welcome back to Au Naturel Naturist Resort."

"Uh, hi." I shoved my hands in the pockets of my cargo pants. "It's nice to see you again, Mara."

"Don't be nervous. We're friends, and all that stuff that happened months ago doesn't matter anymore."

"You honestly are the nicest person on earth. I can see why Ollie loves you."

Mara moved closer, smiling a little. "I get that you're embarrassed about what happened last time you were here, but everything's different now. Think of this as a new beginning."

"I want it to be a fresh start, but crawling back to the scene of the crime doesn't feel like a new beginning."

Mara's smile grew bigger. "But it is, Heidi. Au Naturel is your home away from home, and we're all so happy you're with us again."

She pulled me into a firm hug.

When she let go of me, I tried to smile but only managed to kind of sneer or something. I didn't mean to, but my lips just wouldn't form a real smile.

Mara patted my arm and left.

Eve and Val were helping my friends carry their tents and bags to the camping area on the other side of the clearing. I'd arranged to stay in the guest house, which had disappointed the Kittens. They didn't understand my new outlook on life, but they accepted my decision.

Mara joined Ollie where he was chatting with his best friend, Damian Petrescu. Or, as Damian called himself, the Ludar prince. He claimed to have gypsy ancestry or something, but he was just another arrogant man who thought he was God's gift to women. He hadn't tried to give me that gift yet, but if he made a move, I'd have to disappoint him. My new outlook came with a new dictate—no dating, no sex, nothing but self-reflection until I'd gotten my head screwed on straight again. Men, especially hot ones, had no place in my life right now.

And yeah, Damian Petrescu was hot.

I let my gaze travel up and down his body, taking in his gypsy-chic outfit—black jeans, a long-sleeve black shirt with the top three buttons unhooked, and big black boots with bronze clasps. A necklace that looked like intricately braided rope hung around his neck, and a chunky silver ring glistened on his right hand. Damian hadn't been dressed like that the last time he'd been at the resort, but Mara and Ollie had told me Damian quit his job and joined the team at Au Naturel as concierge and resident gypsy. He did palm readings or whatever and had a "gypsy wagon" parked behind the guest house. That was his home base for peddling hooey to tourists.

But damn, that man was fantastic eye candy. Val Silva had the most ripped body I'd ever seen, while Ollie had a more normal type of muscular physique. Damian was somewhere in the middle. He boasted muscles, a fact I knew because I'd seen him naked. Ollie's best friend had dived right into the naturist lifestyle on his first visit to the resort a few months ago. And okay, maybe I'd loved admiring his sexy bod. With that olive skin and dark hair, he looked every bit the gypsy prince. He'd let his hair grow out some since the last time I'd seen him, so now wild curls framed his masculine face.

I did not have the hots for Damian Petrescu. He was man candy, for sure, but also a player. I couldn't verify that assessment with facts, but I sensed it. Having hooked up with one too many players, I'd developed a sixth sense for detecting them.

Tearing my gaze away from Damian, I retrieved my duffel bag from the RV and headed into the guest house. Once I got inside the building, I froze at the bottom of the stairs. My room was on the second floor, but suddenly, I couldn't make my feet budge another inch. A fresh start? How would I get that when I'd come back to the place where I'd always behaved like a foolish flirt? I tipped my head back, staring up at nothing. Maybe coming here had been a huge mistake.

I should go home. Catch the next flight out.

Had seeing Damian again triggered this sudden anxiety? No, of course not. I was not afraid I might succumb to his charms and revert to my old ways. That was just dumb.

"Hey. Remember me?"

I startled, swerving my gaze to the man who'd sneaked up behind me. "Oh, it's you. Damian, right? You're Ollie's friend."

Why was I acting like I barely remembered his name? So he wouldn't get the wrong idea and decide I might be his next target, that's why.

"Yeah, but I don't think we were ever properly introduced." Damian held out his hand. "Damian Petrescu, proud Rom and descendant of the Ludar line."

I shook his hand cautiously. "Right. I remember now. You're the guy who loves to put on gypsy airs. I'm Heidi Mackenzie." I raked my gaze over his entire body, and my tongue darted out to moisten my bottom lip. Not because I was attracted to him. No way. "Why are you dressed like Dracula's low-rent cousin?"

"Women love the way I dress." He smirked. "You do, that's for sure. I can tell by the way your pupils dilated when you saw me and the way you licked your lips."

"My lips are dry, and it's kind of dark in here. It makes everybody's pupils get bigger."

"Have dinner with me."

I blinked slowly, my brows hiking up. "Excuse me?"

"You heard what I said. Have dinner with me. I give awesome dating."

Oh yeah, this was exactly how I expected Damian to behave. *Player alert.* "Yeah, I'm sure you think you're awesome at everything to do with women. But I'm not interested."

He leaned against the bottom post on the staircase, cocking his hip. "I bet you'll change your mind after a date with me. What have you got to lose? I'll buy you a nice meal, we'll have some laughs, and then you can decide how badly you want to get me naked."

"Oh please. Does that kind of talk really work for you?"

"Usually." He slanted toward me and lowered his voice. "I can give you the best time of your life, and I'll even talk dirty if you beg me for it." He grinned. "Actually, you won't have to beg. I love whispering filthy things into a woman's ear."

"I'm not into that." It was a lie, but sometimes a woman had to deceive a man to protect herself. I crossed my arms over my chest. "I'm not interested in dating or sex at all."

"Come on, you must be joking. Aren't you the girl who loves to be naked and loves to suck every ounce of marrow out of life?"

Hearing him say the word suck sent a hot shiver through me. But that did not mean I wanted to sleep with him. Even if I did want that, I would not do it. "I'm not a silly, wild girl anymore. I've changed, for the better."

"Don't you miss having a good time?" he asked. "I guarantee I can make you feel good."

Oh God, that sounded amazing. Even before I made my celibacy vow, I'd gone without sex for months. A steamy, meaningless fling sounded perfect.

No, it did not. *Focus, Heidi.*

"I'm not having sex with you," I said.

"We can start with a date, then."

I shook my head, trying to frown but not quite succeeding. "You really are persistent, aren't you? Maybe I'm not being clear enough. I'm done with men, at least for a while."

"Have you defected to the other side?"

"What?" For a second, I had no idea what he meant. Then it hit me. I shook my head again, almost smiling. "Oh, I get it. I'm not a lesbian. I'm taking a break from dating, that's all."

"Hmm." Damian inched closer. "We can start with getting it on, and upgrade to dinner once you're over this no-dating thing."

"Do you have concrete for brains?" I made exaggerated lip movements to match my exaggerated enunciation when I informed him, "I am celibate. No sex. No dating. No men, except for platonic friends. Get it?"

"I can read lips, you know. You could've just mouthed all that, and I would've understood."

"You're so pigheaded, I figured you needed extra emphasis."

"How about a kiss?"

"No, Damian." Jeez, why was he so determined to get in my pants? I wore baggy clothes so men wouldn't pay attention to me. That tactic had worked out so well, hadn't it? "We can be friends—platonic, which means no sex, no kissing, no fondling—but that's it."

He sighed with no small measure of sarcasm. "Have it your way."

"Thank you."

"We'll be friends, until you drag me into the woods and ravage me."

I couldn't help it. I smiled. "You're going to be a handful, aren't you?"

"Oh yeah. I always am."

He kissed my hand and walked away.

That man was trouble with a capital T, two exclamation points, and a double underline.

Chapter Two

Damian

I loved my job. Working at Au Naturel Naturist Resort was the best thing that had ever happened to me, and I had my best friend to thank for it. Ollie had convinced me to quit my old job, since I was bored out of my ever-loving mind there, and join him here. He'd been pestering me about it for almost a year, ever since he quit his tech job to move to Oregon. I kept saying no. I mean, a nudist resort? How could I ever concentrate with all those hot, naked girls prancing around? Then I came here for a visit and suddenly understood.

Not that many hot girls on the premises. Well, except when the Kitten Brigade was here. I'd met those girls twice so far, including today, but most of our guests were families or senior citizens.

So yeah, no hordes of nubile hotties to distract me.

Too bad, but also good. I loved women, but this was my job now, not a sexy vacay at an adults-only nudist resort in the Caribbean. But today, my focus had been shattered by the arrival of one woman—Heidi Mackenzie.

She was the sexiest woman on earth, even in cargo pants and a baggy T-shirt with a baseball cap covering all that lush blonde hair. I'd seen her naked, but I had never so much as shaken her hand. We got introduced on my first trip to the resort a few months ago when I showed up for a surprise visit so I could hang with my best friend. Turned out Heidi was Ollie's ex, though they dated for such a short time they barely had a chance to blink before it was over. She still had a thing for him and tried to seduce him away from Mara. It didn't work. Heidi felt humiliated and sneaked out with her tail between her legs.

I would've loved to get between her legs, but no way in hell did I want to become the rebound guy. That sucked, a fact I knew from experience.

While Heidi's girlfriends disrobed and got the party started, I snagged Ollie and Mara so I could get more info about the hottest member of the Kitten Brigade. I already knew they'd been given that nickname because those girls loved to have fun and flirt with any eligible male on the premises. They didn't do anything raunchy—a damn shame, I said—but they did spice up the place.

My polite inquiries about Heidi resulted in Ollie informing me that I should "leave her alone" and "give Heidi some space." Ollie had also told me Heidi needed all the friends she could get.

Well, if sexy little Heidi needed a friend… I volunteered for the job. As long as it came with benefits.

I knew underneath those layers of khaki she had a killer body. Though she'd covered her head with a baseball cap, I knew those long, golden-blonde waves usually tumbled over her shoulders. Every time I'd seen her, I wanted to fist my hands in that hair while I fucked her. She was hiding her curves, but I'd seen every inch of that body the first time we met. She had spectacular breasts and a toned physique, but those curves softened her figure so she didn't look like a bodybuilder.

Christ, I wanted to explore that body from head to toe.

But Heidi had told me to buzz off. Not in those exact words. But yeah, I got the point.

Fortunately, I'd never been that easy to discourage. The way Heidi licked her lips and her pupils enlarged when she looked at me, I knew she felt the same lust I did. But like I'd told Ollie earlier, I wasn't a total dick. I could sense when a woman needed some space, and for now, I'd give it to her. Ollie wouldn't tell me everything about Heidi, like why she threw herself at him when they'd only dated briefly. I'd ask Heidi about that sometime.

Since I couldn't seduce Heidi yet, I decided to watch the naturists playing miniten. They kept trying to get me into their games, but I couldn't see past the wedge-shaped wooden boxes on their hands. They called those things "thugs." Now there was a friendly, fun-sounding word. The thugs looked like medieval torture devices designed to help the guy who wanted to lop off your hand get his ax lined up right. Not that I thought people actually did that with thugs.

I kicked back on a lawn chaise so I could observe the miniten game. Most of the players I knew, like the senior citizens who came here often. Ruth and Sylvester Norris had basically taken up residence at the resort, and Eve and Val let them have a permanent lock on the bungalow behind the guest house. Anyway, I watched while Ruth and Sly led their team, the Silver Foxes, to victory despite the younger crew giving it their all. The old farts had stamina and the killer instinct, but the guests who were my age always underestimated the Silver Foxes.

Heidi emerged from the guest house a few minutes after the miniten game ended.

Unfortunately, that was right when I had to go to the office on the second floor of the guest house to perform my concierge duties. Guests left notes in the box beside the office doorway or they submitted their requests on our mobile app. Yeah, we had one of those now. Ollie created the app himself since he had all the computer creds required to do mind-numbingly boring stuff like that.

So I schlepped up to the office and snagged the few pieces of paper that were in the request box, then I sat down at the desk and accessed the app. Not much going on. Nudists were surprisingly easy-going. They didn't have prima donna demands, which meant I had more free time than I suspected the average concierge at a normal resort might have had. I changed into my uniform and took care of every request, delivering bottles of sunscreen and insect repellent, dropping off extra towels and pillows, and finally, helping a guy my age get his locked suitcase open. The dude lost his key. Luckily, I knew a thing or two about picking locks.

Strictly in case of an emergency. I wasn't a criminal or anything, though I did learn lock-picking from a pro. He was behind bars, but I didn't hold that against him.

After completing every concierge task, I headed out to the lawn again.

The Kitten Brigade was about to play volleyball, and one of Heidi's friends seemed to be trying to convince her to participate. Heidi hunched her shoulders and kept shaking her head.

I remembered the last time the Kittens had visited. Heidi played every game with gusto—miniten, tennis, volleyball, whatever—and she didn't wear a sports bra. I'd followed the movements of her bouncing tits instead of the bouncing ball. Man, she had fabulous jugs. It was weird that I'd seen her completely naked, many times, but I had never so much as kissed her cheek.

That was nudism. Hot girls on display, but no touching allowed.

Heidi's friends gave up and started the volleyball game without her. Heidi shuffled over to an Adirondack chair, the one farthest away from the game in progress. Her chair sat under the bows of a large pine tree, so she had plenty of shade. Since nobody else was on that side of the lawn, she had privacy too.

I marched over there and dropped onto the chair beside hers. "Thought you liked sports. Why aren't you playing with your friends?"

She raised her brows. "You really don't believe in easing into a conversation, do you? It's straight to the intrusive questions."

"Why not answer? Maybe I'll go away if you satisfy my curiosity."

"Doubtful. You seem like the kind of guy who has an insatiable curiosity about things that are none of your business."

I might've thought I'd annoyed her if not for the calm, almost sultry tone of her voice. Her lips curled up a touch too. And her blue eyes sparkled, even though the sun didn't hit them directly.

She was beautiful. Was it any surprise I wanted to seduce this girl?

"You're right about one thing," I said, leaning over the arm of my chair to get closer to her. "I am insatiable."

"Hmm." She roved her gaze over my entire body. "Why aren't you dressed like a Dracula knockoff anymore? Thought that was your shtick."

"I'm not a knockoff of anyone. I'm an original. Johnny Cash always wore black, you know, but he wasn't a vampire."

She turned slightly sideways, toward me. "You like country music? I would've thought you'd be more into death metal."

Her lips curled up even more when she said that. Heidi was teasing me. *Score one for the Dracula knockoff.*

"I like good music," I said. "Don't care if it's country, classical, or jazz fusion. What about you?"

"What music do I like?" She shrugged. "Not into music except at parties. Then I don't care what it sounds like as long as I can dance to it."

Now there was the Heidi Mackenzie I expected to see. Except I wasn't seeing it. She told me she loved to dance, but she sat there in an Adirondack chair wearing khaki cargo pants and a baggy T-shirt. She still had that baseball cap on too. Carefree Heidi was still in hiding.

I jumped up and held out my hand to her. "Let's dance."

"What?" She drew her head back like she thought I might've been concealing metal spikes in my palm. "There's no music. And nobody else is dancing."

"Let's be trailblazers. Maybe we can inspire other people to get off their asses and do the rumba." Not that I had one single clue how to rumba, but that wasn't the point. "Come on, Heidi. Have a little fun."

She shook her head. "I don't dance anymore."

"Why not? Did you join one of those cults where every guy has ten wives and the women have to wear ugly brown dresses?" I glanced at her clothes. "Or maybe the cult uniform is cargo pants."

"I am not in a cult." She gave me the once-over, puckering her lips like she was trying not to smile. "You're the one who usually looks cult-ready. You probably want to sleep with me just so you can make me your satanic sacrifice."

"People wear uniforms at work. It's not a cult thing."

"I was talking about your fake-gypsy outfit."

Fake gypsy? She was trying to annoy me, but I wouldn't fall for it. "Relax, Heidi, I'm not into sacrificing beautiful women. I might bite your neck, though, and suck on various parts of your body."

"Celibate, Damian. I've told you already there will be no sex, no kissing, no anything that you're thinking about right now."

I chuckled. "You read thoughts? That's supposed to be my shtick."

"Don't need a crystal ball to know what you're thinking."

How could I convince Heidi to have fun? Maybe I should've been asking myself why I cared if she didn't have any fun. It was a challenge, I supposed, and I'd always loved those.

"Okay, no sex," I said. "But let's at least go for a walk. That'll be a lot more entertaining than sitting around watching other people have fun. And besides, I have a secret place to show you."

"A secret place?" She said that like she thought I was going to drag her off to my satanic-sacrifice lair.

"You'll like it, I promise." I held out my hand again. "Come on, Heidi, it's just a walk."

She chewed on her lip for a few seconds, then she placed her hand in mine. "Okay. Show me your secret place."

Chapter Three

Heidi

Damian led me around the edge of the lawn, where my friends were playing volleyball, and along the tree line until we came to a narrow trail that headed into the woods. He strode down that path. I'd never seen this trail before, despite having visited the resort many times over the years. Had I somehow missed it every single time I came here?

The path might've been narrow, but we still managed to walk side by side. I didn't mind that. Company was nice, even if my new "friend" wanted to get me naked. He hadn't said anything overly suggestive since he tried to talk me into dating with a possible upgrade to sex.

Damian was hot, but I had a plan and I would stick to it. Maybe it was more like penance than a plan. I had some serious penance to do to make up for all my mistakes.

So yeah, no sex. Not with Damian. Not with anyone. No kissing either. And absolutely no flirting, not even if Damian started it.

"Where are we going?" I asked. "I've never seen this trail before."

"That's because it didn't exist until recently. I talked Eve and Val into starting a pilot program for something new we can offer to our guests. It's still in the developmental phase."

"I hope you're not taking me to your secret sex house."

He chuckled. "Interesting that your mind went straight to sex. But no, this is G-rated entertainment."

"Okay. That's good." I considered him for a moment while we kept strolling down the trail, and my brain kept dreaming up questions I wanted to ask him. Before I did that, I needed to decide if I wanted to be friends with Damian. If not, then I didn't need to ask him personal questions. But my curiosity was pushing me to find out more about the man who liked to dress like a sexy vampire. Not that I would ever admit to him that I liked his Dracula-gypsy shtick.

Right now, he was wearing his work uniform. But damn, he looked hot in that too.

Stop thinking about how hot he is. No sex for six months, remember?

"You look like you want to say something," Damian told me. "Go on, I don't mind. You might've noticed I'm not shy. Shameless might be a better description."

"No kidding? I never would've guessed, Mr. I Love to Talk Dirty."

"Would you want me to lie and say all I want to do is hold your hand and recite sonnets to you? I'm honest and upfront about what I want. You can feel free to slap me if you don't like it."

Feel free to slap him? Damian was the weirdest man I'd ever met.

"No thanks," I said, "count me out. Emotional torture is more than enough for me to handle."

He raised his brows. "Torture? I don't want to do that."

"Oh. Good." Maybe he meant that, maybe he didn't. I had no idea. But my brain kept urging me to ask questions and satisfy my curiosity, so I gave in. "What did you do for a living before you took a job here?"

"I was a corrections officer at a state prison in Idaho."

My feet stopped moving. My eyes refused to blink. I stared at him for several seconds, trying to digest his response. Damian seemed like the type of guy who would be a massage therapist or the owner of a cigar shop, not a prison guard. Maybe I had misjudged him.

"Wow, that sounds crazy stressful," I said.

"It could be, but there were never any incidents at the facility where I worked." He smirked. "You expected me to have some kind of sleazy job, didn't you?"

"No, I was thinking either massage therapist or cigar shop owner."

"Hmm. That's better than what most people assume I would do for a job." He swept his gaze over me from head to toe and back again. "What do you do? For work, I mean."

"I'm a pharmacy technician."

"Really? I never would've guessed that."

He didn't sound disappointed like most men were when I revealed my career choice to them. They often responded by lamenting the fact they'd hoped I was a model or a stripper.

Damian studied me again, tipping his head to the side. "I would've guessed geologist."

"Ha-ha."

"Not joking. You seem smart, and the last time you were here, I noticed you kept picking up pebbles on the beach and examining them like you were figuring out what kind of rock they were. Everybody else was swimming in the lake or relaxing on the beach, but you were busy with rocks."

He noticed that? Weird. Either he'd been stalking me or... I didn't want to think about the other option. It meant he was interested, and I didn't want to attract anyone's interest right now.

"I do love rocks," I said, "but it's a hobby, not my job."

The fact that he assumed I had a serious job instead of being a stripper gave me an odd sensation in my tummy. Not quite fluttering. Something similar, but not that. It didn't mean I liked him.

"Here's the deal," Damian said. "I'm attracted to you, Heidi, but I won't push it. You made it clear you think you don't want to date, so I'll respect that. But we can be friends. Right? Just friends."

"Um, okay. Friends might be nice."

"Awesome. Now, let me show you my pilot project."

Damian wasn't a jerk who only cared about what his dick wanted. Huh. I never would've guessed that, but I supposed my checkered past with guys had colored my outlook. Having a new friend sounded kind of nice.

I could keep my libido in check. No problem.

He reached for my hand, then pulled his away. "Sorry. Force of habit."

"Don't worry about it." Wasn't I the one who said no sex, no kissing, no fondling? Now I'd just excused him for attempting to touch me. Well, hand-holding wasn't exactly a felony offense. But it did imply intimacy, so yeah, he shouldn't do that. I might've been flip-flopping on the whole touching thing. Not on the dating thing, though. No way. So no touching either, just to be safe.

But I had always loved going for walks hand in hand.

Cut that out, girl.

I followed Damian down the trail, trying very hard not to stare at his ass. Men's tushes had never been my favorite part of the male anatomy, but I'd seen Damian's naked rear a few months ago when he'd first visited the resort. He walked around in the nude for a long, long time. Even while I'd been insanely determined to win Ollie back, I couldn't stop myself from admiring his best friend's bod. I mean, I was a heterosexual woman and Damian was a hot man. He must've worked out. Not so much that he had giganto muscles like Val Silva. Damian's physique was somewhere between Ollie's subdued muscles and Val's totally ripped body.

His ass flexed under his pants with every leisurely step he took. The fabric clung to his glutes, accentuating every movement of those muscles.

Why did I say I wouldn't have sex for six months?

Because you don't want to make a fool of yourself again, you idiot.

Right. I had this plan that involved celibacy. But I could still ogle Damian's tush. No harm in that.

Damian moved to the side as we entered a grassy clearing that was ensconced in the forest. Two horses grazed inside a large field that had a wooden fence around it and a metal gate. Part of the field nearest to us had been fenced off to form a small, round paddock.

"What is this?" I asked.

"My pilot project." He swept his outstretched arm to indicate the entire clearing. "I want to offer riding lessons and horseback tours. Val and Eve suggested I try it out first to make sure having horses out here is feasible, and to make sure I really want to do this. I know I do, absolutely, but I respect their opinions. That's why I started my pilot project."

"You ride horses?"

"Of course. I'm a gypsy, after all." One side of his mouth ticked upward. "Oh wait, that's wrong. I'm a low-rent Dracula knockoff."

"I'm sorry I said that."

He shrugged. "I've been called worse. Dracula's cool, anyway. Must be, considering how many movies have been made about him and his kind. Vamps are supposed to be very erotic and enticing to women." He bared his teeth. "Want to find out if it's true? I'd love to bite your neck and suck on it."

"There you go again, mouthing off. And I was just starting to think you might be a nice guy after all."

"It was a joke. I'm not a total dick, you know."

"Doesn't change the fact that I'm celibate. No kissing, fondling, or neck-sucking."

He sighed. "Is this no-sex thing permanent? Or can I make a reservation to seduce you on the day your celibacy plan ends?"

I rolled my eyes, but I couldn't help laughing. "Is this how you prove you're not a dick? It's less than convincing."

"Okay, I give. Let's go play with the horses."

My gaze shifted to the horses out in the field, chomping on grass and swishing their tails. They looked serene right now, but I tried to steer clear of the big four-legged beasties. My history with horses wasn't pleasant.

"I'd rather not," I told Damian. "Horses and me... We don't get along."

"These two are sweethearts. You'll like them."

Staring out at the horses, I suddenly realized I was hugging myself.

"Are you afraid of horses?" Damian asked.

"Um...maybe. A little." I forced myself to lower my arms, and instead, I stuffed my hands in my pants pockets. "I got bitten by a horse when I was eight."

"You're with me this time, and I won't let anything happen to you."

I might've thought he was being arrogant when he said that, but his tone of voice belied that. He sounded like he genuinely meant to protect me. Once upon a time, I'd loved horses and wanted to learn to ride. After the biting incident, I hadn't gone near a horse ever again, not even a miniature one.

"How about this," Damian said. "I'll go in there and catch the boys, then bring them over here so you can pet them over the fence. We can call it a soft launch for your riding lessons."

"What's a soft launch?"

"A limited preview before a product launches."

"Oh." I bit my lip, studying the horses. Didn't I want to change my life? Become a better person who wasn't terrified of being alone or making bad decisions? Facing one of my fears might kick-start that plan. I cleared my throat and straightened my spine. "Okay. Let's do the soft launch."

"Awesome."

He walked over to a small shed I hadn't noticed before. It was made of wood and almost the same color as the tree trunks around it. Plus, shadows darkened the area, making the little building blend in even more. Damian pulled out a key ring and unlocked the shed, then retrieved two halters and lead ropes from inside it.

"Be right back," he said as he went through the gate and closed it behind him.

I watched Damian sauntering out into the pasture. Hunching my shoulders, I wondered if I was ready for this. What, I could stalk Ollie but I couldn't pet a horse? Sheesh.

Time to face my fears—starting with horses.

Chapter Four

Damian

I caught the horses and put their halters on, then led them back to the fence where Heidi was waiting. She was biting her lip pretty hard and gripping the wood fence like it might fly away. I got that she was anxious around horses, but I also had a feeling she'd get over that faster if she faced her fear instead of hiding from it. Heidi Mackenzie didn't strike me as the cowering type. But facing fears could be hard, so I'd take it easy with her.

Not just with the horses. But with dating too.

Heidi took one step away from the fence when I brought the horses up to it.

"Meet Lenny and Georgie," I said. "They're geldings, which means they've been castrated so they won't be big-time assholes like stallions can be. These guys are laid-back. That's what makes them great riding horses."

"Okay," Heidi said carefully, eying the horses like they might leap over the fence to maul her.

"Georgie and Lenny are lovable. Give them a chance, and you'll see." I held both leads in one hand and stretched my arm out to Heidi, offering her my other hand. "Come on, it'll be okay. They won't stampede over you."

She took a baby step toward me, just enough that she could grasp my hand. "Isn't this close enough?"

"You can't pet them from there. Come a little closer." I gently pulled on her hand until she tiptoed to within a foot of the fence. "Good. Now just reach out your hand to touch Georgie's neck."

I patted him with my free hand, trying to show her Georgie wasn't a wild beast. He nuzzled my cheek.

Heidi almost smiled.

"Give it a try," I said. "He won't bite, I promise."

She moved closer, inches from the fence, and slowly raised a hand, stretching it out toward Georgie's neck. Her fingertips grazed him, but she pulled her hand away.

"It's okay," I said, "try again. Take all the time you need. You're not the first horse-o-phobe I've met. Ollie hadn't been super comfortable around horses—got kicked once on a pony ride at a county fair—but I talked him into letting me teach him how to ride. Not long after, we started going on trail rides whenever he visited me. If Ollie can get over the fear, so can you."

Heidi glanced at me, surprise in her eyes, but she quickly diverted her attention to Georgie. She touched her fingertips to his neck again, but this time, she moved her fingers in a faint petting motion. After a minute or two of that, she laid her palm on his neck and glided it up and down.

"Look, he's smiling," I said. "That means he likes you."

"How can you tell he's smiling?"

"Ludar lidar."

Her lips kinked into a slight smile. "Yeah, I remember your Ludar lidar. It told you Mara wasn't the right woman for Ollie."

"No system is perfect."

She kept petting Georgie, running her hands along the length of his neck, while she looked at me. "What is Ludar lidar, anyway? Doesn't sound very gypsy-ish."

"Lidar is like radar, except it uses lasers instead of microwaves. I just thought Ludar lidar sounded cooler than Ludar radar." I realized I was still holding her hand, but I didn't want to let go. She seemed to have forgotten her hand was still in mine, or maybe she knew but didn't care. "When I say I'm using my Ludar lidar, it just means that I have an intuition about something."

"I get it." Heidi skimmed her hands up to Georgie's ears to scratch behind them, which he loved, though I wasn't sure she knew she was doing that. "I might've been wrong about you, and I'm sorry."

"No need to apologize. I know I can come on kind of strong. It's my way."

"The Ludar way?"

I winked. "Wouldn't you love to find out?"

Heidi laughed, the sound soft and delicate. Georgie nuzzled her arm with his lips, and she laughed again. "He's a real sweetie."

"Yep. And I think he's smitten." I nodded over my shoulder. "Want to try petting Lenny too? Mara and Eve both say Lenny has a muzzle as soft as velvet."

Heidi moved sideways to get closer to Lenny, but she kept holding my hand. That meant she had to angle her other arm across me to pet the horse, but I didn't mind. I liked having her hand in mine. Heidi stroked Lenny's neck and scratched behind his ears.

"Look," she said, "his bottom lip is hanging down."

"Means he's relaxed and happy—and he likes you."

How could any male, human or beast, not like Heidi Mackenzie?

After a few more minutes of watching Heidi pet the horses, I decided she'd probably had enough immersion therapy for today. She just got here a few hours ago, so she must've been tired from the long ride in an RV. I had to let go of her hand to take the halters off Lenny and Georgie, and I didn't plan on trying to reclaim her hand while we walked back to the resort.

But Heidi slipped her palm into mine.

What happened to "no dating"? Holding hands felt like dating behavior to me, but I wouldn't complain about it.

Once we reached the lawn, Heidi and I went our separate ways. But before we did that, I stopped us at the edge of the lawn.

"Are you any less afraid of horses now?" I asked.

"Yeah, your idea helped. Thank you, Damian."

"We can do more horse therapy anytime you want. Just call me or come find me."

She kissed my cheek. "You're not as much of a player as I used to think."

"Thanks." I'd take any compliment from Heidi, even a half-assed one. "I'll be in the gypsy wagon if you want a palm reading. I give great readings."

"I bet you do."

She started to walk away, but I caught her arm to stop her. When she glanced at me, I said, "For the record, I don't think I'm awesome at everything. I suck at geometry. Squeaked by with a C minus in high school."

Heidi's brows tightened as if I'd confused her.

Then she headed for her girlfriends who were relaxing on chaises, while I went back to the office to change into my gypsy uniform.

I spent the next two hours doing my shtick, reading palms and tarot cards, though I didn't gaze into any crystal balls. Maybe I couldn't prove my tarot and palm readings were accurate, but even I didn't stoop to crystal-ball bullshit. The big crystal orb in my wagon was there strictly for show. Tourists loved the way I'd decorated the interior, and they loved my gypsy routine, though I was sure ninety-nine point nine percent of them realized it was just for fun.

At lunch, I looked for Heidi in the dining hall but didn't see her, so I ate in my wagon. Ollie, Mara, Eve, and Val wanted me to join them in the caretaker's house, but I preferred to have lunch alone. It gave me time to think—about Heidi, of course. I wanted her, and I liked the side of her I got to see when we visited the horses, but I didn't know if I should pursue anything with her. She claimed she didn't want to date or have sex, so I guessed what I wanted didn't matter.

Maybe I was arrogant and persistent, but I never tried to push a woman into being with me.

Just as I went back into the guest house to check on my concierge duties, my cell phone rang. I dug it out of my pocket, but before I could say hello, my mom started speaking.

"Damian, are you still slumming it at the nudist camp?"

"No, I'm working at a naturist resort. It's beautiful here, Mom, not a slum." Which I'd told her many times over the past couple of months, but she didn't listen any of those times. My mom wasn't a snob, not really. She just didn't understand my desire to live and work at a nudist resort. "Ollie works here too, you know. Your 'precious, sweet little Oliver' is a nudist."

I didn't say that like I was offended by how much my mom loved Ollie. It didn't bother me. She loved me too, but Mom had always had a soft spot for my best friend. Seemed like the geek thing actually worked. Even mothers fell for it.

But Heidi Mackenzie liked my gypsy thing.

She also crushed on Ollie for a while, so I probably shouldn't have gotten smug about the way Heidi almost drooled over me. Yeah, I did not want to be the rebound guy.

"Maybe we should come there," Mom said, "to see what our boy is doing in the wilderness with a bunch of hippies."

Yep, my mother thought hippies were gauche, but being a gypsy was high class. Where did I get my Ludar prince routine? From my mother. She liked to dress up as "Ileana the Ludar queen" and do highly entertaining palm and tarot readings for our neighbors at birthday parties, weddings, bar mitzvahs, whatever. People loved it.

And they knew it was bullshit. My mom was born and raised in Brooklyn, and her real name was Monica.

"You don't need to come here, Mom," I said. "Unless you're suddenly itching to get rid of your clothes. A lot of the naturists here are your age or older, so all you codgers can commiserate about how your asses hurt while enjoying a little nude sunbathing."

She huffed. "I'm fifty-six, not eighty. Don't lump me in with the codgers just yet."

"I know, Mom, it was a joke."

"But I was serious about visiting you. I need to make sure my sweet Ludar prince hasn't gotten himself into trouble."

Maybe I had gotten myself into trouble—just a little, with Heidi the celibate sex kitten—but it wasn't anything I couldn't handle. Definitely nothing my mom needed to know about. I was an adult, not a dumb kid.

I'd just reached the bottom of the stairs, about to climb up to the second floor. "Gotta go, Mom. Say hi to Dad."

"Be careful, Damian."

We hung up.

Of course my mother couldn't say "have a good day." No, she had to tell me to be careful. I didn't know if Mom would ever accept the idea that I lived and worked at a nudist resort, I loved it, and I would never quit. This was my dream job.

So yeah, I might've been crazy. But in a good way.

After I took care of the concierge requests, I resolved to find Heidi. Probably a bad idea, but then, I'd always enjoyed a challenge—and a dirty-hot bad idea.

Chapter Five

Heidi

I lay on the bed in my room, staring up at the ceiling, counting the little acoustic balls stuck to it. I kept losing count, though. The balls had no pattern to follow, so I was pretty sure I counted the same ones five or six times. What did it matter? Why was I staring at the ceiling?

Because of Damian Petrescu, that was why.

The man was trouble. I didn't care how sexy he was, or how surprisingly sweet he could be, I would never, never, never sleep with him. Six months of celibacy. I'd made that vow, and I refused to break it on my first day at the resort. I had willpower. Somewhere. Probably buried way down under a lot of hooey like all that silly stuff I used to love to do.

No more chasing butterflies. No more playing miniten in the nude with no sports bra. And absolutely no more flirting with every guy who walked past me. Time to dig out that willpower because Damian would push me to the limits of my self-control. I wasn't blaming him, not directly. After I told him I planned to be celibate, he hadn't pushed me at all. He'd barely flirted with me after that. But our time at the horse pasture had shown me a side of him that left me stunned and confused. Sweet, patient Damian didn't jibe with the Ludar prince who offered to "upgrade" me to dating if we had sex first. Or maybe he had said he'd upgrade me from dating to sex. Ugh, I couldn't remember. Didn't matter since I was never going to get naked with him.

Avoiding Damian seemed like the best solution to the problem of my MIA willpower.

Someone knocked on the door.

I moaned like a miserable coward. "Who is it?"

"Damian."

Oh shit. Why had he appeared two seconds after I thought about him? Maybe he did have Ludar lidar or whatever the hell it was. And what on earth did Ludar mean? He explained lidar, but that other word was a mystery to me, one I did not need to solve.

"Are you going to open the door?" he asked. "I brought you a surprise."

Great. He probably brought me lingerie.

I moaned again and heaved myself off the bed to trudge over to the door. Taking a deep breath, like that would quell my lust at all, I opened the door.

Damian stood there wearing his gypsy outfit. He held out his hand. "Give me your phone."

"Excuse me?"

"It's for your surprise. I promise I'm not trying to hack your phone. Ollie would know how to do that, but I haven't got a clue." He kept holding his hand out, and when I didn't move a muscle, he gave me an amused smile. "Trust me, Heidi. You'll like this."

Grumbling, I got my phone from the bedside table and gave it to him.

His thumbs flew over the screen, and his focus was zeroed in on whatever he was doing. After a minute, he handed the phone back to me. "There you go. Jams to lift your spirits, everything from Mozart to Miles to Minogue."

"Huh? I know who Mozart is, but the rest made no sense."

"Miles and Minogue." Damian chuckled. "That means Miles Davis, the jazz musician, and Kylie Minogue, the Australian pop singer."

"Oh, right, I get it."

"I was trying to be clever with my alliteration, but I guess my efforts tanked."

"No, it's not you. I'm still feeling kind of off-kilter." Why did I tell him that? Since I didn't want to date him, he didn't need to know. But he had suggested we could be friends. Maybe it was okay to blab that stupid confession to him.

"Being back at the resort is weird for you," Damian said. "I get that. After the stuff with Ollie the last time you were here, I'm sure it'll take time for you to get comfortable."

"Yeah, I think so."

"Don't hide in your room all day. Listen to the music I gave you, then take a chance and get out there with your friends."

I couldn't understand why he cared about making me feel better. We didn't know each other, not really. But he did care, and that gave me a strangely comforting sensation of warmth on my skin. "Thank you, Damian. It was so sweet of you to give me this music."

"No problem. I'll leave you alone, but I hope you'll come outside later."

He turned to walk away.

And for some reason, I grabbed his arm to stop him.

Damian raised his brows. "Something wrong?"

"No." I let go of his arm and bit my lip. "Would you, um, like to talk?"

"About what?"

I hunched my shoulders. "Anything, I guess. When we talked earlier, it was nice."

"Sure, I can hang with you for a while. I promised Ollie I'd take the new guests out to the pilot project later, since they've got a horse-crazy kid, but I've got some time to kill."

He sat down in the chair by the window while I relaxed on the bed—sitting up this time, not lying flat on my back staring at the ceiling balls.

"What does Ludar mean?" I asked. "You called yourself a Ludar prince, and you mentioned your Ludar lidar."

Damian rested his feet on the bedside table, his ankles crossed, and clasped his hands over his belly. "The Ludar people came from Eastern Europe, mainly Bosnia but also Romania. My mother is descended from that line. My dad is of Rom heritage, which means Eastern Europe and Russia. Both Ludar and Rom are known as gypsies. We call ourselves that, but I think it's mostly because that's easier for most normal people to remember. Rom, Ludar, Romnichels, it all gets kind of confusing."

"Okay. So you are a genuine gypsy."

"By heritage and by choice, yeah, I am. But nobody in my family has ever been to the old country. We're all Americans who love football and apple pie." His mouth slid into a sexy smile. "But we do have gypsy powers. Want me to read your palm?"

I didn't know how he did it, but he managed to make that simple question sound erotic.

"You don't actually believe you have psychic powers or whatever, do you?" I asked. "The gypsy thing is cool and fun, but you can't actually divine my thoughts."

"No." He winked. "Or maybe I can."

He planned to keep up this "I'm a mysterious gypsy thing" for as long as possible, didn't he? Maybe he was teasing me, but I couldn't tell for sure. Did I want him to tease me? Friends could do things like that, so it wouldn't necessarily mean he was trying to seduce me.

I felt a twinge of disappointment when I realized that.

No, I didn't. *Get a grip, Heidi.*

So what if Damian looked extra sexy in that black outfit, kicking back in a chair like he owned the place. I didn't even care that the way he'd smiled a minute ago made my tummy flutter. I had willpower, if I could ever find it.

"Do you speak Romanian or whatever language the Ludar speak?" I asked.

"I don't know much Romanian, not like my mom. She's fluent. I took French in high school, but I don't remember anything except how to ask where the bathroom is."

"Yeah, I took Spanish, but I've forgotten all of that too. Can't even ask where the bathroom is."

He smiled, and even though he wasn't trying to be sexy, he was.

And my tummy fluttered again. Dammit.

"Where does your family live?" I asked.

"St. Paul, Minnesota. My mom was born and raised in Brooklyn, my dad too, but they moved to St. Paul when I was in eighth grade. Dad got a job there. My brother and his wife and kids live there too."

"How did you wind up in Idaho?"

He smirked. "You mean how did I wind up in the potato state working at a prison. It's simple. After college, I wanted an adventure, so I joined a circus run by gypsies, mostly Ludar and Rom. By the time we got to Idaho, I'd had enough of the vagabond lifestyle, so I applied for a job as a prison guard. They hired me, and I kept that job until Ollie convinced me to work here instead."

Damian had told me that part this morning, but he hadn't mentioned his circus job.

"What did you do in the circus?" I asked.

"I was an animal trainer. Horses, mostly, but I also helped out the elephant and monkey trainers whenever they needed it." He sighed like he was remembering good times. "I also did some palm reading, though it's my mom who's the best at that stuff. Our friends and neighbors always love it when Ileana the Ludar Queen entertains them."

How was I supposed to reconcile all these different sides to him? Circus trainer, prison guard, concierge at a nudist resort, gypsy showman. Damn, this guy was confusing.

Surprising was a better word.

"What about you?" Damian asked. "Tell me about your family."

"My parents are divorced. Bitterly divorced. Holidays are lots of fun, with my parents griping at each other and my grandmother smacking her spoon on the table to make everyone shut up. Last Thanksgiving, Mom threw a big lump of mashed potatoes at Dad."

Damian's face went blank. He just looked at me like that for a long time.

Finally, he took his feet off the table and sat forward. "Christ, Heidi, I'm sorry. That must be awful. And here I was telling you how awesome my family is."

"I'm glad you have parents like that. And I don't need any sympathy. I'm used to Mom and Dad acting that way. They got divorced when I was ten."

"Do you have any brothers or sisters?"

"Only child."

He watched me with a strange expression that I couldn't figure out. Pity? Sympathy? Disgust? I had no idea.

Damian got up and walked to the bed, sitting down near my feet. "I think I'm starting to understand you—your behavior, anyway. You've got scars, don't you? Lots of them, I'd say."

"Yeah. Doesn't everybody?"

"Most people don't have as many as you seem to." He patted my leg. "Scoot over. I'd like to sit next to you if that's okay."

"Um, sure." I scooted over to make room for him.

Damian sat beside me, though not touching me. "Don't take this the wrong way, but you seem like you could use a hug."

How did he know that? Because yeah, a hug would've been awesome. But I shouldn't let him do that. He might get the wrong idea—or I might. Sitting this close to him, I started to feel warm again, but not in the comforting way I'd experienced earlier. I felt warm in a completely different way, one that skirted dangerously close to desire.

"Guess that's a no to the hug," Damian said, not sounding annoyed, just mildly disappointed.

"Actually, a hug would be nice." Why had I said that? My mouth insisted on telling him the truth, even while I tried to deny it in my own mind.

He draped an arm across my shoulders, tugging me closer until I could've rested my cheek on his shoulder if I'd wanted. God, did I want to, but I fought the urge. Fought it like crazy. He smelled good, like woodsy cologne or potpourri or something.

Damian stroked my upper arm with his fingertips.

I couldn't stop myself. I rested my cheek on his shoulder.

We sat there like that for several minutes, not speaking, just enjoying the easy intimacy of the moment. I'd told him about my family. Ollie didn't know about that. Even my ex, the one I'd gone back to over and over despite his cheating, never met my parents or asked me about them. So I never told him. But today, I'd needed to tell Damian.

He cleared his throat. "Sorry to cut this short, but I need to do my job for a while. I'd much rather stay here with you, but..."

"I get it. You can leave, it's fine." I lifted my head to look at him. "Besides, I've got those jams you gave me, the ones you promised will make me feel better."

"Guaranteed to lift your spirits."

We gazed into each other's eyes. It wasn't a conscious decision on my part, and I didn't think it was for him either. Our gazes gravitated to each other all on their own, like our subconscious minds craved the connection. He still had his arm around me. I was still leaning into him. Our faces hovered a foot apart at most, and suddenly, I needed to be closer, needed to feel his lips on mine.

I couldn't make myself move or speak. Just as well since I *really* shouldn't kiss him.

But God, I wanted to.

Damian slanted his head down, leaning in a touch, bringing his mouth to within millimeters of mine. His breaths ghosted over my lips, tantalizing my skin with a sultry warmth. I couldn't tear my focus away from his eyes, couldn't catch my breath, couldn't make myself pull away.

"I want to kiss you," he murmured. "But only if you want it too."

Oh yes, I wanted that. But my voice wouldn't work, so I gave my consent the only way I could. I closed my eyes and pressed my mouth to his. Damian's lips were soft and warm, and I couldn't stop myself from moaning with pleasure. He kissed me back, tugging me closer with the arm he'd draped around me. I laid a hand on his shoulder, sliding it up to his neck, and moaned even more deeply when he slipped his tongue between my lips. Heat rushed through me from head to toe, settling in my lower belly, igniting a fire between my thighs. He explored my mouth with leisurely strokes of his tongue while I thrust my hand into his hair to pull his head even closer.

No one had ever kissed me like Damian did, like he had endless lifetimes to spend doing nothing but kissing me.

When he pulled away, he was breathing harder, like he couldn't catch his breath either. "As much as I'd love to keep kissing you…"

"Guests need you. It's fine. I'm fine, promise." After that kiss, yeah, I felt fantastic. "Go do your horse whisperer thing."

"I don't whisper to them." He slid off the bed and winked. "Don't need to. I've got Ludar magic, remember?"

Oh, he definitely had some kind of magical powers, at least when he kissed.

Damian walked out the door.

And I listened to the music he'd given me, but I didn't need songs to lift my spirits anymore. Making out with Damian had erased all my worries.

But I still wouldn't sleep with him. We shared one hot moment, that was all. My Damian cravings would be gone now, for sure. One hundred percent gone.

Until I saw him again, at least.

Chapter Six

Damian

Heidi kissed me. Sure, I had suggested it, but I expected her to remind me again that she's celibate and there would be no dating or sex. Instead, she kissed me. Damn, I'd loved kissing her. I hadn't meant to do it, hadn't meant to say I wanted to do it, but our conversation had made me feel the need to comfort her. And that somehow turned into a lip-lock.

Not that I was complaining. No way. Feeling her lips on mine, tasting her… That had made me crave Heidi even more.

I managed to focus on my job for the rest of the day, but once I clocked out, the urge to find Heidi and kiss her again got stronger. Okay, I didn't actually clock out since we didn't have time cards or even strictly set hours. But anyway, I was done for the day. And I needed to see Heidi.

The dining hall was packed, as usual, full of naturists enjoying the buffet and conversation. All those voices chattering away might've made the dining hall a noisy place, but people who loved to go nude could be surprisingly polite. Out in the wider world, most people weren't that thoughtful. Another reason I loved it here.

I spotted Heidi sitting at a table near the back with Ollie, Mara, Eve, and Val. I would've expected Heidi to hang out with her girlfriends, but she surprised me again. I noticed an empty chair at the employees table where the five of them sat. They weren't eating, didn't even have plates yet. Were they waiting for me? Was Heidi waiting for me?

Yeah, suddenly I'd become a girl, worrying about whether my crush had a crush on me too.

Ollie saw me and waved, urging me to go over there.

I jogged across the dining hall and sat down beside Heidi. Had she saved this chair for me? Christ, I really had become a girl.

"Hey, guys," I said to the others. Then I glanced at the sexy woman sitting beside me. "Hey, Heidi. How was your afternoon?"

"Good. How was yours?"

"Fine." What a nice awkward conversation we were having. I never felt weird around a girl after I kissed her. I never got nervous around girls either. The awkwardness had the bizarre effect of making me spout inane things. "Hey, uh, you can visit the horses anytime you want."

"Thanks. Not sure I'm ready for a solo visit yet."

"Yeah, I get it."

I glanced around and realized the other two couples at the table were staring at me and Heidi. Ollie smirked. Val seemed vaguely amused. Mara and Eve both smiled with their lips sealed and their cheeks dimpled.

"Aw," Mara said, "you two are so cute together."

"We're not together," Heidi said.

She didn't have to say that quite so fast, did she? Like she needed to make sure everyone, including me, knew we weren't dating. Was it my imagination, or had she almost shouted that statement?

I needed to have sex with her soon, before my balls shriveled up and I actually turned into a woman.

"Let's get our food," Ollie said. He got a sneaky look on his face and added, "Damian and Heidi better stay here to make sure nobody steals our table. We'll bring you guys some food."

All the guests were already here and already seated at other tables, so I knew he was full of crap. Since when did he try to play matchmaker? Ollie had hated it when my mom tried to set him up with the daughter of one of her friends. But now he was trying to maneuver me and Heidi into…something.

True love, marriage, and babies. That was what my best friend had suddenly decided I needed.

Once the others had hurried off to the buffet, Heidi and I enjoyed the most awkward silence in history. Yeah, I was pretty sure not even cavemen and cavewomen who spoke in grunts ever suffered through a silence as awkward as this one. I scratched my neck. Heidi clasped her hands on the table. I cleared my throat and set my hands on my thighs. She toyed with one of her little stud earrings.

Those little studs were blue like her eyes. Staring at her earring made me want to look into her eyes since they were almost the same shade, but she kept staring at the wall.

Finally, I couldn't stand the cavepeople awkwardness anymore. "We had a good talk earlier, so this shouldn't be so hard now."

Heidi swerved her gaze to me but kept her head aimed straight at the wall. "I know, but it is weird. We, you know, kissed."

"Yeah, I remember." That kiss was something I would never forget, not even when I got old and couldn't remember how to zip up my pants.

"About what happened earlier," she said, "it can't ever happen again."

"You kissed me."

"A gentleman wouldn't point that out."

Now I wasn't a gentleman? Because I let her kiss me? Jeez, this girl was wound up even tighter than I'd realized.

"I'm sorry," I told her. "I wasn't trying to be a dick. But you're acting like it's my fault you kissed me."

"Well, it kind of is. You said you wanted to kiss me."

"But I didn't—"

I stopped myself before I argued more with her about who instigated that kiss. We shouldn't have been fighting about this, but clearly, our kiss had unsettled her. I didn't know everything her ex had done to her, though I knew the story about how she kept going back to the cheating jerk over and over. Heidi had told me about her parents, and I got the feeling their hostile relationship had affected her in ways even she probably didn't understand.

That meant I needed to be gentle with her. Not my strong suit.

"Listen," I said, "I don't want to argue about it. The kiss happened, but it doesn't matter who started it. I won't try to kiss you again unless you tell me that's what you want, and I'll do my best not to flirt with you either. Honestly, I'm not that good at stopping myself from flirting, but I promise to try."

She stared blankly at me, without blinking, for several seconds while all around us people were talking and laughing, having a good time.

Maybe I said too much. Or not enough. Either way, all I could do was wait.

Heidi sighed and glanced down at her lap, then aimed her baby blues at me. "Sorry I got mad at you. I don't mind the flirting. Actually, I kind of like that. It's the intimate stuff that freaks me out. You know, kissing and dating and...other stuff."

"By 'other stuff,' you mean sex."

"Not just that." She wriggled on her chair and hunched her shoulders, seeming like she couldn't get comfortable. "Relationships too. That's 'other stuff,' I mean."

"Oh, right. I get it."

"We don't know each other that well, but I'd like it if we could be friends."

"Thought we already were. I suggested it this morning, and you said being friends might be nice."

She almost smiled. "Forgot I said that. So we are friends already."

"Yep." I reached out, intending to touch her leg, but then I realized that was a bad impulse. She might've taken it as a come-on, though that wasn't what I meant. I started to pull my hand away.

Heidi grasped my hand and laid it on her thigh.

"Uh, what are you doing?" I asked.

"Putting your hand on my leg."

"But you just said—I'm confused, Heidi. What the hell do you want me to do or not do?"

"I..." She pushed my hand off her leg, and I swore her cheeks turned faintly pink. "That was completely inappropriate. I'm sorry."

She jumped up, clearly about to flee.

"Where are you going?" Mara asked as she and Ollie returned to the table. "Heidi, we brought you food."

Mara held up the two plates she had in her hands. Ollie held up two plates too.

Heidi hurried around to the other side of the table. "I'd rather sit by you and Eve. You know, girls on one side, boys on the other. Doesn't that sound like fun?"

Though Mara seemed less than convinced by Heidi's announcement, she carried her two plates to the opposite side of the table, setting one down in front of Heidi. Mara sat down with her plate.

Ollie scrunched up his eyebrows, clearly confused.

Yeah, I was right there with him.

Mara gave Ollie a stern look, nodding her head in a gesture I was pretty sure meant she was ordering him to sit down on the boys' side of the table.

Ollie shook his head and took the chair beside me, handing me a plate. He leaned toward me and whispered, "What did you do?"

"Nothing. I think Heidi's got a Jekyll-and-Hyde thing going on."

"I told you to leave her alone."

"She's an adult, Ollie. Neither of us gets to tell Heidi what to do or who to do it with." Not that I'd done much of anything. She kissed me, and somehow, I became the bad guy. "Chill out, man. Let me worry about Heidi. We're friends now."

"Friends?" Ollie said, sounding way too baffled by that idea.

Was it so bizarre for me to be friends with a woman?

I gave up trying to explain myself to Ollie just as Eve and Val came back to the table. We ate our meals and talked, though not about much of anything. Pointless small talk seemed to be all any of us could manage. After dinner, I went to my room and Heidi went to hers.

For hours, I tossed and turned in bed, trying to figure out what to do about Heidi Mackenzie.

I had no frigging idea.

Chapter Seven

Heidi

I behaved like a completely insane person at dinner last night. Damian had been so nice, but I freaked out because our friends conspired to push us together by abandoning us while they went to get the food. Seriously? That was the best plan four adults could come up with. Well, at least their ineptitude made me feel better about my screwy behavior.

Why had I freaked when Damian got confused by me putting his hand on my leg? Why had I grabbed his hand, anyway? Jeez, I was a mess.

But I had an inkling of why I kept acting like a crazy person around Damian.

I liked him. I was attracted to him. My celibacy vow had made perfect sense until I saw Damian yesterday, right after I'd stepped out of the RV. He'd kind of flirted with me months ago when I first met him. But now, he'd ramped up the flirtation to a whole new level. Damian didn't do anything obnoxious. He was surprisingly sweet underneath the cocky exterior. But I'd been fooled before by a man who convinced me he wasn't a jerk, and I'd been dumb enough to keep going back to him. Grant never helped me face my fear of horses, though, and he never told me he wanted to kiss me but then waited for me to say it was okay.

Not that I had said that. I kissed Damian instead.

Maybe I was having such a hard time because I kept fighting my true nature. I'd always loved flirting with guys, loved the build-up to the first kiss, loved that free-fall sensation when I realized I had feelings for a guy. I hadn't experienced the free-fall with Damian—jeez, I hardly knew him—but I had enjoyed the flirtation. And when we sat on my bed and he said he wanted to kiss me...

I hadn't felt anticipation like that in years.

After a fitful night's sleep, I didn't feel like showering or brushing my teeth, or changing out of my pajamas. When had I become a slob and a coward? Cargo pants were one thing, but loafing in my PJs... That was an alternate universe version of me. So I made myself get clean, get dressed, and go out into the world. I'd chosen jeans and a loose-fitting blouse with short sleeves and a flower print. My blue sneakers matched the flowers on my shirt. For too long, I'd been wearing frumpy stuff like cargo pants and baggy T-shirts. It had been a way to kind of punish myself for my past transgressions, I guessed. Today, I suddenly wanted to wear something feminine again.

But that impulse had nothing to do with Damian.

Seriously, nothing.

The second I stepped into the dining hall, Mara ran up and hugged me. "Heidi, you look beautiful this morning." She stepped back, grasping my upper arms. "Are you wearing makeup?"

Yeah, maybe I had put on a teeny bit of eye shadow and mascara, and my lip balm had a slight tint to it that made my lips look pretty. For about half a second, I wondered if Damian would like the way I looked today, then I resisted the urge to smack myself on the forehead for thinking about that—about him.

So of course, Damian walked into the dining hall right then.

He had to squeeze past me since I was standing a foot inside the threshold, but he didn't stop to flirt with me. He nodded and said hello to me and Mara, then he wandered off toward a table where some of the Silver Foxes were eating.

Damian wanted to eat with the senior citizens?

"Are you okay?" Mara asked.

"Huh? Yeah, I'm fine." The fact that I'd kept staring at Damian until she asked me that question didn't mean a thing. I was confused by his decision to dine with the seniors, that was all.

Mara glanced toward the self-proclaimed Ludar prince. "If you like Damian, go for it. You don't need anyone's permission, and he's a good man."

"Not interested in Damian. He's weird. Besides, I barely know him."

"That didn't stop me. I slept with Ollie the day after we met." She grinned. "And look how that turned out."

"Uh-huh." I couldn't think of anything meaningful to say. Why did my eyes insist on making me look at Damian? I'd done it again when Mara told me he was a good guy, and I was doing it again right now. *Get hold of yourself, woman. No man is so hot you can't keep your eyes off him.*

Except Damian kind of was.

I ate breakfast with Mara, Ollie, Val, and Eve. They did not pester me about Damian, thank goodness, and kept the conversation limited to everything else not related in any way to the gypsy who had the softest lips I'd ever felt.

After breakfast, I headed outdoors to hang out with the Kitten Brigade. Every single one of them was naked. They had decided to play miniten, Kittens versus Kittens. Shelby tried to talk me into playing, but I wasn't up for that yet. Sure, I felt better. Not better enough to strip naked and shove a wooden box over my hand. Nudity was required for miniten, at least according to my friends. So instead, I relaxed on a chaise and watched them having a good time.

The first game ended with Shelby and Allison beating Jane and Heather. Leah rushed over to me, pleading for me to join them so the other Kittens could play a match, but they needed one more person since each side had two players.

"Not a nudist anymore," I told Leah. "Get Mara or Eve. They love miniten."

"But we want you, Heidi. You're the best player, our reigning champion."

I'd won my fair share of miniten matches, but I couldn't participate now. Maybe never. At least, not until I figured out why I kept screwing up my life.

Leah glanced past my chair, and her lips stretched into a slow, sneaky smile. "Oh, I've got a fabulous idea."

She ran away before I could ask what her idea was. Honestly, I doubted I wanted to know considering her sneaky smile. She and the rest of the Kittens gathered in a huddle like they were football players or something. After a minute, they pulled out of the huddle.

Leah shoved two fingers into her mouth and whistled. The sound echoed off the buildings and the trees. "Listen up, naturists. We're playing a miniten mixed doubles match. We need two hot guys to volunteer. Come on, studs, man up! Or are you afraid the girls will make you look like wusses?"

Sylvester Norris, one of the Silver Foxes, jogged up to Leah. "I'm in. But you know I like to play aggressive."

Leah laughed. "Oh yeah, we all know how you old farts get about miniten." She looked at someone further away, someone I couldn't see. "Come on, join the game. You know you want to."

Damian traipsed past my chair, flashing me a sexy smirk and winking. He stopped in front of Leah and stripped naked.

Her jaw dropped. Not an exaggeration. Her eyes bulged, and her mouth fell open while she ogled Damian's body, making no attempt to disguise her appreciation.

Sylvester was already naked, but Leah hadn't gaped at him like that.

I could see only his backside, but wow, that man had gorgeous glutes.

He turned sideways to follow Leah's hand movements while she explained something. Probably which team would take which side of the grass court.

Oh my God. From this angle, I had a perfect view of his dick, the way it hung slack between his hips. His cock was sleek and thick, but not too thick, just right for closing my mouth around it. Damn, I wanted to feast on that beefstick for hours. Months ago, I'd seen Damian naked and felt only the slightest sexual interest in him. Today, I couldn't stop staring at his naked body, and I experienced a wave of heat that stole my breath for a few seconds. The muscles on his chest made me want to lick a trail over every single one of them, moving lower and lower while I kissed his defined abs and inched my way closer and closer to that beautiful dick.

I wanted to fan myself, but I didn't have a fan. Not even a piece of paper I could fold over and use to cool myself down. That wouldn't work, anyway. The only thing that might cool me down was sex with Damian. I couldn't do that. Wouldn't do that. *Celibacy vow, remember?*

But I hadn't been with a man since before my stalking-Ollie nonsense.

No sex with Damian. No way. So what if he had the hottest body I'd ever seen? No sex, no way, period.

Sylvester and Taylor took one side of the court while Damian and Leah took the other. They started batting the tennis ball around in the laid-back way most people played miniten. Nudists liked the game because it wasn't as strenuous as tennis, though sometimes guests got a little overexcited—guests like Sylvester. He and his wife, Ruth, could turn a laid-back game into a death match. Nobody minded, though. They never did anything lewd or got too aggressive.

Damian leaped up to whack the ball.

And his dick flapped.

I usually thought men's flapping members were silly, but I found myself getting tingly and slick while I watched Damian's manly bits waving around with every graceful, athletic move he made to hit the ball. His muscles flexed, from his thighs to his biceps and everywhere in between.

Leah missed her shot—on purpose, it looked like—and stumbled, holding her knee like it really hurt. "Timeout. I twisted my knee."

Damian rushed over to check her supposedly injured knee, but Leah shooed him away. "I just need to sit down for a while. It's fine, I swear." She glanced at me. "Heidi can fill in for the rest of the match."

I groaned, though I doubted she could hear it. "For the umpteenth time, I am not a nudist anymore."

"We'll make an exception to the nakedness rule for you." Leah fake pouted. "You can't let us lose the match. You're the best player."

"Yeah," Sylvester said. "Get in there and show 'em how it's done, kiddo."

The entire Kitten Brigade looked at me with hopeful expressions.

How was I supposed to say no when they looked like that? I could keep my clothes on, though I'd be playing alongside Damian the naked gypsy.

Leah clasped her hands under her chin and grinned at me, hopping up and down on her tippy toes.

Oh jeez. She'd be so disappointed if I didn't do this, they all would, but I knew Leah had faked hurting her knee as a means to push me and Damian together. Did everyone think I liked him? Or had Mara told Leah—

For heaven's sake, what was wrong with me? Now I was thinking like a teenager. I was an adult, and I could handle playing miniten with Damian, even if he was buck naked.

I pushed up out of my chaise and headed for the miniten court.

Leah handed me her thug as I walked past her.

And we played miniten.

Sylvester and Taylor had skills, but Damian played the game like he'd been born with a thug on his hand. I'd been playing for years, but he hadn't tried the game until recently. With all those muscles, he had the equipment to rock miniten. And rock other things too. Naked, sweaty, dirty things.

I missed my swing. The ball shot past me, but Damian whacked it over the net.

Never in my life had I gotten so distracted by lustful thoughts that I couldn't concentrate on winning a game of miniten.

Taylor hit the ball over the net, but when I raised my racket, my foot slipped. I fell down, landing on my side.

Damian knelt to sling an arm around my waist and hoist me up. "You okay?"

"Fine, thanks." That was a lie. I hadn't injured myself, but I was nothing close to fine with my body crushed to his naked muscles.

He let go and picked up my racket, handing it to me.

We ended up winning the game, but I couldn't concentrate on that fact. The feel of his body, his arm around me, his dick pressed against me... It had made me almost lightheaded. He hadn't been aroused, not at all, but I could still feel his dick. Watching Damian play miniten had been the most erotic thing I'd ever seen, but not because he did anything unseemly. He played like a gentleman—a determined, focused gentleman. Maybe it was his attitude and his determination that got me so hot and bothered. Whatever the cause, I'd gotten so turned on I could feel the slickness between my thighs. It had drenched my panties, and my clitoris throbbed every time I glanced at him.

Oh yeah, miniten had been the worst idea ever. I should've gone back to my room before Damian took his clothes off.

He walked up to me, took my hand, and kissed it. "You're an expert player, Heidi. We won because of you."

That was baloney. I'd been distracted most of the time—by his body.

"You did most of the work," I said. "How did you pick up the game so fast? I thought you hadn't played until you came here."

"I hadn't, but it only took a few weeks to understand the rules and strategy. Ollie and Eve took turns teaching me."

He hadn't let go of my hand, and now he rubbed the back of it with his thumb.

I resisted the urge to clear my throat because I didn't have any reason to do that. It was a dumb impulse. But standing here with naked Damian inches away from me and his hand holding mine, I couldn't think straight.

He kissed my hand again, this time letting his lips linger on my skin. "I have to get back to work, but I'll see you at lunch."

Damian sauntered away.

And I went back to my room. I tried to watch TV, even listened to some of the songs Damian had given me, but I couldn't relax. My thoughts kept returning to Damian in the nude, whacking a tennis ball around with a thug, his muscles flexing and his dick bouncing.

My body thrummed with a need I could not quench. Not with Damian. But I could do something to alleviate this craving.

I unzipped my jeans and slid my hand inside them, inside my panties, until my palm rested over my mound.

My mind conjured a vision of Damian naked, sweat drizzling down his skin.

I pushed my longest finger between my folds, into the hot slickness there, and began to brush that finger up and down in an easy rhythm. While I fantasized about Damian's muscles and imagined his body positioned over me, his hips thrusting, I slid another finger down there to rub myself harder and faster. God, I was getting wetter. Every time I pictured Damian on top of me, I got so hot I could barely breathe. Panting, gasping, I worked myself into a need so intense I thought I'd go insane if I didn't come soon.

Another vision flared in my mind, of Damian kissing me.

My back bowed into the mattress, my head snapped forward, and every muscle in my body went rigid—except my fingers. I couldn't breathe, but I couldn't stop rubbing and rubbing until the climax overtook me. My mind wouldn't let me stop picturing Damian thrusting into me, and I came so hard I would've cried out if I'd had any breath left. My free hand fisted in the blanket. I kept scraping my fingers over my clit until the last wave of my orgasm faded.

Wow. I hadn't experienced a climax like that in… I wasn't sure I'd ever come that hard before.

And Damian hadn't even touched me yet.

I would keep quenching my lust the solo way. It was the safest sex. Getting involved with Damian would only lead to more humiliation and heartbreak.

Chapter Eight

Damian

I stood outside the door to Heidi's room with my fist raised like I was about to knock. I had been about to do that, but I stopped when I heard strange noises coming from inside her room. After about two seconds of listening, I'd realized what those noises were.

Heidi was masturbating.

Really enjoying it, by the sound of things. All her gasps and groans made me want to barge in there and take over for her fingers or her vibrator, whatever she was using to get off. The bed creaked faintly, which made me picture that bed thumping and creaking like crazy while I fucked her.

Just when my brain decided to divert all the blood in my body to my cock, the noises stopped. I could still barge in and—

No, I wouldn't be that kind of asshole. I might've been a bit of an ass sometimes, but I wasn't a complete jerk. Still, I couldn't decide whether to knock or leave and pretend I hadn't heard anything. If I knocked now, it might've been obvious I'd been hovering outside her door. Plus, I had an erection, so she'd notice that for sure.

I'd come here to invite Heidi to the picnic Eve and Val had organized for the guests. Some people preferred to eat lunch in the dining hall, but others loved the idea of eating alfresco in the most natural way imaginable.

Well, now that I'd been standing here like a moron for several minutes, I supposed Heidi wouldn't know I'd overheard her. So I knocked, then held my linked hands in front of my groin, casually, like I was doing that for no reason.

The door opened, and Heidi's eyes went wide. "Damian? What are you doing here?"

She sounded slightly panicked. Oh great, had she somehow guessed I must have heard all those hot noises she made? Her gaze flicked down to my groin, and her eyes flared wider for a heartbeat. Then she looked at my face, though not my eyes. She seemed to be staring at my nose.

"Eve and Val organized a picnic for lunch," I told her. "Wanna come? We're going to the lake."

"Um…" She bit her lip, and her gaze traveled down my body and back up again, hesitating at my groin. "Think I'll eat in my room."

"Are you sure? It's a beautiful afternoon. About a dozen guests are joining the picnic, so this isn't a trick to get you alone."

"I never thought it was."

Why had I said that? Trying to convince Heidi to come along on the picnic, while I had the hardest hard-on ever, was messing with my head and making me say stupid things.

She looked so damn good in those jeans and that flowery shirt.

"The guests will probably be naked," I said, "but you can keep your clothes on. I'll keep mine on too. That way, you won't be the only non-naturist."

"I don't know…"

"You can hang out with Val and Eve the whole time. I won't be offended if you'd rather not talk to me." I held out my hand, palm up. "Fresh air is good for you, Heidi."

How stupid had that sounded? Had I actually said "fresh air is good for you"? Christ, she must've thought I'd suffered a head injury during the miniten game that turned me into a ninety-year-old grandpa.

She took a deep breath, making her breasts rise and fall. "Okay. I'll go on the picnic."

"Great. Eve made sandwiches with her secret sauce on them."

"Ooh, I love that." She slipped her hand into mine. "And I'm starving. Ravenous, actually. Miniten burns more calories than I realized."

Ravenous. I wish she hadn't said that word with so much…hunger. I was doing my damnedest to get rid of my erection, but the way she said that word had sent more blood rushing south.

Heidi didn't seem to care that I had a hard-on.

The feel of her hand in mine wasn't helping matters. I couldn't stroll down the trail to the lake, surrounded by a dozen other people, while I had a raging stiffy. I needed to alleviate the problem somehow. Since I was pretty sure Heidi wouldn't let me get naked with her right now, I went for the only feasible option.

When we got to the bottom of the stairs, I said, "Need to use the restroom. I'll meet you outside."

Before she could say anything, I ran to the restroom and slammed the door, locking it. Being an employee had its perks. I could lock the door to keep everyone else out.

Maybe I should've checked to see if anyone was in here first.

Peeking under the stall doors proved I was alone.

I leaned against the wall beside the sinks, unzipped my pants, and pulled my dick out. My mind went straight to a fantasy of Heidi touching herself, writhing and moaning. I closed my hand around my cock and glided it up and down, over and over, while I imagined sneaking into her room late at night when she was getting off on her own. I'd take over that task with my mouth on her clit, gorging myself on the luscious flavor of her cream.

"Fuck," I growled, working myself faster.

My fantasy escalated to Heidi thrashing, grasping my head, and bucking her hips while she screamed my name.

I slapped a hand on the nearest sink, gripping its edge so hard my fingers hurt. I couldn't breathe, and the only part of my body I seemed to have any control over was my hand pumping my cock. The pressure mounted, ramped up by the hottest fantasies I'd ever had. Heidi writhing, screaming my name while I gave her the best orgasm in history. I came so hard and fast that my knees almost buckled.

Only when I'd finished did I realize I'd, um, spewed all over the sink.

"Shit," I muttered, then I yanked a bunch of paper towels out of the dispenser on the wall and did what I could to clean things up. The janitor left all the cleaning supplies in a locked cabinet in the corner, so I used my master key to get out some disinfectant. Once I'd cleaned everything up, I finally remembered to zip my pants.

When I walked out of the restroom, I looked reasonably normal. My uniform wasn't even wrinkled.

Heidi stood just outside the restroom door.

I froze. Did she know what I'd done? I didn't care. So what if I jerked off after hearing her do the same thing? I was a man, not a robot. Of course I got turned on by overhearing her orgasm, and of course I needed to relieve the pressure. I had no reason to feel embarrassed.

So why was I scratching the back of my neck and avoiding her gaze?

"Are you okay?" Heidi asked. "You ran off so fast, I was worried you were having some kind of…medical problem."

Was that a euphemism for jerking off? I'd never heard anyone call it a "medical problem" before.

"I'm fine," I told her. "Just, uh, really needed to go."

Not exactly a lie. I had needed to "go," just not in the way people usually meant when they said that.

"Better get a move on," I said. "Everybody's waiting."

We walked outside and met the rest of the gang on the lawn. Ollie carried a big picnic basket, but Val carried two of those. I offered to take one, and though Val didn't seem to mind lugging both baskets, he let me help out. I was reasonably sure Val could bench press a small car. Maybe a midsize sedan. He didn't need help with two picnic baskets, but I would've felt like a jackass if I hadn't offered to take one.

Guests had blankets slung over their shoulders or arms. I hadn't thought to bring one for Heidi. Damn.

I must've looked annoyed with myself because Ollie sidled up to me and said, "Got an extra blanket for you and your new girlfriend." He lifted the blanket he had over his arm, revealing another one underneath it. "So relax, you're covered. Got condoms too."

Luckily, he said that too softly for Heidi or anyone to overhear.

Condoms? I'd barely kissed Heidi, and she had way too many hang-ups for me to seduce her today.

"Guess you're planning to do your fiancée in the woods," I told Ollie. "Those condoms aren't for me, that's for sure."

My best friend smirked and wagged his eyebrows.

I had no idea what that was supposed to mean.

We all enjoyed our picnic by the lake, though I didn't see any couples sneaking off to have a little alone time in the woods, not even Val and Eve who were the two horniest people I'd ever met. They loved to make noise too. I couldn't count how many times I'd heard them getting it on in the caretaker's house. They lived there, so they had every right to be doing whatever the hell they wanted in their own home. I'd stumbled onto them at the hot spring last week too, and that was one awkward moment.

But I now knew Eve had great tits.

Heidi decided to hang out with the Kittens instead of having a private picnic with me. I lay on the blanket Ollie had brought for me, gazing out across the lake. I did not fall asleep, though Ollie shoved me once to make sure I was awake.

"Don't want you to get sunburned," he'd told me with a smirk. "Heidi doesn't go for guys who look like roasted pigs."

"I used sunblock, Ollie. That means I won't burn even if I do fall asleep."

"Oh-ho, you know what that means. You do care what Heidi likes in a man."

"Go jump in a lake." I pointed toward the water. "It's right over there."

Ollie kept smirking, but he went back to his own blanket with his own girl and didn't harass me about Heidi anymore.

I did notice Heidi watching me even while she was hanging out with her friends. She was wearing sunglasses, so I couldn't tell for sure if she was ogling me. I had stripped off everything except my boxer shorts. Maybe I'd told Heidi I wouldn't go naked as some kind of solidarity thing, but I hadn't been lying. Boxers were clothes. Promise kept.

Once, I glanced in Heidi's direction just as she lifted her sunglasses to look at me. She roamed her gaze over my entire body and licked her lips. When she noticed me noticing her, she lowered her sunglasses again and turned back to her friends.

Everybody tromped back to the resort, then split off to do their own thing.

I jogged to my room to change into my other work outfit, what Heidi said made me look like "Dracula's low-rent cousin." Her sort-of insult hadn't bothered me in the least. I could tell she liked my Ludar prince costume. But I wasn't wearing it to impress Heidi. I had actual work to do—in my gypsy wagon, for paying customers who loved my palm readings and all that other stuff average people expected from a gypsy.

Trotting out to my wagon, I opened the padlock on the door and went inside to get set up for the afternoon's entertainment.

Maybe Heidi would take me up on my offer for a palm reading.

I wouldn't hold my breath.

Chapter Nine

Heidi

What was I doing on this beautiful afternoon? Sunbathing? Having fun of any kind? Nope. My friends had wanted me to play Monopoly with them in the entertainment room, but I couldn't get into the idea. I loved board games, but I was too distracted to enjoy it right now. So instead, I was lying on my bed again, staring up at the ceiling balls again, thinking about Damian again. For two hours.

Yes, it was entirely his fault I couldn't have fun.

How could I think about anything except him when he stretched out on a towel on the beach wearing nothing but a pair of boxers? Honestly, the man had no shame. I mean, sure, other guys had gone naked—including Ollie and Val, two super hotties—but I couldn't have cared less about them. My eyes insisted I had to gawk at Damian. Damn, he had the kind of body any woman would drool over. Not that I drooled. Maybe my mouth had gotten a teeny bit overly salivated, but that did not mean I wanted to get naked with the Dracula knockoff.

Maybe I should've stopped thinking of him that way. Vampires were hot, after all. I'd watched enough movies and read enough romance novels to understand the allure of a man in black. Even Johnny Cash was kind of hot in that color. But Damian Petrescu… He could set the entire state of Oregon on fire just by stripping naked on the beach.

He hadn't gotten naked, though. He'd worn those boxers, which only made me want to go over there, rip those shorts off, and drag him into the woods.

If Damian were a player, like I'd always assumed, I wouldn't want him this much. He just had to go and be a nice guy. *Damn him.*

Laughter outside my window made me sit up. I'd left the window open to get some fresh air, so I could hear whatever went on out there. My room was on the backside of the guest house, and there wasn't much out there except for the bungalow where Ruth and Sylvester slept. Well, that and Damian's gypsy wagon.

More laughter echoed off the trees.

I slid off the bed and leaned out the window.

Shelby and Heather stood just outside Damian's wagon. Leah was descending the steps. All three of my friends laughed some more, grinning.

Damian followed Leah out of the wagon.

Heather kissed his cheek. Shelby squeezed his biceps and pretended to swoon. At least, I thought she was pretending. Damian kissed Leah's hand, and she giggled. The girls trotted around the guest house, out of sight. What had those three been doing in Damian's wagon?

Damian saw me and waved.

I waved back.

He made a come-hither gesture.

No, I would not go down there. Considering how much I liked the way he looked in that black outfit, I knew I'd only get myself into trouble if I went downstairs and climbed into his wagon. What did he have in there? Chairs? Cushions on the floor? I would've loved to lie on a pile of pillows while Damian—

Oh no, I would not go there, not even in my fantasies.

I shut the window.

For twelve minutes and thirteen seconds, I stopped myself from rushing out there. Finally, I couldn't stand it anymore, what with my curiosity prodding me to go to him. I didn't rush, though. I walked.

Damian wasn't outside anymore. A sign on the wagon's door said, "Knock, please. The spirits appreciate politeness."

Oh yeah, that sounded like a Damian thing to say.

I knocked on the door.

Damian swung it open a split second after I knocked. His lips curved into an enticing smile. "Glad you came, Heidi. Welcome to my lair."

He stepped back enough to make room for me and offered me his hand.

I accepted it, and he helped me into the wagon, shutting the door.

Whatever I'd expected to find in here, I'd been dead wrong. The space was cozy and homey, but with an elegant gypsy style that made it intriguing. The entire interior was composed of wood in warm, rich shades of honey, from the floor to the walls to the ceiling. A blue velvet curtain cordoned off the front section, the part furthest from the door. The rest of the space featured a padded bench upholstered in shades of gold, blue, and green, as well as a small round table fashioned from honey-colored wood and topped with a gold tablecloth. I saw shelves of knickknacks too, everything from a crystal ball to little figurines of magical creatures. A long window behind the bench let in the natural light, but I saw a lamp and an overhead light fixture too.

The table sat low to the floor, surrounded by pillows.

Earlier, I'd fantasized about Damian and a stack of pillows, but this was nothing like what I'd imagined. These pillows clearly served as seats.

"Sit down," Damian said. "The bench or the pillows, whichever you prefer."

I settled onto the bench, loving the cushy padding. "What's behind the curtain?"

"The Great and Powerful Oz, of course."

"Cute. But seriously, what's back there?"

Damian walked to the curtain, hunched over a little since the wagon wasn't as tall as he was. He pulled back one side of the curtain, revealing a bed accessed by wooden steps. Cream-colored sheets and a scarlet blanket covered the bed, with cream-colored pillows scattered across the length of it up against the wall. Sunlight shined through a small window at the center of the wagon's back wall.

"Your love nest?" I asked.

"The wagon came this way. I didn't ask for a bed." He let the curtain fall shut. "I do occasionally sleep in here, but I've never seduced a woman on that bed—or anywhere in this wagon."

I shouldn't have cared whether he had done that or not, but I felt bizarrely relieved to hear him declare he hadn't. "You seduce women outdoors, then? Or in your room?"

"No, Heidi, I don't. I haven't had sex since before the first time I came here."

He'd been celibate? Why? Damian seemed like the kind of passionate man who would never go without sex for long. But it had been months for him?

"I shocked you," he said, sitting down at the table, cross-legged on a royal-blue pillow. "You've been assuming I'm the kind of guy who screws a woman every night, haven't you? I'm not like that."

"Yeah, I, um, can see that now. Sorry I leaped to that assumption."

"Don't worry about it. What other people think doesn't matter to me." He folded his hands on the tabletop. "Except for you."

He cared what I thought. That was weird and slightly disturbing.

But it also made me feel warm all over like I'd drunk a glass of brandy. Yeah, Damian was intoxicating—and I hadn't even slept with him yet.

Not that I would sleep with him.

"Did you want a palm reading?" he asked. "Or maybe tarot? You must've come here for a reason."

"I wanted to see your wagon, the inside of it." I glanced around to admire the lush surroundings again, then I ran my palms over the velvet cushions beneath me. "It's beautiful. Very cozy."

"No other reason? Just wanted to get a look at my secret den of mystical sorcery?"

He smiled with his lips sealed, the expression sexy and mysterious, worthy of the Ludar prince he claimed to be.

And God, I wanted him.

"I should go," I told him. "You must have paying customers waiting for you."

"My gypsy hours are over. I'm all yours." He patted the pillow next to his on the floor. "Come over here, Heidi. Let me read your palm."

His voice had gotten lower and rougher, so enticing that I couldn't stop myself from sliding off the bench and crawling onto that cushion. I sat cross-legged like he did. No more than a foot separated us, and the proximity sent a warm tingle of excitement rushing over my skin. The hairs on my arms shivered erect. So did my nipples.

"Are you right-handed or left-handed?" he asked.

"Right."

"We'll start with the left, then. It can tell me more about your character and personality than your dominant hand. Though I don't need to read your palm to know what kind of woman you are." He held out his hand, palm up. "Trust me, this won't hurt."

I wasn't worried about that. If he touched me, even my hand, I didn't know if I could stop myself from kissing him again. I should've walked out the door, but I couldn't move except to hold out my left hand to him.

He turned it palm up and cradled my hand in his. "Ready?"

"Uh, sure. Never done anything like this before."

"I'd love to be the one who pops your palm-reading cherry."

Why did he have to phrase it like that? Spoken in his sexy rumble, those words sounded like the most erotic come-on ever.

With my hand cupped in his, he bowed his head and lifted his free hand to skim his fingertips over my palm, moving them slowly, focused on the task of…whatever it was he was doing. The sensation of his fingers on my skin elicited a shiver of the sensual kind. I'd been acutely aware of him before this moment, but now, my body awakened in ways I'd never experienced before. I swore the touch of his hand and his fingers reached beneath my skin, like he was already inside me, thrusting with leisurely strokes of his cock while his skin brushed over my entire body. The memory of kissing him replayed in my mind. The heat of his mouth. The softness of his lips. The sensuous way his tongue coiled around mine and flicked out to taste me. I loved kissing him, and I hungered to do it again, right here, right now.

Damian turned my hand over and began caressing the backside.

I couldn't catch my breath. Everything between my thighs tingled and ached, desperate for his touch. God, I needed him to fuck me, like I'd never needed anything before—and he'd only touched my hand.

He turned it palm up again, gazing up at me without lifting his head. "You have long palms and fingers, and your skin is silky soft. That means you have water hands, Heidi. Souls like yours are full of compassion, imagination, and curiosity. You're also sensitive, emotionally."

"Yeah, I'm a flake. I already knew that."

"Being sensitive isn't a bad thing. Unless you get too wrapped up in the emotion of every moment and forget to take care of yourself."

He must have guessed that based on the things I'd told him earlier. Palm reading was hooey, right? But the feel of his skin on mine made it hard to breathe or think or do anything except watch him while he examined my palm.

Damian swirled his longest finger over the center of my palm, then glided it up to the base of my index finger, massaging the fleshy spot there. "Your Mount of Jupiter is hard to figure out. It's not large, but not sunken either. You have confidence, but sometimes you forget that, and you have a connection to the spiritual world."

"Are you talking about ghosts?"

"Not necessarily. There are many forms of spirits." He moved his fingertip to the base of my middle finger and skated it in a circle. "Your Mount of Saturn is average, I'd say, but it shows you have integrity." He shifted to the next finger over and glanced up at me, his head still bowed. "The Mount of Apollo signifies optimism and the strength of your life essence. Your vitality burns inside you like a smoldering fire, just waiting for a chance to erupt."

I cleared my throat, unable to make my vocal cords work. My breasts felt heavy, my skin tight, and the strength of my lust for him made my breaths shallower and faster.

"Ah, the Mount of Mercury," he said, his tone hushed and so damn sexy as he moved his finger to the spot just under my pinky. "This one is well-developed, which tells me what I already knew. You're a smart, capable woman."

He dragged his finger across the center of my palm, teasing the most sensitive part and making me suck in a sharp breath, then he slid it toward the bottom of my hand, below my pinky. He rubbed that area with his thumb in gentle circles until my skin grew so sensitized to his touch that I bit down on my bottom lip to stave off a whimper.

"Just like I thought," he said, "you have incredible compassion and imagination, though you don't harness that power to its full potential. Not yet."

"Oh." That syllable was partly a reply to what he said, but mostly it was my breathless response to the way he touched me. How could massaging my hand feel so sensual that I'd lost all capacity for thought? With anyone else, it wouldn't. I knew that, though I couldn't explain how.

"And now, the Mount of Venus." He glided his thumb over to the base of mine and massaged that fleshy area while he spoke. "Can you guess what this region signifies?"

"I...don't know." My brain shut down a few minutes ago, so yeah, I had no clue about anything. "Tell me, please."

He leaned toward me, still massaging the base of my thumb, bringing his face to within inches of mine. "Passion, sensuality, attraction, and magnetism." He gazed straight into my eyes. "You have all of those qualities. That's why you're so anxious these days, isn't it? Because you're fighting your natural instincts, the ones that drive you to indulge your desires."

Indulge my desires? I used to do that, too much, and it got me into trouble. Maybe I did burn to indulge my lust for Damian, but it was a horrible idea. Another round of humiliation wouldn't do me any good. Still, I couldn't stop myself from gazing into his eyes, letting myself sink into the depths of this heady desire for him. His mouth hovered so close to mine that I could've kissed him if I slanted in a touch.

"You're a special woman, Heidi," he murmured. "Don't hide behind cargo pants and a baseball cap. Let your inner goddess come out to play."

Oh God, I wanted to do that. Strip naked, crawl over his entire body, take his cock into my mouth and—

No, not again. No, no, no, no. I was tumbling head over heels into another mistake, and this time, I didn't know if I could claw my way out again.

I jumped up. "Sorry, I can't—This is—I just can't."

"Take it easy. I didn't mean to upset you, but I got a little carried away. I apologize." He patted the cushion I'd been sitting on. "Come on, don't leave yet. Please."

"No, I can't. Sorry. It's me, not you."

I staggered to the door and flung it open. As I clambered down the steps, Damian called out to me.

"We haven't even gotten to Mars or the lines yet."

No idea what that meant, but it didn't matter. I ran to the guest house, heading for my room.

Chapter Ten

Damian

What was that about? Heidi panicked and bolted, all because of a palm reading. I'd stuck to the principles of palmistry, but okay, maybe I got a little too invested in the process. Touching Heidi felt so good I couldn't stop myself. She smelled good too. And looked good. I should have kept my head down, focused on the reading, instead of looking into her eyes. Her pupils had gotten bigger, a sure sign of desire, and she kept licking her lips, though I was positive she didn't realize she was doing that.

I didn't see Heidi for the rest of the afternoon or in the evening. She must've been hiding in her room. Ruth Norris told me Heidi had "skulked" into the dining hall to grab some dinner, then took her meal somewhere else to eat it. Her room, I was sure. This was my fault, though I couldn't quite figure out why. I hadn't done anything more salacious than massaging her hand and talking about the mounts, those fleshy little mounds on her palm. Maybe the word mount had freaked her out. Could she have thought I meant I wanted to "mount" her right there in my gypsy wagon?

No, she was too smart not to realize "mount" had other meanings unrelated to sex. I did want to use that word in its dirty meaning, but not until Heidi got comfortable with the idea of sleeping with me. Maybe she'd panicked because I talked about the Mount of Venus and how it represented passion and sexuality. I hadn't invented that stuff to get her horny. It was a genuine part of palmistry.

I could drive myself crazy trying to figure out why Heidi ran away, so I stopped trying.

Eve and Val were hosting a staff dinner at their place tonight, and I never missed those, even though I kind of felt like a fifth wheel. Eve and Val, Mara and Ollie, they'd coupled up big time. Me? I couldn't convince Heidi not to freak out when I massaged her palm. So yeah, I attended the staff dinner as the obligatory fifth wheel stuck at the end of the table. Both couples sat side by side, exchanging loving glances and affectionate smiles while I pushed food around on my plate and tried to talk my stomach into wanting noodle omelet and spinach.

Vegetarian wasn't my thing. But mostly, I couldn't work up any enthusiasm for food because I kept thinking about Heidi.

"What's wrong with you tonight?" Ollie asked. He was sitting beside me, though he faced across the table instead of facing me.

"Nothing's wrong."

"You've been frowning at your food and moving it around like you think an alien creature will burst out of your noodle omelet any second to strangle you."

"Shouldn't you be making goo-goo eyes at your fiancée? She's probably feeling neglected since you haven't looked at her in at least ten seconds."

Ollie's brows hiked up. "Since when do you get grumpy? Something's definitely up with you tonight."

"I am fine," I said, emphasizing each word so maybe he'd believe me. Yeah, sounding grumpy might not have been the best tactic to refute his claim.

"Did you and Heidi have a fight?"

"We're not dating, so we can't have a fight. Not the kind you mean."

I suddenly realized everyone was looking at me. Looking and listening. Damn.

Eve, who sat opposite Ollie, touched my hand. "We all saw Heidi fleeing from your gypsy wagon this afternoon. Seemed like you must've had a fight."

"Why can't any of you grasp the concept that Heidi and I are not a couple?"

"But you like her a lot. Don't you?"

I did like Heidi, but this wasn't the kind of thing I wanted to talk about at the dinner table with Eve, Val, and Mara. Ollie was my best friend, so I would've talked about it with him. It shouldn't have been a group discussion, though.

"Can we talk about something else?" I asked.

Eve patted my hand. "Go talk to her. You two can work things out, I know."

My first impulse was to remind Eve, and everyone else, that I was not dating Heidi Mackenzie. But more grumpiness would only convince them I had a thing going on with Heidi. Maybe I did, sort of. I couldn't force her to want to have a thing with me.

She kissed me. Didn't that mean she wanted to be with me?

Forget about Heidi, you idiot.

Everyone was still staring at me.

"I'll talk to Heidi," I said.

That seemed to satisfy my friends, and they went back to exchanging lovey-dovey gazes and enjoying their meal. I managed to eat my food, though I didn't enjoy it. I might as well have scarfed down a plateful of Styrofoam peanuts since I didn't taste the food at all.

Maybe I ought to go see Heidi.

No, that would be stupid. Only if we were dating would I feel the need to "work things out," as Eve put it. Since I wasn't involved with Heidi, I did not need to see her.

When I tried to volunteer for clearing the table and loading the dishwasher, four people told me emphatically "no" and all but shoved me out the door. "Talk to Heidi," they said, almost at the same time, like a chorus of meddling friends.

I should've gone to my room and forgotten about Heidi. I intended to do that. Honestly, I did.

But my feet had plans of their own.

That was how I wound up standing in front of the door to Heidi's room with my fist raised to knock. I froze then, staring at the metal numbers attached to the door. Heidi must've been inside. If I came here to see her, I ought to knock. Why was I hesitating?

Because I had become a brainless idiot.

I rapped on the door.

When it opened a few seconds later, Heidi gaped at me. "Damian?"

"Yeah, that's still my name. Glad you remember it." If I'd tried really hard maybe I could've come up with something even dumber to say. "How are you? Ruth said you grabbed some food and took off without talking to anyone."

"I wanted to eat alone. Is that a crime?"

"No, but—"

"Good night, Damian." She slammed the door in my face.

What the hell?

I banged on the door until she opened it again. "What is wrong with you? I came here to make sure you're okay, but you're acting like I'm a criminal trying to break into your room."

"Go away, please. I don't want to sleep with you."

"What part of anything I just said implied I want to sleep with you?"

She flattened her lips, one hand on the door, one foot tapping furiously. "Just leave, okay? I don't have to explain myself to you."

"No, but—"

Heidi slammed the door. Again.

To hell with this. She had clearly gone insane since the last time I saw her, and I didn't feel like trying to talk her down. If she wanted to behave like a lunatic, she could go for it.

But not with me. I was done. No more fantasizing about Heidi or trying to make Heidi feel better or massaging Heidi's palm. It was over.

Not that we'd ever had a thing in the first place.

I stalked out of the guest house, veering toward my wagon. Whenever I needed a little peace and quiet, I retreated into my little gypsy home. I got about halfway there when someone ran up behind me and seized my arm, forcing me to stop. I half-turned to face that person.

Heidi was breathing hard, her tits heaving. "I'm sorry, Damian."

"For which part? Slamming the door in my face twice, or announcing out of frigging nowhere that you don't want to sleep with me?"

"All of it." She still had her hand on my arm, but now she slid it down to my hand, slipping her fingers between mine. "I panicked when I saw you, which has kind of become my signature move lately."

"What did I do? A palm reading was supposed to be fun, but I must've screwed it up somehow."

"No, it's not you. I've made a lot of mistakes with men, and I'm terrified I'll screw up this time too."

This time? That almost sounded like she was saying… No, she couldn't have meant *that*.

"I like you, Damian," she said, "and it scares me. So I panicked."

"Because I knocked on your door."

She moved closer, clasping my hand more firmly. "Because I'd been thinking about you ever since the palm-reading thing. I've been, um…fantasizing about you."

"I fantasize about you too."

"When I opened the door, and you were there, I wanted you. I still want you." She inched even closer, her breasts grazing my chest. "I want you all the time. Maybe I should stop fighting it."

"Maybe we both should." I wrapped my free arm around her waist, tugging her closer. "Come with me to the wagon."

"Thought you never seduced anyone in there."

"I haven't, not until now." I touched my lips to hers, a soft, gentle kiss. "Assuming you come with me. I'd love to spend the night with you in my gypsy sanctuary."

She laid a hand on my cheek. "Yes, Damian, I will."

"We can just talk if that's what you want. Talk and sleep together, and I mean 'sleep' as in catching some Z's."

"I want more than that."

"Me too." I led her toward the wagon, holding her hand the whole time, letting go only so I could open the door. As she climbed up the steps, her ass was inches away from my face. "Already loving the view."

She smiled at me over her shoulder. "You'll get a much better view in a few minutes."

Naked Heidi. Sure, I'd seen her naked before, but this time would be different. No comparison, actually. I would have her nude body underneath mine.

I climbed into the wagon and shut the door, stopping just past the threshold.

Heidi stood by the table, gazing down at it. She traced her fingertips over the surface, then laid her palm on it. "Later, I'd love for you to finish that palm reading." She looked at me. "If you don't mind."

"Love to—later." I strode up to her, laying my palm over her hand on the table. "This is your night, Heidi. You set the pace, you decide what you want to do, and you tell me what you want me to do."

"That's sweet, but it's unnecessary. I trust you, Damian."

"You trust me so much that you ran away from a palm reading. I'm not being sarcastic or grumpy. I'm stating a fact."

"I know. But I didn't run away because of you. I did it because you make me feel so good that I want more than friendship with you." She fingered the lapel of my shirt. "I want you, period. And that scares me, but I refuse to keep being a coward who's too afraid to admit what I want. So if you still want me—"

"Hell yes, I want you."

"Good." She pointed at the bench. "Sit down, please."

"The bed is a lot more comfortable for having sex."

"You said you'd do what I want."

I had said that, and I never reneged on a promise. So I dropped onto the bench and spread my arms across its back. "I'm all yours."

"Got any music? The steamy kind, preferably."

"Absolutely." I dug my phone out of my pocket and found a good playlist, one of my favorites, then I started the music. It played through a Bluetooth speaker embedded in the wall, thanks to an app I'd installed on my phone. "Steamy enough for you?"

"Mm, I like this. Belly dancing music."

While the Middle Eastern style music played, Heidi began to sway her hips. She got her whole body into it, like a real belly dancer, moving her sexy body in ways that made the blood in my brain pour down into my dick. She pulled her shirt off over her head, then unzipped her pants and got rid of them too.

I stroked my hardening cock through my jeans, imagining all the things I wanted to do with her tonight.

Heidi undid her bra and let it fall away from her body. She kept shimmying and gyrating while she removed her panties, and I couldn't tear my gaze away from her, couldn't stop myself from following every movement. Her tits swayed, her eyes fluttered shut, and she skimmed her hands up and down her body the way I wanted to do to her.

She knelt in front of me, pushed my knees apart, and positioned herself between them. "I've wanted to do this for so long, maybe since the first time I saw you. Can't wait anymore."

I reached for my shirt, about to unbutton it, but she stopped me with her hand on mine.

"Let me do that," she purred, her voice so sultry the sound of it made my balls tighten.

"Well, it is your night." I lowered my hand.

She unhooked the buttons on my shirt one by one while seductive music played, her movements synced with the rhythm of the song. Her hips kept swaying, despite being wedged between my legs. Her fingers grazed my skin as she made her way down my chest until she'd undone every button and my shirt hung open. Humming with pleasure, she glided her palms up my chest and then dragged her nails back down it. When her fingers found the fly on my jeans, she undid that too and pulled the zipper down, down, down until she'd exposed my cock.

"I love that you don't wear anything under your pants," she said in that hot-as-hell purr. With one hand, she pulled my dick out and cupped it in her palm. "This is what I've wanted to do so badly I had to make myself come every time I fantasized about it. Like this morning. You heard me, didn't you?"

"Yeah. That's why I ran to the restroom. I needed to make myself come too."

She slid her hand up and down my length. "Yeah, I figured out what you were doing even before I heard you come."

"You heard me?" I sucked in a breath when she flicked her thumb over the head of my erection. "Fuck, Heidi, that's hot."

"Things are about to get even hotter."

She grasped the base of my erection and bent to take me into her mouth.

I set a hand on her shoulder to stop her. "Are you sure about this? Ten minutes ago, you told me to go away and you don't want to sleep with me."

"Yeah, I know. But I only said that because I do want you, so damn much, and that scares me. My history with men isn't the greatest." She peeled my hand away from her shoulder and massaged my palm with her thumb. "You're not like anyone else, though, and I suddenly realized I don't want to fight this anymore. Can't promise I'll want a candlelight dinner with you, but for tonight, all I know is that I need to be with you. Okay?"

"Sure. I want that too." I glanced down at my hard-on. "I'd love to have your mouth on me, but you shouldn't make me come. Takes me a while to get up and running again."

"That's okay. We have all night."

"Do you mean you're staying until morning?"

"Yes. Now shut up and let me taste you."

I relaxed against the bench.

Heidi lowered her mouth and licked my crown, then blew air across it. She'd hardly done anything to me, but already I had trouble catching my breath. When she swept her tongue up my cock and back down to the crown, I gripped the bench's edge hard enough to crush the cushioning. She did that again, slowly raking her tongue up my entire length and then down the other side, her damp tongue leaving a cool trail in its wake.

"Fuck, Heidi, that feels—"

My voice died when she took me into her mouth, one hand grasping the base of my erection while she massaged my inner thigh with her other hand. She pumped me while her tongue darted out to tease my skin, and she gently sucked, moving her mouth up and down, over and over, spurring me to clench the cushions harder and gasp for breath. Her mouth felt hot and wet, her tongue velvety soft, and God, the way she rubbed my thigh, inching her fingers closer and closer to my balls...

She skimmed her fingers past my balls and massaged the skin behind them.

I'd never experienced anything like this before. No one had ever touched me in that spot, but it felt incredible.

Heidi sped up her movements, pumping me faster, sucking me harder. I threw my head back and groaned, and I swore my eyes rolled back in my head for a second. Pressure built inside me as an electric current rushed down my spine, making every hair on my body stiffen, and I knew I'd lose it soon. I couldn't manage to groan, let alone speak, but I couldn't stop myself from grasping the back of her head and fisting one hand in her hair. She grunted out ravenous little noises like she loved having me in her mouth.

I came like a bomb going off. My back bowed, and the only sound I could make was a strangled gasp. She kept sucking, taking everything I had without flinching or even letting up, not until I'd spent everything inside her mouth.

She sat back on her heels and wiped her lips with one hand. "I loved doing that for you."

"Yeah," I said, still breathing hard, "I loved you doing that for me too."

Laughing, she leaned in to wrap her arms around my neck. "Mind if kiss you? Most guys don't want to kiss me when I've just given them head."

"I don't mind."

"Maybe I should drink something first."

"Don't worry about it."

I took hold of her face and tugged her closer, mashing my mouth to hers and plunging my tongue between her lips to get a deeper taste of her. Maybe I did taste myself a little, but it was only a hint of a salty tang, and I didn't care. I'd kiss her if she'd just eaten a big plateful of raw garlic and onions, or even sauerkraut. I hated that stuff.

When I finally relinquished her lips, I smiled and rubbed the corner of her mouth with my thumb. "About time I got to taste you."

Chapter Eleven

Heidi

Damian was nothing like any man I'd ever known before. Ollie was a great guy, but we just weren't right for each other, a fact I realized way too late to avoid humiliating myself. But here in this lushly decorated wagon, I knew I wouldn't make a mistake—not with Damian. Not tonight, anyway. If this didn't last beyond one night, I knew at least I'd walk away with an amazing memory.

I couldn't decide if I wanted it to last longer.

He needed a few minutes after the blow job to recover, but he let me undress him while he lay there watching me do that. I swore he enjoyed seeing me take his clothes off more than he enjoyed my little striptease. Maybe he loved it because I let my fingers graze his skin as often as possible, and I showered kisses over his chest and biceps before I moved on to getting rid of his pants. I kissed his thighs too, and his hips, and I tickled his belly button with my tongue.

"You're getting me going again in record time," he said. "Damn, Heidi, you are the sexiest, most passionate woman on earth."

"We haven't had sex yet. How do you know I'm passionate?"

"By the way you gave me head. No woman has ever done it like that."

I'd loved feasting on him, more than I'd ever loved giving a man oral sex before tonight. What was it about Damian that made me crave him with a hunger so deep and all-consuming that I couldn't stand the thought of not being with him? Maybe tomorrow I'd worry about that. Tonight, I wanted to be with him.

He led me to the curtain that concealed his mini-bedroom and held it open so I could climb onto the bed. The covers were already pulled back. The plush padding of the mattress cradled my body and made me feel like I was floating on the ocean. Maybe I felt that way because I knew Damian would touch me any second. Maybe I always felt weightless when I was with him, like the burden of all my worries had lifted off me.

Damian crawled onto the bed, straddling me. "Don't be shy. If there's something you want me to do that I'm not doing, tell me."

How many guys would say something like that during sex? I would've bet Ollie did, though I'd never slept with him. Nobody else would—except for Damian.

"You're so sweet," I told him. "And so damn hot."

He chuckled. "Thanks. You're smokin' hot too."

I moved my arms above my head on the pillow, linking my hands.

"Love these tits," he said, smirking right before he took my nipple into his mouth and suckled it.

"Oh yes, please keep doing that."

He curled his tongue around my stiff peak, then tugged it with his teeth.

I arched my back, loving the sensation of electricity zinging through me, from my breast down to my sex. He kept tormenting my nipple, licking, sucking, and scraping it while I writhed and moaned, sending more jolts of electric pleasure straight down to my core. When he pulled his mouth away, I made an impatient noise.

"Don't worry," he said, patting my hip. "I'm nowhere near done with you."

He slid his lips down my belly, swirled his tongue inside my navel, and kissed his way down to my hip. I moaned, or maybe I said "please," couldn't swear to anything right now. His mouth and the feel of his body sliding down mine destroyed my willpower and my ability to think. Screw thinking. What did I need a brain for right now? Only to deliver more of those delicious waves of electric pleasure.

Damian placed an open-mouth kiss on the hollow of my hip, his warm tongue dampening my skin. The coolness when he pulled his mouth away made me shiver the tiniest bit. With one hand, he exerted gentle pressure on my inner thigh, urging me to spread my legs for him. I couldn't resist anything he wanted me to do, so I opened for him. He shimmied backward until his face hovered over my mound, then he dropped onto his elbows. With his mouth almost touching the hairs down there, his breaths excited my skin.

He pushed his mouth between my folds.

I felt his breaths on my slick skin first, followed by the roughness of his evening stubble, and finally, his tongue scraping over my flesh as he dragged it up one side of my folds and then the other. He licked his way down to my opening, swirling his tongue around the rim. I needed him to touch my clit, needed it so intensely that I bucked my hips, silently pleading with him to devour me the way I wanted him to the most.

"Not yet," he said, lifting his head to peek up at me over my hips. "I want to keep you on the edge until you're a wild, thrashing animal. Only then will I let you come. Relax, I won't push you too far. I'll know when you really need it and give you exactly what you want."

I already burned for him, after the way he'd stroked his tongue over my flesh. Whatever he might do to me tonight, I knew it would leave me breathless and satisfied. How did I know that? No idea, but it didn't matter. For one night, I needed to experience sex with this man and know exactly how much satisfaction he could give me.

One night only. No spooning. No hand-holding tomorrow. One night of mind-blowing sex, nothing more.

Damian dipped his head between my thighs again, and I couldn't worry about anything anymore. He traced his tongue around my rigid nub without contacting it, teasing me with his agile tongue and his heated breaths. My skin came alive, starting at my clitoris and blossoming outward until my entire body felt more awake and alive than ever before. I couldn't catch my breath, and he'd barely done anything to me. He watched me over my mound, his gaze capturing mine and refusing to let me glance away for even half a second. I swore he looked straight into my soul with those searing brown eyes. My breathing grew heavier, like the most delicious weight had settled on top of me and now it bore down on my body. I wanted him on top of me like that, thrusting inside me while his weight pressed me into the mattress.

He flicked his tongue across my nub.

I jerked and gasped, stunned by the power of the sensations that raced down my nerves, sharp and electric. My clit pulsed, my sex too, and I prayed any second he would send me hurtling over the edge. I clenched my fingers in the silky sheets, panting while he slowly dragged his tongue around my taut bud, eliciting more little shocks, making me cry out.

"Oh God, Damian, please." I couldn't stop the whimper that burst out of me. "Please, I need—oh God."

He latched on to my clit and sucked it hard.

My body froze, every muscle taut and ready, and even my lungs couldn't function. My gaze stayed glued to his while he nipped and suckled my nub, and the pleasure escalated higher and higher, my ears ringing because I couldn't breathe.

Then I came. The climax detonated inside me, so intense that choked gasps were the only sounds I could make. It felt like a thousand tiny explosions under my skin, setting me on fire from head to toe with ricocheting waves of pleasure inside my body. My sex yearned for his cock inside me, clenching again and again but with nothing to fill the void.

He didn't stop tormenting my flesh until he'd wrung every last spasm from my body.

I was breathing so hard I almost hyperventilated. Ridiculous. But I couldn't deny the truth of it. Was it only the way he'd touched me that drove me wild? Or was it *him*?

His tongue, that was all. His tongue and his piercing gaze.

And his incredible body. And his sexy smile.

No, it was only his tongue, nothing more.

Damian rose onto hands and knees, straddling me with his face above mine. He bent his elbows a little, just enough to bring his face closer to mine. "Don't panic yet. Save that for tomorrow."

"You want me to panic in the morning?"

"No, but I realize you probably will. We're about to shatter that celibacy vow of yours."

"Think we already did."

He smirked, and even that expression was devastatingly erotic. "What we've done so far was only blowing off steam. Now, we're going to turn that steam engine up so high it'll shatter."

"Yes, please, I need super-hot sex."

"It will be super hot, but not the way you mean." He bent his head to nuzzle my nose. "There are many kinds of hot sex, and I'm about to give you the kind you need the most, even if you don't realize it yet."

What did that mean? The hormones flooding my body made it hard to concentrate on anything, especially his words. "Hot sex" were the only words I could understand.

He leaned over the bed's edge, stretching an arm down to reach under the bed. His face tightened while he struggled to get whatever it was he wanted down there. Then he grinned and held up a condom packet. "Ready to go."

"You keep condoms under your bed? Thought you never seduced women in this wagon."

"That's true. I bought some condoms today in the resort gift shop because I hoped you might want to do more than flirt with me, eventually." He ripped the condom packet open with his teeth. "Thought it would take longer. Damn, I'm even better than I thought, getting you to beg me for sex."

I couldn't deny I'd begged with my actions and my intentions, though I hadn't outright begged for it. The implications of my need for him might hit me later, but for now, I wouldn't think about anything except having Damian inside me.

He rolled the condom on and knelt over me again on all fours. "I won't hurt you, not ever."

Why was he saying that? If he meant physically, I never thought he'd hurt me like that. "What happened to 'I love to talk dirty'? We're having sex, not going to a couples therapy group."

"No talking, not tonight. Next time, I'll talk dirty to you for as long as you want."

But not tonight? Why? I was on fire for him, and he kept saying things that sounded...like things he shouldn't be saying.

He kissed me, soft and slow, his tongue slipping between my lips with such gentleness that it made my throat ache. But when he toyed with my tongue, all that delicious excitement I'd felt a few minutes ago came rushing back, enlivening every part of me. When he positioned his knees between my legs, I couldn't stop my knees from bending and my thighs from parting, like my body wanted him so badly it had to offer me up to him in the most blatant way.

Damian settled his body on top of mine.

My breaths quickened. My pulse accelerated. I wanted him so much, but I didn't know if I could handle the way he would make me feel. *I won't hurt you*, he'd said. I clutched his biceps, where he'd planted his elbows on the mattress at either side of me.

"Shh," he murmured, brushing his lips over mine. "Forget about everything else and be with me tonight."

He pushed inside me inch by inch, his cock gliding deeper with such exquisite slowness that my breaths became pants and my heartbeat pounded in my ears and my chest. I gripped his arms tighter while he thrust in and out, taking his time like he relished every second of making love to me. The easy pace made it impossible for me to block out all the things I didn't want to feel, like the sensation of his body on mine, warm and strong, or the scent of him that enveloped me. With his head alongside mine, his hair tickled my cheek, and every time he exhaled it sent a rush of warm air over my earlobe.

My body cradled his, inside and out.

Damian groaned softly like this was the best thing he'd ever felt. Every thrust aroused me more, little by little, until the feel of him sliding in and out, his body grazing my nub, had me gasping and lashing my arms around him. My stiff nipples scraped against his chest, the friction so delicious that I dug my nails into his back.

"Faster," I pleaded. "Please, faster, harder."

"Not this time," he whispered into my ear, his voice strained and rough.

"But I—"

He covered my mouth with his.

And still, he moved his hips in that easy rhythm. In slow, out slow, over and over, oh so patient that even while he kept his lips glued to mine, he didn't try for a deeper kiss. Lips on lips, nothing more. How could that be so intensely erotic? He took my body with a gentleness no man had ever shown me before, and my chest tightened from the knowledge of what that might mean, but my mind couldn't decipher anything more complex than the need to come that built inside me second by second.

I wrapped my legs around him, my ankles locked behind his ass.

The climax rippled through me like no orgasm I'd ever experienced before. It came over me as slowly as he'd taken my body, the intensity of it growing with every thrust of his cock until my gasps became throaty moans and the moans turned into strangled cries. I gripped him with every part of my body, from my arms and legs to the muscles deep inside me that milked him with spasms that grew stronger with each wave of pleasure.

My heart thrashed in my chest. Desperate noises erupted out of me.

He pulled his hips back and plowed into me, his cock throbbing as he let go, releasing everything he had inside me. After two gentler thrusts, he let his body go slack on top of me. He raised his head, gazing at me with a soft expression that conveyed things I didn't want to think about right now.

"Damian, I—"

With two fingers, he sealed my lips. "Hush. We don't need to talk. You can tell me to go to hell in the morning."

"I wasn't going to say that."

"Glad to hear it." He claimed my mouth in a kiss that was soft and slow and full of longing. Then he slid off my body to lie beside me, one arm draped over my belly. "Let's get some sleep."

"Okay."

I rolled onto my side facing away from him.

He tugged me into his body, one hand on my belly.

We were spooning. Oh no, we couldn't do that. It was too...intimate.

But I couldn't make myself tell him to move or make my muscles work so I could move away from him. I should've gotten up and left, but I didn't want to leave. For one night, I could let myself enjoy sleeping with Damian.

Tomorrow... I'd worry about that in the morning.

Chapter Twelve

Damian

Iwoke up in the best way imaginable, with Heidi Mackenzie snuggled up to me. We'd fallen asleep with my front to her back, but now we lay face to face. She had her arm hanging over me, her sweet body tucked against mine, and her silky hair brushing against my face. Her nose brushed me too. And her lips. Was that an unconscious invitation for me to wake her with a kiss? Sure looked like one to me.

Laying a hand on her hip, I pressed my lips to hers and let them linger there until she sighed delicately. Then I gave her ass a quick squeeze. "Good morning, Heidi."

Her lids fluttered open, and a lazy smile curved her lips. "Good morning, Damian."

She hadn't seemed this relaxed when we fell asleep last night. I'd kind of expected her to panic the instant she woke up and realized she'd spent the night with me. Instead, she was smiling in the sweetest sleepy-sexy way.

And of course, my dick decided now was the right time for some morning wood.

Heidi screwed up her mouth. "Is there a live snake between our bodies, or is that *your* snake stiffening up?"

"It's me. Sorry, it happens every morning." But I was sure I'd get much stiffer this morning than I ever had before. How could I not? Heidi's luscious body was touching mine and the scent of her, that indescribable feminine aroma, made my cock wake up even faster than usual.

She laughed. "I've slept with other men, so I know all about morning hard-ons."

"Good. Then you won't mind taking care of the problem for me like you did last night."

"Mm-mm, no can do." She sat up and stretched, making her gorgeous tits lift and jiggle. "One time only, Damian. Last night was amazing, but we will never do that again."

Oh damn. I'd hoped making love to her, really making love to her, would banish that stupid idea. She'd broken her celibacy vow, but only for one night. Yeah, right. I'd believe that on the day Bigfoot walked out of the woods and introduced himself. He'd have a southern accent. Why not? It was my stupid fantasy.

No, my fantasy had unfolded last night, with Heidi.

But she wanted my body and nothing else. Well, she thought she did. I knew it was bullshit. We'd talked and shared personal stuff before we had sex, before last night when she ran after me to ask me to fuck her. She liked me, but she was terrified of getting hurt again.

I had no idea how to convince her I wouldn't be like her douchebag ex.

"We like each other," I said. "It's not a crime, and you don't need to run away from me because of what happened last night."

She slid off the bed, standing on the top step. "Thank you for the mind-blowing orgasms, but we will never have sex again. We are not dating."

"But we're friends, right?" Friends with the best benefits ever. I wanted more than that, but I wouldn't push. Heidi needed gentle nudges in the right direction, though.

"No, we're not friends." She hopped off the steps, bending over to hunt around on the floor for her clothes. "I'm a guest, and you're the concierge. That's it."

Okay, last night had freaked her out even more than I thought.

I jumped off the bed and over the steps, landing a few feet from Heidi.

She startled and yelped.

"Didn't mean to scare you," I said. "But I don't want you to leave until we've talked about this. Please, Heidi, let's have a real conversation like we did before."

"I'm hungry, and the food is in the dining hall."

"Stay here. I'll go get some food for us."

"No, Damian," she said firmly, managing to look resolute and stubborn while she was naked and struggling to get her bra clasps hooked.

"At least let me help you with that." I moved closer and reached for the back of her bra.

She batted my hand away. "I can do it myself."

"Okay, fine." I raised my hands. "I surrender."

Heidi's gaze swept over me from head to toe. She licked her lips when her focus landed on my groin.

Yeah, the morning wood had arrived.

She cleared her throat and tore her gaze away from my dick. "Get dressed, please."

"I know nudity doesn't bother you in general. I mean, you used to be a naturist. So I'm assuming you want me to get dressed because *my* nudity bothers you—in a sexy way."

"Don't flatter yourself." She finally got her bra done up and started pulling on the rest of her clothes. "You aren't so hot that I can't keep my hands off you, or my eyes off you."

But she had watched me lately. A lot. Especially when I was naked.

I wouldn't point that out to her. Only an asshole did something like that.

"Get dressed," she said again, notably without the "please" this time.

"Yeah, okay, relax." While I found my clothes and put them on, Heidi hurried out of the wagon. I called out, "Your clothes are wrinkled, Heidi, and I think your shirt is on backwards."

She froze mid-step, threw me an annoyed look over her shoulder, then stomped off.

Maybe I shouldn't have told her that, but I figured she'd want to know if she looked like she just got back from a night of hot sex. I couldn't seem to do anything right with her. Not this morning, at least.

I headed for my room in the guest house and changed into casual clothes. Today was my day off, so I didn't need to wear either of my work uniforms—the resort version or the gypsy version. Jeans and a T-shirt would do fine today. Maybe I'd go nude later. Then again, maybe I shouldn't. Heidi was upset about last night, and seeing my nakedness might make her panic again.

Why did I care? She'd made it clear we weren't dating and never would be.

Maybe I wasn't a Casanova type, but I could get a date if I wanted one. No woman had ever turned me down, for a date or sex. Maybe that sounded a tad arrogant, but I didn't mean it that way. Could I help it if women lusted for me? Like I'd told Heidi, I gave awesome dating.

But Heidi wouldn't go on a date with me.

Had I ever actually asked her for a date? "Have dinner with me," I'd said when I approached Heidi minutes after she'd arrived at the resort. That wasn't a question. It was a statement, like I planned to throw her over my shoulder and take her back to my cave for a dinner of barbecued squirrel with pine nuts on the side. Was I being a dick today? No, I'd treated Heidi with kid gloves because I worried about freaking her out.

Maybe that was the problem. I was being too nice. She'd liked me yesterday when I'd told her "have dinner with me" and when I'd announced I loved whispering filthy things into a woman's ear. Last night, I held back and tried to show her my tender side. Maybe I was going about this the wrong way. Heidi might respond better to my rakish side since making sweet love to her had resulted in panic.

Couldn't hurt to try.

But I'd relished making love to her.

I went to Heidi's room, but she either wasn't there or refused to let on that she was. Knocking, even banging, on her door resulted in silence. Since I'd already changed into my off-duty clothes, I trotted downstairs to eat breakfast. Heidi wasn't there. I ate fast and split.

Outside the guest house, I bumped into Ollie. "Have you seen Heidi?"

He smirked. "Only when she was running out of your wagon with her clothes on backwards."

"You better not have said anything to her about that."

"I'm the good one, Damian, remember? You're the bad boy."

"Does that mean you haven't said anything to Heidi about how she, uh, was in my wagon with her clothes on the wrong way?"

My best friend snickered. "I kind of doubt she went into your little love nest with her clothes like that. But no, I didn't say a thing to Heidi."

I let out the breath I hadn't realized I was holding. "You don't know where she is now."

"No." He tipped his head to the side, studying me. "You like her a lot, don't you?"

"Mind your own business, Ollie."

I walked away—okay, stomped away—without giving Ollie a chance to say anything else that would make me irritable. Some guests were already on the lawn, including Ruth and Sylvester. I flopped onto a chaise beside them.

"Good morning, sunshine," Ruth said. She scrutinized me for a moment, then said, "I see storm clouds brewing around you. What's wrong? Did you and Heidi have a fight?"

"We're not dating, Ruth."

"You can have an argument even if you're not dating."

"I don't want to talk about Heidi."

Ruth clucked her tongue. "You two definitely had a fight."

Grumbling, I shoved myself up out of the chair. "I'm going for a walk."

"If we see Heidi, we'll let her know where you went."

I might've actually growled, like a wild animal.

Rather than heading for the nature trail, I veered across the lawn to take the almost-hidden path to my pilot project. Lenny and Georgie nickered when they saw me, but oddly, they were already standing at the fence near the gate.

Then I noticed why.

Heidi stood at the fence, half-hidden in the shadows of the surrounding trees. She kept a six-inch gap between her and the fence and bit her lip while she watched the horses. And she'd gotten her clothes on the right way.

"There you are," I said.

She swung her head around to stare at me. "Damian? I thought it was your day off."

"It is. How did you know that?"

"Well, I…" She hunched her shoulders. "I asked Ollie."

"Because you're dying to spend more time with me, alone. That's cool." I rested an arm on the top bar of the fence, facing Heidi. "Ever have sex in the woods?"

"No dating, Damian."

"I mentioned sex, not dating." Leaning toward her, I gave her my best suggestive smile. "Unless you're ready for that upgrade."

"What upgrade?"

"From sex to dating. I told you we could start with getting it on, then you can upgrade to having dinner with me."

She crossed her arms over those gorgeous tits. "I'm done with men."

"But you had your way with me last night. That was the best blow job in history."

"This was a bad idea."

Heidi started to walk away, but I snagged her arm. "What was a bad idea?"

"Coming here to see the horses. I should've guessed you'd show up. Are you stalking me?"

"I had no idea you would be here. You're terrified of horses."

"Thought I'd try a little more immersion therapy."

Georgie nudged my arm, so I scratched under his chin. "Did you even pet one of these guys?"

"No, I've only been here for a couple minutes."

"At least give Georgie some love before you go." I wanted her to give me some too, but I kind of doubted that would happen.

Heidi stretched out a hand to stroke Georgie's neck, then scratched under his chin.

She turned to walk away again.

"I'll see you later, Heidi, when you get desperate to kiss me." I said those words in a teasing tone, and I knew she got that because she threw me a grudging smile over her shoulder.

And I watched her ass while she walked away.

Chapter Thirteen

Heidi

I stalked back to the lawn and flumped onto an Adirondack chair. Nobody was playing miniten or any other game at the moment, though a handful of people sat in chairs or on the grass in small groups, talking and laughing. I didn't feel like laughing. Damian had me feeling…uncomfortable. Why had he felt the need to turn a night of mind-blowing sex into an intensely intimate encounter? Why couldn't he just give me amazing orgasms and leave it at that? No, he had to say sweet, sexy things and look at me like I was the most beautiful woman he'd ever seen. Instead of getting his rocks off and saying good night, he'd made love to me with a kind of tenderness no other man had ever shown me.

That bastard.

How was I supposed to keep pretending we weren't involved, that all I wanted was meaningless sex, if he wouldn't cooperate? Caring and sharing had never been a part of any relationship I'd ever had with a man. Even the nicest ones didn't want to cuddle after sex. None of them had ever been as patient with me or as concerned with my pleasure. I'd told Damian I trusted him, and I meant it. Even when I slammed a door in his face, he didn't get angry. He worried he'd done something wrong. And all the other things he'd said to me last night…

We can just talk if that's what you want. Talk and sleep together, and I mean 'sleep' as in catching some Z's.

Men never wanted that. Bang and run, that was the usual way things went. Either that or bang and fall asleep.

This is your night, Heidi. You set the pace, you decide what you want to do, and you tell me what you want me to do.

Damian had kept that promise. He never did anything I didn't want. If I had told him not to make love to me, I was sure he would've stopped. But I hadn't wanted him to. Even while part of me panicked, the rest of me reveled in the sweet, sensual glory of Damian loving my body.

"Don't be shy," he'd said last night. "If there's something you want me to do that I'm not doing, tell me."

Then he'd assured me he would never push me too far sexually, and he'd know exactly what I needed and when. I couldn't deny he had known, almost like he could read my mind. Maybe a palm reading genuinely did provide supernatural insight.

There are many kinds of hot sex, and I'm about to give you the kind you need the most, even if you don't realize it yet.

Had I needed sweet, sensual, loving sex? Since I'd never experienced that kind before, I couldn't say for sure whether I'd needed it. Oh, who was I kidding? I'd needed it, he gave it to me, and now I had to deal with the consequences of letting him make love to me.

One of the last things he'd said to me before we fell asleep replayed in my mind, as clearly as if he were whispering it into my ear right now. *I won't hurt you, not ever.*

God, I wished he hadn't been so…wonderful. Walking away from him had been way too hard, and it gave me a sharp pain in the back of my throat. I barely knew Damian, but I felt like he knew me, for sure. Should I give him a chance?

A chill shivered over my skin, but a luxurious warmth swept in behind it.

If that indicated something, I refused to think about what it was.

Damian sauntered out of the woods.

That man looked as steamy-hot in jeans and a gray T-shirt as he did in his gypsy-vampire outfit. The way he had his shirt untucked made me want to push my hands up under the fabric and run them over his smooth chest. God, I loved his body. Even seeing him with clothes on made me want to lick him from head to toe, especially that beautiful dick.

Okay, I wanted him. The slickness between my thighs would've contradicted me if I'd claimed I didn't want him anymore. Getting it on with Damian had only intensified my lust for him. Avoiding the man seemed like the only prudent choice.

But I didn't want to stay away. I wanted him naked, this time with me on top. The thought terrified me, but also got me even wetter. Maybe I could have sex with him again, just once, purely to satisfy my craving for his body.

Yeah, right, I'd screw him one more time and then I'd be over it. *What kind of idiot have you become, woman?*

Damian started to turn left, toward the far end of the lawn. But then he saw me, and his mouth slid into a sexy smile. He waved.

I waved back without thinking about it, spurred by a politeness reflex.

He took it as an invitation and jogged across the lawn toward where I sat.

Oh crap. I could not see or speak to Damian when I was still turned on by fantasies of him.

"What's up, Heidi?" Damian asked as he stopped beside my chair.

"Nothing. You waved, so I waved. It wasn't an invitation."

"But you wanted me to come over here." He bent to rest his hand on my chair's arm, his face way too close to mine. "Let's go for a walk. Just the two of us. I promise not to do anything you don't want me to do." He slanted in more, moving his lips to within millimeters of my ear. "I may not be awesome at everything, but I will give you the best dating you've ever had. My hand-holding will make you shiver with anticipation, and when I put my arm around your shoulders, you'll get so hot for me it'll make you weak in the knees."

"That's silly. Holding hands is not erotic."

"It is the way I do it. And I haven't even gotten to the kissing yet. One peck on the cheek will have you begging me to make you come."

My sarcastic laugh came out as a splutter. "Does this kind of thing work for you? Dirty hand-holding? Seriously? That's ridiculous."

"It's all in the delivery."

He picked up my hand, simply cradling it in his.

Warmth rushed through me.

But when he touched his lips to my cheek, I almost gasped. Which was idiotic. A chaste kiss on the cheek did not make me weak with lust. Except my legs did feel a touch wobbly like if I tried to stand up, I'd fall back onto the chair.

"Come with me," Damian murmured. "Please, Heidi, say yes."

"I… What are we going to do on this so-called walk?"

He chuckled. "Walk and talk, that's all."

"Well, in that case… all right."

Damian straightened and offered me his hands, helping me get up. He settled a palm on my lower back as we strolled toward the nature trail.

And damn, that gentle touch sent a delicate tingle chasing over my skin.

"What did you mean 'it's all in the delivery'?" I asked while we headed into the woods. "You barely kissed my cheek."

"But the things I said and the way I said them got you worked up. That's what I meant." He danced his fingertips over my spine, the touch light and teasing. "Sometimes the right words spoken the right way are more enticing than actions."

I couldn't deny that was true, but only with Damian had I ever experienced it.

"When I talk dirty to you," he said, "you'll feel it inside your body like I'm fucking you."

After the way he so easily turned me on with his words a minute ago, I couldn't deny he might do exactly what he suggested. My body awakened at the mere thought of Damian whispering dirty things in my ear.

We strolled down the main trail hand in hand like he'd suggested, and I found myself relaxing even though we didn't speak a word to each other. It felt nice to spend time with a guy without the pressure of expectations. Damian didn't expect anything, I knew that. But I kept assuming he'd turn into a dick like my ex—like all my exes. Why did I keep picking losers?

I hadn't picked Damian. He had chosen me, though he let me set the pace.

Maybe we were kind of—almost, but not quite—dating.

"Which trail do you want to take now?" he asked as we approached a fork in the path.

One fork led to the hot spring. The other path, the main trail, headed toward the lake but had some offshoots that led to areas that were great for seeing the wildlife and scenery. If I chose the hot spring trail, that might imply I wanted to get naked with Damian in the steamy blue water. Okay, I did want that. The second I thought of it, I needed to go there with him. But I shouldn't. Not yet.

"Straight ahead," I told him. "But you can choose after that."

"Okay."

We ambled down the trail a little further, then turned onto a side path that I knew led to a small meadow where wildflowers bloomed. Still, we didn't talk. Damian held my hand, that was all. He smiled at me too, whenever I glanced at him, but it was a soft, sweet smile. I'd never been a big fan of holding hands, but with Damian, I found I loved it. He kept rubbing the back of my hand with his thumb, gently, and while we wandered toward the meadow, he threaded his fingers through mine.

Once we got to the meadow, he suggested we lie in the grass, amid the wildflowers, and relax. I already felt super relaxed, thanks to his sweetness, but I didn't tell him so.

We stretched out on the grass with a blue sky above us.

His hand stayed linked with mine.

Damian shifted in place like he was getting more comfortable. "Can I ask you a personal question?"

"Since when do you need permission? I told you all kinds of personal stuff the other day."

"But you're still dealing with last night, so I figured I'd be a nice guy instead of an asshat and ask permission before grilling you."

"That's very considerate," I said with only part sarcasm. He was a genuinely nice guy. "Fine, grill away."

"Why did you dump Ollie to go back to your ex? Why did you break up with that other guy in the first place?"

A wave of cold swept through me, raising all the hairs on my arms and sinking deep under my skin. Nobody had asked me those questions before. I'd never wanted to talk about it except to tell Mara and Ollie that I kept going back to Grant because he always seemed sincere when he begged me to forgive him. Should I tell Damian everything? What if, after hearing about it, he didn't want to be with me anymore?

Not that it mattered. I couldn't get involved with him.

So, uh, why was I holding his hand?

My voice had a mind of its own and decided to tell him everything. "I have a habit of picking the wrong guys. I convinced myself I should be with Ollie because he's such a sweetie, and I knew he'd never hurt me the way other guys have. But I had no business getting involved with him when I'd just broken up with Grant."

"Ollie says things were good when he was with you."

"Yeah, it was good. So of course, I trashed it." I pulled my hand free of Damian's and hugged myself. "Grant can be very charming, especially when he's making me believe he loves me even when I know how many times he's cheated. Shelby told her boyfriend about me and Ollie, and her boyfriend told somebody else who happened to know Grant. When Grant found out I was with someone else, he called me and begged me to take him back."

"He used his charm to convince you."

"Like I said, Grant is good at that. It was the fifth time he'd cheated on me, that I know of, but I believed it when he said he loved me and he'd never do it again." I levered my body up into a sitting position but kept hugging myself. "Like an idiot, I fell for his lies again. For six months, I struggled to make it work with him, until I realized I'd made a huge mistake. I should never have broken up with Ollie, that's what I thought. So when the Kitten Brigade came back here for a vacation, I convinced myself I needed to win Ollie back. I think you know the rest of that story."

"Uh-huh." Damian sat up, braced with one hand on the ground. He studied me for a moment like he was considering how to tell me what a pathetic moron I was. He didn't say that, though. Instead, he laid a hand on my knee and said, "You don't have to tell me, but I'd like to know the real reason you dumped Ollie and kept going back to Grant. It's not only because of his charm, is it?"

Damn, sometimes I hated how perceptive Damian was. How could I hide from the truth when he kept gently guiding me toward it? Maybe I should've told him to buzz off, but instead, I did the last thing I should've wanted to do.

I told him the truth.

"Guess I've always felt like I don't deserve a good man," I said. "Whenever I find one, I shove him away. Ollie wasn't the first nice guy I dumped for no good reason. I have a bad habit of ditching the good ones and latching on to the assholes who have charm and sweet words on their side."

"Why do you think you don't deserve someone who appreciates you?"

"Because…" I dropped my face into my hands, feeling the sting of tears trying to form. I did not want to cry in front of Damian—or anyone, but especially not him.

He pried my hands away from my face and held them sandwiched between his palms. "You don't have to tell me. But if you want to, I'll listen. I'm your friend, if you want me to be."

Gazing into his earnest eyes, I couldn't remember why I kept pushing him away and telling him I didn't want more than friendship. Damian was so kind and patient and thoughtful. He was also drop-dead sexy and amazing in bed, not to mention a great kisser. The only other guy I'd known who had all those qualities was Ollie, though I'd never slept with him. And I'd never wanted him the way I wanted Damian.

"I don't want to blame my parents," I said, "but they have used me as a pawn in their arguments. It always feels like they want me to choose between them. I can't do that. Whatever their faults are, they're still my parents, and I won't get rid of one of them to make the other happy. So I've tried to please them both, which just winds up with both of them getting mad, at each other and me. Guess I made up for not being able to make my parents happy by trying to make men happy. Maybe that's why I pick jerks. Maybe that's all I deserve because I'm so damn screwed up."

"You are not screwed up, Heidi."

"Of course I am. I let you make love to me, then I ran away." I tore my hands free of his. "You're a nice guy. You should go find a girl who won't drive you insane with her neurotic behavior."

"If you're trying to dump me, you can't do that. We're not a couple, right? That's what you keep saying. And that means you can't give me the big heave-ho." He leaned in, his mouth a breath from mine. "You're stuck with me."

"So you're going to stalk me because I had sex with you."

"No." He brushed his thumb over my bottom lip. "I'm going to be the best friend you've ever had. I'll give you so much awesome friendship that you won't be able to live without me."

"Why do you bother with me? I'm a mess."

He sighed, regarding me in silence while keeping his lips within kissing distance. Then he picked me up and stood, cradling me in his arms. "Let's go to the lake and swim."

"I don't have my swimsuit."

"This is a nudist resort, Heidi. No swimsuit required." He set me down, settling his hands on my hips. "But we can walk on the beach if you'd rather."

"Okay."

While he led me away from the meadow, I tried to figure out what Damian was really after. He couldn't want to date me. I told him what a mess I was, and he responded by sighing and staring at me, right before he suggested a nude swim. Would I ever understand Damian Petrescu?

Not likely.

Chapter Fourteen

Damian

I took Heidi for a walk down the beach, but we didn't swim, with or without clothes. She seemed edgy after sharing her anxieties with me, so I didn't push for more than a walk. I couldn't remember the last time I'd done something like this, just walking and talking with a woman, no flirting or sex involved. It felt good. Heidi clearly thought she was a flake, but I never saw her that way, not even when we'd first met months ago. Nobody who worked as a pharmacy technician could be a flake.

Heidi was smart and together, but she didn't seem to realize it.

Though I hadn't thought she would want to hear more about my happy family, she asked me to tell her stories about them. So I did. She seemed to like that, which surprised me, though maybe it shouldn't have. Maybe hearing about my family made her feel better or…something. She got more relaxed and at ease the longer we strolled down the beach and talked. She did tell me more about her family too—good things this time. Her parents weren't total jerks, I learned. When she was a kid, Heidi's parents always gave her everything she wanted for Christmas, except for the year when she wanted a hot-air balloon.

Yeah, I could understand not wanting to give a kid that for a present.

But I would never understand why her parents made her the center of their marital problems and made her feel like their divorce was her fault. Maybe they hadn't meant to, but everything they'd done made her feel that way.

On the way back to the resort, I told her funny stories about my parents and my brother.

"Does your family like Halloween?" Heidi asked after I'd finished one of my stories. "Or is that not part of gypsy culture?"

"We love Halloween, but it's not a gypsy tradition. We're Americans as well as gypsies, and Americans love dressing up and trying to scare each other."

Heidi smiled. "Yeah, we do. Well, not me, but lots of other people."

"You don't dress up for Halloween?"

"Sure, I do. But my costumes are sexy, not scary." Her smile turned teasing, and she bumped her shoulder into me. "Do you wear your hot gypsy outfit for Halloween?"

"No, I didn't start dressing that way until I came here and decided to play up my Ludar heritage for the tourists. Honestly, I haven't done the Halloween-costume thing in years."

"Seriously? I would've thought you'd love that holiday."

"I used to, but I kind of grew out of it."

She arched her brows. "Damian the gypsy vampire doesn't like Halloween anymore? Maybe you need to loosen up a little too."

I let go of her hand to sling my arm around her shoulders. "Maybe I do. A little. I have spent years working at a prison, which isn't the most relaxing environment."

As we reached the edge of the woods, with the lawn in sight, she stopped and looked at me. "Want to finish that palm reading?"

"Maybe later. Why don't we go into the entertainment room and play a game?"

"Like what?"

"Anything you want. Poker, Monopoly, Go Fish, Twister."

She laughed. "Does anybody play Twister anymore? I'm not sure that's a safe game to play with you."

We wandered across the lawn and into the guest house, with my arm still around her, and we played silly games for two hours. Nobody bothered us because Eve and Val had taken a big group into town for shopping and sightseeing. The rest of the guests were either in their rooms or on the lawn enjoying the sunshine. Heidi and I had the entertainment room to ourselves. I could've taken advantage of that fact and turned it into an afternoon of naughty games, but I didn't. Spending time with Heidi felt even better than sex.

Yeah, I actually thought that. Playing board games with Heidi was better than making love to her. Nobody would believe I could feel that way.

I wanted to take Heidi into town and buy her dinner at a nice restaurant, but I figured that might trigger her anxiety again. So instead, we got our food from the dining hall and took it outside for a moonlight picnic. I got a battery-powered lantern from the supply closet so we wouldn't need to hunt around in the dark for our food. After we ate, we turned off the lantern and enjoyed lying on our blanket on the lawn with the stars and the moon above us.

After that, I escorted her back to her room.

Yeah, there was a good-night kiss. A chaste one.

How long could I last without tasting her again? The flavor of her mouth drove me crazy, but the taste I hungered for the most was her luscious cream.

In the morning, I brought her breakfast in bed. Turned out she slept in short-sleeve pajamas, not sexy lingerie. Still, seeing her in PJs got me just as turned on as lingerie might have. We sat on the bed, side by side, to enjoy our meal and tease each other.

After we'd finished our French toast and bacon, Heidi turned to me. "You don't have to hold back. I'm not as fragile as you think. I know I acted like I am, but honestly, that's not the real me. I'd kind of forgotten who I am until you helped me remember."

"I didn't do anything. You found your way again all on your own."

She feigned shock. "Damian Petrescu is refusing to take credit for giving awesome dating and awesome sex?"

"Very funny. I take full credit for the sex, but the rest was all you." I raised my brows. "Thought we weren't dating, anyway. Friends only, you said."

"Oh, forget about that. We're dating."

I stared at her. Probably with a blank expression. Or possibly with my mouth hanging open. Maybe both.

She gave my shoulder a little shove. "Why are you catatonic because I admitted we're dating? I thought you'd be happy."

"I am happy, but I feel rightfully shocked. Thought you'd need a lot more time to get over your anxieties." I couldn't help smiling with smug satisfaction, though it was the sarcastic kind. "Damn, I'm even better than I realized. One night of hot sex and two days of wooing, and you're begging me to be your boyfriend."

"There's been no begging. Don't turn back into arrogant Damian. I'm starting to like the sweet guy under the Dracula-knockoff exterior."

"Now you're back to calling me a knockoff?" I wrapped an arm around her, tugging her against my side, bringing our faces to within a hair's breadth of each other. "Maybe it's time I give you my awesome dirty talk. You'll never insult me again once you've heard me whisper filthy things into your ear."

"Go on. I'm ready for that."

"Maybe later. This is a workday for me, so I need to get into concierge mode."

"Okay. What about tonight?" She snuggled up to me, running her palm over my chest. "I need you to talk dirty and fuck me, Damian."

I coughed, like that would ever stop my dick from getting hard. Which it was. Right now. "Tonight, for sure. I swear a solemn Ludar oath to fuck you senseless tonight."

She grinned.

And I went to work.

I wanted to spend my lunch break with Heidi, but her friends commandeered her for a girlie shopping trip in town. Instead, I ate alone in the office.

My cell phone rang while I was wolfing down a big bite of my turkey club sandwich. I fished it out of my pocket and answered while still chewing.

"Damian, don't speak while eating. How many times have I told you that's uncouth?"

"Mom?" I swallowed and cleared my throat. "It's my lunch break, so yeah, I was eating. Pardon my rudeness for not wanting to starve."

She clucked her tongue. "My sweet boy is becoming a heathen out there in the woods."

"Did you call to give me a verbal spanking? Or was there a genuine reason?"

"Of course there's a reason." She paused, probably for dramatic effect. My mother had always loved doing that. "We're coming for a visit, to see what about the Oregon woods has lured our son into the nudist lifestyle."

"I work here, Mom. It's a legitimate job, not an excuse for getting naked and sleeping with hot girls. And for your information, I keep my clothes on during work hours."

"We need to check on you. Your father is booking our flight as we speak."

"No, Mom, you will not invade the resort. I'm a big boy, and I can take care of myself. I think we're all booked up, anyway." I had no idea if that was true, but I hoped so. I loved my family, but they—especially my mom—could be a bit much. Heidi would panic for sure if my mother showed up and started grilling her like a shish kebab.

"Ollie reserved rooms for us," Mom said. "And he told Mary you have a girlfriend, so she told me. I should have heard that from you, Damian, not from Ollie's mother."

Yeah, my mom and Ollie's mom were good friends, and sometimes Ollie inadvertently told his mom something I didn't want my parents to know, and then Mary would tell my mom. I couldn't blame Ollie, though. He'd always sucked at lying, and besides, it was my problem, not his.

"Who is she?" Mom asked.

"I, uh, well…" Was it wrong to tell my mother to go suck a lemon? "I only just started seeing this girl, and I don't need you guys getting in the middle of things. Please hold off on your visit until later."

Maybe I should've begged. Or shouted. Or begged in a shouty voice. But no, that wouldn't have worked. Once my mother made up her mind, there was no stopping the runaway train.

"We'll see you tomorrow," she said. "I can't wait to meet your girl."

Given the tone of her voice, I knew she meant "I can't wait to aim my evil stare at your girl while giving her a full physical including a pelvic exam." My mother was a good person, but she could do the evil-stare thing better than anyone. She also tended to get overprotective.

What was it about this resort that made our families decide to invade the place for surprise visits? Eve's family had done it. So had Mara's. Now my mom was planning a "visit" I was sure would match the Invasion of Normandy in scale and drama.

Since I seemed to have no choice in the matter, I told her, "Fine, I'll see you guys tomorrow."

"Your brother is coming too. With Emily and the kids."

A total family invasion? Somehow, some way, I had to prepare Heidi for this.

Yeah, no problem. She freaked when I made love to her, but she'd handle the invasion of the Ludar horde, no problem.

I said goodbye to my mother, then dropped my head onto the desktop, facedown, and groaned.

Chapter Fifteen

Heidi

Shopping had sounded like a good idea when my friends suggested it, but it turned into the longest retail torture session ever. I didn't care about push-up bras or novelty T-shirts. Even cute skirts couldn't drag my attention back to the present. No, I kept remembering the other night when Damian made love to me. Memories of our nature walk tormented me too—the way he'd held my hand, the feel of his lips on mine, our conversations, his patience and kindness. All of that affected me with almost as much strength as the lovemaking had.

I liked Damian. A lot. I told him we're dating.

My tummy fluttered, and my pulse accelerated. Was it fear or excitement? Maybe both. Being with Damian felt like a dangerous and thrilling adventure, one I didn't want to end, not yet. Being here at the resort gave us a chance to explore this whatever-it-was between us without the distraction of our families getting involved. Sure, we had lots of friends here, but I remembered the fiascoes that happened when Eve's family and Mara's family had turned up, on separate occasions, to push their noses into their budding relationships with Val and Ollie. Mara and Ollie had survived her parents' visit. Eve and Val got through it too when her parents, her brother, and her sister showed up.

But I didn't know if I'd survive something like that. My parents would never in a million billion years show up here, at a nudist resort. I barely talked to them anymore except on holidays and birthdays. Damian's parents wouldn't come here, would they? No, of course not. I was being paranoid, worrying about something that wouldn't happen.

Even lunch at a nice restaurant didn't rouse me from my Damian daydreams.

When my friends and I got back to the resort, I told them I was tired and wanted to go back to my room. They probably believed me since I'd been yawning a lot today. Staying awake half the night fantasizing about Damian had left me at less-than-optimal wakefulness.

I trudged into the guest house, shoulders hunched, hands jammed into the pockets of my cargo pants.

And I ran straight into Damian.

"Sorry," he said, grasping my shoulders when I teetered. "Are you okay? I wasn't looking where I was going."

"I'm fine. And I wasn't looking either."

"Did you not have a good time in town?"

Shrugging, I took a step backward. The feel of his hands on my body had set off a faint tingle on my skin. "It was okay. Guess I'm not in a shopping mood today."

His features tightened into a pained expression. "I need to tell you something, and it might make you anxious again. Please don't panic. It's not as big a deal as it sounds like."

I was getting anxious just listening to him say that. But I would not panic. No way. I was done with that. So I pulled my hands out of my pockets, rolled my shoulders back, and said like a mature, level-headed woman, "Whatever it is, you can tell me. I'll be fine, promise."

"Okay." He said that like he wasn't at all sure he believed me, not that I could blame him for being skeptical. "My mom called me earlier. Turns out Ollie mentioned to his mom that you and I are dating, and she told my mom, so now the whole family knows, and…" He winced. "My parents and my brother are coming for a visit."

"Here?" I was so proud of myself for not shrieking that word. It had come out sounding a touch surprised, but in a mature and level-headed way.

"Yeah, here."

"When? Like, next week or something?"

He winced again, harder. "Tomorrow."

I swore every ounce of blood in my body evaporated, leaving behind an icy chill. Damian's family? The gypsies who read palms and who-knew-what-else? What if his mother put a curse on me? *Get a grip, woman, you will not panic again, absolutely not.* I pulled in a slow, deep breath and exhaled it little by little.

Damian grasped my shoulders again, gazing into my eyes with the sweetest look of concern. "It'll be okay. My mom likes to put on a show of being a mystical gypsy, but she's actually a tax accountant, and she's a nice person deep down. Once she gets to know you, she'll love you."

"Are you lying through your teeth to make me feel better?"

He winced for a third time. "Yes. But only a little. My mother takes…getting used to."

"Uh-huh."

"I tried to talk her out of coming here, but she's determined. Mom can be pigheaded, especially when it comes to me and my brother."

"Really?" I said with a smirk. "That's a shocker. I mean, you're so not pigheaded."

His lips kicked up at one corner. "I prefer to call it sexy determination."

"I suppose that's a mostly accurate description." I kissed him. "I'll be okay, even if your mom curses me to be frigid just to stop you from dating me."

"Nothing will make me do that." He pulled me into his arms. "But I want to make sure you're okay with this. You are wearing cargo pants again, after all."

"I like them. They're comfortable."

He gave me a skeptical look. "Are you sure it's not because you're anxious again and trying to hide that gorgeous body?"

"Yes, I'm sure. Maybe I'm not quite ready to go nude again, but I'm telling the truth about cargo pants. I have decided I like them." I patted one of the many pockets on my pants. "Lots of places to stash lip gloss and mascara."

He squinted like he was scrutinizing me. "You don't look like you're wearing either of those."

"No, but I could keep them in these pockets if I wanted to wear them."

"Right." He stroked my back with his palms. "Are you absolutely sure you want to be here when my parents show up?"

"Yes. I'm positive." It was my turn to wince. "Though I can't promise I won't get a teeny bit anxious when I meet your mom. I will not panic, though. I've made a vow to myself."

"Is that like your celibacy vow? Because you kind of ditched that one."

"And it was your fault." I wriggled against him, loving the way he hissed in a breath. I was rubbing myself on the bulge in his pants, after all. "If you weren't so damn sexy, I would've kept that vow for six months."

"But you won't break your no-panicking vow."

"That's right. I understand if you don't believe me, though."

He kissed my forehead. "I believe you, Heidi. I have to get back to work, but we could have dinner tonight. In my wagon. The atmosphere will be sensual and seductive."

"Just like you. Please say you'll make love to me tonight."

"That's a certainty." He kissed me, taking his time, making me feel warm and liquid in all the best ways before he peeled his lips away from mine. "Meet me in the wagon at eight."

"Okay."

He walked out the guest-house door.

And I went upstairs to take a nap. Yeah, I actually slept. Despite knowing Damian's parents were coming tomorrow, I felt more relaxed and at ease after talking to him. When he held me in his arms, all my anxieties melted away. Maybe that meant something, and maybe I'd panic if I let myself examine it more closely, but I'd worry about that later. Tonight, I planned to revel in the pleasure of making love with Damian.

Tomorrow… Well, I hoped his mom didn't lay that frigidity curse on me because I needed to have sex with Damian. Lots of sex. And talking too.

If his mom cursed me to silence, that might be even worse than no sex.

Wow. I loved talking more than screwing. Who knew that could happen?

Chapter Sixteen

Damian

I would've loved to say I cooked dinner for Heidi, but I didn't have that kind of skill. Making mac and cheese from a box was about all I'd ever done in the kitchen. I lived on frozen dinners and takeout, so I couldn't impress Heidi with my culinary prowess. Maybe I didn't cook for her, but I did go to the guest house and grab two trays full of food for us, then hauled it all back to the wagon. I had our meal set out on the little table by the time Heidi knocked on the door. The interior always had subdued lighting, produced by a single lamp, so the atmosphere was ready to go.

When I opened the door, Heidi smiled.

"Come on in," I said. "Your romantic dinner is hot and ready."

"Are you talking about the food?" she asked as she ducked inside. "Or are you describing yourself?"

"Both, in whichever order you prefer."

Heidi wore a short, tight dress that accentuated her breasts and hips. The sapphire color of the fabric brought out her eyes, even in this light. She looked good enough to fuck, but then, she always looked like that, even in cargo pants.

"Would you like to eat right away or do the palm reading first?" I asked. "Or if you can't wait to get me naked, we could have sex first."

"Let's eat." She glanced down at my groin, then peeked up at me through her lashes. "Food, I mean. I'll have you for dessert."

"You stole my line. I was about to say the same thing to you."

"I'm sure you can come up with something even better. When you talk dirty to me."

We sat down on the cushions at the table, side by side, and talked while we enjoyed our dinner. The food wasn't fancy, but that didn't matter. It smelled good, tasted good, and filled our bellies. What more did we need?

The longer we sat here in this cozy little wagon, the more I needed to get her naked. Dinner and conversation were awesome, but I knew what it felt like to be inside her, watching her expressions and listening to her noises while she edged toward climax. And when she came… Christ, I loved that. As much as I'd enjoyed making love to her, I wanted something else tonight.

She had implied she wanted me to talk dirty to her. I wanted that too.

Once we'd finished eating, I took hold of her hand. "Time to finish your reading."

"I'd love that."

Cradling the bottom of her hand in my palm, I traced the lines on her skin, avoiding the thumb, letting my fingertips graze her flesh as I explored her palm. "Last time, we never got to Mars or the lines."

"Go all the way, Damian. Read me good and hard."

Yeah, I was hard now for sure. Heidi could do that to me so easily.

I swirled my finger over the skin just above her thumb. "This is Inner Mars. I can see you have tenacity and boldness, but in moderation." I slid my finger across her palm to the outer edge, below her pinky. "Outer Mars shows me your perseverance and emotional strength." I moved my finger to the lower center of her palm. "The Plain of Mars is trickier to interpret. This is where the lines come into it. I'll need to explore them to lay bare your inner truths."

"Do it, Damian. Lay me bare."

"Are you starting the dirty talk without me?"

"Sorry." She made a zipper motion across her mouth. "I'll just listen. Your voice makes me so hot."

"I need to examine the length, depth, and curvature of every line. Where they cross mounts. The intersections of the creases. Everything matters when I'm delving inside you." I traced the lines with my fingertips like I had earlier, but this time I did it slowly and kept my touch light to tease her skin. I loved the way she ran her tongue over her lips and caught the bottom one between her teeth. Her reactions had my dick getting even harder every second. "These lines tell me a lot about you. I know you're smarter than you want everyone to think, you have a big heart, and you relish every minute of your life. You're independent, but your restlessness has left you unsatisfied."

Pink speckled her cheeks, and I swore I could smell her desire.

With one finger, I followed the line at the center of her palm. "I sense changes coming in your life. Embrace them, don't hide from your fate."

"And what do you think my fate is?"

"To scream my name all night long."

She turned her palm over, so it lay flush with mine. "I'm ready, Damian. Talk to me."

I set her hand on her lap. "No touching, not yet. First, I need to tell you everything I plan on doing to your body tonight."

"You don't want me to touch you?"

"Of course I want that, but not yet." I turned sideways to the table and stretched my legs out. "Sit on my lap, Heidi, facing me. Wrap those sexy thighs around me but keep your hands and your lips to yourself. For now."

She straddled me, her ass resting on my thighs, and hugged my hips with her legs. She set her hands on her thighs.

"Perfect," I said. Leaning back, I set my hands on the floor behind me to hold myself up. "I love your body, Heidi, every inch of it. Tonight, I'm going to explore your skin from head to toe, with my tongue and my lips and hands, until you're moaning and gasping. I've been fantasizing about you all day, about all the things I want to do to you and with you. Take that dress off, Heidi. I want to look at you."

She peeled the dress off, revealing...her, completely naked.

"No underwear this time?" I said. "You must want me bad, like you're desperate for me to make you come."

"I do, and I am."

With her on my lap, I had trouble focusing on all the naughty things I wanted to say to her. So I let myself drink in the vision of her, nude and straddling my thighs, and the words tumbled out of me. "I love your tits. They're the perfect size for my hands, and I know your nipples taste so damn good. I love sucking on them and making you squirm."

"Oh yes, please do that to me."

I surged forward, latching my hands behind her back, just above that sweet ass, but I kept my mouth several inches away from hers. "Not yet, baby. I haven't finished telling you my plans for your luscious body."

She bit her lip, letting it go little by little. "Tell me, please, Damian. Tell me all of it in your panty-melting voice."

"You don't have any panties for me to melt, which is too bad. I would've loved to shred your underwear." I tipped my head closer, but not too close, enough that I could exhale a soft, teasing breath onto her lips. "Have you ever worn silk lingerie?"

"No."

"I've got a silk scarf, one I bought for you."

"When did you buy that? You haven't left the resort."

I let my lips spread into a slow, sensual smile as I tugged her closer. "I ordered it overnight delivery, just for you, so I could drag it across your soft skin and make you wild for me. You'll shiver and moan and beg me to fuck you."

"But I'm ready to do that right now."

"Patience, baby. There's no rush." I traced my tongue over her bottom lip, loving the way she sucked in a breath. "I need to touch you, tease you, taste you for so long that you'll feel like you're losing your mind, but in the best way. I want to hear you beg me to make you come, but I won't, not until you're so wet it's dribbling down your inner thighs and you can barely breathe because you're so damn excited."

"I already feel that way." She spread her palms on my chest, swirling them in circles. "As for being outrageously wet for you... Well, feel it for yourself."

My cock throbbed, letting me know it couldn't wait much longer to be inside her. I couldn't wait either. Something about this woman made me harder than ever before and hot enough to melt steel. I slid my fingers down between her ass cheeks, feeling her slick heat.

She grabbed my hand, shoving it between her thighs. "Feel how much I want you."

"Fuck," I growled, like an animal. I felt like a wild beast right now, with her cream coating my fingers and the heat of her body penetrating my jeans. "We're skipping the rest of the dirty talk. I need to have you right now."

I stripped off my shirt and unzipped my jeans.

"Condom?" Heidi said.

"Shit." I leaned over to grab one from the box I'd left on the steps that led to the bed. Screw the bed. This time, I needed her right here on the floor.

Heidi started to move off my lap.

I grasped her hips to hold her in place. "Don't move. I want you here."

"Oh God, yes."

"This will be fast and hard." I pulled her snug against me and got to my knees, then dropped us onto the cushions on the floor with her underneath me. In seconds, I had the condom on. "Scream for me, baby."

I braced my hands at either side of her head and thrust into her, hard and fast like I'd promised I would. Couldn't go slow. Couldn't be the gentle lover, not tonight.

She wrapped her legs around me.

And I couldn't have held back even if I'd wanted to. Every pounding thrust made her tits jiggle, and when I pumped faster, the wagon started to shake. The heat of her surrounded my cock while the scent of her cream drowned my senses, and I couldn't stop myself from pummeling her like a mad man. She clutched my arms, her nails piercing my skin and scraping down my biceps. I lunged my head to seize her nipple and suck on it. She threw her head back and let out a sharp cry.

Words burst out of me, but I had no idea what I was saying.

Her body tensed, and she stopped breathing, her mouth gaping open and her eyes squeezed shut.

"Come for me, baby," I snarled.

She came like she was following my command. Her body clenched my cock over and over, making me growl like a beast again and grit my teeth. A bolt of white-hot lightning shot down my spine, and I couldn't hold it back anymore. I came so hard I couldn't see or do anything other than punch into her twice more until I had nothing left to give.

I collapsed on top of her, gasping for breath.

Heidi folded her arms around me, breathing as hard as I was. After a few minutes, she whispered in my ear, "Holy shit, Damian. That was… Oh God, you're amazing."

"Thanks." I lifted my head to look at her. "You were totally amazing too. I thought I was the master of dirty talk, but you outmatched me."

"Let's call it even. We both rocked."

"Definitely." I rolled off her, though all I could manage to do was lie sprawled on my back. "Good thing we ate first. I needed all those calories. Think I burned at least ninety percent of them in the last few minutes."

"Me too." She turned onto her side and kissed my shoulder. "Sorry I scratched you up. Does it hurt?"

I lifted my arms to examine them. I had red slashes on my biceps. "A few scratches, that's all. I'll survive, and it was totally worth the pain."

"Maybe I should kiss it better."

"After what just happened, I think I need sleep more than tender loving care."

"Yeah, I'm wiped out too. Let's go to bed and snuggle up."

I kissed the tip of her nose. "Sounds like a plan."

Chapter Seventeen

I woke up but couldn't convince myself to open my eyes, much less get out of bed. Damian had his arm draped over my belly, his body cradling mine from behind, and his gentle breaths fluttered my hair. I loved lying here like this. It was peaceful and sensual at the same time. How could I love being with Damian, the last man on earth I ever wanted to get involved with? He was strange and cocky, sweet and sexy, dirty and funny. Okay, maybe I did see why I enjoyed spending time with him and making love with him.

So yeah, my celibacy vow lasted less than two days after I arrived at the resort. Months of no sex, and all it took to shatter my willpower was a palm reading. Why had I thought celibacy would cure me of my insecurities? That had to be the dumbest idea I'd ever come up with. Here with Damian, in this cozy little bed inside a cozy little wagon, I felt freer and stronger and more alive than ever before.

Damian stirred behind me, his cock stiffening.

I couldn't resist wriggling my bottom to rub it against his dick.

He pulled me tighter against his body and chuckled softly. "Good morning, sex kitten."

"Are you calling me that because we had awesome sex or because I'm part of the Kitten Brigade?"

"Both." He nuzzled my throat while his dick got even stiffer. "How about a quickie before breakfast?"

"Uh-uh." I turned my head to look at him, which put our faces an inch apart. "This morning, I need it long and slow and hot as hell."

"I can do that." He glided his hand down my belly to tease the hairs on my mound with his fingertips. "Should I let your screams echo through the resort, or do you want me to swallow them for you with a deep, thrusting kiss?"

My sex pulsed at his suggestion, and I no longer had any reason to pretend I didn't want him like crazy. "Deep and thrusting, please. Drive me crazy with your mouth and your dick."

"Anything for you, baby."

He'd started calling me baby last night, and I loved it. When other men had called me that, I didn't like it so much. But Damian knew how to shape those two syllables into the sweetest, sexiest pet name I'd ever heard. I even liked it when he called me sex kitten.

"It's weird," I said while he kept teasing me with his fingers, "but I don't feel anxious anymore. I'm not worried I'll make a fool of myself again, and I don't care if everyone finds out we're sleeping together. I want to be your girlfriend, but that's not terrifying anymore. I love it when you call me baby and sex kitten." I settled my hand over his on my mound and bent one knee, my foot planted on the bed, so I could push his hand between my folds. "Touch me everywhere, Damian. Touch me with your hands, your mouth, your tongue, every part of you. I'm done fighting how much I want you."

He chuckled again. "I figured that out last night."

"Good, then I don't need to explain it to you."

"No, I understand everything." He stroked me with his longest finger, making me suck in a sharp breath. "And I know how much you love dirty talk."

"Oh God, yes. Whisper filthy things to me, please."

"Every time you beg, it makes me want to fuck you until you can't walk anymore."

"Keep going. Touch me, talk to me, anything you want."

He slid his hand out from under my palm, laying it on top of mine. "I'm going to make you come with your own hand, but you won't move a muscle. I'll do everything."

I moaned because it was all I could manage to do. He'd hardly said anything, and already I was throbbing for him, in my clitoris and deep inside my body. With his erection plastered to my backside, he moved my fingers like I was an instrument and he was the virtuoso plucking my strings, drawing pleasure out of me like a song. I thrust my hips in time with his movements, feeling my own slickness on my fingers and the heat of his palm on the back of my hand.

"Damian," I whispered while he used my fingers to toy with my clit. "Damian, yes."

"Kiss me, Heidi."

I twisted my head around, seized his nape, and pulled him in for a deep kiss. Our tongues thrust in time with the movements of our joined hands, and when he pushed our fingers inside me, I cried out. Just like he'd promised, he swallowed my cry while plunging his tongue in time with the thrusts of our fingers.

Someone knocked on the door. "Damian? Are you in there?"

Damian tore his mouth away from mine and shouted, "Go away, Ollie. We're busy."

He never stopped pumping into me with our fingers, even while he shouted those words. The man had skills, for sure. Awesome skills, like he'd told me.

I moaned, then he sealed his mouth over mine again.

"Sorry to interrupt," Ollie called out, "but I thought you'd want to know your parents and your brother are here. Your mom seems awfully determined to barge into wherever you are. I told her to check in your room first, but she'll be back any minute."

Damian froze with his tongue in my mouth and our fingers inside me.

We both opened our eyes, our gazes locked.

He groaned so deeply I felt the vibrations in his chest. He sat up and rubbed his eyes with the heels of his hands. "Okay, we'll be out in a minute. Keep Mom away from the wagon for as long as possible."

"I'll try. But you know how she is."

"Sorry, Heidi," Damian said. "Looks like my family showed up early. I wasn't expecting them until this afternoon."

"That's okay. Maybe I should be gone before she storms the wagon."

"Why?"

His look of genuine confusion made me want to hug him, but I didn't understand why he seemed baffled.

"Your family is here," I said. "Your mom is here. I shouldn't be lying naked in your bed when she shows up, should I? Don't want to make this any more awkward for you than it has to be."

"My mother can be overprotective, but she isn't a monster. She's not about to throw a hex on you or something." He leaned over me, held up by one bent arm, his face so close I felt his breaths whispering over my lips. "You might want to get dressed, but not until after I finish what I started."

"We can't have sex now."

His lips kinked into a devilish smirk. "But I can finish you off."

"There's no time. Your family—"

My voice died the instant he shoved his hand between my folds and plunged three fingers inside me, pumping hard and fast. He stretched his thumb up to rub my hard nub.

And I came. Just like that. My back arched, my mouth fell open, and my entire body went rigid for a split second before the climax pulsated deep inside me and stole my breath. I clenched the sheets.

Damian covered my open mouth with his, silencing the single sharp cry that burst out of me.

"There," he said, "you're all done."

He jumped off the bed, grabbed my dress, and tossed it at me.

"Are you kidding me?" I asked. "You can't give me an orgasm, then take me out there to meet your mother."

"Get dressed, Heidi. She'll be here any second."

He didn't sound or look panicked. The idea of his mom finding us in flagrante didn't seem to bother him at all. I felt a little shaky, but that might've been from the climax I'd experienced seconds ago. It had been like a bomb exploding inside my body.

I got dressed.

So did Damian, and he found a hairbrush for me too. At least my hair wouldn't flash like a neon sign announcing, "Just got fucked by a hot gypsy." My dress was a little rumpled, that was all.

He gave me a quick kiss. "You look beautiful, baby."

"You're full of it, but your bullshit is sweet."

The door burst inward.

A dark-haired woman stood on the second step, her mouth tight. Her gaze locked onto Damian, then swerved to me. She lifted one perfectly plucked brow, staring at me for a second or two before zeroing her attention in on Damian again. "*Bună ziua, fiu.* Are you going to introduce us?"

"*Mamă,*" Damian said, "you can't barge in like you own the place. It's my wagon, not yours."

"If my boy has taken up with a sallow blonde, it's my responsibility to make sure he's not in over his head."

"You're being rude, *Mamă*. Heidi is my girlfriend, and she's not sallow."

The woman stepped into the wagon and marched straight to me. "*Scuze*, child, but I need to speak with my son alone."

Damian slung an arm around my shoulders. "No, you don't. Since you haven't bothered to ask, this is Heidi Mackenzie. We're dating. I like her, a lot, and you are not chasing her away."

The woman scanned me up and down, then offered her hand to me. While she shook it, she said, "I am Monica Petrescu, royal seer of the Ludar and divine conduit to the spirit world."

"Cut the crap, Mom," Damian said, though he didn't sound angry.

I leaned in close to him and whispered, "I thought your mother's name was Ileana."

"No, that's her stage name when she's doing her shtick for the neighbors."

His mother shouted over her shoulder, "Adrian, what in heaven's name are you doing out there? Come meet the foreigner our son has taken up with."

A man with salt-and-pepper hair mounted the steps, halting at the threshold. He smiled when he saw Damian. "Hey, kiddo, what's up? Is this your new girl? She's a looker, for sure."

Monica Petrescu shook her head, her lips ticking up into a faint smile. "Introduce yourself, dear."

The man climbed into the wagon and offered me his hand. "Adrian Petrescu. I'm not a royal anything or a conduit, and neither is my wife."

"It's nice to meet you," I said as we shook hands.

Adrian glanced at his wife. "She doesn't sound foreign to me."

Monica huffed. "She is clearly not Ludar. Her skin is so pale."

"Stefan's wife isn't Ludar either. We love her anyway."

Damian tightened his arm around my shoulders, and I let him tug me closer.

This was going to be one doozy of a day.

Chapter Eighteen

Damian

I could've wasted hours on trying to convince my mother that Heidi was not a foreigner just because she didn't have Ludar ancestry. Mom loved to trot out the Romanian phrases whenever I introduced her to a girl. How many Ludar women were there in the world? Probably not that many these days, at least not many who knew they were Ludar. There weren't exactly hordes of Rom of any ilk these days.

Heidi took it all in stride despite Mom's attempts to unsettle her. She might've looked a touch anxious now and then, but I stayed close to offer silent support. I also provided vocal support when my mother got too involved in her gypsy royalty routine.

Like when she waved a hand in a grand gesture and said, "Give me your hand, child. I need to read the lines and determine whether you are the right woman for my boy."

"Stop that, Mom," I said. "It's up to me to decide if Heidi is the right woman. Besides, I've already given her a palm reading, and it told me she has a beautiful heart. That's all I need to know."

Mom squinted at Heidi, roving her gaze over my girlfriend like she was checking for signs of demonic possession. "All right. If you read her, then I accept your assessment. Provisionally."

"Gee, thanks, Mom." Yeah, there was sarcasm in that statement. I loved my mother, but she seriously needed an editor to review every word she wanted to speak before she spoke it.

We all climbed out of the wagon.

My brother and his wife were waiting nearby, and they hurried over to us.

Before my mom could speak again, I barged in. "Heidi, this is my brother, Stefan, and his wife, Emily. Where are the kids, Stef?"

"We left them with Emily's parents. This sounded like an adults-only reunion, and I'm not talking about the nudist thing."

He threw a meaningful glance toward our mother.

Yeah, we both knew she was going to keep harassing Heidi, all in the name of protecting her full-grown son who knew how to take care of himself.

Stefan shook Heidi's hand, then looked at me. "Wow, you hit it outta the park this time, didn't you? This girl's wicked hot."

"And also a very nice person and very smart," I said pointedly.

My brother grinned. "You must have it bad. Should we start thinking about wedding dates?"

"No," our mother said. "I have not fully approved her yet."

I sighed. "Mom, you don't get to pick my girlfriends anymore. I haven't let you do that since I was fifteen, and we both know why."

Stefan chuckled. "Yeah, Mom only wanted us to date Ludar girls, but the only ones she could find had buck teeth and hairy moles on their faces, or they dressed like vampires." He glanced at my clothes, his brows lifting. "Guess you're into that now, though, huh? Does Heidi bite your neck, or do you bite hers?"

I rolled my eyes.

"Damian looks good in black," Heidi said. "But he dresses that way strictly for the tourists. The rest of the time, he wears a uniform."

"Uniform?" Stefan said, looking way too pleased about that. "Thought you quit the prison-guard thing so you could get away from that stuff."

"No, I quit to get away from the prison."

Heidi, who was standing next to me, slipped her arm around mine and leaned in to whisper, "Sorry. I didn't know the uniform thing was a secret."

"It's not, but I hadn't mentioned it to my family yet."

"Maybe we should show them your pilot project."

Would that appease my mother? Probably not, but it might distract her for a while. My mom wasn't an evil queen, but I knew she'd keep up the act for as long as possible to see how Heidi reacted.

"Okay," I said, "let's do it."

Heidi kissed my cheek.

Mom raked her assessing gaze over Heidi from head to toe. "Is her dress on backwards?"

I probably growled. "Mom, cut it out."

Heidi's dress was wrinkled and not exactly on straight, but it wasn't backwards.

My mother harrumphed, but then something past my shoulder caught her attention. Her expression brightened. "There's my darling Ollie. I have to say hello to that dear boy. *Scuze.*"

She marched toward Ollie with Dad trailing after her.

"Don't worry about Mom," Stefan said to Heidi. "She's testing you, that's all. As long as you don't run away screaming or whack her with a baseball bat, you'll do fine."

"Thanks," Heidi said, sounding less than convinced.

"Ignore my brother," I said. "He's on strong meds to keep him from seeing leprechauns under every tree."

"Not leprechauns," Stefan said. "Vampires. I have erotic hallucinations about a sexy female vamp sucking on my…" He glanced down at his groin. "Neck."

"I don't think your 'neck' is big enough for anybody to suck on it."

Stefan threw an arm around his wife and hugged her close. "Oh wait, it wasn't a vampire. It's Emily who likes to sink her teeth into me."

Heidi smiled and laughed. "Guess naughtiness runs in the family, huh?"

I glanced at Mom and Ollie to see her holding his head with both hands and kissing his cheeks. Dad slapped Ollie's arm. Mom dragged Mara into a bear hug, then performed some kind of made-up gypsy blessing by waving her hands and tipping her head up.

Yeah, Mom loved to do that. It was part of her "Ileana the Gypsy Queen" act. Why she needed a stage name, I had no idea. When I was ten, I asked her. She told me she was "building the fantasy" for the neighbors and other people who asked her to entertain them at parties.

And people thought I was a show-off.

Well, I must have inherited it from Mom.

My parents came back over to us, and I led them all into the guest house to show them their rooms. Heidi rushed off to change clothes, but when she rejoined us, she stayed right by my side and didn't seem disquieted at all by my mom's antics.

Since her change of heart happened after we had sex, I could've convinced myself I was just that good in bed. Sure, I was good. But sex with me had never cured a woman of her insecurities. The first time I'd met Heidi, she had been a vivacious, carefree girl who loved to go nude and play miniten. Then she'd embarrassed herself with Ollie and, combined with all the times she'd forgiven her cheating ass of an ex, she'd lost her self-confidence.

Maybe screwing me hadn't cured her, but the time we'd spent getting to know each other must have played a part in her ongoing transformation. It was more like a return to her true self. She didn't need to change, just to get back to that carefree, fun girl she'd once been.

After my family got settled in, Heidi and I took them out to the pilot project. While we petted the horses and talked about my plans for horseback nature tours, Mom gradually let go of her haughty act and turned back into a semi-normal person. Like me, she could never quite be normal—and like me, she didn't want to be. But Mom started smiling and joking with the rest of us, so I knew she wouldn't harass Heidi too much more.

My family might have surprised me with their visit and their early arrival, but nobody surprised me more than Heidi. When Georgie nuzzled her cheek, she not only didn't freak, but she kissed his nose too and scratched under his chin. She also started a conversation with my mother, and they talked about everything from horses to palm reading to embarrassing stories from my childhood. Heidi told her own childhood stories, but she left out the stuff about her parents being such dicks.

I didn't blame her for omitting that.

Not once did Heidi seem anxious. I hadn't seen her this relaxed and outgoing since that day months ago when I'd first seen her.

Watching Heidi with my family, I got a strange pain in my chest. Her eyes sparkled in the sun, and whenever she smiled, I swore the entire world got brighter. I wanted to pull her into my arms and just hold her.

Was I falling for Heidi Mackenzie? I didn't know, but the idea that I might have been didn't bother me at all.

Chapter Nineteen

Heidi

At first, Damian's mom had seemed like a tough cookie who would rather spit at me and curse me to become a toad than call me "sweetie" and hug me. She hadn't done the latter yet, but she hadn't done the former either. That seemed like a good sign.

Monica Petrescu was a performer, like her son, though she played up the magic aspect while Damian relied more on sex appeal. They shared the same charisma and charm, though. I liked seeing him through the lens of his family. It showed me different sides to him that I might not have noticed otherwise and proved to me that he wasn't patient and sweet with only me. He treated his family the same way, even when he was a touch frustrated with his mom's antics.

I liked Monica, but I wasn't sure if she liked me until she cornered me in the hallway of the guest house. Since it was lunchtime, Damian had escorted us to the dining hall, but his mom waylaid me. Damian saw it and raised his eyebrows at me, like he was asking if I needed help. I smiled, and he seemed to get the picture that I could handle his mom.

Compared to my parents, the Petrescus were the perfect mom and dad.

Once the others had disappeared into the dining hall, Monica faced me. "You are not Ludar."

"No, I'm an average American girl."

She squinted at me. "My son doesn't know it yet, but he's in love with you."

Damian in love with me? I kind of doubted that. Sure, we liked each other—a lot—but love seemed like a giant leap. Being with Damian made me feel more like myself than I had in years, since before I hooked up with a cheating loser. Damian would never cheat on me. I had no facts to back up that belief, but I trusted him so much more than I'd trusted any other man in my entire life. I loved being with him, and I loved the way he made me feel, but I had no idea if I might fall for him.

Even if I did, I shouldn't let Damian feel that way about me. After meeting his family, I realized exactly how screwed up mine was. I couldn't drag him into my mess of a life. He deserved happiness and love, but I didn't know if I could give him that, or if my family would drain it out of him.

What if I was too screwed up to save? Damned by my parents' toxic relationship?

"I like Damian a lot," I said to Monica. "He's a great guy. But I think it's too early to start talking about love, especially with his mother. That's something he and I need to talk about, alone. No offense."

"I'm not offended, dear." She took my hand, turning it over so the palm faced up. Head down, she ran her fingers over the lines on my palm. "I like you, Heidi, but I can't give your relationship with Damian my blessing until I've spent more time with you."

"My relationship with him is something Damian and I should discuss without anyone else involved. I hope you and I can be friends, but honestly, the only person whose opinion matters to me is Damian."

She peered up at me, her head still bowed. "Your lines tell me a lot about you, but what you've said tells me even more."

My mouth had gotten dry, and I couldn't think of any response. What had I said? I wasn't sure which words that came out of my mouth had told her what she needed to know.

She clasped my hand in both of hers and met my gaze. "Your loyalty and spirit are a comfort to me."

Monica released my hand, then walked into the dining hall.

What on earth had she been talking about? I had no idea what our conversation had proved to her. Maybe she'd been reading my palm, and that had comforted her. Whatever.

I wandered into the dining hall, to the table where the Petrescus had gathered. The only empty seat was right next to Damian, so I sat down there.

Damian laid his hand on my thigh and murmured, "Mom saved that seat for you."

"What?"

"Stefan wanted to sit there, but she told him to move his ass. Well, she told him to 'relocate your derriere,' but it's the same thing. She wanted you to sit beside me." He squeezed my thigh, aiming his sweet smile at me. "Mom likes you."

"Oh. I'm glad."

"But not as much as I like you."

Warmth blossomed in my chest, blooming outward until it suffused my entire body. It wasn't lust, though. This feeling stemmed from something softer and sweeter, something that touched a part of me no one had ever managed to touch before. How did Damian always know the right thing to say? How did he pull off being arrogant and dirty but tender and caring too? The contradictions somehow made sense because he was…Damian.

I didn't get a chance to respond to what he'd said. His brother started talking to him, and I enjoyed listening to their banter. They loved to tease each other, but underneath the sarcasm, I could tell they loved each other. They loved their parents too, and Monica and Adrian adored their sons.

My parents had worried more about whose fault this or that was than about whether I had a happy childhood.

A lump hardened in my throat.

But then Damian squeezed my thigh again, flashing me his heart-melting smile, and I forgot to worry about the past.

Everyone chatted during lunch, with lots of good-natured teasing and laughter thrown in too, but I couldn't make myself get as involved in the conversation as I used to do. Maybe the old me would come back eventually, or maybe that version of me had been an illusion. Recent events had made me gun shy about pretty much everything, so I probably shouldn't condemn myself as a lost cause until I'd recovered from my own mistakes and come to terms with my opposite-of-perfect family.

Damian kept squeezing my thigh occasionally and giving me supportive smiles. Tender smiles. The kind that made my tummy flutter.

I couldn't help smiling at him too. Whenever our eyes met, our lips curved up. I wondered if he felt the same chest tightness and tummy flutters every time we looked at each other. I hadn't spent much time around Damian until this week, yet I'd started to feel like I'd known him forever. Which was crazy. But it felt too good to fight it.

After lunch, as we exited the dining hall, Damian pulled me aside and waited for everyone else to file out of the building. They were headed for the lawn where Eve and Val had arranged to hold a soccer match. Once they had all departed, Damian grasped my hands and tugged me closer, our bodies almost touching.

"I need to have you all to myself," he said, "at least for a while. Family time is great, but we're still figuring out this thing between us, and having everybody else hanging around makes that more difficult."

"Yeah, it kind of does." I inhaled a deep breath just so I could enjoy the enticing scent of him. Why did he always smell so damn good? It wasn't cologne. He had a naturally delicious scent. "What did you have in mind?"

"Let's go to the hot spring."

"You mean the place where couples like to go to get it on?"

His lips twitched upward the tiniest bit, and he tugged me even closer, wrapping his arms around me. "No, I mean the hot spring where people who aren't total horndogs go to relax. The getting-it-on part is optional."

"I'd love to go there with you, with or without sex."

"Good. I haven't gone there much since I started working here. Too busy."

Hand in hand, we left the guest house and ambled past the lawn toward the nature trail. The soccer game was in full swing, with Val and the younger guests competing against the Silver Foxes. Val had been a professional soccer star—though in the rest of the world they called it football—and his team even won the Olympics. Still, the Silver Foxes always made him work for every goal.

Damian accelerated his pace as we entered the woods.

"In a hurry?" I asked.

"Of course I am. You won't strip naked for me until we get to the hot spring." He eyed me sideways. "Unless you aren't going to do that at all."

"You didn't give me a chance to grab my swimsuit, so I won't have much choice, will I?" Smiling, I bumped my shoulder into his. "Planned it that way, didn't you?"

"No, I would never do that. I'm not, like, an exhibitionist or anything." He wrapped an arm around my shoulders, strapping me to his side. "Okay, yeah, I am an exhibitionist."

"Uh-uh. You're a sexy Ludar prince with magic palm-reading skills, but I haven't seen you do anything that might qualify as exhibitionism."

He grinned. "Not yet. Maybe I've been holding back for professional reasons."

I spotted the sign that announced the hot spring was to the right, and I broke into a dead run, sprinting down the offshoot path. Over my shoulder, I shouted, "Catch me if you can."

Damian grinned again and took off after me. "The chase is the best part."

Our laughter echoed through the woods as we raced down the trail. I kept glancing back to see how close Damian was getting, but I decided he must've been holding back because he never got closer than fifteen feet or so behind me. The second I burst into the little clearing around the hot spring, I tore my clothes off and flung them away, not caring where they landed. I was breathing hard, but smiling too, and I hadn't felt this exhilarated…ever. How could letting Damian chase me become the best time I'd ever had? It was a silly, frivolous thing to do.

Maybe that was why I loved it. Silly and frivolous used to be my forte.

Damian dashed into the clearing, stopped a few feet from me, and got rid of his clothes. He was still grinning, like he had during our entire chase, and he breathed even harder than I did. He bent over, hands on his thighs. "Gimme a minute. I'm too old for high-speed pursuit."

He turned his head to the side to smirk at me.

"Yeah, sure," I said, "you're totally wiped out. Guess you aren't as manly and athletic as I thought. Oh well, we can put off swimming in the hot spring until you're feeling better. I'll get dressed."

I leaned over like I was about to pick up my shirt.

Damian straightened and pulled me into his arms. "No clothes. Once you take them off, they stay off until we go back to the resort."

"Is that the Ludar prince's royal decree?"

"You're damn straight it is." He shuffled toward the hot spring, forcing me to back up to it until my heels reached the rocky edge. "Dive in, Heidi. The water's warm, but not as hot as you."

He pulled his arms away.
And I dived backward into the blue water.

Chapter Twenty

Damian

Heidi and I did not have sex in the hot spring. She was game, but I suggested we should wait awhile before we got it on again. Yeah, I said that. Me. I'd never taken a celibacy vow, and I wasn't exactly known for my restraint when it came to sex, but I'd never pestered a woman to sleep with me either. Still, not doing it when the girl wanted to wasn't my style either. What about Heidi made me want to do anything, even go without sex, just to be with her?

When Heidi dived backward into the hot spring, her face had lit up with the most beautiful, joyful smile I'd ever seen. I got a weird tightness in my chest, like I was having a high blood-pressure attack or something. For a minute, maybe longer, I stood there and watched her paddling around in the blue waters with steam curling up from the surface. Her joy softened into a look of blissful satisfaction, but that didn't make sense. How could she feel blissfully happy from swimming?

The more important question was, why did I feel blissfully happy watching her?

When she dunked her head under the water, I jumped in feet first. Water sprayed up around me.

Heidi surfaced, drenched and grinning. "Took you long enough. I thought you'd gone catatonic the way you were staring at me. Or maybe you think I'm crazy."

"You're crazy-hot, that's for sure." I swam to her and hugged her body to mine. "I like watching you have fun. Nobody does fun better than Heidi Mackenzie."

"I kind of forgot how to enjoy myself." She swept wet hair away from her face, then clasped her hands at my nape. "You helped me remember. Thank you, Damian."

"Nah. All I did was seduce you. The 'fun' part you did all by yourself."

Her lips curled into a sexily teasing smile. "Seduction is the fun part."

That was when I made my insane announcement. "Let's not have sex for a while."

Her brows shot up. "Are you serious?"

"Yeah. I'd like us to get to know each other and spend sex-free time together." Yeah, I must've gone stark-raving bonkers. I had a gorgeous, incredible woman in my arms, and I told her we shouldn't sleep together.

Heidi snuggled up to me, her slick, naked body mashed to mine and those beautiful tits mounded against my chest. "But I want you, Damian. Right now."

"We kind of rushed into the whole naked-and-grunting phase of our relationship. Let's hold off for a little while, okay?"

She blinked slowly, twice. "You're serious, aren't you?"

"Yes."

"Okay." She wriggled away from me, paddling backward. "Wanna chase me in the water?"

"That wouldn't be a fair race. I mean, I've got muscles." I raised my arms, elbows bent, and flexed my biceps. "See? I'll catch you in five seconds at most."

"I'm in great shape, so you'll lose that bet."

"Bet? Guess we should have stakes, then. Five bucks?"

She shook her head, giving me that teasing smile again. "If I win, you take me—the dirty way. Right here, right now."

Those sounded like dangerous stakes, but I could swim faster than a girl. Couldn't I? "Okay. And if I win, you play miniten in the nude, but we don't have sex."

"You're on."

Heidi spun around and started swimming.

I hoisted myself out of the water onto the ledge and leaped into the pool. Even without a springboard, I could propel myself pretty far.

Heidi glanced back and shrieked—with joy, not terror.

Splashing down a foot behind Heidi, I lashed an arm around her waist and tugged her into me. "I win."

She splashed me. "Cheater."

"I said I could catch you in less than five seconds. Never claimed I'd do it by swimming."

"Yeah, I should've written a contract that spelled out the rules of our wager." She wriggled around until she was facing me. "You're way too smart. I'll have to be more careful in the future when we make bets."

I cleared my throat. "You do realize that now you have to play miniten, clothes-free."

"Yep. I never welch on a promise."

We swam in the spring for a little while longer, but we didn't make any more bets. Instead, we did goofy things like diving in cannonball style, splashing each other mercilessly, and chasing each other just for the hell of it. I let Heidi catch me twice. Gotta give a girl a chance, right? It wasn't her fault I had masculine prowess on my side.

Heidi rolled her eyes and splashed me when I said that out loud. "Are all Ludar princes arrogant and sexist?"

"No, only the ones you beg to fuck you."

She splashed me again.

When we finally left the hot spring, Heidi didn't put her clothes back on.

I raised one brow. "Does this mean Heidi the hot naturism enthusiast is back?"

"Maybe. I did promise I'd play miniten in the nude if you caught me."

Had I expected her to renege on our bet? Maybe I had, but not because I thought she was a coward. Overcoming fears usually took longer than a couple of days. Didn't it? I couldn't say for sure since I'd never had any anxieties as strong as hers. I would've loved to believe I'd been the reason she came out of her khaki-clad shell, but even I wasn't a big enough dick to do that.

I threw our clothes over my shoulder, and we walked back to the resort while holding hands. When we emerged from the woods, both naked, and sauntered over to the lawn, everyone stopped to stare at us. Ollie grinned. Mara clapped and grinned. Eve waved and grinned. Val folded his arms over his chest and nodded appreciatively.

Sylvester Norris hollered, "Way to go, Damian! You got our girl out of her funk."

"Watch it, Sly," I hollered back. "Might use my mystical gypsy powers to curse you if you don't stop harassing Heidi."

"Harassing her?" Sly waggled his eyebrows. "Our boy Damian's in love, eh?"

I had no idea how not wanting Sylvester to make Heidi feel weird about going nude equated to me being in love with her. A screw must've popped loose in the old fart's head.

Heidi and I played against Sly and his wife, Ruth, and beat them in two miniten games. Then we whupped Heidi's friends Shelby and Taylor, and after that, we creamed Val and Eve. Heidi grinned and laughed and shouted cheerfully sarcastic comments at our opponents, like I'd heard she used to do. I'd met her during the peak of her get-Ollie-back craziness, so I never got to see her in full-on Heidi mode—happy, carefree, and enjoying life with zeal. Did I have zeal? I wasn't sure, but nobody had ever described me that way. "Zeal" seemed like the appropriate way to describe Heidi, though. I couldn't wait until she climbed out of her funk all the way and became the girl everyone had described to me, the girl who lived every moment to the fullest and burned with the brightest candle on earth.

After miniten, we got dressed and headed out to the horse pasture. Heidi had suggested it. She wanted to spend more time with Lenny and Georgie, not only to keep her immersion therapy going but also because she loved the boys and they loved her. Maybe Heidi wasn't ready for a trail ride, but she got more and more comfortable with the horses every day.

"Wanna brush them?" I asked about ten minutes after we got to the pasture. We were outside the fence, but Heidi had spent the entire time petting and talking to the boys. "It'll mean going through the gate, but I'll be right beside you the whole time. What do you say?"

She stopped blinking for a few seconds, her gaze trained on me, then she blew out a breath that relaxed her tensed shoulders. She smiled. "Yeah, I'd love to brush them."

"Awesome." I got a brush out of the shed and brought it to Heidi. "Here. You hold on to this while I open the gate."

I swung the gate open just enough to accommodate us and sidled through it first, then waved for Heidi to come in.

Georgie walked right past me and ambled over to Heidi to nuzzle her cheek.

She giggled. "His whiskers tickle."

"He's definitely in love." I scratched Lenny behind his ears. "At least this guy still likes me. I was starting to feel rejected."

Lenny walked over to Heidi and nuzzled her hand, the one holding the brush.

I shook my head. "Damn, I *have* been rejected. How can I compete with two big strapping males who could trample me?"

Georgie wiggled his lips over hers.

"Jeez," I said, pretending to be offended, "no way can I compete with a Georgie kiss. He's never done that to me."

She grinned, the brilliant expression aimed at me. "You're the only big strapping male I let kiss me with tongue."

"Well, at least I've got one thing on them." I laid a hand on Lenny's chest and pushed. "Back, Lenny. Come on, back up." When the horse walked backward a few paces, I patted his neck. "Good boy. Now, let Georgie have his turn first. I know Heidi's irresistible, but she can only brush one of you at a time."

"I'm irresistible?" Heidi said.

"Absolutely." I rubbed Georgie's forehead. "Males of any species are putty in your hands."

"Maybe I'll test that hypothesis later and knead you like putty."

Oh yeah, that sounded wonderful. My dick definitely loved the idea since it jerked the second I pictured Heidi kneading my body with those sexy hands.

"Start brushing," I told her. "To these guys, it's like a day at the spa. I'll be right beside you the entire time."

Heidi began brushing Georgie's neck, tentatively at first, then she relaxed into the task. She looked at ease, like skimming a brush over a horse's coat was the most soothing thing she'd ever done. I loved brushing animals. It always made me feel the way Heidi looked right now. Once Heidi had brushed Georgie all over, even his rump, she walked over to Lenny and gave him the same treatment.

I stayed with Georgie, to keep him out of the way.

Once Heidi finished with Lenny, we walked back out the gate.

"You brushed a horse all by yourself," I said. "That's a big step."

She shrugged one shoulder. "You were right next to me the whole time."

"Not when you brushed Lenny. I stayed with Georgie then."

"I know. But you were close by." She kissed my cheek. "Thank you, Damian. It's good to get over at least one fear, but I know I still have more of them to deal with."

"One step at a time, that's the best way to do it."

She wrapped her arms around my waist, pressing her body to mine. "Let's go play chess."

I pulled my head back, gazing at her with a new appreciation. "You really aren't an airhead bimbo, are you?"

She gave my ankle a gentle kick. "Hey, that's not a very nice thing to say. Did you ever think I was an airhead bimbo?"

"No, but I'm sure that's what a lot of the dickwads you dated thought. From what you've said, they sure didn't treat you like a mature, intelligent, sexy-as-hell woman."

"What does 'sexy as hell' have to do with being smart?"

"Nothing. I threw that in there because you've got your hot body glued to mine." I linked my hands at the small of her back. "Not that I'm complaining."

"Have you changed your mind about sex?"

"No. So we'd better play chess. Anything sexier than that will give me a hard-on for sure."

"Okay." She kissed me on the mouth this time. "Prepare to be annihilated on the chessboard."

She took off down the trail.

And I raced after her with Heidi's laughter echoing through the woods.

Chapter Twenty-One

Heidi

I slept with Damian that night, in my room, naked, though we didn't do anything remotely sexual. I loved lying in his arms, listening to his shallow, even breaths and feeling them whispering against my neck. Ever since the first night we had sex in his wagon, I'd been sleeping better than I had in years. The more time I spent with him, the less I worried about making a fool of myself or doing something dumb like going back to my ex. No, Grant could never convince me to do that. Never again.

Damian had to go back to work in the morning, so after breakfast, we kissed goodbye. I spent the morning hanging out with my friends. I had kind of ignored the Kitten Brigade a lot of the time, caught up in pretending I didn't want Damian, then sleeping with Damian, and now wishing I were with him instead of with my friends. I loved these girls, but I felt like my best self when I was with him.

A morning full of Kitten Brigade craziness kept me occupied, and I did have fun. But my thoughts always gravitated back to Damian. Sweet, sexy, naughty, tender Damian. I'd only been half teasing when I told him I'd love to knead him like putty.

I ate lunch in the dining hall with Damian and the Kittens. They made lots of suggestive, teasing comments about the two of us, but Damian took it all in stride. He never got annoyed with any-body, not even when Sylvester stopped by our table to give Da-mian a box of glow-in-the-dark condoms so he wouldn't, as Sly put it, "get confused in the dark and forget where you put that saber."

That had to be the dumbest joke ever, but Damian laughed and said, "When was the last time you even pulled your saber out of its sheath, Sly?"

"More often than you might think." Sylvester winked. "I'm old, not dead."

I'd gotten used to senior citizens making sex jokes. But I tried not to visualize the Silver Foxes doing the bump-and-grind.

Damian handed the condom box back to Sly. "In that case, maybe you better hold on to these."

The senior citizen winked again. "You can get your own box in the gift shop."

Sylvester opened the package to bring out a handful of packets, which he gave to Damian. Then he walked away with the box of rubbers.

Damian stuffed the glow-in-the-dark condoms in his pocket.

I leaned in to whisper in his ear, "Those could be fun."

"Mm-hm." He glanced at me sideways. "Maybe we'll try them out tonight."

Oh God, I hoped he meant that.

Damian studied me the way he often did when he wanted to ask me something. "Do you like working as a pharmacy technician?"

"Huh?" I snapped back to reality, shattering the fabulous fantasy I'd been enjoying that involved him naked on his stomach while I licked my way up his backside. "No, I don't love my job. It's okay, and the pay is decent, but I only became a pharmacy technician to try to appease my parents. They wanted me to be a doctor. I wanted to be an event planner. So we compromised, and I became a pharmacy technician."

"How is that a compromise? Event planning has nothing to do with medicine."

I shrugged. "At least I didn't have to go to medical school."

"Event planner makes a lot more sense for you. I bet you'd rock that job."

His statement made me feel glowy inside, but I also got a tight-ness in my throat. "Your food is getting cold."

Neither of us mentioned my job again.

When lunch was over, Damian went back to work, and I played rummy with the Kittens in the entertainment room. Yesterday, Damian and I had played chess in here by ourselves, and I'd beaten him twice. He beat me once. Though I'd always liked chess, the game had never been so much fun before. Damian would occasionally hold a chess piece to his forehead, shut his eyes, and make ghost-like moaning noises for a few seconds. Then he'd slap the piece down on the board and declare, "I have seen the future. I'm going to win, so you might as well surrender now."

"You don't surrender in chess. You resign."

"I never give up."

"No kidding." I made my move, taking his pawn. "It's one of the sexiest things about you."

"Let's make this a little more interesting and play strip chess."

"Maybe next time."

Playing rummy with my girlfriends wasn't as much fun as doing anything with Damian, but I enjoyed it anyway. I lost every game, though. Thinking about the Ludar prince who had pursued me with tenderness and sensuality kept me distracted. I hoped he'd meant it when he said we could have sex tonight. Making love with Damian felt so good, and not just because of the orgasms involved. It felt right. The intimacy we shared meant more than lust.

After the card games, my friends wanted to go on a nature hike, but I wanted to stick closer to the resort. Yeah, okay, I was hoping to catch a glimpse of Damian while he performed his concierge duties. All morning, I'd kept seeing him walking from the guest house to the caretaker's house, or from the guest house to one of the other buildings. He always noticed me and waved, flashing me a sexy grin. All his smiles were hot, from the subdued ones to the I-want-your-body-now variety.

Every time he smiled at me, I smiled back, overcome by a giddy sensation.

While my friends marched down the nature trail, I hung out on the lawn, relaxing in an Adirondack chair. I didn't see Damian for an hour. Then he walked out of the guest house wearing his Ludar prince garb, looking so damn lickable. Maybe I'd told him on the day I arrived that his Dracula-chic outfit didn't do anything for me, but I had lied. We both knew it, even then. Now that I was done fighting my attraction to him, I could say it out loud.

I wanted to do more than simply say it, though. I wanted to shout it to the rooftops, through the sky, and straight into outer space.

I cupped my hands like a megaphone and hollered, "Woo-hoo, Damian, strut that gypsy-vampire sex appeal."

He grinned and blew me a kiss.

So I blew him one too.

Everyone else on the lawn gave me knowing smiles. Ruth Norris clapped and said, "You go, girl. About time you found the right man, and a hot one too. Bet he's a god in bed."

"He sure is," I shouted loud enough everyone, including Damian, could hear it.

Damian blew me another kiss, smiling with so much sizzling sweetness that my heart stuttered. Only he could be sweet and naughty at the same time.

I watched Damian unlock his wagon and bring out the sandwich board that advertised "a genuine Rom experience" and listed his specialties—palm reading and tarot reading. He set the sign up a few yards in front of the wagon's door, which he left open.

As soon as he disappeared inside, I wandered toward the guest house.

I ran into Mara just coming out of it. She almost collided with me since she had her head down, focused on the clipboard she held.

"Oh!" Mara said, her head jerking up. "Sorry. I wasn't looking, was I?"

"No problem. What's got you so distracted? Must be some heavy marketing stuff." Though Mara was the marketing director at Au Naturel, I didn't think she'd be pondering pay-per-click advertising while walking out of the guest house.

Mara shook her head. "Wedding stuff. Ollie and I are getting married in three weeks, and I still haven't nailed down all the details. Ollie offered to help, but I know he's super busy with work. Besides, men don't get all the wedding stuff."

"Yeah, I guess not. Maybe I can help."

"Oh no, I couldn't ask you to do that. You're a guest."

"I'm a friend too, right? So I absolutely can volunteer to assist the bride."

Mara gave me a grateful smile. "That would be wonderful, but honestly, you don't have to."

"Once upon a time, I wanted to be an event planner. Even interned with a real expert. And I would be honored to take some of the wedding load off your shoulders, Mara. It's the least I can do after how sweet you've been to me, even when I was trying to steal Ollie from you."

She stared at me for several seconds. "That would be amazing, Heidi. Thank you."

I took the clipboard from her. "Let's go sit on the lawn and see what we can work out for you."

Mara and I spent two hours hashing out the details, first while sitting on the lawn, then in my room in the guest house. We didn't have the entire wedding mapped out, but we had a plan. I insisted we split the duties, not only to keep Mara from sinking under the weight of it all, but also to get things done faster. We had a lot of calls to make, but the most important task required a trip into town.

"We have to get you a gorgeous dress," I said while Mara and I walked down the stairs, heading for the main doors of the guest house. "Isn't there a dress shop in town? I think I remember seeing one."

"Yeah, there is a shop." At the bottom of the stairs, Mara stopped and bit her lip. "Um, would you mind going with me to find a dress? Eve is so busy, and I don't want to bother her."

"Sure, I'll go with you."

Mara smiled. "Thank you, Heidi. You are such a wonderful friend."

Her compliment made me feel a little weird, but I knew she meant it. Mara Severins was the kindest person on earth, and I was lucky to have her as a friend. I told her that out loud too, which made her blush. Yeah, I completely understood why Ollie fell for Mara. They were so perfect for each other.

Were Damian and I right for each other? I tried not to think about that too much. Not yet.

He found me at dinnertime and suggested we should take our meal to go and "dine in Ludar splendor inside the mystical gypsy wagon where pleasure is always on hand." Then he'd winked and added, "Or by mouth, whichever you prefer."

"Maybe I prefer the cock method of receiving gypsy pleasure."

"I was hoping you'd say that."

"Does this mean you'll make love to me tonight?"

He molded his lips to mine, holding them there for a moment that felt like a blissful eternity. Then he held my hand to his forehead, shut his eyes, and made those ghost-moan noises again. When he looked straight into my eyes, he murmured, "I foresee nudity, sweat, the scent and flavor of your cream, and multiple orgasms."

If anyone else had told me that, I would've laughed and walked away. But whenever Damian talked that way, I got wet and tingly between my thighs. And whenever he smiled at me in that sweetly understanding way, I got an ache in a different place altogether—in my heart. It was the best kind of pain. Maybe I was falling for him. Here, tonight, in his gypsy wagon, I suddenly realized I wouldn't mind if I did tumble head over heels for him.

No, I wouldn't mind at all.

Chapter Twenty-Two

Damian

Okay, so I lasted less than forty-eight hours before I crumbled and made love to Heidi again. I never claimed to be a bastion of willpower, did I? Besides, she seemed to be better and better every minute, dealing with her anxieties faster than I could've ever dreamed she might. Was it temporary? No, I didn't believe that. Heidi had suppressed her natural tendencies for months out of shame and fear, but now she was unleashing them one by one. It was real and permanent. I believed that.

My prediction for last night came true. And the wagon might've been rocking and rolling, which I hadn't foreseen with my bogus hand-on-the-forehead prediction. That might've been only a ploy to get her to touch me, not that I needed an excuse.

This morning, I woke up with Heidi sprawled on top of me, her cheek on my chest and her hair spilling over my skin. Gently, I brushed enough hair away so that I could see her face.

She was smiling in her sleep.

Yeah, my heart melted when I saw that. She looked so…at peace.

I lay there covered in Heidi for ten minutes before she finally roused, fluttering her lids and sighing. Her body writhed on top of mine as she tried to stretch, though she couldn't quite do it from that position.

She lifted her head to gaze at me with a dreamily satisfied smile. "Good morning."

"Any morning when I wake up with you is the best morning ever."

"For me too." She wriggled, and my already stiff dick twitched. "Ready for wake-up sex?"

"I'm always ready for you." I rolled us over onto our sides and skimmed my hand over her hip to her thigh. "Wish I could spend the day with you, but I'm on duty again."

"That's okay. I can entertain myself." She rolled onto her back to stretch her entire body, her arms above her head, and moaned. "You really do work hard, don't you? I watched you running here, there, and everywhere for hours yesterday."

"You watched me for hours? Sounds like stalking. Maybe I should lock you up in my private jail cell so I can interrogate you the Ludar way."

"Only if the Ludar way means lots and lots of sex. I wouldn't mind handcuffs."

"Sorry, I don't have any of those." But maybe I could order some online, the kind with padded cuffs designed for sexy playtime.

Heidi stared into space for a few seconds, then she pushed up onto her elbows. "Where was your family yesterday? I didn't see them at all."

"They went sightseeing. I gave them a map of all the best attractions in the area, including restaurants, so they could have the full tourist experience."

"Aren't they disappointed you didn't go with them?"

"Nah, they understand I have a job to do. Besides, they came for a surprise visit, which means I didn't have a chance to beg for time off. They get it." I sat up, allowing myself five seconds to admire her breasts before I got back to business. "My family will be hanging around the resort today, so you might have to submit to more of my mom's well-meaning, if misplaced, protective harassment."

"I like Monica. She's a tough cookie but with a soft center, like a caramel-filled sugar cookie."

"Sugar cookie?" I chuckled. "Let's not tell Mom you described her that way. She likes to think she's a force to be reckoned with."

"Oh, she is. But considering what my parents are like, Monica is a breath of fresh, cool air."

"Well, I hope you still feel that way after today."

She sat up and tickled my chin. "Relax, Damian. I'm not a basket case anymore."

"You never were one."

I grabbed my phone off the top step and checked the time. "Afraid we'll have to skip wake-up sex. I need to be at work in twenty minutes. Didn't realize I'd slept so late."

She kissed me. "You go on. I might relax in your bed for a while if that's okay."

"You can rub yourself all over my bed for as long as you want. I love having your scent all over me and my sheets."

"I'll make sure to cover this bed with me." She pulled the sheet up and rubbed it over her belly, then up to her breasts, massaging them with the soft fabric. "Have fun at work."

The last thing I wanted to do right now was to walk away from the beautiful, naked, horny woman in my bed, but I had to go. I'd never missed a day of work at any of my jobs. So I kissed Heidi and said, "Call me if you're still tangled up in my sheets at lunchtime. We can eat in bed."

"Even if I'm not still in your bed at lunch, we can eat here."

"It's a date. Now, I need to get dressed and go."

Heidi watched me while I climbed off the bed, found my clothes, and pulled them on. She kept rubbing the sheet over her belly and chest while licking her lips. Damn, she was the sexiest woman in the universe. So what if I'd never visited another planet? I knew without any doubt that not even the naughtiest alien sex kitten could've been hotter than Heidi Mackenzie.

I left her in the wagon, on my bed, naked and willing. And I went to work.

Yesterday had seemed like a blur, with one guest after another asking for my help. I must've run back and forth between the guest house and the caretaker's house two dozen times, not to mention all the trips to the daycare center on the opposite side of the guest house. Kids made so many messes, but that wasn't my job. I had to ferry stuff over there because the parents forgot their diaper bags, or they left the kid's medication in their room, or Mommy needed her Xanax. I only got one call like that. Mostly, I brought aspirin to those moms and dads. Considering how loud their kids loved to scream, for no reason I could see, I understood why their parents needed headache medicine.

Today turned out to be no less exhausting. Ollie and Mara were supposed to take a group of guests on a guided nature hike, but I got a call from Ollie not five minutes before the hike was scheduled to begin. The second I picked up the call, before I even said hello, Ollie started talking.

"Help," he moaned, doing a totally fake anguished voice. He added a sarcastic whimper at the end of his moan. "Mara just told me she can't co-lead the hike because Heidi's helping her with the wedding plans. You can't leave me alone with these old farts. They're crazy."

I'd forgotten the hike was a special event for seniors. And why was Heidi playing wedding planner for Mara?

"You love the fogies," I said. Since he'd used his sarcastic fake moan to make me feel sorry for him, I decided to use my sarcastic baby-talk voice to irritate him. "And they think you're the cutest wittle thing in the whole wide world. Sing a song for them, wittle Awee."

"Awee? What in the world is that supposed to mean?"

"It's your name in baby talk. Better get used to that kind of thing. I'm sure you'll have Mara knocked up any day now, if you haven't already."

"We're waiting until after the wedding and the honeymoon."

"Uh-huh. You know what they say about best-laid plans."

He snorted. "You are so not funny, man. Get out here and help me before the gray-hair brigade jumps on me like a horde of zombies."

"Why don't you get Val or Eve to help?"

"Val went into town to buy bathroom supplies. Man, these people use a lot of toilet paper. Anyway, Eve is busy teaching an arts-and-crafts class. I think it's how to make shit out of duct tape or something."

"Hey, don't knock duct-tape shit. I had a girlfriend who made me a wallet out of that stuff, and not only was it waterproof, but it lasted forever."

"I remember that wallet. The duct tape was rainbow-colored." Ollie sighed, sounding genuinely miserable. "Please lead this hike with me. I hate doing it alone, and we haven't had a chance to hang lately."

Yeah, we were both too busy with work and women.

"Okay, fine," I said. "I'll be your bodyguard."

I tucked my phone into my pocket and hurried to my room to swap my uniform sneakers for a pair of hiking boots and to grab my favorite baseball cap, then I headed out to the lawn. Ollie and the fogies were waiting there. My best friend was laughing at something one of the older guests had said. He slapped the guy on the arm and started talking while making big hand gestures.

Yeah, he looked stressed-out and desperate for help.

When Ollie saw me approaching, he grinned. "The D-Man is here! Let's get this party started."

"Party?" I said when I reached him. "I thought it was a nature hike and you were about to drop dead from stress if I didn't show up to lend a hand."

Ruth and Sylvester Norris pushed past the other guests to get to me and Ollie. Ruth patted Ollie's cheek. "This dear sweet boy needs all the help he can get."

"Hey, I'm not helpless," Ollie said. "Damian needs fresh air. That's the only reason I conned him into doing this. Excuse me, I talked him into it, not conned."

My best friend was smirking. Oh yeah, he had totally conned me into this.

"You didn't need me at all, did you?" I asked, pretending to be offended. I raised my hands, fingers spread, and tipped my head back like I was communing with the sky. "I call upon the ancient gods of the Ludar to lay a horrendous curse on Oliver Jackson. May he lose his sense of smell forever."

"Awesome," Ollie said, grinning. "I'll never again get nauseous when I smell liverwurst."

One of the older guests, who I didn't recognize, raised his hand. "Can you curse my ex-wife? She got the Boca Raton house in the divorce, but she only wanted it because I loved that place. She hates Florida."

I stifled a laugh. "Sorry, man, I only curse people who annoy *me*."

Ollie gave the introductory speech about the rules of the hike and the things we might see along the way. We both strapped on hefty backpacks stuffed full of snacks and water bottles, plus a few outdoor essentials like bug spray and calamine lotion. For the next half hour, we explained nature to a dozen senior citizens. Well, Ollie did the explaining. I wasn't anywhere near as well-versed in the wildlife and plant life as he was.

We had lunch at the lake, on the beach. While the guests broke off into three groups and entertained each other, Ollie and I set up our picnic blanket a short distance away from everybody else.

A hummingbird buzzed past us, and Ollie smiled like he was reminiscing about something.

I elbowed him in the side. "Are you ever going to tell me why you get sentimental about hummingbirds?"

"Sorry, I've been sworn to secrecy. It's a private thing between me and Mara."

"Whatever." I ate a bite of my sandwich before I asked the question I'd wanted to ask him since he tricked me into going on this hike. "Why did Mara bail on you at the last minute? That's not like her at all."

"She bailed on me last night. I couldn't say no. She's super stressed about all that wedding junk."

"You do realize you can never speak the phrase wedding junk when you're within earshot of Mara. Practice saying 'yes, dear, I'd love to pick out place settings with you.' Then ooh and ah over that crap when you're shopping with her."

Ollie threw a potato chip at me, which bounced off my nose. "What do you know about weddings? You're a confirmed bachelor."

I wasn't feeling confirmed anymore. The more time I spent with Heidi, the more I wanted to do lots of things that didn't involve sex. Cuddling sounded awesome. Maybe some adoring gazes too. Hand-holding would be perfect. I could recite a poem or something like that too. Maybe I'd love to just hold her in my arms for a long, long time.

"Whoa-ho," Ollie said, looking genuinely surprised. "Were you just daydreaming lovey-dovey thoughts about Heidi? Never seen that look on your face before. Is Damian Petrescu, the Ludar playboy, finally ready to settle down?"

"What if I am? It's not a crime."

"No, it's awesome. We could have a double wedding."

"Double what? Whoa, slow down there, Ollie. I've been with Heidi for a few days, and you're getting married in less than three weeks."

He shrugged. "Okay. We can plan your wedding later."

"Aren't the girls supposed to do the planning?"

Ollie snorted. "You really don't understand women, do you? They expect us guys to act like we enjoy talking about stuff like who sits at which table at the reception and whether to have a buffet or a formal dinner."

"Which did you decide on?"

"Haven't decided anything. That's why Mara is panicking." He swigged some water, wiping his mouth with his hand. "Thank goodness Heidi offered to help her with all that. Mara's a lot more relaxed now that she has an unofficial wedding planner."

"I'm sure Heidi will love taking care of the details."

We went back to eating and enjoying the sunshine, and Ollie didn't harass me anymore about Heidi and whether I wanted to settle down. The rest of the nature hike seemed to drag by, though, probably because I kept thinking about Heidi and wondering what she was doing, if she was having fun, whether she would be happy to see me when I got back from the hike. Would she wonder where I'd been? Would she miss me?

Those thoughts made me feel anxious and a little giddy.

I stifled a groan, realizing exactly what that meant. Oh yeah, Ollie would love this.

The Ludar playboy was falling in love.

When we walked out of the woods, our group of seniors wandered off in various directions. Ollie spotted Mara on a chaise and jogged across the lawn to kiss her and sit on the grass beside her chair. Those two were perfect for each other, and they had something I never used to think I wanted—real, soul-deep, forever love. The idea of that kind of connection had always sounded like baloney to me, but the more time I spent with Heidi, the less dumb it all sounded. I guessed that was because I was falling for her.

And I liked it.

I saw Heidi at the instant she saw me. She was with her girlfriends, whose names I couldn't remember offhand, laughing and making hand gestures, probably to go along with whatever jokes they were telling each other. When Heidi noticed me, her face went blank for a second, then her expression lit up with the most brilliant smile I'd ever seen.

A pang stabbed into my chest, and my throat went thick.

Heidi sprinted across the lawn to me, flung her arms around my neck with her feet off the ground, and kissed me. When she unglued her lips from mine, she slid down my body until her feet touched the ground, but she kept her arms wrapped around my neck. "I missed you, Damian."

She felt so damn good crushed against me that I couldn't stop myself from admitting, "I missed you too."

And I grinned as wide as she was still doing.

No doubt about it. I was in love.

Chapter Twenty-Three

Heidi

For the rest of the week, I hung out with Damian as much as possible. Whenever he needed to work, I spent time with the Kittens or with Mara. The wedding plans came together quickly, and we got all the right venues booked and ordered all the right flowers and other accoutrements. Mara and I had been friends for a while now but working with her on the wedding stuff made us even closer. I couldn't have been happier for her and Ollie. Better still, I'd stopped feeling guilty over my half-assed attempt to steal Ollie from Mara all those months ago.

The past was the past. No point in dwelling on it.

Wow, was that me thinking those words? Guess I'd changed more than I realized.

No, not changed. I got back to being myself, and a large part of the reason for that was Damian.

The Petrescus went home after four days, but before they left, Monica took me aside for a little chat. I'd realized a few days ago that she wasn't trying to scare me off. She simply wanted to make sure her son ended up with the right woman. I'd kind of assumed since she'd announced she accepted me provisionally that she would hold off on welcoming me to the family until I had a proven track record with her son.

But on day four, Monica and I stood under the bows of a big pine tree on the far side of the lawn, alone.

She eyed me up and down, her expression indecipherable. "Do you love Damian?"

"What?" The question surprised me, but I collected myself and gave her the most honest answer I could. "I don't know yet. We haven't been together for very long. I like Damian so much, and I want to get to know him better. He means a lot to me."

Monica nodded slowly. "That's good. My son is in love with you, but I'm sure you've realized that on your own since the first time I told you that. If you break his heart, I will lay a hex on you."

"Do whatever you feel you need to do. But I have no intention of hurting him." When I was with Damian, I felt more like myself than I ever had in my entire life, but I couldn't tell Monica that, not unless I told Damian first. "He's the sweetest, kindest, smartest man I've ever known. Whatever happens between us, I'll always care about him."

"I'm glad to hear it." She picked up my hand, sandwiching it between her palms. "I sense you're a good, strong woman, but I'd feel better knowing more about your soul. With your permission, I'd like to do a tarot reading for you."

"Sure, I'm cool with that." I doubted Monica's tarot reading would be as much fun as Damian's palm reading, but I would do whatever it took to win over his mom. If she wanted to hypnotize me and make me grunt like a monkey, I'd go along with that too.

Monica pulled a boxed deck of cards out of her pocket. "We can do it right here. Let's sit cross-legged on the ground."

We sat down facing each other, and she slid the deck out of its box and onto her palm. "This is the old-style Rider-Waite deck. I've tried newer, fancier ones, but the old-school version works best for me."

"Tradition is good."

"I'm glad you feel that way because tradition is extremely important to my family."

"Yeah, I figured it was based on the things Damian has said. It's nice that you guys all get along so well."

While she shuffled the deck, Monica studied me again, though this time her lips curled at the corners the tiniest bit. "You are a clever girl, Heidi. I'm sure that's part of the reason Damian adores you. But what you just said makes me think you and your family don't get along well. Is that true?"

"Yeah." Would that be a black mark against me in Monica's book? Even if it were, even if she rejected me, I would stay with Damian for as long as he'd have me.

"That's a shame." Monica cradled the shuffled deck in her palm, her free hand hovering over it. "But there are different kinds of family, you know. The one you're born with might not always be the best one for you. I'm not insulting your parents, that's not my intent. I'm sure they mean well deep in their souls, and all I'm saying is that you shouldn't feel limited by your past."

I couldn't think of anything to say in response. Monica was a wise woman, but I'd need time to digest her comments. Another kind of family? I didn't know about that.

Monica patted my hand. "Relax, dear, there's nothing to worry about. I'll do a three-card spread."

She dealt three cards, laying them on the grass one by one from left to right, pausing between each card to explain it. The first card showed a woman seated on a throne, wearing flowing robes and a big crown.

"The High Priestess," Monica said. "She symbolizes the mystery of a future that hasn't yet been revealed as well as the wisdom, tenacity, and passion of the querent." With her head bowed, she moved only her eyes to glance up at me. "The querent is you, dear."

"I have wisdom?" A nervous laugh bubbled out of me. "Think you picked the wrong card."

She shook her head. "No, dear, the tarot never lies."

Monica dealt the second card, which featured a naked man and woman with a sun-being hovering above them. She studied it for a moment, then gave me that head-bowed look again, this time with a faint smile on her lips. "The Lovers. This card suggests attraction and obstacles overcome, but it also indicates choices must be made in a relationship and sacrifice may be required."

Was she trying to scare me away after all? I would not sacrifice Damian because of what a few dumb cards claimed to know.

She dealt the third and final card, which showed a compass and a strange humanoid creature plus a winged angel-like being and a bird. "The Wheel of Fortune. This means your destiny awaits if you choose to accept it."

"Does it happen to say what my destiny is?" Not that I believed in this crap, but I appreciated the beauty of the cards and Monica's interpretation of them.

"The tarot does not give specifics. All will be revealed at the appropriate moment."

"What if I don't notice when that happens?"

She smiled gently and touched my hand. "Trust yourself, dear. Be open to the possibilities, and when the time comes, you will understand."

I couldn't help smiling a little. "You really are good at this stuff. I can see where Damian gets it from. He's amazing at palm reading."

"Yes, he's always had a flair for it. Damian sometimes does tarot readings, but it's not his first choice." She held the Wheel of Fortune card out to me. "Keep this. Maybe it will remind you of the potential for happiness and keep you open to the possibilities."

I accepted the card, cradling it in my palm. "Thank you, Monica. I'm glad I got to meet you, and Adrian and Stefan too. I hope we'll see more of each other in the future."

"We will." She rose, offering a hand to help me up. She winked and smiled. "I foresee many future meetings for the two of us, dear."

"Looking forward to that." And I meant it. In the space of a few minutes, Monica Petrescu had made me feel better in ways I couldn't describe. Damian made me feel the best, but his mom had done something for me I couldn't even explain, not yet.

We headed for the driveway where the rest of the Petrescus, and Ollie and Mara, waited alongside a station wagon that served as a taxicab. The driver was shutting the rear door where I could see he'd stashed the family's luggage. It was time to say goodbye.

Damian's dad and brother hugged him, then they shook my hand to say goodbye. My honey hugged his sister-in-law too. But while Ollie and Mara wished the rest of the Petrescus a safe trip home, Damian's mom pulled him into a bear hug and whispered something to him. He looked slightly surprised by whatever she'd told him. She kissed his cheek and came over to me.

Monica hugged me.

I tried not to seem stunned. After the conversation we'd had earlier, I shouldn't have been surprised, I guessed. But I was.

She shocked me even more when she whispered, "You will make a fine addition to the Petrescu family."

Monica kissed my cheek and got into the taxi with her husband. Stefan and his wife climbed in too.

Damian slipped his hand into mine while we waved and watched the vehicle drive away.

Ollie slapped Damian's arm. "What did Mommy say, D-Man? Is she planning the wedding?"

"Shut up," Damian said with a smile. "Don't you need to go assistant-manage something?"

"Uh-huh. We'll leave you and Heidi to talk about…whatever."

Ollie and Mara left us.

Damian slung an arm around my waist, settling his hand on my hip. "Mom whispered to me that she gave you a tarot reading, and it showed good things ahead for us."

"Yeah, but she also said I might need to make a sacrifice."

"In tarot, that can mean a lot of things. Besides, that stuff's a bunch of bunk, right?"

"Sure, yeah, a bunch of bunk."

He tugged me more snugly to him. "Let me give you a palm reading. That'll make you feel so good you won't worry about any-thing for at least three days."

"That will only work if it's a naughty palm reading."

"For you, there's no other kind." He kissed my forehead. "Let's grab lunch and sequester ourselves in the wagon for a good, long reading."

"Can't be too long. Your lunch break is only an hour."

"I'll make up any overrun by working late. Come on, say yes."

"Okay. Yes."

He grinned.

I grinned.

Damn, we were a pair of lovestruck fools, but I didn't care. It felt beautiful and hot and sweet and sexy, all the things that made me forget about everything else in the world.

We stole some food from the lunch buffet in the dining hall, then hid out in the gypsy wagon to eat and…do other things. Mul-tiple orgasms were on the menu for sure. Damian didn't get half-way through the palm reading before I dragged him down onto the pillows and rode him like a wild gypsy cowgirl.

He was half an hour late getting back to work, but nobody cared.

That night, after another round of palm-reading steaminess, I lay sprawled over Damian on the bed inside the wagon, satisfied in more ways than I could count. I'd never felt so at ease or so happy in my entire life, and I wanted to explain to him how much it meant to me, how much he meant to me. But I couldn't make the words come out, not yet.

In my mind, I told him. *I love you, Damian.*

Chapter Twenty-Four

Damian

A week after my family went home, it was time for the Kitten Brigade to leave too. Heidi had been a member of that group since the first time they came to Au Naturel, and I assumed she would go home with them. I didn't want her to leave. Heidi and I had grown so close lately that just the thought of watching her ride away in that pink RV got me choked up. Real manly, right? At least nobody saw me doing that.

We hadn't talked about where we would go from here, so I had no reason to expect her to stay with me. She had a job back home, after all, even if she didn't love it. Mara raved about everything Heidi had done to help her prepare for the wedding, but the prep work wasn't done yet. I supposed Heidi could still help out from home, with video calls or whatever.

I wanted to beg her to stay. Seriously. Me. I wanted to beg on my hands and knees.

Heidi came out of the guest house with her friends, and they piled into the RV, each giving Heidi a hug. She had her purse over her shoulder, but she didn't climb in with them.

I stood at the front of the vehicle, in the gravel driveway, staring at her like a desperate moron and praying she wouldn't get on that RV.

The door closed. Heidi stayed on the ground.

She was about to bang on the door so they'd let her in. Right?

Heidi backed up to get out of the way as the RV's engine revved up.

I lingered there paralyzed until Shelby, who was driving the bus, honked the horn and waved for me to get out of the way. Shouting "sorry," I hustled over to where Heidi stood. She gave me a strange look while the RV turned around and rolled off down the driveway, out of sight.

"Are you okay?" she asked. "You almost got mowed down by a giant, lumbering RV."

"I'm fine." I scratched the back of my neck, head down. "You must be, uh, taking a cab to somewhere to meet up with your friends later, right?"

That did not sound at all pathetic. What in the world was wrong with me?

Heidi stared at me for a minute, then she laughed. Holding my face in her hands, she urged me to raise my head and look at her. "You were worried I was leaving you. That's so cute, Damian. You're always confident and smooth, but it's nice to know you have an anxious side too."

"You like my anxiety? That's crazy."

"I like that you care enough to worry about losing me. You're not, by the way. I'm staying."

"But you have your purse, like you're going somewhere."

She rubbed her thumbs over my lips. "Relax. I'm taking Mara into town so she can buy a wedding dress."

"Oh." How dumb did I feel? Thumb-sucking, babbling, drooling-lunatic dumb. "You're sticking around until the wedding, then."

"I'm sticking around, period."

"What about your job?"

She shrugged one shoulder. "I quit."

"What? When?"

"This morning. Didn't get a chance to tell you yet because I was helping my friends get ready to leave." She draped her arms around my neck, brushing her fingertips through my hair. "I've got enough money in the bank to get by for a couple months, which gives me time to figure out what my next step is. Val and Eve offered me a job here—a nonspecific, whatever-I-want job—but I need to think about it."

"The resort needs an event planner."

"Let's talk about that later. Right now, I need to go with Mara."

"Was her mom upset that you're taking over the wedding planning?"

Heidi leaned her body against me, her fingers still toying with my hair. "No, Sheryl understood. She wants Mara to be happy, and she only became the wedding dictator because Mara didn't want to make her mom feel bad. She was afraid to say what she wanted. Naturally, Sheryl assumed her daughter needed the most expensive, designer everything."

"But she doesn't. Mara wants something cozier and more relaxed."

"That's right. How did you know?"

"I've been working with Mara for months now."

"Right. I almost forgot." She danced her fingertips down my neck, spreading her hand over my shoulder, then she dragged her palm down to my chest. "What should we do this evening, after you get off work?"

I cupped her ass with both hands. "How about we go into town and have dinner at a real restaurant? No buffet, no senior citizens poking their noses into our business, just the two of us."

"Are you asking me out on a date?"

"Yeah, I guess I am."

She smiled. "I'd love to go on a date with you, Damian."

The urge to fist-pump was strong, but I ignored it. "I'll pick you up at eight, at your room. Okay?"

"I'll be ready." She eyed my work uniform. "Are you going to, like, wear a suit or something? Should I dress up?"

I hadn't even considered how we might dress, but nudity was pretty much off the table. The authorities frowned on naked people strolling into a restaurant. I did own a suit, for special occasions. For years, I'd worn a prison-guard uniform, and now I wore the resort uniform. To wear a nice suit again might feel weird, but I looked forward to it. And I couldn't wait to see Heidi in whatever fancy dress she decided to wear.

"Yes, we're dressing up," I said. "The only restaurant in town is the steak house, but I hear it's nice."

"It is. And they usually have live music. A string quartet or something like that."

"Sounds perfect. Have you been to the steak house before?"

Heidi bit her lip again and swerved her gaze away from mine. "Um, once. Back when I was trying to steal Ollie away from Mara. Her ex-husband showed up, and he took me on a date strictly to make Mara jealous. It didn't work. I thought it was a real date, though. Stupid, right?"

"No, that's not stupid. Ollie told me about Nico the Numbskull, and I'm sure he did a bang-up job of sweet-talking you into going out with him."

"He did that all right."

I moved my hands up to her back and tugged her closer. "You're a smart cookie, but everybody gets duped once in a while. Now, let's stop talking about other people and focus on tonight." I bent my head to murmur in her ear, "No underwear, please."

"Not even a bra?"

"Wear one if you'll feel more comfortable that way, but definitely no panties."

"Yes, sir." She caught my earlobe between her teeth, tickling it with her tongue. "No underwear for you either."

"I never bother with those, you know that."

"Just making double sure."

Since I still had my mouth almost touching her ear, I flicked my tongue out to tease the skin under the lobe, loving the way she sucked in a breath. "I never got to use that silk scarf I bought for you. Tonight, I'm going to strip you naked and drag that silk over you so slowly, skimming it across your skin over and over until you beg me to fuck you."

"Oh God, I can't wait for that. I want to go down on you in the restaurant."

I froze as the meaning of what she'd said filtered through my lust-drunk brain. "Are you just saying that, or would you actually do that sometime? Have you done something like it before?"

"No, never. But yes, I want to do that to you." She skated her tongue up my throat. "Tonight."

Damn, and I thought I was the master of dirty talk. My dick jerked the second she spoke the word "tonight" in her sultry voice.

"I, uh, better get back to work," I said, taking a step backward. "But we're on for tonight, and I'm game for anything you want to try."

Mara emerged from the guest house, heading this way. She waved to Heidi.

"See you tonight," I said.

Heidi lunged forward to kiss me. "I'll put my mouth on a different part of you at dinner."

She grinned and trotted toward Mara.

I watched the two girls get into Mara's car, then I waved as they drove off. I went back to work, but it took all my willpower to focus on my job instead of fantasizing about tonight with Heidi. Still, I behaved like a diligent employee and got things done. Sure, I might've locked the office door for five minutes while I jerked off to a fantasy of Heidi going down on me in the restaurant, but that happened during my lunch break. No shirking of duties involved.

At precisely eight o'clock, I approached the door to Heidi's room and knocked.

The door swung open half a second later.

She started to smile, froze, and then went slack-jawed. "Holy cow, Damian, you look like James Bond. You own that color, like the universe invented black just for you."

I'd worn a black suit with a pale-blue shirt and a black tie. I even had shiny black shoes. But I couldn't have guessed she would love my outfit this much. I loved hers too. Like, jaw-droppingly loved it. "You look absolutely incredible, Heidi."

Fuckable, actually, but I was trying to be a gentleman.

Heidi wore a cherry-red dress that clung to her body like a second skin. It featured a halter top that tied behind her neck and a peekaboo cutout that let me glimpse the slopes of her gorgeous breasts. When she twirled so I could see all of her, I discovered the dress was backless. Her red stilettos gave her ankles a sexy curve and made me want to fall to my knees at her feet so I could unhook the slender straps with my teeth and lick my way up her calf.

"Glad you like it," she said. "I bought this dress today for our date. Didn't want to wear something any of those jerks I used to date had seen."

She bought a dress for me. A hot dress.

"I didn't buy this suit for you," I said, "but none of the girls I've dated ever saw it."

Heidi fingered the lapels of my suit jacket. "I like being the first one to see you looking like James Bond."

I offered her my hand. "Shall we go? I made a reservation, so we'd get the perfect table."

"You think of everything." She slipped her hand into mine. "Sweep me off my feet, Damian."

"Anything for you." I swept her into my arms. "I'll carry you to the car like those guys in movies do."

And I did exactly that.

She giggled the entire time.

We walked into the restaurant arm in arm, and every man in the place stopped to stare at Heidi, even the ones who looked like they were ninety. I couldn't blame them. She was stunning.

A waiter took us to our table. The booth nestled in the corner farthest from the entrance, in a shadowy area, behind a brick planter full of small palm trees. That seemed like a weird choice for a steak house in Oregon, but whatever. When I'd made the reservation, I'd asked for a secluded table. This was it, for sure.

Once we ordered, I turned halfway toward Heidi and draped an arm across the back of the booth behind her. "Time for an appetizer."

"The waiter said it would take ten minutes."

"Not talking about that kind of appetizer." I slid closer to her, laying my hand on her thigh. "I need to taste you."

"A gentleman lets the lady go first."

I pushed my fingers under the hem of her dress, gliding them up her skin. "A real gentleman knows the lady always *comes* first."

"Oh, I see."

"Pull your dress up for me, please, and spread your legs."

Elsewhere in the restaurant, people laughed and chattered. Through the branches of those baby palm trees, I could see the movements of people at another table.

Heidi shimmied her hips, hiking up her dress until she'd exposed herself from the waist down. She parted her legs.

I caressed her inner thigh. "When you come, I'll swallow your scream with my mouth over yours."

Her breathing had grown heavier, making her breasts rise and fall. She gripped my thigh with one hand, curling her fingers over the seat's edge with the other.

"Watch what I'm doing to you," I said. "Watch me fuck you with my fingers."

She lowered her head, her gaze trained on my hand.

I slid my hand higher up her thigh and stretched out one finger to tease her mound. When she gasped, I covered those curly hairs with my hand.

Heidi spread her legs even more.

The scent of her cream inundated my senses, and my dick jumped like it couldn't wait to get inside her. *Not yet, bro, not yet.* I sucked in a deep breath through my nostrils, reveling in the aroma of her lust. Fuck, I wanted to shove my head down there and devour her. But I reined in the impulse and kept to the plan, thrusting one finger between her slick lips to massage her clit. She gripped my thigh harder while I skated my finger down one side of her folds and back up the other, coating my finger with her cream.

I lifted that finger to my mouth and licked it clean.

She choked back a moan.

God, I loved the way her cheeks had turned slightly pink and her eyes had gone hooded. There was nothing more beautiful in the world than Heidi Mackenzie at full arousal. I shoved two fingers between her folds, pushing them down until the heel of my hand rested on her taut nub. I rubbed it with my hand while I brushed my fingers up and down, up and down, slowly at first but speeding up little by little as she got more turned on. Her breaths became rhythmic gasps as her nails dug into my thigh.

"How badly do you need to come?" I whispered.

"So damn bad," she said between panting breaths.

I drove my middle finger into her channel as far as it would go, still massaging her clit with my palm and stroking her with my other fingers.

"Oh—God," she hissed under her breath, her gaze riveted to my hand.

Blood was rushing to my cock, but I couldn't focus on anything except the look on her face, a cross between intense pleasure and pain. I ground my hand into her nub, moving my fingers faster and faster and faster. Her body tensed, and her mouth fell open. The second I felt the first hint of a spasm inside her, I sealed my mouth over hers and thrust my tongue deep, swallowing the cry that erupted from her throat. Her body gripped my finger again and again while I kept working her flesh until she was done.

I broke the kiss, breathing almost as hard as she was.

"Wow," she said, her voice breathy. "That was...wow."

"I love it when a woman comes so hard she can't manage a complete sentence." I pulled my hand away from her body and raised my fingers to my mouth, licking them one by one with deliberate slowness, groaning at the flavor of her. "Not sure I need food. The taste of you could sustain me for days."

"But you promised me dinner." She didn't sound breathless anymore, though her cheeks were still pink. "And for the record, I spoke a whole sentence. I said, 'that was wow.' I wasn't incapable of speech."

"I don't think 'wow' counts as part of a sentence, but I'll be a gentleman and give you that one."

"Thank you." She laid a hand on my cheek. "And I mean thank you for the orgasm too."

"My pleasure."

"No, that's what comes next." She cupped my dick through my pants. "I did promise."

"Better fix your dress first."

She wriggled until she had her dress back in position, then she took hold of the zipper on my pants.

The waiter marched up to our table carrying the actual appetizers we had ordered. While he set the food down, another waiter ushered a party of four to the table beside ours. Though a partial wall separated the booths, the two guys sitting right behind me were tall enough to see us if they looked this way.

I leaned close to Heidi and murmured, "Think we better hold off on that thing you wanted to do."

She feigned a pout.

The waiter left, and we stuck to talking and eating.

Chapter Twenty-Five

Heidi

Rats. I had so wanted to give Damian head in the res-taurant, especially after what he did to me. But fate inter-vened in the form of four obnoxious men who got seated right beside our booth and who kept laughing too loudly and glancing in our direction. Well, glancing at me. At my breasts.

Damian and I ignored them as much as possible. He even gave me his jacket so I could cover up my breasts in hopes that would make those twerps give up on leering at me. The tactic worked, thank goodness. We enjoyed our steak dinners and talked, then ordered a yummy, gooey dessert that we fed to each other. I'd never had a more perfect date in my life, despite the loud twerps in the next booth.

Between dinner and dessert, we danced. A jazz quartet played a lazy, sensual song while we shuffled around like two people who had no idea how to dance and didn't care. Damian held me in his arms while I rested my cheek on his shoulder. It was so romantic, and I wanted to commit this entire night to memory so I could relive it in my mind.

I kept Damian's jacket on until we walked out of the restau-rant, not because I worried about men leering at me, No, I'd only thought about that for a few minutes, when those jerks were at their most obnoxious. I kept his jacket because I loved having the scent of him around me and the fabric that had touched him touching me. Once we walked out the doors, I gave it back to him.

"You can keep it," he said. "Looks better on you."

"But I want the whole Ludar James Bond experience on the drive home."

"How can I say no to that?" He took the jacket and slipped it on. "Sorry I don't have an Aston Martin to take you home in style."

"Your Ford Explorer is sexy enough for me."

As we headed into the parking lot, he pushed the button on his key fob to unlock the SUV. "If I'd known all I needed to get you in bed was a Ford Explorer and a suit, I would've given you that the first time we met."

"I wasn't ready for you yet. Now I am."

He opened the passenger door for me. "You were worth the wait."

I settled onto the seat, gazing up at him. "It wasn't the car or the suit that made me want you. It was the palm reading."

"Ludar seduction at its finest."

He shut the door and hustled around to the driver's side, climbing in. When he shoved the key into the ignition, I leaned over to place my hand over his, stopping him from turning the key.

"Not yet," I said. "Got a promise to keep."

"You don't have to—"

I sealed his lips with two fingers. "I want you, Damian. Right now. So I'm adjusting the plan. Got a condom?"

"When I'm with you, always." He dug a packet out of his pants.

"You're the best." I crawled onto his lap, straddling him. "And I do mean that in every way."

Smirking, he reached for the lever under the seat and pulled it. The seat back tipped down at a forty-five-degree angle. "Now we're ready."

I undid his belt and unzipped his pants, freeing his stiff cock.

He lunged forward, wrapped his arms around me, and dragged me down onto the seat with him. Grasping the back of my head, he pulled me in for a deep kiss. While our tongues tangled, he ran his hands up and down my back, and I shoved a hand between our bodies to fondle his cock. Oh wow, he was so hard. When he closed a hand over my breast and kneaded it, I moaned and writhed on top of him, desperate for more of everything—more kissing, more fondling, more of him.

A bright light flared on. Knuckles rapped on the window.

I sprang upright, bashing my head on the ceiling, and cursed under my breath. Squinting at the bright light, I struggled to understand what I was seeing. "Oh shit, Damian, it's a cop."

He sprang upright too, one arm around me, and fumbled with the button that lowered the window. "Hey, officer, what's up?"

The young cop eyed us with narrowed eyes, his flashlight aimed at us, but his mouth twitched into a faint smirk. He nodded toward Damian's lap where his dick was still visible. "You got a permit for that loaded weapon?"

Damian stared at the cop, his mouth open.

I suddenly realized Damian had pulled my tit out of my dress. Tucking it back inside the halter, I cleared my throat. "Are we breaking some kind of law, officer?"

"Yeah, you are. It's called public indecency."

Damian laughed nervously. "Sorry, man, we didn't think. Won't happen again."

"Uh-huh. I'll let you two off with a warning this time." The cop gave us a hard look. "Behave yourselves, kids."

"Will do," Damian said.

The cop ambled away.

I scrambled off Damian's lap. "Guess we better wait till we get home."

"Home?" Damian was just zipping up his pants. "I thought you were a guest."

Why had I called the resort home? The truth hit me, and I had to tell him. "Not anymore. The resort is my home, and I want to work there with you, Ollie, Mara, Eve, and Val. This is where I belong, with the kind of family that loves me no matter what."

"Everybody loves you, Heidi. Your parents are the only dicks in the room."

I leaned over the center console to kiss him. "You're so sweet. Thank you for tonight, and for everything else."

"You're welcome." He turned the key in the ignition, and the vehicle grumbled to life. "Now let's get home so I can make love to you the right way, without any risk of us getting arrested."

"Guess you better obey the speed limit in case that cop keeps tabs on us. We are degenerate criminals, after all."

"We haven't been arrested, so we're not criminals. Unless there's something you haven't told me."

I buckled up my seatbelt. "Nope. What you see is what you get."

Maybe that hadn't been true for the past few months, but it was now. I'd stopped hiding my natural tendencies and gotten back to being my truest self, the woman who took work seriously but loved life and knew how to cut loose. Damian had helped me get there. On the ride home, I couldn't think about anything else except how much this man I'd known for only a short time had changed my life. He meant more to me than any of the other guys I'd dated. Suddenly, I needed to tell him that.

But we had just pulled up in front of the guest house, and he was just getting out of the car, coming around to my side. When he opened the door for me, Damian offered me his hand to help me out. He was such a wonderful man and a gentleman to the core.

I clasped both his hands before he could even close the car door.

His brows crinkled. "Is something wrong?"

"No, everything is just right." I gazed into his eyes, my throat thickening. "I love you, Damian."

For a few seconds, his expression stayed frozen in that crinkled-brows look of worried confusion. Then the corners of his mouth kicked up, and his lips eased into a smile that gradually broadened into a grin. "I love you too, Heidi."

I grinned too.

He pulled me into his arms and kissed me. It was a long, slow, deliciously hot kiss, but it was also more than that. We imbued into it everything we felt for each other and so much more.

Once we finally forced ourselves to stop making out in the driveway, we headed into the gypsy wagon and made love for a long, long time. I fell asleep in Damian's arms.

In the morning, I woke up first and lay there luxuriating in the bliss of having his body entangled with mine. I listened to him breathing in a shallow, steady rhythm and combed my fingers through his hair while I reminisced about all the incredible times I'd had with him. Our relationship had barely begun. We had a lifetime to enjoy even better times. Life would bring bad days too, but for the first time in my life, I knew the good times would outweigh the bad ones from here on.

Damian had just started to rouse when my phone rang.

I tried to wriggle out from under him, but he was too sleepy to help much. So I resorted to gently smacking his cheek a few times until he woke up all the way.

"What?" he asked drowsily, pushing up onto one elbow. "Why are you hitting me? Spousal abuse can't start until we're married."

"Ha-ha. My phone is ringing." I clambered off the bed and snagged my phone from where I'd left it on the top step, near the head of the bed. I swiped right to take the call an instant before it would've gone to voice mail. "Hello?"

"Help!" Mara said, not actually screaming it but fake screaming instead, drawing the word out in one long exhalation.

"What's wrong, sweetie? Did something happen to Ollie?"

"No," she moaned, almost whimpering. "The wedding is in six days, and I suddenly realized I don't have any bridesmaids because I don't have any friends."

Oh boy, the wedding jitters had started early, and in true Mara fashion, she was freaking out. As her wedding planner, I supposed it was my job to calm her down. She was my friend too, despite what she'd just said, so it absolutely was my job to be there for her.

"Relax, Mara," I said. "Everything's okay. Why don't I come to your room? We can talk it all through, and you'll see there's nothing to panic about. How's that sound?"

"Yeah, okay. Thank you, Heidi."

I hung up and started hunting for my clothes. Damian had kind of ripped them off me and flung them wherever. And yeah, I'd done the same thing with his clothes. That suit lay here, there, and everywhere.

"What's up with Mara?" Damian asked.

"Oh, it's wedding anxiety, that's all. I need to take care of her this morning, so I won't be able to have breakfast with you."

"That's okay. The bride takes precedence." He sat up and stretched, yawning. "I'll check on Ollie. See if he's panicking on the inside. You know, the manly way men do."

"Uh-huh, sure. You boys go bang drums or measure your dicks or whatever."

We both got dressed—me in my dress from last night, since it was all I had, and him in his work uniform—and climbed out of the wagon. We both headed into the guest house, but we kissed goodbye on the first landing. Damian strode off toward the office while I continued up to the third floor where Mara and Ollie had taken up residence in one of the rooms ever since they got engaged. Yesterday, Mara had told me she and Ollie wanted to buy a little house near town, but they'd hadn't started looking yet.

After stopping off at my room to change clothes, I knocked on the door to Ollie and Mara's room.

Ollie swung the door open, looking harried. "Oh thank God. Maybe another woman can calm her down. Please, Heidi, she won't listen to me."

Poor Ollie. I wanted to hug him, in a friend way, but he pushed past me and hustled toward the stairs.

Mara sat on the bed hugging her knees and biting her lip. Her eyes were red and puffy.

I shut the door and walked over to sit on the bed next to her. "Did you guys have a fight?"

"No, it's nothing like that. I told him I don't have any friends, and I'll have to stand at the altar all by myself." She grabbed a tissue from a box on the bedside table and blew her nose. "Ollie said I won't be alone because he and Damian and Val will be standing there too, and so will the minister. That's when I started crying. And you know how guys are about tears. He told me to call my mom, but I called you instead."

"I'm glad you did."

"Ugh. I'm such a lunatic." She wadded up the tissue and tossed it into the wastebasket. "Ollie suggested it's hormones. What did I do? I managed to weep uncontrollably and shout at him at the same time."

"Ollie understands, I'm sure. Getting married is a big deal and comes with all kinds of stressful stuff that needs to be done."

She stretched her legs out, leaned back, and laid a hand over her lower belly. "It's more than that. Ollie doesn't mind if I tell you, so, um…" Mara sucked in a big breath and blew it out. "I'm pregnant."

"What? Mara, that's wonderful."

"I know, it really is. We found out yesterday, and at first, we were both over the moon." She shut her eyes and sighed. "But all this wedding craziness is getting to me. The hormonal mood swings aren't helping."

"Don't worry about any of that." I sat up straighter and pointed at myself. "You've got a crack wedding coordinator who's going to handle absolutely everything so the bride can take it easy."

"I can't make you do everything. I'm not even paying you."

"Forget about money. You are my best friend and seeing you and Ollie tie the knot is all the payment I need."

She half-smiled. "Thank you so much, Heidi. You're my best friend too."

I patted her knee. "And as for you not having bridesmaids, that's taken care of too. Eve and I will stand at the altar with you." I glanced at her red, puffy eyes, and realized I needed to do my best-friend job. "Let me get you a cool, damp cloth for your eyes and some chamomile tea to soothe your nerves."

Mara smiled a little more than she had a minute ago. "You're the best, Heidi. I love you."

"Love you too, Mara."

I hustled into the bathroom and got a cool cloth for her, then I insisted she lie down to rest. I settled the cloth over her forehead and partially over her face, so it covered her eyes. After that, I jogged downstairs to get the tea. Maybe I didn't have a paying job at the moment, but helping Mara made me feel useful in a way I hadn't experienced before. I couldn't regret quitting my job.

As I brewed the tea in the kitchen, I wondered if I might have found my new career path after all.

Chapter Twenty-Six

Damian

"Do women always go insane right before the wedding?" Ollie asked, though he didn't give me a chance to respond. "I mean, it's just a wedding, not a presidential inauguration. How could Mara think she doesn't have friends? Of course she does. I tried to calm her down, but no, she had to cry and sniffle and get all puffy-eyed and miserable. She wouldn't even let me hug her, and every time I tried to say something, she'd burst out crying again. She's gone totally nuts."

Ollie had stormed into the office a few minutes ago in a state of half panic, half misery, and flumped onto the chair beside the desk. I sat here in the big chair listening to him vent.

Now, my best friend threw his head back and moaned.

He wasn't angry with Mara. No, he had a much worse problem than that. He was so completely in love with her that he did the worst possible thing any man could do when a woman was upset for what, to us guys, seemed like absolutely nothing. He'd told her it was nothing.

Yeah, Ollie was freaking out too, but in a different way from how Mara had done it.

I was positive Ollie had told her it was nothing in a calm, patient, loving tone. But in my experience, that was also a bad thing to do when a woman started crying. When I'd told Ollie my opinion a minute ago, he had huffed and thrown his hands up, then said, "Then what *is* the right thing to do?"

"No idea, man," I told him. "Women are a mystery."

Ollie genuinely wanted to make his fiancée feel better, but being a guy, he didn't have a frigging clue how to do that.

Since he'd just finished his second diatribe and seemed to be taking a breather, I tried again to settle him down with a bad joke. "Maybe it's PMS. Girls go bananas when it's that time of the month. They can be like that chick in *The Exorcist*, so watch out if Mara's head starts to spin."

Ollie looked at me, suddenly calm and serious. "It's not PMS. Mara is pregnant."

"Are you serious?"

He nodded slowly.

I leaned across the distance between us and slapped his arm. "Congratulations, man. You're gonna be a dad. That's awesome."

"Yeah, awesome," Ollie said in a tone that suggested the news was the opposite of awesome.

"What's wrong? You're head-over-heels in love with Mara, and you've both been talking about having kids practically since the day you met."

"I know, but…" He squirmed in his chair. "What if I screw up?"

"Come on, Ollie, that's nerves talking. Wedding jitters, isn't that what they call it?"

He shrugged. "I guess."

We both needed some booze. Yeah, that would help. Okay, maybe booze wasn't the smartest plan to help my best friend, but I couldn't think of anything better. Desperate times called for desperate measures, right?

That was probably one of the worst excuses for a bender ever invented.

I stood up and slapped his arm again. "Get your butt outta that chair, Ollie. We're going to the pantry."

"What?" Ollie compressed his lips and glared at me. "How is a visit to the food pantry going to make me feel better?"

"You'll see when we get there."

He grumbled, rolling his eyes.

I kicked his foot. "Up. Now."

Ollie grumbled again but pushed out of the chair.

And we trundled downstairs, through the kitchen, to the locked door at the back. I had a key, naturally, being the concierge, so I unlocked the door and swung it open.

"Computer nerds first," I said, hoping a friendly jibe might get a smile from Ollie. It didn't, so I walked into the pantry first. "What are you in the mood for this morning? Bourbon? Beer? Vodka?"

"Isn't it kind of early for drinking?"

"Not when the groom is having a panic attack."

Ollie scowled at me. "I am not having a panic attack."

"When sweet little Ollie gives me a dirty look, I know he's freaking out."

"I'm as tall as you are, which means I'm not little."

"Sensitive this morning, aren't you?" I started browsing the bottles on the shelves. "I noticed you didn't dispute the 'sweet' comment."

"Women like nice guys."

"Mara says you're a snuggly-wuggly wittle cuddle bear." If I couldn't tempt him to drink, maybe some ribbing would work.

Ollie came up beside me, arms locked over his chest. "When did Mara ever tell you that?"

"She didn't. I read between the lines." I threw him a sideways glance and couldn't resist smirking. "When she calls you a stud muffin, I translate that as 'soft and squishy snuggly-wuggly Awee the cuddle bear.' My Ludar lidar confirmed it."

"Maybe you shouldn't harass me when I'm panicking."

"Oh-ho," I said, pointing a finger at him, "you admitted you're freaking out."

"No, I—Well, it's—" He flung his hands up and snarled. "You are such an asshole, Damian."

"That's my job. To piss off the groom so he stops worrying about every little thing." I grabbed a bottle off the shelf. "Well, that and get booze for you."

Ollie eyed the bottle with a hint of suspicion. "You can't seriously think booze is the answer."

"Couldn't hurt."

"It's not even nine a.m. I haven't had breakfast yet."

"Okay, let's get some food to go with our gigantic stash of liquor." I spread an arm to indicate our surroundings. "While we eat, we get hammered. Deal?"

He studied me for a moment, an exceptionally long one. Then Ollie smacked my arm and grinned. "Let's do it. I mean, Mara might dump me for doing this, but so what? I'll crawl back and beg forgiveness like a true cuddly-wuddly computer nerd."

"Sounds like a plan."

We walked back into the kitchen and started rummaging around for the manliest foods available. That's what Ollie said, not me.

"We need manly macho man food," he'd announced as we exited the pantry, aka the Big Closet of Booze.

I didn't even try to figure out what "manly macho man food" was and let Ollie scrounge up whatever he wanted. This was his panic-attack binge, so I decided to stand back and watch while he tore open cupboards and practically climbed inside them in search of the elusive "manly macho man food."

My best friend had probably lost his mind, but it was kind of fun to witness it firsthand.

Our breakfast wound up looking like the fridge had barfed up the contents of a buffet restaurant. Four kinds of sausage. Bacon. Hamburgers. Oh wait, that was bacon cheese hamburgers, so kind of all one thing. What else? Steak fajitas, guacamole, queso, several kinds of chips, baked beans, ham sandwiches, French fries, sweet potato fries, hash browns... I kind of lost track of things after that, partly because we'd raided every cupboard and the fridge but also because we had started drinking somewhere between frying up burgers and scarfing down deviled eggs.

We did not eat all of everything. No, we kind of...sampled everything.

Except for the booze. We might've guzzled that. One shot every time we found something else to eat. First bite of guacamole? *Have a shot of tequila, man.* First taste of sweet potato fries? Time for some Jack Daniels. *Hey, bro, is that some cheesecake in the fridge? Grab it while I steal a bottle of vodka from the pantry.*

Maybe the rest of the morning would've gone better if we'd eaten too much and thrown up the food and the booze. Unfortunately, we sampled but did not gorge ourselves. Not on the food. The liquor... Well, that was a different story.

Ollie glanced at the food littering the island. He blinked in slow motion. "Whoa, dude. Who's gonna clean piss—I mean clean this up."

Every time he spoke the letter S, it sounded kind of like a snake hissing.

I slapped my palm down on the island and burped loudly. "We're, like, you know, in charge or something. Aren't we? Con-sssseee-erge and... What the hell are you?"

"Uhhhh... Assistant manger?" He busted out in guffaws, covering his mouth with one hand. When he pulled his hand away, it had spittle on it. "Did you ever notice assistant manger starts with 'ass'?"

"Dude, you're not a manger. You're a manager." I snorted out a laugh. "Unless you plan on having Mara pop out that kid on your tummy. Get it? Like a manger or…whatevers."

Ollie thrust a bottle at me. "You need more of piss. This. What was I saying?"

I held up a hard-boiled egg. "Ever notice how these look like tits?"

"No, they don't," Ollie said with a laugh that came out like a pig snort. "They've got eggs inside 'em, not on the ousside. Outside. Ugh, I can't talk anymore."

"Do too look like tits. These, I mean." I picked up two eggs and held them to my chest. "See? Hard-boiled titties."

He started guffawing again. "You need a bra, man."

Thinking about tits made me think about Heidi. Yeah, she had the awesomest, fabulosiest boobs on earth. I glanced down at the eggs I was still holding to my chest, and the most awesomest idea ever hit me.

I punched Ollie's arm. "Got a wicked-amazing idea."

"Ow," Ollie said, clutching his arm. "That hurt, dude."

"Don't be a wuss-face." I slid off my stool and snagged a half-empty bottle of Jack Daniels. "Let's go find our woman-girls and, like, kiss them."

"Yeah, we should. Smack some love on 'em." Ollie sort of oozed off his stool and stumbled into me. "Let's do it."

We started for the door, but Ollie froze on the threshold. "Don't we, ya know, have to work or something today?"

"Nah."

"Awesome."

Yeah, two drunk morons thought it was a fantastic idea to find their girlfriends and show off how drunk they were.

At the time, it sounded like the best plan ever.

I grabbed Ollie's arm to stop him halfway down the hall. "We should change clothes first."

"Yeah," he said with a stupid grin. "And I know exactly what we should wear. The girls'll go nutso for it."

Chapter Twenty-Seven

Heidi

Mara and I were sitting on chaises watching Val and Sylvester playing kickball. They weren't concerned with who won but only with having a good time ribbing each other. Val wore his work uniform, but Sly went nude. Well, he was here to enjoy the naturist lifestyle.

Suddenly, Val froze with his foot on the ball. Something past our chairs had captured his attention and made his brows furrow.

"What's wrong?" Sly asked, then he tracked Val's gaze past us, and his face took on a similar expression. "Is that… No, it can't be."

"It is," Val said.

Mara sat forward. "What are you two talking about?"

"Look." Val pointed toward the guest house behind us.

Both Mara and I twisted around on our chaises to see what had caught the men's attention.

Damian and Ollie were walking toward us. Well, staggering toward us. They would move in a straight line for a couple of seconds, then list one way or the other while laughing and slapping each other's arms. Ollie tripped—over grass, it seemed like—and Damian seized his friend's arm to keep him from tumbling over. Just when Ollie regained his balance, sort of, Damian stumbled and staggered sideways.

Oh no. It couldn't be. They wouldn't. Not this early.

They each wore some type of skirt that seemed to be made of hand towels held together by a band of purple duct tape around the waist. No shirts, no shoes, no socks, nothing but those skirts.

Mara leaped off her chaise. "Ollie! What's wrong with you?"

I knew she hadn't figured out what her fiancé's problem was because she looked panicky and worried. If she'd recognized the truth, she'd probably be yelling at him instead of racing toward him.

Damian and Ollie aimed lopsided grins at…no one in particular.

Oh yeah, no doubt about. They were wasted.

I jumped up and hurried after Mara.

The boys halted, waiting for Mara to reach them. I got there two seconds after her.

Ollie swayed, grinning like the drunken fool he was. "Mara, babycakes, you're so friggin' hot."

He slurred those words.

"Pshaw," Damian slurred. "She's nothin' next to Hi-dee-ho-ho-ho."

Ollie rolled his eyes at Damian.

Mara's gaze flicked back and forth between the two men. "What's going on? Ollie, why are you acting this way?"

Jeez, had Mara never seen a drunk person before? Considering the snobby circles her family socialized in, maybe she really hadn't.

Damian tried to put an arm around me but missed and almost fell over.

I slapped a hand on his shoulder to steady him. "What are you doing? You two are wasted. At ten o'clock in the morning."

"Knew you were smart," he said, slapping his hand on top of mine on his shoulder. "You're so perty. Can we have sex now?"

Maybe I should've been more annoyed about their current state, but there wasn't any point in getting upset. Not until they sobered up. "Yeah, sure, let's go into your wagon of love and get it on. If you can crawl up the steps without vomiting."

He thrust out his free hand to me, turning it upside down. "Read my palm, hey? Tell me the foocher."

I assumed he meant "future," but it was hard to tell for sure. I patted his cheek. "That's easy. Your future involves a good long nap, lots of aspirin, and at least three days of groveling for forgiveness." I threw a sharp look at Ollie. "For both of you."

Mara was standing perfectly still, her gaze nailed to Ollie, her expression blank.

"You okay, Mara?" I asked.

She nodded. "I've never seen him like this. Why did you get drunk, Ollie? Don't you want to marry me?"

"Like crazy I do," he said, then he dropped to his knees and hugged hers. "I'm sorry, Mary—Mara. That's your name, right? I'm Awee. Sweet wittle pudgy-wudgy Awee."

Mara covered her face with her hands.

I thought she might be crying—until she lowered her hands.

Her lips were puckered, clearly because she was trying not to laugh.

"No, no, no," Damian said. "It's sweet wittle cuddly wuddly Awee, fuddly muddly...something."

I looked at Mara. "Why don't you take Ollie to your room so he can sleep it off?"

"Good idea." She peeled Ollie's hands away from her knees and convinced him to stand up. "Time for bed, honey."

He let her lead him away, leaning against her the whole time.

Damian latched his arms around my waist. "Is it my bedtime too?"

"Yes, it is." I half dragged him toward the guest house but changed my mind partway there and took him to the wagon. "Naughty little Damian needs some beddy-bye time."

"Oh yeah," he said, "lots and lots of that. Will you tuck me in, Heidi-hi-ho?"

"Uh-huh." After that, he'd have some serious explaining to do.

I managed to get him up the steps and into the wagon, but he careened toward the bench and fell onto it face-first—and promptly passed out. I pushed him onto his side, then grabbed a blanket and draped it over him. By then, he was snoring. What else could I do? I stretched out on the pillows on the floor and waited for him to wake up. Luckily, he had a laptop computer that was hooked into the resort's wi-fi, so I streamed movies while he snored.

Three hours later, he woke up.

Damian yawned loudly, stretched without moving much at all, and groaned. He squinted at me. "On a scale of one to ten, how mad are you?"

"Zero."

His brows rose, but then he winced as if that little action hurt. "Guess I should explain."

I shut the laptop and sat up, holding the computer on my lap. "Yeah, that might be a good idea."

"You see, Ollie was stressed out. And I couldn't think of a way to help him relax and stop worrying so much." He wriggled around until he was lying on his back and rubbed his forehead. "Admittedly, this wasn't my best idea ever."

"No kidding? Huh." I splayed my palms on the computer, tapping my fingertips on it. "So tell me, Your Ludar Highness, what exactly did you hope to accomplish by getting the two of you hammered? I'm assuming that was the plan."

"Yeah, it was." He shrugged. "I wasn't doing much thinking at the time. My best friend needed help, so I, uh…helped." Damian glanced at me sideways, looking almost sheepish. "Ollie was a lot happier after we pigged out and got smashed."

"Of course he was happier. Ollie was high as a kite." I leaned forward, my face a foot from his. "You were too."

"I'm sorry. Trust me, I'm regretting it now. And by the way, I knew it was a bad idea, but I did it anyway. For my friend."

"Mara was stressed too, but I didn't hand her a keg of beer."

"It's different for women. Guys don't do the whole heart-to-heart, let's-share-our-innermost-feelings bullshit."

"Well, at least you didn't hire a hooker." I shimmied closer. "What was Ollie so stressed about? I know why Mara's anxious, but what has Ollie got to be worried about?"

"He's scared he won't be a good father or husband. And he feels guilty for not knowing how to make Mara feel better."

"Do you know about her, um, condition?"

He stared at me for a moment. "Do you know?"

"Yes."

"So do I, if we're talking about the same thing."

We were both trying not to divulge a secret that we each thought the other knew, but we didn't want to betray a confidence from a friend. Mara told me, so Ollie must have told Damian. They'd been best friends since childhood.

"Mara's pregnant," I said. "That's what Ollie told you, right?"

Damian nodded.

I sighed. "She's got her hormones going crazy, but what's Ollie's excuse? He can't honestly believe he'll be a bad father. He'll be great at it."

"They'll both be great parents. We know that, but they're too anxious to realize it. They are getting married in five days."

"And they just found out they're having a baby. That is a lot of stress piled on them. Wish I could do more to help."

Damian raised a hand to cup my cheek. "You've done more than anybody to help Mara. Taking care of all the wedding details must've been a huge weight off her shoulders. You've done way more to help them than I have."

"Getting Ollie drunk might not have been the smartest idea ever, but you did it because you love your best friend."

"Ollie might be my best friend, but you're the best everything to me."

I wasn't sure that statement made sense, but I understood what he meant. If we hadn't said we loved each other last night, maybe I wouldn't have gotten it. But we had, and I did.

"You're my best everything too," I said, turning my face into his palm to kiss it.

He pulled his hand away and grimaced. "Need some water."

"Let's get you into bed first."

I helped him sit up, then hooked an arm around his waist while he laid his arm across my shoulders. We got him into bed without too much trouble, and I tucked him in.

"Be back in a few minutes," I said, kissing his forehead. "You rest. I'll bring water and some saltines."

"Thanks, baby. You're the best."

When I came back ten minutes later, he was still awake and sitting up. I'd brought him water but also a sports drink, for the electrolytes. He sipped that while I opened the box of saltines. I'd brought aspirin too, which he swallowed with the sports drink.

"Nibble on this," I said as I offered him a cracker.

After a few minutes of sipping and nibbling, he waved away any more. "My head's pounding. Think I need another nap."

"Lie on your back. I'll give you my patented headache relief massage."

"You patented it?"

"Not literally. I mean it's guaranteed to work."

He stretched out on his back, his head on the pillow.

I sat beside him, near his head, and began to massage his scalp with my fingertips.

"Mm," he moaned, "that feels so good."

For a few minutes, I massaged his scalp and his temples while humming softly. Then he drifted off, his lips curled up in the sweetest little smile. While he slept, I wandered outside to check on Mara and Ollie, but I ran into Eve first while she was exiting the guest house.

"Ollie's fine," she said when I reached her. "Mara is taking care of him, and she's not even upset about it."

"Mara's a lot stronger than even she knows."

"That's for sure. How's Damian?"

I couldn't help laughing a little. "Wishing he'd come up with a better plan to help Ollie relax."

Eve laughed a bit too. "Val thought it was a great idea. Men. They all think the answer to any problem is booze or sex."

"Good thing they have us to straighten them out, or they'd kill every brain cell they've got."

"So true." Eve tipped her head to the side like she was considering me. "Mara told me how you stepped up to take care of the wedding stuff. Sounds like you've done an amazing job in a short time."

"I owed Mara. After my stupid behavior when we first met."

"You aren't still feeling guilty about that, are you? We all understand what you were going through back then."

"No, I'm not feeling guilty." I shoved my hands into the pockets of my shorts. "But Mara has been such a good friend to me, and I want her to have the wedding of her dreams."

"She told me what you've done. The wedding will be perfect." Eve gave me that head-tipped look again. "Have you ever considered doing that sort of thing for a living?"

"I wanted to be an event coordinator, but my parents thought I should be a doctor. So I became a pharmacy technician instead. Thought that might make them happy, but it didn't."

"You're happy here, aren't you? We certainly love you."

"And I love all you guys too. I love this resort. It feels like home to me."

Damian felt like home too. Even when he got wasted.

Eve set her hands on her hips. "How would you like to become the event coordinator for Au Naturel Naturist Resort? You could do freelance jobs on the side too, like Mara does with the apartment complexes she owns."

For a moment, I could do nothing except stare at her. Had Eve just offered me my dream job? Yeah, she had.

"Are you serious?" I asked. "Because if you are, my answer is yes, yes, yes."

"The job is yours."

I shrieked and leaped up and down, grinning like an idiot. I even clapped my hands and did a little celebration dance.

All the naturists on the lawn turned to look this way, and every one of them smiled and cheered, though they had no idea why I was so happy. I recognized every face. These people were like family to me.

Maybe that's what Damian and Monica had both been trying to tell me. Family was what you made it, and my family was here—with a bunch of naked people.

I hugged Eve. "Thank you so much. This is my dream come true, and I won't let you down."

"Never for a second thought you might."

"Damian will be so happy." I wrinkled my nose. "Unless his hangover is still in high gear."

"Go tell him, sweetie. And welcome to the family."

I raced back into the wagon and leaped onto the bed.

Damian opened his eyes. "What's going on? Is the room actually spinning?"

"No, it's not. Sorry I woke you up, but I have amazing news and I couldn't wait to share it with you."

He yawned and scrubbed his face with both hands, then sat up. "What's the news?"

"I'm the new event coordinator at Au Naturel Naturist Resort."

Damian grinned and kissed me.

Chapter Twenty-Eight

Damian

Heidi must've loved me a lot if she could forgive me for getting drunk with Ollie. She understood why I did it, even if she disagreed with my methods. Once she found out she had a job here at the resort, she didn't care about my dumb idea anymore. Val and Eve did not fire me, though the next morning, they gave me and Ollie a speech about priorities and duties. We nodded at every point they made and promised never again to get drunk on a day when we were supposed to be working.

They weren't angry. But they ran a business, not a home for idiots who thought getting hammered was a reasonable solution for stress relief. Of course they had to give us both a talking-to. We deserved it.

Heidi and I spent the rest of that day lounging in bed while I nursed my hangover. Even after I recovered from my bender, we didn't feel like leaving the wagon except to get food. I wasn't up for sex, literally, so we watched movies and talked.

The next day, we teamed up to finish the wedding prep and keep the bride and groom from going nuts again. Val and Eve decided that was part of our jobs this week, so we didn't get in trouble for not doing our usual jobs. Well, my usual job. Heidi didn't officially start hers until after the wedding.

Two days before the big event, Ollie's family arrived, and an hour later, Mara's parents arrived. My family showed up too. The rest of the guests would be here in the afternoon, but we had lots to do today to get the three families settled in and prepared for the big day. Tonight would be the rehearsal dinner, but the bride and groom had decided against having a bachelor party or a bachelorette party. Instead, we would have one big celebration on the lawn.

Somehow, we survived those two days without any hitches. Mom and I offered free palm and tarot readings to everyone, and we put on a good show for the guests. I'd learned my flair for drama from my mother, so when the two of us collaborated on a show, it was the most fun anyone could have. Heidi was our sexy assistant. Though this wasn't a magic show, we included Heidi just because we wanted to. Mom had suggested it, and I loved having my girl with me while I did my Ludar prince shtick.

Afterward, she called me "the hottest gypsy on earth" and declared I was not a Dracula knockoff after all. I bit her neck just to prove her wrong, but it was only a love bite.

The party Friday night included music, both recorded songs and a live performance by Ollie. He played guitar and sang. Mara even joined him for one song, helping him croon "Bridge Over Troubled Water," which had become their song ever since the day Ollie had sung it to her when they had a private picnic not long after they met.

Heidi and I led a round of charades that resulted in plenty of raucous laughter.

Ollie spent the night in my room to keep up the tradition of the bride and groom not seeing each other until the ceremony.

I slept in the wagon with Heidi. Yeah, we did more than just sleep. When I made love to Heidi that night, I realized I'd fallen even deeper in love with her. Watching this woman wrangle the families and wedding guests, not to mention making sure every last detail got taken care of so Mara and Ollie would have their dream wedding, proved to me what I'd known all along. Heidi Mackenzie was one hell of a woman.

Saturday came so fast. The big day was here.

I didn't see Heidi until we got to the church. Ollie and Mara had considered holding their wedding at the resort, but they decided to go the traditional route instead and have it at the same church where Eve and Val had tied the knot. It was a beautiful building, with stained-glass windows and classic architecture.

Heidi came running up to me in the vestibule. "Can I talk to you alone for a minute?"

"Sure. Is something wrong?"

"No. Just come with me."

I excused myself, telling my parents I'd see them after the ceremony, and followed Heidi into what turned out to be a supply closet.

"What are we doing here?" I asked. "Please don't tell me Mara's getting cold feet."

"No, she's fine. Feeling cold isn't the problem." She backed me up to the wall, pressing her body against me. "I'm having a weird reaction to being the maid of honor."

"Are you getting hives?"

"No, I'm getting hot." She hooked a finger inside my waistband and tugged. "Fuck me, Damian."

"We're in a church. Isn't it a sin or something?"

"Do you care?"

I thought about the question for a few seconds, then wondered why the hell I was thinking about it. Heidi wanted sex. I was a guy, so of course, I wanted that too. My dick was firming up, so it wanted that for sure. But I still had this weird feeling that I shouldn't desecrate a sacred place or something like that.

Maybe falling in love had softened my naughty side, because I found myself easing Heidi away from my body. "I'll fuck you at the reception, okay? Not here in the church. It's Mara and Ollie's big day, after all."

"You'll do it at the reception? Promise?"

I couldn't help laughing. "You have my solemn word. I will drag you into the nearest closet and make you scream—at the reception."

Heidi took a big breath and let it out slowly. "Wow. Who knew a wedding could make me so horny?"

"Everybody reacts differently to big life events." I cradled her face in my hands and kissed the tip of her nose. "Let's go do our wedding jobs. Can't leave Ollie without a best man or Mara without a maid of honor."

"I love you so much, Damian."

Smirking, I slapped her ass. "I kinda like you too, Heidi."

We left the closet hand in hand but said goodbye in the vestibule so we could attend to our duties as maid of honor and best man. Since Ollie and Mara didn't have a flower girl or ring bearer, just the bridesmaids and groomsmen, Ollie led us guys into the chapel and straight to the altar where we would wait for the ladies to do their thing. First, the guests had to file in and take their seats, with Sylvester Norris as the usher. Yeah, he seemed kind of old for the job, but Sly was like family to all of us. He had a great time executing his duties, though he did more than show people to their seats. He told jokes and made a grand, sweeping gesture with his arm to let the guests know where to sit. He also said, in a booming voice, "Please be seated here. It has the best view in the house."

Yeah, every guest got the best view. Amazing, right?

Sly was full of it, but at least he was enjoying himself.

I let my gaze wander over the decorations that had transformed this simple chapel into a dream venue for a wedding. Heidi was responsible for all of it. Garlands of fresh greenery and daisies draped over the backs of the pews and around the edges of the altar, not to mention the doorways and the vestibule. The garlands didn't just have flowers and leafy stuff, though. I also saw sprays of baby's breath and sprigs of fern leaves. Heidi had gone all out. It was the perfect backdrop for the wedding of two naturists who worked at a rural nudist resort.

Once everyone had taken their seats, a violin began to play. The bridesmaids ambled down the aisle toward us with Heidi in front, all of them wearing pale-green dresses that had small daisies sewn onto the neckline. Heidi wore her hair up in a loose style that let tendrils hang down to kiss her cheeks. Eve followed Heidi to the altar. She looked pretty too, but not as beautiful as the maid of honor.

They took their places opposite us guys. I stood beside Ollie with Val Silva on my other side.

Any second, Mara would enter the chapel.

The violin music stopped, and for two seconds, we all waited in silence.

An organ began to play the wedding march.

Mara walked through the doors holding a bouquet of daisies and baby's breath, guided down the aisle by her dad. Peter Severins looked like he was fighting back tears, and when I glanced at where Sheryl Severins sat in the first pew, she was doing more than fighting back tears. They streamed down her cheeks. Ollie's mom sat right next to Sheryl, and she was crying too while the moms clasped each other's hands.

Mara looked like an angel in her flowing white dress and lacy veil that draped down her back and covered most of her hair, though it didn't cover her face. She smiled at Ollie with the most beautiful look of pure love on her face as she slowly approached the altar.

Would Heidi ever look at me that way? I glanced at her, and as if fate had inspired us both, she looked at me at the same time. Maybe I was gazing at her the way Mara had gazed at Ollie. I couldn't say for sure, but I felt a strangely good pressure in my chest and a gentle warmth that spread through me from head to toe.

Heidi blinked away tears, or tried to, and sniffled. She kept smiling at me almost the same way Mara had gazed at Ollie.

I hardly noticed the rest of the ceremony. Ollie and Mara said their vows, both of them crying, and promised to love and respect each other from this day forward. I watched them exchange rings. Why did I get choked up when they did that? I'd never been the sentimental type, but to see my best friend marrying the only woman he'd ever really loved, who loved him too... Okay, I got sentimental. I turned my head to the side and wiped my eyes so no one else would see.

Finally, the big moment came—the kiss.

Ollie cradled Mara's face in his hands and pressed his mouth to hers.

Cheers and clapping erupted inside the chapel, echoing off the high ceiling.

Ollie pulled Mara into his arms, still kissing her. They kept kissing for so long that somebody shouted, "Come on, Ollie, we want to eat. You can make out with Mara later."

Who shouted that? Sylvester, of course.

The newly minted husband and wife trotted down the aisle and out the doors, with the rest of us close behind. They raced across the vestibule and out the main doors, then climbed into a waiting limousine.

Another, bigger limo waited to ferry the bridesmaids and groomsmen to the reception venue.

Heidi and I sat beside each other during the ride, holding hands.

Like a real gentleman, Val had offered to be Bailey Jackson's "date" for the reception since the teenager was the only kid in attendance. Eve was his "secondary date," but she didn't mind coming in number two. Bailey was thrilled to be included in the wedding party and to see her brother get hitched. We arrived seconds after the bride and groom, but the party was already in full swing.

Music. Laughter. Dancing. And yeah, food. Sylvester wouldn't starve today.

Everyone was having a great time. Val danced with Bailey and showed her some classy moves, then he danced with Eve. I danced with lots of women but kept missing out on taking Heidi for a whirl since every other guy here wanted to hold the blonde bombshell in his arms. We glimpsed each other on the dance floor, but I'd have to wait awhile longer for my chance.

But it was my turn to dance with Mara.

"You're the most beautiful bride ever," I told her as I took her hand and we assumed the appropriate pose, moving slowly to the music.

"Thank you, Damian. But I'm sure you'll change your mind about that when you and Heidi get married."

Though I kept dancing, her statement stunned me. Maybe it shouldn't have, but then, Heidi and I hadn't been a couple for long.

"Married?" I said. "We're nowhere near that point yet."

"But you're moving toward it faster every day. Aren't you?"

"I don't know. Not thinking about that stuff."

Mara's lips curved upward in a knowing smile. "Oh yes, you are."

"No, I—"

She nodded past my shoulder and stepped back. "Heidi's ready for you."

I glanced over my shoulder and saw Heidi, standing alone at the edge of the dance floor and smiling at me.

"Go," Mara said. "And think about what I said. There's no such thing as too soon when you're with the right person."

Mara kissed my cheek and trotted off to find her husband.

I walked over to Heidi and held out my hand. "May I have this dance?"

"Yes, please." She settled her hand in mine. "I've been waiting for this dance forever."

And I'd been waiting for her forever. I just hadn't realized that until today.

Chapter Twenty-Nine

Heidi

Damian guided us around the dance floor, one hand on the small of my back and the other clasping mine. He looked gorgeous in his tuxedo, even better than when he'd worn his black suit. The expression on his face made me feel warm in the sweetest way and made my throat tighten. Was I giving him that same adoring look? I did adore him, so yeah, I must've been gazing at him that way.

The wedding had been beautiful, emotional, perfect. I loved watching Ollie and Mara speak their vows, but I loved dancing with Damian even more. Somehow, I could feel blissfully at peace and so damn horny all at the same time.

He bent his head to whisper in my ear, "Still want to get it on? I saw a closet in the hallway."

"Can you read my mind? I was just thinking about how horny I am." I slid my hand up to his neck and tickled his nape. "You make me feel every kind of good there is. And yes, I'd love to get it on with you in a closet or anywhere."

"Glad to hear it." He led me off the dance floor and toward the double doors that opened into the main hallway of the community center, which tonight served as a wedding reception hall. He glanced around as we exited the room, and the doors swung shut behind us. "You did such an amazing job with the decorations, and it's even more impressive considering how little time you had."

My cheeks warmed up. No one had ever complimented a job I'd done, certainly not the way he just did. "Thank you, but Mara and her mom had already done some of the work."

"They say you did ninety-nine percent of it."

"No, I just—"

He pulled us to a stop in the middle of the vestibule and turned toward me, grasping both my hands. "Don't do that, Heidi."

"What?"

"Don't downplay how much work you put into this. You did it. You." He tugged me closer. "You are an amazing woman. That's why I love you. That's why everyone loves you, but me most of all."

Gazing into his eyes, I knew he meant every word. "Thank you, Damian."

He took hold of a lock of my hair, twining it around his finger. "Marry me, Heidi."

"Huh?" Yeah, that was my response. One grunted syllable. I couldn't make any other sounds, not with him looking at me with so much love and sincerity on his face and in his eyes. My pulse pounded in my ears, my heart thudded in my chest, and the sweetest warmth I'd ever experienced glowed inside me. I loved him. I wanted to marry him. Now, if I could only get those words to come out of my mouth. But again, I could speak only one syllable. "Yes."

He cradled my face in his hands. "Are you sure? 'Huh, yes' isn't the most definitive answer."

"Sorry. I was surprised, that's all." I laid my hands over his, where he still held them on my cheeks. "Yes, Damian, my answer is yes. I love you, and I can't wait to marry you."

He smiled, and though it wasn't a big grin, it conveyed all the emotions he felt for me better than the most exuberant grin could. When he kissed me, he did it with the same heartfelt emotion, pressing his lips to mine but not deepening the kiss. He held his mouth to mine for a moment that seemed to last forever, but only in the best way.

Then he pulled away, his lips curving into another heartfelt smile. "Didn't mean to blurt out the question like that, but I suddenly couldn't wait."

"I'm glad you blurted it out."

"Maybe we shouldn't tell everyone until later. This is Mara and Ollie's big night."

"Yeah, we should wait." I looped my arms around his neck. "We'll have the best wedding planner ever, huh?"

"Definitely." He linked his hands at the small of my back. "And I'll have the best partner for the rest of my life."

"Me too."

He hugged me tight and kissed me.

The doors to the reception room swung open.

We turned our heads in that direction.

Val and Eve locked the doors in the open position, then finally noticed us. Eve smiled. Val arched one brow and smirked.

"The bride and groom are ready to head out," Eve said. "If you two can press pause on the make-out session for a few minutes."

Damian peeled our bodies apart and straightened his tux jacket.

He and Val opened the main doors and held them, each leaning back against a door. Eve and I stood beside them.

The happy couple walked out of the reception hall hand in hand, grinning and whispering to each other, while their parents and Ollie's sister followed close behind. Once everyone exited through the main doors, the rest of us hurried down the steps after them, heading for the waiting limo. Sunset glowed pink and purple in the western sky, providing just enough light for the big goodbye.

Everyone hugged Mara and Ollie and wished them the best of everything.

When I hugged Mara, she whispered in my ear, "I know you and Damian will be the next to say 'I do,' and it won't be long at all." She drew her head back to aim a knowing smile at me. "Maybe he's already popped the question?"

How did she know? Maybe it showed on my face. "Don't worry about me and Damian. Go, have a fabulous honeymoon. I expect Ollie to be completely exhausted when you guys get home."

Val opened the limo door.

Ollie held out his hand to help Mara into the car.

While the limo drove away, and the ubiquitous tin cans rattled along behind it, I slipped an arm around Damian's waist and leaned my head against his shoulder. My throat went thick. Tears stung my eyes. Ollie and Mara, the two sweetest people on earth, had found their happily ever after, and so had I. Damian gave it to me.

And we were engaged.

Oh. My. God.

Damian kissed the top of my head. "Don't worry. We can get married tomorrow or wait five years. I don't care as long as I have you."

"Let's not wait five years, but tomorrow might be a bit too soon. I need to plan our wedding, you know. Plus, I've got my awesome new job."

"No rush. I'll wait forever for you."

God, I loved him.

After the limo drove out of sight, everyone went back inside to enjoy the party. Damian and I didn't run off to that closet after all. We stayed with our friends to celebrate. I wasn't disappointed at all because, hey, I loved a party. Everybody knew that. Maybe I hadn't let myself really cut loose in way too long, but tonight, I got back to being the old me—the real me. I partied hearty, doing every dance move I could pull off in this dress, and Damian joined me for every single silly thing I wanted to do. He came up with ideas of his own too, like juggling deviled eggs. Seriously, he did that. Damian called it "an old Ludar wedding tradition," but everyone knew he was making that up because he smirked and winked when he issued his proclamation.

That night, Damian and I slept in my room in the guest house.

After that, the days went by so fast. The families hung around for a couple more days to kick back, which gave us more time to spend with the Petrescus. Damian and I debated whether to tell them our happy news yet, but we finally decided they should hear it from us in person. So we took Damian's parents, his brother, his sister-in-law, and their two kids for a nature walk. Once we got well away from the resort, with no one else around, we stopped the group and faced them, hand in hand.

"We have some news," Damian said.

Monica raised her hands in a grand gesture and smiled. "You're engaged."

"Jeez, Mom, you could've at least let us tell you ourselves."

Adrian Petrescu chuckled. "Mothers always know these things."

Monica held two fingers to each of her temples and squinted. "I foresee children. Many children." She smiled and winked at us. "I foresee that happening soon."

Stefan grinned. "Better hope the kids look like Heidi, not my rat-faced brother."

"Uncle Damian is cute," said the niece of the man in question. "That's what my friends keep saying, anyway."

Damian rolled his eyes. "Is anybody going to congratulate us?"

"Of course, dear," Monica said. She threw her arms around both of us. "Congratulations. I knew from the moment I saw you two together that this would happen. You're destined for a long and happy life together. The spirits have assured me of that." Monica kissed Damian's cheek, then mine. "And your union will produce many grandchildren for me to spoil."

Damian half-scowled, half-smiled. "Mom, would you get off the 'many children' prophecy already? You're scaring Heidi."

"No, she's not," I said with a laugh. "Bring on the army of Ludar babies. I can handle it. They'll only be half Ludar, though."

"Nonsense," Monica said, patting my cheek. "You are one of us now. Ludar by desire, if not by blood."

"Thank you, Monica. That's so kind of you to say."

"Call me Mom. You're joining the family, after all."

My throat tightened. She wanted me to call her Mom. How would my actual mother feel about me marrying a gypsy and joining his family? I'd have to tell my parents, but just thinking about that made me slightly nauseous.

Damian's mother hugged me. "Don't worry, dear. Your parents will see the light one day."

The families went home the next day, but we hadn't shared our news with anyone other than Damian's family. When Ollie and Mara came home a week later, we knew it was time to break the news.

Damian being, well, Damian, he decided to make a big splash. He waited until everyone was gathered in the dining hall, including Val, Eve, Mara, and Ollie. We were seated at the same table with them. Our friends had gotten a touch suspicious when Damian insisted we all must eat in the dining hall tonight, but they went along with it.

Now, Damian jumped onto the table and hollered, "May I have your attention, please. Heidi and I have an announcement to make."

Everyone stopped talking. All eyes turned to us.

Damian bent to offer me his hand.

I accepted it and climbed onto the table with him.

He slipped his arm around me and announced, "We're getting married."

Cheers and whoops filled the hall, the noise almost deafening but filled with real joy.

Damian scooped me up in his arms and leaped off the table, landing flat on his feet inches behind the chairs we had occupied thirty seconds earlier. He kissed me, quick and hard. Then he hoisted me above his head. "The Ludar prince has claimed his mate."

When I glanced down at him, he winked at me.

Damian set me down amid even louder cheers and whoops.

At that moment, I knew our wedding would be one wild event. And I couldn't wait for that.

Chapter Thirty

Damian

A few days after we announced our engagement to our friends and a crowd of naturists, Heidi and I got on a plane to go visit her parents. She had suggested it. Though she was keeping up a brave face, I knew she dreaded telling her mom and dad about us, especially since she'd never mentioned me to them. Heidi admitted to me she hadn't spoken to her parents in months, not since they chastised her for dumping that douchebag cheater she'd kept going back to every time he begged her to forgive him. Well, every time until the last time. Heidi had found her inner strength at last.

We had one last hurdle to jump over. I was about to meet her parents.

Heidi had told them she was bringing her new boyfriend, but she'd wanted to hold off on sharing the engagement news until we were there in person to tell them.

Ethan and Janice Mackenzie lived in Omaha, Nebraska, though separately since they were divorced. Janice still lived in the same cookie-cutter house inside the same cookie-cutter gated community where Heidi had grown up. Nothing wrong with that, but I couldn't see Heidi feeling happy and free in a place like this. They had rules for what people could do with their yards, how often they had to mow and prune the bushes, what kind of Christmas lights they could put up, and lots more stuff. No wonder Heidi had needed to escape to the naturist resort.

I knew she'd been living in a small apartment in Omaha for years. She gave up that apartment a few days after we got engaged. Heidi Mackenzie belonged at the resort where everyone loved her, and where she could be herself without fear of offending anyone.

Yeah, I had a feeling her parents would be offended big time when they met me.

Heidi rang the doorbell and started wringing her hands.

I clasped her left hand, giving it a reassuring squeeze, and glanced at the engagement ring sparkling on her finger. Then I kissed her cheek. "Relax. If they act like dicks, you've got backup."

She smiled tightly. "I know. Thank you for coming with me."

"Just think of me as your Ludar knight, ready to defend your honor to the death."

The door opened, and a gray-haired man furrowed his brows at us. "You brought a man with you."

"Yeah, Dad," Heidi said. "I told you Damian was coming."

Ethan Mackenzie grunted. "Guess you better come inside. Not sure how your mother will react. You know she doesn't do well with the sorts of men you like to take up with. Whatever happened to Grant? He was the only good one."

I could see Heidi was clenching her jaw, but she maintained her polite demeanor.

Ethan led us inside and straight to the dining room where the table had been set up with places for four people. If they'd forgotten Heidi was bringing a guest, why had they set the table for us? I guessed Ethan and Janice just liked making their daughter feel as if she'd done something wrong.

Heidi's mom walked through the swinging door to the kitchen. She was carrying a roast on a platter, which she set down on the table. "At least you're here on time for dinner, Heidi."

As we got closer to the table, I saw name cards in front of each plate. I was supposed to sit across the table from Heidi.

Screw that.

I pretended not to notice the name cards and sat down in the chair next to Heidi's. She bit her lip for half a second, then settled onto the chair beside me, the one reserved for her. Ethan sat at the head of the table beside Heidi. His wife took the chair across from her daughter. I grabbed the place setting meant for me and moved it over to this side of the table.

Janice pursed her lips.

Neither of Heidi's parents had bothered with introductions.

I decided what the hell, I'd do it for them. "I'm Damian Petrescu, by the way. And you are Janice and Ethan Mackenzie. It's nice to meet you. Thank you for cooking such a nice meal for us."

The rest of the meal had already been laid out on the table before Janice brought in the roast. We had broccoli and cauliflower, mashed potatoes, and hot rolls. She really had made a nice meal, so I hadn't been lying when I thanked her for that. Now if she would only start acting like a decent human being, the night would be perfect.

"Petrescu," Janice said, pronouncing my last name as if she'd never heard anything so alien. "Is that Eastern European?"

"Romanian."

"How interesting." Her stiff tone and stiff posture suggested she didn't like having to converse with me. "Isn't that interesting, Ethan?"

"Yeah, it's damn fascinating." Heidi's dad shoved a forkful of meat into his mouth and talked while chewing, his gaze on me. "You one of those commies from the Eastern Bloc?"

"No, I'm descended from a long line of proud Ludar."

He paused in the middle of hacking off another piece of the roast. "Loo-what?"

"Ludar. My family, on both my mother's and my father's side, can trace our lineage back hundreds of years to the earliest Rom tribes."

"You're from Italy? Thought you said Romania."

I couldn't help smiling. Lots of people got confused when I talked about my heritage. "Rom is spelled R-O-M. It's not the city in Italy. It's who we are. The Ludar came from the Rom tribes, which most people call gypsies."

Janice's eyes flew wide. "Gypsies? Oh dear lord, what sort of man have you taken up with this time, Heidi?"

My fiancée slammed her fork down on her plate, making it wobble and smack back down. "Damian is a good man. The best I've ever met, way better than Grant, who you and Dad thought was the perfect match for me."

"He was. I'm sure he'd take you back if—"

"Grant cheated on me repeatedly. I kept taking him back, but never again. Damian is a thousand times the man Grant Busch will ever be."

"But this…gentleman is a gypsy." Janice spoke that word like it was the worst kind of swearing.

"Damian is a wonderful man." She raised her left hand, aiming that sparkling diamond toward her mom. "You guys didn't even notice this, did you? Damian and I are engaged."

Both her parents gaped at her.

I clasped her hand and kissed her ring.

"We know nothing about this man," Ethan said. "You can't marry a complete stranger."

"He's not a stranger to me," Heidi told him.

"Does he even have a job? Or will you be traveling around like hobos?"

"I'm the concierge at a resort," I said.

"What kind of resort?" Ethan asked.

Heidi and I glanced at each other, and I knew from her expression that she wanted me to tell them the truth, no matter how they reacted. "I work at Au Naturel Naturist Resort."

Janice contorted her face into an expression of genuine horror. "Isn't that the unseemly place where Heidi insists on taking her vacations? That's a nudist resort."

"Yeah, it is. We both work there now."

"My daughter cannot work at a place like that. Taking vacations there is bad enough, but—"

"Stop it, Mom," Heidi said. "I work there, and I'm marrying Damian. Get over it."

I was so proud of Heidi that I wanted to hug her.

But she wasn't done yet. The powerhouse hidden inside that easygoing exterior had lots more to say.

Chapter Thirty-One

Heidi

I pushed my chair back and got up, needing to stand tall while I told my parents all the things I should've told them a long time ago. Damian had helped me see how much I'd let my mom and dad affect my life and my choices, and he'd shown me I was done with that garbage. I loved him so much for getting the ball rolling, but now I needed to finish it.

"Yes, my favorite place on earth is a nudist resort," I said, my voice calmer than I could've hoped. I felt calm too, surprisingly so considering what I intended to do. "I feel more at home there than I ever did here with you two. The friends I've made at the resort have become like family to me. Honestly, they *are* my family now, more than my own parents have ever been."

"Heidi—"

I cut my mom off with a raised hand. "Let me finish. You're my parents, and I love you despite all the ways you've made me feel unworthy of your love. Every time you put me in the middle of one of your arguments, I thought it was my fault you couldn't get along. I thought it was my fault you got divorced. No boyfriend I ever had was good enough for you except for the creep who slept with every woman he met and told me it was my fault for not satisfying his needs."

My parents stared at me like I'd grown five extra heads.

But I had a bit more to say. "I should've told you all of this years ago, but I was afraid you'd never speak to me again if I did. Well, I don't care about that anymore. Cut me out of your lives if you want. You've pretty much done that already, but I'll keep the hope alive that one day you will take a hard look at your behavior and decide to end the cycle. When you do that, I'll welcome you back into my life."

They still stared at me.

Good. Maybe that meant I'd shocked them enough that they might actually think about what I'd told them.

"Let's go, Damian," I said. "I'm not hungry anymore."

He got up. "Neither am I."

From my purse, I pulled out the little pad of paper I always carried with me. After scribbling my new phone number and address on the pad, I tore off the page and set it on the table. "This is where you can find me. Good night, Mom. Good night, Dad."

Damian and I walked out of the house and drove to our hotel. We didn't get much sleep that night, though not because of stress or anxiety. He made love to me for hours, and in between each session, we talked and ate snacks and sipped wine. Confronting my parents should have been the most stressful thing I'd ever done, but instead, it had turned into a cathartic moment. The fears I'd lived with for so long melted away. Whether my parents ever wised up didn't matter. I was free.

The next morning, we flew home and got back to our life. And it was "ours" now, not mine or his. We shared a room in the guest house and wound up hunting for a house to buy in tandem with Ollie and Mara. Joint house hunting was a lot more fun than doing it by ourselves. Ollie and Mara found their dream house first, but then Damian and I realized we'd found ours too without even thinking about it.

We bought the house next door to theirs.

The two homes were separated by a few hundred feet, but it seemed appropriate to live so nearby considering that Ollie was Damian's best friend and Mara was mine. The houses sat on the outskirts of town, bordered by woods and fields on three sides, so it felt a lot like how we'd lived at the resort. The commute to work didn't bother us at all. The four of us carpooled.

A few weeks later, I handled my first event for a guest. I organized a birthday party for Ruth Norris. It was a hoot and a half, and it gave me more confidence in my ability to coordinate events for strangers since I'd managed to do two for my friends. My family. That's what they were. Not just friends, but the family I'd chosen for myself.

I still held out hope for my parents, but I didn't dwell on them. I had too much of my own life to keep me busy—and happy.

One day, Eve found me in the resort office. She marched straight up to the desk, where I was sitting while I plotted out a calendar of daily events for our guests. Eve bounced on her toes, biting her lip while she seemed to struggle not to grin. Her eyes shined with excitement too.

"What's up, Evie?" I asked. "You look like you've got amazing news. Are you pregnant?"

"No, not yet." She clasped her hands in front of her chest, bouncing even more. "We have a huge opportunity that could boost the resort's image and expand our demographics big time."

"That's amazing." I stood up. "What is this huge opportunity?"

"A wedding. Here at the resort." Though she still seemed excited, her almost grin turned slightly anxious as she bit down harder on her lip. "But it relies on you. I know you're still settling into your new job, and you haven't done anything this big yet, but..." She grabbed my hands and stopped bouncing. "Please don't say no until you've talked to him."

"Who?"

"The groom. He's British, and his fiancée is Scottish, and they have lots of relatives and friends in America and the UK." Eve gripped my hands tighter. "They have a *lot* of relatives on the bride's side. I mean a *lot*. They want to get married here, but we'll need to arrange for accommodations in town too since we don't have the capacity for this big a gathering. Then there will be events in the week leading up to the wedding, but the bride's sister wants to help out with that. The rest is up to us—and you."

The bride and groom had so many relatives and friends that we'd need to put some of them up in town. How many people would there be? Sheesh, it must be one enormous family.

"Um, well," I started, biting my lip much the way Eve had bitten hers, "you know I'm new at this event coordinator stuff. This sounds like a huge deal, and I don't want to screw it up. Maybe you should hire a professional."

"I have hired one. You." She grasped my shoulders. "You can do this, Heidi. We all believe in you. Plus, Mara and I can handle the logistics. The boys can help out too, with the heavy lifting and stuff. You will be the big boss, the one making the plans that we execute."

"Well… I don't know. What if I screw up our big chance to expand our demographics?"

"You won't. Talk to Damian. He'll convince you." Eve hugged me. "You can do this, Heidi. Trust me, you can."

How could I say no? Eve and Val had given me a job that I had no experience or training to do and trusted me to do it right. So far, I had. But a huge event like this ratcheted up my anxiety. Still, I refused to shy away from a challenge. And I had my new family to stand by me.

"Okay," I said. "I'll do it."

Eve, the level-headed resort owner, shrieked and leaped up and down. She dragged me into a bear hug, then bolted out the door.

Wow, this event must've been a doozy. Maybe it would flush the resort with cash so we could make even more improvements.

I found Damian at the gypsy wagon. He'd just finished up with a young couple and was standing outside the wagon shaking their hands and wishing them a good stay at the resort. When they walked away, I approached him.

"Did you hear about the massively huge event Eve set up?" I asked.

"Yeah, Ollie told me. You're nervous about coordinating the whole thing, aren't you?"

"Of course I am. But I'll do it anyway. I need to do it, to prove I can handle this job."

He slung an arm around my waist and tugged me close. "You can deal with anything, baby. After the way you stood up to your parents, I know there's nothing you can't handle."

"I really, really love you."

"Good. Because it's time to arrange our wedding."

Maybe I should've felt anxious about that since I had this other huge event to plan, but thinking about our wedding relaxed me. I couldn't wait to organize that. Couldn't wait to marry Damian.

Eve came running up from the direction of the guest house. She stopped a few feet from us, breathing hard. "Almost forgot. That British guy is coming tomorrow to check out the resort and talk to us in person about what events he and his fiancée would like to have here."

"We'll be ready," I said. "The Au Naturel Reserve Army is ready for action. And by that I mean me, Damian, Ollie, Mara, and Val."

"Guess that makes me the general."

I saluted her. "Yes, ma'am."

Eve grinned and sprinted for the caretaker's house.

"Ready to plan two weddings at once?" I asked Damian.

"Absolutely. I'm your slave, so order me to do anything you want." He bent his head until his nose bumped mine. "And I do mean anything. I'd love to be your personal masseur, strictly for stress relief."

"You are fantastic at relieving my stress."

We headed back to the office and got to work.

The next morning, we hosted our own little British invasion. Our guest didn't sing pop songs, but he was from that other country over there. He arrived in a rented car. Though Eve had offered to pick him up at the airport, he had declined their offer, saying he preferred to drive himself. His fiancée wasn't coming with him, Eve had said.

Val, Eve, Ollie, Mara, Damian, and I waited in the driveway as our guest parked and got out.

Wow, if all Brits were as hot as this guy, I'd have to drag Damian over to the UK for our honeymoon just so I could enjoy the eye candy. This Brit had a muscular body and a beautiful face, with whiskey-brown eyes and hair to match.

He strode up to our little army. "Which of you is Eve?"

"I am," our fearless leader said. She offered the man her hand. "Welcome to Au Naturel Naturist Resort, Dr. Thorne."

"Call me Alex." He shook her hand. "It's a pleasure to meet you, Eve, after the phone discussions we've had. Catriona would've loved to meet all of you too, but I haven't told her about this place yet. I wanted to see it for myself first and surprise her with the news."

"Let me introduce you to everyone." Eve turned sideways to us. "Guys, this is Dr. Alex Thorne. He's an archaeologist, and so is his fiancée. Alex, meet the Au Naturel team."

Eve introduced us one by one, starting with Val, and we had a group chat before Eve and Val took Alex Thorne on a tour of the grounds. That gave the rest of us a break before we would be asked to chat with our guest about what he and fiancée might like for their wedding and when that would be.

Since we had free time, Damian and I headed for the horse pasture. While I brushed the boys, Damian went over to the shed that held all the horsey stuff. I got engrossed in my grooming duties and didn't notice what he was doing until he came up beside me.

"Ready for a ride?" he asked.

I glanced at him. He was holding a saddle in his arms.

For two seconds, I panicked on the inside.

"You don't have to if you're not ready for it yet," he said. "But you've gotten comfortable with Lenny and Georgie. You lead them around and make them back up and stop. They love and respect you almost as much as I do, so I know you're ready for this. But it's up to you."

The panic had evaporated almost as quickly as it set in, and I knew one thing for certain. I was always safe when I was with Damian.

"Sure," I said. "It's about time I tried riding."

Damian put the saddle on Georgie and did up all the complicated doohickeys that held it in place. He would need to teach me about all that eventually, but for now, I just wanted to overcome my last remaining fear. I wanted to ride a horse.

Georgie nuzzled me when I approached him, like he wanted me to climb onto his back.

Damian half crouched and cupped his hands, linking his fingers. "I'll give you a boost."

I stepped into his waiting hands, and he pushed up while I grasped the saddle horn and swung my leg over. I slipped my boots into the stirrups and picked up the reins.

"How's it feel?" Damian asked.

"Good. A little weird, since I've never done this before. But mostly good."

"I'll lead him around until you get comfortable with everything."

Damian took hold of the reins and guided Georgie around in the paddock.

I was on a horse. Holy cow.

After a few minutes, Damian let go. He gave me advice on how to make Georgie do what I wanted, and I rode him around and around inside the paddock, feeling more at ease with every passing moment. Maybe I wasn't an expert rider, not yet, but I had the best teacher to guide me. And the sweetest horse too.

Whatever life threw at me now, I could handle it.

And as for the massive wedding... Yeah, I could deal with that too.

Chapter Thirty-Two

Damian

After Heidi's first ride, we returned to the resort for the big meeting with Alex Thorne. This was when we would all present our ideas for his wedding and listen to his thoughts so we could hash out the details. We had two months to get it done, but Eve wanted to have as much nailed down as possible before our guest flew home tomorrow. To accommodate all seven of us, we gathered in the dining hall and pushed two tables together.

Our guest sat at the head of the table. The ladies occupied one side while the guys took the other.

I'd never met a British person before, or a Scottish person either. But soon, I'd meet more Brits and a whole honking horde of Scots.

Eve and Heidi took the lead in our discussion.

Alex Thorne seemed to like that.

"Aren't I a lucky bloke?" he said. "Two beautiful women ready to cater to my every whim." He winked at me. "Don't worry. I have my hands full with a fiery Scots lass, so I don't have time to seduce your fiancée away from you."

"What about Eve?" I asked. "She's not your type?"

He chuckled. "Every woman is my type, but I'm strictly a window-shopper these days. I've waited fourteen bloody years to marry Catriona MacTaggart, and I won't bollocks it up. Not that I have eyes for anyone but her. She is my soul mate, which is something I used to think was rubbish."

"But now you're into it. I get that. Never believed in soul mates either until I fell for Heidi."

My fiancée glanced at me, her eyes widening briefly right before she smiled. "Yeah, I believe in that sappy stuff now too. Love changes your perspective on everything."

Alex sighed, his lips forming a soft smile. "Yes, it does. And to think I never would've found Cat again after all these years if her meddling family hadn't gotten involved."

"Is that the mob of Scots you mentioned earlier?" Ollie asked. "Can't wait to meet them. They sound like a crazy bunch."

"Oh yes, that they are," Alex said with what I could only describe as a devious smile. "Most of them want to murder me, but marrying Cat ought to keep their homicidal impulses at bay. She will beat to death anyone who lays a finger on me."

Were all Brits as weird as this guy? I kind of liked him, but damn, he had the most bizarre sense of humor. At least I thought he was kidding about Scots wanting to murder him.

Ollie seemed confused too. "You're joking, right? There won't seriously be Scottish people trying to off you while you're all here for the wedding."

"Yes, of course I'm joking," Alex said. "My parents did kidnap us recently, but Cat and I outwitted them. Now they're both locked up."

No one spoke. We all stared at Alex Thorne. Had that been another joke?

"I can see I've stunned the lot of you," Alex said. "It's true, though. My mother is in prison, and my father resides in a psychiatric facility."

Eve regained her ability to speak before the rest of us. "Do you tell everyone you meet about your, um, parents being…"

"Incarcerated? No, I don't spread that around." Alex clasped his hands behind his head. "But it was in the papers and on the telly a few months ago, at least in Scotland. So it's hardly a state secret these days."

"Telly?" I asked.

Val explained, "He means television. Brits call it the telly. I spent some time in England when I was on the Brazilian national football team."

"You're a footballer?" Alex said. "Have you ever tried shinty?"

"I have never heard of it."

"Not surprising. It's a Scottish game that I like to call the bastard child of lacrosse and field hockey."

The conversation continued from there, with Alex making strange jokes while he discussed the wedding preparations and the differences between the UK and America. We all got used to Alex's sense of humor and wound up laughing a lot. The wedding would take place in eight weeks, but when Eve told Alex we already had guests booked for that week, he offered to pay those people to take a vacation anywhere in the world they wanted to go, no matter the cost.

He wasn't kidding. He seriously would do that.

After the group confab, Eve and Val went into the caretaker's house to call those guests and tell them the plan. I had a feeling nobody would balk. I mean, Alex had vowed to spend "any amount of money" to send those people on "their dream holiday." Ollie and Mara went to the office to study the list of wedding guests Alex had given them.

Heidi and I took Alex out to the horse pasture. When I'd mentioned my pilot project, he had wanted to see it "purely for the sake of curiosity but potentially for more." I had no idea what he meant by "more," but hey, if the guy wanted to see the horse pasture, I'd show it to him. He was paying an obscene amount of money for a week-long "wedding extravaganza," as he called it.

We stood at the fence, petting the horses while we talked. He told us a bit about his life, and we shared funny stories from the resort.

"I saw a gypsy wagon out there," Alex said. "Is that owned by a guest or the resort?"

"The resort paid for it, but it's my thing."

"You would be the Ludar prince referenced on the sign."

"That's right."

Alex scratched under Georgie's chin. "Are you a genuine Ludar, or is that strictly an act for the tourists?"

My Ludar lidar was pinging, but in a good way. I had a feeling Alex knew about this stuff. "I'm descended from a long line of proud Ludar, that's what my mom likes to say. I've got Rom genes on both sides of the family tree."

"Your ancestors must've fled Eastern Europe in the late eighteen hundreds during the great migration."

"That's right."

"I'm not well-versed in the history of the gypsies, but it has always fascinated me. Everything historical interests me."

"Happy to give you a palm reading while you're here."

Alex raised one brow. "Don't think I'll risk finding out what the Fates have in store for me. I prefer to live in blissful ignorance believing only good things will come my way now that I have Catriona. The past is prologue, but it's not the denouement."

I had no idea what that meant, but it sounded cool.

Heidi cleared her throat. "Can I ask you a personal question, Alex?"

"Go on. I'm not at all shy. Shameless is more accurate."

The Brit and I had something in common. Who knew?

"Okay," Heidi said. She hesitated before asking, "How did you deal with having bad parents?"

Alex studied her for a moment, his head tipped to the side. "Am I sensing a bit of a kindred spirit in you, Heidi? Are your parents not the sweet, doting sort?"

"No. They're not as bad as yours, but they aren't ideal either. They've always made me the center of their arguments, even when I was a kid, and even after they got divorced."

I draped an arm around her shoulders. "Heidi told them off a while back. I think they're still recovering from the shock."

Alex braced his arm on the fence, tapping one finger on the board. "My best advice for dealing with rubbish parents is to pretend they don't exist. If your mother and father should ever want back in your life, you'll have to decide whether to let them in. Unless and until that happens, make your own family with the friends you have here. It seems as if they're already like family to you."

"Yeah, we're all super close. And you're not the first person who's told me family is what you make it, that blood isn't everything."

"That's true. I'm about to have parents-in-law, three brothers-in-law, and two sisters-in-law, not to mention an army of Catriona's cousins. Then there's my half-brother, though I had no idea he existed, and vice versa, until a few months ago. My brother has cousins too, and they've sort of adopted me." Alex smirked. "I'm positively swimming in family."

Heidi wasn't swimming in family yet, but she had plenty of people who loved her. I got why she'd asked Alex how he dealt with having jerks for parents, but I was also pretty sure she wouldn't have gotten upset if he'd told her he had never made peace with his past. Heidi had moved beyond all that too. I still hoped one day her mom and dad would get over their issues and start acting like adults. I wouldn't hold my breath, though.

We talked to Alex for a little while longer, then we returned to the resort to check in with what the rest of the gang had done in our absence concerning Alex's big wedding. Heidi went to the office to sort through all the ideas the gang had come up with and start formulating a plan. I had my concierge stuff to do, so I left Alex with Eve and Val.

Halfway through the afternoon, I stopped by the office to check on Heidi. She was poring over the information on several pieces of paper that were stapled together.

I settled onto the chair beside the desk. "How's it going?"

"Okay." She held up the stapled sheets so I could see the text printed on them. "This is the guest list. It's four pages long. Of course, some of that is explanations of how each guest is related to Alex or Cat or if they're just friends, plus details about their occupations and ages and how many kids they're bringing. This is more than a huge event. It's like Woodstock and the Super Bowl put together."

"You'll get it all sorted out. But if there's anything I can do to help, just ask." I spread a hand over her thigh. "The only payment I ask for is a blow job."

"Yeah, you're the easiest employee to handle."

"I'm not your employee, but I am your willing slave."

"Thanks, but I'm doing okay on my own." She leaned over to gaze into my eyes from inches away. "But I'll give you head anytime you want."

"Ditto." I slid my hand between her thighs. "Don't forget about our wedding plans. It's only two weeks away."

"I haven't forgotten. It's all sewn up."

"Seriously? Heidi, you are amazing."

"You know, I don't mind if you want to have a bachelor party."

"Got a better idea." I bent toward her to clasp her hands. "Let's ditch the traditional crap about not seeing each other the night before the wedding. I want to give you a full-body reading instead."

"Ooh, I'd love that. It's a date."

I rose and kissed her softly. "Don't work too hard."

Then I left Heidi to sort out the arrangements for the big event while I got back to work.

And in two weeks, I'd be married to that incredible woman.

Chapter Thirty-Three

Heidi
Two weeks later

I got married. Wow. The ceremony was mostly a blur of sounds and motion, but I remembered Eve and Mara fussing over my hair and my dress, then I walked down the aisle toward Damian—and I lost my breath. He looked gorgeous in a tux, but I'd already known that. What stole the air from my lungs wasn't his outfit. It was the expression on his face. He looked at me like I had a glowing golden aura around me and a sparkling halo over my head. When I reached the altar, I realized his eyes were glistening like he might cry any minute.

Yeah, I'd gotten choked up too, but I started crying the instant we faced each other and the minister started reciting the wedding spiel. I had only the haziest memory of speaking my vows and of exchanging the rings. The guests had clapped and cheered, and Sylvester Norris whistled, when Damian and I kissed. It wasn't a hot kiss, but we held our lips pressed to each other for a long moment, savoring the knowledge that we had bound our lives together. Euphoria had swept through me because I suddenly realized I had everything I'd always wanted.

Oh, did I forget to mention my parents showed up? Yeah, they had. My dad even asked if he could accompany me down the aisle and give me away. I said yes. I mean, my parents had gotten a lot better lately. Each of them had called me several times over the past two weeks, and they knew about the wedding. I'd sent them invitations, though I included a note saying I would understand if they didn't want to come.

Damian had bet me fifty bucks they would come.

He won. Was it thanks to Ludar lidar?

Mom and Dad arrived two days before the ceremony, and they hadn't argued once in all that time—at least, not so anyone heard or saw them. My parents were seeing a therapist, together and separately, to work through their issues. They had no plans to get back together, but they wanted to become better parents. All it took was for me to finally stand up and tell them how much they had hurt me over the years. Jeez, if I'd known that... I still wouldn't have done it any earlier. My parents were trying to change, but I'd had my transformation already, thanks to the amazing man I'd just married.

The reception was held at the resort since that was where we'd met and fallen in love. Damian and I stayed at the party for twenty minutes, just long enough for me to dance with my dad and my new husband. Then we retreated to the gypsy wagon. Sure, we had a Hawaiian honeymoon planned, but for tonight, my husband owed me a full-body reading.

I lay on the bed on my stomach, naked.

He straddled my legs and ran his hands over my body, starting with my shoulders, exploring my skin with his fingertips and painting a path of tingling warmth in their wake. I always got hot and bothered when Damian touched me. But the way his fingers trailed over my skin made me shiver too and suck in a breath. My nipples ached. Slick heat gathered between my thighs, and I knew I couldn't survive much longer without him inside.

"Your body tells me everything I need to know," he said while he skimmed his palms over my ass. "But I can't read you the right way unless I'm inside you."

"The whole body-reading thing was just a ploy to get me naked, then."

"I don't need tricks to do that." He dragged his tongue down my spine, swirling it as he moved. "All I have to do is look at you."

"Mm, that's true. For you, I'm the easiest lay on the planet."

"Ditto." He patted my hip. "Turn over, baby. I want to look into your eyes while we make love."

I flipped over, which took a little finagling since he was still straddling me. His dick waved above me, hard and thick, the crown damp. I couldn't resist lunging up to lick the moisture off it and flick my tongue across the slit underneath.

Damian hissed in a breath. "You can do that later. I need to be inside you now, baby."

He reached for a condom.

I grasped his wrist. "Skip that. Let's work on making a baby."

A grin slowly spread across his face. "Love to."

"We can skip foreplay too. I'm so damn ready."

"I can smell how ready you are." He knelt over me, pushing my thighs apart with his knee. "Let's make a rug rat tonight."

"You're supposed to say 'bundle of joy,' not rug rat."

"Right." He thrust into me with one long, swift stroke, filling me completely. "Might need to do this at least three times if we want to get you knocked up tonight."

"As long as it takes. I can't get enough of you, Damian."

He braced his hands at either side of my head and thrust in a measured rhythm, sucking in a breath every time he withdrew and blowing it out with a long groan when he pushed deep inside me again. I grasped his biceps and bent my knees, lifting my hips every time he plunged in. My gaze stayed riveted to his as our breaths quickened and his movements accelerated. The wet sound of our bodies merging mingled with our grunts and gasps and the groans that resonated in his chest. He punched into me faster and harder, making me bounce, and I latched my legs around him, clutching his arms, my neck arched and my back bowed, my mouth open though I couldn't draw in a breath, not anymore. The need to come bore down on me as every muscle in my body tensed.

Damian reached down to pinch my clit.

And I came. Thrashing, writhing, screaming his name, while my sex wrung his cock in wave after wave of pleasure. I was still climaxing when I felt his release pulse inside me. His back bowed too, and strangled shouts burst out of him.

He dropped onto the bed beside me. "That was—Holy shit."

"I know." I rolled over to cuddle up to him. "Imagine doing that over and over and over…"

"Gimme a few minutes, and I'll be ready for round two."

We did make love twice more, then Damian sneaked back to the reception to grab us some food and a bottle of champagne. Celebrating alone, in the wagon, seemed like the most appropriate way to start our marriage. The party continued for us even after the reception ended because we hopped on a plane the next morning to start our Hawaiian honeymoon. Though our honeymoon was fabulous, we were ready to come home after six days. Good thing we'd arranged to stay in Hawaii for only that long.

My parents visited the resort a few weeks later, and though they didn't go nude, they did see naked people. At first, they were freaked out, but they quickly got used to it and even made some new friends.

We still had the big wedding event to handle, but I wasn't worried at all. I had a blueprint for the entire week-long extravaganza, plus I had a bunch of amazing friends to help me. This event would prove to the world that a rural nudist resort could handle any kind of get-together. Alex Thorne had sent us a massive check that was way more than the contract for the wedding called for, but he included a note to explain.

"This is for the pilot project," he wrote, "and I fully expect to see more horses on the premises when I arrive for the wedding."

Damian was thrilled, but being a guy, he had to play it cool.

And the next day, we heard more good news. Eve was pregnant. Damian swore his Ludar lidar assured him I'd be a mom too, very soon. Having a baby would be amazing, but even if that never happened, I had everything I wanted. I had a real family—my parents, my friends, and all the other wonderful people who had come to mean the world to me. I'd been blessed. The future looked more than bright, it shined with the brilliance of a thousand stars. What else was there to say? Well, maybe just one more thing…

And we all lived happily ever after.

Anna Durand is a bestselling, multi-award-winning author of contemporary and paranormal romance. Her books have earned bestseller status on every major retailer and wonderful reviews from readers around the world. But that's the boring spiel. Here are the really cool things you want to know about Anna!

Born on Lackland Air Force Base in Texas, Anna grew up moving here, there, and everywhere thanks to her dad's job as an instructor pilot. She's lived in Texas (twice), Mississippi, California (twice), Michigan (twice), and Alaska—and now Ohio.

As for her writing, Anna has always invented stories in her head, but she didn't write them down until her teen years. Those first awful books went into the trash can a few years later, though she learned a lot from those stories. Eventually, she would pen her first romance novel, the paranormal romance *Willpower*, and she's never looked back since.

To get exclusive content, join Anna's Facebook group, Anna's Romance Addicts, or sign up for her newsletter.

Visit AnnaDurand.com to sign up.